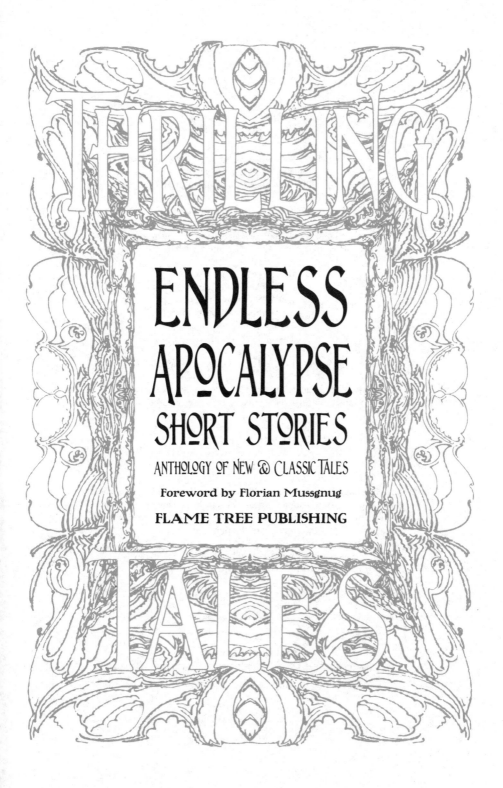

THRILLING

ENDLESS APOCALYPSE SHORT STORIES

ANTHOLOGY OF NEW & CLASSIC TALES

Foreword by Florian Mussgnug

FLAME TREE PUBLISHING

TALES

This is a FLAME TREE Book

Publisher & Creative Director: Nick Wells
Project Editor: Josie Mitchell
Editorial Board: Gillian Whitaker, Laura Bulbeck, Catherine Taylor

Publisher's Note: Due to the historical nature of the classic text, we're aware that
there may be some language used which has the potential to cause offence to
the modern reader. However, wishing overall to preserve the integrity of the text,
rather than imposing contemporary sensibilities, we have left it unaltered.

FLAME TREE PUBLISHING
6 Melbray Mews, Fulham,
London SW6 3NS, United Kingdom
www.flametreepublishing.com

First published 2018

The cover image is created by Flame Tree Studio
based on artwork by Slava Gerj and Gabor Ruszkai.

A copy of the CIP data for this book is available from the British Library.

Printed and bound in China

And Coming Soon
FLAME TREE PRESS | FICTION WITHOUT FRONTIERS
New and original writing in Horror, Crime, SF and Fantasy

THRILLING

ENDLESS APOCALYPSE SHORT STORIES

ANTHOLOGY OF NEW & CLASSIC TALES

Foreword by Florian Mussgnug

FLAME TREE PUBLISHING

TALES

Contents

Foreword: Endless Apocalypse Short Stories

THE FUTURE has always seemed a dangerous place. To resist the inescapable apocalyptic mood of our age, it is good to recall that the end of the world has been with us since the beginnings of human history. But how did other periods and cultures imagine man's final hour?

Apocalypse, in the Biblical context, means 'revelation': the ultimate disclosure of God's will and purpose at the end of time. In this overtly Christian guise, global catastrophe has exercised a powerful fascination down the centuries, and continues to do so in our more secular world. Yet, as this magnificent collection reminds us, modern figurations of apocalypse have many roots, including the *Epic of Gilgamesh* – retold here as 'The Deluge' – as well as the Norse cosmogony laid out in the medieval, Icelandic tales of 'The Fooling of Gylfe' and the rest of the *Prose Edda*. These texts mark the emergence of an expectation that continues to shape our fears, hopes and stories: what would it be like to survive the end of everything we once took for granted?

The darkly sublime visions of Mary Shelley's *The Last Man* or Lord Byron's 'Darkness' – two of the earliest works of secular apocalypse fiction – reveal that end time stories are more than an expression of sordid pessimism. They astonish and delight, make us aware of the extreme fragility of our lives and institutions, and send shivers of metaphysical horror down our spines. Edgar Allan Poe and H.P. Lovecraft, in particular, relished this sense of profound vulnerability. Their influence, and the influence of their successors, continues to be felt in many major works of apocalyptic science fiction, in literature and film. Ranging from Romanticism to the Edwardian period, the stories collected in this volume are terrifying, but they also remind us that fear is not the only response to apocalypse. We can laugh at the curious mishaps of J.D. Beresford's solitary, post-apocalyptic survivors, be puzzled by Stephen Vincent Benét's riddles, or gasp at the heroic – but, thankfully, anachronistic – masculinity of M.P. Shiel and George Allan England's protagonists. Or, like Arthur Conan Doyle's Professor Challenger, we can sigh with relief when the supposed end of the world turns out, against all odds, to be just another crisis.

Apocalypse fiction may even teach us a lesson. In 1914, when H.G. Wells made his most striking forecast – predicting a worldwide atomic war by 1953 – even he could not have imagined the role that *The World Set Free* would play for Leo Szilard, the physicist who in 1933 conceived the nuclear chain reaction and who later claimed that the Bomb was directly inspired by his experience of reading Wells as a teenager. Apocalypse literature, then, can conjure real threats, but it also prepares us for real emergencies. More optimistically, the wonderful texts in this collection remind us that past risks, including those most feared by our ancestors, now make for good stories. Let us enjoy their dark flights of fancy, and hope that we and our children may enjoy their stories endlessly, without being distracted by the actual end of the world.

Florian Mussgnug

Publisher's Note

Stories about the end of the world have always fascinated us, throughout history, from ancient myths to the very latest popular apocalypse fiction. Many of these stories come in the form of warnings, others grip with scientific knowledge of future eras or survival tactics but all speak to a place of curiosity and fear that is in all of us. We have represented the origins of the genre with an extract from Snorri Sturluson's Norse myth 'The Fooling of Gylfe' featuring Ragnarök as well as later works by writers such as J.D. Beresford, Jules Verne and M.P. Shiel. Some of these stories are well known but we hope there are some undiscovered gems too.

Every year the response to our call for submissions seems to grow and grow, giving us a rich universe of stories to choose from, but making our job all the more difficult in narrowing down the final selection. We've loved delving into such secret worlds, and ultimately chose a selection of stories we hope sit alongside each other and with the classic selection, to provide a fantastic *Endless Apocalypse* book for all to enjoy.

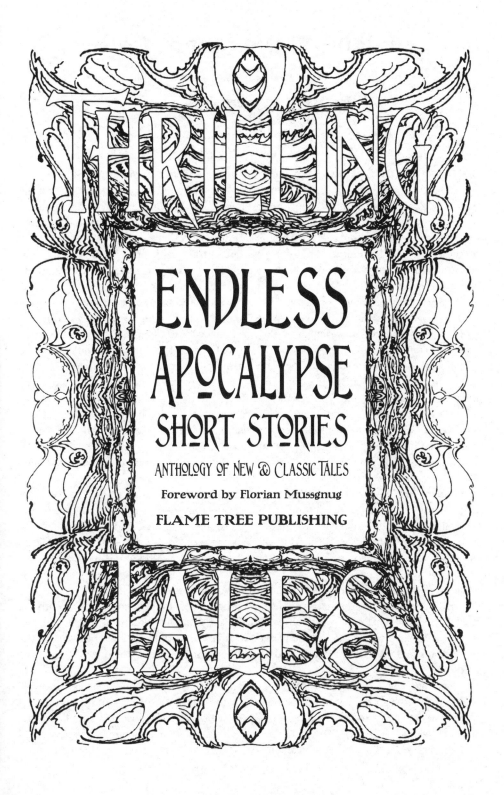

THRILLING

ENDLESS
APOCALYPSE
SHORT STORIES

ANTHOLOGY OF NEW & CLASSIC TALES

Foreword by Florian Mussgnug

FLAME TREE PUBLISHING

TALES

Flight of the Storm God

Mike Adamson

SOMETIMES THE DREAMS are wonderful, and sometimes they are living hell.

There are times I walk in the Eden of olden times, when the world was green and the wind made racing waves across the steppes. I was there not long ago, it seems, standing in the clean wind under a warm sun, looking across the land, rolling away to the spine of the Urals, white against the sky, the mountains that bisect Europe from Asia. I could forget for a while the reality of matters, luxuriate in the sense of the primal Earth, its air so kind upon my skin. There were birds on the wing, horses upon the green sea, and the world was good.

I remember those dreams fondly, and know the AI tries valiantly to foster such memories, to damp down the nightmares – for when they break through it seems they endure for months, years, and my sanity staggers in the grip of images I would sooner forget. Only when I am fully conscious can I deal with reality by a philosophic feat, for who could endure the ongoing vision of those green lands made desert, dunes where there had been rivers, a world of stinging wind filled with grit, and where the cities of old were swallowed down deep by the marching sands?

Heat and dust now define the Earth, a scorching planet with a broken food web, largely dead oceans and only the tropical forests persist in the carbon dioxide-rich air. The oceans encroached upon the coastal plains, 130 meters of onlap worked its relentless destruction upon the doings of humankind, and cities above those elevations are eerie necropoli filled with the bleached bones of billions.

I think it was this horror, more than any other aspect, that taxed my sanity in the endless night of waiting. The AI bridge into my consciousness was linked via the dream cortex, and those dreams dominated me in ways they were never meant to. A clean passage through the alpha brainwave range as I ascended to consciousness or down into the untroubled sleep of ages would have made the process simple, but actually waking was something I could never do.

None of us could, we, the 29,000 souls who survived here.

That was the trick, coming close enough to consciousness for my mind to be in control of itself without my physical body actually waking; the infiltration of dreams was the price, and technicians long ago had warned me I risked madness. But someone must be aware of the world to make the decision to wake, and as director of the project I would leave the task to no other.

How long? The AI whispered to me of decades flowing by, of conditions above slowly changing. Forty years ago it noticed an anomaly on the external visual pickups and correlated observations to reach the astonishing conclusion that energy reaching the ground from the sun had fractionally reduced, as if solar output had lessened. No known mechanism could account for it but recalculation now assumed a slow but genuine cooling trend in our over-hot world.

As the hundred drones went about their repetitive tasks, maintaining the biostasis modules, I saw through their eyes, walked the chill corridors of the redoubt, and consoled myself with the thought that all was *in the green* – we were alive, and would stay so for as long as it took. My machine memory told me I had paced the catwalks to their modules – Eleyna and Talia – 176 times; each pilgrimage was to stand for a while and look down on their faces, unchanging in the gentle arms of stasis, and heave a mental sigh, longing for the moment the march of the years was over and we would be together again.

One can acclimate to anything, and I had come to understand my lot was eternity, gliding from year to year and decade to decade. Thus it was with strange disquietude I felt myself roused from the deeper layers where dreams came less frequently, piloted up through vivid cycles toward the edges of wakefulness, where my mind could reach through and phase with the world once more.

Things have changed, the AI whispered, *faster than we ever anticipated. The air is breathable once more.*

How – I stammered mentally, but had no time to complete the thought before the real message drove home to me with the force of a commentary impact.

We have visitors.

* * *

Not in more than seven decades had any living thing walked these halls, and I was perturbed by the thought of coming face to face with whoever it may be.

I phased in a smooth, cool dive into the perceptive envelope of a maintenance drone, breathed mentally as if I still had a body of flesh and blood, and flexed powerful metal hands. My vision cleared and I knew at once I was in sub-maintenance bay 12, the machine vault where the drones repaired each other. No lights were required, my senses were multiple layers of thermoscan and lidar, supplementing empirical knowledge of the redoubt layout. I had an immediate feed via the AI from the external sensors on the energy towers far above, and a passive imaging system fed me a scene such as I had imagined down the long, dark years but never truly dared expect.

The wind-tormented desert was its dirty red-brown self, the slope down to the dry meanders of the Ural River, here to the west of lost Orenburg, a rippled field of low dunes. A hundred meters from the slowly-corroding towers that rose, squat and obtuse, from the desert, stood a craft of unknown design; wing-mounted engines were obviously rotated for vertical landing performance, and from it had emerged four people.

People!

Human beings – living human beings! My heart flip-flopped and I zoomed the lens to examine them one by one. Two men, two women – a tall, broad, Slavic male, a Caucasian male with more western features; one of the women was small, petite and Chinese, the other a flaxen-haired European. The latter was dressed in a rugged jumpsuit of dusty white fabric, the others in what seemed a uniform of simple cut and grey-green tone. They walked with care in the slithery sands, panning instruments as they examined the towers, and I knew at once they had no knowledge of the redoubt – zero information had come down to them, and my curiosity was doubled when I matched this to the mystery of how the external environment had veered back toward human-habitable inside the same century as its downfall.

The signal sky was quiet in all the bands we were tuned to monitor, but clearly we had been listening in the wrong regions of the spectrum. These people were technological and appeared healthy enough, healthier than the oxygen-poor air and still high temperatures should have permitted. Perhaps – my digital heart fluttered at this notion – perhaps those who had abandoned the Earth had returned at last.

I was unsure how I felt about it, but a current of resentment made itself known. We had held our ground, cloven to Mother Earth, not run away from the mess our ancestors made. It was *ours* to inherit, and we had every tool and resource in our vast underground chambers to do so when the time was right. But these strangers' presence posed uncomfortable questions, thoughts which placed our survival strategy in doubt, and this was unacceptable.

With a whine of servos I stepped out of my service dock and headed for the vertical access. After a seeming eternity of sleeping darkness, I was back – and before all else I was my people's protector. I rose to a command node on a higher level and woke systems with silent, lightning-fast commands, standing in a ring of projection screens on which data streamed and images played from a dozen perspectives. Here I contented myself to watch; after three quarters of a century, what did a few hours matter? If they were smart, they would find their way in.

As the day aged toward evening I watched them scanning the towers as if they had no notion of such designs – likely checking for ionizing radiation, and chemo and biohazards. The structures were merely the upper extremities of a thermal-differential energy installation, whose endlessly circulating freon gas, between the heat of the upper world where it expanded violently and the chill of bedrock where it re-condensed, drove generators and provided all the power the redoubt would ever need. It was engineering no more complicated than a refrigerator, but on the scale of a skyscraper, and its sheer simplicity guaranteed longevity. These people from the sky must be looking for something more complex, I guessed, and their perplexity struck me as amusing. But they brought tools from their craft and spent an hour shovelling sand and grit from the base of one of the stacks, and at last uncovered an access hatch.

Now it got interesting and I watched with keen attention as the tall Slav pried open the command panel by the hatch, dismantled the code keypad and scanned the reverse side, obviously analysing the circuitry. I knew it was just a matter of time before he worked out how to circumvent the entry lockout. I smiled mentally, acknowledging the smarts of our guests, as motors turned for the first time since the complex was sealed, withdrawing tooled steel lugs, and the door swung inward. I felt motion sensors detect the intruders and systems swung into action – LED strips blinked on and fans began to circulate the stale, hot air.

In the sight of discrete cameras, the four penetrated the service way surrounding the heat-exchanger ducting at the core of the tower and began their descent. Now I nodded to myself. It was time. I strode to meet them, aware clearly as they encountered other drones in their rounds, and I ordered the machines to remain impassive at the intrusion.

The long metal halls were chill and echoed dully to footfalls. My sensors picked up voices as I approached, a Russian accent commenting in English as service panels were read: "High-pressure air line... Condensation recovery duct... Main A/C harness... Caution: Hot... Robot access only..."

At once the four intruders whirled as I strode purposefully from a turning and eased to a halt before them. The moment was more laden with meaning than even my processors could calculate and I registered their apprehension as they took in my form, head and shoulders taller than any of them, my dull metallic casing stencilled with Cyrillic characters. My optical pickups glowed softly as I scanned them in return, while my human heart sang to behold the living.

"I don't think it's hostile," the Chinese woman whispered after a few moments, and my reaction was a very human twitch of my shoulders.

"*Privetstvuyu*," I said, amiably enough, to the Slavic man, who smiled at once.

"*Zdravstvuyte*," he returned easily, as I placed my hands together in human manner.

A moment later I switched languages. "Chinese, Russian, European... I sense English is your *lingua franca*." I read their expressions and moved on, my voice slightly metalicised and with a soft Russian accent. I spoke easily but with a reserve perhaps only I appreciated. "Welcome to the South Urals Survival Redoubt... We have waited a *very* long time."

The silence was difficult, and the fair-haired European woman stepped forward. "Doctor Sondra Cullaine, of Prometheus City, out by the Moon. I'm in command."

I extended my hand gently and an emotion for which I was not ready filled me as I pronounced my name for the first time. "Doctor Anton Mikhailov. My body lies sleeping with the rest, but my mind is very much here."

With the strangest feelings in my heart and belly, I felt her clasp my cold metal hand, and I shook with a soul from my personal future.

* * *

They had torn apart asteroids for the raw materials to build their cities, powered by the sun and the atom, and controlled by EM drives. I wished my drone body was more expressive as I struggled to keep up with the revelations. Using the same technologies, they had placed a vast obstruction in space between the sun and Earth, generating an eternal eclipse which mediated in a very controlled way the precise amount of energy striking the planet at any latitude, at any time. This was what the AI had detected decades ago, explaining the trend to a cooler environment. I accepted their explanations, if not uncritically, as the AI surged in its cybernetic vaults, examining the data, cross-matching and modelling.

"Outside oxygen levels are our indicator of the recovery of the planet," I replied as I lead our guests along an interminable corridor in the cool depths of the complex. "The redoubt was designed to survive for many centuries if need be. The terrain is geologically reasonably stable, minor disturbances the engineering can cope with. A hundred drones look after the systems and themselves, while the power will flow as long as the heat differential lasts." I paused by a long gallery and passed a hand over a control. Metal window shields ground slowly upward to reveal a vista of systems in multiple repetitions – and I felt a hand brush my spine at our guest's expressions as they realized they looked out upon tier after tier of casket-sized capsules.

"Are they biostasis modules?" The European man, Travers, whispered.

"Twenty-nine thousand people lie sleeping below," I replied simply. "When the O_2/CO_2 balance comes even 10% closer to pre-industrial levels, it will be time for them to wake and build a new home." I gestured with a hydraulic arm. "There I am, on that uppermost tier, number 28062. Beside my wife and daughter... My consciousness drifts in a shallow sleep, my dream cortex linked to the complex's AI and interfaced with this drone. I am the eyes and ears of the project." My voice faded, became introspective. In a flurry I recalled the nightmares, filled with thoughts of a burning, angry desert, the decades drifting by with the sand on the wind, the lost race asleep amid the bones of perished nations. My metallic whisper trailed off and Cullaine shared a difficult glance with the Chinese woman, Chan. I pulled myself together. "Still, when this redoubt was built in the first years of this century, we were sure we were not alone. There are others in Russia, more in China, in Scandinavia and

Japan, and probably elsewhere also. As millions fled into the sky, those who remained knew any hope of survival lay here, not in the vain dream of joining you Hi-Techers at L5." I slapped the railing below the windows. "This is the low-tech solution, and we have always believed it was the right one."

Zaitsin, my countryman, was unreservedly proud of all he saw. He was an engineer by trade, and appreciated the elegance of our solution. "A race in being – people of the late 21st century who will return and make the 23rd their own." He nodded with quiet satisfaction. "The continuity is amazing, and unexpected."

I nodded silently in return, but raised a cautioning finger. "Be warned, many resented those in the sky.… You ran away from the problems our ancestors caused, and left the rest of the human race to suffer the consequences." The silence was difficult, and I filled it with a coughing sound. "That was before all your times, I know. But not mine. Though your lives are much extended by technology, none of you was born before 2100, and The End. I have been *sleeping* since 2105. It is a sad reminder of the chaos of those last terrible years as the world became unable to support animal life, that your people and ours lost track of each other so thoroughly we now meet as strangers."

Cullaine checked the time display in the corner of her tablet and lay a hand on my arm, the human familiarity making my heart ache and underlining the loneliness I had endured. I recognized her expression as compassion and in that moment found I could believe it was genuine. "Anton… we can't speak for those who built the cities in which we were born. But it is our mission and purpose to restore what was lost. The atmospheric balances you are monitoring are responding to *our* efforts. Do you not monitor the signal traffic between the space cities?"

"We have no means. We were… unconcerned with the doings of those who turned their backs on us."

"Then let us show you something amazing," Cullaine said softly, gestured to the world above, and offered me her hand.

* * *

Evening thickened over the wastelands, a reddish sunset building through the dust, when we emerged on the surface. I looked up at the sky and stretched, the human expressing through the machine; if I could have wept I would have done so now, for never before had I left the redoubt. But my attention was drawn to the east, where clouds boiled in slow motion, and a shape beyond all reckoning lay at their heart.

"We call them *Genesis Ships*," Cullaine said softly, my hand still in hers. "This is the *Perun*."

"Perun?" I returned in some small surprise, scanning the AI's database. "God of storms and head of the ancient Slavic pantheon."

"Just so. It was rather apt, we felt. In ancient times, storms were understood to be the harbingers of life. Nothing grows without water, and thunder and lightning are the bringers of rain, thus storm gods were often patron deities of agriculture. Each continent has its vessel. Thor works Europe, Dian Mu China, Oya cruises Africa and Mamaragan Australia. The Americas are tended by Thunderbird and Baka'b."

As we watched, a great fork of lightening played through the clouds and stroked the vessel, mirrored a moment later from another angle, then multiple strikes to the earth below the craft's oblate belly.

"The hull is charged," I observed in an awed whisper.

"The whole vessel is a lightning rod.... In her holds are the systems which read DNA and write out proteins, turning raw materials into life. The seeds of the hardiest grasses, able to stabilize these sands, are made in that ship and scattered to the world below as she raises the storm. Each seeding run strips the moisture from the clouds, and makes the rivers run. A million storms have been triggered in the right places, a trillion-trillion seeds have rained from the clouds, and little by little, we are winning back the Earth."

"However were they built...?" I murmured

"Each took around a year, much of them 3D printed. 1500 meters long, the largest craft ever to move on the face of this world. They were assembled by drones, much like yours. It took a decade to crack out enough helium to fill them, but time is one thing we have plenty of."

We stood in the last light of day to watch the behemoth creep westward, towing its vortex of cloud and fury, a marching curtain of blue-white strokes writing the furious command to life upon the desert. The rains came in concert, a silver-gray curtain that sent reaching fingers flooding through the dry bed of the Ural River on the slopes below us, and as the titanic craft made its stately passage I nodded my metal head, hands folded before me as my resentment, my apprehensions, melted away and I understood the scope of their achievement.

"The oceans, too, yes?"

"Each has its own vessel," Cullaine said softly. "Named for the sea gods, as you'd guess. They've spent 15 years writing out the genes and proteins for phytoplankton and raining them into the spring seas. When their proliferation has raised the oxygen levels far enough, we'll introduce zooplankton. Then the first fish... From the humblest building blocks of life, the great food web will be rebuilt..."

"Now I understand," I said softly, raising my hands to the vista of the storm and the tremendous, organically curved vessel. "When we sealed ourselves into our redoubt we expected many hundreds of years to go by before natural processes began to repair the damage. A single century now seems more likely." A sudden elation gripped me, edged my voice with joy as the overwhelming image of the sunset-lit titan, wreathed in lightning, filled the sky before us. "Our own gene banks become merely a failsafe, a reserve. Ten years more and I will awaken our people. They will emerge upon steppes already green with a sea of deep grasses, the Kazakh desert driven south once more. We will rebuild Orenburg, and see the first snows return in the highlands. The Ural shall flow once more, to swell and refresh the foul remnants of the Caspian Sea." I spoke with, more than passion, the sense of prayers being answered, and of gratitude for the revelation to have come upon me when faith was long since eroded by the grinding sameness of the decades.

"It's the dream of the age," Cullaine murmured against the near-continuous rumble of thunder, and we felt the first rain spots on our upturned faces. "It's good to think the Earth was never quite as dead as we feared."

"Life persists," I returned quietly, and those two simple words were a summation of the will for Planet Earth to endure and overcome all we had, in our ignorance, inflicted upon it.

By the Waters of Babylon

Stephen Vincent Benét

THE NORTH and the west and the south are good hunting ground, but it is forbidden to go east. It is forbidden to go to any of the Dead Places except to search for metal and then he who touches the metal must be a priest or the son of a priest. Afterwards, both the man and the metal must be purified. These are the rules and the laws; they are well made. It is forbidden to cross the great river and look upon the place that was the Place of the Gods – this is most strictly forbidden. We do not even say its name though we know its name. It is there that spirits live, and demons – it is there that there are the ashes of the Great Burning. These things are forbidden – they have been forbidden since the beginning of time.

My father is a priest; I am the son of a priest. I have been in the Dead Places near us, with my father – at first, I was afraid. When my father went into the house to search for the metal, I stood by the door and my heart felt small and weak. It was a dead man's house, a spirit house. It did not have the smell of man, though there were old bones in a corner. But it is not fitting that a priest's son should show fear. I looked at the bones in the shadow and kept my voice still.

Then my father came out with the metal – good, strong piece. He looked at me with both eyes but I had not run away. He gave me the metal to hold – I took it and did not die. So he knew that I was truly his son and would be a priest in my time. That was when I was very young – nevertheless, my brothers would not have done it, though they are good hunters. After that, they gave me the good piece of meat and the warm corner of the fire. My father watched over me – he was glad that I should be a priest. But when I boasted or wept without a reason, he punished me more strictly than my brothers. That was right.

After a time, I myself was allowed to go into the dead houses and search for metal. So I learned the ways of those houses – and if I saw bones, I was no longer afraid. The bones are light and old – sometimes they will fall into dust if you touch them. But that is a great sin.

I was taught the chants and the spells – I was taught how to stop the running of blood from a wound and many secrets. A priest must know many secrets – that was what my father said.

If the hunters think we do all things by chants and spells, they may believe so – it does not hurt them. I was taught how to read in the old books and how to make the old writings – that was hard and took a long time. My knowledge made me happy – it was like a fire in my heart. Most of all, I liked to hear of the Old Days and the stories of the gods. I asked myself many questions that I could not answer, but it was good to ask them. At night, I would lie awake and listen to the wind – it seemed to me that it was the voice of the gods as they flew through the air.

We are not ignorant like the Forest People – our women spin wool on the wheel, our priests wear a white robe. We do not eat grubs from the trees, we have not forgotten the old writings, although they are hard to understand. Nevertheless, my knowledge and my lack of knowledge burned in me – I wished to know more. When I was a man at last, I came to my father and said, "It is time for me to go on my journey. Give me your leave."

He looked at me for a long time, stroking his beard, then he said at last, "Yes. It is time." That night, in the house of the priesthood, I asked for and received purification. My body hurt but my spirit was a cool stone. It was my father himself who questioned me about my dreams.

He bade me look into the smoke of the fire and see – I saw and told what I saw. It was what I have always seen – a river, and, beyond it, a great Dead Place and in it the gods walking. I have always thought about that. His eyes were stern when I told him he was no longer my father but a priest. He said, "This is a strong dream."

"It is mine," I said, while the smoke waved and my head felt light. They were singing the Star song in the outer chamber and it was like the buzzing of bees in my head.

He asked me how the gods were dressed and I told him how they were dressed. We know how they were dressed from the book, but I saw them as if they were before me. When I had finished, he threw the sticks three times and studied them as they fell.

"This is a very strong dream," he said." It may eat you up."

"I am not afraid," I said and looked at him with both eyes. My voice sounded thin in my ears but that was because of the smoke.

He touched me on the breast and the forehead. He gave me the bow and the three arrows.

"Take them," he said. "It is forbidden to travel east. It is forbidden to cross the river. It is forbidden to go to the Place of the Gods. All these things are forbidden. "

"All these things are forbidden," I said, but it was my voice that spoke and not my spirit. He looked at me again.

"My son," he said. "Once I had young dreams. If your dreams do not eat you up, you may be a great priest. If they eat you, you are still my son. Now go on your journey."

I went fasting, as is the law. My body hurt but not my heart. When the dawn came, I was out of sight of the village. I prayed and purified myself, waiting for a sign. The sign was an eagle. It flew east.

Sometimes signs are sent by bad spirits. I waited again on the flat rock, fasting, taking no food. I was very still – I could feel the sky above me and the earth beneath. I waited till the sun was beginning to sink. Then three deer passed in the valley going east – they did not mind me or see me. There was a white fawn with them – a very great sign.

I followed them, at a distance, waiting for what would happen. My heart was troubled about going east, yet I knew that I must go. My head hummed with my fasting – I did not even see the panther spring upon the white fawn. But, before I knew it, the bow was in my hand. I shouted and the panther lifted his head from the fawn. It is not easy to kill a panther with one arrow but the arrow went through his eye and into his brain. He died as he tried to spring – he rolled over, tearing at the ground. Then I knew I was meant to go east – I knew that was my journey. When the night came, I made my fire and roasted meat.

It is eight suns' journey to the east and a man passes by many Dead Places. The Forest People are afraid of them but I am not. Once I made my fire on the edge of a Dead Place at night and, next morning, in the dead house, I found a good knife, little rusted. That was small to what came afterward but it made my heart feel big. Always when I looked for game, it was in front of my arrow, and twice I passed hunting parties of the Forest People without their knowing. So I knew my magic was strong and my journey clean, in spite of the law.

Toward the setting of the eighth sun, I came to the banks of the great river. It was half-a-day's journey after I had left the god-road – we do not use the god-roads now for they are falling apart into great blocks of stone, and the forest is safer going. A long way off, I had seen the water through trees but the trees were thick. At last, I came out upon an open place at the top of a cliff. There was the great river below, like a giant in the sun. It is very long, very wide. It could eat all the streams we know and still be thirsty. Its name is Ou-dis-sun, the Sacred, the Long. No man of my tribe had seen it, not even my father, the priest. It was magic and I prayed.

Then I raised my eyes and looked south. It was there, the Place of the Gods.

How can I tell what it was like – you do not know. It was there, in the red light, and they were too big to be houses. It was there with the red light upon it, mighty and ruined. I knew that in another moment the gods would see me. I covered my eyes with my hands and crept back into the forest.

Surely, that was enough to do, and live. Surely it was enough to spend the night upon the cliff. The Forest People themselves do not come near. Yet, all through the night, I knew that I should have to cross the river and walk in the places of the gods, although the gods ate me up. My magic did not help me at all and yet there was a fire in my bowels, a fire in my mind. When the sun rose, I thought, "My journey has been clean. Now I will go home from my journey." But, even as I thought so, I knew I could not. If I went to the Place of the Gods, I would surely die, but, if I did not go, I could never be at peace with my spirit again. It is better to lose one's life than one's spirit, if one is a priest and the son of a priest.

Nevertheless, as I made the raft, the tears ran out of my eyes. The Forest People could have killed me without fight, if they had come upon me then, but they did not come.

When the raft was made, I said the sayings for the dead and painted myself for death. My heart was cold as a frog and my knees like water, but the burning in my mind would not let me have peace. As I pushed the raft from the shore, I began my death song – I had the right. It was a fine song.

> "I am John, son of John," I sang. "My people are the Hill People. They are the men.
> I go into the Dead Places but I am not slain.
> I take the metal from the Dead Places but I am not blasted.
> I travel upon the god-roads and am not afraid. E-yah! I
> have killed the panther, I have killed the fawn!
> E-yah! I have come to the great river. No man has come there before.
> It is forbidden to go east, but I have gone, forbidden
> to go on the great river, but I am there.
> Open your hearts, you spirits, and hear my song.
> Now I go to the Place of the Gods, I shall not return.
> My body is painted for death and my limbs weak, but my
> heart is big as I go to the Place of the Gods!"

All the same, when I came to the Place of the Gods, I was afraid, afraid. The current of the great river is very strong – it gripped my raft with its hands. That was magic, for the river itself is wide and calm. I could feel evil spirits about me, I was swept down the stream. Never have I been so much alone – I tried to think of my knowledge, but it was a squirrel's heap of winter nuts. There was no strength in my knowledge any more and I felt small and naked as a new-hatched bird – alone upon the great river, the servant of the gods.

Yet, after a while, my eyes were opened and I saw. I saw both banks of the river – I saw that once there had been god-roads across it, though now they were broken and fallen like broken vines. Very great they were, and wonderful and broken – broken in the time of the Great Burning when the fire fell out of the sky. And always the current took me nearer to the Place of the Gods, and the huge ruins rose before my eyes.

I do not know the customs of rivers – we are the People of the Hills. I tried to guide my raft with the pole but it spun around. I thought the river meant to take me past the Place of the Gods and out into the Bitter Water of the legends. I grew angry then – my heart felt strong. I said aloud, "I am a priest and the son of a priest!" The gods heard me – they showed me how to paddle with the pole on one side of the raft. The current changed itself – I drew near to the Place of the Gods.

When I was very near, my raft struck and turned over. I can swim in our lakes – I swam to the shore. There was a great spike of rusted metal sticking out into the river – I hauled myself up upon it and sat there, panting. I had saved my bow and two arrows and the knife I found in the Dead Place but that was all. My raft went whirling downstream toward the Bitter Water. I looked after it, and thought if it had trod me under, at least I would be safely dead. Nevertheless, when I had dried my bowstring and re-strung it, I walked forward to the Place of the Gods.

It felt like ground underfoot; it did not burn me. It is not true what some of the tales say, that the ground there burns forever, for I have been there. Here and there were the marks and stains of the Great Burning, on the ruins, that is true. But they were old marks and old stains. It is not true either, what some of our priests say, that it is an island covered with fogs and enchantments. It is not. It is a great Dead Place – greater than any Dead Place we know. Everywhere in it there are god-roads, though most are cracked and broken. Everywhere there are the ruins of the high towers of the gods.

How shall I tell what I saw? I went carefully, my strung bow in my hand, my skin ready for danger. There should have been the wailings of spirits and the shrieks of demons, but there were not. It was very silent and sunny where I had landed – the wind and the rain and the birds that drop seeds had done their work – the grass grew in the cracks of the broken stone. It is a fair island – no wonder the gods built there. If I had come there, a god, I also would have built.

How shall I tell what I saw? The towers are not all broken – here and there one still stands, like a great tree in a forest, and the birds nest high. But the towers themselves look blind, for the gods are gone. I saw a fishhawk, catching fish in the river. I saw a little dance of white butterflies over a great heap of broken stones and columns. I went there and looked about me – there was a carved stone with cut – letters, broken in half. I can read letters but I could not understand these. They said UBTREAS. There was also the shattered image of a man or a god. It had been made of white stone and he wore his hair tied back like a woman's. His name was ASHING, as I read on the cracked half of a stone. I thought it wise to pray to ASHING, though I do not know that god.

How shall I tell what I saw? There was no smell of man left, on stone or metal. Nor were there many trees in that wilderness of stone. There are many pigeons, nesting and dropping in the towers – the gods must have loved them, or, perhaps, they used them for sacrifices. There are wild cats that roam the god-roads, green-eyed, unafraid of man. At night they wail like demons but they are not demons. The wild dogs are more dangerous, for they hunt in a pack, but them I did not meet till later. Everywhere there are the carved stones, carved with magical numbers or words.

I went north – I did not try to hide myself. When a god or a demon saw me, then I would die, but meanwhile I was no longer afraid. My hunger for knowledge burned in me – there was so much that I could not understand. After a while, I knew that my belly was hungry. I could have hunted for my meat, but I did not hunt. It is known that the gods did not hunt as we do – they got their food from enchanted boxes and jars. Sometimes these are still found in the Dead Places – once, when I was a child and foolish, I opened such a jar and tasted it and found the food sweet. But my father found out and punished me for it strictly, for, often, that food is death. Now, though, I had long gone past what was forbidden, and I entered the likeliest towers, looking for the food of the gods.

I found it at last in the ruins of a great temple in the mid-city. A mighty temple it must have been, for the roof was painted like the sky at night with its stars – that much I could see, though the colors were faint and dim. It went down into great caves and tunnels – perhaps they kept their slaves there. But when I started to climb down, I heard the squeaking of rats, so I did not go – rats are unclean, and there must have been many tribes of them, from the squeaking. But near there, I found food, in the heart of a ruin, behind a door that still opened. I ate only the fruits from the jars – they had a very sweet taste. There was drink, too, in bottles of glass – the drink of the gods was strong and made my head swim. After I had eaten and drunk, I slept on the top of a stone, my bow at my side.

When I woke, the sun was low. Looking down from where I lay, I saw a dog sitting on his haunches. His tongue was hanging out of his mouth; he looked as if he were laughing. He was a big dog, with a gray-brown coat, as big as a wolf. I sprang up and shouted at him but he did not move – he just sat there as if he were laughing. I did not like that. When I reached for a stone to throw, he moved swiftly out of the way of the stone. He was not afraid of me; he looked at me as if I were meat. No doubt I could have killed him with an arrow, but I did not know if there were others. Moreover, night was falling.

I looked about me – not far away there was a great, broken god-road, leading north. The towers were high enough, but not so high, and while many of the dead-houses were wrecked, there were some that stood. I went toward this god-road, keeping to the heights of the ruins, while the dog followed. When I had reached the god-road, I saw that there were others behind him. If I had slept later, they would have come upon me asleep and torn out my throat. As it was, they were sure enough of me; they did not hurry. When I went into the dead-house, they kept watch at the entrance – doubtless they thought they would have a fine hunt. But a dog cannot open a door and I knew, from the books, that the gods did not like to live on the ground but on high.

I had just found a door I could open when the dogs decided to rush. Ha! They were surprised when I shut the door in their faces – it was a good door, of strong metal. I could hear their foolish baying beyond it but I did not stop to answer them. I was in darkness – I found stairs and climbed. There were many stairs, turning around till my head was dizzy. At the top was another door – I found the knob and opened it. I was in a long small chamber – on one side of it was a bronze door that could not be opened, for it had no handle. Perhaps there was a magic word to open it but I did not have the word. I turned to the door in the opposite side of the wall. The lock of it was broken and I opened it and went in.

Within, there was a place of great riches. The god who lived there must have been a powerful god. The first room was a small ante-room – I waited there for some time, telling the spirits of the place that I came in peace and not as a robber. When it seemed to me that they had had time to hear me, I went on. Ah, what riches! Few, even, of the windows had been broken – it was all as it had been. The great windows that looked over the city had not been broken at all though they were dusty and streaked with many years. There were coverings on the floors, the colors not greatly faded, and the chairs were soft and deep. There were pictures upon the walls, very strange, very wonderful – I remember one of a bunch of flowers in a jar – if you came close to it, you could see nothing but bits of color, but if you stood away from it, the flowers might have been picked yesterday. It made my heart feel strange to look at this picture – and to look at the figure of a bird, in some hard clay, on a table and see it so like our birds. Everywhere there were books and writings, many in tongues that I could not read. The god who lived there must have been a wise god and full of knowledge. I felt I had a right there, as I sought knowledge also.

Nevertheless, it was strange. There was a washing-place but no water – perhaps the gods washed in air. There was a cooking-place but no wood, and though there was a machine to cook food, there was no place to put fire in it. Nor were there candles or lamps – there were things that looked like lamps but they had neither oil nor wick. All these things were magic, but I touched them and lived – the magic had gone out of them. Let me tell one thing to show. In the washing-place, a thing said 'Hot' but it was not hot to the touch – another thing said 'Cold' but it was not cold. This must have been a strong magic but the magic was gone. I do not understand – they had ways – I wish that I knew.

It was close and dry and dusty in the house of the gods. I have said the magic was gone but that is not true – it had gone from the magic things but it had not gone from the place. I felt the spirits about me, weighing upon me. Nor had I ever slept in a Dead Place before – and yet, tonight, I must sleep there. When I thought of it, my tongue felt dry in my throat, in spite of my wish for knowledge. Almost I would have gone down again and faced the dogs, but I did not.

I had not gone through all the rooms when the darkness fell. When it fell, I went back to the big room looking over the city and made fire. There was a place to make fire and a box with wood in it, though I do not think they cooked there. I wrapped myself in a floor-covering and slept in front of the fire – I was very tired.

Now I tell what is very strong magic. I woke in the midst of the night. When I woke, the fire had gone out and I was cold. It seemed to me that all around me there were whisperings and voices. I closed my eyes to shut them out. Some will say that I slept again, but I do not think that I slept. I could feel the spirits drawing my spirit out of my body as a fish is drawn on a line.

Why should I lie about it? I am a priest and the son of a priest. If there are spirits, as they say, in the small Dead Places near us, what spirits must there not be in that great Place of the Gods? And would not they wish to speak? After such long years? I know that I felt myself drawn as a fish is drawn on a line. I had stepped out of my body – I could see my body asleep in front of the cold fire, but it was not I. I was drawn to look out upon the city of the gods.

It should have been dark, for it was night, but it was not dark. Everywhere there were lights – lines of light – circles and blurs of light – ten thousand torches would not have been the same. The sky itself was alight – you could barely see the stars for the glow in the sky. I thought to myself 'This is strong magic' and trembled. There was a roaring in my ears like the rushing of rivers. Then my eyes grew used to the light and my ears to the sound. I knew that I was seeing the city as it had been when the gods were alive.

That was a sight indeed – yes, that was a sight: I could not have seen it in the body – my body would have died. Everywhere went the gods, on foot and in chariots – there were gods beyond number and counting and their chariots blocked the streets. They had turned night to day for their pleasure – they did not sleep with the sun. The noise of their coming and going was the noise of the many waters. It was magic what they could do – it was magic what they did.

I looked out of another window – the great vines of their bridges were mended and god-roads went east and west. Restless, restless, were the gods and always in motion! They burrowed tunnels under rivers – they flew in the air. With unbelievable tools they did giant works – no part of the earth was safe from them, for, if they wished for a thing, they summoned it from the other side of the world. And always, as they labored and rested, as they feasted and made love, there was a drum in their ears – the pulse of the giant city, beating and beating like a man's heart.

Were they happy? What is happiness to the gods? They were great, they were mighty, they were wonderful and terrible. As I looked upon them and their magic, I felt like a child – but a little more, it seemed to me, and they would pull down the moon from the sky. I saw them with wisdom beyond wisdom and knowledge beyond knowledge. And yet not all they did was well done – even I could see that – and yet their wisdom could not but grow until all was peace.

Then I saw their fate come upon them and that was terrible past speech. It came upon them as they walked the streets of their city. I have been in the fights with the Forest People – I have seen men die. But this was not like that. When gods war with gods, they use weapons we do not know. It was fire falling out of the sky and a mist that poisoned. It was the time of the Great Burning and the Destruction. They ran about like ants in the streets of their city – poor gods, poor gods! Then the towers began to fall. A few escaped – yes, a few. The legends tell it. But, even after the city had become a Dead Place, for many years the poison was still in the ground. I saw it happen, I saw the last of them die. It was darkness over the broken city and I wept.

All this, I saw. I saw it as I have told it, though not in the body. When I woke in the morning, I was hungry, but I did not think first of my hunger for my heart was perplexed and confused. I knew the reason for the Dead Places but I did not see why it had happened. It seemed to me it should not have happened, with all the magic they had. I went through the house looking for an answer. There was so much in the house I could not understand – and yet I am a priest and the son of a priest. It was like being on one side of the great river, at night, with no light to show the way.

Then I saw the dead god. He was sitting in his chair, by the window, in a room I had not entered before and, for the first moment, I thought that he was alive. Then I saw the skin on the back of his hand – it was like dry leather. The room was shut, hot and dry – no doubt that had kept him as he was. At first I was afraid to approach him – then the fear left me. He was sitting looking out over the city – he was dressed in the clothes of the gods. His age was neither young nor old – I could not tell his age. But there was wisdom in his face and great sadness. You could see that he would have not run away. He had sat at his window, watching his city die – then he himself had died. But it is better to lose one's life than one's spirit – and you could see from the face that his spirit had not been lost. I knew, that, if I touched him, he would fall into dust – and yet, there was something unconquered in the face.

* * *

That is all of my story, for then I knew he was a man – I knew then that they had been men, neither gods nor demons. It is a great knowledge, hard to tell and believe. They were men – they went a dark road, but they were men. I had no fear after that – I had no fear going home, though twice I fought off the dogs and once I was hunted for two days by the Forest People. When I saw my father again, I prayed and was purified. He touched my lips and my breast, he said, "You went away a boy. You come back a man and a priest." I said, "Father, they were men! I have been in the Place of the Gods and seen it! Now slay me, if it is the law – but still I know they were men."

He looked at me out of both eyes. He said, "The law is not always the same shape – you have done what you have done. I could not have done it my time, but you come after me. Tell!"

I told and he listened. After that, I wished to tell all the people but he showed me otherwise. He said, "Truth is a hard deer to hunt. If you eat too much truth at once, you may die of the truth. It was not idly that our fathers forbade the Dead Places." He was right – it is better the truth should come little by little. I have learned that, being a priest. Perhaps, in the old days, they ate knowledge too fast.

Nevertheless, we make a beginning. It is not for the metal alone we go to the Dead Places now – there are the books and the writings. They are hard to learn. And the magic tools are broken – but we can look at them and wonder. At least, we make a beginning. And, when I am chief priest we shall go beyond the great river. We shall go to the Place of the Gods – the place newyork – not one man but a company. We shall look for the images of the gods and find the god ASHING and the others – the gods Lincoln and Biltmore and Moses. But they were men who built the city, not gods or demons. They were men. I remember the dead man's face. They were men who were here before us. We must build again.

Goslings
Chapters IX–XV
J.D. Beresford

[Publisher's Note: At this point in the story a great plague is spreading across the world, and has now made its way to London.]

Chapter IX
The Devolution of George Gosling

THE PROGRESS of the plague through London and the world in general was marked, in the earlier stages, by much the same developments as are reported of the plague of 1665. The closed houses, the burial pits, the deserted streets, the outbreaks of every kind of excess, the various symptoms of fear, cowardice, fortitude and courage, evidenced little change in the average of humanity between the seventeenth and the twentieth centuries. The most notable difference during these earlier stages was in the enormously increased rapidity with which the population of London was reduced to starvation point. Even before the plague had reached England, want had become general, so general, indeed, as to have demonstrated very clearly the truth of the great economist's contention that England could not exist for three months with closed doors.

The coming of the plague threw London on to its own very limited resources. That vast city, which produced nothing but the tokens of wealth, and added nothing to the essentials that support life, was instantly reduced to the state of Paris in the winter of 1870–71; with the difference, however, that London's population could be decreased rapidly by emigration, and was, also, even more rapidly decreased by pestilence. Yet there was a large section of the population which clung with blind obstinacy to the only life it knew how to live.

There was, for instance, George Gosling, more fortunate in many respects than the average citizen, who clung desperately to his house in Wisteria Grove until forced out of it by the lack of water.

On the ninth day after the first coming of the plague to London – it appeared simultaneously in a dozen places and spread with fearful rapidity – Gosling broke one of the great laws he had hitherto observed with such admirable prudence. The offices and warehouse in Barbican had been shut up (temporarily, it was supposed), and the partners had disappeared from London. But Gosling had a duplicate set of keys, and, inspired by the urgency of his family's need, he determined to dare a journey into the City in order to *borrow* (he laid great stress on the word) a few necessaries of life from the well-stored warehouse of his firm.

In this scheme, planned with some shrewdness, he co-operated with a friend, a fellow-sidesman at the Church of St. John the Evangelist. This friend was a coal merchant, and thus fortunately circumstanced in the possession of wagons and horses.

These two arranged the details of their borrowing expedition between them. Economically, it was a deal on the lines of the revived methods of exchange and barter. Gosling was willing to exchange certain advantages of knowledge and possession for the hire of wagons and horses. It was decided, for obvious reasons, to admit no other conspirator into the plot, and Boost, the coal merchant, drove one cart and Gosling drove the other. Perhaps it should rather be said that he led the other, for, after a preliminary trial, he decided that he was safer at the horses' heads than behind their tails.

The raid was conducted with perfect success. Boost had a head for essentials. The invaluable loads of tinned meats, fruits and vegetables were screened by tarpaulins from the possibly too envious eyes of hungry passers-by – quite a number of vagrants were to be seen in the streets on that day – and Boost and Gosling, disguised in coal-begrimed garments, made the return journey lugubriously calling, "Plague, plague," the cry of the drivers of the funeral carts which had even then become necessary. Their only checks were the various applications they received for the cartage of corpses; applications easily put on one side by pointing to the piled-up carts – they had spent six laborious hours in packing them. "No room; no room," they cried, and on that day the applicants who accosted Boost and Gosling were not the only ones who had to wait for the disposal of their dead.

Gosling arrived at Wisteria Grove, hot and outwardly jubilant, albeit with a horrible fear lurking in his mind that he had been in dangerous proximity to those tendered additions to his load. His booty was stored in one of the downstairs rooms – with the assistance of Mrs. Gosling and the two girls they managed the unpacking without interruption in two hours and a half – and then, with boarded windows and locked doors, the Goslings sat down to await the passing of horror.

Boost died of the plague forty-eight hours after the great adventure, but as he had a wife and four daughters his plunder was not wasted.

* * *

For nearly a fortnight after the raid the Goslings lay snug in their little house in Wisteria Grove, for they, in company with the majority of English people at this time, had not yet fully appreciated the fact that women were almost immune from infection. In all, not more than eight per cent of the whole female population was attacked, and of this proportion the mortality was almost exclusively among women over fifty years of age. When the first faint rumours of the plague had come to Europe, this curious, almost unprecedented, immunity of women had been given considerable prominence. It had made good copy, theories on the subject had appeared, and the point had aroused more interest than that of the mortality among males – infectious diseases were commonplace enough; this new phase had a certain novelty and piquancy. But the threat of European infection had overwhelmed the interest in the odd predilection of the unknown bacterium, and the more vital question had thrown this peculiarity into the background. Thus the Goslings and most other women feared attack no less than their husbands, brothers and sons, and found justification for their fears in the undoubted fact that women had died of the plague.

The Goslings had always jogged along amiably enough; their home life would have passed muster as a tolerably happy one. The head of the family was out of the house from 8.15 a.m. to 7.15 p.m. five days of the week, and it was only occasionally in the evening of some long wet Sunday that there was any open bickering.

Now, confinement in that little house, aggravated by fear and by the absence of any interest or diversion coming from outside, showed the family to one another in new aspects. Before two days had passed the air was tense with the suppressed irritation of these four people, held together by scarcely any tie other than that of a conventional affection.

By the third day the air was so heavily charged that some explosion was inevitable. It came early in the morning.

Gosling had run out of tobacco, and he thought in the circumstances that it would be wiser to send Blanche or Millie than to go himself. So, with an air of exaggerated carelessness, he said:

"Look here, Millie, my gel, I wish you'd just run out and see if you can get me any terbaccer."

"Not me," replied Millie, with decision.

"And why not?" asked Gosling.

Millie shrugged her shoulders, and called her sister, who was in the passage. "I say, B., father wants us to go out shopping for him. Are you on?"

Blanche, duster in hand, appeared at the doorway.

"Why doesn't he go himself?" she asked.

"Because," replied her father, getting very red, and speaking with elaborate care, "men's subject to the infection and women is not."

"That's all my eye," returned Millie. "Lots of women have got it."

"It's well known," said Gosling, still keeping himself in hand, "a matter of common knowledge, that women is comparatively immune."

"Oh, that's a man's yarn, that is," said Blanche, "just to save themselves. We all know what men are – selfish brutes!"

"Are you going to fetch me that terbaccer or are you not?" shouted Mr. Gosling suddenly.

"No, we aren't," said Millie, defiantly. "It isn't safe for girls to go about the streets, let alone the risk of infection." She had heard her father shout before, and she was not, as yet, at all intimidated.

"Well, then, I say you are!" shouted her father. "Lazy, good-for-nothing creatures, the pair of you! 'Oose paid for everything you've eat or drunk or wore ever since you was born? An' now you won't even go an errand." Then, seeing the ready retort rising to his daughters' lips, he grew desperate, and, advancing a step towards them, he said savagely: "If you don't go, I'll find a way to make yer!"

This was a new aspect, and the two girls were a little frightened. Natural instinct prompted them to scream for their mother.

She had been listening at the top of the stairs, and she answered the call for help with great promptitude.

"You ought to be ashamed of yourself, Gosling," she said, on a high note. "The streets isn't safe for gels, as you know well enough; and why should my gels risk their lives for the sake of your nasty, dirty, wasteful 'abit of smoking, I should like to know?"

Gosling's new-found courage was evaporating at the attack of this third enemy. He had been incensed against his daughters, but he had not yet overcome the habit of giving in to his wife, for the sake of peace. She had managed him very capably for a quarter of a century, but on the occasions when she had found it necessary to use what she called the "rough side of her tongue" she had demonstrated very clearly which of the two was master.

"I should have thought I might 'a been allowed a little terbaccer," he said, resentfully. "'Oo risked his life to lay in provisions, I should like to know? An' it's a matter o' common knowledge as women is immune from this plague."

"And Mrs. Carter, three doors off, carried out dead of it the day before yesterday!" remarked Mrs. Gosling, triumphantly.

"Oh, 'ere and there, a case or two," replied her husband. "But not one woman to a thousand men gets it, as every one knows."

"And how do you know I mightn't be the one?" asked Millie, bold now under her mother's protection.

For that morning, the matter remained in abeyance; but Gosling, muttering and grumbling, nursed his injury and meditated on the fact that his daughters had been afraid of him. Things were altered now. There was no convention to tie his hands. He would work himself into a protective passion and defy the three of them. Also, there was an unopened bottle of whisky in the sideboard.

Nevertheless, he would have put off the trial of his strength if he had had to seek an opportunity. He was, as yet, too civilized to take the initiative in cold blood.

The opportunity, however, soon presented itself in that house. The air had been little cleared by the morning's outbreak, and before evening the real explosion came. A mere trifle originated it – a warning from Gosling that their store of provisions would not last for ever, and a sharp retort from Millie to the effect that her father did not stint himself, followed by a reminder from Mrs. Gosling that the raid might be repeated.

"Oh! Yes, you'd be willing enough for *me* to die of the plague, I've no doubt!" broke out Gosling. "*I* can walk six mile to get you pervisions, but you can't go to the corner of the street for my terbaccer."

"Pervisions is necessary, terbaccer ain't," said Mrs. Gosling. She was not a clever woman. She judged this to be the right opportunity to keep her husband in his place, and relied implicitly on the quelling power of her tongue. Her intuitions were those of the woman who had lived all her life in a London suburb; they did not warn her that she was now dealing with a specimen of half-decivilized humanity.

"Oh! Ain't it?" shouted Gosling, getting to his feet. His face was purple, and his pale blue eyes were starting from his head. "I'll soon show you what's necessary and what ain't, and 'oose master in this 'ouse. And *I* say terbaccer is necessary, an' what's more, one o' you three's goin' to fetch it quick! D'ye 'ear – one – o' – you – three!"

This inclusion of Mrs. Gosling was, indeed, to declare war.

Millie and Blanche screamed and backed, but their mother rose to the occasion. She did not reserve herself; she began on her top note; but Gosling did not allow her to finish. He strode over to her and shook her by the shoulders, shouting to drown her strident recriminations. "'Old your tongue! 'Old your tongue!" he bawled, and shook her with increasing violence. He was feeling his power, and when his wife crumpled up and fell to the floor in shrieking hysterics, he still strode on to victory. Taking the cowed and terrified Millie by the arm, he dragged her along the passage, unlocked and opened the front door and pushed her out into the street. "And don't you come back without my terbaccer!" he shouted.

"How much?" quavered the shrinking Millie.

"'Alf-a-crown's worth," replied Gosling fiercely, and tossed the coin down on the little tiled walk that led up to the front door.

After Millie had gone he stood at the door for a moment, thankful for the coolness of the air on his heated face. "I got to keep this up," he murmured to himself, with his first thought of wavering. Behind him he heard the sound of uncontrolled weeping and little cries of the "first time in twenty-four years" and "what the neighbours'll think, I *don't* know."

"Neighbours," muttered Gosling, contemptuously, "there aren't any neighbours – not to count."

A distant sound of slow wheels caught his ear. He listened attentively, and there came to him the remote monotonous chant of a dull voice crying: "Plague! Plague!"

He stepped in quickly and closed the door.

* * *

Millie found the Kilburn High Road deserted. No traffic of any kind was to be seen in the street, and the rare foot-passengers, chiefly women, had all a furtive air. Starvation had driven them out to raid. No easy matter, as Millie soon found, for all shutters were down, and in many cases shop-fronts were additionally protected by great sheets of strong hoarding.

Millie, recovering from her fright, was growing resentful. Her little conventional mind was greatly occupied by the fact that she was out in the High Road wearing house-shoes without heels, in an old print dress, and with no hat to hide the carelessness of her hair-dressing. At the corner of Wisteria Grove she stopped and tried to remedy this last defect; she had red hair, abundant and difficult to control.

The sight of the deserted High Road did not inspire her with self-confidence; she still feared the possibility of meeting some one who might recognize her. How could one account for one's presence in a London thoroughfare at seven o'clock on a bright May evening in such attire? Certainly not by telling the truth.

The air was wonderfully clear. Coal was becoming very scarce, and few fires had been lighted that day to belch forth their burden of greasy filth into the atmosphere. The sun was sinking, and Millie instinctively clung to the shadow of the pavement on the west side of the road. She, too, slunk along with the evasive air that was common to the few other pedestrians, the majority of them on this same shadowed pavement. That warm, radiant light on the houses opposite seemed to hold some horror for them.

So preoccupied was Millie with her resentment that she wandered for two or three hundred yards up the road without any distinct idea of what she was seeking. When realization of the futility of her search came to her, she stopped in the shadow of a doorway. "What *is* the good of going on?" she argued. "All the shops are shut up." But the thought of her father in his new aspect of muscular tyrant intimidated her. She dared not return without accomplishing her errand. "I'll have another look, anyway," she said; and then: "Who'd have thought he was such a brute?" She rubbed the bruise on her arm; her mouth was twisted into an ugly expression of spiteful resentment. Her thoughts were busy with plans of revenge even as she turned to prosecute her search for the tyrant's tobacco.

Here and there shops had been forcibly, burglariously entered, plate-glass windows smashed, and interiors cleared of everything eatable; the debris showed plainly enough that these rifled shops had all belonged to grocers or provision merchants. Into each of these ruins Millie stared curiously, hoping foolishly that she might find what she sought. She ventured into one and carried away a box of soap – they were running short of soap at home. A sense of moving among accessible riches stirred within her, a desire for further pillage.

She came at last to a shop where the shutters were still intact, but the door hung drunkenly on one hinge. A little fearfully she peered in and discovered that fortune had been kind to her. The shop had belonged to a tobacconist, and the contents were almost untouched – there had been more crying needs to satisfy in the households of raiders than the desire for tobacco.

It was very dark inside, and for some seconds Millie stared into what seemed absolute blackness, but as her eyes became accustomed to the gloom, she saw the interior begin to take outline, and when she moved a couple of steps into the place and allowed more light to come in through the doorway, various tins, boxes and packets in the shelves behind the counter were faintly distinguishable.

Once inside, the spirit of plunder took hold of her, and she began to take down boxes of cigars and cigarettes and packets of tobacco, piling them up in a heap on the counter. But she had no basket in which to carry the accumulation she was making, and she was feeling under the counter for some box into which to put her haul, when the shadows round her deepened again into almost absolute darkness. Cautiously she peered up over the counter and saw the silhouette of a woman standing in the doorway.

For ten breathless seconds Millie hung motionless, her eyes fixed on the apparition. She was very civilized still, and she was suddenly conscious of committing a crime. She feared horribly lest the figure in the doorway might discover Millicent Gosling stealing tobacco. But the intruder, after recognizing the nature of the shop's contents, moved away with a sigh. Millie heard her dragging footsteps shuffle past the window.

That scare decided her movements. She hastily looped up the front of her skirt, bundled into it as much plunder as she could conveniently carry, and made her way out into the street again.

She was nearly at the corner of Wisteria Grove before she was molested, and then an elderly woman came suddenly out of a doorway and laid a hand on Millie's arm.

"Whacher got?" asked the woman savagely.

Millie, shrinking and terrified, displayed her plunder.

"Cigars," muttered the woman. "Whacher want with cigars?" She opened the boxes and stirred up the contents of Millie's improvised bundle in an eager search for something to eat. "Gawd's truth! Yer must be crazy, yer thievin' little slut!" she grumbled, and pushed the girl fiercely from her.

Millie made good her escape, dropping a box of cigars in her flight. Her one thought now was the fear of meeting a policeman. In three minutes she was beating fiercely on the door of the little house in Wisteria Grove, and, disregarding her father's exclamations of pleased surprise when he let her in, she tumbled in a heap on to the mat in the passage.

Gosling's first declaration of male superiority had been splendidly successful.

* * *

A few minutes after Millie's return, Mrs. Gosling, red-eyed and timidly vicious, interrupted her husband's perfect enjoyment of the long-desired cigar by the announcement: "The gas is off!"

Gosling got up, struck a match, and held it to the sitting-room burner. The match burned steadily. There was no pressure even of air in the pipes.

"Turned off at the meter!" snapped Gosling. "'Ere, lemme go an' see!" He spoke with the air of the superior male, strong in his comprehension of the mechanical artifices which so perplex the feminine mind. Mrs. Gosling sniffed, and stood aside to let him pass. She had already examined the meter.

"Well, we got lamps!" snarled Gosling when he returned. He had always preferred a lamp to read by in the evening.

"No oil," returned Mrs. Gosling, gloomily. She'd teach him to shake her!

Gosling meditated. His parochial mind was full of indignation. Vague thoughts of "getting some one into trouble for this" – even of that last, desperate act of coercion, writing to the papers about it – flitted through his mind. Plainly something must be done. "'Aven't you got any candles?" he asked.

"One or two. They won't last long," replied his studiously patient partner.

"Well, we'll 'ave to use them tonight and go to bed early," was Gosling's final judgment. His wife left the room with a shrug of forbearing contempt.

When she had gone, the head of the house went upstairs and peered out into the street. The sun had set, and an unprecedented mystery of darkness was falling over London. The globes of the tall electric standards, catching a last reflection from the fading sky, glimmered faintly, but were not illuminated from within by any fierce glare of violet light. Darkness and silence enfolded the great dim organism that sprawled its vast being over the earth. The spirit of mystery caught Gosling in its spell. "All dark," he murmured, "and quiet! Lord! how still it is!" Even in his own house there was silence. Downstairs, three injured, resentful women were talking in whispers.

Gosling, still sucking his cigar, stood entranced, peering into the darkness; he had ventured so far as to throw up the sash. "It's the stillness of death!" he muttered. Then he cocked his head on one side, for he caught the sound of distant shouting. Somewhere in the Kilburn Road another raid was in progress.

"No light," murmured Gosling, "and no fire!" An immediate association suggested itself. "By gosh! And no *water*!" he added. For some seconds he contemplated with fearful awe the failure of the great essential of life.

In the cistern room he was reassured by the sound of a delicious trickle from the ball-cock. "Still going," he said to himself; "but we'll 'ave to be careful. Surely they'll keep the water goin', though; whatever 'appens, they'd surely keep the water on?"

* * *

Nothing but the failure of the water could have driven them from Wisteria Grove. Half-a-dozen times every day Gosling would climb up to the top of the house to reassure himself. And at last came the day when a dreadful silence reigned under the slates, when no delicious tinkle of water gave promise of maintained security from water famine.

"It'll come on again at night," said Gosling to himself. "We'll 'ave to be careful, that's all." He went downstairs and issued orders that no more water was to be drawn that day.

"Well, we must wash up the breakfast things," was his wife's reply.

"You mustn't wash up nothing," said Gosling, "not one blessed thing. It's better to go dirty than die o' thirst. Hevery drop o' the water in that cistern must be saved for drinkin'."

Mrs. Gosling noisily put down the kettle she was holding. "Oh! Very well, my lord!" she remarked, sarcastically. She looked at her two daughters with a twist of her mouth. There were only two sides in that house; the women were as yet united against the common foe.

When Gosling, fatuously convinced of his authority, had gone, his wife quietly filled the kettle and proceeded with her washing up.

"Your father thinks 'e knows everything these days," remarked the mother to her allies. There was much whispering for some time.

Gosling spent most of the day in the roof, but not until the afternoon did he realize that the cistern was slowly being emptied. His first thought was that one of the pipes leaked, his second that it was time to make a demonstration of force. He found a walking-stick in the hall....

But even when that precious half-cistern of water was only called upon to supply the needs of thirst, and the Goslings, sinking further into the degradation of savagedom, slunk furtive and filthy about the gloomy house, it became evident that a move must be made sooner or later. Two alternatives were presented: they might go north and east to the Lea, or south to the Thames.

Gosling chose the South. He knew Putney; he had been born there. He knew nothing of Clapton and its neighbourhood.

So one bright, clear day at the end of May, the Goslings set out on their great trek. The head of the house, driven desperate by fear of thirst, raided his late partner's coal sheds and found one living horse and several dead ones. The living horse was partly revived by water from an adjacent butt, and the next day it was harnessed to a coal cart and commandeered to convey the Goslings' provisions to Putney. It died half-a-mile short of their destination, but they were able, by the exercise of their united strength, to get the cart and its burden down to the river.

They found an empty house without difficulty, but they had an unpleasant half-hour in removing what remained of one of the previous occupants. Gosling hoped it was not a case of plague. As the body was that of a woman, and terribly emaciated, there were some grounds for his optimism.

Gosling was in a state of some bewilderment. When water had been fetched in buckets from the river, and the three women had explored, criticized and sniffed over their new home somewhat in the manner of strange cats, the head of the house settled down to a cigar and a careful consideration of his perplexities.

In the first place, he wondered why those horses of Boost's had not been used for food; in the second, he wondered why he had not seen a single man during the whole of the long trek from Brondesbury to Putney. By degrees an unbelievable explanation presented itself: no men were left. He remembered that the few needy-looking women he had seen had looked at him curiously; in retrospect he fancied their regard had had some quality of amazement. Gosling scratched the bristles of his ten-days'-old beard and smoked thoughtfully. He almost regretted that he had stared so fiercely and threateningly at every chance woman they had seen; he might have got some news. But the whole journey had been conducted in a spirit of fear; they had been defending their food, their lives; they had been primitive creatures ready to fight desperately at the smallest provocation.

"No man left," said Gosling to himself, and was not convinced. If that indeed were the solution of his perplexity, he was faced with an awful corollary; his own time would come. He thought of Barbican, E.C., of Flack, of Messrs Barker and Prince, of the office staff, and the office itself. He had not been able to rid his mind of the idea that in a few weeks he would be back in the City again. He had several times rehearsed his surprise when he should be told of the depredations in the warehouse; he had wondered only yesterday if he dared go to the office in his beard.

But tonight the change of circumstance, the breaking up of old associations, was opening his eyes to new horizons. There might never be an office again for him to go to. If he survived – and he was distinctly hopeful on that score – he might be almost the only man left in London; there might not be more than a few thousand in the whole of England, in Europe....

For a time he dwelt on this fantastic vision. Who would do the work? What work would there be to do?

"Got to get food," murmured Gosling, and wondered vaguely how food was 'got' when there were no shops, no warehouses, no foreign agents. His mind turned chiefly to meat, since that had been his trade. "'Ave to rear sheep and cattle, I suppose," said Gosling. As an afterthought he added: "An' grow wheat."

He sighed heavily. He realized that he had no knowledge on the subject of rearing cattle and growing wheat; he also realized that he was craving for ordinary food again – milk, eggs, and fresh vegetables. He had a nasty-looking place on his leg which he rightly attributed to unwholesome diet.

* * *

After forty-eight hours' residence in the new house, Gosling began to pluck up his courage and to dare the perils of the streets. He was beginning to have faith in his luck, to believe that the plague had passed away and left him untouched.

And as day succeeded day he ventured further afield; he went in search of milk, eggs and vegetables, but he only found young nettles, which he brought home and helped to eat when they had been boiled over a wood fire. They were all glad to eat nettles, and were the better for them. Occasionally he met women on these excursions, and stayed to talk to them. Always they had the same tale to tell – their men were dead, and themselves dying of starvation.

One day at the beginning of June he went as far as Petersham, and there at the door of a farmhouse he saw a fine, tall young woman. She was such a contrast to the women he usually met on his expeditions that he paused and regarded her with curiosity.

"What do *you* want?" asked the young woman, suspiciously.

"I suppose you 'aven't any milk or butter or eggs to sell?" asked Gosling.

"Sell?" echoed the girl, contemptuously. "What 'ave you got to give us as is worth food?"

"Well, money," replied Gosling.

"Money!" came the echo again. "What's the good of money when there's nothing to buy with it? I wouldn't sell you eggs at a pound apiece."

Gosling scratched his beard – it looked quite like a beard by this time. "Rum go, ain't it?" he asked, and smiled.

His new acquaintance looked him up and down, and then smiled in return, "You're right," she said. "You're the first man I've seen since father died, a month back."

"'Oo's livin' with you?" asked Gosling, pointing to the house.

"Mother and sister, that's all."

"'Ard work for you to get a livin', I suppose?"

"So, so. We're used to farm-work. The trouble's to keep the other women off."

"Ah!" replied Gosling reflectively, and the two looked at one another again.

"You 'ungry?" asked the girl.

"Not to speak of," replied Gosling. "But I'm fair pinin' for a change o' diet. Been livin' on tinned things for five weeks or more."

"Come in and have an egg," said the girl.

"Thank you," said Gosling, "I will, with pleasure."

They grew friendly over that meal – two eggs and a glass of milk. He ate the eggs with butter, but there was no bread. It seemed that the young woman's mother and sister were at work on the farm, but that one of them had always to stay at home and keep guard.

They discussed the great change that had come over England, and wondered what would be the end of it; and after a little time, Gosling began to look at the girl with a new expression in his pale blue eyes.

"Ah! Hevrything's changed," he said. "Nothin' won't be the same any more, as far as we can see. There's no neighbours now, f'rinstance, and no talk of what's going on – or anythin'."

The girl looked at him thoughtfully. "What we miss is some man to look after the place," she said. "We're robbed terrible."

Gosling had not meant to go as far as that. He was not unprepared for a pleasant flirtation, now that there were no neighbours to report him at home, but the idea that he could ever separate himself permanently from his family had not occurred to him.

"Yes," he said, "you want a man about these days."

"Ever done any farm work?" asked the girl.

Gosling shook his head.

"Well, you'd soon learn," she went on.

"I must think it over," said Gosling suddenly. "Shall you be 'ere tomorrow?"

"One of us will," said the girl.

"Ah! But shall *you*?"

"Why me?"

"Well, I've took a fancy to you."

"Very kind of you, I'm sure," said the girl, and laughed.

Gosling kissed her before he left.

* * *

He returned the next afternoon and helped to cut and stack sainfoin, and afterwards he watched the young woman milk the cows. It was so late by the time everything was finished that he was persuaded to stay the night.

In the new Putney house three women wondered what had happened to 'father.' They grew increasingly anxious for some days, and even tried in a feeble way to search for him. By the end of the week they accepted the theory that he too had died of the plague.

They never saw him again.

Chapter X
Exodus

IN WEST HAMPSTEAD a Jewess, who had once been fat, looked out of the windows of her gaudy house. She was partly dressed in a garish silk negligé. Her face was exceedingly dirty, but the limp, pallid flesh was revealed in those places where she had wiped away her abundant tears. Her body was bruised and stiff, for in a recent raid on a house suspected of containing provisions she had been hardly used by her sister women. She had made the mistake of going out too well dressed; she had imagined that expensive clothes would command respect....

As she looked out she wept again, bewailing her misery. From her earliest youth she had been pampered and spoilt. She had learnt that marriage was her sole object in life, and she had sold herself at a very respectable price. She had received the applause and favour of her family for marrying the man she had chosen as most likely to provide her with the luxury which she regarded as her birth-right.

Two days ago she had cooked and eaten the absurdly expensive but diminutive dog upon which she had lavished the only love of which she had been capable. She had wept continuously as she ate her idol, but for the first time she had regretted his littleness.

Hunger and thirst were driving her out of the house of which she had been so vain; the primitive pains were awakening in her primitive instincts that had never stirred before. From her window she could see naught but endless streets of brick, stone and asphalt, but beyond that dry, hot, wilderness she knew there were fields – she had seen them out of the corner of her eye when she had motored to Brighton. Fields had never been associated in her mind with food until the strange new stirring of that unsuspected instinct. Food for her meant shops. One went to shops and bought food and bought the best at the lowest price possible. With all her pride of position, she had never hesitated to haggle with shopkeepers. And when the first pinch had come, when her husband had selfishly died of the plague, and her household had deserted her, it was to the shops she had gone, autocratically demanding her rights. She had learned by experience now that she had no longer any rights.

She dressed herself in her least-conspicuous clothes, dabbed her face with powder to cover some of the dirt – there was no water, and in any case she did not feel inclined to wash – carefully stowed away all her money and the best of her jewels in a small leather bag, and set out to find the country where food grew out of the ground.

Instinct set her face to the north. She took the road towards Hendon....

* * *

In every quarter of London, in every great town and city throughout Europe, women were setting their faces towards the country.

By the autumn London was empty. The fallen leaves in park squares and suburban streets were swept into corners by the wind, and when the rain came the leaves clung together and rotted, and so continued the long routine of decay and birth.

When spring came again, Nature returned with delicate, strong hands to claim her own. For hundreds of years she had been defied in the heart of this great, hard, stone place. Her little tentative efforts had been rudely repulsed, no tender thread of grass had been allowed to flourish for an hour under the feet of the crushing multitude. Yet she had fought with a steady persistence that never relaxed a moment's effort. Whenever men had given her a moment's opportunity, even in the very heart of that city of burning struggle, she had covered the loathed sterility with grass and flowers, dandelions, charlock, grounsel and other life that men call weeds.

Now, when her full opportunity came, she set to work in her slow, patient way to wreck and cover the defilement of earth. Her winds swept dust into every corner, and her rain turned it into a shallow bed of soil, ready to receive and nurture the tiny seeds that sailed on little feathered wings, or were carried by bird and insect to some quiet refuge in which they might renew life, and, dying, add fertility to the mother who had brought them forth.

Nature came, also, with her hurricanes, her lightnings and her frosts, to rend and destroy. She stripped slates from roofs, thrust out gables and overturned solid walls. She came with fungi to undermine and with the seeds of trees to split asunder.

She asked for but a few hundred years of patient, continuous work in order to make of London once more a garden; where the nightingale might sing in Oxford Street and the children of a new race pluck sweet wild flowers over the site of the Bank of England....

* * *

The spirit of London had gone out of her, and her body was crumbling and rotting. There was no life in all that vast sprawl of bricks and mortar; the very dogs and cats, deserted by humanity, left her to seek their only food, to seek those other living things which were their natural quarry.

In her prime, London had been the chief city of the world. Men and women spoke of her as an entity, wrote of her as of a personality, loved her as a friend. This aggregate of streets and parks, this strange confusion of wealth and squalor, had stood to men and women for something definitely lovable. It was not her population they loved, not the polyglot crowd that swarmed in her streets, but she herself and all the beauty and intoxication of life she had gathered into her embrace.

Now she was dead. Whatever fine qualities she had possessed, whatever vices, had gone from her. She sprawled in all her naked ugliness, a huge corpse rotting among the hills, awaiting the slow burial which Nature was tediously preparing.

All those wonderful buildings, the great emporiums in the West End, the magnificent banks and insurance offices, museums and picture galleries, regarded as the storehouses of incalculable wealth, vast hotels, palatial private residences, the thundering railway termini, Government offices, Houses of Parliament, theatres, churches and cathedrals, all had become meaningless symbols. All had represented some activity, some ambition of man, and man had fled to the country for food, leaving behind the worthless tokens of wealth that had intrigued him for so many centuries.

Gold and silver grew tarnished in huge safes that none wished to rifle, banknotes became mildewed, damp and fungus crept into the museums and picture galleries, and in the whole of Great Britain there was none to grieve. Every living man and woman was back at the work of their ancestors, praying once more to Ceres or Demeter, working with bent back to produce the first essentials of life.

Each individual must produce until such time as there was once more a superfluity, until barns were filled and wealth re-created, until the strong had seized from the weak and demanded labour in return for the use of the stolen instrument, until civilization had sprung anew from the soil.

Meanwhile London was not a city of the dead, but a dead city.

Chapter XI
The Silent City

JULY CAME IN with temperate heat and occasional showers, ideal weather for the crops; for all the precious growths which must ripen before the famine could be stayed. The sudden stoppage of all imports, and the flight of the great urban population into the country, had demonstrated beyond all question the poverty of England's resources of food supply, and the demonstration was to prove of value although there was no economist left to theorize. England was once again an independent unit, and no longer a member of a great world-body. Indeed England was being subdivided. The unit of organization was shrinking with amazing rapidity. The necessity for concentration grew with every week that passed, the fluidity of the superfluous labour was being resolved by death from starvation.

The women who wandered from one farm to the next died by the way.

In the Putney house, Mrs. Gosling and her daughters were faced by the failure of their food supply. The older woman had little initiative. She was a true Londoner. Her training and all the circumstances of her life had narrowed her imaginative grasp till she was only able to comprehend one issue. And as yet her daughters, and more particularly Millie, were so influenced by their mother's thought that they, also, had shown little evidence of adaptability to the changed conditions.

"We shall 'ave to be careful," was Mrs. Gosling's first expression of the necessity for looking to the future. She had arranged the bulk of her stores neatly in one room on the second floor, and although a goodly array of tins still faced her she experienced a miserly shrinking from any diminishment of their numbers. Moreover, she had long been without such necessities as flour. Barker and Prince had not dealt in flour.

Returning from her daily inspection one morning in the second week of July, Mrs. Gosling decided that something must be done at once. Fear of the plague was almost dead, but fear of invasion by starving women had kept them all close prisoners. That house was a fortress.

"Look 'ere, gels," said Mrs. Gosling when she came downstairs. "Somethin' 'll 'ave to be done."

Blanche looked thoughtful. Her own mind had already begun to work on that great problem of their future. Millie, lazy and indifferent, shrugged her shoulders and replied: "All very well, mother, but what *can* we do?"

"Well, I been thinking as it's very likely as things ain't so bad in some places as they are just about 'ere," said Mrs. Gosling. "We got plenty o' money left, and it seems to me as two of us 'ad better go out and 'ave a look about, London way. One of us could look after the 'ouse easy enough, now. We 'aven't 'ardly seen a soul about the past fortnight."

The suggestion brought a gleam of hope to Blanche. She visualized the London she had known. It might be that in the heart of the town, business had begun again, that shops were open and people at work. It might be that she could find work there. She was longing for the sight and movement of life, after these two awful months of isolation.

"I'm on," she said briskly. "Me and Millie had better go, mother, we can walk farther. You can lock up after us and you needn't open the door to anyone. Are you on, Mill?"

"We must make ourselves look a bit more decent first," said Millie, glancing at the mirror over the mantelpiece.

"Well, of course," returned Blanche, "we brought one box of clothes with us."

They spent some minutes in discussing the resources of their wardrobe.

"Come to the worst we could fetch some more things from Wisteria. I don't suppose anyone has touched 'em," suggested Blanche.

At the mention of the house in Wisteria Grove, Mrs. Gosling sighed noticeably. She was by no means satisfied with the place at Putney, and she could not rid herself of the idea that there must be accessible gas and water in Kilburn, as there had always been.

"Well, you might go up there one day and 'ave a look at the place," she put in. "It's quite likely they've got things goin' again up there."

In less than an hour Blanche and Millie had made themselves presentable. Life had begun to stir again in humanity. The atmosphere of horror which the plague had brought was being lifted. It was as if the dead germs had filled the air with an invisible, impalpable dust, that had exercised a strange power of depression. The spirit of death had hung over the whole world and paralyzed all activity. Now the dust was dispersing. The spirit was withdrawing to the unknown deeps from which it had come.

"It is nice to feel decent again," said Blanche. She lifted her head and threw back her shoulders.

Millie was preening herself before the glass.

"Well, I'm sure you 'ave made yourselves look smart," said their mother with a touch of pride. "They were good girls," she reflected, "if there had been more than a bit of temper shown lately. But, then, who could have helped themselves? It had been a terrible time."

The July sun was shining brilliantly as the two young women, presentable enough to attend morning service at the Church of St John the Evangelist, Kilburn, set out to exhibit their charms and to buy food in the dead city.

* * *

They crossed Putney Bridge and made their way towards Hammersmith.

The air was miraculously clear. The detail of the streets was so sharp and bright that it was as if they saw with wonderfully renewed and sensitive eyes. The phenomenon produced a sense of exhilaration. They were conscious of quickened emotion, of a sensation of physical well-being.

"Isn't it *clean?*" said Blanche.

"H'm! Funny!" returned Millie. "Like those photographs of foreign places."

Under their feet was an accumulation of sharp, dry dust, detritus of stone, asphalt and steel. In corners where the fugitive rubbish had found refuge from the driving wind, the dust had accumulated in flat mounds, broken by scraps of paper or the torn flag of some rain-soaked poster that gave an untidy air of human refuse. Across the open way of certain roads the dust lay in a waved pattern of nearly parallel lines, like the ridged sand of the foreshore.

For some time they kept to the pavements from force of habit.

"I say, Mill, don't you feel adventurous?" asked Blanche.

Millie looked dissatisfied. "It's so lonely, B.," was her expression of feeling.

"Never had London all to myself before," said Blanche.

Near Hammersmith Broadway they saw a tram standing on the rails. Its thin tentacle still clung to the overhead wire that had once given it life, as if it waited there patiently hoping for a renewal of the exhilarating current.

Almost unconsciously Blanche and Millie quickened their pace. Perhaps this was the outermost dying ripple of life, the furthest outpost of the new activity that was springing up in central London.

But the tram was guarded by something that in the hot, still air seemed to surround it with an almost visible mist.

"Eugh!" ejaculated Millie and shrank back. "Don't go, Blanche. It's awful!"

Blanche's hand also had leapt to her face, but she took a few steps forward and peered into the sunlit case of steel and glass. She saw a heap of clothes about the framework of a grotesquely jointed scarecrow, and the gleam of something round, smooth and white.

She screamed faintly, and a filthy dog crept, with a thin yelp, from under the seat and came to the door of the tram. For a moment it stood there with an air that was half placatory, wrinkling its nose and feebly raising a stump of propitiatory tail, then, with another protesting yelp, it crept back, furtive and ashamed, to its unlawful meat.

The two girls, handkerchief to nose, hurried by breathless, with bent heads. A little past Hammersmith Broadway they had their first sight of human life. Two gaunt faces looked out at them from an upper window. Blanche waved her hand, but the women in the house, half-wondering, half-fearful, at the strange sight of these two fancifully dressed girls, shook their heads and drew back. Doubtless there was some secret hoard of food in that house and the inmates feared the demands of charity.

"Well, we aren't quite the last, anyway," commented Blanche.

"What were they afraid of?" asked Millie.

"Thought we wanted to cadge, I expect," suggested Blanche.

"Mean things," was her sister's comment.

"Well! *We* weren't so over-anxious to have visitors," Blanche reminded her.

"*We* didn't want their beastly food," complained the affronted Millie.

The shops in Hammersmith did not offer much inducement to exploration. Some were still closely shuttered, others presented goods that offered no temptation, such as hardware; but the majority had already been pillaged and devastated. Most of that work had been done in the early days of the plague when panic had reigned, and many men were left to lead the raids on the preserves of food.

Only one great line of shuttered fronts induced the two girls to pause.

"No need to go to Wisteria for clothes," suggested Blanche.

"How could we get in?" asked Millie.

"Oh! Get in some way easy enough."

"It's stealing," said Millie, and thought of her raid on the Kilburn tobacconist's.

"You can't steal from dead people," explained Blanche, "besides, who'll have the things if we don't?"

"I suppose it'd be all right," hesitated Millie, obviously tempted.

"Well, of course," returned Blanche and paused. "I say, Mill," she burst out suddenly. "There's all the West-end to choose from. Come on!"

For a time they walked more quickly.

In Kensington High Street they had an adventure. They saw a woman decked in gorgeous silks, strung and studded with jewels from head to foot. She walked with a slow and flaunting step, gesticulating, and talking. Every now and again she would pause and draw herself up with an affectation of immense dignity, finger the ropes of jewels at her breast, and make a slow gesture with her hands.

"She's mad," whispered Blanche, and the two girls, terrified and trembling, hastily took refuge in a great square cave full of litter and refuse that had once been a grocer's shop.

The woman passed their hiding-place in her stately progress westward without giving any sign that she was conscious of their presence. When she was nearly opposite to them she made one of her stately pauses. "Queen of all the Earth," they heard her say, "Queen and Empress. Queen of the Earth." Her hand went up to her head and touched a strange collection of jewels pinned in her hair, of tiaras and brooches that flashed brighter than the high lights of the brilliant sun. One carelessly fastened brooch fell and she pushed it aside with her foot. "You understand," she said in her high, wavering voice, "you understand, Queen and Empress, Queen of the Earth."

They heard the refrain of her gratified ambition repeated as she moved slowly away.

A long submerged memory rose to the threshold of Millie's mind. "Thieving slut," she murmured.

* * *

As they came nearer to representative London the signs of deserted traffic were more numerous. By the Albert Memorial they saw an overturned motor-bus which had smashed into the park railings, and a little further on were two more buses, one standing decently at the curb, the other sprawling across the middle of the road. The wheels of both were axle deep in the dust which had blown against them, and out of the dust a few weak threads of grass were sprouting. There were other vehicles, too, cabs, lorries and carts: not a great number altogether, but even the fifty or so which the girls saw between Kensington and Knightsbridge offered sufficient testimony to the awful rapidity with which the plague had spread. For it seems probable that in the majority of cases the drivers of these deserted vehicles must have been attacked by the first agonizing pains at the base of the skull while they were actually employed in driving their machines. There were few skeletons to be seen. The lull which intervened between the first unmistakable symptoms of the plague and the oncoming of the paralysis had given men time to obey their instinct to die in seclusion, the old instinct so little altered by civilization. Those vestiges of humanity which remained had, for the most part, been cleansed by the processes of Nature, but twice the girls disturbed a horrible cloud of blue flies which rose with an angry buzzing so loud that the girls screamed and ran, leaving the scavengers to swoop eagerly back upon their carrion. Doubtless the thing in the Hammersmith tram had been the body of a woman, recently-dead from starvation. Even from the houses there was now little exhalation.

In Knightsbridge, a little past the top of Sloane Street, Blanche and Millie came to a shop which diverted them from their exploration for a time. Most of the huge rolling shutters had been pulled down and secured, but one had stopped half way, and, beyond, the great plate-glass windows were uncovered. One of ten million tragedies had descended swiftly to interrupt the closing of that immense place, and some combination of circumstances had followed to prevent the completion of the work. The imaginative might stop to speculate on the mystery of that half-closed shutter; the two Goslings stopped to admire the wonders behind the glass.

For a time the desolation and silence of London were forgotten. In imagination Blanche and Millie were once again units in the vast crowd of antagonists striving valiantly to win some prize in the great competition between the boast of wealth and the pathetic endeavour of make-believe.

They stayed to gaze at the 'creations' behind the windows, at dummies draped in costly fabrics such as they had only dreamed of wearing. The silks, satins and velvets were whitened now with the thin snow of dust that had fallen upon them, but to Blanche and Millie they appeared still as wonders of beauty.

For a minute or two they criticized the models. They spoke at first in low voices, for the deep stillness of London held them in unconscious awe, but as they became lost in the fascination of their subject they forgot their fear. And then they looked at one another a little guiltily.

"No harm in seeing if the door's locked, anyway," said Blanche.

Millie looked over her shoulder and saw no movement in the frozen streets, save the sweep of one exploring swallow. Even the sparrows had deserted the streets. She did not reply in words, but signified her agreement of thought by a movement towards the entrance.

The swing doors were not fastened, and they entered stealthily.

They began with the touch of appraising fingers, wandering from room to room. But most of the rooms on the ground floor were darkened by the drawn shutters, and no glow of light came in response to the clicking of the electric switches that they experimented with with persistent futility. So they adventured into the clearly lit rooms upstairs and experienced a fallacious sense of security in the knowledge that they were on the floor above the street.

Fingering gave place to still closer inspection. They lifted the models from the stands and shook them out. They held up gorgeous robes in front of their own suburban dresses and admired each other and themselves in the numerous cheval glasses.

"Oh! Bother!" exclaimed Blanche at last, "I'm going to try on."

"Oh! B." expostulated the more timid Millie.

"Well! Why to goodness not?" asked her elder sister. "Who's to be any the wiser?"

"Seems wrong, somehow," replied Millie, unable to shake off the conventions which had so long served her as conscience.

"Well, I am," said Blanche, and retired into a little side room to divest herself of her own dress. She had always shared a bedroom with her sister, and they observed few modesties before each other, but Blanche was mentally incapable of changing her dress in the broad avenues of that extensive show-room. It is true that the tall casement windows were wide open and the place was completely overlooked by the massive buildings opposite, but even if the windows had been screened she would not have changed her skirt in the publicity of that open place, though every human being in the world were dead.

When she emerged from her dressing-room she was transformed indeed. She went over to her still hesitating sister.

"Do me up, Mill," she said.

Blanche had chosen well; the fine cloth walking dress admirably fitted her well-developed young figure. When she had discarded her hat and touched up her hair before the glass, only her boots and her hands remained to spoil the disguise. Well gloved and well shod, she might have passed down the Bond Street of the old London, and few women and no man would have known that she had not sprung from the ruling classes.

She posed. She stepped back from the mirror and half-unconsciously fell to imitating the manners of the revered aristocracy she had respectfully studied from a distance.

In a few minutes she was joined by Millie, also arrayed in peacock's feathers and anxious to be "fastened."

Their excitement increased. Walking dresses gave place to evening gowns. They lost their sense of fear and ran into other departments searching for long white gloves to hide the disfigurements of household work. They paraded and bowed to each other. The climax came when they discovered a Court dress, immensely trained, and embroidered with gold thread, laid by with evidences of tenderest care in endless wrappings of tissue paper. Surely the dress of some elegant young duchess!

For a moment they wrangled, but Blanche triumphed. "You shall have it afterwards," she said, as she ran to her dressing-room.

Millie followed in an elaborate gown of Indian silk; a somewhat sulky Millie, inclined to resent her duty of lady's maid. She dragged disrespectfully at the innumerable fastenings.

"My!" ejaculated Blanche when she could indulge herself in the glory of full examination before a cheval glass in the open show-room. She struggled with her train and when she had arranged it to her satisfaction, threw back her shoulders and lifted her chin haughtily.

"I ought to have some diamonds," she reflected.

"It drags round the hips," was Millie's criticism.

"You should say 'Your Majesty,'" corrected Blanche.

"Oh! A Queen, are you?" asked Millie.

"Rather –"

"Queen of all the Earth," sneered Millie.

Blanche's face suddenly fell. "I wonder if she began like this," she said, and a note of fear had come into her voice.

Millie's eyes reflected her sister's alarm.

"Oh! Let's get out of this, B.," she said, and began to tear at the neck of her Indian silk gown.

"I wanted diamonds, too," persisted Blanche.

"Oh! B., it *isn't* right," said Millie. "I said it wasn't right and you *would* come."

Silence descended upon them for a moment, and then both sisters suddenly screamed and ducked, putting up their hands to their heads.

"Goodness! What was that?" cried Blanche.

A swallow had swept in through the open window, had curved round in one swift movement, and shot out again into the sunlight.

"Only a bird of some sort," said Millie, but she was trembling and on the verge of hysterics. "Do let's get out, B."

After they had put on their own clothes once more they became aware that they were hungry.

"We *have* wasted a lot of time here," said Blanche as they made their way out.

She did not pause to wonder how many women had spent the best part of their lives in a precisely similar manner.

"And we ought to have been looking for food," she added.

"Come on," replied Millie. "That place has given me the creeps."

* * *

Growing rather tired and footsore they made their way to Piccadilly Circus, and so on to the Strand. Everywhere they found the same conditions: a few skeletons, a few deserted vehicles, young vegetation taking hold wherever a pinch of soil had found an abiding place, and over all a great silence. But food there was none that they were able to find, though it is probable that a careful investigation of cellars and underground places might have furnished some results. The more salient resources of London had been effectively pillaged so far as the West-end was concerned. They were too late.

In Trafalgar Square, Millie sat down and cried. Blanche made no attempt to comfort her, but sat wide eyed and wondering. Her mind was opening to new ideas. She was beginning to understand that London was incapable of supporting even the lives of three women; she was wrestling with the problem of existence. Every one had gone. Many had died; but many more, surely, must have fled into the country. She began to understand that she and her family must also fly into the country.

Millie still sobbed convulsively now and again.

"Oh! Chuck it, Mill," said Blanche at last. "We'd better be getting home."

Millie dabbed her eyes. "I'm starving," she blubbered.

"Well, so am I," returned Blanche. "That's why I said we'd better get home. There's nothing to eat here."

"Is – is every one dead?"

"No, they've gone off into the country, and that's what we've got to do."

The younger girl sat up, put her hat straight, and blew her nose. "Isn't it awful, B.?" she said.

Blanche pinched her lips together. "What are you putting your hat straight for?" she asked. "There's no one to see you."

"Well, you needn't make it any worse," retorted Millie on the verge of a fresh outburst of tears.

"Oh! Come on!" said Blanche, getting to her feet.

"I don't believe I *can* walk home," complained Millie; "my feet ache so."

"You'll have to wait a long time if you're going to find a bus," returned Blanche.

Three empty taxicabs stood in the rank a few feet away from them, but it never occurred to either of the two young women to attempt any experiment with these mechanisms. If the thought had crossed their minds they would have deemed it absurd.

"Let's go down by Victoria," suggested Blanche. "I believe it's nearer."

In Parliament Square they disturbed a flock of rooks, birds which had partly changed their natural habits during the past few months and, owing to the superabundance of one kind of food, were preying on carrion.

"Crows," commented Blanche. "Beastly things."

"I wonder if we could get some water to drink," was Millie's reply.

"Well, there's the river," suggested Blanche, and they turned up towards Westminster Bridge.

In one of the tall buildings facing the river Blanche's attention was caught by an open door.

"Look here, Mill," she said, "we've only been looking for shops. Let's try one of these houses. We might find something to eat in there."

"I'm afraid," said Millie.

"What of?" sneered Blanche. "At the worst it's skeletons, and we can come out again."

Millie shuddered. "You go," she suggested.

"Not by myself, I won't," returned Blanche.

"There you are, you see," said Millie.

"Well, it's different by yourself."

"I hate it," returned Millie with emphasis.

"So do I, in a way, only I'm fair starving," said Blanche. "Come on."

The building was solidly furnished, and the ground floor, although somewhat disordered, still suggested a complacent luxury. On the floor lay a copy of the *Evening Chronicle*, dated May 10; possibly one of the last issues of a London journal. Two of the pages were quite blank, and almost the only advertisement was one hastily-set announcement of a patent medicine guaranteed as a sure protection against the plague. The remainder of the paper was filled with reports of the devastation that was being wrought, reports which were nevertheless marked by a faint spirit of simulated confidence. Between the lines could be read the story of desperate men clinging to hope with splendid courage. There were no signs of panic here. Groves had come out well at the last.

The two girls hovered over this piece of ancient history for a few minutes.

"You see," said Blanche triumphantly, "even then, more'n two months ago, every one was making for the country. We shall have to go, too. I told you we should."

"I never said we shouldn't," returned Millie. "Anyhow there's nothing to eat here."

"Not in this room, there isn't," said Blanche, "but there might be in the kitchens. Do you know what this place has been?"

Millie shook her head.

"It's been a man's club," announced Blanche. "First time you've been in one, old dear."

"Come on, let's have a look downstairs, then," returned Millie, careless of her achievement.

In the first kitchen they found havoc: broken china and glass, empty bottles, empty tins, cooking utensils on the floor, one table upset, everywhere devastation and the marks of struggle; but in none of the empty tins was there the least particle of food. Everything had been completely cleaned out. The rats had been there, and had gone.

Exploring deeper, however, they were at last rewarded. On a table stood a whole array of unopened tins and in one of them was plunged a tin-opener, a single stab had been given, and then, possibly, another of these common tragedies had begun. Had he been alone, that plunderer, or had his companions fled from him in terror?

Here the two girls made a sufficient meal, and discovered, moreover, a large store of unopened beer-bottles. They shared the contents of one between them, and then, feeling greatly reinvigorated, they sought for and found two baskets, which they filled with tinned foods. They only took away one bottle of beer – a special treat for their mother – on account of the weight. They remembered that they had a long walk before them; and they were not over-elated by their discovery; they were sick to death of tinned meats.

In looking for the baskets they came across a single potato that the rats had left. From it had sprung a long, thin, etiolated shoot which had crept under the door of the cupboard and was making its way across the floor to the light of the window. Already that shoot was several feet in length.

"Funny how they grow," commented Millie.

"Making for the country, I expect," replied Blanche, "same as we shall have to do."

It was a relief to them to find their way into the sunlight once more. Those cold, forsaken houses held some suggestion of horror, of old activities so abruptly ended by tragedy. From these interiors Nature was still shut off. That ghostly tendril aching towards the light had no chance for life and reproduction....

* * *

The two Gosling girls had yet one more adventure before they toiled home with their load.

They were growing bolder, despite the gloom and oppression of those human habitations, and some freakish spirit prompted Blanche to suggest that they should visit the Houses of Parliament. After a brief demur, Millie acceded.

That great stronghold was open to them now. They might walk the floor of the House, sit in the Speaker's chair, penetrate into the sacred places of the Upper Chamber.

Gone were all the rules and formulas, the intricacies and precedents of an unwritten constitution, the whole cumbrous machinery for the making of new laws. The air was no longer disturbed by the wranglings, evasions and cunning shifts of those who had found here a stage for their personal ambitions. The high talk of progress had died into silence along with the struggle of parties which had played the supreme game, side against side, for the prize of power. Progress had been defined in this place, in terms of human activity, human comfort. The end in sight had been some vague conception of general welfare through accumulated riches. And from the sky had fallen a pestilence to change the meaning of human terms. In three months the old conception of wealth was gone. Money, precious stones, a thousand accepted forms of value had become suddenly worthless, of no more account than the symbol of power which lay coated with dust on the table of the House of law-makers. Even law itself, that slow growth of the centuries, had become meaningless. Who cared if some mad woman plundered every jeweller's shop in the whole

City? Who was to forbid theft or avenge murder? The place of traffic was empty. Only one law was left and only one value; the law of self-preservation, the value of food.

The sunlight fell in broad coloured shafts upon two half-educated girls come on a plundering expedition, and they might sit in the high places if they would, and make new laws for themselves.

Blanche sat for a few moments in the Speaker's chair.

"It's a fine big place," she remarked.

"Oh! Come on, B., do," replied Millie. "I want to get home."

As they crossed the Square, Millie looked up at Big Ben. "Quarter-past nine," she said. "It must have stopped."

"Well, of course, silly," replied Blanche. "All the clocks have stopped. Who's to wind 'em?"

Chapter XII
Emigrant

FOR SOME TIME Mrs. Gosling was quite unable to grasp the significance of her daughters' report on the condition of London. During the past two months she had persuaded herself that the traffic of the town was being resumed and that only Putney was still desolate. She had always disapproved of Putney; it was damp and she had never known anyone who had lived there. It is true that the late lamented George Gosling had been born in Putney, but that was more than half a century ago, the place was no doubt quite different then; and he had left Putney and gone to live in the healthy North before he was sixteen. Mrs. Gosling was half inclined to blame Putney for all their misfortunes – it was sure to breed infection, being so near the river and all – and she had become hopeful during the past month that all would be well with them if they could once get back to Kilburn.

"D'you mean to say you didn't see no one at all?" she repeated in great perplexity.

"Those three we've told you about, that's all," said Blanche.

"Well, o' course, they're all shut up in the 'ouses, still; afraid o' the plague and 'anging on to what provisions they've got put by, same as us," was the hopeful explanation Mrs. Gosling put forward.

"They ain't," said Millie, and Blanche agreed.

"Well, but 'ow d'you know?" persisted the mother. "Did you go in to the 'ouses?"

"One or two," returned Blanche evasively, "but there wasn't no need to go in. You could see."

"Are you quite sure there was no shops open? Not in the Strand?" Mrs. Gosling laid emphasis on the last sentence. She could not doubt the good faith of the Strand. If that failed her, all was lost.

"Oh! Can't you understand, mother," broke out Blanche petulantly, "that the whole of London is absolutely deserted? There isn't a soul in the streets. There's no cabs or buses or trams or anything, and grass growing in the middle of the road. And all the shops have been broken into, all those that had food in 'em, and –" words failed her. "Isn't it, Millie?" she concluded lamely.

"Awful," agreed Millie.

"Well, I can't understand it," said Mrs. Gosling, not yet fully convinced. She considered earnestly for a few moments and then asked: "Did you go into Charing Cross Post Office? They'd sure to be open."

"Yes!" lied Blanche, "and we could have taken all the money in the place if we'd wanted, and no one any the wiser."

Mrs. Gosling looked shocked. "I 'ope my gels'll never come to that," she said. Her girls, with a wonderful understanding of their mother's opinions, had omitted to mention their raid on the Knightsbridge emporium.

"No one'd ever know," said Millie.

"There's One who would," replied Mrs. Gosling gravely, and strangely enough, perhaps, the two girls looked uneasy, but they were thinking less of the commandments miraculously given to Moses than of the probable displeasure of the Vicar of St John the Evangelist's Church in Kilburn.

"Well, we've got to do something, anyhow," said Blanche, after a pause. "I mean we'll have to get out of this and go into the country."

"We might go to your uncle's in Liverpool," suggested Mrs. Gosling, tentatively.

"It's a long walk," remarked Blanche.

Mrs. Gosling did not grasp the meaning of this objection. "Well, I think we could afford third-class," she said. "Besides, though we 'aven't corresponded much of late years, I've always been under the impression that your uncle is doin' well in Liverpool; and at such a time as this I'm sure 'e'll do the right thing, though whether it would be better to let 'im know we're comin' or not I'm not quite sure."

"Oh! Dear!" sighed Blanche, "I *do* wish you'd try to understand, mother. There aren't any trains. There aren't any posts or telegraphs. Wherever we go we've just got to walk. Haven't we, Millie?"

Millie began to snivel. "It's 'orrible," she said.

"Well I *can't* understand it," repeated Mrs. Gosling.

By degrees, however, the controversy took a new shape. Granting for the moment the main contention that London was uninhabited, Mrs. Gosling urged that it would be a dangerous, even a foolhardy, thing to venture into the country. If there was no Government there would be no law and order, was the substance of her argument; government in her mind being represented by its concrete presentation in the form of the utterly reliable policeman. Furthermore, she pointed out, that they did not know anyone in the country, with the exception of a too-distant uncle in Liverpool, and that there would be nowhere for them to go.

"We shall have to work," said Blanche, who was surely inspired by her glimpse of the silent city.

"Well, we've got nearly a 'undred pounds left of what your poor father drew out o' the bank before we shut ourselves up," said her mother.

"I suppose we *could* buy things in the country," speculated Blanche.

"You seem set on the country for some reason," said Mrs. Gosling with a touch of temper.

"Well, we've got to get food," returned Blanche, raising her voice. "We can't live on air."

"And if food's to be got cheaper in the country than in London," snapped Mrs. Gosling, "my experience goes for nothing, but, of course, you know best, if I *am* your mother."

"There isn't any food in London, cheap or dear, I keep telling you," said Blanche, and left the room angrily, slamming the door behind her.

Millie sat moodily biting her nails.

"Blanche lets 'er temper get the better of 'er," remarked Mrs. Gosling addressing the spaces of the kitchen in which they were sitting.

"It's right, worse luck," said Millie. "We shall have to go. I 'ate it nearly as much as you do."

The argument thus begun was continued with few intermissions for a whole week. A thunderstorm, followed by two days of overcast weather, came to the support of the older woman. One thing was certain among all these terrible perplexities, namely, that you couldn't start off for a trip to the country on a wet day.

Meanwhile their stores continued to diminish, and one afternoon Mrs. Gosling consented to take a walk with Blanche as far as Hammersmith Broadway.

The sight of that blank desert impressed her. Blanche pointed out the house in which she had seen the two women five days before, but no one was looking out of the window on that afternoon. Perhaps they had fled to the country, or were occupied elsewhere in the house, or perhaps they had left London by the easier way which had become so general in the past few months.

When she returned to the Putney house, Mrs. Gosling wept and wished she, too, was dead, but she consented at last to Blanche's continually urged proposition, in so far as she expressed herself willing to make a move of some sort. She thought they might, at least, go back and have a look at Wisteria Grove. And if Kilburn had, indeed, fallen as low as Hammersmith, then there was apparently no help for it and they must try their luck in the waste and desolation of the country. Perhaps some farmer's wife might take them in for a time, until they had a chance to look about them. They had nearly a hundred pounds in gold.

The girls found a builder's trolley in a yard near by, a truck of sturdy build on two wheels with a long handle. It bore marks of having held cement, and there were weeds growing in one end of it, but after it had been brought home and thoroughly scrubbed, it looked quite a presentable means for the transport of the 'necessaries' they proposed to take with them.

They made too generous an estimate of essentials at first, piling their truck too high for safety and overtaxing their strength; but that problem, like many others, was finally solved for them by the clear-sighted guidance of necessity.

They started one morning – a Monday if their calculations were not at fault – about two hours after breakfast. Mrs. Gosling and Millie pushed behind, and Blanche, the inspired one, went before, pulled by the handle of the pole and gave the others their direction.

It is possible that they were the last women to leave London.

By chance they discovered the Queen of all the Earth on a doorstep near Addison Road. She was quite dead, but they did not despoil her of the jewels with which she was still covered.

* * *

Mrs. Gosling was a source of trouble from the outset. She had lived her life indoors. In the Wisteria Grove days, she never spent two hours of the twenty-four out of the house. Some times for a whole week she had not gone out at all. It was a mark of their rise in the world that all the tradesmen called for orders. She had found little necessity to buy in shops during recent years. And so, very surely, she had grown more and more limited in her outlook. Her attention had become concentrated on the duties of the housewife. She had not kept any servant, a charwoman who came for a few hours three times a week had done all that the mistress of the house had not dared, in face of neighbourly criticism – in her position she could not be seen washing down the little tiled path to the gate nor whitening the steps.

The effect of this cramped existence on Mrs. Gosling would not have been noticeable under the old conditions. She had become a specialized creature, admirably adapted to her place in the old scheme of civilization. No demand was ever made upon her resources other than those familiar demands which she was so perfectly educated to supply. Even when the plague had come, she had not been compelled to alter her mode of life. She had made trouble enough about the lack of many things she had once believed to be necessary – familiar foods, soap and the thousand little conveniences that the twentieth century inventor had patented to assist the domestic economy of the small householder; but the trouble was not too great to be overcome. The adaptability required from her was within the scope of her specialized vision. She could learn to do without flour, butter, lard, milk, sugar and the other things, but she could not learn to think on unfamiliar lines.

That was the essence of her trouble. She was divorced from a permanent home. She was asked to walk long miles in the open air. Worst of all, she was called upon for initiative, ingenuity; she was required to exercise her imagination in order to solve a problem with which she was quite unfamiliar. She was expected to develop the potentialities of the wild thing, and to extort food from Nature. The whole problem was beyond her comprehension.

The sight of Kilburn was a great blow to her. She had hoped against hope that here, at least, she would find some semblance of the life she had known. It had seemed so impossible to her that Aiken, the butcher's, or Hobb's, the grocer's, would not be open as usual, and the vision of those two desolated and ransacked shops – the latter with but a few murderous spears of plate-glass left in its once magnificent windows – depressed her to tears.

So shaken was she by the sight of these horrors that Blanche and Millie raised no objection to sleeping that night in the house in Wisteria Grove. Indeed, the two girls were almost tired out, although it was yet early in the afternoon. The truck had become very heavy in the course of the last two miles; and they had had considerable difficulty in negotiating the hill by Westbourne Park Station.

Mrs. Gosling was still weeping as she let herself in to her old home, and she wept as she prowled about the familiar rooms and noted the dust which had fallen like snow on every surface which would support it. And for the first time the loss of her husband came home to her. She had been almost glad when he had vanished from the Putney house – in that place she had only seen him in his new character of tyrant. Here, among familiar associations, she recalled the fact that he had been a respectable, complacent, hard-working, successful man who had never given her cause for trouble, a man who did not drink nor run after other women, who held a position in the Church and was looked up to by the neighbourhood. According to her definition he had certainly been an ideal husband. It is true that they had dropped any pretence of being in love with one another after Blanche was born, but that was only natural.

Mrs. Gosling sat on the bed she had shared with him so long and hoped he was happy. He was; but if she could have seen the nature of his happiness the sight would have given her no comfort. Vaguely she pictured him in some strange Paradise, built upon those conceptions of the medieval artists, mainly Italians, which have supplied the ideals of the orthodox. She saw an imperfectly transfigured and still fleshly George Gosling, who did unaccustomed things with a harp, was dressed in exotic garments and was on terms with certain hybrids, largely woman but partly bird, who were clearly recognizable as the angelic host. If she had been a Mohammedan, her vision would have accorded far more nearly with the fact.

* * *

The successful animal is that which is adapted to its circumstances. Herbert Spencer would appear foolish and incapable in the society of the young wits who frequent the private bar; he might be described by them as an old Johnny who knew nothing about life. Mrs. Gosling in her own home had been a ruler; she had had authority over her daughters, and, despite the usual evidences of girlish precocity, she had always been mistress of the situation. In the affairs of household management she was *facile princeps*, and she commanded the respect accorded to the eminent in any form of specialized activity. But even on this second morning of their emigration it became clear to Blanche that her mother had ceased to rule, and must become a subordinate. A certain respect was due to her in her parental relation, but if she could not be coaxed she must be coerced.

"She'll be better when we get her right away from here," was Blanche's diagnosis, and Millie, who had also achieved some partial realization of the necessities imposed by the new conditions, nodded in agreement.

"She wants to stop here altogether, and, of course, we can't," she said.

"We shall starve if we do," said Blanche.

From that time Mrs. Gosling dropped into the humiliating position of a kind of mental incapable who must be humoured into obedience.

The first, and in many ways the most difficult, task was to persuade her away from Kilburn. She clung desperately to that stronghold of her old life.

"I'm too old to change at my age," she protested, and when the alternative was clearly put before her, she accepted it with a flaccidity that was as aggravating as it was unfightable.

"I'd sooner die 'ere," said Mrs. Gosling, "than go trapesing about the fields lookin' for somethin' to eat. I simply couldn't do it. It's different for you two gels, no doubt. You go and leave me 'ere."

Millie might have been tempted to take her mother at her word, but Blanche never for a moment entertained the idea of leaving her mother behind.

"Very well, mother," she said, desperately, "if you won't come we must all stop here and starve, I suppose. We've got enough food to last a fortnight or so."

As she spoke she looked out of the window of that little suburban house, and for the first time in her life a thought came to her of the strangeness of preferring such an inconvenient little box to the adventure of the wider spaces of open country. Outside, the sun was shining brilliantly, but the windows were dim with dust and cobwebs.

Yet her mother was comparatively happy in this hovel; she would find delight in cleaning it, although there was no one to appraise the result of her effort. She was a specialized animal with habits precisely analogous to the instincts of other animals and insects. There were insects who could only live in filth and would die miserably if removed from their natural surroundings. Mrs. Gosling was a suburban-house insect who would perish in the open air. After all, the chief difference between insects and men is that the insect is born perfectly adapted to its specialized existence, man finds, or is forced into, a place in the scheme after he has come to maturity....

"I can't see why you shouldn't leave me behind," pleaded Mrs. Gosling.

"Well, we won't," replied Blanche, still looking out of the window.

"It's wicked of you to make us stop here and starve," put in Millie. "And even you must see that we *shall* starve."

Mrs. Gosling wept feebly. She had wept much during the past twenty-four hours. "Where can we go?" she wailed.

"There's country on the other side of Harrow," said Blanche.

The thought of Harrow or Timbuctoo was equally repugnant to Mrs. Gosling.

Then Millie had an idea. "Well, we only brought four bottles of water with us," she said, "where are we going to get any more in Kilburn?"

Mrs. Gosling racked her brain in the effort to remember some convenient stream in the neighbourhood. "It may rain," she said feebly at last.

Blanche turned from the window and pointed to the blurred prospect of sunlit street. "We might be dead before the rain came," she said.

They wore her out in the end.

* * *

With Harrow as an immediate objective, they toiled up Willesden Lane with their hand-cart early the next morning. Blanche took that route because it was familiar to her, and after passing Willesden Green, she followed the tram lines.

As they got away from London they came upon evidences of the exodus which had preceded them. Bodies of women, for the most part no longer malodorous, were not infrequent, and pieces of household furniture, parcels of clothing, boxes, trunks and smaller impedimenta lay by the roadside, the superfluities of earlier loads that had been lightened, however reluctantly.

Mrs. Gosling blenched at the sight of every body – only a few of them could be described as skeletons – and protested that they were all going to their death, but Blanche kept on resolutely with a white, set face, and as Millie followed her example, if with rather less show of temerity, there was no choice but to follow. When the gradients were favourable the girls helped their mother on to the truck and gave her a lift. She was a feeble walker.

Not till they reached Sudbury did they see another living being of their own species, or any sign of human habitation in the long rows of dirty houses.

The great surge of migration had spread out from the centre and become absorbed in circles of ever-widening amplitude. The great entity of London had eaten its way so far outwards in to arable and pasturage that within a ten-mile radius from Charing Cross not a thousand women could be found who had been able to obtain any promise of security from the products of the soil. And although there were great open spaces of land, such as Wembley Park, which had to be crossed in the journey outwards, the exiles had been unable to wait until such time as seed could be transformed into food by the alchemy of Nature. So the pressure had been continually outwards, forcing the emigrants toward the more distant farms where some fraction of them, at least, might find work and food until the coming of the harvest. In Kent, vegetables were comparatively plentiful. In Northern Middlesex and Buckinghamshire the majority had to depend upon animal food. But in all the Home Counties and in the neighbourhood of every large town, famine was following hard upon the heels of the plague, and 70 per cent of the town-dwelling women and children who had escaped the latter visitation died of starvation and exposure before the middle of August.

In the first inner ring, still sparsely populated, were to be found those who had had vegetable gardens and had been vigorous enough to protect themselves against the flood of migration which had swept up against them.

It was the first signs of this inner ring that the Goslings discovered at Sudbury.

*   *   *

They came upon a little row of cottages, standing back a few yards from the road. All three women had been engaged in pushing their trolly up an ascent, and with heads down, and all their physical energies concentrated upon their task, they did not notice the startling difference between these cottages and other houses they had passed, until they stopped to take breath at the summit of the hill.

Mrs. Gosling had immediately seated herself upon the sloping pole of the trolly handle. She was breathing heavily and had her hands pressed to her sides. Millie leaned against the side of the trolly, her eyes still on the ground. But Blanche had thrown back her shoulders and opened her lungs, and she saw the banner of smoke that flew from the middle of the three chimney-stacks – smoke, in this wilderness, smoke the sign of human life! To Blanche it seemed the fulfilment of a great hope. She had begun to wonder if all the world were dead.

"Oh!" she gasped. "Look!"

They looked without eagerness, anticipating some familiar horror.

"Ooh!" echoed Millie, when she, too, had recognized the harbinger. But Mrs. Gosling did not raise her eyes high enough.

"What?" she asked stupidly.

"There's some one living in that cottage," said Blanche, and pointed upwards to the soaring pennant.

Mrs. Gosling's face brightened. "Well, to be sure," she said, "I wonder if they'd let me sit down and rest for a few minutes? And perhaps they might be willing to sell me a glass of milk. I'm sure I'd pay a good price for it."

"We can see, anyway," replied Millie, and they roused themselves and pushed on eagerly. The cottage was not more than thirty yards away.

Before they reached it, a woman came to the doorway, stared at them for a moment and then came down to the little wooden gate.

She was a thick-set woman of fifty or so, with iron grey hair cut close to her head. She wore a tweed skirt which did not reach the tops of her heavily soled, high boots. She looked capable, energetic and muscular. And in her hand she carried about three feet of stout broomstick.

She did not speak until the little procession halted before her gate, and then she pointed meaningly up the road with her broomstick and said: "Go on. You can't stop here." She spoke with the voice and inflection of an educated woman.

Blanche paused in the act of setting down the trolly handle. Mrs. Gosling and Millie stared in amazement; they had been prepared to weep on the neck of this human friend, found at last in the awful desert of Middlesex.

"We only wanted to buy a little milk," stammered Blanche, no less astonished than her mother and sister.

The big woman looked them over with something of pity and contempt. "I can see you're not dangerous," she sneered and crossed her great bare fore-arms over the top of the gate. "Only three poor feckless idiots going begging."

"We're *not* begging," retorted Blanche. "We've got money and we're willing to pay."

"Money!" repeated the woman. She looked up at the sky and nodded her head, as though beseeching pity for these feeble creatures. "My dear girl," she went on, "what do you suppose is the good of money in this world? You can't eat money, nor wear it, nor use it to light a fire. Now, if you'd offered me a box of matches, you should have had all the milk I can spare."

"Well, I never," put in Mrs. Gosling, who had feebly come to rest again on the handle of the trolly.

"No, my good woman, you never did," said the stranger. "You never could and I should say the chances are that you never will."

Millie was intimidated and shrinking, even Blanche looked a little nervous, but Mrs. Gosling was incapable of feeling fear of a fellow-woman. "You can't mean as you won't sell us a glass of milk?" she said.

"Have you got a box of matches you'll exchange for it?" asked the stranger. "I've got a burning glass I stole in Harrow, but you can't depend on the sun."

"No, nor 'aven't 'ad, the last three weeks," said Mrs. Gosling. "But if you've more money a'ready than you know what to do with, I should 'ave thought as you'd 'a been willing to spare a glass o' milk for charity's sake."

The stranger regarded her petitioner with a hard smile. "Charity's sake?" she said. "Do you realize that I've had to defend this place like a fort against thousands of your sort? I've killed three madwomen who fought me for possession and buried 'em in the orchard like cats. I held out through the first rush and I can hold out now easily enough. You three are the first I've seen for a month, and before that they'd begun to get weak and poor. These are your daughters, I suppose, and the three of you had always depended upon some fool of a man to keep you. Yes? Well, you deserve all you've got. Now you can start and do a little healthy, useful work for yourselves. I've no pity for you. I've got a damned fool of a sister and an old fool of a mother to keep in there," she pointed to the cottage with her broomstick. "Parasitic like you, both of 'em, and pretty well all the use they are is to keep the fire alight. No, my good woman, you get no charity from me."

When she had finished her speech, which she delivered with a fluency and point that suggested familiarity with the platform, the stranger crossed her arms again over the gate and stared Mrs. Gosling out of countenance.

"Come along, my dears," said that outraged lady, getting wearily to her feet. "I wouldn't wish your ears soiled by such language from a woman as 'as forgotten the manners of a lady. But, there, poor thing, I've no doubt 'er 'ead's been turned with all this trouble."

The stranger smiled grimly and made no reply, but as the Goslings were moving away, she called out to them suddenly: "Hi! You! There's a witless creature along the road who'll probably help you. The house is up a side road. Bear round to the right."

"What a beast," muttered Blanche when they had gone on a few yards.

"One o' them 'new' women, my dear," panted Mrs. Gosling, who remembered the beginning of the movement and still clung to the old terminology. "'Orrible unsexed creatures! I remember how your poor father used to 'ate 'em!"

"I'd like to get even with her," said Millie.

They bore to the right, and so avoided two turnings which led up repulsive-looking hills, but they missed the side road.

"I'm sure we must have passed it," complained Mrs. Gosling at last. Her sighs had been increasing in volume and poignancy for the past half-mile, and the prospect of uninhabited country which lay immediately around her she found infinitely dispiriting.

"There isn't an 'ouse in sight," she added, "and I really don't believe I *can* walk much farther."

Blanche stopped and looked over the fields on her right towards London. In the distance, blurred by an oily wriggle of heat haze, she could see the last wave of suburban villas which had broken upon this shore of open country. They had left the town behind them at last, but they had not found what they sought. This little arm of land which cut off Harrow and Wealdstone from the mother lake of London had not offered sufficient temptation to delay their forerunners in the search for food. Most of them, with a true instinct for what they sought, had followed the main road into the Chiltern Hills, and those who for some cause or another had wandered into this side track had pushed on, even as Blanche and Millie would have done had they not been dragged back by their mother's complaints. The sun was falling a little towards the west, and bird and animal life, which had seemed to rest during the intenser heat of mid-day, was stirring and calling all about them. A rabbit lolloped into the road, a few yards away, pricked up its ears, stared for an instant, and then scuttled to cover. A blackbird flew out of the hedge and fled chattering up the ditch. The air was murmurous with the hum of innumerable insects, and above Mrs. Gosling's head hovered a group of flies which ever and again bobbed down as if following some concerted plan of action, and tried to settle on the poor woman's heated face.

"Oh! Get away, do!" she panted, and flapped a futile handkerchief.

"How quiet it is!" said Blanche; and although the air was full of sound it did indeed appear that a great hush had fallen over the earth. No motor-horn threateningly bellowed its automatic demand for right of way; there was no echo of hoofs nor grind of wheels; no call of children's voices, nor even the bark of a dog. The wild things had the place to themselves again, and the sound of their movements called for no response from civilized minds. The ears of the Goslings heard, but did not note these, to them, useless evidences of life. They were straining and alert for the voice of humanity.

"I don't know when I've felt the 'eat so much," said Mrs. Gosling suddenly, and Blanche and Millie both started.

"Hush!" said Blanche, and held up a warning finger.

In the distance they heard a sound like the closing of a gate, and then, very clear and small, a feminine voice. "*Chuck!* Chuck! Chuck!" it said. "Chuck! Chuck! *Chuck!!!*"

"I told you we'd passed it," said Mrs. Gosling triumphantly. They turned the trolly and began to retrace their footsteps. Their eager eyes tried to peer through the spinney of trees which shut them off from the south. Once or twice they stopped to listen. The voice was fainter now, but they could hear the squawk of greedily competitive fowls.

Chapter XIII
Differences

THE ONLY side road they could find proved to be no more than a track through the little wood. They almost passed it a second time, and hesitated at the gate – a sturdy five-barred gate bearing 'Private' on a conspicuous label – debating whether this "could be right." They still suffered a spasm of fear at the thought of trespass, and to open this gate and march up an unknown private road pushing a hand-cart seemed to them an act of terrible aggression.

"We might leave the cart just inside," suggested Blanche.

"And get our food stole," said Mrs. Gosling.

"There's no one about," urged Blanche.

"There's that broomstick woman," said Millie. "She may have followed us."

"I'm sure I dunno if it's safe to go foragin' in among them trees, neither," continued Mrs. Gosling. "Are you sure this is right, Blanche?"

"Well, of course, I'm not sure," replied Blanche, with a touch of temper.

They peered through the trees and listened, but no sign of a house was to be seen, and all was now silent save for the long drone of innumerable bees about their afternoon business.

"Oh! Come on!" said Blanche at last. She was rapidly learning to solve all their problems by this simple formula…

In the wood they found refuge from those attendant flies which had hung over them so persistently.

Mrs. Gosling gave a final flick with her handkerchief and declared her relief. "It's quite pleasant in 'ere," she said, "after the 'eat."

The two girls also seemed to find new vigour in the shade of the trees.

"We *have* got a cheek!" said Millie, with a giggle.

"Well! Needs must when the devil drives," returned Mrs. Gosling, "and our circumstances is quite out of the ordinary. Besides which, there can't be any 'arm in offerin' to buy a glass of milk."

Blanche tugged at the trolley handle with a flicker of impatience. Why would her mother be so foolish? Surely she must see that everything was different now? Blanche was beginning to wonder at and admire the marvel of her own intelligence. How much cleverer she was than the others! How much more ready to appreciate and adapt herself to change! They could not understand this new state of things, but she could, and she prided herself on her powers of discrimination.

"Everything's different now," she said to herself. "We can go anywhere and do anything, almost. It's like as if we were all starting off level again, in a way." She felt uplifted: she took extraordinary pleasure in her own realization of facts. A strange, new power had come to her, a power to enjoy life, through mastery. "Everything's different now," she repeated. She was conscious of a sense of pity for her mother and sister.

* * *

The road through the wood curved sharply round to the right, and they came suddenly upon a clearing, and saw the house in front of them. It was a long, low house, smothered in roses and creepers, and it stood in a wild garden surrounded by a breast-high wall of red brick. At the edge of the clearing several cows were lying under the shade of the trees, reflectively chewing the cud with slow, deliberate enjoyment, while one, solitary, stood with its head over the garden gate, motionless, save for an occasional petulant whisp of its ropey tail.

"Now, then, what are we going to do?" asked Mrs. Gosling.

The procession halted, and the three women regarded the guardian cow with every sign of dismay.

"Shoo!" said Millie feebly, flapping her hands; and Blanche repeated the intimidation with greater force; but the cow merely acknowledged the salutation by an irritable sweep of its tail.

"'Orrid brute!" muttered Mrs. Gosling, and flicked her handkerchief in the direction of the brute's quarters.

"I know," said Blanche, conceiving a subtle strategy. "We'll drive it away with the cart." She turned the trolly round, and the three of them grasping the pole, they advanced slowly and warily to the charge, pushing their siege ram before them. They made a slight detour to achieve a flank attack and allow the enemy a clear way of retreat.

"Oh, dear! What *are* you doing?" said a voice suddenly, and the three startled Goslings nearly dropped the pole in their alarm – they had been so utterly absorbed in their campaign.

A young woman of sixteen or seventeen, very brown, hot and dishevelled, was regarding them from the other side of the garden wall with a stare of amazement that even as they turned was flickering into laughter.

"It's that great brute by the gate, my dear," said Mrs. Gosling, "and we've just –"

"You don't mean Alice?" interrupted the young woman. "Oh! You couldn't go charging poor dear Alice with a great cart like that! Three of you, too!"

"Is its name Alice?" asked Blanche stupidly. She did not feel equal to this curious occasion.

"*Its* name!" replied the young woman, with scorn. "*Her* name's Alice, if that's what you mean." She shook back the hair from her eyes and moved down to the gate. The cow acknowledged her presence by an indolent toss of the head.

"Oh! But my sweet Alice!" protested the young woman; "you must move and let these funny people come in. It really isn't good for you, dear, to stand about in the sun like this, and you'd much better go and lie down in the shade for a bit!" She gently pulled the gate from under the cow's chin, and then, laying her hands flat on its side, made as if to push it out of the way.

"Well, I never!" declared Mrs. Gosling, regarding the performance with much the same awe as she might have vouchsafed to a lion-tamer in a circus. "'Oo'd 'ave thought it'd 'a been that tame?"

The cow, after a moment's resistance, moved off with a leisurely walk in the direction of the wood.

"Now, you funny people, what *do* you want?" asked the young woman.

Mrs. Gosling began to explain, but Blanche quickly interposed. "Oh! Do be quiet, mother; you don't understand," she said, and continued, before her mother could remonstrate, "We've come from London."

"Goodness!" commented the young woman.

"And we want –" Blanche hesitated. She was surprised to find that in the light of her wonderful discovery it was not so easy to define precisely what they ought to want. As the broomstick woman had said, they were "beggars." Fairly confronted with the problem, Blanche saw no alternative but a candid acknowledgment of the fact.

"You want feeding, of course," put in the young woman. "They all do. You needn't think you're the first. We've had dozens!"

A solution presented itself to Blanche. "We don't really want food," she said. "We've got a lot of tinned things left still, only we're ill with eating tinned things. I thought, perhaps, you might be willing to let us have some milk and eggs and vegetables in exchange?"

"That's sensible enough," commented the young woman. "If you only knew the things we have been offered! Money chiefly, of course" – Mrs. Gosling opened her mouth, but Blanche frowned and shook her head – "and it does seem as if money's about as useless as buttons. In fact, I'd sooner have buttons – you *can* use them. But the other funny things – bits of old furniture, warming-pans, jewellery! You should have heard Mrs. Isaacson! She was a Jewess who came from Hampstead a couple of months ago, and she had a lot of jewels she kept in a bag tied round her waist under her skirt; and when Aunt May and I simply had to tell her to go she tried to bribe us with an old brooch and rubbish. She was a terror. But, I say" – she looked at the sun – "I've got lots of things to do before sunset." She paused, and looked at the three Goslings. "Look here," she went on, "are you all right? You seem all right."

Again Mrs. Gosling began to reply, but Blanche was too quick for her. "Tell me what you mean by 'all right'?" she asked, raising her voice to drown her mother's "Well, I never did 'ear such –"

"Well, of course, mother'll give you any mortal thing you want," replied the young woman at the gate. "Dear old mater! She simply won't think of what we're going to do in the winter; and I mean, if you come in for tonight, say, and we let you have a few odd things, you won't go and plant yourselves on us like that Mrs. Isaacson and one or two others, because if you do, Aunt May and I will have to turn you out, you know."

"What we 'ave we'll pay for," said Mrs. Gosling with dignity.

The young woman smiled. "Oh, I dare say!" she said; "pay us with those pretty little yellow counters that aren't the least good to anyone. You wait here half a jiff. I'll find Aunt May."

She ran up the path and entered the house. A moment later they heard her calling "Aunt May! Auntie – Aun-*tee*!" somewhere out at the back.

"Let's 'ope 'er Aunt May'll 'ave more common sense," remarked Mrs. Gosling.

Blanche turned on her almost fiercely. "For goodness sake, mother," she said, "do try and get it out of your head, if you can, that we can buy things with money. Can't you see that everything's different? Can't you see that money's no good, that you can't eat it, or wear it, or light a fire with it, like that other woman said? *Can't* you understand, or *won't* you?"

Mrs. Gosling gaped in amazement. It was incredible that the mind of Blanche should also have been distorted by this terrible heresy. She turned in sympathy to Millie, who had taken her mother's seat on the pole of the trolly, but Millie frowned and said:

"B.'s right. You can't buy things with money; not here, anyway. What'd they do with money if they got it?"

Mrs. Gosling looked at the trees, at the cows lying at the edge of the wood, at the sunlit fields beyond the house, but she saw nothing which suggested an immediate use for gold coin.

"Lemme sit down, my dear," she said. "What with the 'eat and all this walkin' – Oh! What wouldn't I give for a cup o' tea!"

Millie got up sulkily and leaned against the wall. "I suppose they'll let us stop here tonight, B.?" she asked.

"If we don't make fools of ourselves," replied Blanche, spitefully.

Mrs. Gosling drooped. No inspiration had come to her as it had come to her daughter. The older woman had become too specialized. She swayed her head, searching – like some great larva dug up from its refuse heap – confused and feeble in this new strange place of light and air.

And as Blanche had repeated to herself "Everything's different," so Mrs. Gosling seized a phrase and clung to it as to some explanation of this horrible perplexity. "I can't understand it," she said; "I *can't* understand it!"

* * *

Aunt May appeared after a long interval – a thin, brown-faced woman of forty or so. She wore a very short skirt, a man's jacket and an old deerstalker hat, and she carried a pitchfork. She must have brought the pitchfork as an emblem of authority, but she did not handle it as the other woman had handled her broomstick. The murderous pitchfork appeared little more deadly in her keeping than does the mace in the House of Commons, but as an emblem the pitchfork was infinitely more effective.

Aunt May's questions were pertinent and searching, and after a few brief explanations had been offered to her she drove off the young woman, her niece, whom she addressed as "Allie," to perform the many duties which were her share of the day's work.

Allie went, laughing.

"You can sleep here tonight," announced Aunt May. "We shall have a meal all together soon after sunset. Till then you can talk to my sister, who's an invalid. She's always eager for news."

She took charge of them as if she were the matron of a workhouse receiving new inmates.

"You'd better bring your truck into the garden," she said, "or Alice will be turning everything over. Inquisitive brute!" she added, snapping her fingers at the cow, who had returned, and stood within a few feet of them, eyeing the Goslings with a slow, dull wonder – a mournfully sleepy beast whose furiously wakeful tail seemed anxious to rouse its owner out of her torpor.

The invalid sister sat by the window of a small room that faced west and overlooked the luxuriance of what was still recognizably a flower-garden.

"My sister, Mrs. Pollard," said Aunt May sharply, and then addressing the woman who sat huddled in shawls by the window, she added: "Three more strays, Fanny – from London, Allie tells me." She went out quickly, closing the door with a vigour which indicated little tolerance for invalid nerves.

Mrs. Pollard stretched out a delicate white hand. "Please come and sit near me," she said, "and tell me about London. It is so long since I have had any news from there. Perhaps you might be able –" she broke off, and looked at the three strangers with a certain pathetic eagerness.

"I'll take me bonnet off, ma'am, if you'll excuse me," remarked Mrs. Gosling. She felt at home once more within the delightful shelter of a house, although slightly overawed by the aspect of the room and its occupant. About both there was an air of that class dignity to which Mrs. Gosling knew she could never attain. "I don't know when I've felt the 'eat as I 'ave today," she remarked politely.

"Has it been hot?" asked Mrs. Pollard. "To me the days all seem so much alike. I want you to tell me, were there any young men in London when you left? You haven't seen any young man who at all resembles this photograph, have you?"

Mrs. Gosling stared at the silver-framed photograph which Mrs. Pollard took from the table at her side, stared and shook her head.

"We haven't seen a single man of any kind for two months," said Blanche, "not a single one. Have we, Millie?"

Millie, sitting rather stiffly on her chair, shook her head. "It's terrible," she said. "I'm sure I don't know where they can have all gone to."

Mrs. Pollard did not reply for a moment. She looked steadfastly out of the window, and tears, which she made no attempt to restrain, chased each other in little jerks down her smooth pale cheeks.

Mrs. Gosling pinched her mouth into an expression of suffering sympathy, and shook her head at her daughters to enforce silence. Was she not, also, a widow?

After a short pause, Mrs. Pollard fumbled in her lap and discovered a black-bordered pocket-handkerchief – a reminiscence, doubtless, of some earlier bereavement. Her expression had been in no way distorted as she wept, and after the tears had been wiped away no trace of them disfigured her delicate face. Her voice was still calm and sweet as she said:

"I am very foolish to go on hoping. I loved too much, and this trial has been sent to teach me that all love but One is vain, that I must not set my heart upon things of the earth. And yet I go on hoping that my poor boy was not cut off in Sin."

"Dear, dear!" murmured Mrs. Gosling. "You musn't take it to 'eart too much, ma'am. Boys will be a little wild and no doubt our 'eavenly Father will make excuses."

Mrs. Pollard shook her head. "If it had only been a little wildness," she said, "I should have hope. He is, indeed, just and merciful, slow to anger and of great kindness, but my poor Alfred became tainted with the terrible doctrines of Rome. It has been the greatest grief of my life, and I have known much pain...." And again the tears slowly welled up and fell silently down that smooth, unchanging face.

Mrs. Gosling sniffed sympathetically. The two girls glanced at one another with slightly raised eyebrows and Blanche almost invisibly shrugged her shoulders.

The warm evening light threw the waxen-faced, white-shawled figure of the woman in the window into high relief. Her look of ecstatic resignation was that of some wonderful medieval saint returned from the age of vision and miracle to a recently purified earth in which the old ideas of saintship had again become possible. Her influence was upon the room in which she sat. The sounds of the world outside, the evening chorus of wild life, the familiar noise of the farm, seemed to blend into a remote music of prayer – "Kyrie Eleison! Christe Eleison!" Within was a great stillness, as of a thin and bloodless purity; the long continuance of a single thought found some echo in every material object. While the silence lasted everything in that room was responsive to this single keynote of anaemic virtue.

Mrs. Gosling tried desperately to weep without noise, and even the two girls, falling under the spell, ceased to glance covertly at one another with that hint of criticism, but sat subdued and weakened as if some element of life had been taken from them.

The lips of the woman in the window moved noiselessly; her hands were clasped in her lap. She was praying.

* * *

Firm and somewhat clumsy steps were heard in the passage, the door was pushed roughly open, banging back against the black oak chair which was set behind it, and Aunt May entered carrying a large tray.

"Here's your dinner, Fanny," she said. "We've done earlier tonight, in spite of interruptions." She bustled over to the little table in the window, pushed back the Bible and photograph with the edge of the tray until she could release one hand, and then, having driven the tray into a position of safety, moved Bible and photograph to the centre table.

There was something protestingly vigorous about her movements, as though she endeavoured to combat by noise and energy the impoverished vitality of that emasculate room.

"Now, you three!" she went on. "You had better come out into the kitchen and take your things off and wash."

As the Goslings rose, Mrs. Pollard turned to them and stretched out to each in turn her delicate white hand. "There is only one Comforter," she said. "Put your trust in Him."

Mrs. Gosling gulped, and Blanche and Millie looked as they used to look when they attended the Bible-classes held by the vicar's wife.

Blanche gave a shiver of relief as they came out into the passage. Her mind was suddenly filled by the astounding thought that everything was not different....

Supper was laid on the kitchen table – cold chicken, potatoes and cabbage, stewed plums and cream, and warm, new milk in a jug; no bread, no salt, and no pepper.

As the three Goslings washed at the scullery sink they chattered freely. They felt pleasure at release from some cold, draining influence; they felt as if they had come out of church after some long, dull service, into the air and sunlight.

"I'm sure she's a very 'oly lady," was Mrs. Gosling's final summary.

Blanche shivered again. "Oh! Freezing!" was her enigmatic reply.

Millie said it gave her "the creeps."

They were a party of seven at supper – the meal was referred to as 'supper,' although to Mrs. Pollard it had been dignified by the name of 'dinner' – including two young women whom the Goslings had not hitherto seen; strong, brown-faced girls, who spoke with a country accent. They had something still of the manner of servants, but they were treated as equals both by Allie and Aunt May.

There was little conversation during the meal, however, for all of them were too intent on the business in hand. To the Goslings that meal was, indeed, a banquet.

When they had all finished, Aunt May rose at once. "Thank Heaven for daylight," she remarked; "but we must set our brains to work to invent some light for the winter. We haven't a candle or a drop of oil left," she went on, addressing the Goslings, "and for the past five weeks we have had to bustle to get everything done before sunset, I can tell you. Last night we couldn't wash up after supper."

"We know," replied Blanche.

Aunt May nodded. "We all know," she said. "Now, you three girls, get busy!" And Allie and the two brown-faced young women rose a little wearily.

"I'm getting an old woman," remarked Aunt May, "and I'm allowed certain privileges, chief of them that I don't work after supper. She paused and looked keenly at the three Goslings. "Which of you three is in command?" she asked.

"Well, it seems as if my eldest, Blanche, that is, 'as sort o' taken the lead the past few days," began Mrs. Gosling.

"Ah! I thought so," said Aunt May. "Well, now, Blanche, you'd better come out into the garden and have a talk with me, and we'll decide what you had better do. If your mother and sister would like to go to bed, Allie will show them where they can sleep."

She moved away in the direction of the garden and Blanche followed her.

Chapter XIV
Aunt May

THE SUN had set, but as yet the daylight was scarcely faded. Under the trees the fowls muttered in subdued cluckings, and occasionally one of them would flutter up into the lower branches with a squawk of effort and then settle herself with a great fluttering and swelling of feathers, and all the suggestion of a fussy matron preparing for the night – preparing only, for these early roosters sat open-eyed and watchful, as if they knew that there was no chance of sleep for them until every member of that careless crowd below had found its appointed place in the dormitory.

"We put 'em inside in the winter," remarked Aunt May, as she and Blanche paused, "but they prefer the trees. We haven't any foxes here, but I've noticed that the wild things seem to be coming back."

Blanche nodded. She was thinking how much there was to learn concerning those matters which appertained to the production of food.

"They're rather a poor lot," Aunt May continued, "but they have to forage for themselves, except for the few bits of vegetable and such things we can spare them. We've no corn or flour or meal of any kind for ourselves yet. But a farmer's wife about a mile from here has got a few acres of wheat and barley coming on, and we shall help her to harvest and take our share later. We shall be rich then," she added, with a smile.

"I'm town-bred, you know," said Blanche. "We've got an awful lot to learn, Millie and me."

"You'll learn quickly enough," was the answer. "You'll have to."

"I suppose," returned Blanche.

At the end of the orchard through which they had been passing they came to a knoll, crowned by a great elm. Round the trunk of the elm a rough seat had been fixed, and here Aunt May sat down with a sigh of relief.

"It's a blessed thing to earn your own bread day by day," she said. "It's a beautiful thing to live near the earth and feel physically tired at night. It's delightful to be primitive and agricultural, and I love it. But I have a civilized vice, Blanche. I have a store of cigarettes I stole from a shop in Harrow, and every night when it's fine I come out here after supper and smoke three; and when it's wet I smoke 'em in my own bedroom, and – I dream. But tonight I'm going to talk to you, because you want help."

She produced a cigarette case and matches from a side pocket of her jacket, lit a cigarette, inhaled the smoke with a long gasp of intensest enjoyment, and then said: "Men weren't fools, my dear; they had pockets in their coats."

"Yes?" said Blanche. She felt puzzled and a little awkward. She knew that this woman was a friend, but the girl's town-bred, objective mind was critical and embarrassed.

"Do you smoke?" asked Aunt May. "I can spare you a cigarette, though I know the time must come when there won't be any more. Still, it's a long way off yet. Bless the clever man who invented air-tight tins!"

"No, I don't smoke, thanks," replied Blanche, conventionally; and, try as she would, she could not keep some hint of stiffness out of her voice. Modern manners take a long time to influence suburban homes of the Wisteria Grove type.

"Ah! Well, you miss a lot!" said Aunt May; "but you're better without it, especially now, when tobacco isn't easy to get, and will soon be impossible."

"But do you think," asked Blanche, drawing her eyebrows together, "that this sort of thing is going on always?"

"I dare say. Don't ask me, my dear; the problem's beyond me. What we poor women have got to do is to keep ourselves alive in the meantime. And that's what we've come out here to talk about. What about your mother and you two girls? Where are you going? And what are you proposing to do?"

"*I* don't know," said Blanche. "I – I've been trying to think."

"Good!" remarked Aunt May. "I believe you'll do. I'm doubtful about your sister."

"We'll have to work on a farm, I suppose."

"It's the only way to live."

"Only where?"

"That's what I've been trying to worry out," said Aunt May. "We do get news here, of a sort. Our girls work in Mrs. Jordan's fields, and meet girls and women who come from Pinner, and the Pinner people hear news from Northwood, and the Northwood people from somewhere else; and so we get into touch with half a county. But, coming to your affairs; you see, we here are just the innermost circle. Most of the women who came from London missed this place and passed us by, thanks be!... Now, that poor unfortunate Miss Grant, down the road, had to defend herself with weapons. Fortunately she's strong."

"Is Miss Grant the awful woman with the broomstick?" asked Blanche.

"She's not really awful, my dear," said Aunt May, smiling; "she's a very good sort. A little rough in her manners, perhaps, and quite mad about the uselessness of the creatures we used to know as men, but a fine, generous, unselfish woman, if she does boast of her three murders. Did she tell you that, by the way?"

Blanche nodded.

"She would, of course; and I believe it's true; but her theory was to defend her own people. She said they'd *all* have died if she hadn't. I'm not sure about the ethic, but I know dear old Sally Grant meant well. However, I'm wandering – I often do when I talk like this. The point was that just this little circle here, close to London, is very thickly populated, and there's precious little food ready to be got any way; but you'll have to pass through the country beyond Pinner before you'll find a place where they'll give you work and keep you. There's a surplus in the next ring, I gather, too much labour and too little to grow. You'll have to push out into the Chilterns, out to Amersham at the nearest. It's all on the main road, of course, which is bad in a general way, because that's the road they all took. But I think if you'll cut across towards Wycombe you might, perhaps, find a place of some sort, though whether they'll feed your mother free gratis I can't say. Women are of all sorts, but this plague hasn't made 'em more friendly to one another, or perhaps it is we notice it more, and the worst of the lot are the farmers' wives and daughters who've got the land. They get turned out, though, sometimes. We hear about it. The London women have made raids; only, you see, the poor dears don't know what to do with the land when they get it, so they have to keep the few who do know to teach 'em – when they're sensible enough – the raiders, I mean. They aren't always."

"It'll be an adventure," remarked Blanche.

Aunt May threw away the very short end of her second cigarette and lighted her third. "Adventure will do you good," she said.

It was nearly dark under the elm. The things of the night were coming out. Occasionally a cockchafer would go humming past them, the bats were flitting swiftly and silently about the orchard, and presently an owl swept by in one great stride of soundless flight.

"How they are all coming back!" murmured Aunt May. "All the wild things. I never saw an owl here before this year."

"I should be frightened if you weren't here," said Blanche.

"Nothing to be frightened of, yet."

"Yet?"

"In a few years' time, perhaps. I don't know. We killed a wild cat who came after the chickens a few days ago. The cats have gone back already, and the dogs aren't so respectful as they used to be. The dogs'll interbreed, I suppose, and evolve a common form – strike some kind of average in a beast which will be somewhere near the ancestral type, smaller, probably, I don't know. It's a wonderful world, and very interesting. I could almost wish man wouldn't return for twenty years or so – just to see how much of his handiwork Nature could undo in the interval. I often think about it out here in the evenings."

"I wish I knew more about it," said Blanche timidly. "Are there any books, do you know, that –"

"You won't want books, my dear. Keep your eyes open and think."

They lapsed into silence again. The third cigarette was finished, but Aunt May gave no indication of a desire to get back to the house, and Blanche's mind was so excited with all the new ideas which were pouring in upon her that she had forgotten her tiredness.

"It's awfully interesting," she said at last. "It's all so different. Mother and Millie hate it, and they'd like all the old things back; but I don't think I would."

"You're all right. You'll do," replied her companion. "You're one of the new sort, though you might never have found it out if it hadn't been for the plague. Now, your sister will do one of two things, in my opinion; either she'll stop in some place where there's a man – there's one at Wycombe, by the way – and have children, or she'll turn religious."

Blanche was about to ask a question, but Aunt May stopped her. "Never mind about the man, my dear," she said. "You'll learn quickly enough. It's like Heaven now, you see – no marrying or giving in marriage. With one man to every thousand women or so, what can you expect? It's no good kicking against it. It's got to be. That's where Fanny –" She broke off suddenly, with a little snort of impatience. "I think tonight's an exception," she went on. "I like talking to you, and one simply can't talk to Allie yet, so just tonight I'll have one more." She took out her cigarette case with a touch of impatience.

It was dark under the elm now, and she had to hold up her cigarette case close to her face in order to see the contents. "Two more," she announced. "It's a festival, and for once I can speak my mind to some one. An imprudence, perhaps, like this habit of smoking, but I shall probably never see you again, and I'm sure you won't tell."

"Oh, no!" interposed Blanche eagerly.

"You're not tired? You don't want to go to bed?"

"Not a bit. I love being out here."

"I can't see you, but I know you're speaking the truth," said Aunt May, after a pause. "In the darkness and silence of the night I will make a confession. I look weather-worn and fifty, I know, but I feel absurdly romantic, only there's no man in this case. I used to write novels, my dear – an absurd thing for any spinster to do, but they paid, and I've got the itch for self-expression. That's the one outlet I miss in this new world of ours. Sally Grant and I can't agree, and, in any case, she wants to do all the talking. And sometimes I'm idiot enough to go on writing little bits even now when I have become a capable, practical woman with at least four lives dependent upon me. Well, it shows, anyhow, that we writing women weren't all fools...." She hung on that for a moment or two, and then continued.

"Are you religious?"

"I don't know – I suppose so. We always went to Church at home," said Blanche. "I thought every one was, almost. Not quite like Mrs. Pollard, of course."

"Oh, well!" said Aunt May. "There's no harm and a lot of good in being religious, if you go about it in the right way. I don't want to change your opinions, my dear. It's just a question to me of the right way. And I *can't* see that Fanny's way is right. Here we are, and we've got to make the best of it; and to my mind that means facing life, and not shutting yourself into one room with a Bible and spending half your time on your knees. Fanny never was good for much. She brought up Alfred – my nephew, you know – with only one idea, and she stuffed him so full of holiness that the English Church couldn't hold him, and he had to work some of it off by going over to Rome. He thought he'd have better chances of saintship there. He was a poor, pale thing, anyway. Of course, that was anathema to Fanny. She might have forgiven him for committing a murder, but to become a Roman Catholic! Oh, Lord! She's been praying for him ever since. And, my dear, what difference can it make? Alfred's apostasy, I mean. Do you think it matters what particular form of worship or pettifogging details of belief you adopt? Why can't the Churches take each other for granted, and be generous enough to suppose that all roads lead to Heaven, which is, according to all accounts, a much better place than Rome? But, oh! Above all, if you have a religion, do be practical! Come out and do your work, instead of sighing and psalm-singing, and wearying dumb Heaven with fulsome praise and lamentations of your unworthiness, as if you were trying to propitiate a rich customer!

"There, my dear, I won't say any more. My last cigarette's done, and wasted, because I was too excited to enjoy it. I know I've been disloyal; but it's my temperament. I could slap Fanny sometimes. And she shan't have Allie.... It's the night that has affected me. Tomorrow I shall be just as practical as ever, and you'll forget that you've seen this side of me. Come along. We must go to bed."

"This is the greatest night of my life," thought Blanche as they walked back in silence to the house.

Even when she was in bed, she did not go to sleep at once. She lay and listened to the heavy breathing of her mother and Millie, and she wondered. Everything, indeed, was different, but everybody was just the same, only, in some curious way, individualities seemed more pronounced.

Could it be that everybody was more natural, that there was less restraint?

Blanche was not introspective. She did not test the theory on herself. She thought of the women she had met that day, and of her mother and Millie.

She fell asleep, determined to be more like Aunt May.

Chapter XV
From Sudbury to Wycome

ALLIE KNOCKED on the Goslings' door at sunrise the next morning, and Blanche, who had come to bed two hours after her mother and sister, was the only one to respond. She woke with the feeling that she had something important to do, and that the affair was in some way pleasant and inspiring.

Millie was not easily roused. She had slept heavily, and did not approve the suggestion that she should get up and dress herself.

"All right, B., all right!" she mumbled, and cuddled down under the bedclothes like a dormouse into its straw.

"Oh! Do get up!" urged Blanche, impatiently, and at last resorted to physical force.

"What *is* the matter?" snapped Millie, struggling to maintain her hold of the blankets. "Why *can't* you leave me alone?"

"Because it's time to get up, lazy!" said Blanche, continuing the struggle.

"Well, I said I'd get up in a minute."

"Well, get up then."

"In a minute."

"No – now!"

"Oh, bother!" said Millie.

Blanche succeeded at last in obtaining possession of the blankets.

"You'll wake mother!" was Millie's last, desperate shaft.

"I'm going to try," replied Blanche.

Millie sat up in the bed and wondered vaguely where she was. These scenes had often been enacted at Wisteria Grove, and her mind had gone back to those delightful days of peace and security. When full consciousness returned to her, she was half inclined to cry, and more than half inclined to go to sleep again.

Mrs. Gosling was quite as difficult.

"What's the time?" was her first question.

"I don't know," said Blanche.

"I'm sure it's not seven," murmured Mrs. Gosling.

Millie, still sitting on the bed, wondered whether Blanche would let her get to the blankets which were tumbled on the floor a few feet away.

"No, you don't!" exclaimed Blanche, anticipating the attempt.

Finally she lost her temper and shook her mother vigorously.

At that, Mrs. Gosling sat up suddenly and stared at her. "What in 'eaven's name's wrong, gel?" she asked. Her instinct told her with absolute certainty that it was still the middle of the night by Wisteria Grove standards.

"Oh! My goodness! I'm going to have my hands full with you two!" broke out Blanche impatiently. Her imagination pictured for her in that instant how great the trouble would be. She would never be able to wake them up...

They took the road before eight o'clock. Aunt May was generous in the matter of eggs and fruit, and she left her many urgent duties to point the way for the inexperienced explorers.

"Get right out as far as you can," was her parting word of advice.

They did not see Mrs. Pollard again. She was still in bed when they set out.

* * *

Despite the promise of another cloudless day, none of the three travellers set out in high spirits. To all of them, even to Blanche, it seemed a return to weariness and pain to start out once more pushing that abominable truck. That truck represented all their troubles. It had become associated with all the discomforts they had endured since they left the Putney house. It indicated the paucity of their possessions, and yet it was intolerably heavy to push. After their brief return to the comfort and stability of a home and natural food, this adventuring out into the inhospitable country appeared more hopeless than ever. If they could have gone without the truck, they might, at least, have avoided that feeling of horrible certainty. They might have cheated themselves into the belief that they would return. The truck was the brand of their vagabondage.

Mrs. Gosling did not spare her lamentations concerning the hopelessness of their endeavour, and gave it as her opinion that they had been most heartlessly treated by Aunt May.

"Turning out a woman of my age into the roads," she grumbled. "She might 'ave kept us a day or two, I should 'ave thought. It ain't as if we were beggars. We could 'ave paid for what we 'ad."

She had, indeed, made the suggestion and been repulsed. Aunt May had firmly put the offer on one side without explanation. She understood that explanations would be wasted on Mrs. Gosling.

Millie was inclined to agree with her mother.

Blanche, at the handle, did not interrupt the statement of their grievances. She was occupied with the problem of the future, trying to think out some plan in her own confused inconsecutive way.

Their progress was tediously slow. Against the combined brake of the truck and Mrs. Gosling, they did not average two miles an hour; and even before they came to Pinner it was becoming obvious to the two girls that they might as well let their mother ride on the trolly as allow her to lean her weight upon it as she walked.

They took the road through Wealdstone to avoid the hill and found that they were still in the track of one wing of the foraging army which had preceded them. That first rush of emigrants had ravaged the stores and houses as locusts will ravage a stretch of country. The suburb of regular villas and prim shops had been completely looted. Doors stood open and windows were smashed; the spread of ugly houses lay among the fields like an unwholesome eruption, awaiting the healing process of Nature. Wealdstone also was deserted by humanity. The flood had swept on towards the open country.

But as they approached Pinner the signs of devastation and desertion began to give way. Here and there women could be seen working in the fields; one or two children scuttled away before the approach of the Goslings and hid in the hedges, children who had evidently grown furtive and suspicious, intimidated by the experiences of the past two months; and when the outlying houses were reached – detached suburban villas, once occupied by relatively wealthy middle-class employers – it was evident that efforts were being made to restore the wreckage of kitchen gardens.

The Goslings had reached the point at which the wave had broken after its great initial energy was spent. Somewhere about this fifteen-mile limit, varying somewhat according to local conditions, the real disintegration of the crowd had begun. As the numerous tokens of the road had shown, a great number of women and children – possibly one-fifth of the whole crowd – had died of starvation and disease before any harbour was reached. From this fifteen-mile circle outwards, an increasing number had been stayed in their flight by the opportunities of obtaining food. Work was urgently demanded for the future, but the determining factor was the present supply of food, and the constriction of immediate supply had decided the question of how great a proportion of the women and children should remain. Here, about Pinner, was more land than the limited number of workers could till, but little of it was arable, and this year there would be almost no harvest of grain.

Vaguely, Blanche realized this. She remembered Aunt May's advice to keep her eyes open, and looking about her as she walked she found little promise of security in the grass fields and the rare signs of human activity.

Mrs. Gosling, eager to find some home at any price, expressed her usual optimistic opinion with regard to the value of money. She saw signs of life again, at last, conditions familiar to her. She thought that they were returning once more to some kind of recognizable civilization, and began, with some renewal of her old vigour, to advise that they should find an hotel or inn and take 'a good look round' before going any further.

Millie, heartened by her mother's belief, was of much the same opinion, and Blanche was summoned from the pole to listen to the proposition.

She shook her head stubbornly.

"I'm not going to argue it out all over again," she said. "You can just look round and see for yourselves that there's no food to be got here. We must get further out."

Mrs. Gosling refused to be convinced, and advanced her superior knowledge of the world to support her judgment of the case.

"Oh! Very well," said Blanche, at last. "Come on to the inn and see for yourselves."

The inn, however, was deserted. All its available supply of food, solid and liquid, had long been exhausted, and the gardenless house had offered no particular attractions as a residence. Houses were cheap in that place, the whole population of Pinner, including children, did not exceed three hundred persons.

They found a woman working in a garden near by, and she, with perhaps unnecessary harshness, warned them that they could not stay in the village. "There's not enough food for us as it is," she said, and made some reference to "silly Londoners."

That was an expression with which the Goslings were to become very familiar in the near future.

The appeal for pity fell on deaf ears. Mrs. Gosling learned that she was only one of many thousands who had made the same appeal.

The sun was high in the sky as they trudged out of Pinner on the road towards Northwood. It was then Blanche suggested that her mother should always ride on the trolly, except when they were facing a hill; and after a few weak protestations the suggestion was accepted. The trolly was lightened of various useless articles of furniture – a grudging sacrifice on the part of Mrs. Gosling – and the party pushed on at a slightly improved pace.

After her disappointment in Pinner, Mrs. Gosling's interest in life began rapidly to decline. Seated in her truck, she fell into long fits of brooding on the past. She was too old and too stereotyped to change, the future held no hope for her, and as the meaning and purpose of her existence faded, the life forces within her surely and ever more rapidly ebbed. Reality to her became the discomfort of the sun's heat, the dust of the road, the creak and scream of the trolly wheels. She was incapable of relating herself to the great scheme of life, her consciousness was limited, as it had always been limited, to her immediate surroundings. She saw herself as a woman outrageously used by fate, but to fate she gave no name; the very idea, indeed, was too abstract to be appreciated by her. Blanche, Millie and that horrible truck were all that was left of her world, and in spirit she still moved in the beloved, familiar places of her suburban home.

* * *

As the Goslings trudged out into the Chilterns they came into new conditions. Soon they found over-crowding in place of desolation. The harvest was ripening and in a month's time the demand for labour would almost equal the supply, for the labour offered was quite absurdly unskilled and ten women would be required to perform the work of one man equipped with machines. But at the end of July the surplus of women, almost exclusively Londoners, had no employment and little food, and many were living on grass, nettles, leaves, any green stuff they could boil and eat, together with such scraps of meat and vegetables as they could steal or beg. Their experiments with wild green stuffs often resulted in some form of poisoning, and dysentery and starvation were rapidly increasing the mortality among them. Nevertheless, in Rickmansworth houses were still at a premium, and many of those who camped perforce in fields or by the roadside were too enfeebled by town-life to stand the exposure of the occasional cold, wet nights. The majority of the women in this ring were those who had been too weak to struggle on. They represented the class least fitted to adapt themselves to the new conditions. The stronger and more capable had persisted, and left these congested areas behind them; and it was evident that in a very few months a balance between labour and supply would be struck by the relentless extermination of the weakest by starvation and disease.

Blanche, if she was unable to grasp the problem which was being so inevitably solved by the forces of natural law, was at least able to recognize clearly enough that she and her two dependents must not linger in the district to which they had now come. Aunt May had warned her that she must push out as far as Amersham at the nearest, but Millie was too tired and footsore to go much further than Rickmansworth that night, and after a fruitless search for shelter they camped out half a mile from the town in the direction of Chorley Wood.

They made some kind of a shield from the weather by emptying and tilting the trolly, and they hid their supply of food behind them at the lowest point of this species of lean-to roof. The two girls had realized that that supply would soon be raided if the fact of its existence were to become known. They had been the object of much scrutiny as they passed, and their appearance of well-being had prompted endless demands for food, from that pitiful crowd of emaciated women and children. It had been a demand quickly put on one side by lying. Their applicants found it only too easy to believe that the Goslings had no food hidden in the truck.

"I hated to refuse some of 'em," Blanche said as they carefully hid what food was left to them, before turning in for the night, "but what good would our little bit have done among all that lot? It would have been gone in half a jiff."

"Well, of course," agreed Millie.

Mrs. Gosling had taken little notice of the starving crowd. "We've got nothin' to give you," was her one form of reply. She might have been dealing with hawkers in Wisteria Grove.

She was curiously apathetic all that afternoon and evening, and raised only the feeblest protestation against the necessity for sleeping in the open air. But she was very restless during the night, her limbs twitched and she moved continually, muttering and sometimes crying out. And as the three women were all huddled together, partly to make the most of their somewhat insufficient lean-to, and partly because they were afraid of the terrors of the open air, both Blanche and Millie were constantly aroused by their mother's movements. Once they heard her calling urgently for "George."

"Mother's odd, isn't she?" whispered Blanche after one such disturbance. "Do you think she's going to be ill?"

"Shouldn't wonder," muttered Millie. "Who wouldn't be?"

In the morning Blanche was very careful with their food. For breakfast they ate only part of a tin of condensed beef between them – Mrs. Gosling indeed ate hardly anything. The eggs which they had brought from Sudbury they reserved, chiefly because they had neither water nor fire.

They drank from a stream, later, and at midday Blanche and Millie each ate one of the eggs raw. Mrs. Gosling refused all food on this occasion. She had been very quiet all the morning, and had made little complaint when she had been forced to walk the many hills which they were now encountering.

Blanche was uneasy and tried to induce her mother to talk. "Do you feel bad, mother?" she asked continually.

"I wish I could get 'ome," was all the reply she received.

"She'll be all right when we can get settled somewhere," grumbled Millie. "If such a time ever comes."

* * *

They came to Amersham in the afternoon. The signs of misery and starvation were here less marked. They were approaching the outer edge of this ring of compression, having passed through the node at Rickmansworth. The faint relief of pressure was evidenced to some extent in the attitude of the people they addressed. It is true that no immediate hope of food and employment were held out to them, but on the one hand Blanche's inquiries were answered with less acerbity and on the other they were less besieged by importunate demands for charity. Blanche gave an egg to one precocious girl of thirteen or so, who insisted on helping them to push the truck uphill, and she and Millie watched the deft way in which the child broke the shell at one end and sucked out the contents. Their own methods had been both unclean and wasteful.

They turned off the Aylesbury Road, towards High Wycombe late in the afternoon and about a mile from Amersham came to a farm where they made their last inquiry that day.

Blanche saw signs of life in the outbuildings and went to investigate, leaving Millie and her mother to guard the truck. She found three women and a girl of fourteen or so milking. For some minutes she stood watching them, the women, after one glance at her, proceeding with their work without paying her any further attention. But, at last, the eldest of the three rose from her stool with a sigh of relief, picked up her wooden bucket of milk, gave the cow a resounding slap on the side, and then, turning to Blanche, said, "Well, my gal, what's for you?"

"Will you change two pints of milk for a small tin of tongue?" asked Blanche. It was the first time she had offered any of their precious tinned meats in exchange for other food, but she wanted milk for her mother, who had hardly eaten anything that day.

The two other women and the girl looked round and regarded Blanche with the first signs of interest they had shown.

"Tongue, eh?" said the older woman. "Where from did you get tongue, my gal?"

"London," replied Blanche tersely.

"When did you leave there?" asked the woman, and then Blanche was engaged in a series of searching questions respecting the country she had passed through.

"You can have the milk if you've anything to put it in," said the woman at last, and Blanche went to fetch the tongue and the two bottles that they had had from Aunt May.

The bottles had to be scalded, a precaution that had not occurred to Blanche, and one of the other women was sent to carry out the operation.

"Well, your tale don't tell us much," said the woman of the farm, "but we always pass the news here, now. Where are you going to sleep tonight?"

Blanche shrugged her shoulders.

"You can sleep here in the outhouses, if you've a mind to," said the woman, "but I warn you we get a crowd. Silly Londoners like yourself for the most part, but we find a use for 'em somehow, though I'd give the lot for three labourers."

She paused and twisted her mouth on one side reflectively. "Ah! Well," she went on with a sigh, "no use grieving over them that's gone; all I was goin' to say was, if you sleep here you'd better keep an eye on what food you've got with you. My lot'll have it before you can say knife, if they get half a chance."

"It isn't us girls, me and my sister," explained Blanche. "It's my mother. She's bad, I'm afraid. If she could sleep in your kitchen...? *She* wouldn't steal anything."

After a short hesitation the woman consented.

Yet neither the glory of being once more within the four walls of a house, nor the refreshment of the milk which she drank readily enough, seemed appreciably to rouse Mrs. Gosling's spirits.

The woman of the farm, a kindly enough creature, plied the old lady with questions, but received few and confused answers in reply. Mrs. Gosling seemed dazed and stupid. "A touch of the sun," the farmer's widow thought.

"The sun's been cruel strong the past week," she said, "but she'll be all right in a day or two, get her to shelter."

"Ah! That's the trouble," said Blanche.

That night the farmer's widow said no more on that subject. She allowed the three Goslings to sleep in an upstair room, in which there was one small bed for the mother, and the two girls slept on the floor. Exchanging confidence for confidence, they brought their truck into the kitchen; and then the farmer's widow proceeded to lock up for the night, an elaborate business, which included the fastening of all ground-floor windows and shutters.

"It's a thievin' crowd we've got about here," she explained, "and you can't blame them or anyone when there ain't enough food to go round. But we have to be careful for 'em. Let 'em go their own way and they'd eat up everything in a week and then starve. It looks like you're being hard on 'em, but it's for their own good. There's some, of course," she went on, "as you have got to get shut of. Only yesterday I had to send one of 'em packing. A Jew woman she was, called 'erself Mrs. Isaacson or something. She was a caution."

Blanche wondered idly if this were the same Mrs. Isaacson who had stayed too long with Aunt May.

The woman of the farm roused the Goslings at sunrise, and she, like Aunt May, had a brisk, practical, morning manner.

She gave the travellers no more food, but when they were nearly ready to take the road again she gave them one valuable piece of information.

"If I was you," she said, "I'd make through Wycombe straight along the road here, and go up over the hill to Marlow. Mind you, they won't let every one stop there. But you look two healthy gals enough and it's getting on towards harvest when there'll be work as you *can* do."

"Marlow?" repeated Blanche, fixing the name in her memory.

The farmer's widow nodded. "There's a man there," she said. "A queer sort, by all accounts. Not like Sam Evans, the butcher at Wycombe, he ain't. Seems as this Marlow chap don't have no truck with gals, except setting 'em to work. However, time'll show. He may change his mind yet."

They had some difficulty with Mrs. Gosling. She refused feebly to leave the house. "I ain't fit to go out," she complained, and when they insisted she asked if they were going home.

"Best say 'yes,'" whispered the woman of the farm. "The sun's got to her head a bit. She'll be all right when you get her to Marlow."

Blanche accepted the suggestion, and by this subterfuge Mrs. Gosling was persuaded into the truck. The girl found the ruins of an umbrella, which they rigged up to protect her from the sun.

Blanche and Millie were quite convinced now that their mother was suffering from a slight attack of sunstroke.

Both the girls were still footsore, and one of Millie's boots had worn into a hole, but they had a definite objective at last, and only some ten or twelve miles to travel before reaching it.

"We shall be there by midday," said Blanche, hopefully.

Unconsciously, every one was using a new measure of time.

The complete and unabridged text is available online, *from flametreepublishing.com/extras*

Darkness

Lord Byron

I HAD A DREAM, *which was not all a dream.*
The bright sun was extinguished, and the stars
Did wander darkling in the eternal space,
Rayless, and pathless, and the icy Earth
Swung blind and blackening in the moonless air;
Morn came and went – and came, and brought no day,
And men forgot their passions in the dread
Of this their desolation; and all hearts
Were chilled into a selfish prayer for light:
And they did live by watchfires – and the thrones,
The palaces of crownéd kings – the huts,
The habitations of all things which dwell,
Were burnt for beacons; cities were consumed,
And men were gathered round their blazing homes
To look once more into each other's face;
Happy were those who dwelt within the eye
Of the volcanos, and their mountain-torch:
A fearful hope was all the World contained;
Forests were set on fire – but hour by hour
They fell and faded – and the crackling trunks
Extinguished with a crash – and all was black.
The brows of men by the despairing light
Wore an unearthly aspect, as by fits
The flashes fell upon them; some lay down
And hid their eyes and wept; and some did rest
Their chins upon their clenchéd hands, and smiled;
And others hurried to and fro, and fed
Their funeral piles with fuel, and looked up
With mad disquietude on the dull sky,
The pall of a past World; and then again
With curses cast them down upon the dust,
And gnashed their teeth and howled: the wild birds shrieked,
And, terrified, did flutter on the ground,
And flap their useless wings; the wildest brutes
Came tame and tremulous; and vipers crawled
And twined themselves among the multitude,
Hissing, but stingless – they were slain for food:
And War, which for a moment was no more,

Did glut himself again: – a meal was bought
With blood, and each sate sullenly apart
Gorging himself in gloom: no Love was left;
All earth was but one thought – and that was Death,
Immediate and inglorious; and the pang
Of famine fed upon all entrails – men
Died, and their bones were tombless as their flesh;
The meagre by the meagre were devoured,
Even dogs assailed their masters, all save one,
And he was faithful to a corse, and kept
The birds and beasts and famished men at bay,
Till hunger clung them, or the dropping dead
Lured their lank jaws; himself sought out no food,
But with a piteous and perpetual moan,
And a quick desolate cry, licking the hand
Which answered not with a caress – he died.
The crowd was famished by degrees; but two
Of an enormous city did survive,
And they were enemies: they met beside
The dying embers of an altar-place
Where had been heaped a mass of holy things
For an unholy usage; they raked up,
And shivering scraped with their cold skeleton hands
The feeble ashes, and their feeble breath
Blew for a little life, and made a flame
Which was a mockery; then they lifted up
Their eyes as it grew lighter, and beheld
Each other's aspects – saw, and shrieked, and died –
Even of their mutual hideousness they died,
Unknowing who he was upon whose brow
Famine had written Fiend. The World was void,
The populous and the powerful was a lump,
Seasonless, herbless, treeless, manless, lifeless –
A lump of death – a chaos of hard clay.
The rivers, lakes, and ocean all stood still,
And nothing stirred within their silent depths;
Ships sailorless lay rotting on the sea,
And their masts fell down piecemeal: as they dropped
They slept on the abyss without a surge –
The waves were dead; the tides were in their grave,
The Moon, their mistress, had expired before;
The winds were withered in the stagnant air,
And the clouds perished; Darkness had no need
Of aid from them – She was the Universe.

A Brief Moment of Rage

Bill Davidson

I KEEP THE GUN hidden. The gun keeps me alive. It's a fair exchange.

Apart from having a loaded Glock in my jacket, the only plan I'd had since killing the old man was to avoid survivors and keep moving south. South was as good as any, but you run out of it, after a while.

I was the outskirts of a seaside town, moving quietly between houses, when somebody behind me said, "Hey."

I turned, slowly. A very young man, maybe only eighteen, something like that. I could have imagined that Jake might have grown up to look very like this tall, skinny boy. I was thinking of him now as a boy, shivering in his jeans and hoodie, messy dark hair flopped across his brow.

"Hey yourself."

He jerked, nervous. Not used to speaking to people, I guessed. He bobbed his head and said, "You're alive, then."

Nine months earlier

It started just like any morning, with the Pure DAB showing 6:45 and playing Classic FM down low; 'The Lark Ascending'. Jeff, without really waking, rolled over and tapped the handle to give us five minutes, coming back to pull me in, my big warm bear.

He snored like he was enjoying the racket, then muttered, "We need another alarm."

"What, one that goes off in the afternoon?"

"One with bigger numerals."

That surprised me. "You can't read the display? Really?"

"Hit forty and everything goes to shit."

I pushed my face into his chest and breathed him in. Then pulled my head up, hearing Abbie starting, not crying yet, but it would get there in a hurry.

I pushed myself against him, "Your turn."

"I was up in the night."

I tried to remember that, and maybe could. It was all blending into one, hard not to wish your baby's life away, wanting her to sleep through. Get out of bed herself. She was coming to the end of this stage anyway, a toddler rather than a baby now. I still called her my baby.

Just a normal morning. Normal, normal, normal.

Half an hour later we were in the kitchen. I had been trying to get Abbie to eat a boiled egg, but she had other uses for it. Breakfast News was on in the background, Steph and Charlie sitting on the red couch, but I wasn't taking any of it in. Normal.

I stood to look out of the window, down at the street four floors below, already busy with cars and bicycles. Pedestrians walking, others standing at the bus stop, looking tired. And, as usual, it made me feel itchy, lives being lived out there while I would be killing the hours, tied to Abbie. Get myself out for coffee at Angela's house, so the babies could hit each other with spoons and we could bitch about Marcus and Jeff, the brothers we married. Maybe waste some time at the Borough gardens if it didn't rain. I'd forgotten to notice the weather forecast, as usual.

Jake had put his school uniform on but still couldn't manage his tie, no matter how hard he tried. Jeff knelt in front of him, telling how he couldn't do it when he was six either, talking him through the steps as he tied, using his patient voice that wasn't patient at all. Jake caught my eye over his Father's back and waggled his eyebrows.

I said, "Wait a damned minute here. I got up in the night. Me. You did it Saturday."

"What, are you sure?"

"Yes, I'm sure. Christ, Jeff, I'm going to be here all day while you…"

I caught myself, about to accuse him of going out gallivanting. I honestly couldn't understand how he stuck that job, that horrible woman who was his boss.

I remember the next moments like they are branded on my consciousness, seared in, so they can come at me again and again, any time, bring me to my knees. Abbie, see her, big blue eyes looking round to make sure she had our attention before her hand comes out and opens, quite deliberately. The egg hitting the floor. Jeff pressing his lips together in a failed effort to stop himself from laughing. Me coming over and being unable to resist pressing my face into her lovely curly head for a second to catch that unbelievable brand-new scent, the skin of her brow so soft under my lips it was almost like powder. She waved her Pooh Bear fork, smiling her triumphant, two-toothed smile.

As I picked the spilled egg from the floor, I was suddenly angry. Not just angry, furious, enraged in a scalding way I had never been before and had no idea I could be. That little shit and her fucking egg. Did she think I was her slave?

Instead of putting the mess on the table, I squeezed it in a tight fist before hurling it across the floor. Then I stood, with my teeth bared, *wanting* this anger. Loving the liberating heat of it, sizzling its ferocious way from my head to the burning tips of my fingers.

Abbie was still in her high chair, but had half clambered out, her face a red mask of fury. She swiped with her Winnie the Pooh fork, raking my forearm. I was going to hit her, was pulling back to do it, but suddenly Jeff was there, huge and crazy in his anger. I screamed at him and he roared back and, as he closed, I threw a chair with everything I had, knocking him back and giving myself time to go for the knife. He hadn't gotten up in the night, that was me, the selfish bastard.

Jeff was coming on again, his face contorted with fury but Jake was on his Father's back, biting his neck, and I saw my chance and stabbed my husband, the carving knife going most of the way into his belly. I pulled the knife out, ready to plunge it in again, when he caught me with a roundhouse punch that smacked my head against the wall. Only my incredible burning fury kept me upright to stab him again, but his next punch caught me square in the face and my legs buckled. I was on my knees and he was beating me, pummeling me with his club like fists as blood from his belly and chest sprayed me.

* * *

I came to, my head on the kitchen floor. I was looking at Abbie, lying broken only inches from my face. There was no doubt that my baby was dead. I could hear a noise coming from my mouth as I pulled myself shakily to my knees, a keening note that I hadn't known I had. I stopped as I caught sight of Jeff. He wasn't dead, but was sitting glazed eyed at the base of the fridge freezer, in a pool of blood that widened even as I watched.

I whispered his name and he had to make an effort to make his eyes focus on me. The ones that needed spectacles now, just to see the time on our clock radio. Pink froth bubbled onto his lips as he spoke. "Thought I'd killed you."

Then he said, "I killed Abbie. Jake too."

But Jake was getting to his feet, looking sick and bloody, but not dead. The television screen was just behind his head and my eyes swept past it and then snapped back. A guy in a bloody shirt was sprawled across the BBC Breakfast couch. The screen went blank.

I put out my arms and Jake stumbled towards me, crying out as he saw his sister, but falling into me, sobbing. Jeff said, "I don't know what came over me. I… I…"

He closed his eyes against the horror and agony and, as I watched, his face relaxed and went slack. His hands fell from his belly.

Jake was crying into my neck and I hushed him, stroking his hair. I couldn't think, couldn't move beyond rocking my little boy. Couldn't believe any of this was real. Two minutes ago, I had been trying to feed Abbie egg that she wanted to push into her ears. Jake whispered, "I wanted to hurt you, Mummy."

I tried to talk but all that came out was "M-m-m-m. T-t-t-t." Like my mouth had lost the ability to form words.

But Jake was crying out and pulling himself into me and I needed to do something for him, my boy. I got myself onto my shaky legs and picked him bodily up, thinking to dial 999. Instead, I glanced out of the window.

The street was in chaos. There had been accidents, cars on the pavement, bodies strewn about the road. People, some injured, were stumbling about, confused, distraught. Like survivors of a bomb or an earthquake.

I slumped back down onto the slippery floor, pulled my live child to my chest and my dead baby into my lap and howled.

* * *

After a while I had to get us out of there. TV was still dead but someone was sobbing quietly on Radio 2. No luck raising anybody on my phone and the few Facebook posts were of people saying they had killed their partners or children or parents.

Jeff was lying dead and so was my beautiful baby. But I had to leave them, get out of that blood smelling house. The electricity had died so the lifts were out, and there were people on the landings, looking stunned, some of them as bloody as me. One or two tried to talk to me as I hurried past, asking what had happened or for help, but most didn't.

I had it in mind to drive to Marcus and Angela's house, thinking Marcus, the policeman, would know what to do. But driving wasn't an option. I pulled Jake close and we walked fast, avoiding looking at the faces around us.

That walk was a horror in itself, but we finally reached the detached house in the suburbs. Nobody answered my knock, so I opened the door onto the neat little hall. Nobody answered my call either, so I walked tentatively inside, keeping Jake close.

Angela was in the bedroom, strangled, I was sure, with Little Mark beside her. I hurried Jake away, even though he had seen much worse carnage on the way, these deaths were more intimate. Then Marcus was coming through the front door, a big man with a crazy look in his eye, holding a pistol.

He asked, "Have you been in the bedroom?"

Not sure what to say to be safe, I just nodded. He held the gun out, butt first.

"This happens again, don't hesitate. Not for a second. Shoot me."

Then he asked, "Is Jeff here?"

I took the gun before answering. Didn't answer while I looked at it, making sure of where the safety was.

I said, "Sorry."

The shudder that went through him came close to taking his legs away. Then he rallied. "Just the two of you? You and Jake?"

"Yea."

"Looks like Jeff caught you a couple of good ones before... whatever."

He pushed past me then, going into the kitchen, saying we should drink whiskey. A lot of it. Coming behind him, I asked about the Police, but he waved it away. "I walked into the station, right to the gun room, got the Glock and walked away."

I can't remember if we did drink whiskey, but I recall him going into the garden and Jake saying, "Uncle Marcus is digging."

We buried his wife and child. My husband and baby were still lying in the flat and I couldn't imagine doing anything about that.

The next day Marcus took the pistol from me, taking it into the garden, to where his family were. He said, "Come and get it, after. Keep it hidden, OK?"

I ran after him and grabbed his arm, suddenly angry. I was briefly terrified of my rage, but, no, this was just normal anger. "We need you! We need you to be the policeman."

He looked at me as if I had lost my mind, and threw my arm off.

The following day, we walked out, Jake and I. We met people in the street, none of whom knew I had the gun and some of whom asked what was going on, like I might know. We made our way to the Council offices, hoping someone would be there, someone who knew something and could be in charge. Smoke was billowing from the big, blocky, ugly building. Someone standing nearby said, "Well, at least something good has come out of this."

We walked to a church, seeing people milling around. I didn't really believe in a God, but we went in. The person standing in front of the altar was a nun, with a badly battered face. She was saying none of us knew God's mind, sobbing as she spoke, but managing to speak loudly enough that I could hear right at the back. Then she said, "But we know he must have a reason. Why we survived when so many others didn't."

That didn't go down well, people were shouting. Somebody calling out that all us survivors were murderers. We had murdered our own families, for fuck's sake. Only the killers had been spared.

That kicked something off and suddenly fighting erupted. We got out of there.

Two days later, the electricity came back on. The day after that, the television, constantly tuned to BBC 1, displayed the banner, 'Public Service announcement to follow shortly.'

It didn't follow shortly, but at least it followed. A Government spokesman behind a desk, somebody I had never seen before. He spent several minutes noisily sorting the hand-written papers in front of him, frowning, as though he didn't know he was being broadcast. Then he cleared his throat and told us...

What did he tell us? That they knew next to fuck all apart from, on 3rd August at 08:14 hours GMT everybody in the whole world seemed to have an episode of uncontrollable rage. It was not known how many had died, but it was a lot. Military personnel were particularly badly hit, what with them having weapons. No truth to the rumor that it was a plot originating in Russia; they were hit as badly as anyone else.

Government was beginning to re-form, but it was patchy and not known when basic services would be returned. He urged people in certain jobs like police and medical services to return to work, saying he knew how hard that would be but we had to get back on our feet, as communities, as a nation.

Then he said, it is not known if this episode is a one-off anomaly, or if it will be repeated. His composure, which had been fairly good up to that point, cracked. But he got it back together and said, the episode took us all by surprise. It may be different if we are prepared for it.

He didn't look like he believed that and I wondered who he had killed.

Over the following weeks, a new normal came close to taking hold. The electricity was sporadic and the city reeked but trucks appeared with food and water. I was torn between keeping Jack by me at all times and wanting to lock him away. I thought, if I feel it coming again I'll blow my own brains out.

Twenty-two days after the first episode, I shot my Jack to death.

I can't remember much about the weeks and months that followed and it's a wonder that I survived. I wandered, my head scoured clear of coherent thought. I walked under clouded moons and clear stars and bright suns and through rain and snow. I slept in wet ditches and stately homes and supermarkets. I was shot at and chased by dogs and half-starved and once someone burned down the house I was sleeping in and I spent a day chasing her down to shoot her like a dog.

I drank wine and vodka till I was unconscious then woke up and started again. I woke one day in a bed in a chintzy bedroom and being warm, an alien feeling by that time. I was hooked up to a clear drip.

I sat up and found I was wearing old style pajamas, blue striped cotton, men's. No gun in sight. The room had floral wallpaper and smelled vaguely musty. I tore the line from my arm and wobbled to the door, but found it locked. I was about to kick and hit it, but knocked instead.

As soon as the person on the other side of the door spoke, I knew it was an elderly man.

"You're awake."

"The door is locked."

"Ah, yes, I'm sorry. How are you feeling?"

"Pretty rough, to be honest. But not murderous in any way, if that's what you're worrying about."

I could almost hear him thinking, this old man who had dressed me in his own pajamas and hooked me to a saline drip. Taken my gun away. Finally, the door opened.

He was hairless, small, smaller than me, and looked about eighty. I could have knocked him over easily, even in my current state.

I said, "Why aren't you pointing the pistol at me?"

He shrugged, "Do I need to, do you think?"

"No."

"You were badly dehydrated. Malnourished. I thought you were dead, when I found you."

When I shrugged again he said, "What we've all been through..." It seemed he couldn't find the right words to end the sentence, so asked, "Are you hungry?"

It turned out I was. Afterwards I said, "I better go. Before the next..."

"Episode?"

"That seems a weedy kind of word for it."

He sat back and laced his fingers together. "I think we're safe enough, for a few days yet."

He said it with such confidence that I had to ask why.

"I've been tracking the episodes and, although there's a wide range, there is definitely a pattern. It always happens between seven and nine a.m., for a start."

"What time is it now?"

"Nearly eleven."

"Ok. I'm still not sure I trust it."

"The time between episodes has been between 21 and 27 days. Always within that range, do you see?"

"But hang on, how many times has it happened?"

He laughed at that, and clapped his hands. Like this was fun.

"Very good, very good! You are quite correct, we are working from a very limited sample. It has occurred twelve times."

"What were you, a statistician?"

"Lucky for you, a retired GP."

Then he said, "You are the first live person I've seen since January."

"What happened to the last one?"

I expected him to say, I killed them, but he threw his hands in the air. "I waved, but he wouldn't come near, not even within shouting distance. There can't be many of us left."

Tim and I lived together then, and it worked in its way. It was easy to find food and I put some weight back on. During the danger periods, I decamped to another house, too far away for us to reach each other. He had managed to record himself in a rage, or episode as he called it. It lasted 32 seconds.

Tim had been an environmental activist, before, and had theories about why this had happened; the Earth taking steps to put itself in balance. He rigged up a radio set and would broadcast regularly, but never managed to contact anyone. One evening, when we were drinking wine after a meal, he said, "Something you should know. I can still manage an erection and I ejaculate."

I was staring at him, my wine glass in my hand. "Congratulations."

"I'm serious."

"What are you saying?"

"That it's not beyond us to find a way to rear children. To manage our condition."

The thought of becoming pregnant, having a baby, bringing it into a world where I would be its mother. I didn't make it to the sink in time.

Still gasping and choking, I rounded on him. "Is that why you saved me?"

Not long after, during one of Tim's safe periods, we attacked each other and I killed him with my bare hands.

It was two months later when I met my next living person, a boy who stepped out behind me to say, "Hey."

"Hey yourself."

"You're alive then."

He took a couple of paces closer so he was only about ten feet away. It hurt to look at him, just a young boy, ducking his head, shy. If Jake had lived… I shook that away.

I asked, "Do you always do this? Make contact?"

"You think that's crazy?"

"Depends on if you want to stay alive."

"I have a question that I like to ask."

OK, something about this seemed wrong, the sideways way this kid was looking at me, sly, like he expected something. I said, "Let me guess. Why, oh why did this terrible thing happen?"

He was shaking his head, irritated. "No! No, not why. Who. Who has done this to us."

I let my hand wander to my chest, almost touching the pistol. "You think this is being done to us?"

"And you think I'm the crazy one? Jesus Christ!"

"Well, who then, Mr. answers?"

"It's obvious. Aliens."

"Really. You think?"

He threw his hand at me, annoyed. "Yes, I think. They've been doing their research on us for years."

"None of that was ever…"

It was as if he couldn't stay still. I wondered if maybe he had been taking drugs, you could just walk into any pharmacy. "You expected they were going to be our chums? Or maybe come down here and shoot it out with us?"

"OK. I see your point. Calm down, though, eh?"

He caught himself. Then he looked at me slit eyed, nodding, like I had just confirmed something for him. "See how it works? We're finished. Easy as pie."

I took a step back, away from him "I knew a wise old man. He thought it was the Earth, having had enough of us. Getting rid of us before we destroyed it."

"Is he still alive?"

"He wasn't that wise." I took another step away. "And I met a holy woman who thought that this was God's judgement. And a guy who said we were a failed experiment, that we had an inbuilt self-destruct button."

"That's all shit."

"Probably. My point is, the only thing we know for sure, is that it happened."

The way the boy was looking at me now. I took another step away. He took a step forward. "Tell yourself that, if it helps."

"OK, how's this? If aliens do land, I'll come find you. Give you a high five."

Another step forward, two more, and we were only a few feet apart, so he could whisper and still be heard. "How long till we lose it next, d'you think?"

I'd had enough of this creepy boy. "I've no idea why you're still alive."

I slid my hand inside my jacket, but he was already pointing his gun at me, grinning.

"That's easy. I was fucking furious from the start."

The Poison Belt

Arthur Conan Doyle

Chapter I
The Blurring of Lines

IT IS IMPERATIVE that now at once, while these stupendous events are still clear in my mind, I should set them down with that exactness of detail which time may blur. But even as I do so, I am overwhelmed by the wonder of the fact that it should be our little group of the 'Lost World' – Professor Challenger, Professor Summerlee, Lord John Roxton, and myself – who have passed through this amazing experience.

When, some years ago, I chronicled in the Daily Gazette our epoch-making journey in South America, I little thought that it should ever fall to my lot to tell an even stranger personal experience, one which is unique in all human annals and must stand out in the records of history as a great peak among the humble foothills which surround it. The event itself will always be marvellous, but the circumstances that we four were together at the time of this extraordinary episode came about in a most natural and, indeed, inevitable fashion. I will explain the events which led up to it as shortly and as clearly as I can, though I am well aware that the fuller the detail upon such a subject the more welcome it will be to the reader, for the public curiosity has been and still is insatiable.

It was upon Friday, the twenty-seventh of August – a date forever memorable in the history of the world – that I went down to the office of my paper and asked for three days' leave of absence from Mr. McArdle, who still presided over our news department. The good old Scotchman shook his head, scratched his dwindling fringe of ruddy fluff, and finally put his reluctance into words.

"I was thinking, Mr. Malone, that we could employ you to advantage these days. I was thinking there was a story that you are the only man that could handle as it should be handled."

"I am sorry for that," said I, trying to hide my disappointment. "Of course if I am needed, there is an end of the matter. But the engagement was important and intimate. If I could be spared –"

"Well, I don't see that you can."

It was bitter, but I had to put the best face I could upon it. After all, it was my own fault, for I should have known by this time that a journalist has no right to make plans of his own.

"Then I'll think no more of it," said I with as much cheerfulness as I could assume at so short a notice. "What was it that you wanted me to do?"

"Well, it was just to interview that deevil of a man down at Rotherfield."

"You don't mean Professor Challenger?" I cried.

"Aye, it's just him that I do mean. He ran young Alec Simpson of the Courier a mile down the high road last week by the collar of his coat and the slack of his breeches. You'll have read of it, likely, in the police report. Our boys would as soon interview a loose alligator in the zoo. But you could do it, I'm thinking – an old friend like you."

"Why," said I, greatly relieved, "this makes it all easy. It so happens that it was to visit Professor Challenger at Rotherfield that I was asking for leave of absence. The fact is, that it is the anniversary of our main adventure on the plateau three years ago, and he has asked our whole party down to his house to see him and celebrate the occasion."

"Capital!" cried McArdle, rubbing his hands and beaming through his glasses. "Then you will be able to get his opeenions out of him. In any other man I would say it was all moonshine, but the fellow has made good once, and who knows but he may again!"

"Get what out of him?" I asked. "What has he been doing?"

"Haven't you seen his letter on 'Scientific Possibeelities' in today's *Times*?"

"No."

McArdle dived down and picked a copy from the floor.

"Read it aloud," said he, indicating a column with his finger. "I'd be glad to hear it again, for I am not sure now that I have the man's meaning clear in my head."

This was the letter which I read to the news editor of the Gazette:

"SCIENTIFIC POSSIBILITIES"

"Sir, – I have read with amusement, not wholly unmixed with some less complimentary emotion, the complacent and wholly fatuous letter of James Wilson MacPhail which has lately appeared in your columns upon the subject of the blurring of Fraunhofer's lines in the spectra both of the planets and of the fixed stars. He dismisses the matter as of no significance. To a wider intelligence it may well seem of very great possible importance – so great as to involve the ultimate welfare of every man, woman, and child upon this planet. I can hardly hope, by the use of scientific language, to convey any sense of my meaning to those ineffectual people who gather their ideas from the columns of a daily newspaper. I will endeavour, therefore, to condescend to their limitation and to indicate the situation by the use of a homely analogy which will be within the limits of the intelligence of your readers."

"Man, he's a wonder – a living wonder!" said McArdle, shaking his head reflectively. "He'd put up the feathers of a sucking-dove and set up a riot in a Quakers' meeting. No wonder he has made London too hot for him. It's a peety, Mr. Malone, for it's a grand brain! We'll let's have the analogy."

"We will suppose," I read, "that a small bundle of connected corks was launched in a sluggish current upon a voyage across the Atlantic. The corks drift slowly on from day to day with the same conditions all round them. If the corks were sentient we could imagine that they would consider these conditions to be permanent and assured. But we, with our superior knowledge, know that many things might happen to surprise the corks. They might possibly float up against a ship, or a sleeping whale, or become entangled in seaweed. In any case, their voyage would probably end by their being thrown up on the rocky coast of Labrador. But what could they know of all this while they drifted so gently day by day in what they thought was a limitless and homogeneous ocean?

"Your readers will possibly comprehend that the Atlantic, in this parable, stands for the mighty ocean of ether through which we drift and that the bunch of corks represents the little and obscure planetary system to which we belong. A third-rate sun, with its rag tag and bobtail of insignificant satellites, we float under

the same daily conditions towards some unknown end, some squalid catastrophe which will overwhelm us at the ultimate confines of space, where we are swept over an etheric Niagara or dashed upon some unthinkable Labrador. I see no room here for the shallow and ignorant optimism of your correspondent, Mr. James Wilson MacPhail, but many reasons why we should watch with a very close and interested attention every indication of change in those cosmic surroundings upon which our own ultimate fate may depend."

"Man, he'd have made a grand meenister," said McArdle. "It just booms like an organ. Let's get doun to what it is that's troubling him."

"The general blurring and shifting of Fraunhofer's lines of the spectrum point, in my opinion, to a widespread cosmic change of a subtle and singular character. Light from a planet is the reflected light of the sun. Light from a star is a self-produced light. But the spectra both from planets and stars have, in this instance, all undergone the same change. Is it, then, a change in those planets and stars? To me such an idea is inconceivable. What common change could simultaneously come upon them all? Is it a change in our own atmosphere? It is possible, but in the highest degree improbable, since we see no signs of it around us, and chemical analysis has failed to reveal it. What, then, is the third possibility? That it may be a change in the conducting medium, in that infinitely fine ether which extends from star to star and pervades the whole universe. Deep in that ocean we are floating upon a slow current. Might that current not drift us into belts of ether which are novel and have properties of which we have never conceived? There is a change somewhere. This cosmic disturbance of the spectrum proves it. It may be a good change. It may be an evil one. It may be a neutral one. We do not know. Shallow observers may treat the matter as one which can be disregarded, but one who like myself is possessed of the deeper intelligence of the true philosopher will understand that the possibilities of the universe are incalculable and that the wisest man is he who holds himself ready for the unexpected. To take an obvious example, who would undertake to say that the mysterious and universal outbreak of illness, recorded in your columns this very morning as having broken out among the indigenous races of Sumatra, has no connection with some cosmic change to which they may respond more quickly than the more complex peoples of Europe? I throw out the idea for what it is worth. To assert it is, in the present stage, as unprofitable as to deny it, but it is an unimaginative numskull who is too dense to perceive that it is well within the bounds of scientific possibility.

"Yours faithfully,

"George Edward Challenger.

"The Briars, Rotherfield."

"It's a fine, steemulating letter," said McArdle thoughtfully, fitting a cigarette into the long glass tube which he used as a holder. "What's your opeenion of it, Mr. Malone?"

I had to confess my total and humiliating ignorance of the subject at issue. What, for example, were Fraunhofer's lines? McArdle had just been studying the matter with the aid of our tame scientist at the office, and he picked from his desk two of those many-coloured spectral bands which bear a general resemblance to the hat-ribbons of some young and ambitious cricket club. He pointed out to me that there were certain black lines which formed crossbars upon the series of brilliant colours extending from the red at one end through gradations of orange, yellow, green, blue, and indigo to the violet at the other.

"Those dark bands are Fraunhofer's lines," said he. "The colours are just light itself. Every light, if you can split it up with a prism, gives the same colours. They tell us nothing. It is the lines that count, because they vary according to what it may be that produces the light. It is these lines that have been blurred instead of clear this last week, and all the astronomers have been quarreling over the reason. Here's a photograph of the blurred lines for our issue tomorrow. The public have taken no interest in the matter up to now, but this letter of Challenger's in the *Times* will make them wake up, I'm thinking."

"And this about Sumatra?"

"Well, it's a long cry from a blurred line in a spectrum to a sick nigger in Sumatra. And yet the chiel has shown us once before that he knows what he's talking about. There is some queer illness down yonder, that's beyond all doubt, and today there's a cable just come in from Singapore that the lighthouses are out of action in the Straits of Sundan, and two ships on the beach in consequence. Anyhow, it's good enough for you to interview Challenger upon. If you get anything definite, let us have a column by Monday."

I was coming out from the news editor's room, turning over my new mission in my mind, when I heard my name called from the waiting-room below. It was a telegraph-boy with a wire which had been forwarded from my lodgings at Streatham. The message was from the very man we had been discussing, and ran thus:

Malone, 17, Hill Street, Streatham. – Bring oxygen. – Challenger.

"Bring oxygen!" The Professor, as I remembered him, had an elephantine sense of humour capable of the most clumsy and unwieldly gambollings. Was this one of those jokes which used to reduce him to uproarious laughter, when his eyes would disappear and he was all gaping mouth and wagging beard, supremely indifferent to the gravity of all around him? I turned the words over, but could make nothing even remotely jocose out of them. Then surely it was a concise order – though a very strange one. He was the last man in the world whose deliberate command I should care to disobey. Possibly some chemical experiment was afoot; possibly – Well, it was no business of mine to speculate upon why he wanted it. I must get it. There was nearly an hour before I should catch the train at Victoria. I took a taxi, and having ascertained the address from the telephone book, I made for the Oxygen Tube Supply Company in Oxford Street.

As I alighted on the pavement at my destination, two youths emerged from the door of the establishment carrying an iron cylinder, which, with some trouble, they hoisted into a waiting motor-car. An elderly man was at their heels scolding and directing in a creaky, sardonic voice. He turned towards me. There was no mistaking those austere features and that goatee beard. It was my old cross-grained companion, Professor Summerlee.

"What!" he cried. "Don't tell me that *you* have had one of these preposterous telegrams for oxygen?"

I exhibited it.

"Well, well! I have had one too, and, as you see, very much against the grain, I have acted upon it. Our good friend is as impossible as ever. The need for oxygen could not have been so urgent that he must desert the usual means of supply and encroach upon the time of those who are really busier than himself. Why could he not order it direct?"

I could only suggest that he probably wanted it at once.

"Or thought he did, which is quite another matter. But it is superfluous now for you to purchase any, since I have this considerable supply."

"Still, for some reason he seems to wish that I should bring oxygen too. It will be safer to do exactly what he tells me."

Accordingly, in spite of many grumbles and remonstrances from Summerlee, I ordered an additional tube, which was placed with the other in his motor-car, for he had offered me a lift to Victoria.

I turned away to pay off my taxi, the driver of which was very cantankerous and abusive over his fare. As I came back to Professor Summerlee, he was having a furious altercation with the men who had carried down the oxygen, his little white goat's beard jerking with indignation. One of the fellows called him, I remember, "a silly old bleached cockatoo," which so enraged his chauffeur that he bounded out of his seat to take the part of his insulted master, and it was all we could do to prevent a riot in the street.

These little things may seem trivial to relate, and passed as mere incidents at the time. It is only now, as I look back, that I see their relation to the whole story which I have to unfold.

The chauffeur must, as it seemed to me, have been a novice or else have lost his nerve in this disturbance, for he drove vilely on the way to the station. Twice we nearly had collisions with other equally erratic vehicles, and I remember remarking to Summerlee that the standard of driving in London had very much declined. Once we brushed the very edge of a great crowd which was watching a fight at the corner of the Mall. The people, who were much excited, raised cries of anger at the clumsy driving, and one fellow sprang upon the step and waved a stick above our heads. I pushed him off, but we were glad when we had got clear of them and safe out of the park. These little events, coming one after the other, left me very jangled in my nerves, and I could see from my companion's petulant manner that his own patience had got to a low ebb.

But our good humour was restored when we saw Lord John Roxton waiting for us upon the platform, his tall, thin figure clad in a yellow tweed shooting-suit. His keen face, with those unforgettable eyes, so fierce and yet so humorous, flushed with pleasure at the sight of us. His ruddy hair was shot with grey, and the furrows upon his brow had been cut a little deeper by Time's chisel, but in all else he was the Lord John who had been our good comrade in the past.

"Hullo, Herr Professor! Hullo, young fella!" he shouted as he came toward us.

He roared with amusement when he saw the oxygen cylinders upon the porter's trolly behind us. "So you've got them too!" he cried. "Mine is in the van. Whatever can the old dear be after?"

"Have you seen his letter in the *Times*?" I asked.

"What was it?"

"Stuff and nonsense!" said Summerlee harshly.

"Well, it's at the bottom of this oxygen business, or I am mistaken," said I.

"Stuff and nonsense!" cried Summerlee again with quite unnecessary violence. We had all got into a first-class smoker, and he had already lit the short and charred old briar pipe which seemed to singe the end of his long, aggressive nose.

"Friend Challenger is a clever man," said he with great vehemence. "No one can deny it. It's a fool that denies it. Look at his hat. There's a sixty-ounce brain inside it – a big engine, running smooth, and turning out clean work. Show me the engine-house and I'll tell you the size of the engine. But he is a born charlatan – you've heard me tell him so to his face – a born charlatan, with a kind of dramatic trick of jumping into the limelight. Things are quiet, so friend Challenger sees a chance to set the public talking about him. You don't imagine that he seriously believes all this nonsense about a change in the ether and a danger to the human race? Was ever such a cock-and-bull story in this life?"

He sat like an old white raven, croaking and shaking with sardonic laughter.

A wave of anger passed through me as I listened to Summerlee. It was disgraceful that he should speak thus of the leader who had been the source of all our fame and given us such an experience as no men have ever enjoyed. I had opened my mouth to utter some hot retort, when Lord John got before me.

"You had a scrap once before with old man Challenger," said he sternly, "and you were down and out inside ten seconds. It seems to me, Professor Summerlee, he's beyond your class, and the best you can do with him is to walk wide and leave him alone."

"Besides," said I, "he has been a good friend to every one of us. Whatever his faults may be, he is as straight as a line, and I don't believe he ever speaks evil of his comrades behind their backs."

"Well said, young fellah-my-lad," said Lord John Roxton. Then, with a kindly smile, he slapped Professor Summerlee upon his shoulder. "Come, Herr Professor, we're not going to quarrel at this time of day. We've seen too much together. But keep off the grass when you get near Challenger, for this young fellah and I have a bit of a weakness for the old dear."

But Summerlee was in no humour for compromise. His face was screwed up in rigid disapproval, and thick curls of angry smoke rolled up from his pipe.

"As to you, Lord John Roxton," he creaked, "your opinion upon a matter of science is of as much value in my eyes as my views upon a new type of shot-gun would be in yours. I have my own judgment, sir, and I use it in my own way. Because it has misled me once, is that any reason why I should accept without criticism anything, however far-fetched, which this man may care to put forward? Are we to have a Pope of science, with infallible decrees laid down *ex cathedra*, and accepted without question by the poor humble public? I tell you, sir, that I have a brain of my own and that I should feel myself to be a snob and a slave if I did not use it. If it pleases you to believe this rigmarole about ether and Fraunhofer's lines upon the spectrum, do so by all means, but do not ask one who is older and wiser than yourself to share in your folly. Is it not evident that if the ether were affected to the degree which he maintains, and if it were obnoxious to human health, the result of it would already be apparent upon ourselves?" Here he laughed with uproarious triumph over his own argument. "Yes, sir, we should already be very far from our normal selves, and instead of sitting quietly discussing scientific problems in a railway train we should be showing actual symptoms of the poison which was working within us. Where do we see any signs of this poisonous cosmic disturbance? Answer me that, sir! Answer me that! Come, come, no evasion! I pin you to an answer!"

I felt more and more angry. There was something very irritating and aggressive in Summerlee's demeanour.

"I think that if you knew more about the facts you might be less positive in your opinion," said I.

Summerlee took his pipe from his mouth and fixed me with a stony stare.

"Pray what do you mean, sir, by that somewhat impertinent observation?"

"I mean that when I was leaving the office the news editor told me that a telegram had come in confirming the general illness of the Sumatra natives, and adding that the lights had not been lit in the Straits of Sunda."

"Really, there should be some limits to human folly!" cried Summerlee in a positive fury. "Is it possible that you do not realize that ether, if for a moment we adopt Challenger's preposterous supposition, is a universal substance which is the same here as at the other side of the world? Do you for an instant suppose that there is an English ether and a Sumatran ether? Perhaps you imagine that the ether of Kent is in some way superior to the ether of Surrey, through which this train is now bearing us. There really are no bounds to the credulity and ignorance of the average layman. Is it conceivable that the ether in Sumatra should be so deadly as to cause total insensibility at the very time when the ether here has had no appreciable effect upon us whatever? Personally, I can truly say that I never felt stronger in body or better balanced in mind in my life."

"That may be. I don't profess to be a scientific man," said I, "though I have heard somewhere that the science of one generation is usually the fallacy of the next. But it does not take much common sense to see that, as we seem to know so little about ether, it might be affected by some local conditions in various parts of the world and might show an effect over there which would only develop later with us."

"With 'might' and 'may' you can prove anything," cried Summerlee furiously. "Pigs may fly. Yes, sir, pigs *may* fly – but they don't. It is not worth arguing with you. Challenger has filled you with his nonsense and you are both incapable of reason. I had as soon lay arguments before those railway cushions."

"I must say, Professor Summerlee, that your manners do not seem to have improved since I last had the pleasure of meeting you," said Lord John severely.

"You lordlings are not accustomed to hear the truth," Summerlee answered with a bitter smile. "It comes as a bit of a shock, does it not, when someone makes you realize that your title leaves you none the less a very ignorant man?"

"Upon my word, sir," said Lord John, very stern and rigid, "if you were a younger man you would not dare to speak to me in so offensive a fashion."

Summerlee thrust out his chin, with its little wagging tuft of goatee beard.

"I would have you know, sir, that, young or old, there has never been a time in my life when I was afraid to speak my mind to an ignorant coxcomb – yes, sir, an ignorant coxcomb, if you had as many titles as slaves could invent and fools could adopt."

For a moment Lord John's eyes blazed, and then, with a tremendous effort, he mastered his anger and leaned back in his seat with arms folded and a bitter smile upon his face. To me all this was dreadful and deplorable. Like a wave, the memory of the past swept over me, the good comradeship, the happy, adventurous days – all that we had suffered and worked for and won. That it should have come to this – to insults and abuse! Suddenly I was sobbing – sobbing in loud, gulping, uncontrollable sobs which refused to be concealed. My companions looked at me in surprise. I covered my face with my hands.

"It's all right," said I. "Only – only it *is* such a pity!"

"You're ill, young fellah, that's what's amiss with you," said Lord John. "I thought you were queer from the first."

"Your habits, sir, have not mended in these three years," said Summerlee, shaking his head. "I also did not fail to observe your strange manner the moment we met. You need not waste your sympathy, Lord John. These tears are purely alcoholic. The man has been drinking. By the way, Lord John, I called you a coxcomb just now, which was perhaps unduly severe. But the word reminds me of a small accomplishment, trivial but amusing, which I used to possess. You know me as the austere man of science. Can you believe that I once had a well-deserved reputation in several nurseries as a farmyard imitator? Perhaps I can help you to pass the time in a pleasant way. Would it amuse you to hear me crow like a cock?"

"No, sir," said Lord John, who was still greatly offended, "it would *not* amuse me."

"My imitation of the clucking hen who had just laid an egg was also considered rather above the average. Might I venture?"

"No, sir, no – certainly not."

But in spite of this earnest prohibition, Professor Summerlee laid down his pipe and for the rest of our journey he entertained – or failed to entertain – us by a succession of bird and animal cries which seemed so absurd that my tears were suddenly changed into boisterous laughter, which must have become quite hysterical as I sat opposite this grave Professor and saw him – or rather heard him – in the character of the uproarious rooster or the puppy whose tail had been trodden upon. Once Lord John passed across his newspaper, upon the margin of which he had written in pencil, "Poor devil! Mad as a hatter." No doubt it was very eccentric, and yet the performance struck me as extraordinarily clever and amusing.

Whilst this was going on, Lord John leaned forward and told me some interminable story about a buffalo and an Indian rajah which seemed to me to have neither beginning nor end. Professor Summerlee had just begun to chirrup like a canary, and Lord John to get to the climax of his story, when the train drew up at Jarvis Brook, which had been given us as the station for Rotherfield.

And there was Challenger to meet us. His appearance was glorious. Not all the turkey-cocks in creation could match the slow, high-stepping dignity with which he paraded his own railway station and the benignant smile of condescending encouragement with which he regarded everybody around him. If he had changed in anything since the days of old, it was that his points had become accentuated. The huge head and broad sweep of forehead, with its plastered lock of black hair, seemed even greater than before. His black beard poured forward in a more impressive cascade, and his clear grey eyes, with their insolent and sardonic eyelids, were even more masterful than of yore.

He gave me the amused hand-shake and encouraging smile which the head master bestows upon the small boy, and, having greeted the others and helped to collect their bags and their cylinders of oxygen, he stowed us and them away in a large motor-car which was driven by the same impassive Austin, the man of few words, whom I had seen in the character of butler upon the occasion of my first eventful visit to the Professor. Our journey led us up a winding hill through beautiful country. I sat in front with the chauffeur, but behind me my three comrades seemed to me to be all talking together. Lord John was still struggling with his buffalo story, so far as I could make out, while once again I heard, as of old, the deep rumble of Challenger and the insistent accents of Summerlee as their brains locked in high and fierce scientific debate. Suddenly Austin slanted his mahogany face toward me without taking his eyes from his steering-wheel.

"I'm under notice," said he.

"Dear me!" said I.

Everything seemed strange today. Everyone said queer, unexpected things. It was like a dream.

"It's forty-seven times," said Austin reflectively.

"When do you go?" I asked, for want of some better observation.

"I don't go," said Austin.

The conversation seemed to have ended there, but presently he came back to it.

"If I was to go, who would look after 'im?" He jerked his head toward his master. "Who would 'e get to serve 'im?"

"Someone else," I suggested lamely.

"Not 'e. No one would stay a week. If I was to go, that 'ouse would run down like a watch with the mainspring out. I'm telling you because you're 'is friend, and you ought to know. If I was to take 'im at 'is word – but there, I wouldn't have the 'eart. 'E and the missus would be like two babes left out in a bundle. I'm just everything. And then 'e goes and gives me notice."

"Why would no one stay?" I asked.

"Well, they wouldn't make allowances, same as I do. 'E's a very clever man, the master – so clever that 'e's clean balmy sometimes. I've seen 'im right off 'is onion, and no error. Well, look what 'e did this morning."

"What did he do?"

Austin bent over to me.

"'E bit the 'ousekeeper," said he in a hoarse whisper.

"Bit her?"

"Yes, sir. Bit 'er on the leg. I saw 'er with my own eyes startin' a marathon from the 'all-door."

"Good gracious!"

"So you'd say, sir, if you could see some of the goings on. 'E don't make friends with the neighbors. There's some of them thinks that when 'e was up among those monsters you wrote about, it was just ''Ome, Sweet 'Ome' for the master, and 'e was never in fitter company. That's what *they* say. But I've served 'im ten years, and I'm fond of 'im, and, mind you, 'e's a great man, when all's said an' done, and it's an honor to serve 'im. But 'e does try one cruel at times. Now look at that, sir. That ain't what you might call old-fashioned 'ospitality, is it now? Just you read it for yourself."

The car on its lowest speed had ground its way up a steep, curving ascent. At the corner a notice-board peered over a well-clipped hedge. As Austin said, it was not difficult to read, for the words were few and arresting:

> WARNING.
> Visitors, Pressmen, and Mendicants are not encouraged.
> G. E. CHALLENGER.

"No, it's not what you might call 'earty," said Austin, shaking his head and glancing up at the deplorable placard. "It wouldn't look well in a Christmas card. I beg your pardon, sir, for I haven't spoke as much as this for many a long year, but today my feelings seem to 'ave got the better of me. 'E can sack me till 'e's blue in the face, but I ain't going, and that's flat. I'm 'is man and 'e's my master, and so it will be, I expect, to the end of the chapter."

We had passed between the white posts of a gate and up a curving drive, lined with rhododendron bushes. Beyond stood a low brick house, picked out with white woodwork, very comfortable and pretty. Mrs. Challenger, a small, dainty, smiling figure, stood in the open doorway to welcome us.

"Well, my dear," said Challenger, bustling out of the car, "here are our visitors. It is something new for us to have visitors, is it not? No love lost between us and our neighbors, is there? If they could get rat poison into our baker's cart, I expect it would be there."

"It's dreadful – dreadful!" cried the lady, between laughter and tears. "George is always quarreling with everyone. We haven't a friend on the countryside."

"It enables me to concentrate my attention upon my incomparable wife," said Challenger, passing his short, thick arm round her waist. Picture a gorilla and a gazelle, and you have the pair of them. "Come, come, these gentlemen are tired from the journey, and luncheon should be ready. Has Sarah returned?"

The lady shook her head ruefully, and the Professor laughed loudly and stroked his beard in his masterful fashion.

"Austin," he cried, "when you have put up the car you will kindly help your mistress to lay the lunch. Now, gentlemen, will you please step into my study, for there are one or two very urgent things which I am anxious to say to you."

Chapter II
The Tide of Death

AS WE CROSSED the hall the telephone-bell rang, and we were the involuntary auditors of Professor Challenger's end of the ensuing dialogue. I say 'we,' but no one within a hundred yards could have failed to hear the booming of that monstrous voice, which reverberated through the house. His answers lingered in my mind.

"Yes, yes, of course, it is I…. Yes, certainly, *the* Professor Challenger, the famous Professor, who else? … Of course, every word of it, otherwise I should not have written it…. I shouldn't be surprised…. There is every indication of it…. Within a day or so at the furthest…. Well, I can't help that, can I? … Very unpleasant, no doubt, but I rather fancy it will affect more important people than you. There is no use whining about it…. No, I couldn't possibly. You must take your chance…. That's enough, sir. Nonsense! I have something more important to do than to listen to such twaddle."

He shut off with a crash and led us upstairs into a large airy apartment which formed his study. On the great mahogany desk seven or eight unopened telegrams were lying.

"Really," he said as he gathered them up, "I begin to think that it would save my correspondents' money if I were to adopt a telegraphic address. Possibly 'Noah, Rotherfield,' would be the most appropriate."

As usual when he made an obscure joke, he leaned against the desk and bellowed in a paroxysm of laughter, his hands shaking so that he could hardly open the envelopes.

"Noah! Noah!" he gasped, with a face of beetroot, while Lord John and I smiled in sympathy and Summerlee, like a dyspeptic goat, wagged his head in sardonic disagreement. Finally Challenger, still rumbling and exploding, began to open his telegrams. The three of us stood in the bow window and occupied ourselves in admiring the magnificent view.

It was certainly worth looking at. The road in its gentle curves had really brought us to a considerable elevation – seven hundred feet, as we afterwards discovered. Challenger's house was on the very edge of the hill, and from its southern face, in which was the study window, one looked across the vast stretch of the weald to where the gentle curves of the South Downs formed an undulating horizon. In a cleft of the hills a haze of smoke marked the position of Lewes. Immediately at our feet there lay a rolling plain of heather, with the long, vivid green stretches of the Crowborough golf course, all dotted with the players. A little to the south, through an opening in the woods, we could see a section of the main line from London to Brighton. In the immediate foreground, under our very noses, was a small enclosed yard, in which stood the car which had brought us from the station.

An ejaculation from Challenger caused us to turn. He had read his telegrams and had arranged them in a little methodical pile upon his desk. His broad, rugged face, or as much of it as was visible over the matted beard, was still deeply flushed, and he seemed to be under the influence of some strong excitement.

"Well, gentlemen," he said, in a voice as if he was addressing a public meeting, "this is indeed an interesting reunion, and it takes place under extraordinary – I may say unprecedented – circumstances. May I ask if you have observed anything upon your journey from town?"

"The only thing which I observed," said Summerlee with a sour smile, "was that our young friend here has not improved in his manners during the years that have passed. I am sorry to state that I have had to seriously complain of his conduct in the train, and I should be wanting in frankness if I did not say that it has left a most unpleasant impression in my mind."

"Well, well, we all get a bit prosy sometimes," said Lord John. "The young fellah meant no real harm. After all, he's an International, so if he takes half an hour to describe a game of football he has more right to do it than most folk."

"Half an hour to describe a game!" I cried indignantly. "Why, it was you that took half an hour with some long-winded story about a buffalo. Professor Summerlee will be my witness."

"I can hardly judge which of you was the most utterly wearisome," said Summerlee. "I declare to you, Challenger, that I never wish to hear of football or of buffaloes so long as I live."

"I have never said one word today about football," I protested.

Lord John gave a shrill whistle, and Summerlee shook his head sadly.

"So early in the day too," said he. "It is indeed deplorable. As I sat there in sad but thoughtful silence –"

"In silence!" cried Lord John. "Why, you were doin' a music-hall turn of imitations all the way – more like a runaway gramophone than a man."

Summerlee drew himself up in bitter protest.

"You are pleased to be facetious, Lord John," said he with a face of vinegar.

"Why, dash it all, this is clear madness," cried Lord John. "Each of us seems to know what the others did and none of us knows what he did himself. Let's put it all together from the first. We got into a first-class smoker, that's clear, ain't it? Then we began to quarrel over friend Challenger's letter in the *Times*."

"Oh, you did, did you?" rumbled our host, his eyelids beginning to droop.

"You said, Summerlee, that there was no possible truth in his contention."

"Dear me!" said Challenger, puffing out his chest and stroking his beard. "No possible truth! I seem to have heard the words before. And may I ask with what arguments the great and famous Professor Summerlee proceeded to demolish the humble individual who had ventured to express an opinion upon a matter of scientific possibility? Perhaps before he exterminates that unfortunate nonentity he will condescend to give some reasons for the adverse views which he has formed."

He bowed and shrugged and spread open his hands as he spoke with his elaborate and elephantine sarcasm.

"The reason was simple enough," said the dogged Summerlee. "I contended that if the ether surrounding the earth was so toxic in one quarter that it produced dangerous symptoms, it was hardly likely that we three in the railway carriage should be entirely unaffected."

The explanation only brought uproarious merriment from Challenger. He laughed until everything in the room seemed to rattle and quiver.

"Our worthy Summerlee is, not for the first time, somewhat out of touch with the facts of the situation," said he at last, mopping his heated brow. "Now, gentlemen, I cannot make my point better than by detailing to you what I have myself done this morning. You will the more easily condone any mental aberration upon your own part when you realize that even I have had moments when my balance has been disturbed. We have had for some years in this household a housekeeper – one Sarah, with whose second name I have never attempted to burden my memory. She is a woman of a severe and forbidding aspect, prim and demure in her bearing, very impassive in her nature, and never known within our experience to show signs of any emotion. As I sat alone at my breakfast – Mrs. Challenger is in the habit of keeping her room of a morning – it suddenly entered my head that it would be entertaining and instructive to see whether I could find any limits to this woman's inperturbability. I devised a simple but effective experiment. Having upset a small vase of flowers which stood in the centre of the cloth, I rang the bell and slipped under the table. She entered and, seeing the room empty, imagined that I had withdrawn to the study. As I had expected, she approached and leaned over the table to replace the vase. I had a vision of a cotton stocking and an elastic-sided boot. Protruding my head, I sank my teeth into the calf of her leg. The experiment was successful beyond belief. For some moments she stood paralyzed, staring down at my head. Then with a shriek she tore herself free and rushed from the room. I pursued her with some thoughts of an explanation, but she flew down the drive, and some minutes afterwards I was able to pick her out with my field-glasses travelling very rapidly in a south-westerly direction. I tell you the anecdote for what it is worth. I drop it into your brains and await its germination. Is it illuminative? Has it conveyed anything to your minds? What do *you* think of it, Lord John?"

Lord John shook his head gravely.

"You'll be gettin' into serious trouble some of these days if you don't put a brake on," said he.

"Perhaps you have some observation to make, Summerlee?"

"You should drop all work instantly, Challenger, and take three months in a German watering-place," said he.

"Profound! Profound!" cried Challenger. "Now, my young friend, is it possible that wisdom may come from you where your seniors have so signally failed?"

And it did. I say it with all modesty, but it did. Of course, it all seems obvious enough to you who know what occurred, but it was not so very clear when everything was new. But it came on me suddenly with the full force of absolute conviction.

"Poison!" I cried.

Then, even as I said the word, my mind flashed back over the whole morning's experiences, past Lord John with his buffalo, past my own hysterical tears, past the outrageous conduct of Professor Summerlee, to the queer happenings in London, the row in the park, the driving of the chauffeur, the quarrel at the oxygen warehouse. Everything fitted suddenly into its place.

"Of course," I cried again. "It is poison. We are all poisoned."

"Exactly," said Challenger, rubbing his hands, "we are all poisoned. Our planet has swum into the poison belt of ether, and is now flying deeper into it at the rate of some millions of miles a minute. Our young friend has expressed the cause of all our troubles and perplexities in a single word, 'poison.'"

We looked at each other in amazed silence. No comment seemed to meet the situation.

"There is a mental inhibition by which such symptoms can be checked and controlled," said Challenger. "I cannot expect to find it developed in all of you to the same point which it has reached in me, for I suppose that the strength of our different mental processes bears some proportion to each other. But no doubt it is appreciable even in our young friend here. After the little outburst of high spirits which so alarmed my domestic I sat down and reasoned with myself. I put it to myself that I had never before felt impelled to bite any of my household. The impulse had then been an abnormal one. In an instant I perceived the truth. My pulse upon examination was ten beats above the usual, and my reflexes were increased. I called upon my higher and saner self, the real G.E.C., seated serene and impregnable behind all mere molecular disturbance. I summoned him, I say, to watch the foolish mental tricks which the poison would play. I found that I was indeed the master. I could recognize and control a disordered mind. It was a remarkable exhibition of the victory of mind over matter, for it was a victory over that particular form of matter which is most intimately connected with mind. I might almost say that mind was at fault and that personality controlled it. Thus, when my wife came downstairs and I was impelled to slip behind the door and alarm her by some wild cry as she entered, I was able to stifle the impulse and to greet her with dignity and restraint. An overpowering desire to quack like a duck was met and mastered in the same fashion.

"Later, when I descended to order the car and found Austin bending over it absorbed in repairs, I controlled my open hand even after I had lifted it and refrained from giving him an experience which would possibly have caused him to follow in the steps of the housekeeper. On the contrary, I touched him on the shoulder and ordered the car to be at the door in time to meet your train. At the present instant I am most forcibly tempted to take Professor Summerlee by that silly old beard of his and to shake his head violently backwards and forwards. And yet, as you see, I am perfectly restrained. Let me commend my example to you."

"I'll look out for that buffalo," said Lord John.

"And I for the football match."

"It may be that you are right, Challenger," said Summerlee in a chastened voice. "I am willing to admit that my turn of mind is critical rather than constructive and that I am not a ready convert to any new theory, especially when it happens to be so unusual and fantastic as this one. However, as I cast my mind back over the events of the morning, and as I reconsider the fatuous conduct of my companions, I find it easy to believe that some poison of an exciting kind was responsible for their symptoms."

Challenger slapped his colleague good-humouredly upon the shoulder. "We progress," said he. "Decidedly we progress."

"And pray, sir," asked Summerlee humbly, "what is your opinion as to the present outlook?"

"With your permission I will say a few words upon that subject." He seated himself upon his desk, his short, stumpy legs swinging in front of him. "We are assisting at a tremendous and awful function. It is, in my opinion, the end of the world."

The end of the world! Our eyes turned to the great bow-window and we looked out at the summer beauty of the country-side, the long slopes of heather, the great country-houses, the cozy farms, the pleasure-seekers upon the links.

The end of the world! One had often heard the words, but the idea that they could ever have an immediate practical significance, that it should not be at some vague date, but now, today, that was a tremendous, a staggering thought. We were all struck solemn and waited in silence for Challenger to continue. His overpowering presence and appearance lent such force to the solemnity of his words that for a moment all the crudities and absurdities of the man vanished, and he loomed before us as something majestic and beyond the range of ordinary humanity. Then to me, at least, there came back the cheering recollection of how twice since we had entered the room he had roared with laughter. Surely, I thought, there are limits to mental detachment. The crisis cannot be so great or so pressing after all.

"You will conceive a bunch of grapes," said he, "which are covered by some infinitesimal but noxious bacillus. The gardener passes it through a disinfecting medium. It may be that he desires his grapes to be cleaner. It may be that he needs space to breed some fresh bacillus less noxious than the last. He dips it into the poison and they are gone. Our Gardener is, in my opinion, about to dip the solar system, and the human bacillus, the little mortal vibrio which twisted and wriggled upon the outer rind of the earth, will in an instant be sterilized out of existence."

Again there was silence. It was broken by the high trill of the telephone-bell.

"There is one of our bacilli squeaking for help," said he with a grim smile. "They are beginning to realize that their continued existence is not really one of the necessities of the universe."

He was gone from the room for a minute or two. I remember that none of us spoke in his absence. The situation seemed beyond all words or comments.

"The medical officer of health for Brighton," said he when he returned. "The symptoms are for some reason developing more rapidly upon the sea level. Our seven hundred feet of elevation give us an advantage. Folk seem to have learned that I am the first authority upon the question. No doubt it comes from my letter in the *Times*. That was the mayor of a provincial town with whom I talked when we first arrived. You may have heard me upon the telephone. He seemed to put an entirely inflated value upon his own life. I helped him to readjust his ideas."

Summerlee had risen and was standing by the window. His thin, bony hands were trembling with his emotion.

"Challenger," said he earnestly, "this thing is too serious for mere futile argument. Do not suppose that I desire to irritate you by any question I may ask. But I put it to you whether there may not be some fallacy in your information or in your reasoning. There is the sun shining as brightly as ever in the blue sky. There are the heather and the flowers and the birds. There are the folk enjoying themselves upon the golf-links and the laborers yonder cutting the corn. You tell us that they and we may be upon the very brink of destruction – that this sunlit day may be that day of doom which the human race has so long awaited. So far as we know, you found this tremendous judgment upon what? Upon some abnormal lines in a spectrum – upon rumours from Sumatra – upon some curious personal excitement which we have discerned in each other. This latter symptom is not so marked but that you and we could, by a deliberate effort, control it. You need not stand on ceremony with us, Challenger. We have all faced death together before now. Speak out, and let us know exactly where we stand, and what, in your opinion, are our prospects for our future."

It was a brave, good speech, a speech from that stanch and strong spirit which lay behind all the acidities and angularities of the old zoologist. Lord John rose and shook him by the hand.

"My sentiment to a tick," said he. "Now, Challenger, it's up to you to tell us where we are. We ain't nervous folk, as you know well; but when it comes to makin' a weekend visit and finding you've run full butt into the Day of Judgment, it wants a bit of explainin'. What's the danger, and how much of it is there, and what are we goin' to do to meet it?"

He stood, tall and strong, in the sunshine at the window, with his brown hand upon the shoulder of Summerlee. I was lying back in an armchair, an extinguished cigarette between my lips, in that sort of half-dazed state in which impressions become exceedingly distinct. It may have been a new phase of the poisoning, but the delirious promptings had all passed away and were succeeded by an exceedingly languid and, at the same time, perceptive state of mind. I was a spectator. It did not seem to be any personal concern of mine. But here were three strong men at a great crisis, and it was fascinating to observe them. Challenger bent his heavy brows and stroked his beard before he answered. One could see that he was very carefully weighing his words.

"What was the last news when you left London?" he asked.

"I was at the Gazette office about ten," said I. "There was a Reuter just come in from Singapore to the effect that the sickness seemed to be universal in Sumatra and that the lighthouses had not been lit in consequence."

"Events have been moving somewhat rapidly since then," said Challenger, picking up his pile of telegrams. "I am in close touch both with the authorities and with the press, so that news is converging upon me from all parts. There is, in fact, a general and very insistent demand that I should come to London; but I see no good end to be served. From the accounts the poisonous effect begins with mental excitement; the rioting in Paris this morning is said to have been very violent, and the Welsh colliers are in a state of uproar. So far as the evidence to hand can be trusted, this stimulative stage, which varies much in races and in individuals, is succeeded by a certain exaltation and mental lucidity – I seem to discern some signs of it in our young friend here – which, after an appreciable interval, turns to coma, deepening rapidly into death. I fancy, so far as my toxicology carries me, that there are some vegetable nerve poisons –"

"Datura," suggested Summerlee.

"Excellent!" cried Challenger. "It would make for scientific precision if we named our toxic agent. Let it be daturon. To you, my dear Summerlee, belongs the honour – posthumous, alas, but none the less unique – of having given a name to the universal destroyer, the Great Gardener's disinfectant. The symptoms of daturon, then, may be taken to be such as I indicate. That it will involve the whole world and that no life can possibly remain behind seems to me to be certain, since ether is a universal medium. Up to now it has been capricious in the places which it has attacked, but the difference is only a matter of a few hours, and it is like an advancing tide which covers one strip of sand and then another, running hither and thither in irregular streams, until at last it has submerged it all. There are laws at work in connection with the action and distribution of daturon which would have been of deep interest had the time at our disposal permitted us to study them. So far as I can trace them" – here he glanced over his telegrams – "the less developed races have been the first to respond to its influence. There are deplorable accounts from Africa, and the Australian aborigines appear to have been already exterminated. The Northern races have as yet shown greater resisting power than the Southern. This, you see, is dated from Marseilles at nine-forty-five this morning. I give it to you verbatim:

"'All night delirious excitement throughout Provence. Tumult of vine growers at Nimes. Socialistic upheaval at Toulon. Sudden illness attended by coma attacked population this morning. *Peste foudroyante*. Great numbers of dead in the streets. Paralysis of business and universal chaos.'

"An hour later came the following, from the same source: –

"'We are threatened with utter extermination. Cathedrals and churches full to overflowing. The dead outnumber the living. It is inconceivable and horrible. Decease seems to be painless, but swift and inevitable.'

"There is a similar telegram from Paris, where the development is not yet as acute. India and Persia appear to be utterly wiped out. The Slavonic population of Austria is down, while the Teutonic has hardly been affected. Speaking generally, the dwellers upon the plains and upon the seashore seem, so far as my limited information goes, to have felt the effects more rapidly than those inland or on the heights. Even a little elevation makes a considerable difference, and perhaps if there be a survivor of the human race, he will again be found upon the summit of some Ararat. Even our own little hill may presently prove to be a temporary island amid a sea of disaster. But at the present rate of advance a few short hours will submerge us all."

Lord John Roxton wiped his brow.

"What beats me," said he, "is how you could sit there laughin' with that stack of telegrams under your hand. I've seen death as often as most folk, but universal death – it's awful!"

"As to the laughter," said Challenger, "you will bear in mind that, like yourselves, I have not been exempt from the stimulating cerebral effects of the etheric poison. But as to the horror with which universal death appears to inspire you, I would put it to you that it is somewhat exaggerated. If you were sent to sea alone in an open boat to some unknown destination, your heart might well sink within you. The isolation, the uncertainty, would oppress you. But if your voyage were made in a goodly ship, which bore within it all your relations and your friends, you would feel that, however uncertain your destination might still remain, you would at least have one common and simultaneous experience which would hold you to the end in the same close communion. A lonely death may be terrible, but a universal one, as painless as this would appear to be, is not, in my judgment, a matter for apprehension. Indeed, I could sympathize with the person who took the view that the horror lay in the idea of surviving when all that is learned, famous, and exalted had passed away."

"What, then, do you propose to do?" asked Summerlee, who had for once nodded his assent to the reasoning of his brother scientist.

"To take our lunch," said Challenger as the boom of a gong sounded through the house. "We have a cook whose omelettes are only excelled by her cutlets. We can but trust that no cosmic disturbance has dulled her excellent abilities. My Scharzberger of '96 must also be rescued, so far as our earnest and united efforts can do it, from what would be a deplorable waste of a great vintage." He levered his great bulk off the desk, upon which he had sat while he announced the doom of the planet. "Come," said he. "If there is little time left, there is the more need that we should spend it in sober and reasonable enjoyment."

And, indeed, it proved to be a very merry meal. It is true that we could not forget our awful situation. The full solemnity of the event loomed ever at the back of our minds and tempered our thoughts. But surely it is the soul which has never faced death which shies strongly from it at the end. To each of us men it had, for one great epoch in our lives, been a familiar presence. As to the lady, she leaned upon the strong guidance of her mighty husband and was well content to go whither his path might lead. The future was our fate. The present was our own. We passed it in goodly comradeship and gentle merriment. Our minds were, as I have said, singularly lucid. Even I struck sparks at times. As to Challenger, he was wonderful! Never have I so realized the elemental greatness of the man, the sweep and power of his understanding. Summerlee drew him on with his chorus of subacid criticism, while Lord John and I laughed at the contest and the lady, her hand upon his sleeve, controlled the bellowings of the philosopher. Life, death, fate, the destiny of man – these were the stupendous subjects of that memorable hour, made vital by the fact that as the meal progressed strange, sudden exaltations in my mind and tinglings in my limbs proclaimed that the invisible tide of death was slowly and gently rising around us. Once I saw Lord John put his hand suddenly to his eyes, and once Summerlee dropped back for an instant in his chair. Each breath we breathed was charged with strange forces. And yet our minds were happy and at ease. Presently Austin laid the cigarettes upon the table and was about to withdraw.

"Austin!" said his master.

"Yes, sir?"

"I thank you for your faithful service." A smile stole over the servant's gnarled face.

"I've done my duty, sir."

"I'm expecting the end of the world today, Austin."

"Yes, sir. What time, sir?"

"I can't say, Austin. Before evening."

"Very good, sir."

The taciturn Austin saluted and withdrew. Challenger lit a cigarette, and, drawing his chair closer to his wife's, he took her hand in his.

"You know how matters stand, dear," said he. "I have explained it also to our friends here. You're not afraid are you?"

"It won't be painful, George?"

"No more than laughing-gas at the dentist's. Every time you have had it you have practically died."

"But that is a pleasant sensation."

"So may death be. The worn-out bodily machine can't record its impression, but we know the mental pleasure which lies in a dream or a trance. Nature may build a beautiful door and hang it with many a gauzy and shimmering curtain to make an entrance to the new life for our wondering souls. In all my probings of the actual, I have always found wisdom and kindness at the core; and if ever the frightened mortal needs tenderness, it is surely as he makes the passage perilous from life to life. No, Summerlee, I will have none of your materialism, for I, at least, am too great a thing to end in mere physical constituents, a packet of salts and three bucketfuls of water. Here – here" – and he beat his great head with his huge, hairy fist – "there is something which uses matter, but is not of it – something which might destroy death, but which death can never destroy."

"Talkin' of death," said Lord John. "I'm a Christian of sorts, but it seems to me there was somethin' mighty natural in those ancestors of ours who were buried with their axes and bows and arrows and the like, same as if they were livin' on just the same as they used to. I don't know," he added, looking round the table in a shamefaced way, "that I wouldn't feel more homely myself if I was put away with my old .450 Express and the fowlin'-piece, the shorter one with the rubbered stock, and a clip or two of cartridges – just a fool's fancy, of course, but there it is. How does it strike you, Herr Professor?"

"Well," said Summerlee, "since you ask my opinion, it strikes me as an indefensible throwback to the Stone Age or before it. I'm of the twentieth century myself, and would wish to die like a reasonable civilized man. I don't know that I am more afraid of death than the rest of you, for I am an oldish man, and, come what may, I can't have very much longer to live; but it is all against my nature to sit waiting without a struggle like a sheep for the butcher. Is it quite certain, Challenger, that there is nothing we can do?"

"To save us – nothing," said Challenger. "To prolong our lives a few hours and thus to see the evolution of this mighty tragedy before we are actually involved in it – that may prove to be within my powers. I have taken certain steps –"

"The oxygen?"

"Exactly. The oxygen."

"But what can oxygen effect in the face of a poisoning of the ether? There is not a greater difference in quality between a brick-bat and a gas than there is between oxygen and ether. They are different planes of matter. They cannot impinge upon one another. Come, Challenger, you could not defend such a proposition."

"My good Summerlee, this etheric poison is most certainly influenced by material agents. We see it in the methods and distribution of the outbreak. We should not *a priori* have expected it, but it is undoubtedly a fact. Hence I am strongly of opinion that a gas like oxygen, which increases the vitality and the resisting power of the body, would be extremely likely to delay the action of what you have so happily named the daturon. It may be that I am mistaken, but I have every confidence in the correctness of my reasoning."

"Well," said Lord John, "if we've got to sit suckin' at those tubes like so many babies with their bottles, I'm not takin' any."

"There will be no need for that," Challenger answered. "We have made arrangements – it is to my wife that you chiefly owe it – that her boudoir shall be made as airtight as is practicable. With matting and varnished paper."

"Good heavens, Challenger, you don't suppose you can keep out ether with varnished paper?"

"Really, my worthy friend, you are a trifle perverse in missing the point. It is not to keep out the ether that we have gone to such trouble. It is to keep in the oxygen. I trust that if we can ensure an atmosphere hyper-oxygenated to a certain point, we may be able to retain our senses. I had two tubes of the gas and you have brought me three more. It is not much, but it is something."

"How long will they last?"

"I have not an idea. We will not turn them on until our symptoms become unbearable. Then we shall dole the gas out as it is urgently needed. It may give us some hours, possibly even some days, on which we may look out upon a blasted world. Our own fate is delayed to that extent, and we will have the very singular experience, we five, of being, in all probability, the absolute rear guard of the human race upon its march into the unknown. Perhaps you will be kind enough now to give me a hand with the cylinders. It seems to me that the atmosphere already grows somewhat more oppressive."

Chapter III
Submerged

THE CHAMBER which was destined to be the scene of our unforgettable experience was a charmingly feminine sitting-room, some fourteen or sixteen feet square. At the end of it, divided by a curtain of red velvet, was a small apartment which formed the Professor's dressing-room. This in turn opened into a large bedroom. The curtain was still hanging, but the boudoir and dressing-room could be taken as one chamber for the purposes of our experiment. One door and the window frame had been plastered round with varnished paper so as to be practically sealed. Above the other door, which opened on to the landing, there hung a fanlight which could be drawn by a cord when some ventilation became absolutely necessary. A large shrub in a tub stood in each corner.

"How to get rid of our excessive carbon dioxide without unduly wasting our oxygen is a delicate and vital question," said Challenger, looking round him after the five iron tubes had been laid side by side against the wall. "With longer time for preparation I could have brought the whole concentrated force of my intelligence to bear more fully upon the problem, but as it is we must do what we can. The shrubs will be of some small service. Two of the oxygen tubes are ready to be turned on at an instant's notice, so that we cannot be taken unawares. At the same time, it would be well not to go far from the room, as the crisis may be a sudden and urgent one."

There was a broad, low window opening out upon a balcony. The view beyond was the same as that which we had already admired from the study. Looking out, I could see no sign of disorder anywhere. There was a road curving down the side of the hill, under my very eyes. A cab from the station, one of those prehistoric survivals which are only to be found in our country villages, was toiling slowly up the hill. Lower down was a nurse girl wheeling a perambulator and leading a second child by the hand. The blue reeks of smoke from the cottages gave the whole widespread landscape an air of settled order and homely comfort. Nowhere in the blue heaven or on the sunlit earth was there any foreshadowing of a catastrophe. The harvesters were back in the fields once more and the golfers, in pairs and fours, were still streaming round the links. There was so strange a turmoil within my own head, and such a jangling of my overstrung nerves, that the indifference of those people was amazing.

"Those fellows don't seem to feel any ill effects," said I, pointing down at the links.

"Have you played golf?" asked Lord John.

"No, I have not."

"Well, young fellah, when you do you'll learn that once fairly out on a round, it would take the crack of doom to stop a true golfer. Halloa! There's that telephone-bell again."

From time to time during and after lunch the high, insistent ring had summoned the Professor. He gave us the news as it came through to him in a few curt sentences. Such terrific items had never been registered in the world's history before. The great shadow was creeping up from the south like a rising tide of death. Egypt had gone through its delirium and was now comatose. Spain and Portugal, after a wild frenzy in which the Clericals and the Anarchists had fought most desperately, were now fallen silent. No cable messages were received any longer from South America. In North America the southern states, after some terrible racial rioting, had succumbed to the poison. North of Maryland the effect was not yet marked, and in Canada it was hardly perceptible. Belgium, Holland, and Denmark had each in turn been affected. Despairing messages were flashing from every quarter to the great centres of learning, to the chemists and the doctors of world-wide repute, imploring their advice. The astronomers too were deluged with inquiries. Nothing could be done. The thing was universal and beyond our human knowledge or control. It was death – painless but inevitable – death for young and old, for weak and strong, for rich and poor, without hope or possibility of escape. Such was the news which, in scattered, distracted messages, the telephone had brought us. The great cities already knew their fate and so far as we could gather were preparing to meet it with dignity and resignation. Yet here were our golfers and laborers like the lambs who gambol under the shadow of the knife. It seemed amazing. And yet how could they know? It had all come upon us in one giant stride. What was there in the morning paper to alarm them? And now it was but three in the afternoon. Even as we looked some rumour seemed to have spread, for we saw the reapers hurrying from the fields. Some of the golfers were returning to the club-house. They were running as if taking refuge from a shower. Their little caddies trailed behind them. Others were continuing their game. The nurse had turned and was pushing her perambulator hurriedly up the hill again. I noticed that she had her hand to her brow. The cab had stopped and the tired horse, with his head sunk to his knees, was resting. Above there was a perfect summer sky – one huge vault of unbroken blue, save for a few fleecy white clouds over the distant downs. If the human race must die today, it was at least upon a glorious death-bed. And yet all that gentle loveliness of nature made this terrific and wholesale destruction the more pitiable and awful. Surely it was too goodly a residence that we should be so swiftly, so ruthlessly, evicted from it!

But I have said that the telephone-bell had rung once more. Suddenly I heard Challenger's tremendous voice from the hall.

"Malone!" he cried. "You are wanted."

I rushed down to the instrument. It was McArdle speaking from London.

"That you, Mr. Malone?" cried his familiar voice. "Mr. Malone, there are terrible goings-on in London. For God's sake, see if Professor Challenger can suggest anything that can be done."

"He can suggest nothing, sir," I answered. "He regards the crisis as universal and inevitable. We have some oxygen here, but it can only defer our fate for a few hours."

"Oxygen!" cried the agonized voice. "There is no time to get any. The office has been a perfect pandemonium ever since you left in the morning. Now half of the staff are insensible. I am weighed down with heaviness myself. From my window I can see the people lying thick in Fleet Street. The traffic is all held up. Judging by the last telegrams, the whole world –"

His voice had been sinking, and suddenly stopped. An instant later I heard through the telephone a muffled thud, as if his head had fallen forward on the desk.

"Mr. McArdle!" I cried. "Mr. McArdle!"

There was no answer. I knew as I replaced the receiver that I should never hear his voice again.

At that instant, just as I took a step backwards from the telephone, the thing was on us. It was as if we were bathers, up to our shoulders in water, who suddenly are submerged by a rolling wave. An invisible hand seemed to have quietly closed round my throat and to be gently pressing the life from me. I was conscious of immense oppression upon my chest, great tightness within my head, a loud singing in my ears, and bright flashes before my eyes. I staggered to the balustrades of the stair. At the same moment, rushing and snorting like a wounded buffalo, Challenger dashed past me, a terrible vision, with red-purple face, engorged eyes, and bristling hair. His little wife, insensible to all appearance, was slung over his great shoulder, and he blundered and thundered up the stair, scrambling and tripping, but carrying himself and her through sheer will-force through that mephitic atmosphere to the haven of temporary safety. At the sight of his effort I too rushed up the steps, clambering, falling, clutching at the rail, until I tumbled half senseless upon by face on the upper landing. Lord John's fingers of steel were in the collar of my coat, and a moment later I was stretched upon my back, unable to speak or move, on the boudoir carpet. The woman lay beside me, and Summerlee was bunched in a chair by the window, his head nearly touching his knees. As in a dream I saw Challenger, like a monstrous beetle, crawling slowly across the floor, and a moment later I heard the gentle hissing of the escaping oxygen. Challenger breathed two or three times with enormous gulps, his lungs roaring as he drew in the vital gas.

"It works!" he cried exultantly. "My reasoning has been justified!" He was up on his feet again, alert and strong. With a tube in his hand he rushed over to his wife and held it to her face. In a few seconds she moaned, stirred, and sat up. He turned to me, and I felt the tide of life stealing warmly through my arteries. My reason told me that it was but a little respite, and yet, carelessly as we talk of its value, every hour of existence now seemed an inestimable thing. Never have I known such a thrill of sensuous joy as came with that freshet of life. The weight fell away from my lungs, the band loosened from my brow, a sweet feeling of peace and gentle, languid comfort stole over me. I lay watching Summerlee revive under the same remedy, and finally Lord John took his turn. He sprang to his feet and gave me a hand to rise, while Challenger picked up his wife and laid her on the settee.

"Oh, George, I am so sorry you brought me back," she said, holding him by the hand. "The door of death is indeed, as you said, hung with beautiful, shimmering curtains; for, once the choking feeling had passed, it was all unspeakably soothing and beautiful. Why have you dragged me back?"

"Because I wish that we make the passage together. We have been together so many years. It would be sad to fall apart at the supreme moment."

For a moment in his tender voice I caught a glimpse of a new Challenger, something very far from the bullying, ranting, arrogant man who had alternately amazed and offended his generation. Here in the shadow of death was the innermost Challenger, the man who had won and held a woman's love. Suddenly his mood changed and he was our strong captain once again.

"Alone of all mankind I saw and foretold this catastrophe," said he with a ring of exultation and scientific triumph in his voice. "As to you, my good Summerlee, I trust your last doubts have been resolved as to the meaning of the blurring of the lines in the spectrum and that you will no longer contend that my letter in the *Times* was based upon a delusion."

For once our pugnacious colleague was deaf to a challenge. He could but sit gasping and stretching his long, thin limbs, as if to assure himself that he was still really upon this planet. Challenger walked across to the oxygen tube, and the sound of the loud hissing fell away till it was the most gentle sibilation.

"We must husband our supply of the gas," said he. "The atmosphere of the room is now strongly hyperoxygenated, and I take it that none of us feel any distressing symptoms. We can only determine by actual experiments what amount added to the air will serve to neutralize the poison. Let us see how that will do."

We sat in silent nervous tension for five minutes or more, observing our own sensations. I had just begun to fancy that I felt the constriction round my temples again when Mrs. Challenger called out from the sofa that she was fainting. Her husband turned on more gas.

"In pre-scientific days," said he, "they used to keep a white mouse in every submarine, as its more delicate organization gave signs of a vicious atmosphere before it was perceived by the sailors. You, my dear, will be our white mouse. I have now increased the supply and you are better."

"Yes, I am better."

"Possibly we have hit upon the correct mixture. When we have ascertained exactly how little will serve we shall be able to compute how long we shall be able to exist. Unfortunately, in resuscitating ourselves we have already consumed a considerable proportion of this first tube."

"Does it matter?" asked Lord John, who was standing with his hands in his pockets close to the window. "If we have to go, what is the use of holdin' on? You don't suppose there's any chance for us?"

Challenger smiled and shook his head.

"Well, then, don't you think there is more dignity in takin' the jump and not waitin' to be pushed in? If it must be so, I'm for sayin' our prayers, turnin' off the gas, and openin' the window."

"Why not?" said the lady bravely. "Surely, George, Lord John is right and it is better so."

"I most strongly object," cried Summerlee in a querulous voice. "When we must die let us by all means die, but to deliberately anticipate death seems to me to be a foolish and unjustifiable action."

"What does our young friend say to it?" asked Challenger.

"I think we should see it to the end."

"And I am strongly of the same opinion," said he.

"Then, George, if you say so, I think so too," cried the lady.

"Well, well, I'm only puttin' it as an argument," said Lord John. "If you all want to see it through I am with you. It's dooced interestin', and no mistake about that. I've had my share of adventures in my life, and as many thrills as most folk, but I'm endin' on my top note."

"Granting the continuity of life," said Challenger.

"A large assumption!" cried Summerlee. Challenger stared at him in silent reproof.

"Granting the continuity of life," said he, in his most didactic manner, "none of us can predicate what opportunities of observation one may have from what we may call the spirit plane to the plane of matter. It surely must be evident to the most obtuse person" (here he glared a Summerlee) "that it is while we are ourselves material that we are most fitted to watch and form a judgment upon material phenomena. Therefore it is only by keeping alive for these few extra hours that we can hope to carry on with us to some future existence a clear conception of the most stupendous event that the world, or the universe so far as we know it, has ever encountered. To me it would seem a deplorable thing that we should in any way curtail by so much as a minute so wonderful an experience."

"I am strongly of the same opinion," cried Summerlee.

"Carried without a division," said Lord John. "By George, that poor devil of a chauffeur of yours down in the yard has made his last journey. No use makin' a sally and bringin' him in?"

"It would be absolute madness," cried Summerlee.

"Well, I suppose it would," said Lord John. "It couldn't help him and would scatter our gas all over the house, even if we ever got back alive. My word, look at the little birds under the trees!"

We drew four chairs up to the long, low window, the lady still resting with closed eyes upon the settee. I remember that the monstrous and grotesque idea crossed my mind – the illusion may have been heightened by the heavy stuffiness of the air which we were breathing – that we were in four front seats of the stalls at the last act of the drama of the world.

In the immediate foreground, beneath our very eyes, was the small yard with the half-cleaned motor-car standing in it. Austin, the chauffeur, had received his final notice at last, for he was sprawling beside the wheel, with a great black bruise upon his forehead where it had struck the step or mud-guard in falling. He still held in his hand the nozzle of the hose with which he had been washing down his machine. A couple of small plane trees stood in the corner of the yard, and underneath them lay several pathetic little balls of fluffy feathers, with tiny feet uplifted. The sweep of death's scythe had included everything, great and small, within its swath.

Over the wall of the yard we looked down upon the winding road, which led to the station. A group of the reapers whom we had seen running from the fields were lying all pell-mell, their bodies crossing each other, at the bottom of it. Farther up, the nurse-girl lay with her head and shoulders propped against the slope of the grassy bank. She had taken the baby from the perambulator, and it was a motionless bundle of wraps in her arms. Close behind her a tiny patch upon the roadside showed where the little boy was stretched. Still nearer to us was the dead cab-horse, kneeling between the shafts. The old driver was hanging over the splash-board like some grotesque scarecrow, his arms dangling absurdly in front of him. Through the window we could dimly discern that a young man was seated inside. The door was swinging open and his hand was grasping the handle, as if he had attempted to leap forth at the last instant. In the middle distance lay the golf links, dotted as they had been in the morning with the dark figures of the golfers, lying motionless upon the grass of the course or among the heather which skirted it. On one particular green there were eight bodies stretched where a foursome with its caddies had held to their game to the last. No bird flew in the blue vault of heaven, no man or beast moved upon the vast countryside which lay before us. The evening sun shone its peaceful radiance across it, but there brooded over it all the stillness and the silence of universal death – a death in which we were so soon to join. At the present instant that one frail sheet of glass, by holding in the extra oxygen which counteracted the poisoned ether, shut us off from the fate of all our kind. For a few short hours the knowledge and foresight of one man could preserve our little oasis of life in the vast desert of death and save us from participation in the common catastrophe. Then the gas would run low, we too should lie gasping upon that cherry-coloured boudoir carpet, and the fate of the human race and of all earthly life would be complete. For a long time, in a mood which was too solemn for speech, we looked out at the tragic world.

"There is a house on fire," said Challenger at last, pointing to a column of smoke which rose above the trees. "There will, I expect, be many such – possibly whole cities in flames – when we consider how many folk may have dropped with lights in their hands. The fact of combustion is in itself enough to show that the proportion of oxygen in the atmosphere is normal and that it is the ether which is at fault. Ah, there you see another blaze on the top of Crowborough Hill. It is the golf clubhouse, or I am mistaken. There is the church clock chiming the hour. It would interest our philosophers to know that man-made mechanisms have survived the race who made it."

"By George!" cried Lord John, rising excitedly from his chair. "What's that puff of smoke? It's a train."

We heard the roar of it, and presently it came flying into sight, going at what seemed to me to be a prodigious speed. Whence it had come, or how far, we had no means of knowing. Only by some miracle of luck could it have gone any distance. But now we were to see the terrific end of its career. A train of coal trucks stood motionless upon the line. We held our breath as the express roared along the same track. The crash was horrible. Engine and carriages piled themselves into a hill of splintered wood and twisted iron. Red spurts of flame flickered up from the wreckage until it was all ablaze. For half an hour we sat with hardly a word, stunned by the stupendous sight.

"Poor, poor people!" cried Mrs. Challenger at last, clinging with a whimper to her husband's arm.

"My dear, the passengers on that train were no more animate than the coals into which they crashed or the carbon which they have now become," said Challenger, stroking her hand soothingly. "It was a train of the living when it left Victoria, but it was driven and freighted by the dead long before it reached its fate."

"All over the world the same thing must be going on," said I as a vision of strange happenings rose before me. "Think of the ships at sea – how they will steam on and on, until the furnaces die down or until they run full tilt upon some beach. The sailing ships too – how they will back and fill with their cargoes of dead sailors, while their timbers rot and their joints leak, till one by one they sink below the surface. Perhaps a century hence the Atlantic may still be dotted with the old drifting derelicts."

"And the folk in the coal-mines," said Summerlee with a dismal chuckle. "If ever geologists should by any chance live upon earth again they will have some strange theories of the existence of man in carboniferous strata."

"I don't profess to know about such things," remarked Lord John, "but it seems to me the earth will be 'To let, empty,' after this. When once our human crowd is wiped off it, how will it ever get on again?"

"The world was empty before," Challenger answered gravely. "Under laws which in their inception are beyond and above us, it became peopled. Why may the same process not happen again?"

"My dear Challenger, you can't mean that?"

"I am not in the habit, Professor Summerlee, of saying things which I do not mean. The observation is trivial." Out went the beard and down came the eyelids.

"Well, you lived an obstinate dogmatist, and you mean to die one," said Summerlee sourly.

"And you, sir, have lived an unimaginative obstructionist and never can hope now to emerge from it."

"Your worst critics will never accuse you of lacking imagination," Summerlee retorted.

"Upon my word!" said Lord John. "It would be like you if you used up our last gasp of oxygen in abusing each other. What can it matter whether folk come back or not? It surely won't be in our time."

"In that remark, sir, you betray your own very pronounced limitations," said Challenger severely. "The true scientific mind is not to be tied down by its own conditions of time and space. It builds itself an observatory erected upon the border line of present, which separates the infinite past from the infinite future. From this sure post it makes its sallies even to the beginning and to the end of all things. As to death, the scientific mind dies at its post working in normal and methodic fashion to the end. It disregards so petty a thing as its own physical dissolution as completely as it does all other limitations upon the plane of matter. Am I right, Professor Summerlee?"

Summerlee grumbled an ungracious assent.

"With certain reservations, I agree," said he.

"The ideal scientific mind," continued Challenger – "I put it in the third person rather than appear to be too self-complacent – the ideal scientific mind should be capable of thinking out a point of abstract knowledge in the interval between its owner falling from a balloon and reaching the earth. Men of this strong fibre are needed to form the conquerors of nature and the bodyguard of truth."

"It strikes me nature's on top this time," said Lord John, looking out of the window. "I've read some leadin' articles about you gentlemen controllin' her, but she's gettin' a bit of her own back."

"It is but a temporary setback," said Challenger with conviction. "A few million years, what are they in the great cycle of time? The vegetable world has, as you can see, survived. Look at the leaves of that plane tree. The birds are dead, but the plant flourishes. From this vegetable life in pond and in marsh will come, in time, the tiny crawling microscopic slugs which are the pioneers of that great army of life in which for the instant we five have the extraordinary duty of serving as rear guard. Once the lowest form of life has established itself, the final advent of man is as certain as the growth of the oak from the acorn. The old circle will swing round once more."

"But the poison?" I asked. "Will that not nip life in the bud?"

"The poison may be a mere stratum or layer in the ether – a mephitic Gulf Stream across that mighty ocean in which we float. Or tolerance may be established and life accommodate itself to a new condition. The mere fact that with a comparatively small hyperoxygenation of our blood we can hold out against it is surely a proof in itself that no very great change would be needed to enable animal life to endure it."

The smoking house beyond the trees had burst into flames. We could see the high tongues of fire shooting up into the air.

"It's pretty awful," muttered Lord John, more impressed than I had ever seen him.

"Well, after all, what does it matter?" I remarked. "The world is dead. Cremation is surely the best burial."

"It would shorten us up if this house went ablaze."

"I foresaw the danger," said Challenger, "and asked my wife to guard against it."

"Everything is quite safe, dear. But my head begins to throb again. What a dreadful atmosphere!"

"We must change it," said Challenger. He bent over his cylinder of oxygen.

"It's nearly empty," said he. "It has lasted us some three and a half hours. It is now close on eight o'clock. We shall get through the night comfortably. I should expect the end about nine o'clock tomorrow morning. We shall see one sunrise, which shall be all our own."

He turned on his second tube and opened for half a minute the fanlight over the door. Then as the air became perceptibly better, but our own symptoms more acute, he closed it once again.

"By the way," said he, "man does not live upon oxygen alone. It's dinner time and over. I assure you, gentlemen, that when I invited you to my home and to what I had hoped would be an interesting reunion, I had intended that my kitchen should justify itself. However, we must do what we can. I am sure that you will agree with me that it would be folly to consume our air too rapidly by lighting an oil-stove. I have some small provision of cold meats, bread, and pickles which, with a couple of bottles of claret, may serve our turn. Thank you, my dear – now as ever you are the queen of managers."

It was indeed wonderful how, with the self-respect and sense of propriety of the British housekeeper, the lady had within a few minutes adorned the central table with a snow-white cloth, laid the napkins upon it, and set forth the simple meal with all the elegance of civilization, including an electric torch lamp in the centre. Wonderful also was it to find that our appetites were ravenous.

"It is the measure of our emotion," said Challenger with that air of condescension with which he brought his scientific mind to the explanation of humble facts. "We have gone through a great crisis. That means molecular disturbance. That in turn means the need for repair. Great sorrow or great joy should bring intense hunger – not abstinence from food, as our novelists will have it."

"That's why the country folk have great feasts at funerals," I hazarded.

"Exactly. Our young friend has hit upon an excellent illustration. Let me give you another slice of tongue."

"The same with savages," said Lord John, cutting away at the beef. "I've seen them buryin' a chief up the Aruwimi River, and they ate a hippo that must have weighed as much as a tribe. There are some of them down New Guinea way that eat the late-lamented himself, just by way of a last tidy up. Well, of all the funeral feasts on this earth, I suppose the one we are takin' is the queerest."

"The strange thing is," said Mrs. Challenger, "that I find it impossible to feel grief for those who are gone. There are my father and mother at Bedford. I know that they are dead, and yet in this tremendous universal tragedy I can feel no sharp sorrow for any individuals, even for them."

"And my old mother in her cottage in Ireland," said I. "I can see her in my mind's eye, with her shawl and her lace cap, lying back with closed eyes in the old high-backed chair near the window, her glasses and her book beside her. Why should I mourn her? She has passed and I am passing, and I may be nearer her in some other life than England is to Ireland. Yet I grieve to think that that dear body is no more."

"As to the body," remarked Challenger, "we do not mourn over the parings of our nails nor the cut locks of our hair, though they were once part of ourselves. Neither does a one-legged man yearn sentimentally over his missing member. The physical body has rather been a source of pain and fatigue to us. It is the constant index of our limitations. Why then should we worry about its detachment from our psychical selves?"

"If they can indeed be detached," Summerlee grumbled. "But, anyhow, universal death is dreadful."

"As I have already explained," said Challenger, "a universal death must in its nature be far less terrible than a isolated one."

"Same in a battle," remarked Lord John. "If you saw a single man lying on that floor with his chest knocked in and a hole in his face it would turn you sick. But I've seen ten thousand on their backs in the Soudan, and it gave me no such feelin', for when you are makin' history the life of any man is too small a thing to worry over. When a thousand million pass over together, same as happened today, you can't pick your own partic'lar out of the crowd."

"I wish it were well over with us," said the lady wistfully. "Oh, George, I am so frightened."

"You'll be the bravest of us all, little lady, when the time comes. I've been a blusterous old husband to you, dear, but you'll just bear in mind that G.E.C. is as he was made and couldn't help himself. After all, you wouldn't have had anyone else?"

"No one in the whole wide world, dear," said she, and put her arms round his bull neck. We three walked to the window and stood amazed at the sight which met our eyes.

Darkness had fallen and the dead world was shrouded in gloom. But right across the southern horizon was one long vivid scarlet streak, waxing and waning in vivid pulses of life, leaping suddenly to a crimson zenith and then dying down to a glowing line of fire.

"Lewes is ablaze!"

"No, it is Brighton which is burning," said Challenger, stepping across to join us. "You can see the curved back of the downs against the glow. That fire is miles on the farther side of it. The whole town must be alight."

There were several red glares at different points, and the pile of *debris* upon the railway line was still smoldering darkly, but they all seemed mere pin-points of light compared to that monstrous conflagration throbbing beyond the hills. What copy it would have made for the Gazette! Had ever a journalist such an opening and so little chance of using it – the scoop of scoops, and no one to appreciate it? And then, suddenly, the old instinct of recording came over me. If these men of science could be so true to their life's work to the very end, why should not I, in my humble way, be as constant? No human eye might ever rest upon what I had done. But the long night had to be passed somehow, and for me at least, sleep seemed to be out of the question. My notes would help to pass the weary hours and to occupy my thoughts. Thus it is that now I have before me the notebook with its scribbled pages, written confusedly upon my knee in the dim, waning light of our one electric torch. Had I the literary touch, they might have been worthy of the occasion. As it is, they may still serve to bring to other minds the long-drawn emotions and tremors of that awful night.

Chapter IV
A Diary of the Dying

HOW STRANGE the words look scribbled at the top of the empty page of my book! How stranger still that it is I, Edward Malone, who have written them – I who started only some twelve hours ago from my rooms in Streatham without one thought of the marvels which the day was to bring forth! I look back at the chain of incidents, my interview with McArdle, Challenger's first note of alarm in the *Times*, the absurd journey in the train, the pleasant luncheon, the catastrophe, and now it has come to this – that we linger alone upon an empty planet, and so sure is our fate that I can regard these lines, written from mechanical professional habit and never to be seen by human eyes, as the words of one who is already dead, so closely does he stand to the shadowed borderland over which all outside this one little circle of friends have already gone. I feel how wise and true were the words of Challenger when he said that the real tragedy would be if we were left behind when all that is noble and good and beautiful had passed. But of that there can surely be no danger. Already our second tube of oxygen is drawing to an end. We can count the poor dregs of our lives almost to a minute.

We have just been treated to a lecture, a good quarter of an hour long, from Challenger, who was so excited that he roared and bellowed as if he were addressing his old rows of scientific sceptics in the Queen's Hall. He had certainly a strange audience to harangue: his wife perfectly acquiescent and absolutely ignorant of his meaning, Summerlee seated in the shadow, querulous and critical but interested, Lord John lounging in a corner somewhat bored by the whole proceeding, and myself beside the window watching the scene with a kind of detached attention, as if it were all a dream or something in which I had no personal interest whatever. Challenger sat at the centre table with the electric light illuminating the slide under the microscope which he had brought from his dressing room. The small vivid circle of white light from the mirror left half of his rugged, bearded face in brilliant radiance and half in deepest shadow. He had, it seems, been working of late upon the lowest forms of life, and what excited him at the present moment was that in the microscopic slide made up the day before he found the amoeba to be still alive.

"You can see it for yourselves," he kept repeating in great excitement. "Summerlee, will you step across and satisfy yourself upon the point? Malone, will you kindly verify what I say? The little spindle-shaped things in the centre are diatoms and may be disregarded since they are probably vegetable rather than animal. But the right-hand side you will see an undoubted amoeba, moving sluggishly across the field. The upper screw is the fine adjustment. Look at it for yourselves."

Summerlee did so and acquiesced. So did I and perceived a little creature which looked as if it were made of ground glass flowing in a sticky way across the lighted circle. Lord John was prepared to take him on trust.

"I'm not troublin' my head whether he's alive or dead," said he. "We don't so much as know each other by sight, so why should I take it to heart? I don't suppose he's worryin' himself over the state of *our* health."

I laughed at this, and Challenger looked in my direction with his coldest and most supercilious stare. It was a most petrifying experience.

"The flippancy of the half-educated is more obstructive to science than the obtuseness of the ignorant," said he. "If Lord John Roxton would condescend –"

"My dear George, don't be so peppery," said his wife, with her hand on the black mane that drooped over the microscope. "What can it matter whether the amoeba is alive or not?"

"It matters a great deal," said Challenger gruffly.

"Well, let's hear about it," said Lord John with a good-humoured smile. "We may as well talk about that as anything else. If you think I've been too off-hand with the thing, or hurt its feelin's in any way, I'll apologize."

"For my part," remarked Summerlee in his creaky, argumentative voice, "I can't see why you should attach such importance to the creature being alive. It is in the same atmosphere as ourselves, so naturally the poison does not act upon it. If it were outside of this room it would be dead, like all other animal life."

"Your remarks, my good Summerlee," said Challenger with enormous condescension (oh, if I could paint that over-bearing, arrogant face in the vivid circle of reflection from the microscope mirror!) – "your remarks show that you imperfectly appreciate the situation. This specimen was mounted yesterday and is hermetically sealed. None of our oxygen can reach it. But the ether, of course, has penetrated to it, as to every other point upon the universe. Therefore, it has survived the poison. Hence, we may argue that every amoeba outside this room, instead of being dead, as you have erroneously stated, has really survived the catastrophe."

"Well, even now I don't feel inclined to hip-hurrah about it," said Lord John. "What does it matter?"

"It just matters this, that the world is a living instead of a dead one. If you had the scientific imagination, you would cast your mind forward from this one fact, and you would see some few millions of years hence – a mere passing moment in the enormous flux of the ages – the whole world teeming once more with the animal and human life which will spring from this tiny root. You have seen a prairie fire where the flames have swept every trace of grass or plant from the surface of the earth and left only a blackened waste. You would think that it must be forever desert. Yet the roots of growth have been left behind, and when you pass the place a few years hence you can no longer tell where the black scars used to be. Here in this tiny creature are the roots of growth of the animal world, and by its inherent development, and evolution, it will surely in time remove every trace of this incomparable crisis in which we are now involved."

"Dooced interestin'!" said Lord John, lounging across and looking through the microscope. "Funny little chap to hang number one among the family portraits. Got a fine big shirt-stud on him!"

"The dark object is his nucleus," said Challenger with the air of a nurse teaching letters to a baby.

"Well, we needn't feel lonely," said Lord John laughing. "There's somebody livin' besides us on the earth."

"You seem to take it for granted, Challenger," said Summerlee, "that the object for which this world was created was that it should produce and sustain human life."

"Well, sir, and what object do you suggest?" asked Challenger, bristling at the least hint of contradiction.

"Sometimes I think that it is only the monstrous conceit of mankind which makes him think that all this stage was erected for him to strut upon."

"We cannot be dogmatic about it, but at least without what you have ventured to call monstrous conceit we can surely say that we are the highest thing in nature."

"The highest of which we have cognizance."

"That, sir, goes without saying."

"Think of all the millions and possibly billions of years that the earth swung empty through space – or, if not empty, at least without a sign or thought of the human race. Think of it, washed by the rain and scorched by the sun and swept by the wind for those unnumbered ages. Man only came into being yesterday so far as geological times goes. Why, then, should it be taken for granted that all this stupendous preparation was for his benefit?"

"For whose then – or for what?"

Summerlee shrugged his shoulders.

"How can we tell? For some reason altogether beyond our conception – and man may have been a mere accident, a by-product evolved in the process. It is as if the scum upon the surface of the ocean imagined that the ocean was created in order to produce and sustain it, or a mouse in a cathedral thought that the building was its own proper ordained residence."

I have jotted down the very words of their argument, but now it degenerates into a mere noisy wrangle with much polysyllabic scientific jargon upon each side. It is no doubt a privilege to hear two such brains discuss the highest questions; but as they are in perpetual disagreement, plain folk like Lord John and I get little that is positive from the exhibition. They neutralize each other and we are left as they found us. Now the hubbub has ceased, and Summerlee is coiled up in his chair, while Challenger, still fingering the screws of his microscope, is keeping up a continual low, deep, inarticulate growl like the sea after a storm. Lord John comes over to me, and we look out together into the night.

There is a pale new moon – the last moon that human eyes will ever rest upon – and the stars are most brilliant. Even in the clear plateau air of South America I have never seen them brighter. Possibly this etheric change has some effect upon light. The funeral pyre of Brighton is still blazing, and there is a very distant patch of scarlet in the western sky, which may mean trouble at Arundel or Chichester, possibly even at Portsmouth. I sit and muse and make an occasional note. There is a sweet melancholy in the air. Youth and beauty and chivalry and love – is this to be the end of it all? The starlit earth looks a dreamland of gentle peace. Who would imagine it as the terrible Golgotha strewn with the bodies of the human race? Suddenly, I find myself laughing.

"Halloa, young fellah!" says Lord John, staring at me in surprise. "We could do with a joke in these hard times. What was it, then?"

"I was thinking of all the great unsolved questions," I answer, "the questions that we spent so much labor and thought over. Think of Anglo-German competition, for example – or the Persian Gulf that my old chief was so keen about. Whoever would have guessed, when we fumed and fretted so, how they were to be eventually solved?"

We fall into silence again. I fancy that each of us is thinking of friends that have gone before. Mrs. Challenger is sobbing quietly, and her husband is whispering to her. My mind turns to all the most unlikely people, and I see each of them lying white and rigid as poor Austin does in the yard. There is McArdle, for example, I know exactly where he is, with his face upon his writing desk and his hand on his own telephone, just as I heard him fall. Beaumont, the editor, too – I suppose he is lying upon the blue-and-red Turkey carpet which adorned his sanctum. And the fellows in the reporters' room – Macdona and Murray and Bond. They had certainly died hard at work on their job, with note-books full of vivid impressions and strange happenings in their hands. I could just imagine how this one would have been packed off to the doctors, and that other to Westminster, and yet a third to St. Paul's. What glorious rows of head-lines they must have seen as a last vision beautiful, never destined to materialize in printer's ink! I could see Macdona among the doctors – 'Hope in Harley Street' – Mac had always a weakness for alliteration. 'Interview with Mr. Soley Wilson.' 'Famous Specialist says "Never despair!"' "Our Special Correspondent found the eminent scientist seated upon the roof, whither he had retreated to avoid the crowd of terrified patients who had stormed his dwelling. With a manner which plainly showed his appreciation of the immense gravity of the occasion, the celebrated physician refused to admit that every avenue of hope had been closed." That's how Mac would start. Then there was Bond; he would probably do St. Paul's. He fancied his own literary touch. My word, what a theme for him! "Standing in the little gallery under the dome and looking down upon that packed mass of despairing humanity, groveling at this last instant before a Power which they had so persistently ignored, there rose to my ears from the swaying crowd such a low moan of entreaty and terror, such a shuddering cry for help to the Unknown, that –" and so forth.

Yes, it would be a great end for a reporter, though, like myself, he would die with the treasures still unused. What would Bond not give, poor chap, to see 'J.H.B.' at the foot of a column like that?

But what drivel I am writing! It is just an attempt to pass the weary time. Mrs. Challenger has gone to the inner dressing-room, and the Professor says that she is asleep. He is making notes and consulting books at the central table, as calmly as if years of placid work lay before him. He writes with a very noisy quill pen which seems to be screeching scorn at all who disagree with him.

Summerlee has dropped off in his chair and gives from time to time a peculiarly exasperating snore. Lord John lies back with his hands in his pockets and his eyes closed. How people can sleep under such conditions is more than I can imagine.

Three-thirty a.m. I have just wakened with a start. It was five minutes past eleven when I made my last entry. I remember winding up my watch and noting the time. So I have wasted some five hours of the little span still left to us. Who would have believed it possible? But I feel very much fresher, and ready for my fate – or try to persuade myself that I am. And yet, the fitter a man is, and the higher his tide of life, the more must he shrink from death. How wise and how merciful is that provision of nature by which his earthly anchor is usually loosened by many little imperceptible tugs, until his consciousness has drifted out of its untenable earthly harbor into the great sea beyond!

Mrs. Challenger is still in the dressing room. Challenger has fallen asleep in his chair. What a picture! His enormous frame leans back, his huge, hairy hands are clasped across his waistcoat, and his head is so tilted that I can see nothing above his collar save a tangled bristle of luxuriant beard. He shakes with the vibration of his own snoring. Summerlee adds his occasional high tenor to Challenger's sonorous bass. Lord John is sleeping also, his long body doubled up sideways in a basket-chair. The first cold light of dawn is just stealing into the room, and everything is grey and mournful.

I look out at the sunrise – that fateful sunrise which will shine upon an unpeopled world. The human race is gone, extinguished in a day, but the planets swing round and the tides rise or fall, and the wind whispers, and all nature goes her way, down, as it would seem, to the very amoeba, with never a sign that he who styled himself the lord of creation had ever blessed or cursed the universe with his presence. Down in the yard lies Austin with sprawling limbs, his face glimmering white in the dawn, and the hose nozzle still projecting from his dead hand. The whole of human kind is typified in that one half-ludicrous and half-pathetic figure, lying so helpless beside the machine which it used to control.

* * *

Here end the notes which I made at the time. Henceforward events were too swift and too poignant to allow me to write, but they are too clearly outlined in my memory that any detail could escape me.

Some chokiness in my throat made me look at the oxygen cylinders, and I was startled at what I saw. The sands of our lives were running very low. At some period in the night Challenger had switched the tube from the third to the fourth cylinder. Now it was clear that this also was nearly exhausted. That horrible feeling of constriction was closing in upon me. I ran across and, unscrewing the nozzle, I changed it to our last supply. Even as I did so my conscience pricked me, for I felt that perhaps if I had held my hand all of them might have passed in their sleep. The thought was banished, however, by the voice of the lady from the inner room crying:

"George, George, I am stifling!"

"It is all right, Mrs. Challenger," I answered as the others started to their feet. "I have just turned on a fresh supply."

Even at such a moment I could not help smiling at Challenger, who with a great hairy fist in each eye was like a huge, bearded baby, new wakened out of sleep. Summerlee was shivering like a man with the ague, human fears, as he realized his position, rising for an instant above the stoicism of the man of science. Lord John, however, was as cool and alert as if he had just been roused on a hunting morning.

"Fifthly and lastly," said he, glancing at the tube. "Say, young fellah, don't tell me you've been writin' up your impressions in that paper on your knee."

"Just a few notes to pass the time."

"Well, I don't believe anyone but an Irishman would have done that. I expect you'll have to wait till little brother amoeba gets grown up before you'll find a reader. He don't seem to take much stock of things just at present. Well, Herr Professor, what are the prospects?"

Challenger was looking out at the great drifts of morning mist which lay over the landscape. Here and there the wooded hills rose like conical islands out of this woolly sea.

"It might be a winding sheet," said Mrs. Challenger, who had entered in her dressing-gown. "There's that song of yours, George, 'Ring out the old, ring in the new.' It was prophetic. But you are shivering, my poor dear friends. I have been warm under a coverlet all night, and you cold in your chairs. But I'll soon set you right."

The brave little creature hurried away, and presently we heard the sizzling of a kettle. She was back soon with five steaming cups of cocoa upon a tray.

"Drink these," said she. "You will feel so much better."

And we did. Summerlee asked if he might light his pipe, and we all had cigarettes. It steadied our nerves, I think, but it was a mistake, for it made a dreadful atmosphere in that stuffy room. Challenger had to open the ventilator.

"How long, Challenger?" asked Lord John.

"Possibly three hours," he answered with a shrug.

"I used to be frightened," said his wife. "But the nearer I get to it, the easier it seems. Don't you think we ought to pray, George?"

"You will pray, dear, if you wish," the big man answered, very gently. "We all have our own ways of praying. Mine is a complete acquiescence in whatever fate may send me – a cheerful acquiescence. The highest religion and the highest science seem to unite on that."

"I cannot truthfully describe my mental attitude as acquiescence and far less cheerful acquiescence," grumbled Summerlee over his pipe. "I submit because I have to. I confess that I should have liked another year of life to finish my classification of the chalk fossils."

"Your unfinished work is a small thing," said Challenger pompously, "when weighed against the fact that my own *magnum opus*, 'The Ladder of Life,' is still in the first stages. My brain, my reading, my experience – in fact, my whole unique equipment – were to be condensed into that epoch-making volume. And yet, as I say, I acquiesce."

"I expect we've all left some loose ends stickin' out," said Lord John. "What are yours, young fellah?"

"I was working at a book of verses," I answered.

"Well, the world has escaped that, anyhow," said Lord John. "There's always compensation somewhere if you grope around."

"What about you?" I asked.

"Well, it just so happens that I was tidied up and ready. I'd promised Merivale to go to Tibet for a snow leopard in the spring. But it's hard on you, Mrs. Challenger, when you have just built up this pretty home."

"Where George is, there is my home. But, oh, what would I not give for one last walk together in the fresh morning air upon those beautiful downs!"

Our hearts re-echoed her words. The sun had burst through the gauzy mists which veiled it, and the whole broad Weald was washed in golden light. Sitting in our dark and poisonous atmosphere that glorious, clean, wind-swept countryside seemed a very dream of beauty. Mrs. Challenger held her hand stretched out to it in her longing. We drew up chairs and sat in a semicircle in the window. The atmosphere was already very close. It seemed to me that the shadows of death were drawing in upon us – the last of our race. It was like an invisible curtain closing down upon every side.

"That cylinder is not lastin' too well," said Lord John with a long gasp for breath.

"The amount contained is variable," said Challenger, "depending upon the pressure and care with which it has been bottled. I am inclined to agree with you, Roxton, that this one is defective."

"So we are to be cheated out of the last hour of our lives," Summerlee remarked bitterly. "An excellent final illustration of the sordid age in which we have lived. Well, Challenger, now is your time if you wish to study the subjective phenomena of physical dissolution."

"Sit on the stool at my knee and give me your hand," said Challenger to his wife. "I think, my friends, that a further delay in this insufferable atmosphere is hardly advisable. You would not desire it, dear, would you?"

His wife gave a little groan and sank her face against his leg.

"I've seen the folk bathin' in the Serpentine in winter," said Lord John. "When the rest are in, you see one or two shiverin' on the bank, envyin' the others that have taken the plunge. It's the last that have the worst of it. I'm all for a header and have done with it."

"You would open the window and face the ether?"

"Better be poisoned than stifled."

Summerlee nodded his reluctant acquiescence and held out his thin hand to Challenger.

"We've had our quarrels in our time, but that's all over," said he. "We were good friends and had a respect for each other under the surface. Goodbye!"

"Goodbye, young fellah!" said Lord John. "The window's plastered up. You can't open it."

Challenger stooped and raised his wife, pressing her to his breast, while she threw her arms round his neck.

"Give me that field-glass, Malone," said he gravely.

I handed it to him.

"Into the hands of the Power that made us we render ourselves again!" he shouted in his voice of thunder, and at the words he hurled the field-glass through the window.

Full in our flushed faces, before the last tinkle of falling fragments had died away, there came the wholesome breath of the wind, blowing strong and sweet.

I don't know how long we sat in amazed silence. Then as in a dream, I heard Challenger's voice once more.

"We are back in normal conditions," he cried. "The world has cleared the poison belt, but we alone of all mankind are saved."

Chapter V
The Dead World

I REMEMBER that we all sat gasping in our chairs, with that sweet, wet south-western breeze, fresh from the sea, flapping the muslin curtains and cooling our flushed faces. I wonder how long we sat! None of us afterwards could agree at all on that point. We were bewildered, stunned, semi-conscious. We had all braced our courage for death, but this fearful and sudden new fact – that we must continue to live after we had survived the race to which we belonged – struck us with the shock of a physical blow and left us prostrate. Then gradually the suspended mechanism began to move once more; the shuttles of memory worked; ideas weaved themselves together in our minds. We saw, with vivid, merciless clearness, the relations between the past, the present, and the future – the lives that we had led and the lives which we would have to live. Our eyes turned in silent horror upon those of our companions and found the same answering look in theirs. Instead of the joy which men might have been expected to feel who had so narrowly escaped an imminent death, a terrible wave of darkest depression submerged us. Everything on earth that we loved had been washed away into the great, infinite, unknown ocean, and here were we marooned upon this desert island of a world, without companions, hopes, or aspirations. A few years' skulking like jackals among the graves of the human race and then our belated and lonely end would come.

"It's dreadful, George, dreadful!" the lady cried in an agony of sobs. "If we had only passed with the others! Oh, why did you save us? I feel as if it is we that are dead and everyone else alive."

Challenger's great eyebrows were drawn down in concentrated thought, while his huge, hairy paw closed upon the outstretched hand of his wife. I had observed that she always held out her arms to him in trouble as a child would to its mother.

"Without being a fatalist to the point of nonresistance," said he, "I have always found that the highest wisdom lies in an acquiescence with the actual." He spoke slowly, and there was a vibration of feeling in his sonorous voice.

"I do *not* acquiesce," said Summerlee firmly.

"I don't see that it matters a row of pins whether you acquiesce or whether you don't," remarked Lord John. "You've got to take it, whether you take it fightin' or take it lyin' down, so what's the odds whether you acquiesce or not?"

"I can't remember that anyone asked our permission before the thing began, and nobody's likely to ask it now. So what difference can it make what we may think of it?"

"It is just all the difference between happiness and misery," said Challenger with an abstracted face, still patting his wife's hand. "You can swim with the tide and have peace in mind and soul, or you can thrust against it and be bruised and weary. This business is beyond us, so let us accept it as it stands and say no more."

"But what in the world are we to do with our lives?" I asked, appealing in desperation to the blue, empty heaven.

"What am I to do, for example? There are no newspapers, so there's an end of my vocation."

"And there's nothin' left to shoot, and no more soldierin', so there's an end of mine," said Lord John.

"And there are no students, so there's an end of mine," cried Summerlee.

"But I have my husband and my house, so I can thank heaven that there is no end of mine," said the lady.

"Nor is there an end of mine," remarked Challenger, "for science is not dead, and this catastrophe in itself will offer us many most absorbing problems for investigation."

He had now flung open the windows and we were gazing out upon the silent and motionless landscape.

"Let me consider," he continued. "It was about three, or a little after, yesterday afternoon that the world finally entered the poison belt to the extent of being completely submerged. It is now nine o'clock. The question is, at what hour did we pass out from it?"

"The air was very bad at daybreak," said I.

"Later than that," said Mrs. Challenger. "As late as eight o'clock I distinctly felt the same choking at my throat which came at the outset."

"Then we shall say that it passed just after eight o'clock. For seventeen hours the world has been soaked in the poisonous ether. For that length of time the Great Gardener has sterilized the human mold which had grown over the surface of His fruit. Is it possible that the work is incompletely done – that others may have survived besides ourselves?"

"That's what I was wonderin'," said Lord John. "Why should we be the only pebbles on the beach?"

"It is absurd to suppose that anyone besides ourselves can possibly have survived," said Summerlee with conviction. "Consider that the poison was so virulent that even a man who is as strong as an ox and has not a nerve in his body, like Malone here, could hardly get up the stairs before he fell unconscious. Is it likely that anyone could stand seventeen minutes of it, far less hours?"

"Unless someone saw it coming and made preparation, same as old friend Challenger did."

"That, I think, is hardly probable," said Challenger, projecting his beard and sinking his eyelids. "The combination of observation, inference, and anticipatory imagination which enabled me to foresee the danger is what one can hardly expect twice in the same generation."

"Then your conclusion is that everyone is certainly dead?"

"There can be little doubt of that. We have to remember, however, that the poison worked from below upwards and would possibly be less virulent in the higher strata of the atmosphere. It is strange, indeed, that it should be so; but it presents one of those features which will afford us in the future a fascinating field for study. One could imagine, therefore, that if one had to search for survivors one would turn one's eyes with best hopes of success to some Tibetan village or some Alpine farm, many thousands of feet above the sea level."

"Well, considerin' that there are no railroads and no steamers you might as well talk about survivors in the moon," said Lord John. "But what I'm askin' myself is whether it's really over or whether it's only half-time."

Summerlee craned his neck to look round the horizon. "It seems clear and fine," said he in a very dubious voice; "but so it did yesterday. I am by no means assured that it is all over."

Challenger shrugged his shoulders.

"We must come back once more to our fatalism," said he. "If the world has undergone this experience before, which is not outside the range of possibility, it was certainly a very long time ago. Therefore, we may reasonably hope that it will be very long before it occurs again."

"That's all very well," said Lord John, "but if you get an earthquake shock you are mighty likely to have a second one right on the top of it. I think we'd be wise to stretch our legs and have a breath of air while we have the chance. Since our oxygen is exhausted we may just as well be caught outside as in."

It was strange the absolute lethargy which had come upon us as a reaction after our tremendous emotions of the last twenty-four hours. It was both mental and physical, a deep-lying feeling that nothing mattered and that everything was a weariness and a profitless exertion. Even Challenger had succumbed to it, and sat in his chair, with his great head leaning upon his hands and his thoughts far away, until Lord John and I, catching him by each arm, fairly lifted him on to his feet, receiving only the glare and growl of an angry mastiff for our trouble. However, once we had got out of our narrow haven of refuge into the wider atmosphere of everyday life, our normal energy came gradually back to us once more.

But what were we to begin to do in that graveyard of a world? Could ever men have been faced with such a question since the dawn of time? It is true that our own physical needs, and even our luxuries, were assured for the future. All the stores of food, all the vintages of wine, all the treasures of art were ours for the taking. But what were we to *do*? Some few tasks appealed to us at once, since they lay ready to our hands. We descended into the kitchen and laid the two domestics upon their respective beds. They seemed to have died without suffering, one in the chair by the fire, the other upon the scullery floor. Then we carried in poor Austin from the yard. His muscles were set as hard as a board in the most exaggerated rigor mortis, while the contraction of the fibres had drawn his mouth into a hard sardonic grin. This symptom was prevalent among all who had died from the poison. Wherever we went we were confronted by those grinning faces, which seemed to mock at our dreadful position, smiling silently and grimly at the ill-fated survivors of their race.

"Look here," said Lord John, who had paced restlessly about the dining-room whilst we partook of some food, "I don't know how you fellows feel about it, but for my part, I simply *can't* sit here and do nothin'."

"Perhaps," Challenger answered, "you would have the kindness to suggest what you think we ought to do."

"Get a move on us and see all that has happened."

"That is what I should myself propose."

"But not in this little country village. We can see from the window all that this place can teach us."

"Where should we go, then?"

"To London!"

"That's all very well," grumbled Summerlee. "You may be equal to a forty-mile walk, but I'm not so sure about Challenger, with his stumpy legs, and I am perfectly sure about myself." Challenger was very much annoyed.

"If you could see your way, sir, to confining your remarks to your own physical peculiarities, you would find that you had an ample field for comment," he cried.

"I had no intention to offend you, my dear Challenger," cried our tactless friend. "You can't be held responsible for your own physique. If nature has given you a short, heavy body you cannot possibly help having stumpy legs."

Challenger was too furious to answer. He could only growl and blink and bristle. Lord John hastened to intervene before the dispute became more violent.

"You talk of walking. Why should we walk?" said he.

"Do you suggest taking a train?" asked Challenger, still simmering.

"What's the matter with the motor-car? Why should we not go in that?"

"I am not an expert," said Challenger, pulling at his beard reflectively. "At the same time, you are right in supposing that the human intellect in its higher manifestations should be sufficiently flexible to turn itself to anything. Your idea is an excellent one, Lord John. I myself will drive you all to London."

"You will do nothing of the kind," said Summerlee with decision.

"No, indeed, George!" cried his wife. "You only tried once, and you remember how you crashed through the gate of the garage."

"It was a momentary want of concentration," said Challenger complacently. "You can consider the matter settled. I will certainly drive you all to London."

The situation was relieved by Lord John.

"What's the car?" he asked.

"A twenty-horsepower Humber."

"Why, I've driven one for years," said he. "By George!" he added. "I never thought I'd live to take the whole human race in one load. There's just room for five, as I remember it. Get your things on, and I'll be ready at the door by ten o'clock."

Sure enough, at the hour named, the car came purring and crackling from the yard with Lord John at the wheel. I took my seat beside him, while the lady, a useful little buffer state, was squeezed in between the two men of wrath at the back. Then Lord John released his brakes, slid his lever rapidly from first to third, and we sped off upon the strangest drive that ever human beings have taken since man first came upon the earth.

You are to picture the loveliness of nature upon that August day, the freshness of the morning air, the golden glare of the summer sunshine, the cloudless sky, the luxuriant green of the Sussex woods, and the deep purple of heather-clad downs. As you looked round upon the many-coloured beauty of the scene all thought of a vast catastrophe would have passed from your mind had it not been for one sinister sign – the solemn, all-embracing silence. There is a gentle hum of life which pervades a closely-settled country, so deep and constant that one ceases to observe it, as the dweller by the sea loses all sense of the constant murmur of the waves. The twitter of birds, the buzz of insects, the far-off echo of voices, the lowing of cattle, the distant barking of dogs, roar of trains, and rattle of carts – all these form one low, unremitting note, striking unheeded upon the ear. We missed it now. This deadly silence was appalling. So solemn was it, so impressive, that the buzz and rattle of our motor-car seemed an unwarrantable intrusion, an indecent disregard of this reverent stillness which lay like a pall over and round the ruins of humanity. It was this grim hush, and the tall clouds of smoke which rose here and there over the country-side from smoldering buildings, which cast a chill into our hearts as we gazed round at the glorious panorama of the Weald.

And then there were the dead! At first those endless groups of drawn and grinning faces filled us with a shuddering horror. So vivid and mordant was the impression that I can live over again that slow descent of the station hill, the passing by the nurse-girl with the two babes, the sight of the old horse on his knees between the shafts, the cabman twisted across his seat, and the young man inside with his hand upon the open door in the very act of springing out. Lower down were six reapers all in a litter, their limbs crossing, their dead, unwinking eyes gazing upwards at the glare of heaven. These things I see as in a photograph. But soon, by the merciful provision of nature, the over-excited nerve ceased to respond. The very vastness of the horror took away from its personal appeal. Individuals merged into groups, groups into crowds, crowds into a universal phenomenon which one soon accepted as the inevitable detail of every scene. Only here and there, where some particularly brutal or grotesque incident caught the attention, did the mind come back with a sudden shock to the personal and human meaning of it all.

Above all, there was the fate of the children. That, I remember, filled us with the strongest sense of intolerable injustice. We could have wept – Mrs. Challenger did weep – when we passed a great council school and saw the long trail of tiny figures scattered down the road which led from it. They had been dismissed by their terrified teachers and were speeding for their homes when the poison caught them in its net. Great numbers of people were at the open windows of the houses. In Tunbridge Wells there was hardly one which had not its staring, smiling face. At the last instant the need of air, that very craving for oxygen which we alone had been able to satisfy, had sent them flying to the window. The sidewalks too were littered with men and women, hatless and bonnetless, who had rushed out of the houses. Many of them had fallen in the roadway. It was a lucky thing that in Lord John we had found an expert driver, for it was no easy matter to pick one's way. Passing through the villages or towns we could only go at a walking pace, and once, I remember, opposite the school at Tonbridge, we had to halt some time while we carried aside the bodies which blocked our path.

A few small, definite pictures stand out in my memory from amid that long panorama of death upon the Sussex and Kentish high roads. One was that of a great, glittering motor-car standing outside the inn at the village of Southborough. It bore, as I should guess, some pleasure party upon their return from Brighton or from Eastbourne. There were three gaily dressed women, all young and beautiful, one of them with a Peking spaniel upon her lap. With them were a rakish-looking elderly man and a young aristocrat, his eyeglass still in his eye, his cigarette burned down to the stub between the fingers of his begloved hand. Death must have come on them in an instant and fixed them as they sat. Save that the elderly man had at the last moment torn out his collar in an effort to breathe, they might all have been asleep. On one side of the car a waiter with some broken glasses beside a tray was huddled near the step. On the other, two very ragged tramps, a man and a woman, lay where they had fallen, the man with his long, thin arm still outstretched, even as he had asked for alms in his lifetime. One instant of time had put aristocrat, waiter, tramp, and dog upon one common footing of inert and dissolving protoplasm.

I remember another singular picture, some miles on the London side of Sevenoaks. There is a large convent upon the left, with a long, green slope in front of it. Upon this slope were assembled a great number of school children, all kneeling at prayer. In front of them was a fringe of nuns, and higher up the slope, facing towards them, a single figure whom we took to be the Mother Superior. Unlike the pleasure-seekers in the motor-car, these people seemed to have had warning of their danger and to have died beautifully together, the teachers and the taught, assembled for their last common lesson.

My mind is still stunned by that terrific experience, and I grope vainly for means of expression by which I can reproduce the emotions which we felt. Perhaps it is best and wisest not to try, but merely to indicate the facts. Even Summerlee and Challenger were crushed, and we heard nothing of our companions behind us save an occasional whimper from the lady. As to Lord John, he was too intent upon his wheel and the difficult task of threading his way along such roads to have time or inclination for conversation. One phrase he used with such wearisome iteration that it stuck in my memory and at last almost made me laugh as a comment upon the day of doom.

"Pretty doin's! What!"

That was his ejaculation as each fresh tremendous combination of death and disaster displayed itself before us. "Pretty doin's! What!" he cried, as we descended the station hill at

Rotherfield, and it was still "Pretty doin's! What!" as we picked our way through a wilderness of death in the High Street of Lewisham and the Old Kent Road.

It was here that we received a sudden and amazing shock. Out of the window of a humble corner house there appeared a fluttering handkerchief waving at the end of a long, thin human arm. Never had the sight of unexpected death caused our hearts to stop and then throb so wildly as did this amazing indication of life. Lord John ran the motor to the curb, and in an instant we had rushed through the open door of the house and up the staircase to the second-floor front room from which the signal proceeded.

A very old lady sat in a chair by the open window, and close to her, laid across a second chair, was a cylinder of oxygen, smaller but of the same shape as those which had saved our own lives. She turned her thin, drawn, bespectacled face toward us as we crowded in at the doorway.

"I feared that I was abandoned here for ever," said she, "for I am an invalid and cannot stir."

"Well, madam," Challenger answered, "it is a lucky chance that we happened to pass."

"I have one all-important question to ask you," said she. "Gentlemen, I beg that you will be frank with me. What effect will these events have upon London and North-Western Railway shares?"

We should have laughed had it not been for the tragic eagerness with which she listened for our answer. Mrs. Burston, for that was her name, was an aged widow, whose whole income depended upon a small holding of this stock. Her life had been regulated by the rise and fall of the dividend, and she could form no conception of existence save as it was affected by the quotation of her shares. In vain we pointed out to her that all the money in the world was hers for the taking and was useless when taken. Her old mind would not adapt itself to the new idea, and she wept loudly over her vanished stock. "It was all I had," she wailed. "If that is gone I may as well go too."

Amid her lamentations we found out how this frail old plant had lived where the whole great forest had fallen. She was a confirmed invalid and an asthmatic. Oxygen had been prescribed for her malady, and a tube was in her room at the moment of the crisis. She had naturally inhaled some as had been her habit when there was a difficulty with her breathing. It had given her relief, and by doling out her supply she had managed to survive the night. Finally she had fallen asleep and been awakened by the buzz of our motor-car. As it was impossible to take her on with us, we saw that she had all necessaries of life and promised to communicate with her in a couple of days at the latest. So we left her, still weeping bitterly over her vanished stock.

As we approached the Thames the block in the streets became thicker and the obstacles more bewildering. It was with difficulty that we made our way across London Bridge. The approaches to it upon the Middlesex side were choked from end to end with frozen traffic which made all further advance in that direction impossible. A ship was blazing brightly alongside one of the wharves near the bridge, and the air was full of drifting smuts and of a heavy acrid smell of burning. There was a cloud of dense smoke somewhere near the Houses of Parliament, but it was impossible from where we were to see what was on fire.

"I don't know how it strikes you," Lord John remarked as he brought his engine to a standstill, "but it seems to me the country is more cheerful than the town. Dead London is gettin' on my nerves. I'm for a cast round and then gettin' back to Rotherfield."

"I confess that I do not see what we can hope for here," said Professor Summerlee.

"At the same time," said Challenger, his great voice booming strangely amid the silence, "it is difficult for us to conceive that out of seven millions of people there is only this one old woman who by some peculiarity of constitution or some accident of occupation has managed to survive this catastrophe."

"If there should be others, how can we hope to find them, George?" asked the lady. "And yet I agree with you that we cannot go back until we have tried."

Getting out of the car and leaving it by the curb, we walked with some difficulty along the crowded pavement of King William Street and entered the open door of a large insurance office. It was a corner house, and we chose it as commanding a view in every direction. Ascending the stair, we passed through what I suppose to have been the board-room, for eight elderly men were seated round a long table in the centre of it. The high window was open and we all stepped out upon the balcony. From it we could see the crowded city streets radiating in every direction, while below us the road was black from side to side with the tops of the motionless taxis. All, or nearly all, had their heads pointed outwards, showing how the terrified men of the city had at the last moment made a vain endeavor to rejoin their families in the suburbs or the country. Here and there amid the humbler cabs towered the great brass-spangled motor-car of some wealthy magnate, wedged hopelessly among the dammed stream of arrested traffic. Just beneath us there was such a one of great size and luxurious appearance, with its owner, a fat old man, leaning out, half his gross body through the window, and his podgy hand, gleaming with diamonds, outstretched as he urged his chauffeur to make a last effort to break through the press.

A dozen motor-buses towered up like islands in this flood, the passengers who crowded the roofs lying all huddled together and across each others' laps like a child's toys in a nursery. On a broad lamp pedestal in the centre of the roadway, a burly policeman was standing, leaning his back against the post in so natural an attitude that it was hard to realize that he was not alive, while at his feet there lay a ragged newsboy with his bundle of papers on the ground beside him. A paper-cart had got blocked in the crowd, and we could read in large letters, black upon yellow, 'Scene at Lord's. County Match Interrupted.' This must have been the earliest edition, for there were other placards bearing the legend, 'Is It the End? Great Scientist's Warning.' And another, 'Is Challenger Justified? Ominous Rumours.'

Challenger pointed the latter placard out to his wife, as it thrust itself like a banner above the throng. I could see him throw out his chest and stroke his beard as he looked at it. It pleased and flattered that complex mind to think that London had died with his name and his words still present in their thoughts. His feelings were so evident that they aroused the sardonic comment of his colleague.

"In the limelight to the last, Challenger," he remarked.

"So it would appear," he answered complacently. "Well," he added as he looked down the long vista of the radiating streets, all silent and all choked up with death, "I really see no purpose to be served by our staying any longer in London. I suggest that we return at once to Rotherfield and then take counsel as to how we shall most profitably employ the years which lie before us."

Only one other picture shall I give of the scenes which we carried back in our memories from the dead city. It is a glimpse which we had of the interior of the old church of St. Mary's, which is at the very point where our car was awaiting us. Picking our way among the prostrate figures upon the steps, we pushed open the swing door and entered. It was a wonderful sight. The church was crammed from end to end with kneeling figures in every posture of supplication and abasement. At the last dreadful moment, brought suddenly face to face with the realities of life, those terrific realities which hang over us even while we follow the shadows, the terrified people had rushed into those old city churches which for generations had hardly ever held a congregation. There they huddled as close as they could kneel, many of them in their agitation still wearing their hats, while above them in the pulpit a young man in lay dress had apparently been addressing them when he and they had been overwhelmed by the same fate. He lay now, like Punch in his booth, with his head and two limp arms hanging over the ledge of the pulpit. It was a nightmare, the grey, dusty church, the rows of agonized figures, the dimness and silence of it all. We moved about with hushed whispers, walking upon our tip-toes.

And then suddenly I had an idea. At one corner of the church, near the door, stood the ancient font, and behind it a deep recess in which there hung the ropes for the bell-ringers. Why should we not send a message out over London which would attract to us anyone who might still be alive? I ran across, and pulling at the list-covered rope, I was surprised to find how difficult it was to swing the bell. Lord John had followed me.

"By George, young fellah!" said he, pulling off his coat. "You've hit on a dooced good notion. Give me a grip and we'll soon have a move on it."

* * *

But, even then, so heavy was the bell that it was not until Challenger and Summerlee had added their weight to ours that we heard the roaring and clanging above our heads which told us that the great clapper was ringing out its music. Far over dead London resounded our message of comradeship and hope to any fellow-man surviving. It cheered our own hearts, that strong, metallic call, and we turned the more earnestly to our work, dragged two feet off the earth with each upward jerk of the rope, but all straining together on the downward heave, Challenger the lowest of all, bending all his great strength to the task and flopping up and down like a monstrous bull-frog, croaking with every pull. It was at that moment that an artist might have taken a picture of the four adventurers, the comrades of many strange perils in the past, whom fate had now chosen for so supreme an experience. For half an hour we worked, the sweat dropping from our faces, our arms and backs aching with the exertion. Then we went out into the portico of the church and looked eagerly up and down the silent, crowded streets. Not a sound, not a motion, in answer to our summons.

"It's no use. No one is left," I cried.

"We can do nothing more," said Mrs. Challenger. "For God's sake, George, let us get back to Rotherfield. Another hour of this dreadful, silent city would drive me mad."

We got into the car without another word. Lord John backed her round and turned her to the south. To us the chapter seemed closed. Little did we foresee the strange new chapter which was to open.

Chapter VI
The Great Awakening

AND NOW I come to the end of this extraordinary incident, so overshadowing in its importance, not only in our own small, individual lives, but in the general history of the human race. As I said when I began my narrative, when that history comes to be written, this occurrence will surely stand out among all other events like a mountain towering among its foothills. Our generation has been reserved for a very special fate since it has been chosen to experience so wonderful a thing. How long its effect may last – how long mankind may preserve the humility and reverence which this great shock has taught it

– can only be shown by the future. I think it is safe to say that things can never be quite the same again. Never can one realize how powerless and ignorant one is, and how one is upheld by an unseen hand, until for an instant that hand has seemed to close and to crush. Death has been imminent upon us. We know that at any moment it may be again. That grim presence shadows our lives, but who can deny that in that shadow the sense of duty, the feeling of sobriety and responsibility, the appreciation of the gravity and of the objects of life, the earnest desire to develop and improve, have grown and become real with us to a degree that has leavened our whole society from end to end? It is something beyond sects and beyond dogmas. It is rather an alteration of perspective, a shifting of our sense of proportion, a vivid realization that we are insignificant and evanescent creatures, existing on sufferance and at the mercy of the first chill wind from the unknown. But if the world has grown graver with this knowledge it is not, I think, a sadder place in consequence. Surely we are agreed that the more sober and restrained pleasures of the present are deeper as well as wiser than the noisy, foolish hustle which passed so often for enjoyment in the days of old – days so recent and yet already so inconceivable. Those empty lives which were wasted in aimless visiting and being visited, in the worry of great and unnecessary households, in the arranging and eating of elaborate and tedious meals, have now found rest and health in the reading, the music, the gentle family communion which comes from a simpler and saner division of their time. With greater health and greater pleasure they are richer than before, even after they have paid those increased contributions to the common fund which have so raised the standard of life in these islands.

There is some clash of opinion as to the exact hour of the great awakening. It is generally agreed that, apart from the difference of clocks, there may have been local causes which influenced the action of the poison. Certainly, in each separate district the resurrection was practically simultaneous. There are numerous witnesses that Big Ben pointed to ten minutes past six at the moment. The Astronomer Royal has fixed the Greenwich time at twelve past six. On the other hand, Laird Johnson, a very capable East Anglia observer, has recorded six-twenty as the hour. In the Hebrides it was as late as seven. In our own case there can be no doubt whatever, for I was seated in Challenger's study with his carefully tested chronometer in front of me at the moment. The hour was a quarter-past six.

* * *

An enormous depression was weighing upon my spirits. The cumulative effect of all the dreadful sights which we had seen upon our journey was heavy upon my soul. With my abounding animal health and great physical energy any kind of mental clouding was a rare event. I had the Irish faculty of seeing some gleam of humor in every darkness. But now the obscurity was appalling and unrelieved. The others were downstairs making their plans for the future. I sat by the open window, my chin resting upon my hand and my mind absorbed in the misery of our situation. Could we continue to live? That was the question which I had begun to ask myself. Was it possible to exist upon a dead world? Just as in physics the greater body draws to itself the lesser, would we not feel an overpowering attraction from that vast body of humanity which had passed into the unknown? How would the end come? Would it be from a return of the poison? Or would the earth be uninhabitable from the mephitic products of universal decay? Or, finally, might our awful situation prey upon and unbalance our minds? A group of insane folk upon a dead world! My mind was brooding upon this last dreadful idea when some slight noise caused me to look down upon the road beneath me. The old cab horse was coming up the hill!

I was conscious at the same instant of the twittering of birds, of someone coughing in the yard below, and of a background of movement in the landscape. And yet I remember that it was that absurd, emaciated, superannuated cab-horse which held my gaze. Slowly and wheezily it was climbing the slope. Then my eye traveled to the driver sitting hunched up upon the box and finally to the young man who was leaning out of the window in some excitement and shouting a direction. They were all indubitably, aggressively alive!

Everybody was alive once more! Had it all been a delusion? Was it conceivable that this whole poison belt incident had been an elaborate dream? For an instant my startled brain was really ready to believe it. Then I looked down, and there was the rising blister on my hand where it was frayed by the rope of the city bell. It had really been so, then. And yet here was the world resuscitated – here was life come back in an instant full tide to the planet. Now, as my eyes wandered all over the great landscape, I saw it in every direction – and moving, to my amazement, in the very same groove in which it had halted. There were the golfers. Was it possible that they were going on with their game? Yes, there was a fellow driving off from a tee, and that other group upon the green were surely putting for the hole. The reapers were slowly trooping back to their work. The nurse-girl slapped one of her charges and then began to push the perambulator up the hill. Everyone had unconcernedly taken up the thread at the very point where they had dropped it.

I rushed downstairs, but the hall door was open, and I heard the voices of my companions, loud in astonishment and congratulation, in the yard. How we all shook hands and laughed as we came together, and how Mrs. Challenger kissed us all in her emotion, before she finally threw herself into the bear-hug of her husband.

"But they could not have been asleep!" cried Lord John. "Dash it all, Challenger, you don't mean to believe that those folk were asleep with their staring eyes and stiff limbs and that awful death grin on their faces!"

"It can only have been the condition that is called catalepsy," said Challenger. "It has been a rare phenomenon in the past and has constantly been mistaken for death. While it endures, the temperature falls, the respiration disappears, the heartbeat is indistinguishable – in fact, it *is* death, save that it is evanescent. Even the most comprehensive mind" – here he closed his eyes and simpered – "could hardly conceive a universal outbreak of it in this fashion."

"You may label it catalepsy," remarked Summerlee, "but, after all, that is only a name, and we know as little of the result as we do of the poison which has caused it. The most we can say is that the vitiated ether has produced a temporary death."

Austin was seated all in a heap on the step of the car. It was his coughing which I had heard from above. He had been holding his head in silence, but now he was muttering to himself and running his eyes over the car.

"Young fat-head!" he grumbled. "Can't leave things alone!"

"What's the matter, Austin?"

"Lubricators left running, sir. Someone has been fooling with the car. I expect it's that young garden boy, sir."

Lord John looked guilty.

"I don't know what's amiss with me," continued Austin, staggering to his feet. "I expect I came over queer when I was hosing her down. I seem to remember flopping over by the step. But I'll swear I never left those lubricator taps on."

In a condensed narrative the astonished Austin was told what had happened to himself and the world. The mystery of the dripping lubricators was also explained to him. He listened with an air of deep distrust when told how an amateur had driven his car and with absorbed interest to the few sentences in which our experiences of the sleeping city were recorded. I can remember his comment when the story was concluded.

"Was you outside the Bank of England, sir?"

"Yes, Austin."

"With all them millions inside and everybody asleep?"

"That was so."

"And I not there!" he groaned, and turned dismally once more to the hosing of his car.

There was a sudden grinding of wheels upon gravel. The old cab had actually pulled up at Challenger's door. I saw the young occupant step out from it. An instant later the maid, who looked as tousled and bewildered as if she had that instant been aroused from the deepest sleep, appeared with a card upon a tray. Challenger snorted ferociously as he looked at it, and his thick black hair seemed to bristle up in his wrath.

"A pressman!" he growled. Then with a deprecating smile: "After all, it is natural that the whole world should hasten to know what I think of such an episode."

"That can hardly be his errand," said Summerlee, "for he was on the road in his cab before ever the crisis came."

I looked at the card: "James Baxter, London Correspondent, New York Monitor."

"You'll see him?" said I.

"Not I."

"Oh, George! You should be kinder and more considerate to others. Surely you have learned something from what we have undergone."

He tut-tutted and shook his big, obstinate head.

"A poisonous breed! Eh, Malone? The worst weed in modern civilization, the ready tool of the quack and the hindrance of the self-respecting man! When did they ever say a good word for me?"

"When did you ever say a good word to them?" I answered. "Come, sir, this is a stranger who has made a journey to see you. I am sure that you won't be rude to him."

"Well, well," he grumbled, "you come with me and do the talking. I protest in advance against any such outrageous invasion of my private life." Muttering and mumbling, he came rolling after me like an angry and rather ill-conditioned mastiff.

The dapper young American pulled out his notebook and plunged instantly into his subject.

"I came down, sir," said he, "because our people in America would very much like to hear more about this danger which is, in your opinion, pressing upon the world."

"I know of no danger which is now pressing upon the world," Challenger answered gruffly.

The pressman looked at him in mild surprise.

"I meant, sir, the chances that the world might run into a belt of poisonous ether."

"I do not now apprehend any such danger," said Challenger.

The pressman looked even more perplexed.

"You are Professor Challenger, are you not?" he asked.

"Yes, sir; that is my name."

"I cannot understand, then, how you can say that there is no such danger. I am alluding to your own letter, published above your name in the *London Times* of this morning."

It was Challenger's turn to look surprised.

"This morning?" said he. "No *London Times* was published this morning."

"Surely, sir," said the American in mild remonstrance, "you must admit that the *London Times* is a daily paper." He drew out a copy from his inside pocket. "Here is the letter to which I refer."

Challenger chuckled and rubbed his hands.

"I begin to understand," said he. "So you read this letter this morning?"

"Yes, sir."

"And came at once to interview me?"

"Yes, sir."

"Did you observe anything unusual upon the journey down?"

"Well, to tell the truth, your people seemed more lively and generally human than I have ever seen them. The baggage man set out to tell me a funny story, and that's a new experience for me in this country."

"Nothing else?"

"Why, no, sir, not that I can recall."

"Well, now, what hour did you leave Victoria?"

The American smiled.

"I came here to interview you, Professor, but it seems to be a case of 'Is this nigger fishing, or is this fish niggering?' You're doing most of the work."

"It happens to interest me. Do you recall the hour?"

"Sure. It was half-past twelve."

"And you arrived?"

"At a quarter-past two."

"And you hired a cab?"

"That was so."

"How far do you suppose it is to the station?"

"Well, I should reckon the best part of two miles."

"So how long do you think it took you?"

"Well, half an hour, maybe, with that asthmatic in front."

"So it should be three o'clock?"

"Yes, or a trifle after it."

"Look at your watch."

The American did so and then stared at us in astonishment.

"Say!" he cried. "It's run down. That horse has broken every record, sure. The sun is pretty low, now that I come to look at it. Well, there's something here I don't understand."

"Have you no remembrance of anything remarkable as you came up the hill?"

"Well, I seem to recollect that I was mighty sleepy once. It comes back to me that I wanted to say something to the driver and that I couldn't make him heed me. I guess it was the heat, but I felt swimmy for a moment. That's all."

"So it is with the whole human race," said Challenger to me. "They have all felt swimmy for a moment. None of them have as yet any comprehension of what has occurred. Each will go on with his interrupted job as Austin has snatched up his hose-pipe or the golfer continued his game. Your editor, Malone, will continue the issue of his papers, and very much amazed he will be at finding that an issue is missing. Yes, my young friend," he added to the American reporter, with a sudden mood of amused geniality, "it may interest you to know that the world has swum through the poisonous current which swirls like the Gulf Stream through the ocean of ether. You will also kindly note for your own future convenience that today is not Friday, August the twenty-seventh, but Saturday, August the twenty-eighth, and that you sat senseless in your cab for twenty-eight hours upon the Rotherfield hill."

And "right here," as my American colleague would say, I may bring this narrative to an end. It is, as you are probably aware, only a fuller and more detailed version of the account which appeared in the Monday edition of the Daily Gazette – an account which has been universally admitted to be the greatest journalistic scoop of all time, which sold no fewer than three-and-a-half million copies of the paper. Framed upon the wall of my sanctum I retain those magnificent headlines:

TWENTY-EIGHT HOURS' WORLD COMA
UNPRECEDENTED EXPERIENCE
CHALLENGER JUSTIFIED
OUR CORRESPONDENT ESCAPES
ENTHRALLING NARRATIVE
THE OXYGEN ROOM
WEIRD MOTOR DRIVE
DEAD LONDON
REPLACING THE MISSING PAGE
GREAT FIRES AND LOSS OF LIFE
WILL IT RECUR?

Underneath this glorious scroll came nine and a half columns of narrative, in which appeared the first, last, and only account of the history of the planet, so far as one observer could draw it, during one long day of its existence. Challenger and Summerlee have treated the matter in a joint scientific paper, but to me alone was left the popular account. Surely I can sing 'Nunc dimittis.' What is left but anti-climax in the life of a journalist after that!

But let me not end on sensational headlines and a merely personal triumph. Rather let me quote the sonorous passages in which the greatest of daily papers ended its admirable leader upon the subject – a leader which might well be filed for reference by every thoughtful man.

"It has been a well-worn truism," said the *Times*, "that our human race are a feeble folk before the infinite latent forces which surround us. From the prophets of old and from the philosophers of our own time the same message and warning have reached us. But, like all oft-repeated truths, it has in time lost something of its actuality and cogency. A lesson, an actual experience, was needed to bring it home. It is from that salutory but terrible ordeal that we have just emerged, with minds which are still stunned by the suddenness of the blow and with spirits which are chastened by the realization of our own limitations and impotence. The world has paid a fearful price for its schooling. Hardly yet have we learned the full tale of disaster, but the destruction by fire of New York, of Orleans, and of Brighton constitutes in itself one of the greatest tragedies in the history of our race. When the account of the railway and shipping accidents has been completed, it will furnish grim reading, although there is evidence to show that in the vast majority of cases the drivers of trains and engineers of steamers succeeded in shutting off their motive power before succumbing to the poison. But the material damage, enormous as it is both in life and in property, is not the consideration which will be uppermost in our minds today. All this may in time be forgotten. But what will not be forgotten, and what will and should continue to obsess our imaginations, is this revelation of the possibilities of the universe, this destruction of our ignorant self-complacency, and this demonstration of how narrow is the path of our material existence and what abysses may lie upon either side of it. Solemnity and humility are at the base of all our emotions today. May they be the foundations upon which a more earnest and reverent race may build a more worthy temple."

The Vacant World
Chapters I–XII
George Allan England

Chapter I
The Awakening

DIMLY, LIKE THE DAYBREAK glimmer of a sky long wrapped in fogs, a sign of consciousness began to dawn in the face of the tranced girl.

Once more the breath of life began to stir in that full bosom, to which again a vital warmth had on this day of days crept slowly back.

And as she lay there, prone upon the dusty floor, her beautiful face buried and shielded in the hollow of her arm, a sigh welled from her lips.

Life – life was flowing back again! The miracle of miracles was growing to reality.

Faintly now she breathed; vaguely her heart began to throb once more. She stirred. She moaned, still for the moment powerless to cast off wholly the enshrouding incubus of that tremendous, dreamless sleep.

Then her hands closed. The finely tapered fingers tangled themselves in the masses of thick, luxuriant hair which lay outspread all over and about her. The eyelids trembled.

And, a moment later, Beatrice Kendrick was sitting up, dazed and utterly uncomprehending, peering about her at the strangest vision which since the world began had ever been the lot of any human creature to behold – the vision of a place transformed beyond all power of the intellect to understand.

For of the room which she remembered, which had been her last sight when (so long, so very long, ago) her eyes had closed with that sudden and unconquerable drowsiness, of that room, I say, remained only walls, ceiling, floor of rust-red steel and crumbling cement.

Quite gone was all the plaster, as by magic. Here or there a heap of whitish dust betrayed where some of its detritus still lay.

Gone was every picture, chart, and map – which – but an hour since, it seemed to her – had decked this office of Allan Stern, consulting engineer, this aerie up in the forty-eighth story of the Metropolitan Tower.

Furniture, there now was none. Over the still-intact glass of the windows cobwebs were draped so thickly as almost to exclude the light of day – a strange, fly-infested curtain where once neat green shade-rollers had hung.

Even as the bewildered girl sat there, lips parted, eyes wide with amaze, a spider seized his buzzing prey and scampered back into a hole in the wall.

A huge, leathery bat, suspended upside down in the far corner, cheeped with dry, crepitant sounds of irritation.

Beatrice rubbed her eyes.

"What?" she said, quite slowly. "Dreaming? How singular! I only wish I could remember this when I wake up. Of all the dreams I've ever had, this one's certainly the strangest. So real, so vivid! Why, I could swear I was awake – and yet –"

All at once a sudden doubt flashed into her mind. An uneasy expression dawned across her face. Her eyes grew wild with a great fear; the fear of utter and absolute incomprehension.

Something about this room, this weird awakening, bore upon her consciousness the dread tidings this was not a dream.

Something drove home to her the fact that it was real, objective, positive! And with a gasp of fright she struggled up amid the litter and the rubbish of that uncanny room.

"Oh!" she cried in terror, as a huge scorpion, malevolent, and with its tail raised to strike, scuttled away and vanished through a gaping void where once the corridor-door had swung. "Oh, oh! Where *am* I? What – *what has – happened?*"

Horrified beyond all words, pale and staring, both hands clutched to her breast, whereon her very clothing now had torn and crumbled, she faced about.

To her it seemed as though some monstrous, evil thing were lurking in the dim corner at her back. She tried to scream, but could utter no sound, save a choked gasp.

Then she started toward the doorway. Even as she took the first few steps her gown – a mere tattered mockery of garment – fell away from her.

And, confronted by a new problem, she stopped short. About her she peered in vain for something to protect her disarray. There was nothing.

"Why – where's – where's my chair? My desk?" she exclaimed thickly, starting toward the place by the window where they should have been, and were not. Her shapely feet fell soundlessly in that strange and impalpable dust which thickly coated everything.

"My typewriter? Is – can *that* be my typewriter? Great Heavens! What's the matter here, with everything? Am I mad?"

There before her lay a somewhat larger pile of dust mixed with soft and punky splinters of rotten wood. Amid all this decay she saw some bits of rust, a corroded type-bar or two – even a few rubber key-caps, still recognizable, though with the letters quite obliterated.

All about her, veiling her completely in a mantle of wondrous gloss and beauty, her lustrous hair fell, as she stooped to see this strange, incomprehensible phenomenon. She tried to pick up one of the rubber caps. At her merest touch it crumbled to an impalpable white powder.

Back with a shuddering cry the girl sprang, terrified.

"Merciful Heavens!" she supplicated. "What – what does all this mean?"

For a moment she stood there, her every power of thought, of motion, numbed. Breathing not, she only stared in a wild kind of cringing amazement, as perhaps you might do if you should see a dead man move.

Then to the door she ran. Out into the hall she peered, this way and that, down the dismantled corridor, up the wreckage of the stairs all cumbered, like the office itself, with dust and webs and vermin.

Aloud she hailed: "Oh! Help, help, *help!*" No answer. Even the echoes flung back only dull, vacuous sounds that deepened her sense of awful and incredible isolation.

What? No noise of human life anywhere to be heard? None! No familiar hum of the metropolis now rose from what, when she had fallen asleep, had been swarming streets and miles on miles of habitations.

Instead, a blank, unbroken leaden silence, that seemed part of the musty, choking atmosphere – a silence that weighed down on Beatrice like funeral-palls.

Dumfounded by all this, and by the universal crumbling of every perishable thing, the girl ran, shuddering, back into the office. There in the dust her foot struck something hard.

She stooped; she caught it up and stared at it.

"My glass ink-well! What? Only such things remain?"

No dream, then, but reality! She knew at length that some catastrophe, incredibly vast, some disaster cosmic in the tragedy of its sweep, had desolated the world.

"Oh, my mother!" cried she. "My mother – *dead?* Dead, now, how long?"

She did not weep, but just stood cowering, a chill of anguished horror racking her. All at once her teeth began to chatter, her body to shake as with an ague.

Thus for a moment dazed and stunned she remained there, knowing not which way to turn nor what to do. Then her terror-stricken gaze fell on the doorway leading from her outer office to the inner one, the one where Stern had had his laboratory and his consultation-room.

This door now hung, a few worm-eaten planks and splintered bits of wood, barely supported by the rusty hinges.

Toward it she staggered. About her she drew the sheltering masses of her hair, like a Godiva of another age; and to her eyes, womanlike, the hot tears mounted. As she went, she cried in a voice of horror.

"Mr. Stern! Oh – Mr. Stern! Are – are *you* dead, too? You *can't* be – it's too frightful!"

She reached the door. The mere touch of her outstretched hand disintegrated it. Down in a crumbling mass it fell. Thick dust bellied up in a cloud, through which a single sun-ray that entered the cobwebbed pane shot a radiant arrow.

Peering, hesitant, fearful of even greater terrors in that other room, Beatrice peered through this dust-haze. A sick foreboding of evil possessed her at thought of what she might find there – yet more afraid was she of what she knew lay behind her.

An instant she stood within the ruined doorway, her left hand resting on the moldy jam. Then, with a cry, she started forward – a cry in which terror had given place to joy, despair to hope.

Forgotten now the fact that, save for the shrouding of her messy hair, she stood naked. Forgotten the wreck, the desolation everywhere.

"Oh – thank Heaven!" gasped she.

There, in that inner office, half-rising from the wrack of many things that had been and were now no more, her startled eyes beheld the figure of a man – of Allan Stern!

He lived!

At her he peered with eyes that saw not, yet; toward her he groped a vague, unsteady hand.

He lived!

Not quite alone in this world-ruin, not all alone was she!

Chapter II
Realization

THE JOY in Beatrice's eyes gave way to poignant wonder as she gazed on him. Could this be *he?*

Yes, well she knew it was. She recognized him even through the grotesquery of his clinging rags, even behind the mask of a long, red, dusty beard and formidable mustache, even despite the wild and staring incoherence of his whole expression.

Yet how incredible the metamorphosis! To her flashed a memory of this man, her other-time employer – keen and smooth-shaven, alert, well-dressed, self-centered, dominant, the master of a hundred complex problems, the directing mind of engineering works innumerable.

Faltering and uncertain now he stood there. Then, at the sound of the girl's voice, he staggered toward her with outflung hands. He stopped, and for a moment stared at her.

For he had had no time as yet to correlate his thoughts, to pull himself together.

And while one's heart might throb ten times, Beatrice saw terror in his blinking, bloodshot eyes.

But almost at once the engineer mastered himself. Even as Beatrice watched him, breathlessly, from the door, she saw his fear die out, she saw his courage well up fresh and strong.

It was almost as though something tangible were limning the man's soul upon his face. She thrilled at sight of him.

And though for a long moment no word was spoken, while the man and woman stood looking at each other like two children in some dread and unfamiliar attic, an understanding leaped between them.

Then, womanlike, instinctively as she breathed, the girl ran to him. Forgetful of every convention and of her disarray, she seized his hand. And in a voice that trembled till it broke she cried:

"What is it? What does all this mean? Tell me!"

To him she clung.

"Tell me the truth – and save me! Is it *real?*"

Stern looked at her wonderingly. He smiled a strange, wan, mirthless smile.

All about him he looked. Then his lips moved, but for the moment no sound came.

He made another effort, this time successful.

"There, there," said he huskily, as though the dust and dryness of the innumerable years had got into his very voice. "There, now, don't be afraid!

"Something seems to have taken place here while – we've been asleep. What? What is it? I don't know yet. I'll find out. There's nothing to be alarmed about, at any rate."

"But – *look!*" She pointed at the hideous desolation.

"Yes, I see. But no matter. You're alive. I'm alive. That's two of us, anyhow. Maybe there are a lot more. We'll soon see. Whatever it may be, we'll win."

He turned and, trailing rags and streamers of rotten cloth that once had been a business suit, he waded through the confusion of wreckage on the floor to the window.

If you have seen a weather-beaten scarecrow flapping in the wind, you have some notion of his outward guise. No tramp you ever laid eyes on could have offered so preposterous an appearance.

Down over his shoulders fell the matted, dusty hair. His tangled beard reached far below his waist. Even his eyebrows, naturally rather light, had grown to a heavy thatch above his eyes.

Save that he was not gray or bent, and that he still seemed to have kept the resilient force of vigorous manhood, you might have thought him some incredibly ancient Rip Van Winkle come to life upon that singular stage, there in the tower.

But little time gave he to introspection or the matter of his own appearance. With one quick gesture he swept away the shrouding tangle of webs, spiders, and dead flies that obscured the window. Out he peered.

"Good Heavens!" cried he, and started back a pace.

She ran to him.

"What is it?" she breathlessly exclaimed.

"Why, I don't know – yet. But this is something big! Something universal! It's – it's – no, no, you'd better not look out – not just yet."

"I must know everything. Let me see!"

Now she was at his side, and, like him, staring out into the clear sunshine, out over the vast expanses of the city.

A moment's utter silence fell. Quite clearly hummed the protest of an imprisoned fly in a web at the top of the window. The breathing of the man and woman sounded quick and loud.

"All *wrecked!*" cried Beatrice. "But – then –"

"Wrecked? It looks that way," the engineer made answer, with a strong effort holding his emotions in control. "Why not be frank about this? You'd better make up your mind at once to accept the very worst. I see no signs of anything else."

"The worst? You mean –"

"I mean just what we see out there. You can interpret it as well as I."

Again the silence while they looked, with emotions that could find no voicing in words. Instinctively the engineer passed an arm about the frightened girl and drew her close to him.

"And the last thing I remember," whispered she, "was just – just after you'd finished dictating those Taunton Bridge specifications. I suddenly felt – oh, so sleepy! Only for a minute I thought I'd close my eyes and rest, and then – then –"

"*This?*"

She nodded.

"Same here," said he. "What the deuce *can* have struck us? Us and everybody – and everything? Talk about your problems! Lucky I'm sane and sound, and – and –"

He did not finish, but fell once more to studying the incomprehensible prospect.

Their view was towards the east, but over the river and the reaches of what had once upon a time been Long Island City and Brooklyn, as familiar a scene in the other days as could be possibly imagined. But now how altered an aspect greeted them!

"It's surely all wiped out, all gone, gone into ruins," said Stern slowly and carefully, weighing each word. "No hallucination about *that*." He swept the sky-line with his eyes, that now peered keenly out from beneath those bushy brows. Instinctively he brought his hand up to his breast. He started with surprise.

"What's this?" he cried. "Why, I – I've got a full yard of whiskers. My good Lord! Whiskers on *me?* And I used to say –"

He burst out laughing. At his beard he plucked with merriment that jangled horribly on the girl's tense nerves. Suddenly he grew serious. For the first time he seemed to take clear notice of his companion's plight.

"Why, *what* a time it must have been!" cried he. "Here's some calculation all cut out for me, all right. But – you can't go that way, Miss Kendrick. It – it won't do, you know. Got to have something to put on. Great Heavens what a situation!"

He tried to peel off his remnant of a coat, but at the merest touch it tore to shreds and fell away. The girl restrained him.

"Never mind," said she, with quiet, modest dignity. "My hair protects me very well for the present. If you and I are all that's left of the people in the world, this is no time for trifles."

A moment he studied her. Then he nodded, and grew very grave.

"Forgive me," he whispered, laying a hand on her shoulder. Once more he turned to the window and looked out.

"So then, it's all gone?" he queried, speaking as to himself. "Only a skyscraper standing here or there? And the bridges and the islands – all changed.

"Not a sign of life anywhere; not a sound; the forests growing thick among the ruins? A dead world if – if all the world is like this part of it! All dead, save *you* and *me!*"

In silence they stood there, striving to realize the full import of the catastrophe. And Stern, deep down in his heart, caught some glimmering insight of the future and was glad.

Chapter III
On the Tower Platform

SUDDENLY THE GIRL started, rebelling against the evidence of her own senses, striving again to force upon herself the belief that, after all, it *could not* be so.

"No, no, no!" she cried. "This can't be true. It mustn't be. There's a mistake somewhere. This simply *must* be all an illusion, a dream!

"If the whole world's dead, how does it happen *we're* alive? How do we know it's dead? Can we see it all from here? Why, all we see is just a little segment of things. Perhaps if we could know the truth, look farther, and know –"

He shook his head.

"I guess you'll find it's real enough," he answered, "no matter how far you look. But, just the same, it won't do any harm to extend our radius of observation.

"Come, let's go on up to the top of the tower, up to the observation-platform. The quicker we know all the available facts the better. Now, if I only had a telescope – !"

He thought hard a moment, then turned and strode over to a heap of friable disintegration that lay where once his instrument case had stood, containing his surveying tools.

Down on his ragged knees he fell; his rotten shreds of clothing tore and ripped at every movement, like so much water-soaked paper.

A strange, hairy, dust-covered figure, he knelt there. Quickly he plunged his hands into the rubbish and began pawing it over and over with eager haste.

"Ah!" he cried with triumph. "Thank Heaven, brass and lenses haven't crumbled yet!"

Up he stood again. In his hand the girl saw a peculiar telescope.

"My 'level,' see?" he exclaimed, holding it up to view. "The wooden tripod's long since gone. The fixtures that held it on won't bother me much.

"Neither will the spirit-glass on top. The main thing is that the telescope itself seems to be still intact. Now we'll see."

Speaking, he dusted off the eye-piece and the objective with a bit of rag from his coat-sleeve.

Beatrice noted that the brass tubes were all eaten and pitted with verdigris, but they still held firmly. And the lenses, when Stern had finished cleaning them, showed as bright and clear as ever.

"Come, now; come with me," he bade.

Out through the doorway into the hall he made his way while the girl followed. As she went she gathered her wondrous veil of hair more closely about her.

In this universal disorganization, this wreck of all the world, how little the conventions counted!

Together, picking their way up the broken stairs, where now the rust-bitten steel showed through the corroded stone and cement in a thousand places, they cautiously climbed.

Here, spider-webs thickly shrouded the way, and had to be brushed down. There, still more bats hung and chippered in protest as the intruders passed.

A fluffy little white owl blinked at them from a dark niche; and, well toward the top of the climb, they flushed up a score of mud-swallows which had ensconced themselves comfortably along a broken balustrade.

At last, however, despite all unforeseen incidents of this sort, they reached the upper platform, nearly a thousand feet above the earth.

Out through the relics of the revolving door they crept, he leading, testing each foot of the way before the girl. They reached the narrow platform of red tiling that surrounded the tower.

Even here they saw with growing amazement that the hand of time and of this maddening mystery had laid its heavy imprint.

"Look!" he exclaimed, pointing. "What this all means we don't know yet. How long it's been we can't tell. But to judge by the appearance up here, it's even longer than I thought. See, the very tiles are cracked and crumbling.

"Tilework is usually considered highly recalcitrant – but *this* is gone. There's grass growing in the dust that's settled between the tiles. And – why, here's a young oak that's taken root and forced a dozen slabs out of place."

"The winds and birds have carried seeds up here, and acorns," she answered in an awed voice. "Think of the time that must have passed. Years and years.

"But tell me," and her brow wrinkled with a sudden wonder, "tell me how we've ever lived so long? *I* can't understand it.

"Not only have we escaped starvation, but we haven't frozen to death in all these bitter winters. How can *that* have happened?"

"Let it all go as suspended animation till we learn the facts, if we ever do," he replied, glancing about with wonder.

"You know, of course, how toads have been known to live embedded in rock for centuries? How fish, hard-frozen, have been brought to life again? Well –"

"But we are human beings."

"I know. Certain unknown natural forces, however, might have made no more of us than of non-mammalian and less highly organized creatures.

"Don't bother your head about these problems yet a while. On my word, we've got enough to do for the present without much caring about how or why.

"All we definitely know is that some very long, undetermined period of time has passed, leaving us still alive. The rest can wait."

"How long a time do you judge it?" she anxiously inquired.

"Impossible to say at once. But it must have been something extraordinary – probably far longer than either of us suspect.

"See, for example, the attrition of everything up here exposed to the weather." He pointed at the heavy stone railing. "See how *that* is wrecked, for instance."

A whole segment, indeed, had fallen inward. Its débris lay in confusion, blocking all the southern side of the platform.

The bronze bars, which Stern well remembered – two at each corner, slanting downward and bracing a rail – had now wasted to mere pockmarked shells of metal.

Three had broken entirely and sagged wantonly awry with the displacement of the stone blocks, between which the vines and grasses had long been carrying on their destructive work.

"Look out!" Stern cautioned. "Don't lean against any of those stones." Firmly he held her back as she, eagerly inquisitive, started to advance toward the railing.

"Don't go anywhere near the edge. It may all be rotten and undermined, for anything we know. Keep back here, close to the wall."

Sharply he inspected it a moment.

"Facing stones are pretty well gone," said he, "but, so far as I can see, the steel frame isn't too bad. Putting everything together, I'll probably be able before long to make some sort of calculation of the date. But for now we'll have to call it 'X,' and let it go at that."

"The year X!" she whispered under her breath. "Good Heavens, am I as old as that?"

He made no answer, but only drew her to him protectingly, while all about them the warm summer wind swept onward to the sea, out over the sparkling expanses of the bay – alone unchanged in all that universal wreckage.

In the breeze her heavy masses of hair stirred luringly. He felt its silken caress on his half-naked shoulder, and in his ears the blood began to pound with strange insistence.

Quite gone now the daze and drowsiness of the first wakening. Stern did not even feel weak or shaken. On the contrary, never had life bounded more warmly, more fully, in his veins.

The presence of the girl set his heart throbbing heavily, but he bit his lip and restrained every untoward thought.

Only his arm tightened a little about that warmly clinging body. Beatrice did not shrink from him. She needed his protection as never since the world began had woman needed man.

To her it seemed that come what might, his strength and comfort could not fail. And, despite everything, she could not – for the moment – find unhappiness within her heart.

Quite vanished now, even in those brief minutes since their awakening, was all consciousness of their former relationship – employer and employed.

The self-contained, courteous, yet unapproachable engineer had disappeared.

Now, through all the extraneous disguise of his outer self, there lived and breathed just a man, a young man, thewed with the vigor of his plentitude. All else had been swept clean away by this great change.

The girl was different, too. Was this strong woman, eager-eyed and brave, the quiet, low-voiced stenographer he remembered, busy only with her machine, her file-boxes, and her carbon-copies? Stern dared not realize the transmutation. He ventured hardly fringe it in his thoughts.

To divert his wonderings and to ease a situation which oppressed him, he began adjusting the 'level' telescope to his eye.

With his back planted firmly against the tower, he studied a wide section of the dead and buried world so very far below them. With astonishment he cried:

"It *is* true, Beatrice! Everything's swept clean away. Nothing left, nothing at all – no signs of life!

"As far as I can reach with these lenses, universal ruin. We're all alone in this whole world, just you and I – and everything belongs to us!"

"Everything – all ours?"

"Everything! Even the future – the future of the human race!"

Suddenly he felt her tremble at his side. Down at her he looked, a great new tenderness possessing him. He saw that tears were forming in her eyes.

Beatrice pressed both hands to her face and bowed her head. Filled with strange emotions, the man watched her for a moment.

Then in silence, realizing the uselessness of any words, knowing that in this monstrous Ragnarök of all humanity no ordinary relations of life could bear either cogency or meaning, he took her in his arms.

And there alone with her, far above the ruined world, high in the pure air of mid-heaven, he comforted the girl with words till then unthought-of and unknown to him.

Chapter IV
The City of Death

PRESENTLY BEATRICE grew calmer. For though grief and terror still weighed upon her soul, she realized that this was no fit time to yield to any weakness – now when a thousand things were pressing for accomplishment, if their own lives, too, were not presently to be snuffed out in all this universal death.

"Come, come," said Stern reassuringly. "I want you, too, to get a complete idea of what has happened. From now on you must know all, share all, with me." And, taking her by the hand he led her along the crumbling and uncertain platform.

Together, very cautiously, they explored the three sides of the platform still unchoked by ruins.

Out over the incredible mausoleum of civilization they peered. Now and again they fortified their vision by recourse to the telescope.

Nowhere, as he had said, was any slightest sign of life to be discerned. Nowhere a thread of smoke arose; nowhere a sound echoed upward.

Dead lay the city, between its rivers, whereon now no sail glinted in the sunlight, no tug puffed vehemently with plumy jets of steam, no liner idled at anchor or nosed its slow course out to sea.

The Jersey shore, the Palisades, the Bronx and Long Island all lay buried in dense forests of conifers and oak, with only here and there some skeleton mockery of a steel structure jutting through.

The islands in the harbor, too, were thickly overgrown. On Ellis, no sign of the immigrant station remained. Castle William was quite gone. And with a gasp of dismay and pain, Beatrice pointed out the fact that no longer Liberty held her bronze torch aloft.

Save for a black, misshapen mass protruding through the tree-tops, the huge gift of France was no more.

Fringing the water-front, all the way round, the mournful remains of the docks and piers lay in a mere sodden jumble of decay, with an occasional hulk sunk alongside.

Even over these wrecks of liners, vegetation was growing rank and green. All the wooden ships, barges and schooners had utterly vanished.

The telescope showed only a stray, lolling mast of steel, here or yonder, thrusting up from the desolation, like a mute appealing hand raised to a Heaven that responded not.

"See," remarked Stern, "up-town almost all the buildings seem to have crumbled in upon themselves, or to have fallen outward into the streets. What an inconceivable tangle of detritus those streets must be!

"And, do you notice the park hardly shows at all? Everything's so overgrown with trees you can't tell where it begins or ends. Nature has her revenge at last, on man!"

"The universal claim, made real," said Beatrice. "Those rather clearer lines of green, I suppose, must be the larger streets. See how the avenues stretch away and away, like ribbons of green velvet?"

"Everywhere that roots can hold at all, Mother Nature has set up her flags again. Hark! What's that?"

A moment they listened intently. Up to them, from very far, rose a wailing cry, tremulous, long-drawn, formidable.

"Oh! Then there *are* people, after all?" faltered the girl, grasping Stern's arm.

He laughed.

"No, hardly!" answered he. "I see you don't know the wolf-cry. I didn't till I heard it in the Hudson Bay country, last winter – that is, last winter, plus X. Not very pleasant, is it?"

"Wolves! Then – there are –"

"Why not? Probably all sorts of game on the island now. Why shouldn't there be? All in Mother Nature's stock-in-trade, you know.

"But come, come, don't let that worry you. We're safe, for the present. Time enough to consider hunting later. Let's creep around here to the other side of the tower, and see what we can see."

Silently she acquiesced. Together they reached the southern part of the platform, making their way as far as the jumbled rocks of the fallen railing would permit.

Very carefully they progressed, fearful every moment lest the support break beneath them and hurl them down along the sloping side of the pinnacle to death.

"Look!" bade Stern, pointing. "That very long green line there used to be Broadway. Quite a respectable Forest of Arden now, isn't it?" He swept his hand far outward.

"See those steel cages, those tiny, far-off ones with daylight shining through? You know them – the Park Row, the Singer, the Woolworth and all the rest. And the bridges, look at those!"

She shivered at the desolate sight. Of the Brooklyn Bridge only the towers were visible.

The watchers, two isolated castaways on their island in the sea of uttermost desolation, beheld a dragging mass of wreckage that drooped from these towers on either shore, down to the sparkling flood.

The other bridges, newer and stronger far, still remained standing. But even from that distance Stern could quite plainly see, without the telescope, that the Williamsburg Bridge had 'buckled' downward and that the farther span of the Blackwell's Island Bridge was in ruinous disrepair.

"How horrible, how ghastly is all this waste and ruin!" thought the engineer. "Yet, even in their overthrow, how wonderful are the works of man!"

A vast wonder seized him as he stood there gazing; a fierce desire to rehabilitate all this wreckage, to set it right, to start the wheels of the world-machinery running once more.

At the thought of his own powerlessness a bitter smile curled his lips.

Beatrice seemed to share something of his wonder.

"Can it be possible," whispered she, "that you and – and I – are really like Macaulay's lone watcher of the world-wreck on London Bridge?"

"That we are actually seeing the thing so often dreamed of by prophets and poets? That 'All this mighty heart is lying still,' at last – forever? The heart of the world, never to beat again?"

He made no answer, save to shake his head; but fast his thoughts were running.

So then, could he and Beatrice, just they two, be in stern reality the sole survivors of the entire human race? That race for whose material welfare he had, once on a time, done such tremendous work?

Could they be destined, he and she, to witness the closing chapter in the long, painful, glorious Book of Evolution? Slightly he shivered and glanced round.

Till he could adjust his reason to the facts, could learn the truth and weigh it, he knew he must not analyze too closely; he felt he must try not to think. For *that* way lay madness!

Far out she gazed.

The sun, declining, shot a broad glory all across the sky. Purple and gold and crimson lay the light-bands over the breast of the Hudson.

Dark blue the shadows streamed across the ruined city with its crowding forests, its blank-staring windows and sagging walls, its thousands of gaping vacancies, where wood and stone and brick had crumbled down – the city where once the tides of human life had ebbed and flowed, roaring resistlessly.

High overhead drifted a few rosy clouds, part of that changeless nature which alone did not repel or mystify these two beleaguered waifs, these chance survivors, this man, this woman, left alone together by the hand of fate.

They were dazed, fascinated by the splendor of that sunset over a world devoid of human life, for the moment giving up all efforts to judge or understand.

Stern and his mate peered closer, down at the interwoven jungles of Union Square, the leafy frond-masses that marked the one-time course of Twenty-Third Street, the forest in Madison Square, and the truncated column of the tower where no longer Diana turned her huntress bow to every varying breeze.

They heard their own hearts beat. The intake of their breath sounded strangely loud. Above them, on a broken cornice, some resting swallows twittered.

All at once the girl spoke.

"See the Flatiron Building over there!" said she. "What a hideous wreck!"

From Stern she took the telescope, adjusted it, and gazed minutely at the shattered pile of stone and metal.

Blotched as with leprosy stood the walls, whence many hundreds of blocks had fallen into Broadway forming a vast moraine that for some distance choked that thoroughfare.

In numberless places the steel frame peered through. The whole roof had caved in, crushing down the upper stories, of which only a few sparse upstanding metal beams remained.

The girl's gaze was directed at a certain spot which she knew well.

"Oh, I can even see – into some of the offices on the eighteenth floor!" cried she. "There, *look?*" And she pointed. "That one near the front! I – I used to know –"

She broke short off. In her trembling hands the telescope sank. Stern saw that she was very pale.

"Take me down!" she whispered. "I can't stand it any longer – I can't, possibly! The sight of that wrecked office! Let's go down where I can't see *that!*"

Gently, as though she had been a frightened child, Stern led her round the platform to the doorway, then down the crumbling stairs and so to the wreckage and dust-strewn confusion of what had been his office.

And there, his hand upon her shoulder, he bade her still be of good courage.

"Listen now, Beatrice," said he. "Let's try to reason this thing out together, let's try to solve this problem like two intelligent human beings.

"Just what's happened, we don't know; we can't know yet a while, till I investigate. We don't even know what year this is.

"Don't know whether anybody else is still alive, anywhere in the world. But we can find out – after we've made provision for the immediate present and formed some rational plan of life.

"If all the rest *are* gone, swept away, wiped out clean like figures on a slate, then why *we* should have happened to survive whatever it was that struck the earth, is still a riddle far beyond our comprehension."

He raised her face to his, noble despite all its grotesque disfigurements; he looked into her eyes as though to read the very soul of her, to judge whether she could share this fight, could brave this coming struggle.

"All these things may yet be answered. Once I get the proper data for this series of phenomena, I can find the solution, never fear!

"Some vast world-duty may be ours, far greater, infinitely more vital than anything that either of us has ever dreamed. It's not our place, now, to mourn or fear! Rather it is to read this mystery, to meet it and to conquer!"

Through her tears the girl smiled up at him, trustingly, confidingly. And in the last declining rays of the sun that glinted through the window-pane, her eyes were very beautiful.

Chapter V
Exploration

CAME NOW THE EVENING, as they sat and talked together, talked long and earnestly, there within that ruined place. Too eager for some knowledge of the truth, they, to feel hunger or to think of their lack of clothing.

Chairs they had none, nor even so much as a broom to clean the floor with. But Stern, first-off, had wrenched a marble slab from the stairway.

And with this plank of stone still strong enough to serve, he had scraped all one corner of the office floor free of rubbish. This gave them a preliminary camping-place wherein to take their bearings and discuss what must be done.

"So then," the engineer was saying as the dusk grew deeper, "so then, we'll apparently have to make this building our headquarters for a while.

"As nearly as I can figure, this is about what must have happened. Some sudden, deadly, numbing plague or cataclysm must have struck the earth, long, long ago.

"It may have been an almost instantaneous onset of some new and highly fatal micro-organism, propagating with such marvelous rapidity that it swept the world clean in a day – doing its work before any resistance could be organized or thought of.

"Again, some poisonous gas may have developed, either from a fissure in the earth's crust, or otherwise. Other hypotheses are possible, but of what practical value are they now?

"We only know that here, in this uppermost office of the Tower, you and I have somehow escaped with only a long period of completely suspended animation. How long? God alone knows! That's a query I can't even guess the answer to as yet."

"Well, to judge by all the changes," Beatrice suggested thoughtfully, "it can't have been less than a hundred years. Great Heavens!" and she burst into a little satiric laugh. "Am *I* a hundred and twenty-four years old? Think of that!"

"You underestimate," Stern answered. "But no matter about the time question for the present; we can't solve it now.

"Neither can we solve the other problem about Europe and Asia and all the rest of the world. Whether London, Paris, Berlin, Rome, and every other city, every other land, all have shared this fate, we simply don't know.

"All we *can* have is a feeling of strong probability that life, human life I mean, is everywhere extinct – save right here in this room!

"Otherwise, don't you see, men would have made their way back here again, back to New York, where all these incalculable treasures seem to have perished, and –"

He broke short off. Again, far off, they heard a faint re-echoing roar. For a moment they both sat speechless. What could it be? Some distant wall toppling down? A hungry beast scenting its prey? They could not tell. But Stern smiled.

"I guess," said he, "guns will be about the first thing I'll look for, after food. There ought to be good hunting down in the jungles of Fifth Avenue and Broadway!

"You shoot, of course? No? Well, I'll soon teach you. Lots of things both of us have got to learn now. No end of them!"

He rose from his place on the floor, went over to the window and stood for a minute peering out into the gloom. Then suddenly he turned.

"What's the matter with me, anyhow?" he exclaimed with irritation. "What right have I to be staying here, theorizing, when there's work to do? I ought to be busy this very minute!

"In some way or other I've got to find food, clothing, tools, arms – a thousand things. And above all, water! And here I've been speculating about the past, fool that I am!"

"You – you aren't going to leave me – not tonight?" faltered the girl.

Stern seemed not to have heard her, so strong the imperative of action lay upon him now. He began to pace the floor, sliding and stumbling through the rubbish, a singular figure in his tatters and with his patriarchal hair and beard, a figure dimly seen by the faint light that still gloomed through the window:

"In all that wreckage down below," said he, as though half to himself, "in all that vast congeries of ruin which once was called New York, surely enough must still remain intact for our small needs. Enough till we can reach the land, the country, and raise food of our own!"

"Don't go *now!*" pleaded Beatrice. She, too, stood up, and out she stretched her hands to him. "Don't, please! We can get along some way or other till morning. At least, *I* can!"

"No, no, it isn't right! Down in the shops and stores, who knows but we might find –"

"But you're unarmed! And in the streets – in the forest, rather –"

"Listen!" he commanded rather abruptly. "This is no time for hesitating or for weakness. I know you'll stand your share of all that we must suffer, dare and do together.

"Some way or other I've got to make you comfortable. I've got to locate food and drink immediately. Got to get my bearings. Why, do you think I'm going to let you, even for one night, go fasting and thirsty, sleep on bare cement, and all that sort of thing?

"If so, you're mistaken! No, you must spare me for an hour or two. Inside of that time I ought to make a beginning!"

"A whole hour?"

"Two would probably be nearer it. I promise to be back inside of that time."

"But," and her voice quivered just a trifle, "but suppose some wolf or bear –"

"Oh, I'm not quite so foolhardy as all that!" he retorted. "I'm not going to venture outside till tomorrow. My idea is that I can find at least a few essentials right here in this building.

"It's a city in itself – or was. Offices, stores, shops, everything right here together in a lump. It can't possibly take me very long to go down and rummage out something for your comfort.

"Now that the first shock and surprise of our awakening are over, we can't go on in this way, you know – h'm! – dressed in – well, such exceedingly primitive garb!"

Silently she looked at his dim figure in the dusk. Then she stretched out her hand.

"I'll go too," said she quite simply.

"You'd better stay. It's safer here."

"No, I'm going."

"But if we run into dangers?"

"Never mind. Take me with you."

Over to her he came. He took her hand. In silence he pressed it. Thus for a moment they stood. Then, arousing himself to action, he said: "First of all, a light."

"A light? How can you make a light? Why, there isn't a match left anywhere in this whole world."

"I know, but there are other things. Probably my chemical flasks and vials aren't injured. Glass is practically imperishable. And if I'm not mistaken, the bottles must be lying somewhere in that rubbish heap over by the window."

He left her wondering, and knelt among the litter. For a while he silently delved through the triturated bits of punky wood and rust-red metal that now represented the remains of his chemical cabinet.

All at once he exclaimed: "Here's one! And here's another! This certainly *is* luck! H-m! I shouldn't wonder if I got almost all of them back."

One by one he found a score of thick, ground-glass vials. Some were broken, probably by the shock when they and the cabinet had fallen, but a good many still remained intact.

Among these were the two essential ones. By the last dim ghost of light through the window, and by the sense of touch, Stern was able to make out the engraved symbols 'P' and 'S' on these bottles.

"Phosphorus and sulphur," he commented. "Well, what more could I reasonably ask? Here's alcohol, too, hermetically sealed. Not too bad, eh?"

While the girl watched, with wondering admiration, Stern thought hard a moment. Then he set to work.

First he took a piece of the corroded metal framework of the cabinet, a steel strip about eighteen inches long, frail in places, but still sufficiently strong to serve his purpose.

Tearing off some rags from his coat-sleeve, he wadded them together into a ball as big as his fist. Around this ball he twisted the metal strip, so that it formed at once a holder and a handle for the rag-mass.

With considerable difficulty he worked the glass stopper out of the alcohol bottle, and with the fluid saturated the rags. Then, on a clear bit of the floor, he spilled out a small quantity of the phosphorus and sulphur.

"This beats getting fire by friction all hollow," he cheerfully remarked. "I've tried that, too, and I guess it's only in books a white man ever succeeds at it. But this way you see, it's simplicity itself."

Very moderate friction, with a bit of wood from the wreckage of the door, sufficed to set the phosphorus ablaze. Stern heaped on a few tiny lumps of sulphur. Then, coughing as the acrid fumes arose from the sputter of blue flame, he applied the alcohol-soaked torch.

Instantly a puff of fire shot up, colorless and clear, throwing no very satisfactory light, yet capable of dispelling the thickest of the gloom.

The blaze showed Stern's eager face, long-bearded and dusty, as he bent over this crucial experiment.

The girl, watching closely, felt a strange new thrill of confidence and solace. Some realization of the engineer's resourcefulness came to her, and in her heart she had confidence that, though the whole wide world had crumbled into ruin, yet *he* would find a way to smooth her path, to be a strength and refuge for her.

But Stern had no time for any but matters of intensest practicality. From the floor he arose, holding the flambeau in one hand, the bottle of alcohol in the other.

"Come now," bade he, and raised the torch on high to light her way, "You're still determined to go?"

For an answer she nodded. Her eyes gleamed by the uncanny light.

And so, together, he leading out of the room and along the wrecked hall, they started on their trip of exploration out into the unknown.

Chapter VI
Treasure-Trove

NEVER BEFORE had either of them realized just what the meaning of forty-eight stories might be. For all their memories of this height were associated with smooth-sliding elevators that had whisked them up as though the tremendous height had been the merest trifle.

This night, however, what with the broken stairs, the débris-cumbered hallways, the lurking darkness which the torch could hardly hold back from swallowing them, they came to a clear understanding of the problem.

Every few minutes the flame burned low and Stern had to drop on more alcohol, holding the bottle high above the flame to avoid explosion.

Long before they had compassed the distance to the ground floor the girl lagged with weariness and shrank with nameless fears.

Each black doorway that yawned along their path seemed ominous with memories of life that had perished there, of death that now reigned all-supreme.

Each corner, every niche and crevice, breathed out the spirit of the past and of the mystic tragedy which in so brief a time had wiped the human race from earth, "as a mother wipes the milky lips of her child."

And Stern, though he said little save to guide Beatrice and warn her of unusual difficulties, felt the somber magic of the place. No poet, he; only a man of hard and practical details. Yet he realized that, were he dowered with the faculty, here lay matter for an Epic of Death such as no Homer ever dreamed, no Virgil ever could have penned.

Now and then, along the corridors and down the stairways, they chanced on curious little piles of dust, scattered at random in fantastic shapes.

These for a few minutes puzzled Stern, till stooping, he stirred one with his hand. Something he saw there made him start back with a stifled exclamation.

"What is it?" cried the girl, startled. "Tell me!"

But he, realizing the nature of his discovery – for he had seen a human incisor tooth, gold-filled, there in the odd little heap – straightened up quickly and assumed to smile.

"It's nothing, nothing at all!" he answered. "Come, we haven't got any time to waste. If we're going to provide ourselves with even a few necessaries before the alcohol's all gone, we've got to be at work!"

And onward, downward, ever farther and farther, he led her through the dark maze of ruin, which did not even echo to their barefoot tread.

Like disheveled wraiths they passed, soundlessly, through eerie labyrinths and ways which might have served as types of Coleridge's 'caverns measureless to man,' so utterly drear they stretched out in their ghostly desolation.

At length, after an eternal time of weariness and labor, they managed to make their way down into the ruins of the once famous and beautiful arcade which had formerly run from Madison Avenue to the square.

"Oh, how horrible!" gasped Beatrice, shrinking, as they clambered down the stairs and emerged into this scene of chaos, darkness, death.

Where long ago the arcade had stretched its path of light and life and beauty, of wealth and splendor, like an epitome of civilization all gathered in that constricted space, the little light disclosed stark horror.

Feeble as a will-o'-the-wisp in that enshrouding dark, the torch showed only hints of things – here a fallen pillar, there a shattered mass of wreckage where a huge section of the ceiling had fallen, yonder a gaping aperture left by the disintegration of a wall.

Through all this rubbish and confusion, over and through a score of the little dust-piles which Stern had so carefully avoided explaining to Beatrice, they climbed and waded, and with infinite pains slowly advanced.

"What we need is more light!" exclaimed the engineer presently. "We've got to have a bonfire here!"

And before long he had collected a considerable pile of wood, ripped from the door-ways and window-casings of the arcade. This he set fire to, in the middle of the floor.

Soon a dull, wavering glow began to paint itself upon the walls, and to fling the comrades' shadows, huge and weird, in dancing mockery across the desolation.

Strangely enough, many of the large plate-glass windows lining the arcade still stood intact. They glittered with the uncanny reflections of the fire as the man and woman slowly made way down the passage.

"See," exclaimed Stern, pointing. "See all these ruined shops? Probably almost everything is worthless. But there must be some things left that we can use.

"See the post-office, down there on the left? Think of the millions in real money, gold and silver, in all these safes here and all over the city – in the banks and vaults! Millions! Billions!

"Jewels, diamonds, wealth simply inconceivable! Yet now a good water supply, some bread, meat, coffee, salt, and so on, a couple of beds, a gun or two and some ordinary tools would outweigh them all!"

"Clothes, too," the girl suggested. "Plain cotton cloth is worth ten million dollars an inch now."

"Right," answered Stern, gazing about him with wonder.

"And I offer a bushel of diamonds for a razor and a pair of scissors." Grimly he smiled as he stroked his enormous beard.

"But come, this won't do. There'll be plenty of time to look around and discuss things in the morning. Just now we've got a definite errand. Let's get busy!"

Thus began their search for a few prime necessities of life, there in that charnel house of civilization, by the dull reflections of the firelight and the pallid torch glow.

Though they forced their way into ten or twelve of the arcade shops, they found no clothing, no blankets or fabric of any kind that would serve for coverings or to sleep upon. Everything at all in the nature of cloth had either sunk back into moldering annihilation or had at best grown far too fragile to be of the slightest service.

They found, however, a furrier's shop, and this they entered eagerly.

From rusted metal hooks a few warped fragments of skins still hung, moth-eaten, riddled with holes, ready to crumble at the merest touch.

"There's nothing in any of these to help us," judged Stern. "But maybe we might find something else in here."

Carefully they searched the littered place, all dust and horrible disarray, which made sad mockery of the gold-leaf sign still visible on the window: "Lange, Importer. All the Latest Novelties."

On the floor Stern discovered three more of those little dust-middens which meant human bodies, pitiful remnants of an extinct race, of unknown people in the long ago. What had he now in common with them? The remains did not even inspire repugnance in him. All at once Beatrice uttered a cry of startled gladness. "Look here! A storage chest!"

True enough, there stood a cedar box, all seamed and cracked and bulging, yet still retaining a semblance of its original shape.

The copper bindings and the lock were still quite plainly to be seen, as the engineer held the torch close, though green and corroded with incredible age.

One effort of Stern's powerful arms sufficed to tip the chest quite over. As it fell it burst. Down in a mass of pulverized, worm-eaten splinters it disintegrated.

Out rolled furs, many and many of them, black, and yellow, and striped – the pelts of the grizzly, of the leopard, the chetah, the royal Bengal himself.

"Hurray!" shouted the man, catching up first one, then another, and still a third. "Almost intact. A little imperfection here and there doesn't matter. Now we've got clothes and beds.

"What's that? Yes, maybe they are a trifle warm for this season of the year, but this is no time to be particular. See, now, how do you like *that?*"

Over the girl's shoulders, as he spoke, he flung the tiger-skin.

"Magnificent!" he judged, standing back a pace or two and holding up the torch to see her better. "When I find you a big gold pin or clasp to fasten that with at the throat you'll make a picture of another and more splendid Boadicea!"

He tried to laugh at his own words, but merriment sat ill there in that place, and with such a subject. For the woman, thus clad, had suddenly assumed a wild, barbaric beauty.

Bright gleamed her gray eyes by the light of the flambeau; limpid, and deep, and earnest, they looked at Stern. Her wonderful hair, shaken out in bewildering masses over the striped, tawny savagery of the robe, made colorful contrasts, barbarous, seductive.

Half hidden, the woman's perfect body, beautiful as that of a wood-nymph or a pagan dryad, roused atavistic passions in the engineer.

He dared speak no other word for the moment, but bent beside the shattered chest again and fell to looking over the furs.

A polar-bear skin attracted his attention, and this he chose. Then, with it slung across his shoulder, he stood up.

"Come," said he, steadying his voice with an effort; "come, we must be going now. Our light won't hold out very much longer. We've got to find food and drink before the alcohol's all gone; got to look out for practical affairs, whatever happens. Let's be going."

Fortune favored them.

In the wreck of a small fancy grocer's booth down toward the end of the arcade, where the post-office had been, they came upon a stock of goods in glass jars.

All the tinned foods had long since perished, but the impermeable glass seemed to have preserved fruits and vegetables of the finer sort, and chipped beef and the like, in a state of perfect soundness.

Best of all, they discovered the remains of a case of mineral water. The case had crumbled to dust, but fourteen bottles of water were still intact.

"Pile three or four of these into my fur robe here," directed Stern. "Now, a few of the other jars – that's right. Tomorrow we'll come down and clean up the whole stock. But we've got enough for now."

"We'd best be getting back up the stairs again," said he. And so they started.

"Are you going to leave that fire burning?" asked the girl, as they passed the middle of the arcade.

"Yes. It can't do any harm. Nothing to catch here; only old metal and cement. Besides, it would take too much time and labor to put it out."

Thus they abandoned the gruesome place and began the long, exhausting climb.

It must have taken them an hour and a half at least to reach their eerie. Both found their strength taxed to the utmost.

Before they were much more than halfway up, the ultimate drop of alcohol had been burned.

The last few hundred feet had to be made by slow, laborious feeling, aided only by such dim reflections of the gibbous moon as glimmered through a window, cobweb-hung, or through some break in the walls.

At length, however – for all things have an end – breathless and spent, they found their refuge. And soon after that, clad in their savage robes, they supped.

Allan Stern, consulting engineer, and Beatrice Kendrick, stenographer, now king and queen of the whole wide world domain (as they feared), sat together by a little blaze of punky wood fragments that flickered on the eroded floor.

They ate with their fingers and drank out of the bottles, *sans* apology. Strange were their speculations, their wonderings, their plans – now discussed specifically, now half-voiced by a mere word that thrilled them both with sudden, poignant emotion.

An so an hour passed, and the night deepened toward the birth of another day. The fire burned low and died, for they had little to replenish it with.

Down sank the moon, her pale light dimming as she went, her faint illumination wanly creeping across the disordered, wrack-strewn floor.

And at length Stern, in the outer office, Beatrice in the other, they wrapped themselves within their furs and laid them down to sleep.

Despite the age-long trance from which they both had but so recently emerged, a strange lassitude weighed on them.

Yet long after Beatrice had lost herself in dreams, Stern lay and thought strange thoughts, yearning and eager thoughts, there in the impenetrable gloom.

Chapter VII
The Outer World

BEFORE DAYBREAK the engineer was up again, and active. Now that he faced the light of morning, with a thousand difficult problems closing in on every hand, he put aside his softer moods, his visions and desires, and – like the scientific man he was – addressed himself to the urgent matters in hand.

"The girl's safe enough alone, here, for a while," thought he, looking in upon her where she lay, calm as a child, folded within the clinging masses of the tiger-skin.

"I must be out and away for two or three hours, at the very least. I hope she'll sleep till I get back. If not – what then?"

He thought a moment; then, coming over to the charred remnants of last night's fire, chose a bit of burnt wood. With this he scrawled in large, rough letters on a fairly smooth stretch of the wall:

"Back soon. All OK. Don't worry."

Then, turning, he set out on the long, painful descent again to the earth-level.

Garish now, and doubly terrible, since seen with more than double clearness by the graying dawn, the world-ruin seemed to him.

Strong of body and of nerve as he was, he could not help but shudder at the numberless traces of sudden and pitiless death which met his gaze.

Everywhere lay those dust-heaps, with here or there a tooth, a ring, a bit of jewelry showing – everywhere he saw them, all the way down the stairs, in every room and office he peered into, and in the time-ravished confusion of the arcade.

But this was scarcely the time for reflections of any sort. Life called, and labor, and duty; not mourning for the dead world, nor even wonder or pity at the tragedy which had so mysteriously – befallen.

And as the man made his way over and through the universal wreckage, he took counsel with himself.

"First of all, water!" thought he. "We can't depend on the bottled supply. Of course, there's the Hudson; but it's brackish, if not downright salt. I've got to find some fresh and pure supply, close at hand. That's the prime necessity of life.

"What with the canned stuff, and such game as I can kill, there's bound to be food enough for a while. But a good water-supply we must have, and at once!"

Yet, prudent rather for the sake of Beatrice than for his own, he decided that he ought not to issue out, unarmed, into this new and savage world, of which he had as yet no very definite knowledge. And for a while he searched hoping to find some weapon or other.

"I've got to have an ax, first of all," said he. "That's mans first need, in any wilderness. Where shall I find one?"

He thought a moment.

"Ah! In the basements!" exclaimed he. "Maybe I can locate an engine-room, a store-room, or something of that sort. There's sure to be tools in a place like that." And, laying off the bear-skin, he prepared to explore the regions under the ground-level.

He used more than half an hour, through devious ways and hard labor, to make his way to the desired spot. The ancient stair-way, leading down, he could not find.

But by clambering down one of the elevator-shafts, digging toes and fingers into the crevices in the metal framework and the cracks in the concrete, he managed at last to reach a vaulted sub-cellar, festooned with webs, damp, noisome and obscure.

Considerable light glimmered in from a broken sidewalk-grating above, and through a gaping, jagged hole near one end of the cellar, beneath which lay a badly-broken stone.

The engineer figured that this block had fallen from the tower and come to rest only here; and this awoke him to a new sense of ever-present peril. At any moment of the night or day, he realized, some such mishap was imminent.

"Eternal vigilance!" he whispered to himself. Then, dismissing useless fears, he set about the task in hand.

By the dim illumination from above, he was able to take cognizance of the musty-smelling place, which, on the whole, was in a better state of repair than the arcade. The first cellar yielded nothing of value to him, but, making his way through a low vaulted door, he chanced into what must have been one of the smaller, auxiliary engine-rooms.

This, he found, contained a battery of four dynamos, a small seepage-pump, and a crumbling marble switch-board with part of the wiring still comparatively intact.

At sight of all this valuable machinery scaled and pitted with rust, Stern's brows contracted with a feeling akin to pain. The engineer loved mechanism of all sorts; its care and use had been his life.

And now these mournful relics, strange as that may seem, affected him more strongly than the little heaps of dust which marked the spots where human beings had fallen in sudden, inescapable death.

Yet even so, he had no time for musing.

"Tools!" cried he, peering about the dimwit vault. "Tools – I must have some. Till I find tools, I'm helpless!"

Search as he might, he discovered no ax in the place, but in place of it he unearthed a sledge-hammer. Though corroded, it was still quite serviceable. Oddly enough, the oak handle was almost intact.

"Kyanized wood, probably," reflected he, as he laid the sledge to one side and began delving into a bed of dust that had evidently been a work-bench. "Ah! And here's a chisel! A spanner, too! A heap of rusty old wire nails!"

Delightedly he examined these treasures.

"They're worth more to me," he exulted; "than all the gold between here and what's left of San Francisco!"

He found nothing more of value in the litter. Everything else was rusted beyond use. So, having convinced himself that nothing more remained, he gathered up his finds and started back whence he had come.

After some quarter-hour of hard labor, he managed to transport everything up into the arcade. "Now for a glimpse of the outer world!" quoth he.

Gripping the sledge well in hand, he made his way through the confused nexus of ruin. Disguised as everything now was, fallen and disjointed, murdering, blighted by age incalculable, still the man recognized many familiar features.

Here, he recalled, the telephone-booths had been; there the information desk. Yonder, again, he remembered the little curved counter where once upon a time a man in uniform had sold tickets to such as had wanted to visit the tower.

Counter now was dust; ticket-man only a crumble of fine, grayish powder. Stern shivered slightly, and pressed on.

As he approached the outer air, he noticed that many a grassy tuft and creeping vine had rooted in the pavement of the arcade, up-prying the marble slabs and cracking the once magnificent floor.

The doorway itself was almost choked by a tremendous Norway pine which had struck root close to the building, and now insolently blocked that way where, other-time many thousand men and women every day had come and gone.

But Stern clambered out past this obstacle, testing the floor with his sledge, as he went, lest he fall through an unseen weak spots into the depths of coal-cellars below. And presently he reached the outer air, unharmed.

"But – but, the sidewalk?" cried he, amazed. "The street – the Square? Where are they?" And in astonishment he stopped, staring.

The view from the tower, though it had told him something of the changes wrought, had given him no adequate conception of their magnitude.

He had expected some remains of human life to show upon the earth, some semblance of the metropolis to remain in the street. But no, nothing was there; nothing at all on the ground to show that he was in the heart of a city.

He could, indeed, catch glimpses of a building here or there. Through the tangled thickets that grew close up to the age-worn walls of the Metropolitan, he could make out a few bits of tottering construction on the south side of what had been Twenty-Third Street.

But of the street itself, no trace remained – no pavement, no sidewalk, no curb. And even so near and so conspicuous an object as the wreck of the Flatiron was now entirely concealed by the dense forest.

Soil had formed thickly over all the surface. Huge oaks and pines flourished there as confidently as though in the heart of the Maine forest, crowding ash and beech for room.

Under the man's feet, even as he stood close by the building – which was thickly overgrown with ivy and with ferns and bushes rooted in the crannies – the pine-needles bent in deep, pungent beds.

Birch, maple, poplar and all the natives of the American woods shouldered each other lustily. By the state of the fresh young leaves, just bursting their sheaths, Stern knew the season was mid-May.

Through the wind-swayed branches, little flickering patches of morning sunlight met his gaze, as they played and quivered on the forest moss or over the sere pine-spills.

Even upon the huge, squared stones which here and there lay in disorder, and which Stern knew must have fallen from the tower, the moss grew very thick; and more than one such block had been rent by frost and growing things.

"How long has it been, great Heavens! How long?" cried the engineer, a sudden fear creeping into his heart. For this, the reasserted dominance of nature, bore in on him with more appalling force than anything he had yet seen.

About him he looked, trying to get his bearings in that strange *milieu*.

"Why," said he, quite slowly, "it's – it's just as though some cosmic jester, all-powerful, had scooped up the fragments of a ruined city and tossed them pell-mell into the core of the Adirondacks! It's horrible – ghastly – incredible!"

Dazed and awed, he stood as in a dream, a strange figure with his mane of hair, his flaming, trailing beard, his rags (for he had left the bear-skin in the arcade), his muscular arm, knotted as he held the sledge over his shoulder.

Well might he have been a savage of old times; one of the early barbarians of Britain, perhaps, peering in wonder at the ruins of some deserted Roman camp.

The chatter of a squirrel high up somewhere in the branches of an oak, recalled him to his wits. Down came spiralling a few bits of bark and acorn-shell, quite in the old familiar way.

Farther off among the woods, a robin's throaty morning notes drifted to him on the odorous breeze. A wren, surprisingly tame, chippered busily. It hopped about, not ten feet from him, entirely fearless.

Stern realized that it was now seeing a man for the first time in its life, and that it had no fear. His bushy brows contracted as he watched the little brown body jumping from twig to twig in the pine above him.

A deep, full breath he drew. Higher, still higher he raised his head. Far through the leafy screen he saw the overbending arch of sky in tiny patches of turquoise.

"The same old world, after all – the same, in spite of everything – thank God!" he whispered, his very tone a prayer of thanks.

And suddenly, though why he could not have told, the grim engineer's eyes grew wet with tears that ran, unheeded, down his heavy-bearded cheeks.

Chapter VII
A Sign of Peril

STERN'S WEAKNESS – as he judged it – lasted but a minute. Then, realizing even more fully than ever the necessity for immediate labor and exploration, he tightened his grip upon the sledge and set forth into the forest of Madison Square.

Away from him scurried a cotton-tail. A snake slid, hissing, out of sight under a jungle of fern. A butterfly, dull brown and ocher, settled upon a branch in the sunlight, where it began slowly opening and shutting its wings.

"Hem! That's a *Danaus plexippus*, right enough," commented the man. "But there are some odd changes in it. Yes, indeed, certainly some evolutionary variants. Must be a tremendous time since we went to sleep, for sure; probably very much longer than I dare guess. That's a problem I've got to go to work on, before many days!"

But now for the present he dismissed it again; he pushed it aside in the press of urgent matters. And, parting the undergrowth, he broke his crackling way through the deep wood.

He had gone but a few hundred yards when an exclamation of surprised delight burst from his lips.

"Water! Water!" he cried. "What? A spring, so close? A pool, right here at hand? Good luck, by Jove, the very first thing!"

And, stopping where he stood, he gazed at it with keen, unalloyed pleasure.

There, so near to the massive bulk of the tower that the vast shadow lay broadly across it, Stern had suddenly come upon as beautiful a little watercourse as ever bubbled forth under the yews of Arden or lapped the willows of Hesperides.

He beheld a roughly circular depression in the woods, fern-banked and fringed with purple blooms; at the bottom sparkled a spring, leaf-bowered, cool, Elysian.

From this, down through a channel which the water must have worn for itself by slow erosion, a small brook trickled, widening out into a pool some fifteen feet across; whence, brimming over, it purled away through the young sweet-flags and rushes with tempting little woodland notes.

"What a find!" cried the engineer. Forward he strode. "So, then? Deer-tracks?" he exclaimed, noting a few dainty hoof-prints in the sandy margin. "Great!" And, filled with exultation, he dropped beside the spring.

Over it he bent. Setting his bearded lips to the sweet water, he drank enormous, satisfying drafts.

Sated at last, he stood up again and peered about him. All at once he burst out into joyous laughter.

"Why, this is certainly an old friend of mine, or I'm a liar!" he cried out. "This spring is nothing more or less than the lineal descendant of Madison Square fountain, what? But good Lord, what a change!

"It would make a splendid subject for an article in the 'Annals of Applied Geology.' Only – well, there aren't any annals, now, and what's more, no readers!"

Down to the wider pool he walked.

"Stern, my boy," said he, "here's where you get an A-1, first-class dip!"

A minute later, stripped to the buff, the man lay splashing vigorously in the water. From top to toe he scrubbed himself vigorously with the fine, white sand. And when, some minutes later, he rose up again, the tingle and joy of life filled him in every nerve.

For a minute he looked contemptuously at his rags, lying there on the edge of the pool. Then with a grunt he kicked them aside.

"I guess we'll dispense with those," judged he. "The bear-skin, back in the building, there, will be enough." He picked up his sledge, and, heaving a mighty breath of comfort, set out for the tower again.

"Ah, but that was certainly fine!" he exclaimed. "I feel ten years younger, already. Ten, from what? X minus ten, equals – ?"

Thoughtfully, as he walked across the elastic moss and over the pine-needles, he stroked his beard.

"Now, if I could only get a hair-cut and shave!" said he. "Well, why not? Wouldn't that surprise *her*, though?"

The idea strong upon him, he hastened his steps, and soon was back at the door close to the huge Norway pine. But here he did not enter. Instead, he turned to the right.

Plowing through the woods, climbing over fallen columns and shattered building-stones, flushing a covey of loud-winged partridges, parting the bushes that grew thickly along the base of the wall, he now found himself in what had long ago been Twenty-Third Street.

No sign, now of paving or car-tracks – nothing save, on the other side of the way, crumbling lines of ruin. As he worked his way among the detritus of the Metropolitan, he kept sharp watch for the wreckage of a hardware store.

Not until he had crossed the ancient line of Madison Avenue and penetrated some hundred yards still further along Twenty-Third Street, did he find what he sought. "Ah!" he suddenly cried. "Here's something now!"

And, scrambling over a pile of grass-grown rubbish with a couple of time-bitten iron wheels peering out – evidently the wreckage of an electric car – he made his way around a gaping hole where a side-walk had caved in and so reached the interior of a shop.

"Yes, prospects here, certainly prospects!" he decided carefully inspecting the place. "If this didn't use to be Currier & Brown's place, I'm away off my bearings. There ought to be *something* left."

"Ah! Would you?" and he flung a hastily-snatched rock at a rattlesnake that had begun its dry, chirring defiance on top of what once had been a counter.

The snake vanished, while the rock rebounding, crashed through glass.

Stern wheeled about with a cry of joy. For there, he saw, still stood near the back of the shop a showcase from within which he caught a sheen of tarnished metal.

Quickly he ran toward this, stumbling over the loose dooring, mossy and grass-grown. There in the case, preserved as you have seen Egyptian relics two or three thousand years old, in museums, the engineer beheld incalculable treasures. He thrilled with a savage, strange delight.

Another blow, with the sledge, demolished the remaining glass.

He trembled with excitement as he chose what he most needed.

"I certainly do understand now," said he, "why the New Zealanders took Captain Cook's old barrel-hoops and refused his cash. Same here! All the money in this town couldn't buy this rusty knife –" as he seized a corroded blade set in a horn handle, yellowed with age. And eagerly he continued the hunt.

Fifteen minutes later he had accumulated a pair of scissors, two rubber combs, another knife, a revolver, an automatic, several handfuls of cartridges and a Cosmos bottle.

All these he stowed in a warped, mildewed remnant of a Gladstone bag, taken from a corner where a broken glass sign, "Leather Goods," lay among the rank confusion.

"I guess I've got enough, now, for the first load," he judged, more excited than if he had chanced upon a blue-clay bed crammed with Cullinan diamonds. "It's a beginning, anyhow. Now for Beatrice!"

Joyously as a schoolboy with a pocketful of new-won marbles, he made his exit from the ruins of the hardware store, and started back toward the tower.

But hardly had he gone a hundred feet when all at once he drew back with a sharp cry of wonder and alarm.

There at his feet, in plain view under a little maple sapling, lay something that held him frozen with astonishment.

He snatched it up, dropping the sledge to do so.

"What? *What?*" he stammered; and at the thing he stared with widened, uncomprehending eyes.

"Merciful God! How – what – ?" cried he.

The thing he held in his hand was *a broad, fat, flint assegai-point!*

Chapter IX
Headway Against Odds

STERN GAZED at this alarming object with far more trepidation than he would have eyed a token authentically labeled: "Direct from Mars."

For the space of a full half-minute he found no word, grasped no coherent thought, came to no action save to stand there, thunder-struck, holding the rotten leather bag in one hand, the spear-head in the other.

Then, suddenly, he shouted a curse and made as though to fling it clean away. But 'ere it had left his grasp, he checked himself.

"No, there's no use in *that*," said he, quite slowly. "If this thing is what it appears to be, if it isn't merely some freakish bit of stone weathered off somewhere, why, it means – my God, what *doesn't* it mean?"

He shuddered, and glanced fearfully about him; all his calculations already seemed crashing down about him; all his plans, half-formulated, appeared in ruin.

New, vast and unknown factors of the struggle broadened rapidly before his mental vision, *if* this thing were really what it looked to be.

Keenly he peered at the bit of flint in his palm. There it lay, real enough, an almost perfect specimen of the flaker's art, showing distinctly where the wood had been applied to the core to peel off the many successive layers.

It could not have been above three and a half inches long, by one and a quarter wide, at its broadest part. The heft, where it had been hollowed to hold the lashings, was well marked.

A diminutive object and a skilfully-formed one. At any other time or place, the engineer would have considered the finding a good fortune; but now – !

"Yet after all," he said aloud, as if to convince himself, "it's only a bit of stone! What can it prove?"

His subconsciousness seemed to make answer: "So, too, the sign that Robinson Crusoe found on the beach was only a human foot-mark. Do not deceive yourself!"

In deep thought the engineer stood there a moment or two. Then, "Bah!" cried he. "What does it matter, anyhow? Let it come – whatever it is! If I hadn't just happened to find this, I'd have been none the wiser." And he dropped the bit of flint into the bag along with the other things.

Again he picked up his sledge, and, now more cautiously, once more started forward.

"All I can do," he thought, "is just to go right ahead as though this hadn't happened at all. If trouble comes, it comes, that's all. I guess I can meet it. Always *have* got away with it, so far. We'll see. What's on the cards has got to be played to a finish, and the best hand wins!"

He retraced his way to the spring, where he carefully rinsed and filled the Cosmos bottle for Beatrice. Then back to the Metropolitan he came, donned his bear – skin, which he fastened with a wire nail, and started the long climb. His sledge he carefully hid on the second floor, in an office at the left of the stairway.

"Don't think much of this hammer, after all," said he. "What I need is an ax. Perhaps this afternoon I can have another go at that hardware place and find one.

"If the handle's gone, I can heft it with green wood. With a good ax and these two revolvers – till I find some rifles – I guess we're safe enough, spearheads or not!"

About him he glanced at the ever-present molder and decay. This office, he could easily see, had been both spacious and luxurious, but now it offered a sorry spectacle. In the dust over by a window something glittered dully.

Stern found it was a fragment of a beveled mirror, which had probably hung there and, when the frame rotted, had dropped. He brushed it off and looked eagerly into it.

A cry of amazement burst from him.

"Do I look like *that*?" he shouted. "Well, I won't, for long!"

He propped the glass up on the steel beam of the window-opening, and got the scissors out of the bag. Ten minutes later, the face of Allan Stern bore some resemblance to its original self. True enough, his hair remained a bit jagged, especially in the back, his brows were somewhat uneven, and the point to which his beard was trimmed was far from perfect.

But none the less his wild savagery had given place to a certain aspect of civilization that made the white bearskin over his shoulders look doubly strange.

Stern, however, was well pleased. He smiled in satisfaction.

"What will *she* think, and say?" he wondered, as he once more took up the bag and started on the long, exhausting climb.

Sweating profusely, badly "blown," – for he had not taken much time to rest on the way – the engineer at last reached his offices in the tower.

Before entering, he called the girl's name.

"Beatrice! Oh, Beatrice! Are you awake, and visible?"

"All right, come in!" she answered cheerfully, and came to meet him in the doorway. Out to him she stretched her hand, in welcome; and the smile she gave him set his heart pounding.

He had to laugh at her astonishment and naive delight over his changed appearance; but all the time his eyes were eagerly devouring her beauty.

For now, freshly-awakened, full of new life and vigor after a sound night's sleep, the girl was magnificent.

The morning light disclosed new glints of color in her wondrous hair, as it lay broad and silken on the tiger-skin.

This she had secured at the throat and waist with bits of metal taken from the wreckage of the filing-cabinet.

Stern promised himself that ere long he would find her a profusion of gold pins and chains, in some of the Fifth Avenue shops, to serve her purposes till she could fashion real clothing.

As she gave him her hand, the Bengal skin fell back from her round, warm, cream-white arm.

At sight of it, at vision of that messy crown of hair and of those gray, penetrant, questioning eyes, the man's spent breath quickened.

He turned his own eyes quickly away, lest she should read his thought, and began speaking – of what? He hardly knew. Anything, till he could master himself.

But through it all he knew that in his whole life, till now self-centered, analytical, cold, he never had felt such real, spontaneous happiness.

The touch of her fingers, soft and warm, dispelled his every anxiety. The thought that he was working, now, for her; serving her; striving to preserve and keep her, thrilled him with joy.

And as some foregleam of the future came to him, his fears dropped from him like those outworn rags he had discarded in the forest.

"Well, so we're both up and at it, again," he exclaimed, common-placely enough, his voice a bit uncertain. Stern had walked narrow girders six hundred feet sheer up; he had worked in caissons under tide-water, with the air-pumps driving full tilt to keep death out.

He had swung in a bosun's-chair down the face of the Yosemite Cañon at Cathedral Spires. But never had he felt emotions such as now. And greatly he marveled.

"I've had luck," he continued. "See here, and here?"

He showed her his treasures, all the contents of the bag, except the spear-point. Then, giving her the Cosmos bottle, he bade her drink. Gratefully she did so, while he explained to her the finding of the spring.

Her face aglow with eagerness and brave enthusiasts, she listened. But when he told her about the bathing-pool, an envious expression came to her.

"It's not fair," she protested, "for you to monopolize that. If you'll show me the place – and just stay around in the woods, to see that nothing hurts me –"

"You'll take a dip, too?"

Eagerly she nodded, her eyes beaming.

"I'm just dying for one!" she exclaimed. "Think! I haven't had a bath, now, for x years!"

"I'm at your service," declared the engineer. And for a moment a little silence came between them, a silence so profound that they could even hear the faint, far cheepings of the mud-swallows in the tower stair, above.

At the back of Stern's brain still lurked a haunting fear of the wood, of what the assegai-point might portend, but he dispelled it.

"Well, come along down," bade he. "It's getting late, already. But first, we must take just one more look, by this fresh morning light, from the platform up above, there?"

She assented readily. Together, talking of their first urgent needs, of their plans for this new day and for this wonderful, strange life that now confronted them, they climbed the stairs again. Once more they issued out on to the weed-grown platform of red tiles.

There they stood a moment, looking out with wonder over that vast, still, marvelous prospect of life-in-death. Suddenly the engineer spoke.

"Tell me," said he, "where did you get that line of verse you quoted last night? The one about this vast city – heart all lying still, you know?"

"That? Why, that was from Wordsworth's Sonnet on London Bridge, of course," she smiled up at him. "You remember it now, don't you?"

"No-o," he disclaimed a trifle dubiously. "I – that is, I never was much on poetry, you understand. It wasn't exactly in my line. But never mind. How did it go? I'd like to hear it, tremendously."

"I don't just recall the whole poem," she answered thoughtfully. "But I know part of it ran:

> *'...This city now doth like a garment wear*
> *The beauty of the morning. Silent, bare,*
> *Ships, towers, domes, theaters, and temples lie*
> *Open unto the fields and to the sky*
> *All bright and glittering in the smokeless air.'"*

A moment she paused to think. The sun, lancing its long and level rays across the water and the vast dead city, irradiated her face.

Instinctively, as she looked abroad over that wondrous panorama, she raised both bare arms; and, clad in the tiger-skin alone, stood for a little space like some Parsee priestess, sun-worshiping, on her tower of silence.

Stern looked at her, amazed.

Was this, could this indeed be the girl he had employed, in the old days – the other days of routine and of tedium, of orders and specifications and dry-as-dust dictation? As though from a strange spell he aroused himself.

"The poem?" exclaimed he. "What next?"

"Oh, that? I'd almost forgotten about that; I was dreaming. It goes this way, I think:

> *'Never did the sun more beautifully steep*
> *In his first splendor valley, rock, or hill,*
> *Ne'er saw I, never felt a calm so deep;*
> *The river glideth at his own sweet will.*
> *Dear God! the very houses seem asleep,*
> *And all this mighty heart is standing still!...'"*

She finished the tremendous classic almost in a whisper.

They both stood silent a moment, gazing out together on that strange, inexplicable fulfilment of the poet's vision.

Up to them, through the crystal morning air, rose a faint, small sound of waters, from the brooklet in the forest. The nesting birds, below, were busy "in song and solace"; and through the golden sky above, a swallow slanted on sharp wing toward some unseen, leafy goal.

Far out upon the river, faint specks of white wheeled and hovered – a flock of swooping gulls, snowy and beautiful and free. Their pinions flashed, spiralled and sank to rest on the wide waters.

Stern breathed a sigh. His right arm slipped about the sinuous, fur-robed body of the girl.

"Come, now!" said he, with returning practicality. "Bath for you, breakfast for both of us – then we must buckle down to work. *Come!*"

Chapter X
Terror

NOON FOUND THEM far advanced in the preliminaries of their hard adventuring.

Working together in a strong and frank companionship – the past temporarily forgotten and the future still put far away – half a day's labor advanced them a long distance on the road to safety.

Even these few hours sufficed to prove that, unless some strange, untoward accident befell, they stood a more than equal chance of winning out.

Realizing to begin with, that a home on the forty-eighth story of the tower was entirely impractical, since it would mean that most of their time would have to be used in laborious climbing, they quickly changed their dwelling.

They chose a suite of offices on the fifth floor, looking directly out over and into the cool green beauty of Madison Forest. In an hour or so, they cleared out the bats and spiders, the rubbish and the dust, and made the place very decently presentable.

"Well, that's a good beginning, anyhow," remarked the engineer, standing back and looking critically at the finished work.

"I don't see why we shouldn't make a fairly comfortable home out of this, for a while. It's not too high for ease, and it's high enough for safety – to keep prowling bears and wolves and – and other things from exploring us in the night."

He laughed, but memories of the spear-head tinged his merriment with apprehension. "In a day or two I'll make some kind of an outer door, or barricade. But first, I need that ax and some other things. Can you spare me for a while, now?"

"I'd *rather* go along, too," she answered wistfully, from the window-sill where she sat resting.

"No, not this time, please!" he entreated. "First I've got to go 'way to the top of the tower and bring down my chemicals and all the other things up there.

"Then I'm going out on a hunt for dishes, a lamp, some oil and no end of things. You save your strength for a while; stay here and keep house and be a good girl!"

"All right," she acceded, smiling a little sadly. "But really, I feel quite able to go."

"This afternoon, perhaps; not now. Goodbye!" And he started for the door. Then a thought struck him. He turned and came back.

"By the way," said he, "if we can fix up some kind of a holster, I'll take one of those revolvers. With the best of this leather here," nodding at the Gladstone bag, "I should imagine we could manufacture something serviceable."

They planned the holster together, and he cut it out with his knife, while she slit leather thongs to lash it with. Presently it was done, and a strap to tie it round his waist with – a crude, rough thing, but just as useful as though finished with the utmost skill.

"We'll make another for you when I get home this noon," he remarked picking up the automatic and a handful of cartridges. Quickly he filled the magazine. The shells were green with verdigris, and many a rust-spot disfigured the one-time brightness of the arm.

As he stepped over to the window, aimed and pulled the trigger, a sharp and welcome report burst from the weapon. And a few leaves, clipped from an oak in the forest, zigzagged down in the bright, warm sunlight.

"I guess she'll do all right!" he laughed, sliding the ugly weapon into his new holster. "You see, the powder and fulminate, sealed up in the cartridges, are practically imperishable. Here, let me load yours, too.

"If you want something to do, you can practice on that dead limb out there, see? And don't be afraid of wasting ammunition. There must be millions of cartridges in this old burg – millions – all ours!"

Again he laughed, and handing her the other pistol, now fully loaded, took his leave. Before he had climbed a hundred feet up the tower stair, he heard a slow, uneven pop – pop – popping, and with satisfaction knew that Beatrice was already perfecting herself in the use of the revolver.

"And she may need it, too – we both may, badly – before we know it!" thought he, frowning, as he kept upon his way.

This reflection weighed in so heavily upon him, all due to the flint assegai-point, that he made still another excuse that afternoon and so got out of taking the girl into the forest with him on his exploring trip.

The excuse was all the more plausible inasmuch as he left her enough work at home to do, making some real clothing and some sandals for them both. This task, now that the girl had scissors to use, was not too hard.

Stern brought her great armfuls of the furs from the shop in the arcade, and left her busily and happily employed.

He spent the afternoon in scouting through the entire neighborhood from Sixth Avenue as far east as Third and from Twenty-Seventh Street down through Union Square.

Revolver in his left hand, knife in his right to cut away troublesome bush or brambles, or to slit impeding vine-masses, he progressed slowly and observantly.

He kept his eyes open for big game, but – though he found moose-tracks at the corner of Broadway and Nineteenth – he ran into nothing more formidable than a lynx which snarled at him from a tree overhanging the mournful ruins of the Farragut monument.

One shot sent it bounding and screaming with pain, out of view. Stern noted with satisfaction that blood followed its trail.

"Guess I haven't forgotten how to shoot in all these x years!" he commented, stooping to examine the spoor. "That may come in handy later!"

Then, still wary and watchful, he continued his exploration.

He found that the city, as such, had entirely ceased to be.

"Nothing but lines and monstrous rubbish-heaps of ruins," he sized up the situation, "traversed by lanes of forest and overgrown with every sort of vegetation.

"Every wooden building completely wiped out. Brick and stone ones practically gone. Steel alone standing, and *that* in rotten shape. Nothing at all intact but the few concrete structures.

"Ha! Ha!" And he laughed satirically. "If the builders of the twentieth century could have foreseen this they wouldn't have thrown quite such a chest, eh? And *they* talked of engineering!"

Useless though it was, he felt a certain pride in noting that the Osterhaut Building, on Seventeenth Street, had lasted rather better than the average.

"*My* work!" said he, nodding with grim satisfaction, then passed on.

Into the Subway he penetrated at Eighteenth Street, climbing with difficulty down the choked stairway, through bushes and over masses of ruin that had fallen from the roof. The great tube, he saw, was choked with litter.

Slimy and damp it was, with a mephitic smell and ugly pools of water settled in the ancient road-bed. The rails were wholly gone in places. In others only rotten fragments of steel remained.

A goggle-eyed toad stared impudently at him from a long tangle of rubbish that had been a train – stalled there forever by the final block-signal of death.

Through the broken arches overhead the rain and storms of ages had beaten down, and lush grasses flourished here and there, where sunlight could penetrate.

No human dust-heaps here, as in the shelter of the arcade. Long since every vestige of man had been swept away. Stern shuddered, more depressed by the sight here than at any other place so far visited.

"And they boasted of a work for all time!" whispered he, awed by the horror of it. "They boasted – like the financiers, the churchmen, the merchants, everybody! Boasted of their institutions, their city, their country. And *now* –"

Out he clambered presently, terribly depressed by what he had witnessed, and set to work laying in still more supplies from the wrecked shops. Now for the first time, his wonder and astonishment having largely abated, he began to feel the horror of this loneliness.

"No life here! Nobody to speak to – except the girl..." he exclaimed aloud, the sound of his own voice uncanny in that woodland street of death. "All gone, everything! My Heavens, suppose I didn't have *her?* How long could I go on alone, and keep my mind?"

The thought terrified him. He put it resolutely away and went to work. Wherever he stumbled upon anything of value he eagerly seized it.

The labor, he found, kept him from the subconscious dread of what might happen to Beatrice or to himself if either should meet with any mishap. The consequences of either one dying, he knew, must be horrible beyond all thinking for the survivor.

Up Broadway he found much to keep – things which he garnered in the up-caught hem of his bearskin, things of all kinds and uses. He found a clay pipe – all the wooden ones had vanished from the shop – and a glass jar of tobacco.

These he took as priceless treasures. More jars of edibles he discovered, also a stock of rare wines. Coffee and salt he came upon. In the ruins of the little French brass-ware shop, opposite the Flatiron, he made a rich haul of cups and plates and a still serviceable lamp.

Strangely enough, it still had oil in it. The fluid hermetically sealed in, had not been able to evaporate.

At last, when the lengthening shadows in Madison Forest warned him that day was ending, he betook himself, heavy laden, once more back past the spring, and so through the path which already was beginning to be visible back to the shelter of the Metropolitan.

"Now for a great surprise for the girl!" thought he, laboriously toiling up the stair with his burden: "What will she say, I wonder, when she sees all these housekeeping treasures?" Eagerly he hastened.

But before he had reached the third story he heard a cry from above. Then a spatter of revolver-shots punctured the air.

He stopped, listening in alarm.

"Beatrice! Oh, Beatrice!" he hailed, his voice falling flat and stifled in those ruinous passages.

Another shot.

"Answer!" panted Stern. "What's the matter *now?*"

Hastily he put down his burden, and, spurred by a great terror, bounded up the broken stairs.

Into their little shelter, their home, he ran, calling her name.

No reply came!

Stern stopped short, his face a livid gray.

"Merciful Heaven!" stammered he.

The girl was gone!

Chapter XI
A Thousand Years!

SICKENED WITH A NUMBING anguish of fear such as in all his life he had never known, Stern stood there a moment, motionless and lost.

Then he turned. Out into the hall he ran, and his voice, re-echoing wildly, rang through those long-deserted aisles.

All at once he heard a laugh behind him – a hail.

He wheeled about, trembling and spent. Out his arms went, in eager greeting. For the girl, laughing and flushed, and very beautiful, was coming down the stair at the end of the hall.

Never had the engineer beheld a sight so wonderful to him as this woman, clad in the Bengal robe; this girl who smiled and ran to meet him.

"What? Were you frightened?" she asked, growing suddenly serious, as he stood there speechless and pale. "Why – what could happen to me here?"

His only answer was to take her in his arms and whisper her name. But she struggled to be free.

"Don't! You mustn't!" she exclaimed. "I didn't mean to alarm you. Didn't even know you were here!"

"I heard the shots – I called – you didn't answer. Then –"

"You found me gone? I didn't hear you. It was nothing, after all. Nothing – much!"

He led her back into the room.

"What happened? Tell me!"

"It was really too absurd!"

"What was it?"

"Only this," and she laughed again. "I was getting supper ready, as you see," with a nod at their provision laid out upon the clean-brushed floor. "When –"

"Yes?"

"Why, a blundering great hawk swooped in through the window there, circled around, pounced on the last of our beef and tried to fly away with it."

Stern heaved a sigh of relief. "So that was all?" asked he. "But the shots? And your absence?"

"I struck at him. He showed fight. I blocked the window. He was determined to get away with the food. I was determined he *shouldn't.* So I snatched the revolver and opened fire."

"And then?"

"That confused him. He flapped out into the hall. I chased him. Away up the stairs he circled. I shot again. Then I pursued. Went up two stories. But he must have got away through some opening or other. Our beef's all gone!" And Beatrice looked very sober.

"Never mind, I've got a lot more stuff down-stairs. But tell me, did you wing him?"

"I'm afraid not," she admitted. "There's a feather or two on the stairs, though."

"Good work!" cried he laughing, his fear all swallowed in the joy of having found her again, safe and unhurt. "But please don't give me another such panic, will you? It's all right this time, however.

"And now if you'll just wait here and not get fighting with any more wild creatures, I'll go down and bring my latest finds. I like your pluck," he added slowly, gazing earnestly at her.

"But I don't want you chasing things in this old shell of a building. No telling what crevice you might fall into or what accident might happen. *Au revoir!*"

Her smile as he left her was inscrutable, but her eyes, strangely bright, followed him till he had vanished once more down the stairs.

* * *

Broad strokes, a line here, one there, with much left to the imagining – such will serve best for the painting of a picture like this – a picture wherein every ordinary bond of human life, the nexus of man's society, is shattered. Where everything must strive to reconstruct itself from the dust. Where the future, if any such there may be, must rise from the ashes of a crumbling past.

Broad strokes, for detailed ones would fill too vast a canvas. Impossible to describe a tenth of the activities of Beatrice and Stern the next four days. Even to make a list of their hard-won possessions would turn this chapter into a mere catalogue.

So let these pass for the most part. Day by day the man, issuing forth sometimes alone, sometimes with Beatrice, labored like a Titan among the ruins of New York.

Though more than ninety per cent. of the city's one-time wealth had long since vanished, and though all standards of worth had wholly changed, yet much remained to harvest.

Infinitudes of things, more or less damaged, they bore up to their shelter, up the stairs which here and there Stern had repaired with rough-hewn logs.

For now he had an ax, found in that treasure-house of Currier & Brown's, brought to a sharp edge on a wet, flat stone by the spring, and hefted with a sapling.

This implement was of incredible use, and greatly enheartened the engineer. More valuable it was than a thousand tons of solid gold.

The same store yielded also a well-preserved enameled water-pail and some smaller dishes of like ware, three more knives, quantities of nails, and some small tools; also the tremendous bonanza of a magazine rifle and a shotgun, both of which Stern judged would come into shape by the application of oil and by careful tinkering. Of ammunition, here and elsewhere, the engineer had no doubt he could unearth unlimited quantities.

"With steel," he reflected, "and with my flint spearhead, I can make fire at any time. Wood is plenty, and there's lots of 'punk.' So the first step in reestablishing civilization is secure. With fire, everything else becomes possible.

"After a while, perhaps, I can get around to manufacturing matches again. But for the present my few ounces of phosphorus and the flint and steel will answer very well."

Beatrice, like the true woman she was, addressed herself eagerly to the fascinating task of making a real home out of the barren desolation of the fifth floor offices. Her splendid energy was no less than the engineer's. And very soon a comfortable air pervaded the place.

Stern manufactured a broom for her by cutting willow withes and lashing them with hide strips onto a trimmed branch. Spiders and dust all vanished. A true housekeeping appearance set in.

To supplement the supply of canned food that accumulated along one of the walls, Stern shot what game he could – squirrels, partridges and rabbits.

Metal dishes, especially of solid gold, ravished from Fifth Avenue shops, took their place on the crude table he had fashioned with his ax. Not for esthetic effect did they now value gold, but merely because that metal had perfectly withstood the ravages of time.

In the ruins of a magnificent store near Thirty-First Street, Stern found a vault burst open by frost and slow disintegration of the steel.

Here something over a quart of loose diamonds, big and little, rough and cut, were lying in confusion all about. Stern took none of these. Their value now was no greater than that of any pebble.

But he chose a massive clasp of gold for Beatrice, for that could serve to fasten her robe. And in addition he gathered up a few rings and onetime costly jewels which could be worn. For the girl, after all, was one of Eve's daughters.

Bit by bit he accumulated many necessary articles, including some tooth-brushes which he found sealed in glass bottles, and a variety of gold toilet articles. Use was his first consideration now. Beauty came far behind.

In the corner of their rooms, after a time, stood a fair variety of tools, some already serviceable, others waiting to be polished, ground and hefted, and in some cases retempered. Two rough chairs made their appearance.

The north room, used only for cooking, became their forge and oven all in one. For here, close to a window where the smoke could drift out, Stern built a circular stone fireplace.

And here Beatrice presided over her copper casseroles and saucepans from the little shop on Broadway. Here, too, Stern planned to construct a pair of skin bellows, and presently to set up the altars of Vulcan and of Tubal Cain once more.

Both of them "thanked whatever gods there be" that the girl was a good cook. She amazed the engineer by the variety of dishes she managed to concoct from the canned goods, the game that Stern shot, and fresh dandelion greens dug near the spring. These edibles, with the blackest of black coffee, soon had them in fine fettle.

"I certainly have begun to put on weight," laughed the man after dinner on the fourth day, as he lighted his fragrant pipe with a roll of blazing birch-bark.

"My bearskin is getting tight. You'll have to let it out for me, or else stop such magic in the kitchen."

She smiled back at him, sitting there at ease in the sunshine by the window, sipping her coffee out of a gold cup with a solid gold spoon.

Stern, feeling the May breeze upon his face, hearing the bird-songs in the forest depths, felt a well-being, a glow of health and joy such as he had never in his whole life known – the health of outdoor labor and sound sleep and perfect digestion, the joy of accomplishment and of the girl's near presence.

"I suppose we do live pretty well," she answered, surveying the remnants of the feast. "Potted tongue and peas, fried squirrel, partridge and coffee ought to satisfy anybody. But still –"

"What is it?"

"I *would* like some buttered toast and some cream for my coffee, and some sugar."

Stern laughed heartily.

"You don't want much!" he exclaimed, vastly amused, the while he blew a cloud of Latakia smoke. "Well, you be patient, and everything will come, in time.

"You mustn't expect me to do magic. On the fourth day you don't imagine I've had time enough to round up the ten thousandth descendant of the erstwhile cow, do you?

"Or grow cane and make sugar? Or find grain for seed, clear some land, plow, harrow, plant, hoe, reap, winnow, grind and bolt and present you with a bag of prime flour? Now really?"

She pouted at his raillery. For a moment there was silence, while he drew at his pipe. At the girl he looked a little while. Then, his eyes a bit far-away, he remarked in a tone he tried to render casual:

"By the way, Beatrice, it occurs to me that we're doing rather well for old people – very old."

She looked up with a startled glance.

"*Very?*" she exclaimed. "You know how old then?"

"Very, indeed!" he answered. "Yes, I've got some sort of an idea about it. I hope it won't alarm you when you know."

"Why – how so? Alarm me?" she queried with a strange expression.

"Yes, because, you see, it's rather a long time since we went to sleep. Quite so. You see, I've been doing a little calculating, off and on, at odd times. Been putting two and two together, as it were.

"First, there was the matter of the dust in sheltered places, to guide me. The rate of deposition of what, in one or two spots, can't have been anything less than cosmic or star-dust, is fairly certain.

"Then again, the rate of this present deterioration of stone and steel has furnished another index. And last night I had a little peek at the pole-star, through my telescope, while you were asleep.

"The good old star has certainly shifted out of place a bit. Furthermore, I've been observing certain evolutionary changes in the animals and plants about us. Those have helped, too."

"And – and what have you found out?" asked she with tremulous interest.

"Well, I think I've got the answer, more or less correctly. Of course it's only an approximate result, as we say in engineering. But the different items check up with some degree of consistency.

"And I'm safe in believing I'm within at least a hundred years of the date one way or the other. Not a bad factor of safety, that, with my limited means of working."

The girl's eyes widened. From her hand fell the empty gold cup; it rolled away across the clean-swept floor.

"What?" cried she. "You've got it, within a hundred years! Why, then – you mean it's *more* than a hundred?"

Indulgently the engineer smiled.

"Come, now," he coaxed. "Just guess, for instance, how old you really are – and growing younger every day?"

"Two hundred maybe? Oh surely not as old as that! It's horrible to think of!"

"Listen," bade he. "If I count your twenty-four years, when you went to sleep, you're now –"

"What?"

"You're now at the very minimum calculation, just about one thousand and twenty-four! Some age, that, eh?"

Then, as she stared at him wide-eyed he added with a smile.

"No disputing that fact, no dodging it. The thing's as certain as that you're now the most beautiful woman in the whole wide world!"

Chapter XII
Drawing Together

DAYS PASSED, busy days, full of hard labor and achievement, rich in experience and learning, in happiness, in dreams of what the future might yet bring.

Beatrice made and finished a considerable wardrobe of garments for them both. These, when the fur had been clipped close with the scissors, were not oppressively warm, and, even though on some days a bit uncomfortable, the man and woman tolerated them because they had no others.

Plenty of bathing and good food put them in splendid physical condition, to which their active exercise contributed much. And thus, judging partly by the state of the foliage, partly by the height of the sun, which Stern determined with considerable accuracy by means of a simple, home-made quadrant – they knew mid-May was past and June was drawing near.

The housekeeping by no means took up all the girl's time. Often she went out with him on what he called his 'pirating expeditions,' that now sometimes led them as far afield as the sad ruins of the wharves and piers, or to the stark desolation and wreckage of lower Broadway and the onetime busy hives of newspaperdom, or up to Central Park or to the great remains of the two railroad terminals.

These two places, the former tide-gates of the city's life, impressed Stern most painfully of anything. The disintegrated tracks, the jumbled remains of locomotives and luxurious Pullmans with weeds growing rank upon them, the sunlight beating down through the caved-in roof of the Pennsylvania station "concourse," where millions of human beings once had trod in all the haste of men's paltry, futile affairs, filled him with melancholy, and he was glad to get away again leaving the place to the jungle, the birds and beasts that now laid claim to it.

"*Sic transit gloria mundi!*" he murmured, as with sad eyes he mused upon the down-tumbled columns along the facade, the overgrown entrance-way, the cracked and falling arches and architraves. "And *this*, they said, was builded for all time!"

It was on one of these expeditions that the engineer found and pocketed – unknown to Beatrice – another disconcerting relic.

This was a bone, broken and splintered, and of no very great age, gnawed with perfectly visible tooth-marks. He picked it up, by chance, near the west side of the ruins of the old City Hall.

Stern recognized the manner in which the bone had been cracked open with a stone to let the marrow be sucked out. The sight of this gruesome relic revived all his fears, tenfold more acutely than ever, and filled him with a sense of vague, impending evil, of peril deadly to them both.

This was the more keen, because the engineer knew at a glance that the bone was the upper end of a human femur – human, or, at the very least, belonging to some highly anthropoid animal. And of apes or gorillas he had, as yet, found no trace in the forests of Manhattan.

Long he mused over his find. But not a single word did he ever say to Beatrice concerning it or the flint spear-point. Only he kept his eyes and ears well open for other bits of corroborative evidence.

And he never ventured a foot from the building unless his rifle and revolver were with him, their magazines full of high-power shells.

The girl always went armed, too, and soon grew to be such an expert shot that she could drop a squirrel from the tip of a fir, or wing a heron in full flight.

Once her quick eyes spied a deer in the tangles of the one-time Gramercy Park, now no longer neatly hedged with iron palings, but spread in wild confusion that joined the riot of growth beyond.

On the instant she fired, wounding the creature.

Stern's shot, echoing hers, missed. Already the deer was away, out of range through the forest. With some difficulty they pursued down a glen-like strip of woods that must have once been Irving Place.

Two hundred yards south of the park they sighted the animal again. And the girl with a single shot sent it crashing to earth.

"Bravo, Diana!" hurrahed Stern, running forward with enthusiasm. The 'deer fever' was on him, as strong as in his old days in the Hudson Bay country. Hot was the pleasure of the kill when that meant food. As he ran he jerked his knife from the skin sheath the girl had made for him.

Thus they had fresh venison to their heart's content – venison broiled over white-hot coals in the fireplace, juicy and savory – sweet beyond all telling.

A good deal of the meat they smoked and salted down for future use. Stern undertook to tan the hide with strips of hemlock bark laid in a water pit dug near the spring. He added also some oak-bark, nut-galls and a good quantity of young sumac shoots.

"I guess *that* ought to hit the mark if anything will," remarked he, as he immersed the skin and weighed it down with rocks.

"It's like the old 'shotgun' prescriptions of our extinct doctors – a little of everything, bound to do the trick, one way or another."

The great variety of labors now imposed upon him began to try his ingenuity to the full. In spite of all his wealth of practical knowledge and his scientific skill, he was astounded at the huge demands of even the simplest human life.

The girl and he now faced these, without the social cooperation which they had formerly taken entirely for granted, and the change of conditions had begun to alter Stern's concepts of almost everything.

He was already beginning to realize how true the old saying was: "One man is no man!" and how the world had *been* the world merely because of the interrelations, the interdependencies of human beings in vast numbers.

He was commencing to get a glimpse of the vanished social problems that had enmeshed civilization, in their true light, now that all he confronted and had to struggle with was the unintelligent and overbearing dominance of nature.

All this was of huge value to the engineer. And the strong individualism (essentially anarchistic) on which he had prided himself a thousand years ago, was now beginning to receive some mortal blows, even during these first days of the new, solitary, unsocialized life.

But neither he nor the girl had very much time for introspective thought. Each moment brought its immediate task, and every day seemed busier than the last had been.

At meals, however, or at evening, as they sat together by the light of their lamp in the now homelike offices, Stern and Beatrice found pleasure in a little random speculation. Often they discussed the catastrophe and their own escape.

Stern brought to mind some of Professor Raoul Pictet's experiments with animals, in which the Frenchman had suspended animation for long periods by sudden freezing.

This method seemed to answer, in a way, the girl's earlier questions as to how they had escaped death in the many long winters since they had gone to sleep.

Again, they tried to imagine the scenes just following the catastrophe, the horror of that long-past day, and the slow, irrevocable decay of all the monuments of the human race.

Often they talked till past midnight, by the glow of their stone fireplace, and many were the aspects of the case that they developed. These hours seemed to Stern the happiest of his life.

For the *rapprochement* between this beautiful woman and himself at such times became very close and fascinatingly intimate, and Stern felt, little by little, that the love which now was growing deep within his heart for her was not without its answer in her own.

But for the present the man restrained himself and spoke no overt word. For that, he understood, would immediately have put all things on a different basis – and there was urgent work still waiting to be done.

"There's no doubt in my mind," said he one day as they sat talking, "that you and I are absolutely the last human beings – civilized I mean – left alive anywhere in the world.

"If anybody else had been spared, whether in Chicago or San Francisco, in London, Paris or Hong-Kong, they'd have made some determined effort before now to get in touch with New York. This, the prime center of the financial and industrial world, would have been their first objective point."

"But suppose," asked she, "there *were* others, just a few here or there, and they'd only recently waked up, like ourselves. Could they have succeeded in making themselves known to us so soon?"

He shook a dubious head.

"There may be some one else, somewhere," he answered slowly, "but there's nobody else in this part of the world, anyhow. Nobody in this particular Eden but just you and me. To all intents and purposes I'm Adam. And you – well, you're Eve! But the tree? We haven't found that – yet."

She gave him a quick, startled glance, then let her head fall, so that he could not see her eyes. But up over her neck, her cheek and even to her temples, where the lustrous masses of hair fell away, he saw a tide of color mount.

And for a little space the man forgot to smoke. At her he gazed, a strange gleam in his eyes. And no word passed between them for a while. But their thoughts – ?

The complete and unabridged text is available
online, *from flametreepublishing.com/extras*

City of Emerald Ash

Michael Paul Gonzalez

THREE HUNDRED days since the incident. Eighteen hours in a shaky helicopter ride. A day and a half on the road. We've been picking our way through the rubble of buildings for the past week. We're here to bury the dead, release the ghosts. Some people were content to accept the loss of their loved ones from the Incident. Others have to experience it. Walk the roads. Touch the ruins. Smell the burnt cinders and chemical stink in the air.

I work for the government, but you could just call me a tour guide. We're a specialized unit, allowed to take small groups of citizens to lay their demons to rest. All of this is off the books. We only work with people who can afford to grieve outrageously.

I have a single escort today, down near Union Street. The rest of the squad pushed further south towards the remains of the stadium. Me and this lady, we're shin-deep in what's left of downtown Seattle, painstakingly following what's left of the roads by GPS, which is still hinky and unreliable because of all the particles in the air. We have to stop every twenty yards so my escort can catch her breath. I put on a tough act, but I'm grateful for the chance to get my wind back too. We have specialized boots for treading through here, about ten pounds each. The pants probably weigh another ten. It sucks, but when you're up to your knees in powdered glass from shattered skyscrapers, you appreciate the little things.

We stop under the skeleton of Ranier Square, the south-facing wall mostly intact. If I climb it, I may be able to spot our destination and speed things along. Gotta be careful with these high-rises. Some of these structures are an optical illusion, ten stories of tightly packed carbon dust just waiting to collapse the instant you touch them. I approach and kick the charred girder. It's solid as stone. So far, so good. No saying what I'll find higher up. There are sections of the building with flooring still intact. The surrounding towers may have taken the brunt of the eruption blast by the time it got to this building. Still, I climb as fast as I can. I reach the top floor – well, I guess you'd just have to call it the highest floor now, the roof being scattered in ashes below us – and survey the area.

Southwest, I can see the landmark we're looking for, the Hammering Man statue. How did that thing survive? Further to the south, the Gutter. Last month, precipitation began to return to the area, pushing away the ash and debris. NASA got their first satellite shots. Like God dragged a fingernail down the entire northwestern seaboard. I have nightmares about this place sometimes. I remember my first trip in, when the air was still dark, and I had to do a high recon like this at night. Seeing the fire coming up from the ground hundreds of miles to the south… thinking about how, even now, there could be survivors out there, starving, choking, burning. What can you do? I slide down to ground level as quickly as I can, my client awaiting me with shiny puppy dog eyes and a voice choked by tears and coal grit.

"What did you see?"

Hell on Earth. The end of my faith in God. What can you say at times like this?

"There's a hump about ten blocks south of here. I think I saw the Hammering Man, looks like most of it is still there. We should get back to base camp before dark."

Of course, she's having none of this. Not when she paid so much and traveled so far, and do I have any idea what she left behind, what she risked to get out here? I was paid to do a job, and we're so close, blah, blah, blah.

Glancing at my wrist, the tattoo of a chain I started after my first trip out, like so many on the squad do. One broken link for each trip where we came back alive. If you find a survivor or any evidence of human life, you get a closed chain link. Me? I've got five broken links. Nobody has a closed link. Nobody ever will.

I remain silent and we push on. I was paid to do a job, after all.

It's a fairly easy walk, all things considered. We stand at the foot of the iron statue, the remains of the Art Museum before us. The hump I saw is a half block away, a collapsed brick wall leaning on a neighboring pile of rubble. If the GPS is reading right, it's what she paid to see. I flick on a halogen lamp and crawl beneath the collapsed wall. Inside, it's bare, charred to nothing. There are lumps of nylon and plastic, blackened glass. Things that used to be a pool table, a beer-themed faux-tiffany lamp, a neon sign, dust that was the calendar of some big-busted women hawking the good life.

I turn around, and my client is behind me, on her knees, sobbing. Rubbing her hands against the gritty dirt on the floor. Pulling her dust mask off. Happens every time.

"Stop crying. Stop crying or you'll suffocate."

She blinks, nods, pulls her mask back on. Flips the bottom up like I showed her when she starts coughing out the particles. I pull a fresh carbon cartridge out of my belt pouch and set it down in front of her.

"I'll be outside."

I leave her to her suffering and the ghosts of her father. Outside, I return to the base of the statue. I wish I could light a cigarette right now. The longer she stays in there, the more my mind starts to wander.

A little over a mile from here, somewhere near the Space Needle. That's where I lost them. I think. They were having a day out, a little mommy-one and daughter time. Mommy-two was serving her country, loading cardboard boxes into a truck somewhere at an outpost in Texas when her cellphone rang and she got to tell her daughter she loved her for the last time, got to tell her wife that... what? That the food here sucked? That we'd talk later about redoing the kitchen after I got back?

Two hours later we were on alert. Something had happened. They explained it to us a half dozen times and it never made sense. Not until the sky started going dark and the ash started raining.

I hear her crying again, and this time the ash catches up to her and she starts to choke and wheeze. It's enough to snap me out of my self-pity time travel. I scuff my foot across the rubble and uncover something startlingly blue. Scuffed, and singed, but mostly readable. It's funny what survives. It's a plastic sign. "Mariner's Cove, Today's Spe–" Another broken link in the chain.

I check my watch. Sunday, June 23rd, 3:46 p.m. Almost a year to the minute after the chain eruption. St. Helens, Ranier, the Yellowstone Caldera, and at least six more that scientists had never seen. I crawl back into the wreckage and find her sitting with her arms wrapped around her knees. I lay the scrap in front of her and she cradles it. Traces the curves of her father's handwriting. It's enough to bring her peace in this house of spirits.

* * *

When we finally make our way back outside, it's solid dark. A few drops of rain smack against the ground.

I ask her if she feels like walking. She says no. We're walking anyway. I make up some bullshit story about needing to find high ground. If the rain picks up, we could get washed out or buried in a tsunami of garbage and debris. Oh yeah, flash floods are a real threat here. We need to get to the Pacific Science Center. Great place to camp for the night. Supplies in the basement, clean, dry, as many lies as I can tell her to get her moving.

I do this to myself sometimes. Every time. If the trip comes anywhere near the city center, I'm first in line to volunteer, especially if it's a single escort. We don't need to rendezvous for extraction until noon tomorrow, so I'll have time to search. I'll find them. I'll find my scrap, my burnt offering, my evidence that they were here.

I know it's dumb. I know I'm not going to find a note that says "FLED TO VANCOUVER, FIND US."

Fifth Avenue is easy to traverse once you climb up the monorail tower. Just one of the many tips I've picked up on my travels here. The monorail tracks survived unscathed, making the walk to Denny Way quick and easy. That's where something else blew through and tore up the tracks. There's a service ladder just before that, a quick and easy descent.

The Space Needle looks like one of those old drinking bird toys, the kind that bobs up and down endlessly. Well, without the bobbing. The tower snapped and the needle came down. Now it looks like a giant A-shaped monument to failed alien aeronautics. Half of the observation deck is spread across the park like confetti. The other half rises up like a discus stuck in the lawn. I came ready for it this time. As soon as I put this lady to bed in the museum, I'm going to explore as much of it as I can.

"What's your pick? You like music? Sci-fi? Flowers?"

"Wha?" She mumbles. She's clearly exhausted.

"Where do you want to sleep? I've done all three. The museum over there has some pretty decent artefacts that survived the blast. Hendrix's guitar. Cobain's sweater, that kind of stuff. There's a sci-fi museum in the basement. Garden across the way if you prefer sleeping under the uh…" I trail off, looking at the blackened sky, "… stars. Nature. Whatever. I wouldn't recommend the garden. It's gutted anyway."

"The music is… fine… museum… whatever."

I trudge ahead to the shattered wall in the museum. I always forget the architect's name, but I figure in a couple hundred years we'll have a tough time convincing people that this is pretty much what the building looked like *before* disaster hit. Like someone crumpled up a big ball of sheet aluminum and told a kid to paint it with magic marker.

There's a fissure in the wall that runs along Fifth Avenue. I take my pack off and motion for her to do the same. I toss them through the opening, then turn sideways and inch my way inside. I reach a hand back and motion for her to follow. Once we clear the walls, there's a couple of tricky spots where the floor has collapsed and the walls have buckled, but eventually we make our way into a vast exhibit hall.

She gasps when she sees a large tent set up in the middle of the space, equipment scattered nearby.

"No big deal," I say. "It's mine. Set it up my third trip here. Nobody else is around. There's a pedal-generator inside. I'm gonna work it for thirty minutes, that'll give you about three hours of light if you feel like reading or something. Bonus, it also pumps air through a filter in the tent so you can sleep without the mask. Take your clothes off out here before you go in."

"Excuse me?"

ENDLESS APOCALYPSE SHORT STORIES

"I'm not telling you to get naked. Outer layers. You wear that stuff in there and it kind of defeats the purpose." I hold my arm out and swat it twice, sending a shower of blackened soot and white powder into the air. "We keep as much of out here *out here* as we can. Dig?"

She nods and steps aside as I set my lightstick on the floor and mount the tiny exercise bike perched next to the tent. It's tough going at first. The dynamo inside provides a huge pushback, but eventually, I find the rhythm, trying to let the weight of the boots do the hard work on the downstroke. The inside of the tent begins to glow like a candle, then eventually becomes so brilliant that it lights the entire cavernous space. In the far shadows, I see old posters, shattered glass cases. People actually tried to loot this place.

When the meter on the battery light goes full green, I dismount. She's already half out of her protective gear. I help her pile it neatly by the tent entrance. She steps inside and looks back at me through the clear plastic door, zipping it closed. She looks like a reverse raccoon, the skin around her eyes and mouth mostly clean while the rest of her face is soot-black. I fixate briefly on her lips, how full they are, how soft they look, and then I cringe. I haven't felt anything near lust since the world blew up.

Still don't. Just admiring the art, I guess.

"Will you be okay if I leave you here?" I ask.

She sits on the floor of the tent and nods.

"Basic safety," I remind her, "Rebreather first, then goggles, then gear. You feel the ground so much as twitch, get out, as fast as you can. Hopefully you'll have time to get dressed."

"Yeah," she says.

"I'll be outside checking the Needle wreckage. Just... you need something, come out and shout, okay?"

She nods and I head back outside, taking a few basic supplies. Collapsible pickaxes, crampons, climbing cams, and ropes. No stone left unturned. Every time we've headed out this way, the Captain tells me to forget about looking for evidence of my family. Needle in a haystack and all that.

The irony is not lost on me, standing beneath the looming shape of the shattered observation deck of the Space Needle. Carri loved it up here, though. Every weekend she'd ask if we could take her up there, and she'd run laps around the deck and shout and look at the mountains and point out the same buildings and shapes and ask the same questions about the ocean and and and...

I used to get exhausted by the 'and'. I would give anything to hear it again. Maybe Tara brought her up here. Maybe she knew they were sunk, that this was it, death was certain, and they could at least be in their favorite place. They would have evacuated the Needle the second the first rumble came, but everything else happened so fast... maybe they stayed? Maybe she dropped something, maybe I'll find her favorite little Fuzzbear up there.

The deck looms above me, canted at a steep angle. I step through one of the shattered windows and shine my light around, looking for a place to start. Nothing's speaking to me in here. Too dark. Too many variables. I head back outside to tackle it from the other direction. It's a steep climb, but a lot more predictable. I traverse the outside of the deck, taking breaks on rusting I-beams. I crest it in about an hour. From the top of the toppled monument, I pull out my walkie-talkie to check in with the rest of the group and get nothing but static and squelch. As expected. That's why we have time limits and meet-up points.

I pop a chemical glowstick and drop it through the open window at my feet. This was the restaurant. The wall, which is now the floor below me, is littered with broken chairs and tables. Everything that shook free when the tower fell is piled there, which includes a few bodies. There's a pile of ash in the corner where a few chair tops poke out along with the bottom half of someone's leg. Crumpled denim, a filthy sock that flaps on desiccated skin and bone like a flag planted on a monument to the dead.

I tie a rope off to the safety rail and descend, looking for somewhere solid to stand. Between the ash and the debris, there's no telling how stable the ground is. One wrong step could shift a mountain of trash and leave my leg pinned. No amount of screaming would get help up here in time. It would take a team of excavators months to properly unpack this place. I let it go and climb out.

I clamber over the top to the upper deck of the observation tower and drop another glowstick in. This level was clear of furniture, so it's just mounds of drifting ash and remains. Maybe a half dozen bodies, maybe more. I descend and take my chances, slowly pushing my legs down until I'm almost knee deep in ash. It feels solid enough, but I'm going to stay tethered. I have enough leash to walk most of this room.

No sense trying to put stories to the bodies here. They're laying where they are because of physics and gravity, not from any romantic notions of love that lasted unto death. A woman folded in half against the far wall, naked legs thrown over her head, her skirt comically covering her upper body. A man curled up against another man, one of them looks asleep, the other drunk. All basically mummies. I shuffle forward a few feet and feel something at my toes. I plunge a hand into the ash, pushing down slowly until I feel something soft. I grasp it, raising it as slowly as I can to avoid kicking up a debris cloud.

When I nearly have the thing raised, I say a silent prayer. Whatever it is, it's light. Could be a bag. Could be a body, maybe a kid, maybe my kid. I know what I want it to be and I pray that it isn't.

I crack a glowstick with my free hand and plant it in the dust nearby. I shake my arm slowly as I pull up, to help the debris clear.

It's cloth, or vinyl. Covered in powder-white. I brush at it a bit, only to smear the ash around. I lift it a little higher and see a streak of color. The white chemical light is enough to pick up colors. It's teal. Ballistic fabric with a bright pink hem. A child's backpack. I lift it a little higher and I hear something snap. I reach my other hand down to support the sack. My brain tells me it's a support frame for the backpack, but I know better. It's a ribcage. It's a child.

I freeze, unsure of what to do. I hate to disturb the dead. If this isn't her I'll feel vile. If it is her, I'll break. If I leave the body now, it'll haunt me forever.

I slide my hand higher until I feel the chin in my palm. I punch my arm deeper into the ash, squatting down until I can cradle the body in the crook of my arm. The whole room goes swimmy. I think dust has leaked into my goggles until I realize no, I'm just crying uncontrollably. I pull, slowly, gently, until the body rises free. I pull the backpack off gently with one hand and turn the body so it lays on a bed of ash.

It takes me a few more minutes to stop crying, and another five after that to follow proper procedure for clearing visual obstructions from my goggles. When you're wearing thick, armored gloves coated in ash and god-knows-what kind of toxic debris, simply wiping your eyes isn't an option. I kneel down next to the body.

It's a girl.

That's all I can tell. The clothes are soaked in ash, the skin is dry and brittle. Her hair was pulled back in a ponytail, but I can't tell what color it was. She's just... grey. Skin sallow, cheeks sunken and dried, eyes closed, lips slightly parted. She's a mummy. She doesn't look sad or scared or in pain. The fact that she's intact means that the needle stood through the initial blast. No way to trace the chain of events, but she most likely suffocated on ash and smoke. Why couldn't they have gotten down? What stopped them? She would have died, the ash would have blown in, and eventually, whether it was aftershocks or structural damage or something else, the Needle toppled much later.

She's not my little girl, not my Carri, but she is. She's everyone's and no one's.

I sweep a few mounds of ash over her and open her backpack. Inside, there's the standard daytrip kit, remarkably preserved. Tissue. A water bottle. A bag from the souvenir store with a coloring book, some postcards, and a miniature snowglobe of the Space Needle. In the outer pocket, I find a treasure that breaks my heart.

A little stuffed vampire bat. Bright orange and black. The stitching on the nose is worn down, and I tell myself that it's just age, not the fact that she rubbed noses with it for comfort at night, and it's not half-flat because she hugged it so tightly so often, and and and…

I tuck the bat in a pouch on the side of my pants and start to climb the rope out. I hear four soft pops and look down to see small puffs of dust rising below. Then another, then too many to count, and it's raining, *proper* raining. A real Pacific Northwest storm.

I swing from the rope and watch it forming puddles and rivers below me, carrying away the mound of ash I made, bringing her back from the grave. The glowsticks below are dying, but I still see her. Her skin is cleaner. Her shirt is bright yellow, with a cartoon elephant on the front.

Would she wear a shirt like that? Did she have a shirt like that? And I don't know, and I can't remember, and the rain blurs my vision as I climb, not the tears. When I reach the top of the rope, I pull myself over the edge and flop onto my back, letting the rain wash me clean. Thunder swallows my screams and erases my apologies.

I return to the museum, strip down and enter the clean tent. I bring the little stuffed bat inside with me, brush noses with it and set it down. I pull a small kit from my travel pack, a sterile needle and some small vials. We always do the chain link tattoos in the field.

While my employer sleeps next to me, I add another link to my chain, broken.

Written on the Skin

Michael Haynes

THE RAISED voice of one of the Community Center's guards down by the road pulled Julianna from the sweat-soaked stupor of her harvesting. The two young men on guard duty, both about her age, were talking to a couple of strangers. Telling them to move along quick, she reckoned.

Julianna closed her eyes for a moment. It was already over a hundred degrees and not even noon. She heard the Singer's voice carrying across the fields through the hot, moist air. With folks being born and dying fairly regularly, the Community's Singer had plenty of work on both ends of life. Today she'd be singing Terry Conner's song; he'd died last night – a heart attack, someone had said – so they'd be burying him today. Getting him in the ground before he could start to stink.

She opened her eyes and saw the guards flanking the two strangers and leading them not away from the Center but up the trail to the large building where everyone in their community now lived. Julianna could see the unfamiliar pair more clearly as they approached, a young man about her age and a girl who looked a few years younger. Their clothes were torn to shit, but he carried a pack on his back that looked surprisingly full. She wondered what was inside and if that had something to do with the welcome they were receiving.

She paid special attention to the unfamiliar man as he walked along the trail, scruffy red beard, hair tucked up into a baseball cap, gray eyes that caught hers and lit up for just a second. Julianna felt a little shiver run through her body in that moment. And then they were past her. The woman with him – his wife, sister, friend? – stumbled just a little, then righted herself.

"Gonna daydream all day, Jules?" Zeke, one of the agricultural coordinators, hollered to her from a few dozen yards away.

"No, sir." She bent back to it and though normally she would've had no mind for anything but the monotony and ache of her job, she couldn't forget those gray eyes.

The dying notes of Terry Conner's song reached her ears and Julianna thought again of her own father whose song had been sung for that final time barely a month ago. He'd taken sick last winter; a pain in the gut that grew worse with frightening quickness. He wasted away and was gone in a matter of months.

She missed her father. Dad had always been the one keeping things together. Back when they still lived at their own home, he was the only one who could settle Gram Mercedes down when she got into one of her spells. She'd ask for her husband, dead decades before in the Oil Wars, for ice cream, a treat Julianna had never experienced, or for someone to please open a God-damned window and let in a cool breeze. And Julianna's father would say smooth as you please that Grandpa Keith would be home soon, that he would dish up the ice cream in a few minutes, that the window could be opened just as soon as the rain stopped. Never mind that it hardly ever rained in Alabama these days. Tell Gram Mercedes it was raining, and she'd believe you.

It wasn't long after Gram had died that the shit truly hit the fan and everyone had moved into the Center, the only building which still had electricity, the only place weapons and food were allowed to be stored. There Julianna's father was still the one keeping things together. He kept the family's spirits up, smoothed over any unpleasantness from so many people close together, and made certain that his children got their share of whatever small luxuries the community did manage to afford.

With him gone, much of that had fallen to Julianna, but she wasn't half as good at it as he was. Many was the time she'd wished she could ask his advice, even just once more.

At lunch break Julianna went inside. Her mother and four younger siblings were already at the table. Lisa, thirteen years old, parceled the family's food among their plates. Julianna's mother looked lost in thought like she had every day since her husband's death.

Elijah, one of the elders, wandered over as Julianna's family ate. Behind him were the young man and girl from outside.

"Got a couple of folks passing through for the night. Their mom's dying down in Mobile and they're trying to get to her before she passes. They need a place to sleep and ya'll got a little extra room in your quarters." He paused just a second. "Since Martin passed, I mean."

He pulled out four large packs of batteries, a couple dozen cells in each pack. "For your trouble," he said, handing them over to Julianna's mother.

Her brothers and sisters eyed the batteries – their promise of a little bit of fun, a little entertainment – with naked hunger. Even Martin Jr., only three years younger than Julianna, couldn't hide his excitement. Julianna kept her face calm, though she craved what the little blue and orange AA cells offered as much as her siblings did. Something at the back of her mind disturbed her, but she couldn't quite put a name to it.

She tugged on her brother's sleeve and whispered in his ear. "MJ, does this feel right to you?"

He looked at her and frowned. "Why you got to worry so much, sis? Don't go and mess this up for all of us by getting nosey."

Julianna touched her cheek, looked at the bright eyes of the three younger children, and nodded though she still felt ill at ease. While her mother and Elijah talked, the two visitors staying several paces back, she started clearing the table.

Turning around from the bins where the refuse was separated into compostables and plain trash, Julianna drew up short. The gray-eyed boy had come up behind her.

"I saw you working outside, didn't I?" He had the same light in his eyes she'd seen earlier and a broad smile. She nodded. "I'm Lee," he said.

"Julianna," she replied, feeling her heart race as they locked eyes again.

"I'll help you finish cleaning up."

Back at the table, Elijah had just turned to leave. Julianna's mother still held the batteries and all of her siblings were squabbling over who would get to play with the old handheld video game first.

Once the table was clear, Lee introduced his sister, Alexis. "But everyone calls her Lexi." Julianna's mom put the two of them to work for the afternoon and Lee and Lexi ate with them that night at dinner. Lee took a seat across from Julianna. During the meal he kept up a steady stream of conversation, most all of it directed at her. His sister hardly spoke. She looked wrung out and Julianna saw Lee nudge her once when she seemed about ready to fall asleep sitting up.

Later that night, it came time for lights out.

"Ya'll don't have to give up two beds, Mrs. Carson," Lee had said. "Lexi and me can share one. We've shared worse." So Paul, the youngest, climbed into Julianna's mother's bed for the night and the two strangers shared his bed.

Julianna was half-asleep when she felt a hand on her shoulder and heard Lee's voice saying her name.

"Lexi's restless, kicking me. Mind if I climb in here with you for a while?"

Even in the near dark of the Center at night, she could see his face and the hint of a smile on it. Julianna didn't believe his reason for coming to her bed for a moment. But he wasn't from here; maybe where he lived people were less open about sex. Here, keeping the population growing was important and it wasn't at all unusual for a couple of older teenagers to find themselves somewhere to be alone for an hour or two. She slid quickly over to make room for him.

Everything was quiet. Lee didn't seem the type to get cold feet but just in case, Julianna leaned over and kissed his cheek. He turned toward her and kissed her lightly on the lips, reaching up as he did so to run his fingers through her short hair.

His touch was as electrifying as his eyes. Julianna led them into a deeper kiss and her own fingers started running up and down his arms and his chest, first slowly and then with more urgency.

When they were finished, he curled up against her. She fell asleep with him like that, the first time she'd ever actually shared a bed for the whole night with a lover.

In the morning Lee and Lexi were packing their gear up, ready to get back out on the road, when the girl just crumpled to her knees. She vomited a black gout across their floor. Julianna's sister Maya shrieked and all the other kids quickly ran away.

"Get her out of here!" Julianna's mother screamed. "Go! Go!"

They went, the Center's guards roughly shoving them out the main door, but it was already too late. Julianna's family was quarantined in a tent outside and one by one, everyone else in her family came down with the bug. Paul was first to die, just several days after the strangers had stayed the night with them. Julianna's mother, her brother Martin Jr., and their sister Lisa stood a hundred yards away and watched the dirt heaped on his corpse while the Singer sang Paul's song, and they sang along. Maya was already too weak for singing. By the time she died five days later, Julianna was the only one who could stand and join the music.

Martin Jr. lasted the longest, passing away on the first day of October, a full week after their mother had died. Before he fell ill, she'd fallen into the delirium, so at least she passed on thinking that two of her children had survived the community's betrayal. For a betrayal it was. Lee and Lexi had bought their night in the Community Center with two dozen packs of batteries like the ones Elijah had given Julianna's mother that night. (Her friend Maryann had said she'd heard there'd been *three* dozen packs of batteries and that the guards and elders split up one dozen just for themselves. Julianna didn't think that made a damned bit of difference and told her so. Maryann hadn't talked to her since.)

A month after MJ's death, two months since the strangers had shown up at the Center, Julianna came back from working in the kitchens and found two more large packs of batteries lying on her pillow in the smaller space she'd been allocated by the elders. Looking at that blood price, Julianna finally realized she had a future; they wouldn't have wasted the batteries on someone about to die.

She stared at the packages and anger welled up inside her. She was angry at whoever brought the batteries for thinking she could be bought off so cheaply, at Lee and Lexi for bringing the bug into their lives, at the elders for assigning them to her family, at her father for dying before this happened and not being there to protect the family. And at herself. For having been the one who lived.

She swept the batteries to the floor and threw herself on the bed. Tears flowed hot down her cheeks.

Julianna was supposed to go back to the kitchens that night, but she stayed in bed, daring anyone to show up and try to shame her into getting back to work. No one came. The sounds of the people living around her rose and then fell. The lights went out. Still Julianna lay awake.

On the cusp of sleep, she realized she hadn't had a cycle since shortly before the day everything went to hell. In the midst of all that death, the concept of life hadn't even occurred to her. Exhausted, even this realization couldn't keep her awake.

She slept and dreamed of her father. In the dream he was walking through the community, humming the songs of her siblings. Julianna tried talking to him but he wouldn't answer her. Each time they approached one of the elders, he would hum louder, and the elder would frown or flinch or hurry away. At the wall of the Center, he passed through it, like a ghost. Julianna stood there in her dream, hands pressed to her belly, and wished she could follow.

* * *

Late November brought Maya's birthday. Julianna woke that morning and hummed her sister's song quietly. The Singer's work was for births and funerals; birthdays were when family and friends would hum or sing the song.

That evening, Julianna went to Jeremiah for the first time. He had ink and needles for tattooing and she brought a scrap of paper which had the melody to Maya's song written on it.

"You can do this?" she asked.

"Oh, yeah, that's a lot easier than some of what folks ask me to draw." He grinned. Somehow Jeremiah always seemed to be happy. "Where do you want it?"

She hadn't thought that far ahead.

"Where would you recommend?"

He reached out a hand and traced down the outside of her left arm. "Here, I'd say, assuming you want to be able to see it easily."

"Yes." Not just for herself to see it, but for others as well. She reached into a pocket and pulled out a half dozen of the AA batteries. "Will this do for payment?"

By way of answer he took them from her and put them in his own pocket. "Let's get to work."

It stung, but not as much as she had expected it to. While Jeremiah worked, she thought about Maya, remembering how she used to giggle when their father told jokes. She remembered the first time her parents had trusted her to hold baby Maya, how light the girl had felt in her arms.

"All done," Jeremiah said, pulling her back from the past.

The birthdays for her other siblings came over the next several months and each time she went to Jeremiah with their song. By the time the last ink was applied to her skin, in late March, both arms to Julianna's elbows, both legs below the knee, and an arc on her back were covered in music.

It was planting season and even though she was visibly pregnant, Julianna was still assigned to work in the fields. An unseasonably hot spell struck, bringing back memories of that day last year when Terry Conner was buried.

The afternoon sun was merciless and sweat ran down Julianna's skin. It flowed over the tattooed songs of her brothers and sisters, the staffs and clefs and notes and rests part of her for ever. A visible reminder, as well, to those who had been a part of dooming her family.

Her child moved inside her, a feeling that was still strange to Julianna. She touched her stomach absently and her mind wandered back to the other half of the idea which had grown inside her alongside her child. The tattoos had only required willingness to accept a bit of pain. This other request, though, might well be denied. Until she asked, she could imagine that it would work out as she imagined. But now, with her child coming soon, she could no longer afford to wait.

That evening, she ate her evening meal quickly so there was time to spare before going back out to the fields to do a bit more work in the dusk. She walked, with a stride that still felt awkward, to where the Singer was finishing her own meal.

The old woman greeted Julianna with a nod but didn't say anything until she finished the last of her bread and vegetables.

"I'll be singing for you soon," she said.

Julianna's song would be sung just before the child's song was heard for the first time. The father's song would normally be heard as well, but Lee wasn't one of them; even if they had Singers where he came from, they wouldn't know his song here. And with what he'd done, bringing Lexi there and risking so many lives, taking the lives of all those closest to Julianna, she was only too glad not to have a reminder of him.

"Yes, Ma'am. My child's song, too."

"True enough." The woman smiled. "I hope it's a happy one."

Julianna swallowed and before she could lose her nerve she pulled off her shirt and turned around slowly, displaying the tattooed music. "I want it to come from their songs."

She stood motionless as the Singer's eyes flicked across her skin, taking in the songs it carried. This wasn't the way of things. The songs came from the Singer's heart and mind, not anyone else's. Seconds passed by that felt like those drawn-out dying minutes from last fall.

The Singer looked back to Julianna's face and their eyes met. Finally, Julianna got her answer in the form of the faintest of nods.

* * *

Pain. Sweat. Tears.

And then crying. Her child's voice, strong and clear.

More tears now, but tears of relief. And above her tears and pain, above her child's cry, she heard her own song in the Singer's dusty voice.

Someone told her it was a boy. Someone else brought her a wrapped bundle and Julianna saw her son's face for the first time.

The singer finished Julianna's song and her son, who she would name Martin in her father's memory, went still listening to his mother's heartbeat.

So it was blessedly silent as the Singer began to sing her child's song. Julianna heard first pieces of Maya's song, then Paul's and Lisa's and finally MJ's. They were wound together around a different rhythm than any of the individual songs and so her son's song was unique, like everyone's was meant to be, but the linkage to the songs of his aunts and uncles was undeniable.

Julianna held her son close and allowed herself to feel a moment's peace, the world shrunk down to just the two of them and her son's – her family's – song.

The Night Land
Chapters I–V
William Hope Hodgson

Chapter I
Mirdath the Beautiful

"And I cannot touch her face
And I cannot touch her hair,
And I kneel to empty shadows –
Just memories of her grace;
And her voice sings in the winds
And in the sobs of dawn
And among the flowers at night
And from the brooks at sunrise
And from the sea at sunset,
And I answer with vain callings…"

IT WAS THE Joy of the Sunset that brought us to speech. I was gone a long way from my house, walking lonely-wise, and stopping often that I view the piling upward of the Battlements of Evening, and to feel the dear and strange gathering of the Dusk come over all the world about me.

The last time that I paused, I was truly lost in a solemn joy of the Glory of the Coming Night; and maybe I laughed a little in my throat, standing there alone in the midst of the Dusk upon the World. And, lo! my content was answered out of the trees that bounded the country road upon my right; and it was so as that some one had said: "And thou also!" in glad understanding, that I laughed again a little in my throat; as though I had only a half-believing that any true human did answer my laugh; but rather some sweet Delusion or Spirit that was tuned to my mood.

But she spoke and called me by my name; and when I had gone to the side of the road, that I should see her somewhat, and discover whether I knew her, I saw that she was surely that lady, who for her beauty was known through all of that sweet County of Kent as Lady Mirdath the Beautiful; and a near neighbour to me; for the Estates of her Guardian abounded upon mine.

Yet, until that time, I had never met her; for I had been so oft and long abroad; and so much given to my Studies and my Exercises when at home, that I had no further Knowledge of her than Rumour gave to me odd time; and for the rest, I was well content; for as I have given hint, my books held me, and likewise my Exercises; for I was always an athlete, and never met the man so quick or so strong as I did be; save in some fiction of a tale or in the mouth of a boaster.

Now, I stood instantly with my hat in my hand; and answered her gentle bantering so well as I might, the while that I peered intent and wondering at her through the gloom; for truly Rumour had told no tale to equal the beauty of this strange maid; who now stood jesting with so sweet a spirit, and claiming kinship of Cousinhood with me, as was truth, now that I did wake to think.

And, truly, she made no ado; but named me frank by my lad's name, and gave laughter and right to me to name her Mirdath, and nothing less or more – at that time. And she bid me then to come up through the hedge, and make use of a gap that was her own especial secret, as she confessed, when she took odd leave with her maid to some country frolic, drest as village maids; but not to deceive many, as I dare believe.

And I came up through the gap in the hedge and stood beside her; and tall she had seemed to me, when I looked up at her; and tall she was, in truth; but indeed I was a great head taller. And she invited me then to walk with her to the house, that I meet her Guardian and give word to my sorrow that I had so long neglected to make call upon them; and truly her eyes to shine with mischief and delight, as she named me so for my amissness.

But, indeed, she grew sober in a moment, and she set up her finger to me to hush, as that she heard somewhat in the wood that lay all the way upon our right. And, indeed, something I heard too; for there was surely a rustling of the leaves, and anon a dead twig cracked with a sound clear and sharp in the stillness.

And immediately there came three men running out of the wood at me; and I called to them sharply to keep off or beware of harm; and I put the maid to my back with my left hand, and had my oak staff ready for my use.

But the three men gave out no word of reply; but ran in at me; and I saw somewhat of the gleam of knives; and at that, I moved very glad and brisk to the attack; and behind me there went shrill and sweet, the call of a silver whistle; for the Maid was whistling for her dogs; and maybe the call was also a signal to the men-servants of her house.

Yet, truly, there was no use in help that was yet to come; for the need did be then and instant; and I nowise loath to use my strength before my sweet cousin. And I stepped forward, briskly, as I have told; and the end of my staff I drove into the body of the left-ward man, so that he dropped like a dead man. And I hit very sharply at the head of another, and surely crackt it for him; for he made instantly upon the earth; but the third man I met with my fist, and neither had he any great need of a second blow; but went instant to join his companions, and the fight thus to have ended before it was even proper begun, and I laughing a little with a proper pride, to know the bewilderment that I perceived in the way that the Lady Mirdath, my cousin, stood and regarded me through the dusk of the hushed even.

But, indeed, there was no time left to us, before there came bounding up, three great boar-hounds, that had been loosed to her whistle; and she had some ado to keep the brutes off me; and I then to beat them off the men upon the earth, lest they maul them as they lay. And directly, there was a noise of men shouting, and the light of lanthorns in the night, and the footmen of the house to come running with lanthorns and cudgels; and knew not whether to deal with me, or not, in the first moment, even as the dogs; but when they saw the men upon the ground, and learned my name and saw me proper, they kept well their distance and had no lack of respect; but, indeed, my sweet cousin to have the most of any; only that she showed no intent to keep distance of me; but to have a new and deeper feeling of kinship than she at first had shown.

And the men-servants asked what should be done with the foot-pads; seeing that they were now recovering. But, indeed, I left the matter, along with some silver, to the servants;

and very sound justice they dealt out to the men; for I heard their cries a good while after we had gone away.

Now, when we were come up to the Hall, my cousin must take me in to her Guardian, Sir Alfred Jarles, an old man and venerable that I knew a little in passing and because our estates abounded. And she praised me to my face, yet quaintly-wise; and the old man, her Guardian thanked me most honourably and with a nice courtesy; so that I was a welcome house-friend from that time onward.

And I stayed all that evening, and dined, and afterward went out again into the home-grounds with the Lady Mirdath; and she more friendly to me than ever any woman had been; and seemed to me as that she had known me always. And, truly, I had the same feeling in my heart towards her; for it was, somehow, as though we knew each the way and turn of the other, and had a constant delight to find this thing and that thing to be in common; but no surprise; save that so pleasant a truth had so natural a discovery.

And one thing there was that I perceived held the Lady Mirdath all that dear fore-night; and this was, indeed, the way that I had my pleasure so easy with the three foot-pads. And she asked me plainly whether I was not truly very strong; and when I laughed with young and natural pride, she caught my arm suddenly to discover for herself how strong I might be. And, surely, she loosed it even the more sudden, and with a little gasping of astonishment, because it was so great and hard. And afterward, she walked by me very silent, and seeming thoughtful; but she went never any great way off from me.

And, truly, if the Lady Mirdath had a strange pleasure in my strength, I had likewise a constant wonder and marvel in her beauty, that had shown but the more lovely in the candle-light at dinner.

But there were further delights to me in the days that came; for I had happiness in the way that she had pleasure of the Mystery of the Evening, and the Glamour of Night, and the Joy of Dawn, and all suchlike.

And one evening, that I ever remember, as we wandered in the park-lands, she began to say – half unthinking – that it was truly an elves-night. And she stopped herself immediately; as though she thought I should have no understanding; but, indeed, I was upon mine own familiar ground of inward delight; and I replied in a quiet and usual voice, that the Towers of Sleep would grow that night, and I felt in my bones that it was a night to find the Giant's Tomb, or the Tree with the Great Painted Head, or – And surely I stopped very sudden; for she gripped me in that moment, and her hand shook as she held me; but when I would ask her what ailed, she bid me, very breathless, to say on, to say on. And, with a half understanding, I told her that I had but meant to speak of the Moon Garden, that was an olden and happy fancy of mine.

And, in verity, when I said that, the Lady Mirdath cried out something in a strange low voice, and brought me to a halt, that she might face me. And she questioned me very earnest; and I answered just so earnest as she; for I was grown suddenly to an excitement, in that I perceived she knew also. And, in verity, she told me that she had knowledge; but had thought that she was alone in the world with her knowledge of that strange land of her dreams; and now to find that I also had travelled in those dear, strange dream lands. And truly the marvel of it – the marvel of it! As she to say time and oft. And again, as we walked, she gave out word that there was little wonder she had been urged to call to me that night, as she saw me pause upon the road; though, indeed, she had learned of our cousin-ship before, having seen me go by on my horse pretty oft, and inquired concerning me; and mayhap daintily irked that I had so little heed of Lady Mirdath the Beautiful. But, indeed, I had thought of other matters; yet had been human enough, had I but met her proper before I see her.

Now you must not think that I was not utter stirred by the wonder of this thing, that we had both a dreamful knowledge of the same matters, of which each had thought none other knew. Yet, when I questioned more, there was much that had been in my fancies that was foreign to her, and likewise much that had been familiar to her, that was of no meaning to me. But though there was this, that brought a little regret to us, there would be, time and again, some new thing that one told, that the other knew and could finish the telling of, to the gladness and amazement of both.

And so shall you picture us wandering and having constant speech, so that, hour by hour, we grew gladly aged in dear knowledge and sweet friendship of the other.

And truly, how the time passed, I know not; but there came presently a hullabaloo, and the shouts of men's voices and the baying of dogs, and the gleam of lanthorns, so that I knew not what to think; until, very sudden, and with a sweet and strange little laughter, the Lady Mirdath to perceive that we had missed the hours utter in our converse; so that her Guardian (made uneasy because of the three foot-pads) had ordered a search. And we all that time a-wander together in happy forgetfulness.

And we turned homeward, then, and came towards the lights; but indeed, the dogs found us before we were come there; and they had grown to know me now, and leaped about me, barking very friendly; and so in a minute the men had discovered us, and were gone back to tell Sir Jarles that all was well.

And this was the way of our meeting and the growing of our acquaintance, and the beginning of my great love for Mirdath the Beautiful.

Now, from that time onward, evening by evening would I go a-wander along the quiet and country road that led from my estate to the estate of Sir Jarles. And always I went inward by the hedge-gap; and oft I should find the Lady Mirdath walking in that part of the woods; but always with her great boar-hounds about her; for I had begged that she do this thing for her sweet safety; and she to seem wishful to pleasure me; but truly to be just so oft utter perverse in diverse matters; and to strive to plague me, as though she would discover how much I would endure and how far she might go to anger me.

And, truly, well I remember how that one night, coming to the hedge-gap, I saw two country-maids come thence out from the woods of Sir Jarles'; but they were naught to me, and I would have gone upward through the gap, as ever; only that, as they passed me, they curtseyed somewhat over-graceful for rough wenches. And I had a sudden thought, and came up to them to see them more anigh; and truly I thought the taller was surely the Lady Mirdath. But, indeed, I could not be sure; for when I asked who she did be, she only to simper and to curtsey again; and so was I very natural all in doubt; but yet sufficient in wonder (having some knowledge of the Lady Mirdath) to follow the wenches, the which I did.

And they then, very speedy and sedate, as though I were some rack-rape that they did well to be feared of alone at night; and so came at last to the village green, where a great dance was a-foot, with torches, and a wandering fiddler to set the tune; and ale in plenty.

And the two to join the dance, and danced very hearty; but had only each the other for a partner, and had a good care to avoid the torches. And by this, I was pretty sure that they were truly the Lady Mirdath and her maid; and so I took chance when they had danced somewhat my way, to step over to them, and ask boldly for a dance. But, indeed, the tall one answered, simpering, that she was promised; and immediately gave her hand to a great hulking farmer-lout, and went round the green with him; and well punished she was for her waywardness; for she had all her skill to save her pretty feet from his loutish stampings; and very glad she was to meet the end of the dance.

And I knew now for certainty that it was Mirdath the Beautiful, despite her plan of disguise, and the darkness and the wench's dress and the foot-gear that marred her step so great. And I walked across to her, and named her, whispering, by name; and gave her plain word to be done of this unwisdom, and I would take her home. But she to turn from me, and she stamped her foot, and went again to the lout; and when she had suffered another dance with him, she bid him be her escort a part of the way; the which he was nothing loath of.

And another lad, that was mate to him, went likewise; and in a moment, so soon as they were gone away from the light of the torches, the rough hind-lads made to set their arms about the waists of the two wenches, not wetting who they had for companions. And the Lady Mirdath was no longer able to endure, and cried out in her sudden fear and disgust, and struck the rough hind that embraced her, so hard that he loosed her a moment, swearing great oaths. And directly he came back to her again, and had her in a moment, to kiss her; and she, loathing him to the very death, beat him madly in the face with her hands; but to no end, only that I was close upon them. And, in that moment, she screamed my name aloud; and I caught the poor lout and hit him once, but not to harm him overmuch; yet to give him a long memory of me; and afterward I threw him into the side of the road. But the second hind, having heard my name, loosed from the tiring-maid, and ran for his life; and, indeed, my strength was known all about that part.

And I caught Mirdath the Beautiful by her shoulders, and shook her very soundly, in my anger. And afterward, I sent the maid onward; and she, having no word from her Mistress to stay, went forward a little; and in this fashion we came at last to the hedge-gap, with the Lady Mirdath very hushed; but yet walking anigh to me, as that she had some secret pleasure of my nearness. And I led her through the gap, and so homeward to the Hall; and there bid her good-night at a side door that she held the key of. And, truly, she bid me goodnight in an utter quiet voice; and was almost as that she had no haste to be gone from me that night.

Yet, when I met her on the morrow, she was full of a constant impudence to me; so that, having her alone to myself, when the dusk was come, I asked her why she would never be done of her waywardness; because that I ached to have companionship of her; and, instead, she denied my need. And, at that, she was at once very gentle; and full of a sweet and winsome understanding; and surely knew that I wished to be rested; for she brought out her harp, and played me dear olden melodies of our childhood-days all that evening; and so had my love for her the more intent and glad. And she saw me that night to the hedge-gap, having her three great boar-hounds with her, to company her home again. But, indeed, I followed her afterwards, very silent, until I saw her safe into the Hall; for I would not have her alone in the night; though she believed that I was then far away on the country road. And as she walked with her dogs, one or another would run back to me, to nose against me friendly-wise; but I sent them off again very quiet; and she had no knowledge of aught; for she to go singing a love-song quietly all the way home. But whether she loved me, I could not tell; though she had a nice affection for me.

Now, on the following evening, I went somewhat early to the gap; and lo! who should be standing in the gap, talking to the Lady Mirdath; but a very clever-drest man, that had a look of the Court about him; and he, when I approached, made no way for me through the gap; but stood firm, and eyed me very insolent; so that I put out my hand, and lifted him from my way.

And lo! the Lady Mirdath turned a bitterness of speech upon me that gave me an utter pain and astonishment; so that I was assured in a moment that she had no true love for me, or she had never striven so to put me to shame before the stranger, and named me uncouth and brutal to a smaller man. And, indeed, you shall perceive how I was in my heart in that moment.

And I saw that there was some seeming of justice in what the Lady Mirdath said; but yet might the man have shown a better spirit; and moreover Mirdath the Beautiful had no true call to shame me, her true friend and cousin, before this stranger. Yet did I not stop to argue; but bowed very low to the Lady Mirdath; and afterward I bowed a little to the man and made apology; for, indeed, he was neither great nor strong-made; and I had been better man to have shown courtesy to him; at least in the first.

And so, having done justice to my own respect, I turned and went on, and left them to their happiness.

Now, I walked then, maybe twenty good miles, before I came to my own home; for there was no rest in me all that night, or ever, because that I was grown deadly in love of Mirdath the Beautiful; and all my spirit and heart and body of me pained with the dreadful loss that I was come so sudden upon.

And for a great week I had my walks in another direction; but in the end of that week, I must take my walk along the olden way, that I might chance to have but a sight of My Lady. And, truly, I had all sight that ever man did need to put him in dread pain and jealousy; for, truly, as I came in view of the gap, there was the Lady Mirdath walking just without the borders of the great wood; and beside her there walked the clever-drest man of the Court, and she suffered his arm around her, so that I knew they were lovers; for the Lady Mirdath had no brothers nor any youthful men kin.

Yet, when Mirdath saw me upon the road, she shamed in a moment to be so caught; for she put her lover's arm from about her, and bowed to me, a little changed of colour in the face; and I bowed very low – being but a young man myself – ; and so passed on, with my heart very dead in me. And as I went, I saw that her lover came again to her, and had his arm once more about her; and so, maybe, they looked after me, as I went very stiff and desperate; but, indeed, I looked not back on them, as you may think.

And for a great month then, I went not near to the gap; for my love raged in me, and I was hurt in my pride; and, truly, neither had a true justice been dealt to me by the Lady Mirdath. Yet in that month, my love was a leaven in me, and made slowly a sweetness and a tenderness and an understanding that were not in me before; and truly Love and Pain do shape the Character of Man.

And in the end of that time, I saw a little way into Life, with an understanding heart, and began presently to take my walks again past the gap; but truly Mirdath the Beautiful was never to my sight; though one evening I thought she might be not a great way off; for one of her great boar-hounds came out of the wood, and down into the road to nose against me, very friendly, as a dog oft doth with me.

Yet, though I waited a good time after the dog had left me, I had no sight of Mirdath, and so passed on again, with my heart heavy in me; but without bitterness, because of the understanding that was begun to grow in my heart.

Now, there passed two weary and lonely weeks, in which I grew sick to have knowledge of the beautiful maid. And, truly, in the end of that time, I made a sudden resolving that I would go in through the gap, and come to the home-grounds about the Hall, and so maybe have some sight of her.

And this resolving I had one evening; and I went out immediately, and came to the gap, and went in through the gap, and so by a long walking to the gardens about the Hall. And, truly, when I was come there, I saw a good light of lanthorns and torches, and a great company of people dancing; and all drest in quaint dress; so that I knew they had a festival for some cause. And there came suddenly a horrid dread into my heart that this might be the marriage-dance of the Lady Mirdath; but, indeed, this was foolishness; for I had surely heard of the marriage, if there had been any. And, truly, in a moment, I remembered that she was come one-and-twenty years of age on that day, and to the end of her ward-ship; and this surely to be festival in honour of the same.

And a very bright and pretty matter it was to watch, save that I was so heavy in the heart with loneliness and longing; for the company was great and gay, and the lights plentiful and set all about from the trees; and in leaf-made arbours about the great lawn. And a great table spread with eating matters and silver and crystal, and great lamps of bronze and silver went all a-down one end of the lawn; and the dance constant upon the other part.

And surely, the Lady Mirdath to step out of the dance, very lovely drest; yet seeming, to mine eyes, a little pale in the looming of the lights. And she to wander to a seat to rest; and, indeed, in a moment, there to be a dozen youths of the great families of the country-side, in attendance about her, making talk and laughter, and each eager for her favour; and she very lovely in the midst of them, but yet, as I did think, lacking of somewhat, and a little pale-seeming, as I have told; and her glance to go odd-wise beyond the grouped men about her; so that I understood in a moment that her lover was not there, and she to be a-lack in the heart for him. Yet, why he was not there, I could not suppose, save that he might have been called back to the Court.

And, surely, as I watched the other young men about her, I burned with a fierce and miserable jealousy of them; so that I could near have stepped forth and plucked her out from among them, and had her to walk with me in the woods, as in the olden days, when she also had seemed near to love. But, truly, what use to this? For it was not they who held her heart, as I saw plain; for I watched her, with an eager and lonesome heart, and knew that it was one small man of the Court that was lover to her, as I have told.

And I went away again then, and came not near to the gap for three great months, because that I could not bear the pain of my loss; but in the end of that time, my very pain to urge me to go, and to be worse than the pain of not going; so that I found myself one evening in the gap, peering, very eager and shaken, across the sward that lay between the gap and the woods; for this same place to be as an holy ground to me; for there was it that first I saw Mirdath the Beautiful, and surely lost my heart to her in that one night.

And a great time I stayed there in the gap, waiting and watching hopelessly. And lo! sudden there came something against me, touching my thigh very soft; and when I looked down, it was one of the boar-hounds, so that my heart leaped, near frightened; for truly My Lady was come somewhere nigh, as I did think.

And, as I waited, very hushed and watchful; yet with an utter beating heart; surely I heard a faint and low singing among the trees, so utter sad. And lo! it was Mirdath singing a broken love song, and a-wander there in the dark alone, save for her great dogs.

And I harked, with strange pain in me, that she did be so in pain; and I ached to bring her ease; yet moved not, but was very still there in the gap; save that my being was all in turmoil.

And presently, as I harked, there came a slim white figure out from among the trees; and the figure cried out something, and came to a quick pause, as I could see in the half-dark. And lo! in that moment, there came a sudden and unreasoned hope into me; and I came up out of the gap, and was come to Mirdath in a moment, calling very low and passionate and eager: "Mirdath! Mirdath! Mirdath!"

And this way I came to her; and her great dog that was with me, to bound beside me, in thought, mayhap, that it was some game. And when I came to the Lady Mirdath, I held out my hands to her, not knowing what I did; but only the telling of my heart that needed her so utter, and craved to ease her of her pain. And lo! she put out her arms to me, and came into mine arms with a little run. And there she bode, weeping strangely; but yet with rest upon her; even as rest was come sudden and wondrous upon me.

And suddenly, she moved in mine arms, and slipt her hands to me, very dear, and held her lips up to me, like some sweet child, that I kiss her; but, indeed, she was also a true woman, and in honest and dear love of me.

And this to be the way of our betrothal; and simple and wordless it was; yet sufficient, only that there is no sufficiency in Love.

Now, presently, she loosed herself out of mine arms, and we walked homeward through the woods, very quiet, and holding hands, as children do. And I then in a while to ask her about the man of the Court; and she laughed very sweet into the silence of the wood; but gave me no answer, save that I wait until we were come to the Hall.

And when we were come there, she took me into the great hall, and made a very dainty and impudent bow, mocking me. And so made me known to another lady, who sat there, upon her task of embroidering, which she did very demure, and as that she had also a dainty Mischief lurking in her.

And truly, the Lady Mirdath never to be done of naughty laughter, that made her dearly breathless with delight, and to sway a little, and set the trembling of pretty sounds in her throat; and surely she must pull down two great pistols from an arm-rack, that I fight a duel to the death with the lady of the embroidering, who held her face down over her work, and shook likewise with the wickedness of her laughter that she could not hide.

And in the end, the Lady of the Embroidering looked up sudden into my face; and I then to see somewhat of the mischief in a moment; for she had the face of the man of the Court suit, that had been lover to Mirdath.

And the Lady Mirdath then to explain to me how that Mistress Alison (which was her name) was a dear and bosom friend, and she it was that had been dressed in the Court suit to play a prank for a wager with a certain young man who would be lover to her, an he might. And I then to come along, and so speedy to offence that truly I never saw her face plain, because that I was so utter jealous. And so the Lady Mirdath had been more justly in anger than I supposed, because that I had put hands upon her friend, as I have told.

And this to be all of it, save that they had planned to punish me, and had met every evening at the gap, to play at lovers, perchance I should pass, so that I should have greater cause for my jealousy, and truly they to have a good revenge upon me; for I had suffered very great a long while because of it.

Yet, as you do mind, when I came upon them, the Lady Mirdath had a half-regret, that was very natural, because even then she was in love of me, as I of her; and because of this, she drew away, as you shall remember, being – as she confessed – suddenly and strangely troubled and to want me; but afterwards as much set again to my punishment, because that I bowed so cold and went away. And indeed well I might.

Yet, truly, all was safe ended now, and I utter thankful and with a mad delight in the heart; so that I caught up Mirdath, and we danced very slow and stately around the great hall, the while that Mistress Alison whistled us a tune with her mouth, which she could very clever, as many another thing, I wot.

And each day and all day after this Gladness, Mirdath and I could never be apart; but must go a-wander always together, here and there, in an unending joy of our togetherness.

And in a thousand things were we at one in delight; for we had both of us that nature which doth love the blue of eternity which gathers beyond the wings of the sunset; and the invisible sound of the starlight falling upon the world; and the quiet of grey evenings when the Towers of Sleep are builded unto the mystery of the Dusk; and the solemn green of strange pastures in the moonlight; and the speech of the sycamore unto the beech; and the slow way of the sea when it doth mood; and the soft rustling of the night clouds. And likewise had we eyes to see the Dancer of the Sunset, casting her mighty robes so strange; and ears to know that there shakes a silent thunder over the Face of Dawn; and much else that we knew and saw and understood together in our utter joy.

Now, there happened to us about this time a certain adventure that came near to cause the death of Mirdath the Beautiful; for one day as we wandered, as ever, like two children in our contentment, I made remark to Mirdath that there went only two of the great boar-hounds with us; and she then told me that the third was to the kennels, being sick.

Yet, scarce had she told me so much; ere she cried out something and pointed; and lo! I saw that the third hound came towards us, at a run, yet very strange-seeming in his going. And in a moment, Mirdath cried out that the hound was mad; and truly, I saw then that the brute slavered as he came running.

And in a moment he was upon us, and made never a sound; but leaped at me in one instant of time; all before I had any thought of such intent. But surely, My Beautiful One had a dreadful love for me, for she cast herself at the dog, to save me, calling to the other hounds. And she was bitten in a moment by the brute, as she strove to hold him off from me. But I to have him instant by the neck and the body, and brake him, so that he died at once; and I cast him to the earth, and gave help to Mirdath, that I draw the poison from the wounds.

And this I did so well as I might, despite that she would have me stop. And afterwards, I took her into mine arms, and ran very fierce all the long and weary way to the Hall, and with hot skewers I burned the wounds; so that when the doctor came, he to say I have saved her by my care, if indeed she to be saved. But, truly, she had saved me in any wise, as you shall think; so that I could never be done of honour to her.

And she very pale; but yet to laugh at my fears, and to say that she soon to have her health, and the wounds healed very speedy; but, indeed, it was a long and bitter time before they were proper healed, and she so well as ever. Yet, in time, so it was; and an utter weight off my heart.

And when Mirdath was grown full strong again, we set our wedding day. And well do I mind how she stood there in her bridal dress, on that day, so slender and lovely as may Love have stood in the Dawn of Life; and the beauty of her eyes that had such sober sweetness in them, despite the dear mischief of her nature; and the way of her little feet, and the loveliness of her hair; and the dainty rogue-grace of her movements; and her mouth an enticement, as that a child and a woman smiled out of the one face. And this to be no more than but an hint of the loveliness of My Beautiful One.

And so we were married.

Mirdath, My Beautiful One, lay dying, and I had no power to hold Death backward from such dread intent. In another room, I heard the little wail of the child; and the wail of the child waked my wife back into this life, so that her hands fluttered white and desperately needful upon the coverlid.

I kneeled beside My Beautiful One, and reached out and took her hands very gentle into mine; but still they fluttered so needful; and she looked at me, dumbly; but her eyes beseeching.

Then I went out of the room, and called gently to the Nurse; and the Nurse brought in the child, wrapped very softly in a long, white robe. And I saw the eyes of My Beautiful One grow clearer with a strange, lovely light; and I beckoned to the Nurse to bring the babe near.

My wife moved her hands very weakly upon the coverlid, and I knew that she craved to touch her child; and I signed to the Nurse, and took my child in mine arms; and the Nurse went out from the room, and so we three were alone together.

Then I sat very gentle upon the bed; and I held the babe near to My Beautiful One, so that the wee cheek of the babe touched the white cheek of my dying wife; but the weight of the child I kept off from her.

And presently, I knew that Mirdath, My Wife, strove dumbly to reach for the hands of the babe; and I turned the child more towards her, and slipped the hands of the child into the weak hands of My Beautiful One. And I held the babe above my wife, with an utter care; so that the eyes of my dying One, looked into the young eyes of the child. And presently, in but a few moments of time; though it had been some ways an eternity, My Beautiful One closed her eyes and lay very quiet. And I took away the child to the Nurse, who stood beyond the door. And I closed the door, and came back to Mine Own, that we have those last instants alone together.

And the hands of my wife lay very still and white; but presently they began to move softly and weakly, searching for somewhat; and I put out my great hands to her, and took her hands with an utter care; and so a little time passed.

Then her eyes opened, quiet and grey, and a little dazed seeming; and she rolled her head on the pillow and saw me; and the pain of forgetfulness went out of her eyes, and she looked at me with a look that grew in strength, unto a sweetness of tenderness and full understanding.

And I bent a little to her; and her eyes told me to take her into mine arms for those last minutes. Then I went very gentle upon the bed, and lifted her with an utter and tender care, so that she lay suddenly strangely restful against my breast; for Love gave me skill to hold her, and Love gave My Beautiful One a sweetness of ease in that little time that was left to us.

And so we twain were together; and Love seemed that it had made a truce with Death in the air about us, that we be undisturbed; for there came a drowse of rest even upon my tense heart, that had known nothing but a dreadful pain through the weary hours.

And I whispered my love silently to My Beautiful One, and her eyes answered; and the strangely beautiful and terrible moments passed by into the hush of eternity.

And suddenly, Mirdath My Beautiful One, spoke, – whispering something. And I stooped gently to hark; and Mine Own spoke again; and lo! it was to call me by the olden Love Name that had been mine through all the utter lovely months of our togetherness.

And I began again to tell her of my love, that should pass beyond death; and lo! in that one moment of time, the light went out of her eyes; and My Beautiful One lay dead in mine arms…. My Beautiful One….

Chapter II
The Last Redoubt

SINCE MIRDATH, My Beautiful One, died and left me lonely in this world, I have suffered an anguish, and an utter and dreadful pain of longing, such as truly no words shall ever tell; for, in truth, I that had all the world through her sweet love and companionship, and knew all the joy and gladness of Life, have known such lonesome misery as doth stun me to think upon.

Yet am I to my pen again; for of late a wondrous hope has grown in me, in that I have, at night in my sleep, waked into the future of this world, and seen strange things and utter marvels, and known once more the gladness of life; for I have learned the promise of the future, and have visited in my dreams those places where in the womb of Time, she and I shall come together, and part, and again come together – breaking asunder most drearily in pain, and again reuniting after strange ages, in a glad and mighty wonder.

And this is the utter strange story of that which I have seen, and which, truly, I must set out, if the task be not too great; so that, in the setting out thereof, I may gain a little ease of the heart; and likewise, mayhap, give ease of hope to some other poor human, that doth suffer, even as I have suffered so dreadful with longing for Mine Own that is dead.

And some shall read and say that this thing was not, and some shall dispute with them; but to them all I say naught, save "Read!" And having read that which I set down, then shall one and all have looked towards Eternity with me – unto its very portals. And so to my telling:

To me, in this last time of my visions, of which I would tell, it was not as if I *dreamed*; but, as it were, that I *waked* there into the dark, *in the future of this world*. And the sun had died; and for me thus newly waked into that Future, to look back upon this, our Present Age, was to look back into dreams that my soul knew to be of reality; but which to those newly-seeing eyes of mine, appeared but as a far vision, strangely hallowed with peacefulness and light.

Always, it seemed to me when I awaked into the Future, into the Everlasting Night that lapped this world, that I saw near to me, and girdling me all about, a blurred greyness. And presently this, the greyness, would clear and fade from about me, even as a dusky cloud, and I would look out upon a world of darkness, lit here and there with strange sights. And with my waking into that Future, I waked not to ignorance; but to a full knowledge of those things which lit the Night Land; even as a man wakes from sleep each morning, and knows immediately he wakes, the names and knowledge of the Time which has bred him, and in which he lives. And the same while, a knowledge I had, as it were sub-conscious, of this Present – this early life, which now I live so utterly alone.

In my earliest knowledge of *that* place, I was a youth, seventeen years grown, and my memory tells me that when first I waked, or came, as it might be said, to myself, in that Future, I stood in one of the embrasures of the Last Redoubt – that great Pyramid of grey metal which held the last millions of this world from the Powers of the Slayers.

And so full am I of the knowledge of that Place, that scarce can I believe that none here know; and because I have such difficulty, it may be that I speak over familiarly of those things of which I know; and heed not to explain much that it is needful that I should explain to those who must read here, in this our present day. For there, as I stood and looked out, I was less the man of years of *this* age, than the youth of *that*, with the natural knowledge of *that* life which I had gathered by living all my seventeen years of life there; though, until that my first vision, I (of this Age) knew not of that other and Future Existence; yet woke to it so naturally as may a man wake here in his bed to the shining of the morning sun, and know it by name, and the meaning of aught else. And yet, as I stood there in the vast embrasure, I had also a knowledge, or memory, of this present life of ours, deep down within me; but touched with a halo of dreams, and yet with a conscious longing for One, known even there in a half memory as Mirdath.

As I have said, in my earliest memory, I mind that I stood in an embrasure, high up in the side of the Pyramid, and looked outwards through a queer spy-glass to the North-West. Aye, full of youth and with an adventurous and yet half-fearful heart.

And in my brain was, as I have told, the knowledge that had come to me in all the years of my life in the Redoubt; and yet until that moment, this *Man of this Present Time* had no knowledge of that future existence; and now I stood and had suddenly the knowledge of a life already spent in that strange land, and deeper within me the misty knowings of this our present Age, and, maybe, also of some others.

To the North-West I looked through the queer spy-glass, and saw a landscape that I had looked upon and pored upon through all the years of that life, so that I knew how to name this thing and that thing, and give the very distances of each and every one from the 'Centre-Point' of the Pyramid, which was that which had neither length nor breadth, and was made of polished metal in the Room of Mathematics, where I went daily to my studies.

To the North-West I looked, and in the wide field of my glass, saw plain the bright glare of the fire from the Red Pit, shine upwards against the underside of the vast chin of the North-West Watcher – The Watching Thing of the North-West.... "That which hath Watched from the Beginning, and until the opening of the Gateway of Eternity" came into my thoughts, as I looked through the glass... the words of Aesworpth, the *Ancient* Poet (though incredibly *future* to this our time). And suddenly they seemed at fault; for I looked deep down into my being, and saw, as dreams are seen, the sunlight and splendour of *this* our Present Age. And I was amazed.

And here I must make it clear to all that, even as I waked from *this* Age, suddenly into *that* life, so must I – *that* youth there in the embrasure – have awakened then to the knowledge of *this* far-back life of ours – seeming to him a vision of the very beginnings of eternity, in the dawn of the world. Oh! I do but dread I make it not sufficient clear that I and he were both *I* – the same soul. He of that far date seeing vaguely the life that *was* (that I do now live in this present Age); and I of this time beholding the life that I yet shall live. How utterly strange!

And yet, I do not know that I speak holy truth to say that I, in that future time, had *no* knowledge of *this* life and Age, before that awakening; for I woke to find that I was one who stood apart from the other youths, in that I had a dim knowledge – visionary, as it were, of the past, which confounded, whilst yet it angered, those who were the men of learning of that age; though of this matter, more anon. But this I do know, that from that time, onwards, my knowledge and assuredness of the Past was tenfold; for this my memory of that life told me.

And so to further my telling. Yet before I pass onwards, one other thing is there of which I shall speak – In the moment in which I waked out of that youthfulness, into the assured awareness of *this* our Age, in that moment the hunger of this my love flew to me across the ages; so that what had been but a memory-dream, grew to the pain of *Reality*, and I knew suddenly that I *lacked*; and from that time onwards, I went, listening, as even now my life is spent.

And so it was that I (fresh-born in that future time) hungered strangely for My Beautiful One with all the strength of that new life, knowing that she had been mine, and might live again, even as I. And so, as I have said, I hungered, and found that I listened.

And now, to go back from my digression, it was, as I have said, I had amazement at perceiving, in memory, the unknowable sunshine and splendour of this age breaking so clear through my hitherto most vague and hazy visions; so that the ignorance of, Aesworpth was shouted to me by the things which now I *knew*.

And from that time, onward, for a little space, I was stunned with all that I knew and guessed and felt; and all of a long while the hunger grew for that one I had lost in the early days – she who had sung to me in those faery days of light, that *had been* in verity. And the especial thoughts of that age looked back with a keen, regretful wonder into the gulf of forgetfulness.

But, presently, I turned from the haze and pain of my dream-memories, once more to the inconceivable mystery of the Night Land, which I viewed through the great embrasure. For on none did it ever come with weariness to look out upon all the hideous mysteries; so that old and young watched, from early years to death, the black monstrosity of the Night Land, which this our last refuge of humanity held at bay.

To the right of the Red Pit there lay a long, sinuous glare, which I knew as the Vale of Red Fire, and beyond that for many dreary miles the blackness of the Night Land; across which came the coldness of the light from the Plain of Blue Fire.

And then, on the very borders of the Unknown Lands, there lay a range of low volcanoes, which lit up, far away in the outer darkness, the Black Hills, where shone the Seven Lights, which neither twinkled nor moved nor faltered through Eternity; and of which even the great spy-glass could make no understanding; nor had any adventurer from the Pyramid ever come back to tell us aught of them. And here let me say, that down in the Great Library of the Redoubt, were the histories of all those, with their discoveries, who had ventured out into the monstrousness of the Night Land, risking not the life only, but the spirit of life.

And surely it is all so strange and wonderful to set out, that I could almost despair with the contemplation of that which I must achieve; for there is so much to tell, and so few words given to man by which he may make clear that which lies beyond the sight and the present and general knowings of Peoples.

How shall you ever know, as I know in verity, of the greatness and reality and terror of the thing that I would tell plain to all; for we, with our puny span of recorded life must have great histories to tell, but the few bare details we know concerning years that are but a few thousands in all; and I must set out to you in the short pages of this my life there, a sufficiency of the life that had been, and the life that was, both within and without that mighty Pyramid, to make clear to those who may read, the truth of that which I would tell; and the histories of that great Redoubt dealt not with odd thousands of years; but with very millions; aye, away back into what they of that Age conceived to be the early days of the earth, when the sun, maybe, still gloomed dully in the night sky of the world. But of all that went before, nothing, save as myths, and matters to be taken most cautiously, and believed not by men of sanity and proved wisdom.

And I... how shall I make all this clear to you who may read? The thing cannot be; and yet I must tell my history; for to be silent before so much wonder would be to suffer of too full a heart; and I must even ease my spirit by this my struggle to tell to all how it was with me, and how it will be. Aye, even to the memories which were the possession of that far future youth, who was indeed I, of his childhood's days, when his nurse of that Age swung him, and crooned impossible lullabies of this mythical sun which, according to those future fairy-tales, had once passed across the blackness that now lay above the Pyramid.

Such is the monstrous futureness of this which I have seen through the body of that far-off youth.

And so back to my telling. To my right, which was to the North, there stood, very far away, the House of Silence, upon a low hill. And in that House were many lights, and no sound. And so had it been through an uncountable Eternity of Years. Always those steady lights, and no whisper of sound – not even such as our distance-microphones could have discovered. And the danger of this House was accounted the greatest danger of all those Lands.

And round by the House of Silence, wound the Road Where The Silent Ones Walk. And concerning this Road, which passed out of the Unknown Lands, nigh by the Place of the Ab-humans, where was always the green, luminous mist, nothing was known; save that it was held that, of all the works about the Mighty Pyramid, it was, alone, the one that was bred, long ages past, of healthy human toil and labour. And on this point alone, had a thousand books, and more, been writ; and all contrary, and so to no end, as is ever the way in such matters.

And as it was with the Road Where The Silent Ones Walk, so it was with all those other monstrous things… whole libraries had there been made upon this and upon that; and many a thousand million mouldered into the forgotten dust of the earlier world.

I mind me now that presently I stepped upon the central travelling-roadway which spanned the one thousandth plateau of the Great Redoubt. And this lay six miles and thirty fathoms above the Plain of the Night Land, and was somewhat of a great mile or more across. And so, in a few minutes, I was at the South-Eastern wall, and looking out through The Great Embrasure towards the Three Silver-fire Holes, that shone before the Thing That Nods, away down, far in the South-East. Southward of this, but nearer, there rose the vast bulk of the South-East Watcher – The Watching Thing of the South-East. And to the right and to the left of the squat monster burned the Torches; maybe half-a-mile upon each side; yet sufficient light they threw to show the lumbered-forward head of the never-sleeping Brute.

To the East, as I stood there in the quietness of the Sleeping-Time on the One Thousandth Plateau, I heard a far, dreadful sound, down in the lightless East; and, presently, again – a strange, dreadful laughter, deep as a low thunder among the mountains. And because this sound came odd whiles from the Unknown Lands beyond the Valley of The Hounds, we had named that far and never-seen Place 'The Country Whence Comes The Great Laughter.' And though I had heard the sound, many and oft a time, yet did I never hear it without a most strange thrilling of my heart, and a sense of my littleness, and of the utter terror which had beset the last millions of the world.

Yet, because I had heard the Laughter oft, I paid not over-long attention to my thoughts upon it; and when, in a little it died away into that Eastern Darkness, I turned my spy-glass upon the Giants' Pit, which lay to the South of the Giants' Kilns. And these same Kilns were tended by the giants, and the light of the Kilns was red and fitful, and threw wavering shadows and lights across the mouth of the pit; so that I saw giants crawling up out of the pit; but not properly seen, by reason of the dance of the shadows. And so, because ever there was so much to behold, I looked away, presently, to that which was plainer to be examined.

To the back of the Giants' Pit was a great, black Headland, that stood vast, between the Valley of The Hounds (where lived the monstrous Night Hounds) and the Giants. And the light of the Kilns struck the brow of this black Headland; so that, constantly, I saw things peer over the edge, coming forward a little into the light of the Kilns, and drawing back swiftly into the shadows. And thus it had been ever, through the uncounted ages; so that the Headland was known as The Headland From Which Strange Things Peer; and thus was it marked in our maps and charts of that grim world.

And so I could go on ever; but that I fear to weary; and yet, whether I do weary, or not, I must tell of this country that I see, even now as I set my thoughts down, so plainly that my memory wanders in a hushed and secret fashion along its starkness, and amid its strange and dread habitants, so that it is but by an effort I realise me that my body is not there in this very moment that I write.

And so to further tellings:

Before me ran the Road Where The Silent Ones Walk; and I searched it, as many a time in my earlier youth had I, with the spy-glass; for my heart was always stirred mightily by the sight of those Silent Ones.

And, presently, alone in all the miles of that night-grey road, I saw one in the field of my glass – a quiet, cloaked figure, moving along, shrouded, and looking neither to right nor left. And thus was it with these beings ever. It was told about in the Redoubt that they would harm no human, if but the human did keep a fair distance from them; but that it were wise never to come close upon one. And this I can well believe.

And so, searching the road with my gaze, I passed beyond this Silent One, and past the place where the road, sweeping vastly to the South-East, was lit a space, strangely, by the light from the Silver-fire Holes. And thus at last to where it swayed to the South of the Dark Palace, and thence Southward still, until it passed round to the Westward, beyond the mountain bulk of the Watching Thing in the South – the hugest monster in all the visible Night Lands. My spy-glass showed it to me with clearness – a living hill of watchfulness, known to us as The Watcher Of The South. It brooded there, squat and tremendous, hunched over the pale radiance of the Glowing Dome.

Much, I know, had been writ concerning this Odd, Vast Watcher; for it had grown out of the blackness of the South Unknown Lands a million years gone; and the steady growing nearness of it had been noted and set out at length by the men they called Monstruwacans; so that it was possible to search in our libraries, and learn of the very coming of this Beast in the olden-time.

And, while I mind me, there were even then, and always, men named Monstruwacans, whose duty it was to take heed of the great Forces, and to watch the Monsters and the Beasts that beset the great Pyramid, and measure and record, and have so full a knowledge of these same that, did one but sway an head in the darkness, the same matter was set down with particularness in the Records.

And, so to tell more about the South Watcher. A million years gone, as I have told, came it out from the blackness of the South, and grew steadily nearer through twenty thousand years; but so slow that in no one year could a man perceive that it had moved.

Yet it had movement, and had come thus far upon its road to the Redoubt, when the Glowing Dome rose out of the ground before it – growing slowly. And this had stayed the way of the Monster; so that through an eternity it had looked towards the Pyramid across the pale glare of the Dome, and seeming to have no power to advance nearer.

And because of this, much had been writ to prove that there were other forces than evil at work in the Night Lands, about the Last Redoubt. And this I have always thought to be wisely said; and, indeed, there to be no doubt to the matter, for there were many things in the time of which I have knowledge, which seemed to make clear that, even as the Forces of Darkness were loose upon the End of Man; so were there other Forces out to do battle with the Terror; though in ways most strange and unthought of by the human mind. And of this I shall have more to tell anon.

And here, before I go further with my telling, let me set out some of that knowledge which yet remains so clear within my mind and heart. Of the coming of these monstrosities and evil Forces, no man could say much with verity; for the evil of it began before the Histories of the Great Redoubt were shaped; aye, even before the sun had lost all power to light; though, it must not be a thing of certainty, that even at this far time the invisible, black heavens held no warmth for this world; but of this I have no room to tell; and must pass on to that of which I have a more certain knowledge.

The evil must surely have begun in the Days of the Darkening (which I might liken to a story which was believed doubtfully, much as we of this day believe the story of the Creation). A dim record there was of olden sciences (that are yet far off in our future) which, disturbing the unmeasurable Outward Powers, had allowed to pass the Barrier of Life some of those Monsters and Ab-human creatures, which are so wondrously cushioned from us at this normal present. And thus there had materialized, and in other cases developed, grotesque and horrible Creatures, which now beset the humans of this world. And where there was no power to take on material form, there had been allowed to certain dreadful Forces to have power to affect the life of the human spirit. And this growing very dreadful, and the world full of lawlessness and degeneracy, there had banded together the sound millions, and built the Last Redoubt; there in the twilight of the world – so it seems to us, and yet to them (bred at last to the peace of usage) as it were the Beginning; and this I can make no clearer; and none hath right to expect it; for my task is very great, and beyond the power of human skill.

And when the humans had built the great Pyramid, it had one thousand three hundred and twenty floors; and the thickness of each floor was according to the strength of its need. And the whole height of this pyramid exceeded seven miles, by near a mile, and above it was a tower from which the Watchmen looked (these being called the Monstruwacans). But where the Redoubt was built, I know not; save that I believe in a mighty valley, of which I may tell more in due time.

And when the Pyramid was built, the last millions, who were the Builders thereof, went within, and made themselves a great house and city of this Last Redoubt. And thus began the Second History of this world. And how shall I set it all down in these little pages! For my task, even as I see it, is too great for the power of a single life and a single pen. Yet, to it!

And, later, through hundreds and thousands of years, there grew up in the Outer Lands, beyond those which lay under the guard of the Redoubt, mighty and lost races of terrible creatures, half men and half beast, and evil and dreadful; and these made war upon the Redoubt; but were beaten off from that grim, metal mountain, with a vast slaughter. Yet, must there have been many such attacks, until the electric circle was put about the Pyramid, and lit from the Earth-Current. And the lowest half-mile of the Pyramid was sealed; and so at last there was a peace, and the beginnings of that Eternity of quiet watching for the day when the Earth-Current shall become exhausted.

And, at whiles, through the forgotten centuries, had the Creatures been glutted time and again upon such odd bands of daring ones as had adventured forth to explore through the mystery of the Night Lands; for of those who went, scarce any did ever return; for there were eyes in all that dark; and Powers and Forces abroad which had all knowledge; or so we must fain believe.

And then, so it would seem, as that Eternal Night lengthened itself upon the world, the power of terror grew and strengthened. And fresh and greater monsters developed and bred out of all space and Outward Dimensions, attracted, even as it might be Infernal sharks, by that lonely and mighty hill of humanity, facing its end – so near to the Eternal, and yet so far deferred in the minds and to the senses of those humans. And thus hath it been ever.

And all this but by the way, and vague and ill told, and set out in despair to make a little clear the beginnings of that State which is so strange to our conceptions, and yet which had become a Condition of Naturalness to Humanity in that stupendous future.

Thus had the giants come, fathered of bestial humans and mothered of monsters. And many and diverse were the creatures which had some human semblance; and intelligence, mechanical and cunning; so that certain of these lesser Brutes had machinery and underground ways, having need to secure to themselves warmth and air, even as healthy humans; only that they were incredibly inured to hardship, as they might be wolves set in comparison with tender children. And surely, do I make this thing clear?

And now to continue my telling concerning the Night Land. The Watcher of the South was, as I have set to make known, a monster differing from those other Watching Things, of which I have spoken, and of which there were in all four. One to the North-West, and one to the South-East, and of these I have told; and the other twain lay brooding, one to the South-West, and the other to the North-East; and thus the four watchers kept ward through the darkness, upon the Pyramid, and moved not, neither gave they out any sound. Yet did we know them to be mountains of living watchfulness and hideous and steadfast intelligence.

And so, in a while, having listened to the sorrowful sound which came ever to us over the Grey Dunes, from the Country of Wailing, which lay to the South, midway between the Redoubt and the Watcher of the South, I passed upon one of the moving roadways over to the South-Western side of the Pyramid, and looked from a narrow embrasure thence far down into the Deep Valley, which was four miles deep, and in which was the Pit of the Red Smoke.

And the mouth of this Pit was one full mile across, and the smoke of the Pit filled the Valley at times, so that it seemed but as a glowing red circle amid dull thunderous clouds of redness. Yet the red smoke rose never much above the Valley; so that there was clear sight across to the country beyond. And there, along the further edge of that great depth, were the Towers, each, maybe, a mile high, grey and quiet; but with a shimmer upon them.

Beyond these, South and West of them, was the enormous bulk of the South-West Watcher, and from the ground rose what we named the Eye Beam – a single ray of grey light, which came up out of the ground, and lit the right eye of the monster. And because of this light, that eye had been mightily examined through unknown thousands of years; and some held that the eye looked through the light steadfastly at the Pyramid; but others set out that the light blinded it, and was the work of those Other Powers which were abroad to do combat with the Evil Forces. But however this may be, as I stood there in the embrasure, and looked at the thing through the spy-glass, it seemed to my soul that the Brute looked straightly at me, unwinking and steadfast, and fully of a knowledge that I spied upon it. And this is how I felt.

To the North of this, in the direction of the West, I saw The Place Where The Silent Ones Kill; and this was so named, because there, maybe ten thousand years gone, certain humans adventuring from the Pyramid, came off the Road Where The Silent Ones Walk, and into that place, and were immediately destroyed. And this was told by one who escaped; though he died also very quickly, for his heart was frozen. And this I cannot explain; but so it was set out in the Records.

Far away beyond The Place Where The Silent Ones Kill, in the very mouth of the Western Night was the Place of the Ab-humans, where was lost the Road Where The Silent Ones Walk, in a dull green, luminous mist. And of this place nothing was known; though much it held the thoughts and attentions of our thinkers and imaginers; for some said that there was a Place Of Safety, differing from the Redoubt (as we of this day suppose Heaven to differ from the Earth), and that the Road led thence; but was barred by the Ab-humans. And this I can only set down here; but with no thought to justify or uphold it.

Later, I travelled over to the North-Eastern wall of the Redoubt, and looked thence with my spy-glass at the Watcher of the North-East – the Crowned Watcher it was called, in that within the air above its vast head there hung always a blue, luminous ring, which shed a strange light downwards over the monster – showing a vast, wrinkled brow (upon which an whole library had been writ); but putting to the shadow all the lower face; all save the ear, which came out from the back of the head, and belled towards the Redoubt, and had been said by some observers in the past to have been seen to quiver; but how that might be, I knew not; for no man of our days had seen such a thing.

And beyond the Watching Thing was The Place Where The Silent Ones Are Never, close by the great road; which was bounded upon the far side by The Giant's Sea; and upon the far side of that, was a Road which was always named The Road By The Quiet City; for it passed along that place where burned forever the constant and never-moving lights of a strange city; but no glass had ever shown life there; neither had any light ever ceased to burn.

And beyond that again was the Black Mist. And here, let me say, that the Valley of The Hounds ended towards the Lights of the Quiet City.

And so have I set out something of that land, and of those creatures and circumstances which beset us about, waiting until the Day of Doom, when our Earth-Current should cease, and leave us helpless to the Watchers and the Abundant Terror.

And there I stood, and looked forth composedly, as may one who has been born to know of such matters, and reared in the knowledge of them. And, anon, I would look upward, and see the grey, metalled mountain going up measureless into the gloom of the everlasting night; and from my feet the sheer downward sweep of the grim, metal walls, six full miles, and more, to the plain below.

And one thing (aye! and I fear me, many) have I missed to set out with particularness:

There was, as you do know, all around the base of the Pyramid, which was five and one-quarter miles every way, a great circle of light, which was set up by the Earth-Current, and burned within a transparent tube; or had that appearance. And it bounded the Pyramid for a clear mile upon every side, and burned for ever; and none of the monsters had power ever to pass across, because of what we did call The Air Clog that it did make, as an invisible Wall of Safety. And it did give out also a more subtile vibration, that did affect the weak Brain-Elements of the monsters and the Lower Men-Brutes. And some did hold that there went from it a further vibration of a greater subtileness that gave a protecting against the Evil Forces. And some quality it had truly thiswise; for the Evil Powers had no ability to cause harm to any within. Yet were there some dangers against which it might not avail; but these had no cunning to bring harm to any *within* the Great Redoubt who had wisdom to meddle with no dreadfulness. And so were those last millions guarded until the Earth-Current should be used to its end. And this circle is that which I have called the Electric Circle; though with failure to explain. But there it was called only, The Circle.

And thus have I, with great effort, made a little clear that grim land of night, where, presently, my listening heard one calling across the dark. And how that this grew upon me, I will set out forthwith.

Chapter III
The Quiet Calling

NOW, OFT HAD I heard tell, not only in that great city which occupied the thousandth floor, but in others of the one thousand, three hundred and twenty cities of the Pyramid, that there was somewhere out in the desolation of the Night Lands a second Place of Refuge, where had gathered, in another part of this dead world, some last millions of the human race, to fight unto the end.

And this story I heard everywhere in my travels through the cities of the Great Redoubt, which travels began when I came upon my seventeenth year, and continued for three years and two hundred and twenty five days, being even then but one day in each city, as was the custom in the training of every child.

And truly it was a great journey, and in it I met with many, whom to know was to love; but whom never could I see again; for life has not space enough; and each must to his duty to the security and well-being of the Redoubt. Yet, for all that I have set down, we travelled much, always; but there were so many millions, and so few years.

And, as I have said, everywhere I went there was the same story of this other Place of Refuge; and in such of the Libraries of those cities as I had time to search, there were great numbers of works upon the existence of this other Refuge; and some, far back in the years, made assertion with confidence that such a Place was in verity; and, indeed, no doubt did there seem in those by-gone ages; but now these very Records were read only by Scholars, who doubted, even whilst they read. And so is it ever.

But of the reality of this Refuge, I had never a sound doubt, from the day of my hearing concerning it from our Master Monstruwacan, who with all his assistants occupied the Tower of Observation in the apex of the Pyramid. And here let me tell that he and I had always an affinity and close friendship one for the other; though he was full grown, and I but a youth; yet so it was; and thus, when I had come to an age of twenty-one years of life, he opened to me a post within the Tower of Observation; and this was a most wondrous good fortune to me; for in all the vast Redoubt, to be appointed to the Tower of Observation was the most desired; for thereby, even as in these days doth Astronomy, was the natural curiosity of Man eased somewhat, even while thwarted.

Now, let me tell here also, lest it be thought that I was unduly favoured because of my friendship with the Master Monstruwacan, that there was a sound justification for his choice, in that to me had been given that strange gift of hearing, which we called Night-Hearing; though this was but a fanciful name, and meant little. Yet the peculiar gift was rare, and in all the millions of the Pyramid, there was none with the gift to a great degree, saving only myself.

And I, because of this gift, could hear the 'invisible vibrations' of the aether; so that, without harking to the calling of our recording instruments, I could take the messages which came continually through the eternal darkness; aye, even better than they. And now, it may be the better understood, how much was to be counted that I had grown to listen for a voice that had not rung in mine ears for an eternity, and yet which sang sweet and clear in my memory-dreams; so that it seemed to me that Mirdath the Beautiful slept within my soul, and whispered to me out of all the ages.

And then, one day, at the fifteenth hour, when began the Sleep-Time, I had been pondering this love of mine that lived with me still; and marvelling that my memory-dreams held the voice of a love that *had been* in so remote an age. And pondering and dreaming thus, as a young man may, I could fancy this aeon-lost One were whispering beauty into my ears, in verity; so clear had my memory grown, and so much had I pondered.

And lo! as I stood there, harking and communing with my thoughts, I thrilled suddenly, as if I had been smitten; for out of all the everlasting night a whisper was thrilling and thrilling upon my more subtile hearing.

Through four long years had I listened, since that awakening in the embrasure, when but a youth of seventeen; and now out of the world-darkness and all the eternal years of that lost life, which now I live in this Present Age of ours, was the whisper come; for I knew it upon that instant; and yet, because I was so taught to wisdom, I answered by no name; but sent the Master-Word through the night – sending it with my brain-elements, as I could, and as all may, much or little, as may be, if they be not clods. And, moreover, I knew that she who called quietly would have the power to hear without instruments, if indeed it were she; and if it were but one of the false callings of the Evil Forces, or more cunning monsters, or as was sometimes thought concerning these callings, the House of Silence, meddling with our souls, then would they have no power to say the Master-Word; for this had been proven through all the Everlasting.

And lo! as I stood, trembling and striving not to be tense, which destroys the receptivity, there came thrilling round and round my spiritual essence the throb of the Master-Word, beating steadily in the night, as doth that marvellous sound. And then, with all that was sweet in my spirit, I called with my brain elements: "Mirdath! Mirdath! Mirdath!" And at that instant the Master Monstruwacan entered that part of the Tower of Observation, where I stood; and, seeing my face, stood very quiet; for though he had not the power of Night-Hearing, he was wise and thoughtful, and took much account of my gift; more-over, he had but come from the Receiving Instrument, and thought vaguely to have caught the throb of the Master-Word, though too faint to come proper through the Instrument, so that he searched for me, in that I, who had the Hearing, might listen for it, I being, as I have said, gifted in that wise.

And to him I told something of my story and my thoughts and my memories, and of that awakening; and thus up to this present happening, and he hearkened with sympathy and a troubled and wondering heart; for in that age a man might talk sanely upon that which, in this age of ours would be accounted foolishness and maybe the breathings of insanity; for there, by the refinement of arts of mentality and the results of strange experiments and the accomplishment of learning, men were abled to conceive of matters now closed to our conceptions, even as we of this day may haply give a calm ear to talk, that in the days of our fathers would have been surely set to the count of lunacy. And this is very clear.

And all the while that I told my story, I listened with my spirit; but save for a sense of faint, happy laughter that wrapped about me, I heard naught. And nothing more all that day.

Here let me put down that, because of my memories and half memories, I would time and again dispute with our learned men; they being in doubt as to the verity of that olden story of the Days of Light, and the existence of the Sun; though something of all this was set out, as of *truth*, in our oldest records; but I, remembering, told them many tales that seemed fairy-like to them, and entranced their hearts, even whilst I angered their brains, which refused to take seriously and as verity that which their hearts accepted gladly, even as we receive the wonder of poetry into our souls. But the Master Monstruwacan would listen to aught I had to tell; aye! though I spoke through hours; and so it would be, odd times, that having talked long, drawing my stories from my Memory-Dreams, I would come back again into the present of that Future; and lo! all the Monstruwacans would have left their instruments and observations and recording, and be gathered about me; and the Master so sunken in interest that he not to have discovered them; neither had I noticed, being so full of the things which had been.

But when the Master came back to knowledge of that present, he would rouse and chide, and they, all those lesser ones, would fly swiftly and guiltily to their various works; and yet, so I have thought since, each with a muddled and bewildered and thoughtful air upon him; and hungry they were for more, and ever wondering and setting questions about.

And so it was also with those others – those learned ones who were not of the Tower of Observation, and who disbelieved even whilst they hungered. Listen would they, though I talked from the first hour, which was the 'dawn,' to the fifteenth hour, which was the beginning of the 'night'; for the Sleep-Time was set thus, after other usage and experiment. And, odd whiles, I found that there were among them, men of extraordinary learning who upheld my tellings as tales of verity; and so there was a faction; but, later, there grew more to believe; and whether they believed, or not, all were ready to listen; so that I might have spended my days in talk; only that I had my work to do.

But the Master Monstruwacan believed from the beginning, and was wise always to understand; so that I loved him for this, as for many another dear quality.

And so, as may be conceived, among all those millions I was singled out to be known; for the stories that I told went downward through a thousand cities; and, presently, in the lowest tier of the Underground Fields, an hundred miles deep in the earth below the Redoubt, I found that the very ploughboys knew something concerning my tellings; and gathered about me one time and another when the Master Monstruwacan and I had gone down, regarding some matter that dealt with the Earth-Current and our Instruments.

And of the Underground Fields (though in that age we called them no more than 'The Fields') I should set down a little; for they were the mightiest work of this world; so that even the Last Redoubt was but a small thing beside them. An hundred miles deep lay the lowest of the Underground Fields, and was an hundred miles from side to side, every way; and above it there were three hundred and six fields, each one less in area than that beneath; and in this wise they tapered, until the topmost field which lay direct beneath the lowermost floor of the Great Redoubt, was but four miles every way.

And thus it will be seen that these fields, lying one beneath the other, formed a mighty and incredible Pyramid of Country Lands in the deep earth, an hundred miles from the base unto the topmost field.

And the whole was sheathed-in at the sides with the grey metal of which the Redoubt was builded; and each field was pillared, and floored beneath the soil, with this same compound of wonder; and so was it secure, and the monsters could not dig into that mighty garden from without.

And all of that Underground Land was lit, where needed, by the Earth-Current, and that same life-stream fructified the soil, and gave life and blood to the plants and to the trees, and to every bush and natural thing.

And the making of those Fields had taken maybe a million years, and the 'dump' thereof had been cast into the 'Crack,' whence came the Earth-Current, and which had bottom beyond all soundings. And this Underground Country had its own winds and air-currents; so that, to my memory, it was in no ways connected to the monstrous air-shafts of the Pyramid; but in this I may be mistaken; for it has not been given to me to know all that is to be known concerning that vast Redoubt; nor by any one man could so much knowledge be achieved.

Yet that there were wise and justly promoted winds in that Underground Country, I do know; for healthful and sweet they were, and in the corn-fields there was the sweet rustle of grain, and the glad, silken laughter of poppies, all beneath a warm and happy light. And here, did the millions walk and take excursion, and go orderly or not, even as in these days.

And all this have I seen, and the talk of a thousand lovers in the gardens of that place, comes back to me; and with it all the memory of my dear one; and of a faint calling that would seem to whisper about me at times; but so faint and attenuated, that even I, who had the Night-Hearing, could not catch its import; and so went, listening ever the more intently. And oft times calling.

Now there was a Law in the Pyramid, tried and healthful, which held that no male should have freedom to adventure into the Night Land, before the age of twenty-two; *and no female ever.* Yet that, after such age, if a youth desired greatly to make the adventure, he should receive three lectures upon the dangers of which we had knowledge, and a strict account of the mutilatings and horrid deeds done to those who had so adventured. And if, after this had passed over him, he still desired, and if he were accounted healthful and sane; then should he be allowed to make the adventure; and it was accounted honour to the youth who should add to the knowledge of the Pyramid.

But to all such as went forth into the danger of the Night Land, there was set beneath the skin of the inner side of the left forearm, a small capsule, and when the wound had healed, then might the youth make the adventure.

And the wherefore of this, was that the spirit of the youth might be saved, if he were entrapped; for then, upon the honour of his soul, must he bite forth the capsule, and immediately his spirit would have safety in death. And by this shall you know somewhat the grim and horrid danger of the Dark Land.

And this I have set down because later I was to make huge adventure into those Lands; and even at this time, some thought of the same had come to me; for always I went listening for that quiet calling; and twice I sent the Master-Word throbbing solemnly through the everlasting night; yet this I did no more, without certainty; for the Word must not be used lightly. But often would I say with my brain-elements "Mirdath! Mirdath!" – sending the name out into the darkness; and sometimes would I seem to hear the faint thrilling of the aether around me; as though one answered; but weakly, as it were with a weakened spirit, or by instrument that lacked of its earth-force.

And thus, for a great while there was no certainty; but only a strange anxiousness and no clear answer.

Then, one day as I stood by the instruments in the Tower of Observation, at the thirteenth hour there came the thrilling of beaten aether all about me, as it were that all the void was disturbed. And I made the Sign for Silence; so that the men moved not in all the Tower; but bowed over their breathing-bells, that all disturbance might cease.

And again came the gentle thrilling, and broke out into a clear, low calling in my brain; and the calling was my name – the old-earth name of this day, and not the name of that age. And the name smote me, with a frightenedness of fresh awakening memories. And, immediately, I sent the Master-Word into the night; and all the aether was full of movement. And a silence came; and later a beat afar off in the void of night, which only I in all that great Redoubt could hear, until the heavier vibrations were come. And in a moment there was all about me the throbbing of the Master-Word, beating in the night a sure answer. Yet, before this I knew that Mirdath had called; but now had surety.

And immediately, I said "Mirdath," making use of the instruments; and there came a swift and beautiful answer; for out of the dark there stole an old love-name, that she only had ever used to me.

And, presently, I minded me of the men, and signed to them that they should continue; for the Records must not be broken; and now I had the communication full established.

And by me stood the Master Monstruwacan, quietly as any young Monstruwacan, waiting with slips to make any notes that were needful; and keeping a strict eye upon those others; but not unkindly. And so, for a space of wonder, I had speech with that girl out in the darkness of the world, who had knowledge of my name, and of the old-earth love-name, and named herself Mirdath.

And much I questioned her, and presently to my sorrow; for it seemed that her name was not truly Mirdath; but Naani; neither had she known my name; but that in the library of that place where she abode, there had been a story of one named by my name, and called by that sweet love-name which she had sent out somewhat ruthless into the night; and the girl's name had been Mirdath; and when first she, Naani had called, there had come back to her a cry of Mirdath, Mirdath; and this had minded her so strangely of that olden story which had stayed in her memory; that she had answered as the maid in that book might have answered.

And thus did it seem that the utter Romance of my Memory-love had vanished, and I stood strangely troubled for sorrow of a love of olden times. Yet, even then I marvelled that any book should have story so much like to mine; not heeding that the history of all love is writ with one pen.

Yet, even then in that hour of my strange, and quaintly foolish pain, there came a thing that set me thrilling; though more afterwards, when I came to think afresh upon it. For the girl who spoke to me through the night made some wonder that my voice were not deeper; yet in quiet fashion, and as one who says a thing, scarce wotting what they say. But even to me then, there came a sudden hope; for in the olden days of this Present Age my voice had been very deep. And I said to her that maybe the man in the book was said to have had a deep tone of speech; but she, seeming puzzled, said nay; and at that I questioned her the more; but only to the trouble of her memory and understanding.

And strange must it seem that we two should talk on so trivial a matter, when there was so much else that we had need to exchange thought upon; for were a man in this present day to have speech with those who may live within that red planet of Mars within the sky, scarce could the wonder of it exceed the wonder of a human voice coming through that night unto the Great Redoubt, out of all that lost darkness. For, indeed, this must have been the breaking of, maybe, a million years of silence. And already, as I came to know later, was the news passing downward from City to City through all the vast Pyramid; so that the Hour-Slips were full of the news; and every City eager and excited, and waiting. And I better known in that one moment, than in all my life before. For that previous calling, had been but vaguely put about; and then set to the count of a nature, blown upon over-easily by spirit-winds of the half-memory of dreams. Though it is indeed true, as I have set down before this, that my tales concerning the early days of the world, when the sun was visible, and full of light, had gone down through all the cities, and had much comment and setting forth in the Hour-Slips, and were a cause for speech and argument.

Now concerning the voice of this girl coming to us through the darkness of the world, I will set out that which she had to tell; and this, indeed, but verified the tellings of our most ancient Records, which had so long been treated over lightly: There was, it would seem, somewhere out in the lonesome dark of the Outer Lands, but at what distance none could ever discover, a second Redoubt; that was a three-sided Pyramid, and moderate small; being no more than a mile in height, and scarce three quarters of a mile along the bases.

When this Redoubt was first builded, it had been upon the far shore of a sea, where now was no sea; and it had been raised by those wandering humans who had grown weary of wandering, and weary of the danger of night attacks by the tribes of half-human monsters which began to inhabit the earth even so early as the days when the half-gloom was upon the world. And he that had made the plan upon which it was builded, was one who had seen the Great Redoubt, having lived there in the beginning, but escaped because of a correction set upon him for his spirit of irresponsibility, which had made him to cause disturbance among the orderly ones in the lowest city of the Great Redoubt.

Yet, in time, he too had come to be tamed by the weight of fear of the ever-growing hordes of monsters, and the Forces that were abroad. And so he, being a master-spirit, planned and builded the smaller Redoubt, being aided thereto by four millions, who also were weary of the harass of the monsters; but until then had been wanderers, because of the restlessness of their blood.

And they had chosen that place, because there they had discovered a sign of the Earth-Current in a great valley which led to the shore; for without the Earth-Current no Refuge could have existence. And whilst many builded and guarded, and cared for the Great Camp in which all lived, others worked within a great shaft; and in ten years had made this to a distance of many miles, and therewith they tapt the Earth-Current; but not a great stream; yet a sufficiency, as was believed.

And, presently, after many years, they had builded the Pyramid, and taken up their refuge there, and made them instruments, and ordained Monstruwacans; so that they had speech daily with the Great Pyramid; and thus for many long ages.

And the Earth-Current then to begin to fail; and though they laboured through many thousands of years, they came to no better resource. And so it was they ceased to have communication with the Great Redoubt; for the current had a lack of power to work the instruments; and the recording instruments ceased to be sensible of our messages.

And thereafter came a million years, maybe, of silence; with ever the birthing and marrying and dying of those lonesome humans. And they grew less; and some put this to the lack of the Earth-Current, which dwindled slowly through the centuries of that Eternity.

And once in a thousand years, maybe, one among them would be Sensitive, and abled to hear beyond ordinary; and to these, at times, there would seem to come the thrilling of the aether; so that such an one would go listening; and sometimes seem to catch half messages; and so awaken a great interest in all the Pyramid; and there would be turning up of old Records, and many words and writings, and attempts to send the Master-Word through the night; in which, doubtless sometimes they succeeded; for there was set down in the Records of the Great Redoubt certain occasions on which there had come the call of the Master-Word, which had been arranged and made holy between the two Redoubts in the early days of that second life of this world.

Yet, now for an hundred thousand years, there had been none Sensitive; and in that time the people of the Pyramid had become no more than ten thousand; and the Earth-Current was weak and powerless to put the joy of life into them; so that they went listlessly, but deemed it not strange, because of so many aeons of usage.

And then, to the wonder of all, the Earth-Current had put forth a new power; so that young people ceased to be old over-soon; and there was happiness and a certain joy in the living; and a strange birthing of children, such as had not been through half a million years.

And then came a new thing. Naani, the daughter of the Master Monstruwacan of that Redoubt had shown to all that she was Sensitive; for she had perceived odd vibrations afloat in the night; and concerning these she told her father; and presently, because their blood moved afresh in their bodies, they had heart to discover the plans of the ancient instruments; for the instruments had long rusted, and been forgotten.

And so they builded them a new instrument to send forth a message; for they had no memory at that time that the brain-elements had power to do thus; though, mayhap, their brain-elements were weakened, through so many ages of starvation of the Earth-Current, and could not have obeyed, even had their masters known all that we of the Great Redoubt knew.

And when the instrument was finished, to Naani was given the right to call first across the dark to discover whether indeed, after that million years of silence, they were yet companied upon this earth, or whether they were in truth lonely – the last poor thousands of the Humans.

And a great and painful excitement came upon the people of the lesser pyramid; for the loneliness of the world pressed upon them; and it was to them as though we in this age called to a star across the abyss of space.

And because of the excitement and pain of the moment, Naani called only vaguely with the instrument into the dark; and lo! in a moment, as it seemed, there came all about her in the night the solemn throb of the Master-Word, beating in the night. And Naani cried out that she was answered, and, as may be thought, many of the people wept, and some prayed, and some were silent; but others beseeched her that she call again and quickly to have further speech with those of their kind.

And Naani spoke the Master-Word into the night, and directly there came a calling all about her: "Mirdath! Mirdath!" and the strange wonder of it made her silent a moment; but when she would have made reply, the instrument had ceased to work, and she could have no further speech at that time.

This, as may be thought, occasioned much distress; and constant work they had between the instrument and the Earth-Current, to discover the reason for this failing; but could not for a great while. And in that time, oft did Naani hear the call of "Mirdath" thrilling about her; and twice there came the solemn beat of the Master-Word in the night. Yet never had she the power to answer. And all that while, as I learned in time, was she stirred with a quaint ache at heart by the voice that called "Mirdath!" as it might be the Spirit of Love, searching for its mate; for this is how she put it.

And thus it chanced, that the constant thrilling of this name about her, woke her to memory of a book she had read in early years, and but half understood; for it was ancient, and writ in an olden fashion, and it set out the love of a man and a maid, and the maid's name was Mirdath. And so, because she was full of this great awakening of those ages of silence, and the calling of that name, she found the book again, and read it many times, and grew to a sound love of the beauty of that tale.

And, presently, when the instrument was made right, she called into the night the name of that man within the book; and so it came about that I had hoped too much; yet even now was I strangely unsure whether to cease from hoping.

And one other thing there is which I would make clear. Many and oft a time had I heard a thrilling of sweet, faint laughter about me, and the stirring of the aether by words too gentle to come clearly; and these I make no doubt came from Naani, using her brain-elements unwittingly and in ignorance; but very eager to answer my callings; and having no knowledge that, far off across the blackness of the world, they thrilled about me, constantly.

And after Naani had made clear all that I have set out concerning the Lesser Refuge, she told further how that food was not plentiful with them; though, until the reawakening of the Earth-Current, they had gone unknowing of this, being of small appetite, and caring little for aught; but now wakened, and newly hungry, they savoured a lack of taste in all that they ate; and this we could well conceive, from our reasonings and theory; but happily not from our knowledge.

And we said unto them, that the soil had lost its life, and the crops therefrom were not vital; and a great while it would take for the earth within their pyramid to receive back the life-elements. And we told them certain ways by which they might bring a more speedy life to the soil; and this they were eager to do, being freshly alive after so long a time of half-life.

And now, you must know that in all the great Redoubt the story went downwards swiftly, and was published in all the Hour-Sheets, with many comments; and the libraries were full of those who would look up the olden Records, which for so long had been forgotten, or taken, as we of this day would say, with a pinch of salt.

And all the time I was pestered with questions; so that, had I not been determined, I should scarce have been allowed to sleep; moreover, so much was writ about me, and my power to hear, and divers stories concerning tales of love, that I had been like to have grown mazed to take note of it all; yet some note I did take, and much I found pleasant; but some displeasing.

And, for the rest, I was not spoiled, as the saying goes; for I had my work to do; moreover, I was always busied Listening, and having speech through the darkness. Though if any saw me so, they would question; and because of this, I kept much to the Tower of Observation, where was the Master Monstruwacan, and a greater discipline.

And then began a fresh matter; though but an old enough trick; for I speak now of the days that followed that re-opening of the talk between the Pyramids. Oft would speech come to us out of the night; and there would be tales of the sore need of the Lesser Redoubt, and callings for help. Yet, when I sent the Master-Word abroad, there would be no answering. And so I feared that the Monsters and Forces of Evil *knew*.

Yet, at times, the Master-Word would answer to us, beating steadily in the night; and when we questioned afresh, we knew that they in the Lesser Redoubt had caught the beat of the Master-Word, and so made reply; though it had not been they who had made the previous talk, which we had sought to test by the Word. And then they would make contradiction of all that had been spoken so cunningly; so that we knew the Monsters and Forces had sought to tempt some from the safety of the Redoubt. Yet, was this no new thing, as I have made to hint; saving that it grew now to a greater persistence, and there was a loathsome cunning in the using of this new knowledge to the making of wicked and false messages by those evil things of the Night Land. And it told to us, as I have made remark, how that those Monsters and Forces had a full awareness of the speech between the Pyramids; yet could they have no power to say the Master-Word; so had we some test left, and a way to sure knowledge of what made talk in the night.

And all that I have told should bring to those of this Age something of the yet unbegotten terror of that; and a quiet and sound thankfulness to God, that we suffer not as humanity shall yet suffer.

But, for all this, let it not be thought that they of that Age accounted it as suffering; but as no more than the usual of human existence. And by this may we know that we can meet all circumstances, and use ourselves to them and live through them wisely, if we be but prudent and consider means of invention.

And through all the Night Land there was an extraordinary awakening among the Monsters and Forces; so that the instruments made constant note of greater powers at work out there in the darkness; and the Monstruwacans were busied recording, and keeping a very strict watch. And so was there at all that time a sense of difference and awakening, and of wonders about, and to come.

And from The Country Whence Comes The Great Laughter, the Laughter sounded constant... as it were an uncomfortable and heart-shaking voice-thunder rolling thence over the Lands, out from the unknown East. And the Pit of the Red Smoke filled all the Deep Valley with redness, so that the smoke rose above the edge, and hid the bases of the Towers upon the far side.

And the Giants could be seen plentiful around the Kilns to the East; and from the Kilns great belches of fire; though the meaning of it, as of all else, we could not say; but only the cause.

And from the Mountain Of The Voice, which rose to the South-East of the South-East Watcher, and of which I have made no telling hitherto, in this faulty setting-out, I heard for the first time in that life, the calling of the Voice. And though the Records made mention of it; yet not often was it heard. And the calling was shrill, and very peculiar and distressful and horrible; as though a giant-woman, hungering strangely, shouted unknown words across the night. And this was how it seemed to me; and many thought this to describe the sound.

And, by all this, may you perceive how that Land was awakened.

And other tricks there were to entice us into the Night Land; and once a call came thrilling in the aether, and told to us that certain humans had escaped from the Lesser Redoubt, and drew nigh to us; but were faint for food, and craved succour. Yet, when we sent the Master-Word into the night, the creatures without could make no reply; which was a very happy thing for our souls; for we had been all mightily exercised in our hearts by this one message; and now had proof that it was but a trap.

And constantly, and at all hours, I would have speech with Naani of the Lesser Redoubt; for I had taught her how she might send her thoughts through the night, with her brain-elements; but not to over-use this power; for it exhausts the body and the powers of the mind, if it be abused by exceeding usage.

Yet, despite that I had taught her the use of her brain-elements, she sent her message always without strength, save when she had use of the instrument; and this I set to the cause that she had not the health force needful; but, apart from this, she had the Night-Hearing very keen; though less than mine.

And so, with many times of speech, and constant tellings of our doings and thoughts, we drew near in the spirit to one another; and had always a feeling in our hearts that we had been given previous acquaintance.

And this, as may be thought, thrilled my heart very strangely.

Chapter IV
The Hushing of the Voice

("Dearest, thine own feet tread the world at night –
Treading, as moon-flakes step across a dark –
Kissing the very dew to holier light...
Thy Voice a song past mountains, which to hark
Frightens my soul with an utter lost delight.")

Now, one night, towards the end of the sixteenth hour, as I made ready to sleep, there came all about me the thrilling of the aether, as happened oft in those days; but the thrilling had a strange power in it; and in my soul the voice of Naani sounded plain, all within and about me.

Yet, though I knew it to be the voice of Naani, I answered not immediately; save to send the sure question of the Master-Word into the night. And, directly, I heard the answer, the Master-Word beating steadily in the night; and I questioned Naani why she had speech with me by the Instrument at that time, when all were sleeping, and the watch set among the Monstruwacans; for they in the little Pyramid had their sleep-time to commence at the eleventh hour; so that by this it was five hours advanced towards the time of waking; and Naani should have slept; nor have been abroad to the Tower of Observation, apart from her father. For I supposed that she spoke by the Instrument, her voice sounding very clear in my brain. Yet, to this question, she made no answer in kind; but gave a certain thing into my spirit, which set me trembling; for she said certain words, that began:

"Dearest, thine own feet tread the world at night –"

And it well may be that she set me to tremble; for as the words grew about me, there wakened a memory-dream how that I had made these same words to Mirdath the Beautiful in the long-gone Eternity of this our Age, when she had died and left me alone in all the world. And I was weak a little with the tumult and force of my emotion; but in a moment I called eagerly with my brain-elements to Naani to give some explaining of this thing that she had spoken to the utter troubling of my heart.

Yet, once more she made no direct answer; but spoke the words again to me across all the dark of the world. And it came to me suddenly, that it was not Naani that spoke; but Mirdath the Beautiful, from out of all the everlasting night. And I called: "Mirdath! Mirdath," with my brain-elements, into the night; and lo! the far, faint voice spoke again to my spirit through all the darkness of eternity, saying again those words. Yet, though the voice was the voice of Mirdath the Beautiful, it was also the voice of Naani; and I knew in all my heart that this thing was in verity; and that it had been given to me to be birthed once more into this world in the living-time of that Only One, with whom my spirit and essence hath mated in all ages through the everlasting. And I called with my brain-elements and all my strength to Naani; but there came no answer; neither sign of hearing, though through hours I called.

And thus at last I came to an utter exhaustion; but neither could be quiet, nor sleep. Yet, presently, I slept.

And when I waked, my first memory was of the wondrous thing which had befallen in the sleep-time; for none in all this world could have known those words; save it had been the spirit of Mirdath, my Beautiful One, looking from above my shoulder in that utter-lost time, as I made those words to her, out of an aching and a broken heart. And the voice had been the voice of Mirdath; and the voice of Mirdath had been the voice of Naani. And what shall any say to this, save that which I had in my heart.

And immediately I called to Naani, once, and again twice; and in a little moment there came all about me the throbbing of the Master-Word, beating solemnly in the night; and I sent the Master-Word to give assurance, and immediately the voice of Naani, a little weak as was it always when she had not the Instrument, but sent the message with her brain-elements.

And I answered her, and questioned her eagerly concerning her sayings of the past time of sleep; but she disclaimed, and made clear to me that she had no knowledge of having spoken; but had slept through all that time of which I made to tell; and, indeed, had dreamed a very strange dream.

And for a little while I was confused, and meditated, not knowing what to think; but came suddenly again to a knowledge that Naani's far voice was thrilling the aether all about; and that she would tell to me her dream; which had set strong upon her mind.

And she told the dream to me, and in the dream she had seen a tall, dark man, built very big, and dressed in unfamiliar clothing. And the man had been in a little room, and very sorrowful, and lonesome; and in her dream she had gone nigh to him.

And presently the man made to write, that he might ease him by giving expression to his sorrow; and Naani had been able to read the words that he wrote; though to her waking spirit the language in which they were writ was strange and unknown. Yet she could not remember what he had writ, save but one short line, and this she had mind of in that he had writ the word Mirdath above. And she spoke of the strangeness of this thing, that she should dream of this name; but supposed that I had fixed it upon her, by my first callings.

And then did I, with something of a tremble in my spirit, ask Naani to tell me what she remembered of the writing of that big, sorrowful stranger. And, in a little moment, her far voice said these words all about me:

"Dearest, thine own feet tread the world at night –"

But no more had she memory of. Yet it was a sufficiency, and I, maybe with a mad, strange triumph in my soul, said unto her with my brain-elements that which remained of those words. And my spirit felt them strike upon the spirit of Naani, and awake her memory, as with the violence of a blow. And for a little while she stumbled, dumb before so much newness and certainly. And her spirit then to waken, and she near wept with the fright and the sudden, new wonder of this thing.

And immediately, all about me there came her voice thrilling, and the voice was the voice of Mirdath, and the voice of Naani; and I heard the tears of her spirit make pure and wonderful the bewildered and growing gladness of her far voice. And she asked me, as one who had suddenly opened the Gates of Memory, whether she might be truly Mirdath. And I, utter weak and shaken strangely because of this splendour of fulfilment, could make no instant answer. And she asked again, but using mine old love-name, and with a sureness in her far voice. And still I was so strangely dumb, and the blood to thud peculiar in mine ears; and this to pass; and speech to come swift.

And this way to be that meeting of our spirits, across all the everlasting night.

And you shall have for a memory-picture, how that Naani stood there in the world in that far eternity, and, with her spirit having speech with mine, looked back through the part-opened gates of her memory, into the past of this our life and Age. Yet more than this she saw, and more than was given to me in that Age; for she had memory now and sight of other instances, and of other comings together, which had some confusion and but half-meanings to me. Yet of this our present Age and life, we spoke as of some yesterday; but very hallowed.

Now, as may be conceived, the wonder of this surety which had come into my life stirred me fiercely to its completion; for all my heart and spirit cried out to be with that one who was Mirdath, and now spoke with the voice of Naani.

Yet, how should this be won; for none among all the learned men of that Mighty Pyramid knew the position of the Lesser Redoubt; neither could the Records and Histories of the World give us that knowledge; only that there was a general thought among the Students and the Monstruwacans that it lay between the North-West and the North-East. But no man had any surety; neither could any conceive of the distance from us of that Refuge.

And counting all this, there was yet the incredible danger and peril of the Night Land, and the hunger and desolation of the Outer Lands, which were sometimes named the Unknown Lands.

And I spoke much with Naani concerning this matter of their position; yet neither she nor her father, the Master Monstruwacan of that Refuge, had any knowing either of our position; only that the Builder of the Lesser Redoubt had come out of the Southward World in the Beginning, as they had knowledge of by the Records.

Also, the father of Naani set that ancient Compass to bear; for, as he made explanation to us through the Instrument, so great a power of the Earth-Current must be ours that, perchance it was our force which did affect the pointer from steadfastness. For, indeed, the needle did swing in an arc, as we heard, that held between the North and the South; within the Westward arc; but this it had done ever with them, and so was a very helpless guide; save that, maybe, as we had thought, the force of the Earth-Current that was with us, had in truth some power to pull the needle towards us. And if this were so of verity, we made a reckoning that set the Lesser Redoubt to the North; and they did likewise, and put us to the South; yet was it all built upon the sand of guess-work; and nothing to adventure the life and soul upon.

Now we, of curiosity; though a million times had it been done in the past ages, set the compass before us, having it from the Great Museum. But, as ever in that age, it did spin if we but stirred the needle, and would stop nowheres with surety, for the flow of the Earth-Current from the 'Crack' beneath the Pyramid had a power to affect it away from the North, and to set it wandering. And this may seem very strange to this present Age; yet to that, it was most true to the seeming nature of things; and harder to believe that ever it did once point steadfastly, to prove a guide of sureness, and unfailing.

For, be it known, we knew the positions of the Land by tradition, coming from that ancient time when, in the Half-Gloom they had builded the Pyramid; they having known the use of that ancient compass, and with sight of the Sun had named the Positions; though we of that far future day had forgotten the very beginnings of those Names of Direction; and used them but because our fathers did a million years and more. And likewise we did the same with the names of the day and the night and the weeks and the months and the years; though of the visible markings of these there was nothing but only and always the everlasting night; yet the same seeming very natural to that people.

Now, Naani, having heed to my constant questions, craved with an utter keen hunger that I might come to her; but yet forbade it, in that it were better to live and commune in the spirit, than to risk my soul, and mayhaps die, in the foolishness of trying to find her in all the darkness of the dead world. Yet, no heed had I taken of her commands, had I but known of a surety the *direction* in which she might be discovered; and gained some knowledge of the space between, for this might be named by thousands of miles, or but by hundreds; though a great distance it was surely.

Yet, one other thing there was, that has point in this place; for when I sent my speech out into the night, using my brain-elements, I came to know that, whether I had a knowledge of the North, or no knowledge at the moment, yet did I turn oft with a sure instinction to that Direction. And of this, the Master Monstruwacan took very great note, and had me to experiment many a time and way, and so enclosed about with screens, or with bandages across mine eyes, that I could not, save by that inward Knowing, have any knowledge to point me the way. Yet would I turn Northwards very frequent, by a certain feeling; and seemed unable of speech, if I were turned otherwise by force.

But when we asked Naani whether she had an unusualness in this matter, she could discover none; and we could but take note curiously of that which affected my habits; and which truly I set to the attracting of her spirit; for I had mind that she did be somewheres out that way in the darkness of the world; but yet was this no more than to suppose, as you perceive.

And the Master Monstruwacan wrote a study of this matter of the Northwardness of my turning; and it was set out in the Hour-Slips of the Tower of Observation; and so it came to be copied by the Hour-Slips of the great cities, and made much comment, and much calling up to me through the home instruments; so that with this, and the speech that went about concerning my powers to hear, I was much in talk, and diversely pleased and oft angered by overmuch attention and importunity.

And now, whilst I pondered this matter in all my spirit and being, how that I should some way come to Naani, there befell a very terrible thing. And in this wise must I tell it:

It was at the seventeenth hour, when all the millions of the Mighty Pyramid slept, that I was with the Master Monstruwacan in the Tower of Observation taking my due turn. And sudden, I heard the thrilling of the aether all about me, and the voice of Naani in my soul, speaking. And I sent the Master-Word into the darkness of the world, and presently, I heard the solemn answer beating steadfastly in the night; and immediately I called to Naani with my brain-elements, to know what thing troubled her in her sleep.

And her voice came into my spirit, weak and far and faint, and so that scarce I could make to hear the words. Yet, in a while I gathered that all the peoples of the Lesser Redoubt were in very deadly trouble; for that the Earth-Current had failed suddenly and mightily; and they had called her from her sleep, that she might listen whether we answered their callings by the Instrument; but, indeed, no calling had come to us.

And they who had been of late so joyful, were now grown old with sorrow in but an hour or two; for they feared that the fresh coming of the Earth-Current had been but the final flicker and outburst before the end. And, even in this short while of our speech, did it seem to me that the voice of Naani grew further off from me; and I felt like to have broken my heart with the trouble of this thing.

And through all that remained of that sleep-time, did I converse with Naani, as might two lovers who shall presently part forever. And when the cities awoke, the news went throughout them, and all our millions were in sorrow and trouble.

And thus was it for, maybe, a little month; and in that time had the voice of Naani grown so weak and far-off that even I that had the Night-Hearing, could scarce make real its meaning. And every word was to me a treasure and a touch upon my soul; and my grief and trouble before this certain parting drove me that I could not eat, neither have rest; and this did the Master Monstruwacan take upon him to chide and correct; for that, if any were to help, how should it be done if I that had the Night-Hearing, and heard even now that the recording Instruments were dumb, came to ill-health.

And because of this, and such wisdom as was mine, I made to eat and order my life that I might have my full powers. Yet was this beyond all my strength; for, presently, I knew that the people of the Lesser Pyramid were threatened by the monsters that beset them; and later I had knowledge from faint, far words whispered in my brain, that there had been a fight with an outside Force that had harmed many in their minds; so that in madness they had opened the gate and had run from the Lesser Pyramid, out into the darkness of the Lands about them; and there had their physical bodies fallen to the monsters of those Lands; but of their souls who may know?

And this, we set assuredly to the failure of the Earth-Current, which had robbed them of all force and power; so that, in those few weeks all life and joy of living had left them; and neither hunger nor thirst had they, much, nor any great desire to live; but yet a new and mighty fear of death. And this doth seem very strange.

And, as may be thought, all this made the Peoples of the Great Redoubt think newly of the Earth-Current that issued from the 'Crack' beneath the Pyramid; and of their latter end; so that much was writ in the Hour-Slips concerning this matter; yet in the main to assure us that we ourselves might each be free from a disturbed heart; though some went foolishly to the other event, and spoke of a speedy danger to us, likewise; as is ever the way. But the truth of our own case lay, maybe, somewhere between.

And all the Hour-Slips were full also of imaginings of the terror of those poor humans out in the darkness of the world, facing that end which must come upon all, even upon our mighty Pyramid; though, as most would believe, so far away in some future eternity, that we have no cause to trouble.

And there were sad poems writ to the peoples of that Lesser Redoubt, and foolish plans set about to rescue them; but none to put them to effect; and no way by which so great a thing might be done; and doth but show how loosely people will speak out of an over-security. Yet to me, there had come a certain knowledge that I must make the adventure, though I achieved naught save mine own end. Yet, it were better to cease quickly, than that I should feel, as now I did feel.

That same night, in the Eighteenth Hour, there was a great disturbance in the aether about the Mighty Pyramid; and I was awakened suddenly by the Master Monstruwacan; that I might use my gift of the Night-Hearing to hearken for the throbbing of the Master-Word, which they had thought to come vaguely through the Instruments; but no one of the Monstruwacans was sensitive enough of soul to account truly whether this was so.

And lo! as I sat up in the bed, there came the sound of the Master-Word, beating in the night about the Pyramid. And immediately there was a crying in the aether all about me: "We are coming! We are coming!"

And mine inwards leaped and sickened me a moment, so shaken was I with a sudden belief; for the message seemed some ways to come to me from very near to the Great Redoubt; as that they who sent it were nigh to hand.

And, forthwith, I called the Master-Word into the night; but no answer did there come for a while, and then a faint thrilling of the aether about me, and the weak pulse of the Master-Word in the night, sent by a far voice, strangely distant. And I knew that the voice was the voice of Naani; and I put a question through all the darkness of the dead world, whether she were within the Lesser Redoubt, and safe thus far.

And presently, there came a faint disturbance about me, and a small voice in my soul, speaking weakly and out of an infinite distance; and I knew that far away through the night Naani spoke feebly, with her brain-elements; and that she abode within the Lesser Pyramid; but that she too had heard that strange pulse of the Master-Word in the night, and that message: "We are coming! We are coming!" And vastly had this thing disturbed her, waking her within her sleep; so that she knew not what to think; save that we were devising some method to come to them. But this I removed from doubt, saying that she must not build on vain hoping; for I would not have her doubly tortured by the vanity of such believing. And, thereafter, having said such things as I might, though few they were, to comfort her, I bade her, gently, to sleep; and turned therewith to the Master Monstruwacan, who waited in quiet patience; and had no knowledge of that which I had heard and sent; for his hearing was but the normal; though his brain and heart were such as made me to love him.

And I told the Master Monstruwacan many things as I put my clothing about me; how that there had indeed been the calling of the Master-Word; but not by any of that Lesser Redoubt; but that, to my belief, it had come from nigh about the Great Pyramid. Moreover, it was sent by no instrument; as I wotted that he did guess; but, as it seemed to me, by the brain-elements of many, calling in unison.

And all this did I set out to the Master Monstruwacan; and with something uncertain of fear and trouble in my heart; yet with a blind expectation; as, indeed, who would not. Though, no longer was I shaken by that first thought of Her nearness.

And I said to the Master Monstruwacan that we should go to the Tower of Observation, and search the Night Lands with the great spy-glass.

And we did this, and lo! presently, we saw a great number of men pass over the Electric Circle that went about the Pyramid; yet they came not *to* us; but went outwards towards the blackness and the strange fires and hideous mysteries of the Night Land. And we ceased from spying, and looked swiftly at one another, and knew in our hearts that some had left the Mighty Pyramid in the Sleep-Time.

Then the Master Monstruwacan sent word to the Master Watchman that his wardership had been outraged, and that people left the great Pyramid in the Sleep-Time; for this was against the Law; and none ever went out into the Night Land, save the Full Watch were posted to the Great Door; and at a due time, when all were wakeful; for the Opening Of The Door was made known to all the Millions of the Great Redoubt; so that all might be aware; and know that no foolishness was done without their wotting.

Moreover, ere any had power to leave the Pyramid, they must pass The Examination, and Be Prepared; and some of this have I set out already. And so stern was the framing of the Law, that there were yet the metal pegs upon the inner side of the Great Gate, where had been stretched the skin of one who disobeyed; and was flayed and his hide set there to be a warning in the Early Days. Yet the tradition was remembered; for, as I might say it, we lived very close about the place; and Memory had no room whereby she might escape.

Now the Master Watchman, when he heard that which the Master Monstruwacan had to tell, went hastily with some of the Central Watch from the Watch-Dome, to the Great Gate; and he found the men of the Sleep-Time Watch, with the Warder of the Gate, all bound, and stopt in the mouth, so that none could make outcry.

And he freed them, and learned that nigh five hundred young men, from the Upper Cities, by the bigness of their chests, had come upon them suddenly, and bound them, and escaped into the night through the Eye-Gate in the top of the Great Gate.

And the Master Watchman was angry, and demanded why that none had called by the instruments of the Watch House; but lo! some had made to call thus, and found them unable to wake the recorders which lay in the central Watch-Dome; for there had been tampering.

Now, after this, they made certain new rules and Laws concerning the order of Watching, and made tests of the lesser instruments of the inward Pyramid, nightly, upon the coming of the Sleep-Time, which was, even in that strange age, by tradition called the Night, as I have given hint; though hitherto, until the way of my story was known, I have used a word for the sleep hours that was yet not of that time; but somewhat an invention to make this history free from the confusion of 'night' and 'day,' when, in truth, it was always night without upon the world. Yet, after this, shall I keep to mine use the luxury of the true names of that time; and yet, how strange is it that the truth should be of so little to our thinking.

And so to go forward with my telling; for, though all this care were now taken, it had no force until afterward; and at this moment were those poor foolish youths out in all the danger of the Night Land, and no way by which they might be succoured, or called back; save that Fear or Wisdom should come to them quickly, that they cease from so wild an attempt. For it was to make rescue of those in that other, unknown Pyramid, out in all the darkness of the World's Night that was their intent, as we had speedy knowledge from those boon friends that had been in the secret of their plot, which had seemed to them great and heroic; and was so, in verity, but that neither they who went, nor they who stayed, had a true awareness of the danger they had dealing with, being all naught but raw and crude youths; yet, doubtless, with the makings of many fine and great men among them.

And because some had thus abetted that which they knew to be against the Law, which was framed to the well-being and safety of all, there were certain floggings, which might the better help their memories in the future as to the properness of their actions and wisdom.

Moreover, they who returned, if any, would be flogged, as seemed proper, after due examination. And though the news of their beatings might help all others to hesitation, ere they did foolishly, in like fashion, yet was the principle of the flogging not on this base, which would be both improper and unjust; but only that the one in question be corrected to the best advantage for his own well-being; for it is not meet that any principle of correction should shape to the making of human signposts of pain for the benefit of others; for in verity, this were to make one pay the cost of many's learning; and each should owe to pay only so much as shall suffice for the teaching of his own body and spirit. And if others profit thereby, this is but accident, however helpful. And this is wisdom, and denoteth now that a sound Principle shall prevent Practice from becoming monstrous.

Yet, now I must hasten that I set down how it fared with those five hundred youths that had made so sad an adventure of their lives and unprepared souls; and were beyond our aid to help them, who might not so much as make any calling to them, to bid them to return; for to do this would have been to tell to all the Monsters of the Land that humans were abroad from the Mighty Pyramid.

And this would have been to cause the monsters to search the youths out to their destruction, and maybe even to awaken the Forces to work them some dread Spiritual harm, which was the chief Fear.

Now, presently, through all the cities of the Great Redoubt, the news had gone how that five hundred foolish Youths had adventured out into the despair of the Night Land; and the whole Pyramid waked to life, and the Peoples of the South came to the Northern sides, for the Great Gate lay in the North-West side; and the Youths had made from there, not straightly outwards, but towards the North; and so were to be seen from the North-East embrasures, and from those within the North-West wall.

And thus, in a while were they watched by all the mighty multitudes of the Great Pyramid, through millions of spy-glasses; for each human had a spying-glass, as may be thought; and some were an hundred years old, and some, maybe ten thousand, and handed down through many generations; and some but newly made, and very strange. But all those people had some instrument by which they might spy out upon the wonder of the Night Land; for so had it been ever through all the eternity of darkness, and a great diversion and wonder of life was it to behold the monsters about their work; and to know that they plotted always to our destruction; yet were ever foiled.

And never did all that great and terrible Land grow stale upon the soul of any, from birth until death; and by this you shall know the constant wonder of it, and that *sense of enemies in the night about us,* which ever filled the heart and spirit of all Beholders; so that never were the embrasures utterly empty.

Yet, many beheld not the Land from the embrasures; but sat about the View-Tables, which were set properly in certain places throughout the cities, and so beheld the Night Land, without undue cranings, or poising of spy-glasses, though less plain-seen. And these same tables were some form of that which we of this age name Camera Obscura; but made very great, and with inventions, and low to the floor, so that ten thousand people might sit about them in the raised galleries, and have comfortable sight. Yet this attracted not the young people, save they were lovers; and then, in truth, were they comfortable seats for quietness and gentle whisperings.

Yet now, as may be supposed, with all the Peoples of the Mighty Pyramid grown eager to look towards one part of the Night Land, the embrasures were hid in the crowds; and such as could gain no view therethrough, thronged about the View-Tables. And so was it in all the hours of leisure; so that women had scarce patience to attend their children; but must hasten to watch again, that lonesome band of foolish youths making so blind and unshaped a trial to come upon that unknown Lesser Redoubt, somewhere out in all the night of the world.

And in this wise passed three days and nights; yet both in the sleep-time and the time of waking did great multitudes cease not to watch; so that many went hungry for sleep, as in truth did I. And sometimes we saw those Youths with plainness; but other times they were lost to our sight in the utter shadows of the Night Land. Yet, by the telling of our instruments, and the sense of my hearing, there was no awaredness among the Monsters, and the Forces of Evil, that any were abroad from the Pyramid; so that a little hope came into our hearts that yet there might be no tragedy.

And times, would they cease from their way, and sit about in circles among the shadows and the grey moss-bushes, which grew hardly here or there about. And we knew that they had food with them to eat; for this could we see with plainness, as some odd, grim flare of light from the infernal fires struck upon one or another strangely, and passed, and left them in the darkness.

And who of you shall conceive what was in the hearts of the fathers, and the mothers that bore the youths, and who never ceased away from the Northward embrasures; but spied out in terror and in tears, and maybe oft with so good glasses as did show them the very features and look upon the face of son and son.

And the kin of the watchers brought to them food, and tended them, so that they had no need to cease from their watching; and beds were made in the embrasures, rough and resourceful, that they might sleep quickly a little; yet be ever ready, if those cruel Monsters without made discovery of those their children.

Thrice in those three days of journeying to the Northward, did the Youths sleep, and we perceived that some kept a watch, and so knew that there was a kind of order and leadership among them; also, they had each his weapon upon his hip, and this gave to us a further plea to hope.

And concerning this same carrying of weapons, I can but set out here that no healthful male or female in all the Mighty Pyramid but possessed such a weapon, and was trained to it from childhood; so that a ripe and extraordinary skill in the use thereof was common to most. Yet some breaking of Rule had there been, that the Youths had each achieved to be armed; for the weapons were stored in every tenth house of the cities, in the care of the charging-masters.

And here I must make known that these weapons did not shoot; but had a disk of grey metal, sharp and wonderful, that spun in the end of a rod of grey metal, and were someways charged by the Earth-Current, so that were any but stricken thereby, they were cut in twain so easy as aught. And the weapons were contrived to the repelling of any Army of Monsters that might make to win entrance to the Redoubt. And to the eye they had somewhat the look of strange battle-axes, and might be lengthened by the pulling out of the handles.

Now, the Youths made, as I have told, to the Northward; but had first to keep a long way to the North-East, that they might come clear of the Vale of Red Fire. And this wise they journeyed, and kept the Vale about seven miles to the North-West of them, and so were presently beyond the Watcher of the North-East, and going with a greater freedom, and having less care to hide.

And this way, it may be, certain of the giants, wandering, perceived them, and went swiftly to make attack and destroy them. But some order went about among the youths, and they made a long line, with a certain space between each, because of the terror of their weapon, and immediately, it seemed, the Giants were upon them, a score and seven they were, and seeming to be haired like to mighty crabs, as I saw with the Great Spy-Glass, when the great flares of far and mighty fires threw their fierce light across the Dark Lands.

And there was a very great and horrid fight; for the Youths broke into circles about each of the Giants, and many of those young men were torn in pieces; but they smote the Monsters from behind and upon every side, and we of the Mighty Pyramid could behold at times the grey, strange gleam of their weapons; and the jether was stirred about me by the passing of those that died; yet, by reason of the great miles, their screams came not to us, neither heard we the roars of the Monsters; but into our hearts, even from that great distance and safety, there stole the terror of those awesome Brutes; and in the Great Spy-Glass I could behold the great joints and limbs and e'en, I thought, the foul sweat of them; and their size and brutishness was like to that of odd and monstrous animals of the olden world; yet part human. And it must be borne to mind that the Fathers and the Mothers of those Youths beheld all this dread fight from the embrasures, and their other kin likewise watched, and a very drear sight was it to their hearts and their human, natural feelings, and like to breed old age, ere its due.

Then, in a time, the fight ceased; for of those seven and twenty Giant Brutes there remained none; only that there cumbered the ground seven and twenty lumbering hillocks, dreadful and grim. For the lesser dead we could not see proper.

And we that were within the Pyramid saw the Youths sorted together by their leaders, all in the dim twilight of that place; and with the Great Spy-Glass I made a rough count, and found that there lived of them, three hundred; and by this shall you know the power of those few monstrous things, which had slain full two hundred, though each youth was armed with so wondrous a weapon. And I set the word through the Pyramid, that all might have some knowledge of the number that had died; for it was better to know, than to be in doubt. And no spy-glass had the power of The Great Spy-Glass.

After this fight, the youths spent a time having a care to their bodies and wounds; and some were made separate from the others, and of these I counted upon fifty; and whilst the others made to continue their march towards the Road Where The Silent Ones Walk, these were constrained by one who was the Leader, to return to the Pyramid. And in a little, I saw that they came towards us, wearily and with many a halt, as that they suffered great wounds and harm of the fight.

But those others (maybe two hundred and fifty Youths) went onwards into the Night Land; and though we sorrowed at this thing; yet was there come a huge pride into our hearts that those raw ones, who yesterday were but children, had so held themselves in the battle, and done a great deed that day. And I wot that whilst their mothers wept, easeless, their fathers' hearts swelled within them, and held somewhat of their Pain away from them for a time.

And all this while, those wounded Youths came slowly, and rested, and came on again, the better helping the worse; and a great excitement and trouble there was in all the Mighty Pyramid, to learn which were they that came, and they that went, and who lay out there quietly among the slain. But none might say anything with surety; for, even with that great spy-glass in the Tower of Observation, they were not overplain; save when some light from the fires of the Land flared high, and lit them. For they stood not up into the glare of the fires, as had the Giants. And though I saw them with clearness, yet I knew them not; for there was so mighty a multitude in that Vast Redoubt, that none might ever know the half even of their rulers.

And about this time, there came a fresh matter of trouble to our minds; for one of the Monstruwacans made report that the instruments were recording an influence abroad in the night; so that we had knowledge that one of the Evil Forces was Out. And to me there came an awareness that a strange unquiet stole over the Land; yet I knew it not with mine ears;

but my spirit heard, and it was as though trouble and an expectation of horror did swarm about me.

And once, listening, I heard the Master-Word beating strangely low, and I knew the aether to thrill about me, and a faint stirring was there in my soul, as of a faint voice, speaking; and I knew that Naani called to me some message across the night of the world; yet weak and coming without clear meaning; so that I was tormented and could but send comfort to her, with my brain-elements. And presently I knew that she ceased to speak.

And, later, I heard that there was a new matter forward in the Redoubt; for ten thousand men had assembled to attend the Room of Preparation for the Short Preparation; and by this we knew that those poor Youths who stumbled towards us through the dark, were presently to have help.

And through all that Sleep-Time, there went forward the Spiritual and the Physical Preparation of the ten thousand; and upon the morrow they slept, whilst an hundred thousand made ready their arms.

And in this space of time the two hundred and fifty Youths that went towards the Road Where The Silent Ones Walk, had come very nigh thereto; having gone very warily and with some slowness, because, as may be, of the lesson of the Giants.

And to us in the Pyramid, the instruments made known constantly that Influence which was abroad, and which all those of the Tower of Observation thought to proceed from the House of Silence. Yet, nothing could we see with the Great Spy-Glass, and so could come to no sure knowing; but only to fear and wonder.

And, presently, the Youths were upon the Great Road, and turned to the Northward. And beyond them, a great way, stood the House of Silence, upon a low hill at a certain distance to the right of the Road.

By now, they that were wounded had come to within, maybe, fifteen miles of the Great Redoubt; and the news went through all the Cities, that the ten thousand men that were Prepared, made to arm themselves. And I went down by the Tower Lift, and saw them come down by thousands from the Room of Preparation; and none might go nigh to them, or cause them to speak; for they were made Ready, and were, as it might be, holy.

And all the millions of the Mighty Pyramid stood in their cities about certain of the Main Lifts, and watched those thousands go downwards, all in their armour of grey metal, and each one armed with the Diskos, which was that same very terrible weapon, which all had training to.

And I doubt not but that the Young Men of the Pyramid looked, with longing in their hearts, that they might have been among those that went forth to succour. Yet, the older men had graver thoughts in their hearts; for the blood ran more soberly in them, and they had knowledge and memory of the Peril. And by this, I would make clear that I speak less of the peril of the body, which is common to every state of life; but of the peril of the spirit.

And it may be thought by those of this age, that it was most strange that they of that, having all the knowledge of eternity to aid them, had no weapon by which to shoot, and kill at a distance.

But, indeed, this had not been so in the past; as our Histories did show; for some wondrous weapons there had been, that might slay without sound or flash at a full score miles and more; and some we had whole within the Great Museum; and of others but the parts in decay; for they had been foolish things, and reckless to use; for we of that Great Pyramid, wanted not to kill a few of the Monsters that lay at a great distance; but only those which came nigh, to harm us.

And concerning those same weapons that killed silently at a great distance, we had now little knowledge, save that they did waste the Earth-Current; and no practice had we concerning their workings; for it was, maybe, an hundred thousand years gone that they had been used, and found to be of no great worth in a close attack, and harmful otherwise to the peace, in that they angered, unneedful, the Forces of that land, slaying wantonly those monsters which did no more than beset the Mighty Redoubt at a great distance. For, as may be seen by a little thought, we did very gladly keep a reasonable quietness, and refrained from aught that should wake that Land; for we were born to the custom of that strange life, and lived and died in peace, for the most part; and were very content to have security, and to be neutral in all things that did not overbear us; but, as it were, always armed, and ready.

But concerning the great and Evil Forces that were abroad in the Night Land, these we had no power to harm; nor could we hope for more than that we had security from them, which indeed we had; but the hugeness of their power was about us, and we dared not to wake it; save through such extremity as had come to pass by this folly of the Youths; though, even now, we had no thought to attack aught; but only to succour those wounded ones.

And concerning this simplicity of weapons, which excites somewhat even my wonder in this our present age, it may be that the powers of chemistry were someways quaintly limited by conditions in that age; and there to be always a need to spare the Earth-Current; and hence, by this cause and by that, we were brought, by the extreme, nigh to the simplicity of the early world; yet with a strange and mighty difference, as all may know who have read.

Now, presently, the Word was sent to every City throughout the Great Redoubt – as was the Law – that the Great Gate should be opened; and each city sent its Master, to form the Full Watch, as was the Law. And each went clad in grey armour, and carrying the Diskos. And the Full Watch numbered, two thousand; for there were also the Watchmen.

Then the lights in the Great Causeway were made dim; so that the opening of the Gate should cast no great glare from within into the Night Land, to tell the Watcher of the North-West, and all the Monsters, that certain humans went out from the Mighty Pyramid. But whether the vast and hidden Forces of Evil had knowledge, we knew not; and they who went must but chance it, remembering that they were Prepared, and had the Capsule.

And the ten thousand that were Prepared, went out through the Great Gateway, into the night; and the Full Watch stood back from them, and spoke no word, but saluted silently with the Diskos; and they that went, raised each the Diskos a little, and passed out into the dark.

Then the Great Gate was shut; and we made to wait and to watch, with trouble and expectation within our hearts. And at the embrasures many did comfort the women of those men.

And I went back, upwards by miles, until I came to the Tower of Observation; and I looked out from there into the Night Land, and saw that the ten thousand halted at the Circle, and made arrangement of themselves, and sent some before and upon either hand, and so went forward into the Night Land.

And after that, I went to the Great Spy-Glass, and turned it towards the two hundred and fifty Youths that were far off, upon the Road Where The Silent Ones Walk; yet for awhile I could not perceive them, for all the Road seemed empty. But afterward I saw them, and they were clambering back into the Road, having gone aside, as I thought, because of the passing of one of those Silent Ones, that I saw now at a distance to the Southward of them.

There passed then, some three hours; and in that time I varied my watching between those far-off Youths, and the Ten-thousand that went forward to succour the wounded, that were now, maybe, scarce nine miles distant from the Mighty Pyramid, and the Ten-thousand came very close to them. And, in truth, in a little while, they spied one the other, and I gathered, in spirit, something of the rejoicing of those youths; yet weak and troubled were they, because of their wounds, and their knowledge of failure, and their disobedience of the Law.

And, presently, they were surrounded by the Ten-thousand, and carried upon slings; and all that body swung round towards the Pyramid, and came back at a great pace.

And, in the same time, I heard the sound that made them so swift to hasten; for there smote up through the night the Baying of the Hounds; and we knew that they were discovered. And I swept the Great Spy-Glass over the Land, towards the Valley Of The Hounds, that I might discover them quickly; and I saw them come lumbering, at a strange gallop, and great as horses, and it might be only ten miles to the East.

And I looked once upon the Watcher of the North-East, and I saw and marvelled that the great bell-ear quivered constantly; and I knew that it had knowledge, and gave signal to all the Land. Then did one of the Monstruwacans report that a new and terrible Influence was abroad in the Land; and by the instrument, we had knowledge that it approached; and some of the Monstruwacans called foolishly with weak voices to the Ten-thousand to haste; forgetting, and desiring only their safety from that which came near.

Then, looking with the Great Spy-Glass, I saw that there moved across the Land, from the direction of the Plain of Blue Fire, a mighty Hump, seeming of Black Mist, and came with prodigious swiftness. And I called to the Master Monstruwacan, that he come and look through one of the eye-pieces that were about the Great Spy-Glass; and he came quickly, and when he had looked a while, he called to the Monstruwacan that had made report. And the Monstruwacan answered, and replied that the Influence drew nearer, by the reading of the instrument; yet of the thing itself the man had no sight.

And I ceased not to look, and in a little while, the Humped thing passed downwards into the Vale of Red Fire, which lay across the Land that way. But I watched steadfastly, and presently I saw the black Hump climb up from the Vale of Red Fire upon this side, and come through the night, so that in scarce a minute it had come halfway across that part of the Night Land.

And my heart stood quiet with fear, and the utter terror of this Monster, which I knew to be surely one of the Great Forces of Evil of that Land, and had power, without doubt, to destroy the spirit. And the Master Monstruwacan leapt towards the Home-Call, and sent the great Sound down to the Ten-thousand, that they might attend, and immediately, he signalled to them to Beware. Yet, already I perceived that they knew of this Utter Danger that was upon them; for I saw them slay the Youths quickly, that their spirits might not be lost; for they were Unprepared. But the men, being Prepared, had the Capsule, and would die swiftly in the last moment.

I looked again towards the Hump, and saw that it came like a Hill of Blackness in the Land, and was almost anigh. Then there happened a wonder; for in that moment when all had else gone quickly, that they might save their souls, out of the earth there rose a little Light, like to the crescent of the young moon of this early day. And the crescent rose up into an arch of bright and cold fire, glowing but little; and it spanned above the Ten-thousand and the dead; and the Hump stood still, and went backwards and was presently lost.

And the men came swiftly towards the Mighty Pyramid. Yet, ere they were come to safety, the Baying of the Hounds sounded close upon them, and they faced to the danger; yet, as I could know, without despair, because that they yet lived after so enormous a peril.

And the Hounds were very nigh, as now I beheld with the Great Spy-Glass; and I counted five score, running with mighty heads low, and in a pack. And lo! as the Hounds came at them, the Ten-thousand drew apart, and had a space between the men, that they might have full use of that terrible Diskos; and they fought with the handles at length, and I saw the disks spin and glisten and send out fire.

Then was there a very great battle; for the Light that arched above them, and held away The Power from their souls, made not to protect them from this danger of the lesser monsters. And at an hundred thousand embrasures within the Mighty Pyramid, the women cried and sobbed, and looked again. And in the lower cities it was told, after, that the Peoples could hear the crash and splinter of the armour, as the Hounds ran to and fro, slaying; aye, even the sound of the armour between their teeth.

Yet, the Ten-thousand ceased not to smite with the Diskos; and they hewed the Hounds in pieces; but of the men that went forth, there were a thousand and seven hundred slain by the Hounds, ere the men won to victory.

Then came that wearied band of heroes back to the home shelter of the Vast Redoubt; and they bore their dead with them, and the Youths that they slew. And they were received with great honour, and with exceeding grief, and in a great silence; for the thing admitted not of words, until a time had passed. And in the cities of the Pyramid there was mourning; for there had been no sorrow like unto this through, mayhap, an hundred thousand years.

And they bore the Youths to their Mothers and to their Fathers; and the Father of each made thanks to the men that they had saved the soul of his son; but the women were silent. Yet, neither to the Father nor to the Mother, was ever made known the name of the slayers; for this might not be; as all shall see with a little thought.

And some did remember that, in verity, all was due to the unwisdom of those Youths, who had heeded not the Law and their life-teachings. Yet had they paid to the uttermost, and passed outwards; and the account of their Deeds was closed.

And all this while did great numbers spy toward the Road Where The Silent Ones Walk, that they might watch that band of Youths afar in the Night Land, who went forward amid those horrid dangers. Yet, when the dead Youths had been brought in, many had ceased to look out for a time and had turned to questioning, and some had made inspection that they might know which had come back, and which lay out there where the Giants had slain them, or went forward to more dreadful matters.

But who of those that were abroad, were slain, or still went onward, we had but indifferent knowledge; though the men of the Ten-thousand knew somewhat, having had speech with the wounded Youths, ere they slew them. And, as may be thought, these men were sorely questioned by the Mothers and the Fathers of those Youths that were not accounted of; yet I doubt that few had much knowledge wherewith to console them.

Now there was presently, in the Garden of Silence, which was the lowermost of all the Underground Fields, the Ending of those seventeen hundred heroes, and of the Youths that they saved and slew. And the Garden was a great country, and an hundred miles every way, and the roof thereof was three great miles above, and shaped to a mighty dome; as it had been that the Builders and Makers thereof did remember in their spirits the visible sky of this our present age.

And the making of that Country was all set out in a single History of seven thousand and seventy Volumes. And there were likewise seven thousand and seventy years spent to the making of that Country; so that there had unremembered generations lived and laboured and died, and seen not the end of their labour. And Love had shaped it and hallowed it; so that of all the wonders of the world, there has been none that shall ever come anigh to that Country of Silence – an hundred miles every way of Silence to the Dead.

And there were in that roof seven moons set in a mighty circle, and lit by the Earth-Current; and the circle was sixty miles across, so that all that Country of Quiet was visible; yet to no great glare, but a sweet and holy light; so that I did always feel in my heart that a man might weep there, and be unashamed.

And in the midst of that silent Country, there was a great hill, and upon the hill a vast Dome. And the Dome was full of a Light that might be seen in all that Country, which was the Garden of Silence. And beneath the Dome was the "Crack," and within it the glory of the Earth-Current, from which all had life and light and safety. And in the Dome, at the North, there was a gateway; and a narrow road went upward to the gateway; and the Road was named The Last Road; and the Gateway was named by no name, but known to all as The Gateway.

And there were in that mighty Country, long roadways, and hidden methods to help travel; and constant temples of rest along the miles; and groves; and the charm of water, falling. And everywhere the Statues of Memory, and the Tablets of Memory; and the whole of that Great Underground Country full of an echo of Eternity and of Memory and Love and Greatness; so that to walk alone in that Land was to grow back to the wonder and mystery of Childhood; and presently to go upwards again to the Cities of the Mighty Pyramid, purified and sweetened of soul and mind.

And in my boyhood, I have wandered oft a week of days in that Country of Silence, and had my food with me, and slept quietly amid the memories; and gone on again, wrapped about with the quiet of the Everlasting. And the man-soul within would be drawn mightily to those places where the Great Ones of the past Eternity of the World had their Memory named; but there was that within me which ever drew me, in the ending, to the Hills of the Babes; those little hills where might be heard amid the lonesomeness of an utter quiet, a strange and wondrous echo, as of a little child calling over the hills. But how this was I know not, save by the sweet cunning of some dead Maker in the forgotten years.

And here, mayhaps by reason of this Voice of Pathos, were to be found the countless Tokens of Memory to all the babes of the Mighty Pyramid, through a thousand ages. And, odd whiles, would I come upon some Mother, sitting there lonely, or mayhaps companied by others. And by this little telling shall you know somewhat of the quietness and the wonder and the holiness of that great Country hallowed to all Memory and to Eternity and to our Dead.

And it was here, into the Country of Silence, that they brought down the Dead to their Burial. And there came down into the Country of Silence, maybe an Hundred Million, out of the Cities of the Pyramid, to be present, and to do Honour.

Now they that had charge of the Dead, did lay them upon the road which ran up unto The Gateway, even that same road which was named The Last Road. And the Road moved upwards slowly with the Dead; and the Dead went inward through The Gateway; first the poor Youths, and afterward they that had given up life that they might save them.

And as the Dead went upwards, there was a very great Silence over all the miles of the Country of Silence. But in a little while there came from afar off, a sound as of a wind wailing; and it came onwards out of the distance, and passed over the Hills of the Babes, which were a great way off. And so came anigh to the place where I stood. Even as the blowing of a sorrowful wind did it come; and I knew that all the great multitudes did sing quietly; and the singing passed onwards, and left behind it an utter silence; even as the wind doth rustle the corn, and pass onwards, and all fall to a greater seeming quietness than before. And the Dead passed inward through The Gateway, into the great light and silence of the Dome; and came out no more.

And again from beyond the far Hills of the Babes there was that sound of the millions singing; and there rose up out of the earth beneath, the voices of the underground organs; and the noise of the sorrow passed over me, and went again into the distance, and left all hushed.

And lo! as there passed inward to the silence of the Dome the last of those dead Heroes, there came again the sound from beyond the Hills of the Babes; and as it came more nigh, I knew that it was the Song of Honour, loud and triumphant, and sung by countless multitudes. And the Voices of the Organs rose up into thunder from the deep earth. And there was a great Honour done to the glory of the Dead. And afterwards, once more a silence.

Then did the Peoples of the Cities arrange themselves so that from every city whence had come a Hero, were the People of that City gathered together. And when they were so gathered, they set up Tokens of Memory to the Dead of their City. But afterwards did charge Artists to the making of sculpture great and beautiful to that same end; and now did but place Tablets against that time.

And afterwards the People did wander over that Country of Silence, and made visit and honour to their Ancestors, if such were deserving.

And presently, the mighty lifts did raise them all to the Cities of the Pyramid; and thereafter there was something more of usualness; save that ever the embrasures were full of those that watched the Youths afar upon the Great Road. And in this place I to remember how that our spy-glasses had surely some power of the Earth-Current to make greater the impulse of the light upon the eye. And they were like no spy-glass that ever you did see; but oddly shaped and to touch both the forehead and the eyes; and gave wonderful sight of the Land. But the Great Spy-Glass to be beyond all this; for it had the Eyes of it upon every side of The Mighty Pyramid, and did be truly an Huge Machine.

And to me, as I went about my duties, or peered forth through the Great Spy-Glass at the Youths upon the Road Where The Silent Ones Walk, there came at times a far faint thrilling of the aether; so that sometimes I was aware that there was the beating of the Master-Word in the night; but so strange and weak, that the Instruments had no wotting of it. And when this came, then would I call back through all the everlasting night to Naani, who was indeed Mirdath; and I would send the Master-Word with my brain-elements; and afterwards such comfort as I might.

Yet hard and bitter was the truth of my helplessness and weakness, and the utter terror and might of the Evil Forces and Monsters of the Night Land. So that I was like to have brake my heart with pondering.

And the silence would come again; and anon the weak thrilling of the Aether; but no more the far voice speaking in my soul.

Chapter V
Into the Night Land

NOW, AFTER THAT destruction which had come upon the Ten-thousand, and the fresh assurance that was upon us of the terror of the Night Land, it may be known that there could be no more thought to succour. Though, in truth, those Youths that went now upon the Road Where The Silent Ones Walk were far beyond our aid.

Yet might it be thought that we should have signalled to them, calling by the Home-Call, which was that great Voice which went forth from the Machine above the sealed base of the Mighty Pyramid. But this we might not do; for then we gave signal to the Monsters of that Land, that some were even now abroad from the Pyramid; yet we could no more than hope that the Evil Forces had no wotting of them; for, in verity, none might ever know the knowledge or the Ignorance which those Powers did possess.

Yet, it must be kept to the mind that we knew even then there was an Influence abroad in the Land, strange and quiet; so that the Instruments did not more than make record of it. And as I have surely set down ere now, we had belief that it did come from that House of Silence, afar in the Night Land, upon that low hill to the North of the Great Road. And many among the Monstruwacans feared that it was directed upon the Youths; but of this there could be no surety; and we could but wait and watch.

Now, about this time those poor Youths did draw nigh to that part of the Road Where The Silent Ones Walk, where it turned more swiftly to the North; and they to be now at no mighty distance from that grim and horrid House.

And presently we knew that the Influence had a greater Power in the Land; and I had an assuredness that it came from the House; yet no certain proof was this. But I set out my feelings to the Master Monstruwacan; and he had trust in them and in my power; moreover, he also had belief within himself that some secret Power came out from the House of Silence.

And some talk there was at times that we send the Home-Call into the night, to give warning to the Youths of our knowledge and our fear; and to entreat them to make a safe endeavour to return swiftly. Yet was this an error; and refused by the Master Monstruwacan; for it was not meet that we put the souls of those Youths in peril, until such time as we had certainty that they should be lost if we did not bestir ourselves. For, indeed, this Home-Call was as a mighty Voice, calling over the world, and did have so exceeding a noise, that it had immediately told all that Land how that some were yet abroad from the Great Redoubt. And here will I set down how that the Home-Call had no use in those ages; but had been a Call in the olden time when yet the great flying-ships went abroad over the world.

And there passed now a day and a night; and in all that time there ceased not great multitudes to peer forth into the Night Land at the Youths. For it was known concerning the Influence, and all felt that the Youths did draw nigh very speedy to their fate; and much talk there was; and many things said, and much foolish speech, and kind intent; but no courage to go forth to make further attempt to rescue; which, in truth, calls not for great astonishment, as I have surely writ or oft thought.

And in this place let me set down that the Land was, as it might be said, waked, and unquiet, and a sense of things passing in the night, and of horrid watchfulness; and there were, at this time and at that, low roars that went across the Land. And if I have not told the same before this time, it must be set to count against me and my telling; for, indeed, I should have writ it down before this place. Yet is the difficulty of my task great; and all must bear with me, and entreat for me that I have courage, so that I may come at last to strength and wisdom to tell all that I did see.

Now, in the space of this day and night, it was known that the Youths had not slept, neither had they eaten, save once, as they who had the watch through the Great Spy-Glass did affirm. But they to hasten alway at a woeful speed towards the North, along that Great Dismal Road, so that presently they must cease, or slay themselves with their endeavour.

And all this did give surety to our fears that they were under a spell from that horrid House afar in the Land; and we had an assurance that this thing was. For, presently, there came a Monstruwacan to the Master Monstruwacan to report that there had come sudden a mighty Influence into the Land; and in the same moment, as it might be, I spied through the Great Spy-Glass, and did see those Youths break swiftly from the Road Where The

Silent Ones Walk, and begin to run very swift that they might come quickly to the House of Silence.

Then did the Master Monstruwacan hesitate not; but did send the Home-Call across the world, aye, even to those poor doomed ones that hastened, unknowing, to the terror which did compel them. And immediately upon the sound, the Master did send a message to the natural eye, in set language, and made warning that they suffered themselves to be drawn to their destruction by a Force that came from within the House of Silence.

And he besought them to put forth the strength of their spirits, and do battle for their souls; and if they could in no wise compass a victory over *that which drew them onwards*, to slay themselves quickly, ere they went into that House to the horror of utter destruction.

And in all the Pyramid was there a great silence; for the bellowing of the Home-Call bred a quietness, because of that which it did portend; and it was swiftly known by the millions that the Master Monstruwacan did plead for the souls of the Youths; and there went forth, unknowingly, a counter-force from the Mighty Pyramid, by reason of the prayers and soul-wishings of the countless millions.

And the counter-force was plain to my inward hearing, and beat all the aether of the world into a surge of supplication; so that it stunned my spirit with the great power of it. And it seemed to me, as it were, that there was a vast spiritual-noise in all the night; and I spied tremblingly through the Great Spy-Glass, and lo! the Youths did cease from their swift running, and were come together in a crowd, and had a seeming to be confused; as might some who have waked suddenly from sleep, to find that they walked in their sleep, and had come to a strange place.

Then came there a great roar from all the millions that spied from the embrasures – from nigh five hundred thousand embrasures they did look, and I count not the great View-Tables. And the shouting rose up like to the roaring of a mighty wind of triumph, yet was it over-early to sound for victory. For the counter-force which came from the intensity of so many wills blent to one intent, was brake, and the Evil Force which came forth out of the House did draw the Youths again; so that they heeded not their salvation; but turned once again to their running.

And the Mighty Pyramid was full of a shaken silence, and immediately of lamentation and sorrow and horror at this thing. But in that moment there did happen a fresh wonder; for there grew suddenly before those poor Youths, billows of mist – as it had been of pure white fire, shining very chill; yet giving no light upon them.

And the mist of cold fire stayed their way, so that we had knowledge that there fought for the souls of them, one of those sweet Powers of Goodness, which we had belief did strive to ward our spirits at all times from those Forces of Evil and Destruction. And all the millions saw the thing; but some with a great clearness, and many doubtful; yet were all advanced more in spiritual sight and hearing than the normal Peoples of this Age.

But of them all, none had the Night-Hearing, to know a soul having speech in the aether half across the world. Yet, as I have said, some there had been aforetime who were thus given the Hearing, even as was I.

And there came a Monstruwacan to the Master Monstruwacan to make report that the Influence had ceased to work upon the Instruments; and by this thing we knew that in verity the Force which proceeded out from the House of Silence was cut off from us, and from those Youths; and we had assurance that there fought a very mighty Power for the salvation of the souls of the Youths.

And all the Peoples were silent, save for an underbreath of wonder and talk; for all were utter stirred with hope and fear, perceiving that the Youths had some chance given unto them to return.

And whilst the Youths yet wavered in their minds, as I perceived with the Great Spy-Glass, and the knowledge of my soul, and of my natural wit, lo! the Master Monstruwacan sent once more the great Voice of the Home-Call abroad into the Land; and immediately besought those Youths for the sake of their souls and the love which their Mothers had for them, to come swiftly Homewards, whilst they had yet this great Power to shield them, and allow them sweet sanity.

And I thought that some did look towards the Pyramid, as that they answered to the mighty Voice of the Home-Call, and did read the message which the Master Monstruwacan made to them. But in a moment they faced about, seeming to have a good obedience to one who did always lead; and of whom I had inquired, and found to be one named Aschoff, who was a great athlete of the Nine-Hundredth-City. And this same Aschoff, out of the boldness and bravery of his heart, did make, unwitting, to destroy the souls of them all; for he went forward and leapt into the billows of the bright shining fire that made a Barrier in the way of their Destruction.

And immediately the fire ceased from its shining, and gave way and sank and grew to a nothingness; and Aschoff of the Nine-Hundredth-City began again to run towards the House of Silence; and all they that were with him, did follow faithfully, and ceased not to run.

And they came presently to the low Hill whereon was that horrid House; and they went up swiftly – and they were two hundred and fifty, and wholesome of heart, and innocent; save for a natural waywardness of spirit.

And they came to the great open doorway that 'hath been open since the Beginning,' and through which the cold steadfast light and the inscrutable silence of Evil 'hath made for ever a silence that may be felt in all the Land.' And the great, uncased windows gave out the silence and the light – aye, the utter silence of an unholy desolation.

And Aschoff ran in through the great doorway of silence, and they that followed. And they nevermore came out or were seen by any human.

And it must be known that the Mothers and the Fathers of those Youths looked out into the Night Land, and saw that thing which came to pass.

And all the people were silent; but some said presently that the Youths would come forth again; yet the people knew in their hearts that the young men had gone in to Destruction; for, in truth, there was that in the night which spoke horror to the souls of all, and a sudden utter quiet in all the Land.

But unto me (that had the Night-Hearing) there came a great Fear of that which might be whispered into my spirit, out of the Quietness of the night – of the agony of those young men. Yet there came no sound, to the hearing of the soul; neither then nor in all the years that were to come; for, in verity, had those Youths passed into a Silence of which the heart cannot think.

And here will I tell how that the strange Quiet which did fill all the Land, seeming to brood within the night, was horrid beyond all the roarings which had passed over the darkness in the time that went before; so that it had given my spirit some rest and assurance to hear but the far-echoing, low thunder of the Great Laughter, or the whining which was used at times to sound in the night from the South-East, where were the Silver-fire Holes that opened before the Thing that Nods. Or the Baying of the Hounds, or the Roaring of the Giants, or any of those dreadful sounds that did often pass through the night. For they could not have offended me as did that time of silence; and so shall you judge how dreadful was that quiet, which did hold so much of horror.

And surely it will be known that none had thinkings now, even in idle speech, that any should have power to succour the Peoples of the Lesser Redoubt. Neither, as I have said, had any the knowledge of the place where it did stand.

And so was it made plain that those Peoples must suffer and come unhelped and alone to their end; which was a sad and dreadful thought to any. Yet had those within the Great Pyramid come already to much sorrow and calamity because that some had made attempt in this matter. And there had been for gain, only failure, and the sorrow of Mothers, and the loneliness of Wives, and of kin. And now this dread horror upon us, which concerned those lost Youths.

Now, as may be conceived, this *sure knowledge* that we might give no succour to the People of the Lesser Redoubt, weighed heavy upon my heart; for I had, maybe with foolishness, held vague hopes and wonders concerning our power to make expedition secretly into the Night, to discover that Lesser Pyramid, and rescue those poor thousands; and above all, as may be thought, had I the thought of that sweet moment in which I should step forward out of the night and all mystery and terror, and put forth mine arms to Naani, saying: "I am That One." And knowing, in my soul, that she that had been mine in that bygone Eternity, should surely know me upon the instant; and call out swiftly, and come swiftly, and be again unto me in that age, even as she had been in this.

And to think upon it, and to know that this thing should never be; but that, even in that moment of thought, she that had been mine in these olden days of sweetness, might be even then suffering horror in the Power of some foul Monster, was like a kind of madness; so that nearly I could seize the Diskos, and run forth unprepared into the evil and terror of the Night Land, that I should make one attempt to come to that Place where she abode, or else to cast off my life in the attempt.

And oft did I call to Naani; and always I sent the Master-Word beating through the night, that she might have assurance that it was indeed I that did speak unto her spirit, and no foul thing or Monster, spelling evil and lies unto her.

And oft did I make to instruct her that never should she be tempted forth from the shelter of that Redoubt in which she did live, by any message out of the night; but always to await the Master-Word; and, moreover, to have a sure knowledge that none that was her Friend would ever seek to entice her into the night.

And this way and that way would I speak with Naani, sending my words silently with my brain-elements; yet was it doleful and weariful and dreadful always to have speech into the dark, and never to hear the answering beat of the Master-Word, and the sweet, faint voice whispering within my soul. Yet, once and again, would I have knowledge that the aether did thrill about me, weakly, and to mine inward hearing it would seem that the Master-Word did beat faintly in the night; and thereafter would my heart have a little comfort, in that I had assurance, of a kind, that the love-maid of my memory-dreams did still live.

And constant, I put forth my soul to hark; so that my health failed me, with the effort of my harking; and I would chide my being, that I had not a wiser control; and so make a fight to do sanely.

Yet, day by day, did my heart grow more weary and restless; for, indeed, it did seem that life was but a very little matter, against so great a loss as my heart did feel to suffer.

And oft, at this time and that, did there come a Voice speaking plainly out of the night, and did purport to be the voice of Naani; but ever I did say the Master-Word unto the Voice, and the Voice had no power by which it could make the one answer. Yet I jeered not at the Voice, to show contempt of its failing to bewit me; but let the matter bide; and the Voice would be silent a time; and again would make a calling unto me; but never did I make speech with it (for therein lies the danger to the soul), but always did speak the Master-Word to its silencing; and thereafter would shut the thing from my memory, and think only upon sweet and holy matters, as it might be Truth and Courage, but more often of Naani, which was both sweet and holy to my spirit and heart and being.

And so it was as I have set down, there were Monsters without in the Night that did torment me; having, it may be, intent to lure me unto destruction; or indeed it doth chance that they had no hope but to plague me with malice.

And, as may be thought, all this considering of my trouble, and the giving of my strength unto Naani through the night of the world, that she might have comfort and help, did work upon me; so that I grew thin, plainly to the eye of those that loved me.

And the Master Monstruwacan, he that did love me, as I were his son, chid me gently, and had wise speech with me; so that I but loved him the more, yet without having gain of health; for my heart destroyed me, as it doth if love be held back and made always to weep.

And it may be thought strange that my Mother and my Father did not talk also with me; but I had neither Mother nor Father those many years; and this thing I should have set down early; so that none should waste thought pondering to no end. But the blame is to my telling.

Now, concerning my love-trouble, there did happen a certain thing which gave me to decide; for one night I waked from a sore troubled sleep, and it did seem that Naani did call my name, mine olden love name, and in a voice of utter anguish and with beseeching. And I sat up in the bed, and sent the Master-Word into the Night, with my brain-elements; and presently all about me there was the solemn beat of the Master-Word, answering; but weak, and gone faint, that scarce I might hear it.

And I called again with my brain-elements unto Naani, that was Mirdath; and spoke to give her assurance, and to haste to tell unto me that which was so wrong and pitiful with her. And who shall be amazed that I was shaken with the eagerness of my spirit, in that it was so long since Naani had spoken clear within my soul; and now behold, her voice.

Yet, though I did call many a time unto the everlasting night, there came no more the voice of Naani, speaking strangely within my spirit; but only at times a weak thrilling of the aether about me.

And, at the last I grew maddened with the sorrow of this thing, and the sense and knowledge of harm about the maid; and I stood upright upon my feet, and I raised my hands, and gave word and honour unto Naani through all the blackness of the night, that I would no more abide within the Mighty Pyramid to my safety, whilst she, that had been mine Own through Eternity, came to horror and destruction by the Beasts and Evil Powers of that Dark World. And I gave the word with my brain-elements, and bade her to be of heart; for that until I died I would seek her. But out of the Darkness there came naught but the silence.

Then I clothed me swiftly, and went up quickly to the Tower of Observation, that I might speak instant with the Master Monstruwacan; for my heart burned in me to intention, and to be doing speedily that which I had set upon myself to do.

And I came to the Master Monstruwacan, and told all to him; and how that I did mean no more to suffer in quiet and to no end; but to make adventure into the Night Land, that I find Naani, or perchance find a swift peace from this my long troubling.

Now, when the Master Monstruwacan heard that which I had to say, it sat heavily upon him, and he besought me long and many times that I refrain from this thing; for that none might achieve so great a task; but that I should be lost in my Youth before many days were gone by. Yet to all his speech I said naught, save that this thing was laid upon me, and even as I had promised, so should I make to act.

And in the ending, the Master Monstruwacan perceived that I was set to this thing, and not to be moved; and he did put it to me how that I had grown to leanness, with so much troubling, and that I should have wisdom to wait awhile, that I put on my full strength.

But even as I was, so would I go; and this I told to him, gently; and showed how that the thing was meet and helpful to the safety of my soul; for that my strength was still in me; yet was I sweeter in spirit because that I stood lean and pure, and much poor dross and littleness had been burned from me; so that fear was not in me. And all do I lay to the count of my love, which doth purify and make sweet and fearless the human heart.

And because I was even as I have said, so was I the less in trouble of the Forces of Evil; for long and sore had been my Preparation of Spirit; and I wot that none had ever gone forth into the Darkness, so long withholden from that which doth weaken and taint the spirit.

And here let me set down how that the Three Days of Preparation, which were Proper to those that willed to go forth into the Night Land, had for their chief aim the cleansing of the spirit; so that the Powers of Evil did have a less ableness to harm.

But also it was, as I have said, that none should go forth in ignorance of the full dreadfulness of all that held the Night; for it was at the Preparation that there was made known certain horrors that were not told unto the young; and of horrid mutilations, and of abasements of the soul, that did shake the heart with fear, if but they were whispered into the hearing. And these things were not set down in any book that might be lightly come by; but were warded and safe locked by the Master of The Preparation, in the Room of Preparation.

And, indeed, when I did hear that which presently I was to hear, I had wonder in my heart that ever any went out into the Night Land; or that ever the Room of Preparation should have other than Students that meant not to go forth, but only to achieve some knowledge of that which hath been done, and mayhaps shall be once again.

Yet, in verity, is this but the way of the human heart; and hath always been, and will be so in all the years, for ever. For to adventure is the lust of Youth; and to leave Safety is the natural waywardness of the spirit; and who shall reprove or regret; for it were sorrowful that this Spirit of Man should cease. Yet must it not be thought that I do uphold fightings to the death or to mutilation, *between man and man*; but rather do sorrow upon this thought.

Now, when the morrow came, if thus I shall speak of that which was outwardly even as the night, though changing alway within the Mighty Pyramid, I went unto the Room of Preparation; and the Door was closed upon me; and I underwent the Full Preparation; that I might have full power and aid to come to success through all the terror of the Night Land.

And three days and three nights did I abide within the Room of Preparation; and upon the fourth day was mine armour brought unto me; and the Master of the Preparation stood away from me, silent and with sorrow upon his face; but touching me not, neither coming anigh to aid me; nor having any speech with me; for none might crowd upon me, or cause me to answer.

And, presently, was I clad with the grey armour; and below the armour a close-knit suit of special shaping and texture, to have the shape of the armour, and that I might not die by the cold of the Night Land. And I placed upon me a scrip of food and drink, that might keep the life within me for a great time, by reason of its preparation; and this lay ready to me, with the armour, and was stitched about with the Mark of Honour; so that I knew loving women thus to speed me.

And when all was done and made ready, I took up the Diskos, and bowed in silence to the Master of the Preparation; and he went towards the door, and opened it; and signalled that the People stand back; so that I might go forth untouched. And the People stood back; for many had crowded to the door of the Room of Preparation, so that I knew how that my story must be to the heart of all, in all the Cities of the Great Redoubt; for to come unbidden anigh that Door was against the Lesser Law, and that any erred in this matter, betokened much.

And I went out through the Door; and there was a mighty lane of people unto the Great Lift. And about the Great Lift, as I went downwards, did the countless millions stand; and all in a great silence; but having dear sympathy in their souls; yet loyal unto my safety, in that none in all the Mighty Pyramid did make speech unto me, or call out aught. And as I went downward through the miles, lo! all the aether of the world seemed to be surged with the silent prayers and speedings of those quiet multitudes.

And I came at last unto the Great Gate; and behold the dear Master Monstruwacan did stand in full armour, and with the Diskos, to do me honour, with the Full Watch, as I went forth. And I looked at him, quietly, and he looked unto me, and I bent my head to show respect; and he made silent salute with the Diskos; and afterwards I went onwards towards the Great Gateway.

And they made dim the lights in the Great Causeway, that there should no glare go forth into the Land, when the Gate was opened; and behold, they opened not the lesser gate within the greater, for me; but did honour my journey, in that they swung wide the Great Gate itself, through which a monstrous army might pass. And there was an utter silence all about the Gate; and in the hushed light the two thousand that made the Full Watch, held up each the Diskos, silently, to make salute; and humbly, I held up the Diskos reversed, and went forward into the Dark.

The complete and unabridged text is available online, *from flametreepublishing.com/extras*

Silent Night

Liam Hogan

IT WAS the night that everything was silent.

In homes across the country people cowered beneath their Christmas trees. Only real ones would do, the pine scent masking the fear. The trees groaned with brightly coloured baubles, the more the merrier to try and confuse Santa's sensors. It used to be said that he knew if you were naughty or nice and that he'd come for you if you'd been bad, but the truth was much simpler. Any noise, any movement, *anything* that gave away your hiding place and that would be that.

In one living room, made double height by the collapse of the floor above, there were two such trees. Under the larger, a family huddled. The youngest was a mere four years old and small for her age and so, perhaps, the only one among them who would be truly safe. But the sooner she learnt the dangers of this night, the better. Her sister, eighteen months her senior, held her hand and snuggled close, stilling her whimpers. The night was cold and the small fire eating away at the dampened Yule log offered little in the way of either heat or light.

Under the smaller tree the eldest child, Tommy, lay listening to the wind howl, his grandpa beside him. He'd begged and cajoled to be allowed this privilege. Earlier, Gramps had ruined the traditional telling of the holiday tale and had been in disgrace ever since, but, as the long night had dragged on and the danger lurked ever closer, Mother and Father had finally relented. Besides, Tommy was getting bigger every year and there really wasn't that much space under either tree.

After a long while listening to the noises of the night, Tommy finally said, "Gramps...?"

Gramps started and fearfully checked his watch. It was still early; Santa wasn't due for another hour. He let out his breath in a plume of vapour.

"Yes Tommy?" he said quietly. As they were lying close together under the prickly cover of branches and needles, he could speak just above a whisper and still have Tommy hear him.

"That story you told. Is it true?"

Gramps sighed. He'd already gotten into a heap of trouble on that account. And yet he was the oldest person in the village. At 43 he was perhaps the oldest for miles around. It was hard to tell because travelling wasn't as easy as it had once been. When his time came – which could very well be tonight – who then would know the truth?

"About the presents? Yes, Tommy, it's true."

Tommy took a moment to digest the full horror of this. His parents had passed it off as a sick joke, but he'd known it wasn't the sort of thing that Gramps did. Which was why he'd been so eager to leave the family tree for the first time and join Gramps under his.

"What sort of presents?" he asked.

Gramps blinked. Truth be told, he could hardly remember. He'd been younger than Tommy was now, that first year.

"Oh," he muttered, "Wonderful things. Magical things. Games that made moving pictures and sounds. Make believe worlds of bright colours, toy cars..."

Tommy knew all about cars, but couldn't understand why you'd want to make a toy out of them. They were dull, uninteresting things and only good for hiding in or sheltering from the rain.

"Why," Tommy gulped, "Why did he... it... change?"

Gramps thought for a moment. This was the crux of it and he wished he understood it better, but he'd been so young. On that first night, very few kids his age or older had survived; those who had been lucky enough to take shelter beneath the Christmas tree, amongst the presents that would never be opened.

"There was a war," he began tentatively. Of this, he was quite certain. He remembered one of the toys he'd gotten the year before, a tank. He remembered how his mother had not approved of the way he'd lined it up against his other toys, the foam shells knocking them over one by one to the sound of electronic explosions, while his dad looked on beaming.

"There was a war," he repeated, "A war in distant lands, a war won by drones. There were no prisoners, no wounded, and no civilian casualties. Nobody who wasn't a terrorist, wasn't a baddie. The drones went from house to house looking for hidden weapons, seeking out and killing the enemy. And that was that. The war that had lasted for ever came to an end in a single fortnight."

It was amazing how it all came back. For almost 40 years, he'd hardly thought of it, he'd been too busy surviving. They all had. After the adults had gone...

But he was getting ahead of himself.

"It was the first Christmas after. The celebrations were barely over and everyone was happy, everyone was joyous. You know that word? I haven't used it in a long while. Joyous. We all went to bed that Christmas Eve, certain that there were only good things in our future."

"Under the Christmas tree?" asked Tommy.

"What?" Gramps said, a moment of confusion. "No... This was before all of that. We slept in our normal beds, but with stockings hung on the bedposts and a plate of mince pies and carrots put out for Santa."

Tommy looked at him disbelieving. "Carrots? For Santa?"

Gramps laughed, a muffled exhalation that shook the broken red bauble nearest his head and showered them in pine needles. "No, not for Santa. For the reindeers. Donner, and Blitzen. And, of course, good ol' Rudolph!"

Tommy bit his lip. So many things that he didn't understand. It was like a nonsense poem, like the battered copy of *Alice in Wonderland* Gramps used to read to them, until one of the wild dogs ripped it apart. Was this all made up as well, he wondered?

Gramps shook his head, slowly. "But the reindeer didn't come that year, or ever again. Nor did Santa. Not the Santa I remember. The *real* one. Not these killing ones." He patted Tommy's head lightly and fell silent.

Tommy waited for a moment, then another. "What happened?"

Gramps took a deep breath, shaking his head to hide his trembling. "I awoke to the sound of screams, of guns. I didn't know where I was for a moment and then the bedroom door was flung open and a dark figure stood in the doorway. 'Hide!' my father said. 'Quick! They're coming! Hide! For God's sake, hide!'

"It was the last I ever saw of him... alive. I hid under the bed with my brother. I heard more shouts, my mom screaming at my dad for the combination to the gun safe, my dad telling her not to be stupid, that guns wouldn't help, not against *them*. My dad was in the army, before the drones, so I guess he knew. The front door slammed open, or perhaps shut, and there were a couple of loud bangs and then... and then there was silence.

"We could still hear the shots, but they were distant and growing more so. I was shaking and desperately needed to use the bathroom, so I edged out from under the bed while my brother hissed at me to stay put. I crept downstairs. The front room flickered with coloured lights from the tree and, as I looked about wondering where my parents had gone, something red flitted past the window, a strange humming noise that suddenly stopped."

Gramps ran his worn hands over his face. "I dived under the Christmas tree just as the door was blown off its hinges, just as my brother was creeping down the stairs to see where I'd got to. I... I like to think it was quick for him and that from what everyone who survived said, he wouldn't have been safe under the bed anyway. But I sometimes think I should have stayed and shared my brother's fate, whatever it was to be." There was a tremor in Gramps voice and something hot and wet splashed onto Tommy's hand.

"You see, in those days there were so very many targets, they didn't check as closely as they do now. I even pushed aside a branch and *saw* the damned thing hovering over a lifeless body. You don't do that anymore. You see it, it sees you, end of. But somehow I survived. It was a drone, of course, dressed in a red cloak. Someone's sick idea of a Santa."

Tommy gasped. "But... I thought you said we'd *won* the war?"

"We did," Gramps said grimly. "All the drones were ours. They were brought home and put into storage. We don't know for sure what happened next, but smarter boys than I have guessed, and it makes a strange kind of sense."

Gramps levered himself up slightly so he could look Tommy straight in the face. "Some idiot down the depot gets bored of standing guard over a warehouse of tin soldiers. Maybe he's had a Christmas drink or two, so he decides to reprogram them. Decides to turn them into the Military's very own Santas, delivering presents to the whole country.

"Only, he didn't do a very good job of it. We guess he managed to remove most of the safeguards and retarget the drones on the civilians: the children, the adults. Everyone except the very young. Thank God he left that protocol in! The least capable of hiding, of staying quiet; they're the only ones who turned out to be safe.

"He probably tried to disable the weapon systems as well, but... Did they re-arm themselves? Or did he simply mess up?

"I hope he was their first victim, when they awoke as programmed that first Christmas Eve," Gramps said bitterly, shaking his head. "When I think of my parents, my brother and all the many others... I hope he was the first."

He was silent a moment and then, wearily, he finished his tale.

"We survivors didn't know then that Santa would be back. That he would be an annual event. We lost a lot of people that second year: all those who laughed at the childish fears of the more timid kids, or were simply too busy looking after all the little babies to count the days.

"We lost more the year we thought we were grown up enough to attack the depot. I was there, on the fringes. We thought, since it wasn't Christmas, they'd be defenceless. We were wrong. We did manage to kill a few of them and more have fallen by the wayside since. There's no one to repair them, after all. Perhaps, one day, they'll all be dead. Perhaps even in your lifetime. Until then... thank God they weren't programmed to cope with Christmas trees."

"Gramps?" whispered Tommy. "What was Santa like, before?"

"Before? Oh, he was a big, jolly man. Dressed in red, just like the drones, but with a flowing white beard and a hearty laugh. He had a sack of presents slung over his shoulder and everywhere he went, he used to call out, 'Peace and goodwill to all men,' he used to say, 'Peace –'"

Gramps fell abruptly silent and held his roughened finger against Tommy's lips. In the distance, the first shots rang out in the cold night air.

Santa had arrived.

Changed

Jennifer Hudak

FOR MOST people, breath travels unnoticed. I am not most people. I think about every breath. It is hard to think about anything else. My breath is work. I pull each one in with difficulty, then push it out through the same narrow passage. There is never, ever enough of it. It whistles like the wind through the boards we nail over the windows.

The only window left uncovered is the one in the attic, and that's Hector's perch. He's been up there watching for the away team; now he tumbles down the stairs, calling, "They're back! Let 'em in!"

Charles and Philly, the strongest two who've stayed behind, get to work clearing the obstructions in front of the door. The house had been so quiet, but the arrival of the away team punctures that silence with noise: heavy wooden furniture groaning as it's pushed aside, metal screeching against metal, the squeal of rarely-used hinges. Then, voices that carry across the room, words spoken by men and women with lungs full of air.

By the time I reach the entryway, the door is closed again, bookcases and chests pushed back against it, gaping spaces hastily nailed over. The away team gathers into what used to be the kitchen, weighed down with boxes and totes whose contents they dump onto the sturdy island. Hector bobs and weaves among them, eager as a puppy, trying to catch a glimpse of the spoils.

"Chocolate! There's chocolate, Zadie!" Before anyone can stop him, his hand darts in between bodies to snatch a small handful and then withdraws like a rattlesnake, so fast. They barely notice him, but it wouldn't have mattered. They indulge him. He's young and strong, and eager to live. We are all of us living the same day over and over, the same struggle, the same fight; through Hector's eyes, we catch a glimpse of the future. We see what might be when all of this is over.

He presents a chocolate to me, already warm from his hand. It's coin-shaped, and wrapped in gold foil. It's also old, I see when I unwrap it: hardened, with a coating of white crystals. It doesn't matter. Everything is old. I place it on my tongue and it melts slowly, turning soft and slick. The crystals crunch between my teeth.

"Thanks, Hector."

He juts his chin toward the island, now covered with cans and boxes and bags. "Go see if they got inhalers," he says, and then takes the stairs two at a time on his way back up to the attic.

It's always like this, when they come back: a flurry of activity, movement and noise. I'm not like Hector; I wait until the crowd begins to disperse before I sidle up to Frieda. I don't say anything, just lift my eyebrows slightly to ask her a question, *the* question, the same question I ask every time they come back from a supply run.

"I'm sorry, Zee," she says. "I didn't see any; we didn't have much time in there." She murmurs her answer, but Al hears anyway.

"Tell her the truth, Frieda." Al's been leaning against the far wall, but now he stands upright and crosses the room toward us. "Tell her you almost got ambushed looking for those goddamn inhalers."

I look at Frieda in alarm, and she shakes her head. "It wasn't like that. We had to go in there anyway. It wasn't just for the inhalers."

"That's not the point." Al is talking to Frieda but he keeps his eyes on me, moving closer with each sentence. "The question I keep asking is, why the fuck should we risk our lives to keep her breathing? Even with meds she can't do shit. She serves no purpose here. She's a fucking drain on our resources." He's inches away from me now, and so tall that I have to crane my neck so that I can examine his face. Everything is in place. He's an asshole, but he's still Al. His barrel chest rises and falls, his belly expands and contracts over his worn leather belt. It costs him nothing, this easy breath.

"Give it a rest, Al," says Frieda.

Al's eyes flick toward her. Then one side of his mouth lifts in a sneer that exposes the skeleton grin beneath. He turns and strolls back into what used to be the closed-in porch, his boots echoing on the hardwoods. The breath I release is paper-thin. "We'll find some next time," Frieda promises. "Don't worry."

"You were followed!" Hector calls from the top of the stairs. "Just one. Climbing up the hill on the south side."

Charles swears and grabs a crowbar on the way to the living room. He pries a small plank away from the window, creating just enough space for a shotgun and a scope.

"I swear, we were careful," says Frieda. "Nothing followed us."

"Could just be coincidence," says Charles, peering through the scope. "Anyway, it's just a little one. A kid."

The kids are the worst. Early on, when this house still belonged just to Bobby and me, we caught one in a snare trap. It looked just like a regular boy hanging there in the net, dangling a few feet above our heads. "Please help me," it whimpered, reaching its little fingers through the net. "I'm lost."

"Wait," I said, when Bobby shouldered his gun. "How do you know it's changed?"

"We can't take the chance," Bobby said, sounding grim.

"But it's just a child!"

"We don't know that. If it's changed, and we let it go…" The boy swayed back and forth from the tree, watching us with wide, round eyes. "This is the only way." Bobby's voice shook, and he took a breath to steady himself.

I closed my eyes before he did it. The shotgun rang out just once, echoing across the hilltop. Bobby'd been hunting his whole life; he was a good shot. And he was right, we couldn't take the chance. But I always wondered if that kid had just been a kid.

Nowadays, there's no question; anyone wandering around by themselves, especially a child, is changed. Has to be. Charles squeezes the trigger once, then once more. "Got it," he says. He pulls the gun away from the window and Philly steps right in to board up the gap. Even though I can't see it, I can picture the body sprawled on the hillside, where it will stay until the next supply run, unless an animal gets to it first. The kid would have dropped as soon as the bullet hit home, like a light bulb turning off. I wonder if the change is like that, if the transition from living to unliving is that instant and abrupt. I wonder if it hurts, or if it's so subtle that you don't realize what's happened until you're looking out from the other side of the mirror.

My breath is as thin as a whisper, and I edge away from the crowd so that I can count. That's a trick Bobby taught me, when things had just started to get bad and there was no way to refill my prescription. "Relax," he'd say, when the terror made my throat thicken. "It's easier when you relax. Breathe in for a count of three, breathe out for a count of three." He'd place both hands on my shoulders and look into my weepy eyes, and we'd count together.

Leaning against a wall, I count, and I try to remember what it was like before, what *I* was like before. There, on the kitchen island, was where I'd roll out piecrusts. Over in the living room was where Bobby and I would push back the furniture and dance on Saturday nights. One of us would begin to laugh, and the other would join in, and our laughter would tumble and grow like a snowball rolled on a hillside.

Breathe in, one, two, three.

Breathe out, one, two, three.

I pull air in. I push it out. I count the days until the next supply run. I count the breaths I will need to take before then.

* * *

In the beginning, before the mail stopped and the televisions and radios dissolved into static, journalists and reporters devoted all their energy to the change, but you could sum up every article in one word: *why?* Was it a virus escaped from the lab? A medical experiment gone awry? There were those who claimed aliens, demons, punishment from a vengeful god displeased with the world and its creatures. Some people – the poets, the romantics, the very young and the very naïve – claimed that the whole thing was about desire. You had to want to be changed, they said. You had to ask for it. No one really says that anymore.

The truth of the matter is no one knows how it started. No one knows what the changed really are, because anyone who has gotten close enough to one hasn't lived to talk about it. We know that sometimes they kill the people they find instead of changing them – we've seen the bodies they've left behind, ripped apart as if for sport – but no one knows how they decide.

No one knows which is worse, to be killed or to be changed. This is the hardest truth to accept.

Maybe it would have been easier if they stumbled around in tattered clothes and tattered skin; as it is, when someone changes, they don't change all that much. If you know a person, you can almost always tell. It's like looking at a mirror image of someone – things just look *wrong* even if you can't explain why – but it's easy to miss if you're not looking closely. In the beginning we lost a lot of good people because the buddy they thought would keep them safe turned out to be changed. These days, you tend to find a small group of survivors and stick with them. They become your family. After a while, you know each other inside and out, so if someone gets changed, you'll see it right away.

I lucked into this group, and there's no other way to say it. Frieda says they're the lucky ones, to have found me, but what she means is that they're lucky to have found my house. It's way out of town, smack-dab in the center of acres of land, which is why I managed to stay alive for so long by myself. We usually don't see any changed out this far, and any stragglers who try to scrabble up the hill are completely exposed and easy to shoot.

I don't even know how Bobby found this place, back when he first bought it. He didn't tell me he was looking, didn't tell me he was spending hours fixing the place up until the day of our wedding. He barely had any savings, so it must have been a real shithole when he bought it, but by the time he brought me out here it was a beautiful thing: gleaming white with dark green shutters, sitting proudly on its hilltop. I was still in my wedding dress when Bobby carried me over the threshold, and when my train brushed the floor there was no dirt for it to gather. Even during dry spells when the ground was so parched the soil lifted up into the air in sinister particles, Bobby kept our house cleaner than a new penny. He knew what dust did to me even back when I had an inhaler stashed in every room, how it made me cough and wheeze. He took care of me, right up until the day he took the truck to town to find more ammunition and never came back.

No one here asks me what happened to Bobby. They don't have to.

* * *

After Hector has scanned the hillside and given the all clear, he comes back downstairs to try to snatch more chocolate. Everyone else goes back to sorting the supplies, counting cans and boxes, cataloguing jars and tubes. I've tried to help out in the past but I always seem to be in the way. Back when this was my house, mine and Bobby's, the cans were stacked in the cupboard, on the third shelf. Now they're lined up on the large shelves just inside the pantry, and I can't get used to it, just like I can't get used to the people sleeping on couches and floors, and the mess in the bathroom, and the dust: the dust that piles up everywhere, that stays sealed in the house along with all of our exhalations. This is not the house I remember.

The only place that still feels like home is the quilting room, near what used to be the back door, where I sleep. It's not much bigger than a closet, but Bobby built me a piecing table and installed racks to hold my fabric. My old sewing machine is still in the corner, although we can't use it now that the electricity's gone down.

I'm the only one who sleeps here because it's so small. There's no door, but it's cozy enough that it still feels private. I sit cross-legged on the floor, next to the boarded-up window, and I imagine that I can smell the tea roses that used to bloom outside. Maybe they're still blooming, but I have no way of knowing; no one's allowed outside unless it's strictly necessary. I'm not even sure I want to see what the roses look like after years of neglect. They're probably dried-up husks, or eaten by wildlife, or choked by weeds. It's better if I remember the way they used to be.

I hear Al's boots coming down the hallway and I shrink back into the corner, hoping he'll walk on past, that he's just on his way to the back bedroom. But he stops in the quilting room doorway, his eyes scanning until he spots me. Everything about him bristles. "That one that followed us," he says. "That one's on you. You know that, don't you?" He moves into the room. I can feel myself start to panic, can feel my shoulders hitch up every time I inhale. "It's funny," he says. "The changed? They don't breathe. That's one of the things that makes them so hard to kill. We can't drown 'em. Can't choke 'em. Cuz they don't breathe." While he talks, he wanders in casual arcs back and forth, closing in on me with every pass. "*You* don't breathe," he says.

I close my eyes and imagine Bobby's face in front of my own, his rough, calloused hands warming my shoulders. *In, one, two, three. Out, one, two, three.*

"You don't breathe," he says again. "So what really separates you from them?"

"I haven't changed," I say, air whistling through my words.

"See, now, I don't think that's true." Al points at a cluster of photographs on the piecing table, pictures of me and Bobby. On our wedding day. Posing proudly in front of our new truck. In our bathing suits, standing under a waterfall, our mouths wide with laughter. "You think you're still that woman? You're not that woman anymore. No matter which way you look."

The room feels as close as a coffin. The muscles across my chest and neck pull with each inhalation. Al's nearness is a weight pressing the air out of my lungs.

"You've changed, alright. Worthless. Breathless." Al squats down and leans his face so close to mine that all I can see is his mouth, his nose; all I can breathe is his carbon dioxide. He reaches up one finger and drags it down the length of my cheek. I close my eyes and count while air whistles through my windpipe.

Which is why I don't hear the voice right away.

It's airy and soft, like a whisper, like my labored breath. But then it says my name.

"*Zaaaaaaa-die*," it calls.

My eyes snap open. Al is so close I can't see him clearly; he's all gritted teeth and sharply stubbled skin. I place one hand on his chest. "Did you hear that?" I wheeze.

Al looks down at my hand, surprised for an instant, before he grabs my wrist so tightly that I can feel the pressure in my bones.

"*Zaaaaaaa-die*." Al hears it this time; his eyes flick up. The voice is coming from just outside the window. It sounds like a breeze whooshing through a tree full of leaves.

It almost sounds like Bobby.

"*Let me in, Zadie.*"

"Fuck," Al says, stumbling away from me. Released from his grip, I fall heavily to the floor. "Fuck!"

Then the shouting begins throughout the house, getting louder and louder as more people realize what's going on. I hear Hector's feet racing up the attic steps. "They're all around us!" he calls, fear rendering his voice unrecognizable. "Where'd they all come from?"

"Al!" yells Frieda. "Where the hell are you?"

Al is already thundering down the hallway, his footsteps ringing against the wooden floor like gunshots. I can hear the chaos from my room. The sighting of a single one of the changed, or even a small group, wouldn't cause this much confusion and panic. We've practiced the drill but this is the first time it's for real. I know, without looking, what's happening out there: weapons passed from hand to hand. Faces peering at faces, to make sure that none of them have already gotten in. A few boards hastily nailed before everyone retreats into the center of the room, back-to-back, wide-eyed with terror.

I should be out there with them, in the large group. I know this. All alone, I'll be the first one picked off. But I don't move. Moving takes breath, and I have none to spare. I'm sprawled on the floor where Al left me, counting. It doesn't matter. Because Bobby is outside.

"*I've come home*," he's singing in that Bobby but not-Bobby voice. His fingernails scritch against the window-boards like mice in the attic. "*Let me in.*"

In, one, two, three.

Out, one, two, three.

"*Relax*," soothes Bobby, and I look up to see a finger with a ragged nail working its way through a single crack. "*It's easier when you relax.*" Three fingers now, impossibly strong, wiggling the board and prying the nails loose.

In, one, two.

Out, one, two.

"*Things will be just like they used to be. Like nothing ever happened at all.*" The board pulls away and a whole arm comes through the window. One by one, the wooden planks break and splinter, and through the gaping hole comes the scent of freshly-mown grass, rain-soaked soil, and tea roses. I'm weak with relief.

One more push, and the rest of the planks fall away like matchsticks. He steps over the sill with his long, sturdy legs, and he's standing right in front of me. I look into his face. It's like Bobby just took a small step sideways. Like a picture of Bobby hung slightly off plumb.

In, one.

Out, one.

There's more splintering now, coming from the main room of the house, and screaming, and a sound like the roaring of a hurricane. I wonder how many are being changed, how many are just being torn apart, but I know it doesn't really matter. Al was right: I've been living a hair away from death for most of my life. All of us have. A single breath is all that separates me from Bobby. He kneels down and looks me in the eyes, places his hands on my shoulders.

It's just Bobby and me again. Neither of us are who we used to be. But I let him hold me anyway.

In.

Out.

It's like stepping into a mirror. And it's easier than breathing.

In.

The Deluge
The Ancient Sumerian and Babylonian Myth of Apocalypse
Retold by Jake Jackson

Chapter I

ENLIL, FATEGIVER, Lord of Storms and warrior god ruled the realm of Earth, creating kings and great temples for the pure worship and honour of the gods who lived alongside Earth in the great realms of Heaven. Enlil populated the lands with small human creatures made from the clay of the Euphrates, and these people lived long, serving their masters well. In time though they increased vastly in number, and became a source of great noise as they spread across the Earth.

Greatly disturbed, unable to think or sleep Enlil yearned for the eternity of silence that had prevailed across the waters of the deep before the separation of the Heavens from Earth. Where once he had celebrated his noble task, revelling in the worship from his bridge across the worlds, the burgeoning city state of Nippur, and the great harvests of food that were distributed to the gods by these bustling, proliferating creatures, now Enlil suffered in the long nights from the constant noise of busy endeavour. As humans populated the earth, making pots, and striking stoves for fire, clattering their instruments at harvest, carousing and fighting they talked, and talked, and in talking yet more they fuelled a gathering rage in the heart of the Lord of Storms until he could bear it no longer: he declared to rid the world of the pestilence of humankind.

Chapter II

ENLIL CALLED A COUNCIL of the gods in Surupuk a mighty city along the Euphrates. The gods and the people of the earth did dwell in the same places as each other, but the separation of the realms had caused humankind a blindness to the presence of the ancient deities, and so the council of gigantic deities would swirl around and above the people of the city without their notice. Fired into life on the banks of the Euphrates by the hot blood of the gods, the humans otherwise would be terrified by the sight of their creators, their ears would burn in the hearing of the pure and powerful voices, and driven mad their fragile forms would melt back to the muddy rivers of the world. Only the very wise, the prophets and the visionaries, could learn to hear the whispers of the great inhabitants of the heavens, the capricious spirit-giants who sometimes gave instruction, or made demands, sometimes out of wicked amusement, through the form of dreams. Those who received such reports were revered, and became leaders of people, in tribes and cities across the land.

One such, a sage and humble ruler, was Atrahasis, the Lord of Surupuk where he lived amongst his people in the mansions and reed dwellings along the banks of the river. His wisdom was so great that not only was he admired by the people of the city, but the gods themselves acknowledged his exquisite abilities, one whose wisdom might match their own, if not for the fragility of his earthly form. The god Enki, he of the rivers and waters of the world, a virile god who perched under the earth, in the great ocean Abzu, and brother to Enlil, would whisper for hours to the gifted ears of Atrahasis. Although Enlil was worshipped in Surupuk, Enki too was venerated by many, as blessings were requested for their own creations, the mosaics and pottery, the little crafts of wonder that gave splendour to the streets and alleys, the wellsprings and hearths of humankind.

And so, the Gods gathered, hailing from the many realms of the heavens, Bel, Mnip, Ami, Ninurta and Ennugi came together with Hades too leaving his own dark caverns to join his fellows, the gods of rivers, canals, mountains, air and forests. The Great Father Anu presided, and after long discussions, with much regret, it was clear they too shared Enlil's frustrations with the busy noise of humankind. They complained much about the clatter of the creatures fashioned to serve the needs of the gods, that the benefits of humankind no longer outweighed the sins of disturbing their masters, the gods. So, with heavy hearts, they agreed that Enlil should release his storms and together they would overwhelm the Earth with a great deluge, thus sweeping humans from their homes and ending the enemies of silence, returning them to the muds of the rivers, to leave a peaceful land and the Heavens no longer to be troubled. Great Father Anu, as always on such grave matters, required the gods swear a solemn oath to honour their dreadful judgement.

Chapter III

THE GOD ENKI, who had grown to enjoy his connections with the wise and sagacious grew regretful. He remembered the achievements of Atrahasis, and his people, and knew he would miss the gentle visions and dreams, the idle directions cast across the waters for the ears of Atrahasis. He would miss the fascination of watching the people of the city and the banks of the Euphrates as they grew in knowledge, taking the words from his visions, and applying them to the land, to their own creations. He wrestled with the oath he had sworn, and decided it would not stop him whispering at the reed walls of Atrahasis's house, in the night, to tell of the terrors to come, and give instruction, leaving him to find the words by the subtleties of his own mind, for no other human would be wise enough to hear, still less, to understand.

And so he thought greatly, of wood and tar, and methods unknown to the peoples of the land, then he sneaked across and spoke:

> "Reed Wall, Reed Wall, bear my words,
> And if you happen to listen, oh man of Surupak,
> oh son of Ubar-Tutu you must attend, for we gods
> have laid an oath so dread to destroy
> all of man and woman born, to destroy
> all who are deemed to have sinned
> against the gods, and so by their very nature,
> all of mankind born, is destined to be drowned."

Atrahasis felt the rush of words in his dreams, and woke to visions all of destruction if he did not listen.

"You must leave now, forsaking all possessions,
and build, and when the time is right seek all living creatures.
You must make a vessel, in which such seed of life
must be caused to enter. And the boat, she be roofed
from fore to aft, for those you gather must shelter,
as the earth roofs the eternal ocean. And so you must
make a perfect shape, with 600 cubits along its length,
and 60 cubits the measure of its breadth and height.
And once gathered all to its heart, you must launch it forth
and I will shower it with a windfall of birds and a spate of fishes."

Enki shook the reed wall with his urgent whispers, and reaching through he opened the water clock, filled it and showed Atrahasis that the deluge would last seven days and seven nights, and wash all humankind into the seas, and return them to mud.

Atrahasis was frightened, and said, "But how shall I answer the city, the people and our elders? What shall I say to them as they see me build, as you command and gather? They will deride me, young and old alike."

And Enki's voice drifted through the vision, perceived by the wisdom of his servant Atrahasis,

"You will say to them, the gods Enki and Enlil are severed,
and as you are known to follow Enki, Enlil has rejected me,
Say, 'I can reside no longer in this great city, nor in the lands of his creation.
I will go down to Apsu, to the caves below the seas and live with my Lord,
As a great deluge descends upon these lands.'"

Atrahasis was thoughtful, and listened further as his lord Enki continued,

"Once the vessel is made you will it enter and open the door wide
so to bring in thy grain, thy furniture, and thy essential goods,
thy female servants, thy slaves, and the young men,
the beasts and the animals all as I will gather and send to thee,
and they shall all be enclosed within thy doors."

Atrahasis sighed. His head did not feel that a single vessel could rescue him, for surely the Earth was fixed, and from where could all the waters come? But he stilled the doubts and decided to trust the word of the Lord who had yet to mislead or betray him.

Enki whispered on, ignoring the doubts of his servant,

"And while you make the vessel I have commanded of you,
I shall bring you a harvest of true wealth, in the morning
loaves of bread shall shower down, and in evening a rain of wheat.
You shall have your fill while building, and more besides to store."

And so Atrahasis turned and brought about him his family and friends, explaining they must trust his word, for he in turn trusted the whispers of his vision, as they are spoken by his Lord Enki. Even as the vision seemed too fanciful, and beyond the imagination of all around they agreed to obey the instructions, and set about the foundation of the boat amidst a great field. The carpenter brought his hatchet, the reed worker brought his stone, children brought the bitumen to bind the wood, and the weak of limb and breath, they too brought whatever was needed else for all to complete the task.

By the fifth day the framework had been laid, as large as the field; 14 measures all round, 14 measures in height, with walls and frames fixed within its long roof. Six decks, each divided into seven levels were divided further into nine compartments, and so it was ready to be tested.

Atrahasis studied it from within on the sixth day, examined its exterior on the seventh, then once more the inside he checked on the eighth, placing plugs against leaks where they might spring, and where he saw all manner of rents he noted the mends required.

And so in the purpose of this vast task raw bitumen was poured into specially constructed kilns and melted. Three measures of the blackest pitch were then poured over the outside of the vessel to seal the wood, and three more poured over the inside. Three times 3600 porters carried baskets of vegetable oils where they laid down two thirds for storage and kept out the balance for the dedication of the great work. Huge boxes were constructed so that one third of the oxen could be slaughtered for the craftsmen, and a third of the sheep, ready for sacrifice to Enki. And the two thirds then was kept for storage upon the boat.

And so, Atrahasis caused to be gathered beer and wine as free-flowing as the river, and food so plentiful as the grains of dust across the earth. Two thirds were taken into the vast construction, and one third retained for a party of the exhausted, to honour the end of their labours, to celebrate as wild and the joyful as the New Year festival, at the end of all things.

Atrahasis watched the as reed oars too were brought aboard, and saw the final preparations as the sunset saw the boat was finally completed. He fell into deep contemplation about the mighty efforts of all, wondering at the chests of silver and gold hauled in, reflecting the strength and metal of his own purpose, as he had gathered the seed of life into the vessel, his kith and kin, the servants and the beasts, the sons and daughters, the craftsmen, all hailed in. And as night pulled across the skies the huge boat was rolled along long poles until two thirds rested in the waters, awaiting the truth of Atrahasis's vision from his precious Lord.

And while he watched, Great Shamash, known as Utu by some, the God of Justice and Day, of the Sun and Truth Revealed, spoke quietly from behind the reed walls of night into the ears of Atrahasis,

> *"I will cause it to rain so heavily,*
> *You must not linger at the perimeter of your ship.*
> *But flee to its midst; seal all thy doors*
> *And be ready for the crash of waters."*

As the day approached Atrahasis watched with such fear in his heart, and doubt. For his final act he gave his mansion, its goods and lands to Puzur Amurri, a boatman who had decided to stay, and so to seal the final door from the outside, with bitumen.

Chapter IV

AND SO, at the appointed hour, the moment of Enlil's rage arrived. The gods gathered to execute the purpose of their oath and cleanse the lands of noisy humankind; they rose, from the horizon of the Heavens extending and wide arranged themselves, revealed into the realm of Earth to cause utter devastation. Yul in the midst of it thundered, and Nebo and Saru bore ahead, the throne bearers heaved over mountains and plains, the destroyer Nergal burst forth, Ninip surged in front and cast down, the ancient spirits hauled destruction in their glory as they swept across the Earth. Erragal then pulled at the mooring ropes of the world and made the dykes of the Heavens flow, Adad hurled his torrential rain and all the gods set the land ablaze as the light of the emerging day turned to deepest, blackest night.

The bright earth was turned quickly to waste, the surface of the land obliterated by the thunderstorms and floods, with all people blinded by the onslaught draining from the skies, so none could see their fellows sliding from existence all around, or hear them above the roar of the hurricanes.

Everywhere, life was swept from the face of the Earth, overwhelming all people, all creatures, all lands, and so powerful was the cataclysm that it reached to the Heavens and threatened even the gods themselves. Now they too began to fear the tempest, anxious that its wild intensity might destroy them, so they sought refuge and ascended to the highest Heaven of Anu to protest. Like frightened dogs the gods, in droves, fell prostrate at the walls of Anu's Heaven; Ishtar, the goddess of fertility and desire spoke out, distraught as a child, and appealed to the Father of the Gods:

> "All to corruption is turned! I too, in the presence
> of the gods at our Council, professed against evil,
> As evil against us was vent, as sin against us caused
> but now I profess thus: no sooner have I begotten
> my people on the land like the young fishes
> They are scattered as they fill the seas with death."

And the ancient of spirits, the Anunnaki, the lofty redeemers of Fate, echoed Ishtar, and sat lamenting too, their lips covered with evil, slithering, they wretched with distress and regret.

Chapter V

SIX DAYS AND NIGHTS passed, the winds, the deluge, and storm had overwhelmed humankind and swept all away; the waters had closed across and made a single stretch of ocean, with no mountains, islands, and no place for land creatures to dwell, all was lost, but for the single vessel tossed high and higher by the devastating waves.

On the seventh day, with the terrible deed now consummated, the writhing agonies of the deluge began to subside: the whirlwinds abated, the storms retreated, and soon all turmoil fell away to silence.

Atrahasis perceiving the throw of the vessel to have steadied, so ventured to open a hatch, and found daylight breaking across his upturned face. He allowed himself a moment of joy, and relief, before opening his eyes, to observe the whole of mankind, once turned evil to the gods now reduced to clay, and like reeds, corpses floated long on the seas, into the horizon.

Atrahasis fell to his knees and wept, a deluge of his own, his face flowing with tears. Through exhausted eyes he looked out once more and blinked, seeing there a distant shore some twelve leagues away. Land perhaps, he thought, or a cruel illusion.

And so sailed Atrahasis' vessel to the place where once the country of Urartu resided and where, as the seas withdrew slowly, the tips of mountains halted further progress. The first day, and the second, the mountain held the vessel. So too the third day, and the fourth, followed by the fifth, an sixth, the vessel could not move further.

So on the seventh day Atrahasis opened the hatch once more and sent forth a dove. It flew off, but did not find a resting-place, and so returned all to soon.

Next Atrahasis released a swallow into the sky. Joyfully it spun across the air, but did not find a place to rest, so too it returned.

Undeterred, finally Atrahasis sent a raven and watched it leap into the skies. It flew on, across waters that now more visibly slithered back, revealing slowly emerging lands. So, the raven stopped, filled its aching belly, and wandering happily away, did not to return to the one remaining vessel of life on the Earth. Now, Atrahasis saw the great god Utu rise in the sky at last spreading light and warmth once more across the face of the drowned world, revealing the rapid withdrawal of the seas. And Utu, seeing the vessel perched now on a patch dry land, reached out to break the seal on the doors of Atrahasis's huge boat.

Chapter VI

OH, ATRAHASIS wept as he descended from the mighty vessel, pausing only to kiss the ground before the light of Utu. There he built an altar on the peak of the mountain of Urartu: by sevens herbs he cut, at the base of them he placed juniper, the flower of the mountain, with reeds, cedar, and myrtle, then gave sacrifice of oxen and sheep, crumbled barley cakes into the fire, and offered the fragrant libations to the four winds.

Shuddering still in their heavens, quelled by the rage of the deluge the gods received the tribute, and it revived them; they lifted themselves up, shuffling from their hideaways, and gathered like flies over the sacrifice, huge, unseen, consoled, swaying as trees amongst the flickering flames of the sacrifice, casting their shadows, in a ring across the mountain. Atrahasis gazed with wonder at the lights and shadows, the glory of the gods as he perceived them, reflected in the charm of lapis-lazuli around his neck. And so he felt comforted and in those moments he desired with all his being that forever he might not leave them, these strange and complicated gods, and so he spoke in their kind,

> *"May the gods come to my altar,*
> *Though not dread Enlil for he did not consider*
> *Our worth and made such a deluge,*
> *So many of my people he consigned to the deep."*

Indeed the ancient god Enlil finally observed the vessel, and, filled with anger went to the gods and spirits assembled, casting his fury amongst them,

> *"Let not any one come out alive,*
> *let not a man be saved from the deep."*

But, instead of agreeing as before the gods who had cowered from the storms, and saw the world cleansed of humankind, but for these few in the ship and the seeds of fruitful growth within, they resisted Enlil's fury. Before the assembled deities Nintu, the goddess of birth, raised her head and spoke to the warrior Enlil, gesturing to the highest heaven of the Anu:

> *"Who then will ask our Father Anu,*
> *for he knows the Truth of all things,*
> *and the rightness of all deeds done."*

Anu, weary and wise, surveyed the devastation of the land, the people and the creatures of the Earth, then looked to his fellows Utu, Innana, Ishtar and the others, then spoke with great prophesy, and said to the fierce Lord Enlil:

> *"Thou prince of the gods, oh warrior,*
> *when thou art angry a deluge thou makest;*
> *the doer of sin was felled by his own sin,*
> *the doer of evil was felled by his own evil.*
> *But the just survivor let him not be cut off,*
> *The faithful let him not be destroyed.*
> *Instead of thee making a deluge once more,*
> *May lions increase and men be reduced ;*
> *Instead of thee making a deluge once more,*
> *May leopards increase and men be reduced;*
> *Instead of thee making a deluge once more,*
> *May a famine happen and the country be destroyed;*
> *Instead of thee making a deluge once more,*
> *May pestilence increase and men be destroyed."*

Enlil, nodded slowly understanding the words of his father. His own anger was pacified at least that the noise of humankind was abated, that as his father further decreed short lives would also constrict the plague of humankind, that a class of priestess too could remain now celibate, to honour the gods, and further keep down the spread of humanity. Enlil and Enki, with their father, looked across the lands deluged by storms, and saw the bodies clinging to the mud, slowly returning to its succour. Enlil, like the floods he had created, closed his fierce eyes, submitted to the judgement, and withdrew his objections, much to the quiet joy of the gods and spirits gathered there.

Atrahasis could not hear the great debate, but in time Enki sent a dream to him, and the verdict was heard. It made him wonder at his good fortune, and the kind instruction of Enki who had whispered through the reed walls that separates the Heavens of the gods and lands of humankind.

And so in a vision, mighty Enlil, Fategiver and Lord of Storms, made himself appear on the mountainside, huge, contrite and thoughtful as he reached into the midst of the boat. He took the hand of Atrahasis, and gestured him to rise, to bring his wife and all those within to flow out into the lands. With Atrahasis Enlil made a great and rare covenant, and gave this blessing, in the presence of the people and the creatures who had sailed and survived,

> *"So Atrahasis, and your wife, and kin,*
> *to be like the gods will be carried away;*
> *then shall dwell you in a remote place*
> *At a bridge between worlds, at the mouth of the rivers.*
> *And no more shall the gods move to end humankind,*
> *For we have set in motion our means,*
> *So we may have peace and you, life."*

Atrahasis indeed was brought to a remote place at the mouth of the rivers and given a seat amongst the gods, who now he could see and with whom he could converse and there to watch the activities of the people of the Earth, honoured as he was both by his sons and daughters, and by the gods themselves.

Dust Devil

Curt Jeffreys

THE DUNE rose to a height of thirty feet on the north side of the sand fence. Stretching as far as eyes could see, the great mound was a frozen wave of sand with a windblown curlicue on top. Hence the nickname he'd given it, Curly Top. Old Curly Top wasn't really frozen of course. The monstrous pile of sand was on the move, inching its way forward as the wind pushed it along grain by grain, threatening to swallow everything in its path.

Like Ma's shack.

Jubal lay at the bottom of Curly Top, face up to the sun, letting its warmth permeate his thin brown body. High rainless clouds drift overhead as the wind played with the giant dune's curl. Twisted bows of color danced in the sparkling mist of particles flowing towards the squat shack where Ma was sleeping. He should have been fixing the sand fence where last night's storm had knocked it down, but how could anyone be expected to work on a day such as this?

A flash of brown, quick as heat lightning, streaked across the sand, disappearing under a shelf of crumbling gray rock. The boy's hand flicked in and out, returning with the squirming creature in a death grip. The boy's teeth crunched through its skinny reptile neck, putting an end to whatever thought processes tiny lizards possess.

For young Jubal there was nothing better than fresh lizard, all warm, still dripping. He hunkered down behind the fence where he could not see the shack, reasoning that if he couldn't see Ma then she couldn't see him.

Wiping warm goo from his lips he tossed the remains over a dune. Fortified for the moment he took up his hammer, managing to drive in one nail before his tiny attention span failed him once again.

It was nothing, really. A speck, a mere dot, far off on the horizon. Not much to look at, to be sure, but it shouldn't have been there at all, and that was enough to banish all other thoughts from the boy's mind. Chores forgotten, Jubal squatted on his haunches, his unwavering gaze locked on the heat-blurred line between sand and horizon.

Jubal watched, fascinated, as the speck grew under his gaze, resolving itself into a man-shaped form that danced and squirmed in the heat waves like a drunken puppeteer's marionette. A visitor! In all his fifteen years he couldn't recall a single visitor. Not one.

Jubal ran to the shack, disappearing inside. Moments later he emerged, a battered rifle in his hands, his Ma close behind, her ancient shotgun loaded and ready.

Jubal squinted down his barrel, placing his bead square on the man's chest. He'd never shot a man before but it couldn't be much different from shooting anything else – dead's dead, after all.

"Just keep moving," Ma hollered as the man drew closer. She raised her weapon, cocking both barrels with a double click that somehow carried against the wind.

"I'm unarmed."

The man showed his empty hands. Big hands, attached to a big body. A pack nearly the size of the boy sat high on his back.

Jubal figured this to be a lie – no one travels the wastes without some kind of weapon.

"I could use some water," the man's voice rumbled across the sand. "Maybe a place to lay my head. Storm's comin', sure as shootin'."

The wind whipped up a thick cloud of dust, emphasizing his point.

"Please," the wind snatching greedily at his words. "I'll die out here."

Slowly Ma lowered her gun. The man inched forward with all the caution afforded a sleeping rattler. He was big, six feet plus, skin bright and raw from exposure. He removed his hat, pulled down his bandanna. His lips were dried and cracked, his breathing deep and ragged. He wouldn't last another day without shelter and water.

Warily Ma moved from the shadows of the porch.

The man pulled off his goggles, revealing deep-set eyes of brilliant blue. His eyes flicked between Ma's face and her shotgun.

"It's me, Paula," he said cautiously. "Zeb."

"She's not Paula," Jubal laughed. "She's Ma."

Something dark and not at all pleasant flickered across Ma's face. A tight sob squeaked from her throat and she nearly dropped her gun. Gently Jubal took the weapon, looking first to Zeb, then to Ma.

"What's this?" Zeb said, motioning to the boy.

"I'm Jubal."

Zeb frowned. Ma nodded.

Ma wiped at her eyes, the backs of her hands smearing trails of glistening grit down her wrinkled cheeks.

"How'd you find me?" Ma asked, her voice soft and timid.

"Luck," Zeb chuckled. "Pure dumb luck. I was over to Ridgemont couple weeks ago to, um, make a pick up." He looked sideways at Jubal. "Met a fella there said he was from Taylor's Creek. This fella told me a story about a freak kid living with his Ma out in the middle of nowhere. I figured I best come take a look. Imagine my surprise when I seen it was you."

"Then you weren't looking for us?"

"Hell no. Just dumb luck, like I said."

Ma looked like she'd been slapped. Shaking herself she turned to Jubal then back to Zeb.

"We will speak of this later," she said, her voice quivering. "Come, Jubal. It's time for supper."

She disappeared into the shack.

* * *

They ate on the porch, where Ma could catch what little breeze there was. The meal wasn't much to get excited about, a meager mixture of wilted greens, some potatoes and a few beans mother and son had managed to coax from the inhospitable soil. Jubal preferred lizard to lettuce, fresh meat to Ma's gritty vegetables. He pushed the limp mass around his plate with a fork. Ma said nothing. She and Jubal had an unspoken agreement: he pretended to like her veggies and she pretended not to know what he really ate.

Zeb downed three mugs of water like it was no big deal. Maybe it wasn't where he came from, but out here it *was* a very big deal. His rudeness annoyed Jubal to no end. It took days for their little solar still to produce a single gallon of drinkable water. Sure, the cistern under the shack was half full, but that was the point – it was *half* full. Jubal didn't mind the thick brown goo from the well but Ma's stomach couldn't tolerate it.

Zeb pushed back from the table, lit up a fat brown cigar. Ma stole a sideways glance while he was blinded by his match's flame, her sad eyes studying the lines in his face like they were a map to long buried memories. Zeb squinted at Jubal through the haze, studying him.

"Still trying to save the world one stray at time, eh, Paula?" he said, shaking out his match.

"Still ripping babies from their mothers' bosoms, Zeb?" Ma shot back.

Zeb's face turned hard. "I do what needs doing, nothing more."

"Likewise."

They locked eyes, neither saying a word.

The husky smell of wild-weed billowed in noxious white clouds as Zeb exhaled, coughing a deep rattling cough. Ma curled her nose but said nothing.

Zeb coughed, hacked, spat a moist green lump into the desert.

"What happens now?" Ma said.

Zeb flicked ashes into the sand. "You gotta ask?"

"Can't you just leave, pretend you never found us?"

Zeb frowned. "It's not like I have a choice, Paula. It's my job."

"The boy hasn't done a thing to you."

"That hardly matters."

Ma hung her head then started to stand. The boy gave her his arm until she got her balance. Stopping at the door she spoke over her shoulder to the man called Zeb.

"You can sleep in the tool shed. Not much, but it'll keep the sand off you."

Zeb opened his mouth then shut it with a click. He stared off into the night, his face as dark as the desert.

* * *

In the gloom of the shack's single room Ma went about her nightly routine like nothing at all was going on, like there was no strange man sleeping in their tool shed.

Quickly, efficiently, she laid out her bedclothes.

"Ma, who's Zeb?"

Ma pulled the pins holding her hair in a bun. Thin wisps of gray fell across her shoulders.

"Someone I knew," Ma said, "a very long time ago."

She stopped brushing her hair, pulled absently at the tufts stuck in the bristles.

"I'm so tired. We'll talk later." She kissed his cheek. "Good night, my darling."

She snuffed the candle and the room dropped into darkness.

Outside the shack, mere inches from Jubal's head, the wind howled and sang, giving birth to a thousand dust devils twirling and swirling round and round, calling him to join them, to feel the wind on his naked skin, the sand in his face. But he would not be joining the dance tonight. Instead he lay awake, staring into the dark, his mother's soft sobs a forlorn descant to the wind's joyous song.

* * *

The sun rose hard and sharp, burning away all the colors of the world, painting everything in uniform grays and browns. The wind had died in the early morning hours leaving behind rolling mounds of powdery grit that blanketed Ma's vegetable garden. Sighing wearily, her bony shoulders drooping, she took up her hoe and trudged out to inspect the damage.

Ma and Jubal worked silently, efficiently, scooping, shoveling, doing their best to clear the buried furrows without damaging the pitiful plants trapped beneath the fine dry powder.

Zeb emerged from the tool shed, scratching and yawning.

"You want to eat today you best grab a shovel and get to it," Ma hollered.

Zeb joined them, reluctantly bending his back to the task. Jubal was thankful for the extra hands. Ma said nothing.

"Hell of a storm," Zeb said, trying to fill the silence. "Never seen anything like it."

Jubal laughed. "That wasn't a storm."

Zeb looked confused, turned to Ma.

"Boy's right," she said, looking over the sand, deep into the desert. "That was just a little dust up. There is a storm coming, though. How long, Jubal? Another day?"

Jubal closed his eyes, his flat brown nose flaring as he took the desert into his lungs. The desert washed over him, through him. Its wind was his breath, its sand his blood, its rocks his bones.

Opening his eyes he said, "Tomorrow. Storm'll be here tomorrow. Gonna be a big one."

Ma looked amused, Zeb, confused.

"Now come on," he said. "You can't expect me to believe –"

"You best believe it," Ma said. "Jubal knows."

Zeb stared at Jubal. "It just ain't right."

Jubal wanted to ask what wasn't right but Ma's frown hushed him.

Ma and Jubal worked in accustomed silence but before long before Zeb couldn't take it any more. Jubal figured the man could talk a rock's ears off if he thought it was listening.

He'd seen the world, Zeb said. Been to cities with more people than one man can count. He'd seen oceans and seas. Rivers, too. Jubal had never seen a river, let alone an ocean. As far as he knew there wasn't enough water left in the world to fill a whole ocean.

Ma ignored Zeb's rambling tale but Jubal couldn't help laughing, not understanding half the words coming out of the man's mouth. Zeb mistook the boy's laughter as interest and so continued his disjointed soliloquy.

"Here's something I bet you didn't know. My Grandpa Morgan said this place used to be called Kansas." He looked confused for a second. "Or maybe Nebraska. Hell, it don't matter," he laughed. "Point is – and you may find this hard to believe, young Jubal – but back before the world died this land was green, green as Paula's eyes. All a man had to do was drop a seed on the ground and sure as shootin' it would sprout. Wheat, corn, alfalfa, you name it, it'd grow. There was cattle, sheep, horses, birds." He paused, his gaze taking in the ruined landscape. "It must've been something to see," he said softly.

Zeb grew quiet as the morning grew old and died. Each wheezing breath took monumental effort as the desert drained his body of moisture. The heat was getting to Ma as well. The two of them stopped often to drink from their flasks.

Jubal paid no notice to the heat, the wind, the sand. Hatless, shirtless, his brown skin shining in the sun, he hadn't stopped to rest or drink all morning. For him, the hotter it got the stronger he felt.

By midday the garden was uncovered. The scrawny plants could breathe again. But there was no victory here. The desert would win in the end. Even if they succeeded in holding the sand back another season Ma would surely not live to see the next. She'd be better off in Taylor's Creek, where she pass her last days in comfort.

Paula poked and prodded at her sad little plants while Jubal went to fetch water, leaving the two grownups to themselves.

Zeb leaned on his hoe.

"Look at me, Paula."

She turned.

"You're sick," he nodded.

She gave him a sad look. "Is it so obvious?"

"Any fool can see."

"Cancer," she admitted. "Deep in my gut."

"You're dying?"

"We're all dying, Zeb. I'm just real good at it."

"You seen a doctor?"

Paula laughed a graveyard laugh. "Of course. There's a drunken old fart over to Taylor's Creek, but I wouldn't let him embalm me, let alone treat me."

"But what'd he say?"

She shrugged. "Nothing to be done but die, he says."

"You could come back to the city, see a real doctor."

Paula's laugh was deep and hard, like that was just the best joke ever. "There's not a thing in this world worth me going back to the city, Zebulon Meeney. Not one thing."

"It's been fifteen years, Paula. Things've changed. We got electricity again, clean water, schools."

"Do you now?" She squinted out from under her bonnet. "And what about the boy? What happens to him if I go back to the city?"

"You don't want me to answer that, do you?"

"How many have you sent to the camps, Zeb? A hundred? A thousand? Do you even know? Or care?" She shook her head. "You were always a monster."

Zeb's color rose, his face hot and red as the angry sun above them.

"Watch your mouth, Paula, or so help me I'll –"

"What? Hit me?" She spat on the ground. "Still got your temper, I see. You haven't changed, Zeb. You're not able."

Zeb pushed up close, towering over her, chest puffed out, fists clenched. His arm froze mid-swing as Jubal nudged his ribs from behind with his blade. Zeb slowly raised his hands.

"I give, boy. Put your pig sticker away."

Jubal stepped back, his blade glinting in the sun.

"Hear me now woman," Zeb growled. "You can die out here for all I care, but the freak's coming with me and that's the end of it."

Shaking her head Paula went into the cabin to lie down.

* * *

Jubal and Zeb worked in silence, taking turns at the pump, trudging back and forth, dumping buckets of smelly goo along the desiccated furrows of Ma's garden.

"You called me a freak," Jubal said after awhile.

"Yep."

"Why?"

Zeb shook his head, pushing damp hair from his eyes. "It's nothing, kid. Forget it."

But Jubal couldn't, wouldn't forget. "Why'd you call me that?"

"You want the truth?"

The boy nodded.

"Okay, kid. You asked for it." Zeb took off his hat, his goggles, pulled away the bandanna covering his mouth and nose.

"Look at me. Tell me what's different between me and you."

Jubal's eyes moved over the man's face, his beefy body.

"Your face is red and hairy," he said slowly. "Flaky too, like a snake shedding it skin."

"That's sunburn. What about your skin?"

"It's brown. All wrinkly. Shiny."

"That's why you don't burn. What else?"

"Your hair. It's thick. And wet. Mine's thin and dry, like dead grass."

"That's 'cause I'm sweating. Normal folks like your Ma and me sweat to keep our bodies cool. That's why we drink so much water. You haven't had a drink all day. You're not sweating either. Kind of strange, don't you think? And that ain't all. You got thick hairs coming out your ears, over your eyes. You got flaps over your nose holes. Your skin's all oily and slick."

"And that's what makes me a freak?"

"In a nutshell."

Jubal frowned at the desert for a long time, lost in thought. Turning back to Zeb he said, "Is it bad to be a freak?"

"It ain't good, kid," Zeb said, walking away.

* * *

"Ma?" Jubal said from his dark corner that night. "Am I a freak?" He rolled over on his pallet, leaning up on an elbow.

Ma was quiet for a long time before answering. "It's just a word, Jubal. Don't mean a thing."

"Is it because I'm different? Don't say I ain't 'cause I know I am."

"Yes, you're different," she admitted. "And yes, there are some ignorant folks who call your kind freaks."

The boy's heart leaped in his chest. "My kind? There are more like me?"

Ma paused then, "I should've told you a long time ago."

The flickering candlelight threw her lined face into stark relief. She looked ancient, tired. Used up.

"Truth is there's lots like you. Thousands."

"Thousands? Just like me?"

She smiled. "Yes, just like you."

"But why don't I look like you and Zeb?"

She wiped at her puffy eyes with her kerchief. "You know what the world used to be like."

He did know. He'd read Ma's books, studied the pictures of a moist, green world dead and gone years before Ma was even born.

"No one knows for sure how it happened, it was so long ago," she went on. "Some say God took away the rain, poisoned the land and the air to punish us. Others blame ancient enemies, long forgotten now. Me, I believe we did this to ourselves. People can be arrogant children sometimes, wanting things the way they want them, and damn the consequences. They poisoned the world and everybody in it with their greed. Lots of folks get sick and die early nowadays because of it. Lots of babies die quick. Others grow strong."

"Like me?" the boy said eagerly.

"Exactly like you, sweetheart. The world favors your kind, frowns on folks like Zeb and me. Someday we'll be the freaks and your kind'll be the normal ones."

Her moist eyes glistening in the flickering candlelight.

"What I'm trying to say is you're no freak, Jubal. You're my boy. That's all that matters. I'd die for you. I'd – kill for you."

Her smile changed, sad and happy mixed together. She pulled him close, kissed his head. "Blessed are the freaks," she said softly. "For they shall inherit the Earth."

She put out the candle and mother and son settled into the silence of the night.

Jubal's mind whirled at the thought of others like him. He promised himself he'd find them. Meanwhile he had one more question.

"Ma? Are you going to the city with Zeb?"

"Why on earth would you think that?"

"He knows you. Why else would he come all the way out here except for you?"

Ma came to his pallet. Squatting next to him she stroked his hair.

"He didn't come for me," she said. "He came for you."

"Me? Why? He don't know me."

Ma sighed, smoothed her nightclothes.

"I swore I'd never tell. Guess there's no choice now." Her eyes were full of pain. "You aren't my natural born son, Jubal."

The boy started to speak but she hushed him with a finger to his lips.

"Just listen now. Before you were born I lived in Hays with my husband. I was a midwife, a lady who helps other ladies have babies. Your real Ma was not much more than a child, no husband or family of her own. She was scared enough just having a baby. When I showed her her newborn son, well, she went kind of crazy. I didn't know what to do, she was yelling and hollering so. She said to take you away, so I did. I took you home with me.

"My husband, God bless his soul, had a big heart. He loved you as much as I did. We decided to raise you as our own. But we had to keep you a secret, away from prying eyes.

"Daniel, that was my husband's name, he had a brother. As good a man as Daniel was, his brother was dead opposite. A mean, no good, rotten cuss with a heart black as the very pits of Hell."

"Zeb," Jubal said.

Ma nodded. "It was Zeb's job to round up people like you, send them away to places called camps."

"Why?"

"So's they wouldn't have to look at them, I suppose. Anyway, we kept you a secret from Zeb best we could because we were afraid he'd send you away. But someone snitched on us, one of our neighbors, most likely. People are like that sometimes, Jubal. Some can be real nice and others can be nasty as rattle snakes.

"When we found out we'd be snitched on we knew we had to get you somewhere safe before Zeb came around. Daniel, he stayed behind to deal with his brother, kept him busy while I took you and ran."

"What happened to him, to Daniel?"

"I learned later he died," Ma said, her voice flat, emotionless. "I never knew for sure who did it. I like to think it wasn't Zeb who pulled the trigger, killed his own brother. But it's been in the back of my mind all these years."

She shook herself free of the memory.

"Anyways, I knew some folks. Kind, big hearted folks. They helped you and me get away, set us up way out here in the middle of nowhere, far away from the city and men like Zeb. They built this cabin for us, made sure we had a good well, plenty of food, a garden.

"For a long time we were just fine out here, just you and me. But then the well went bad. And the dunes, those damned dunes. Every year they crept a little closer."

She shivered despite the heat.

"It's my fault. I should've packed us up and moved on years ago, before I got so sick." Tears spilled over at last. "Now it's too late. Zeb's found us."

She grabbed Jubal's hand, squeezing tight. "He's going to take you from me," she choked.

Jubal squeezed back. "He can try, but I ain't leaving you. Ever. I promise."

* * *

The storm arrived just as Jubal said. He and Zeb were up on the roof, making ready for the fury to come. The roof was a crazy quilt of sand-blasted sheet metal and wood held together with nails, bailing wire and optimism and in no shape for the coming fury.

The wind rose steadily as the front approached, forcing them to stay low as the gusts tried to hurl them off into space. Beneath them the shack trembled and quivered like a thing alive.

Out of nowhere Jubal said, "Ma says you're scared of me."

Zeb stopped hammering, brushed the grit from his goggles.

"What are you talking about, boy? Nobody'd be afraid of something like you."

"She says you lock up freaks 'cause you're scared of them. Why?"

Zeb wiped a thin layer of crust from his face with the back of a hand. "There's a certain order to things in this world, boy. There's things that should be, and there's things that shouldn't. Folks like me, we're trying to rid the world of things that shouldn't be."

"Like me?"

Zeb nodded. "Nothing personal."

For the first time the boy saw himself as Zeb saw him – as something less than human, as something dangerous.

A freak.

Zeb's voice was hard and sharp. "Soon as this storm blows over you're comin' with me and that's that."

"I ain't leaving Ma. I promised her."

"You got no say, boy," Zeb laughed.

Jubal rose to his full height, ignoring the wind, the stinging sand.

"You think you're man enough to stop me?" Zeb yelled, a nasty grin splitting his face. "C'mon boy, what're you waiting for?"

Jubal didn't move.

"Just as I thought," Zeb sneered. "Your kind ain't got the guts."

Zeb caught the boy's arms, twisting so hard the tendons stretched to near breaking.

"You're coming with me or I'll break your skinny little freak neck," he hissed. "Don't bother me much either way."

"You let my boy go, Zebulon Meeney!" Ma yelled from below, Jubal's rifle aimed at Zeb. "Let him go right now or I'll pop your head clean off your neck."

Zeb laughed, pushing the boy away. Jubal rolled out of reach, rubbing his arms.

Zeb stood, squared himself in defiance, pushing his chest out, giving Ma a bigger target.

"Quit yapping and do it!"

Ma sighted on the man's knee and pulled the trigger.

Click.

Zeb laughed, a humorless, hateful laugh.

"What's the matter, Paula? No bullets? You'll find 'em out there," he waved at the desert. "Shells for the shotgun, too. Can't remember exactly where I threw them, though. It's a big desert."

Jubal struggled to stand. Zeb gave him a swift kick to the ribs. The boy went down with a moan.

"Stay down, freak. This is between me and Paula."

"Let my boy go, Zeb," Ma yelled again. "I mean it!"

Zeb laughed. "Don't be stupid, woman. No point dying for a freak. He'll be better off with his own kind."

He pulled a revolver from deep inside his tunic, pointed it at her.

"I'm taking him. Try and stop me and I'll put a quick end to your suffering."

A gust screamed across the roof, tearing at Zeb's clothes. He staggered sideways, struggling to stay upright.

Jubal moved quickly, diving at his legs, cutting them out from under him. Together they tumbled and twisted in a pile of arms and legs as the boy's momentum carried them both over the edge. For the briefest moment the two hung suspended before gravity claimed them.

Zeb crashed to the ground, Jubal landing on top with a grunt. The revolver skittered off into the sand.

Jubal scrambled for the weapon but Zeb's long arm snagged it first. He smacked the boy's face with the barrel. Jubal's vision exploded in a storm of light and color.

Zeb staggered to his feet, gun in hand. Calmly, deliberately he took aim at the boy's head.

"I'm done playing. Come peaceable or –"

His word's died with a hollow thwack as the butt of Ma's rifle caught the back of his skull.

"Go, Jubal!" she yelled. "Run!"

Jubal sprinted for the sand fence, desperate to reach the safety of the dunes. Ma grappled with Zeb for the revolver, buying her boy precious seconds.

Zeb's pistol barked once, twice.

Looking back Jubal saw Ma drop to her knees, a dark red rose blossoming across the front of her dress.

The boy dove for the top of the dune, rolling up and over Curly Top's crown. Zeb scrambled across the sand in mad pursuit.

Down and down Jubal rolled, faster and faster, letting gravity take him. He hit bottom, scrambling to his feet. Geysers of sand erupted around him in tiny bullet-driven founts. Pop! Pop! Pop!

Diving and rolling, the boy scuttled into a small hollow behind a flat rock.

From high atop Curly Top Zeb shouted against the wind.

"Come on, boy! Stick your head out so I can end this now. Your Ma's dead. You got nothing now!"

The desert boiled and swirled around the lunatic in great gritty clouds as if feeding off his rage, drawn to his fury.

There was a crack and a whap as a slug tunneled into the sand not six inches from Jubal's poorly concealed head. The dust and wind were screwing with Zeb's aim but he was finding his range. Surely he wouldn't miss next time.

Jubal hunkered down, making himself as small as possible.

Zeb ignored the raging wind, reloaded, so focused on murder he didn't notice the monstrous dust devil looming behind him, its swirling funnel wrapped in a viscous brown cloud a hundred feet high.

Laughing, he took aim, squeezed his trigger, then –

* * *

Great waves of sand roiled and swirled over and around Jubal's meager shelter, but he stayed put. Eyes shut tight, not moving, barely breathing, he waited out the storm.

He had no way of knowing how long it lasted. Dust blocked the sun, plunging the desert into an eerie brown twilight.

Hours, days, or weeks later the storm died, dropping its sandy payload to the desert floor.

Warily Jubal crawled out from under his rock, squinting against the hard sun.

It was a strange, unfamiliar world the boy found himself in. Everything rearranged, picked up and put down in random places. The familiar rolling hills and dunes of his childhood were shifted so he couldn't tell one from the other. He scrambled up the highest dune, what surely must have been Curly Top, but there was nothing below.

No Zeb.

No sand fence.

No shack.

No Ma.

Gone. All gone. Not a trace remained, not a clue to testify that any of it had ever existed. The world had been swept clean and now it glowed, all shiny and new.

Motionless high atop the dune Jubal surveyed the vast expanse of his new world. The beauty of it, the sheer power of the desert filled him with wonder. So clean, so pristine, as if he was the first to ever lay eyes on it.

He'd never see Ma again, but her pain was gone now, and surely that was a piece of mercy. Even if it had come at the hands of Zebulon Meeney.

Jubal breathed deeply, bringing the desert into his lungs, feeling the warmth of the sun fill his body. This was how it should be, how it was meant be.

How it always would be.

Two yards off a small brown lizard scurried across the sand in a puff of dust.

Famished, Jubal ran after his supper.

Away They Go or Hurricane Season

Su-Yee Lin

An Introduction

*– **I ALWAYS** thought there was something wonky about those law enforcement officials and I guess, this proves me right.*

Really? How do you figure, Jim?

Have you read the papers, Jim? They've been flocking like geese to Hawaii this past week. Every cop on leave. Every cop enjoying the sunshine, waves, and bikini clad girls dancing in hula skirts.

Every cop?

Yes. Something smells quite fishy here, if I do say so myself.

What will you do about it, Jim?

Wait and see, Jim. Just wait and see.

Waking Silence

WHEN I COME HOME, I am greeted with echoing silence in a space that is too small for echoes. In place of words, there is the tick tock of the clock, the second hand stuck between nine and ten. There is the rustle of leaves against the windowpane. The wind blowing through an open window, ruffling the pages of a book lying on the desk.

The car is in the driveway, the oven is warm and there are fresh muffins on the counter. The fan is blowing away the spring heat. It's late May; I've just gotten home from college and there's no one here.

This is what things should look like:

My mother sitting on the couch, her hands wrapped loosely around a mug of tea, her eyes watching the yellow finches perched on the Echinacea. My father reading a newspaper at the kitchen table, one hand absently holding a muffin. The radio is set to 710 WOR, fuzzy static in the background.

It is early morning and there should be hugs, smiles, rapid words – "How are you? You're home early! Who drove you?" Instead, there is a recent emptiness, as if the room has just been left. As soon as I step in, my key squeaking in the lock, I know that no one's home. I search the rooms as a formality, eat one of the muffins. I stow my bags in the living room, start unpacking, thinking that they'd be back any second. Maybe my mother has run out to get butter at the nearby 7-Eleven. Maybe my father had gone with his friends somewhere. Maybe maybe maybe maybe.

I curl up on my bed with a book and wait for them to come home.

Possibilities

WHEN I WAKE, the sun is slanting through my window and the world outside is bathed in the dim golden light of sunset. When I wake, the house is just as silent as it was when I fell asleep. There is the slow drip, drip of the faucet, the sound of the wind outside. Nothing else.

I get up, pick up the cordless phone in the kitchen. A dull flat dial tone. I call my mother's phone. It rings and rings. I call my father's phone. It rings and rings. Finally, the sound of a woman informing me that the number hadn't set up a voice mailbox. I hang up.

There is this nagging little voice telling me that something's wrong. There is this nagging little voice telling me that I'm being paranoid. There are all these conflicting voices in my mind, telling me what to do, what not to do, and I don't know, I'm worried, I'm confused, I'm ashamed. Should I call the police? Make a sign? Start a bonfire? Shine a giant flashlight across the sky? Wait? Should I ignore the fact that they still aren't home and laugh when they do come back?

What I will do is make a list of possibilities. These are the possibilities:

1. They went out shopping. Walking? By bus? Picked up by someone?

2. They went on a trip somewhere. Maine? New York City?

3. They've been abducted by aliens.

4. They've been kidnapped by the mafia.

5. They went on an epic journey to find themselves.

6. They were eaten by wolves.

I can't think of a 7th possibility so instead, I make myself dinner. Spaghetti with tomato sauce and chunks of mozzarella cheese. While eating, I catch up with email and watch TV. Survivor's on again for their 38th season. I switch the channel and instead, watch the news.

News

– EARLY for hurricane season, Jim?

Yes. Hurricane activity usually peaks in late summer, early autumn here in the northeast. It's pretty surprising that our first hurricane of the season is coming in mid-May. You could even say it's out of season, Jim.

Haha. Yep. And this Tropical Storm Aster looks like it'll be a doozy. It already has 62 mile per hour winds. Florida, be warned. It's heading north from the Gulf of Mexico and making a beeline towards Miami. I'm surprised that the ocean has warm enough waters to sustain the tropical storm, though. What do you think, Jim?

I'd have to agree with you, Jim. It's pretty shocking. Global warming, eh?

Well, that's the weather for the week. A tropical storm heading towards Miami and a week of sunshine and rain. Back to you, Jim, for the evening news.

Thanks, Jim. I definitely wouldn't want to be caught down in Florida right now. As for the evening news, lately, there have been sightings of a mass exodus of rats. Yes, you heard me right, Jim. Rats. They've been –

In Response

IT IS MORNING again and the TV's still on, the reporters jabbering away at each other. My brain is still in its half-asleep state and I think about how the newscasters each have the same exact bald spot on top of their heads, shiny in the heat of the studio lights. My eyes are crusty and my mouth is dry and there's this ache at the back of my head from sleeping on the arm of the couch. I get up and look outside. The car is still in the driveway, the azaleas are still blooming, and everything is exactly the same as it was yesterday.

I play the game of 'If I were my parents, where would I be?' and decide that the answer is: in bed. I look in their bed, under their bed, behind their bed, in front of their bed. I don't find them but instead, find a wedding Barbie with brown hair from the 80s, a pair of scissors, and twenty-eight cents. I get up, shake the dust from my hair, and call my sister.

Miscommunication

"HELLO?" I say.

"Hey, how's home?"

"Do you know –"

"I've been studying –"

"Mom and Dad haven't come back –"

"Crazy thing is that –"

"– seen them?"

"Snow on the ground! And that's not –"

"Otherwise, it's pretty quiet –"

"Gotta study for chem, bye!"

"Bye!"

Unraveling

IT IS LATE afternoon now and there are no signs of where they could be. I call my aunt, my uncles, but their phones ring and ring into the waiting silence, between the miles.

When I was a child, I would go to the mall with my parents and invariably, I would lose them. I would be looking at a toy one second, turn back towards them and they'd be gone. It was a test. I would have to go up to the desk clerk, tell them that I was lost. They'd appear after hearing their names on the intercom, smiling gently, not worried at all. Later on, they told me that they were only making sure I could be independent.

I wonder if this is another test.

I am twenty years old, I should know when to worry and when not to. I should understand fear and its logic and illogic. I should be able to function on my own. I had thought I was independent but when you are forced into independence, you realize exactly how dependent you are. Life is full of shoulds. I should speak, listen, memorize, understand.

I stare around the empty house, the shadows slinking across the floor of the kitchen. I have rarely seen this house empty for more than a few hours; it had always been full of chatter, of siblings and cousins, of the radio or the television. This emptiness is unsettling. It makes me want to leave, want to stay, makes me unsure. I feel trapped and stifled but most of all, confused.

What Now?

IT'S BEEN far too long and I wonder if I should call the police. It's not the first thing to pop into my head. I've always had a fear of cops. Those shiny badges, that big stick. Those hats that stick out a little in front. The guns that they wave in front of your face as if they were toys.

I don't trust them. I also haven't seen one in a while. But I decide to dial the non-emergency line anyway.

There is no answer. 911? Also, no answer. I wonder if perhaps, the phone is dead. I haven't been able to reach anyone for a while although I hear it ringing into the silence.

I look at the phone cord attached to the wall. It's broken, the edges of the tear looking as if mice had gnawed upon them.

I am dumbfounded.

Where did mice come from?

Mice

ONCE WE had cockroaches in our kitchen. We would turn on the lights after coming home and they would scatter, scampering away into the crannies between the cabinets, underneath the floorboards. So we brought out sheets with some kind of strong glue on top and placed them around the kitchen.

Coming into the kitchen the next morning, I found a tiny mouse, its ear and side stuck to the glue. It squirmed, getting itself stuck even more, and squeaked at me, its whiskers twitching. I looked at it, staring straight into its sad black eyes, then looked away. I couldn't save it, no matter how cute it was.

When I returned from school later that day, it was gone, leaving bits of fur in the glue.

Back

USING ELECTRICAL tape, I try to fix the cord but the finished product looks like a botched surgery, a wad of black tape around the cord. Oddly enough, I still hear the phone ringing on the other end when I try dialing. But no one ever picks up. I wonder what space it's ringing into, imagining an empty room in outer space, aliens pressing their faces against the glass windows.

It's dinner time again and as I eat some soup, I browse the headlines of last week's newspaper.

News

LONG DORMANT VOLCANOES ERUPT
– This morning at approximately 10:00am Pacific Time, three volcanoes called the Three Sisters in the Cascade Range in Oregon erupted. None of the three have erupted for thousands of years. The magma from the volcanoes' eruptions covered the nearest town of Sisters, Oregon 15 miles away, burying the two thousand inhabitants. Rescue workers have been unable to help as the ash and magma are still lethal.

Parachute

AS I FALL asleep, I realize that it has been two days or forty-eight hours since I've come home.

I dream of parachutes.

They are falling from the sky, giant parachutes with no one inside the harnesses. I'm watching from below, my face turned to the sky. They start out tiny and I think I can see figures but as they come closer, they disappear so the parachutes are left empty.

Tick Tock, Says the Clock

I WAKE UP again, my dreams disjointed. It's midmorning, the shadows outside inching shorter as the day approaches noon. Tick tock, says the clock, and I wonder what I'm doing in bed. I've spent too much of my time waiting and I don't want to wait anymore.

The watch on my wrist tells me that it's May 25th. May 25th? I distinctly remember that I came home on the 20th, which I thought was two days ago. My watch is telling me that it's been five. I check my computer. Yup, May 25th, 10:48 a.m. I don't know how I could have lost three days but I can't argue with the evidence. And if today is the 25th, then my sister should have returned home yesterday. Could I have missed her?

Again, I search the house and find no signs of anything changed at all. The only sign of habitation are ones that I've made: the mussed bed, the dirty pots on the stove, the dishes on the drying rack. My clothes are still in suitcases scattered in the hall; they have not been joined by any new ones. It's obvious that she's not here.

Maybe something happened on the way here?

News

– AND NOW, to Jim, with the traffic. How are the roads, Jim?

Jim, I gotta admit, you don't want to be out on the roads right now.

Why ever not, Jim?

Well, Jim, there are cars stuck on the roads for miles around. Just stuck.

How are they stuck?

Well, it seems as if their tires have been punctured, Jim. Imagine that. Miles of cars with punctured tires.

Wow, that's pretty bizarre, Jim. Were there nails in the road? Pieces of glass?

As a matter of fact, Jim, there were not. At approximately 8:30 a.m. this morning, every car on the L.I.E. from exit 40 to exit 60 found their tires full of holes. It's a mess, Jim.

An inexplicable mess, for sure, Jim. So what's being done?

Absolutely nothing, Jim. The tow trucks can't get in there. Instead, the drivers are leaving their cars and walking and what we are seeing are just miles of empty cars. No one knows what to do.

Well, Jim, if anyone wants a free car, they know what to do.

Jim, I figure if you can get the car out of there then you deserve it. They're packed like sardines, Jim. Car sardines.

Thank you, Jim. Well, that's the traffic for today. Now onto the stock market –

Good Sister

I TURN OFF the news. Could my sister have gotten stuck in that mess? If so, then she would now be walking home although she was supposed to have been here yesterday, not today. The phone is dead so there's no way to reach her. I decide that I might as well take the car out, try to find her so she wouldn't have to walk the extra miles. I'm just being a good sister.

Three Things

1. THE keys are hanging in the fish.

2. The fish is on the wall.

3. If you want to get the keys, you put your hand in the fish's mouth and press on its tongue. It will then eject the keys.

Leaving, Leaving, Left

I REMOVE the keys from the fish's mouth, throw on a light jacket, grab my wallet, and walk out the door. It feels as if I'm really leaving. But I'm not, I tell myself. I'm just searching for my sister to get her home.

Pulling out of the driveway, I notice something funny. There's frost on the windshield. I get out and start scraping at it. Being inside, maybe I just hadn't noticed a cold spell. A very cold spell.

Once everything is clear, I rev up the engine and I'm gone.

News

THE WEATHER for today is a high of 92 degrees with a low of -15 degrees tonight. The forecast is sun with a light dusting of hail, a sprinkle of lightning. 0 per cent chance of rain. Two clouds. One in the shape of an octopus, the other a regular ol' cumulo-nimbus. Expect bird droppings and birds dropping.

Some Weather

I'M DRIVING west on Middle Country when the sky cracks open and rain comes pouring down. I've never liked the rain. Snow, hail, sun, clouds, I can take. A little drizzle, a little fog is alright. But full-on rain? Not my cup of tea.

Through the frantic swishing of the windshield wipers, I can barely make out the lights of the cars around me, let alone recognize a person on the street. But of course, if she were walking back home, she would've found refuge somewhere from the rain.

I decide that the best place to look for her would be a diner. Warmth, light, greasy fries, late hours all make it the perfect place to wait out a rainstorm.

Cassandra, Are You?

THE DINER I pull up to is quite typical. Garishly reflective walls, neon lights proclaiming it the best diner in Suffolk, a cheery big-bosomed hostess. I take the menu and slide into a booth. It's early but the diner is emptier than I would've expected. There's only one person besides me.

I order home fries and a milkshake and watch the one other person in the diner. He's definitely not my sister. First of all, he's a he. Second of all, he's wearing a hat that my sister would never wear, an Indiana Jones number with a giant crocheted flower sewn on. Third of all, he's mumbling to himself. My sister knows how to project; she would never mumble.

I'm slurping up the dregs of my milkshake when this man slides into the seat across from me. "Hey!" I say; I can't really think of what else to say.

He looks me in the eye and enunciates clearly. "The world is falling apart."

"Yeah, so?"

He seems nonplussed. But honestly, who hasn't known that for years now? The world tends toward entropy, after all. "I mean it. Today, I saw a frog drop from the sky."

I think about that. "Well, it was raining pretty hard." I glance out the window. "Still is, as a matter of fact."

"It will stop raining in two hours."

I shrug. The waitress comes over and I slide some cash into the checkbook. I get up, tell the guy, "Nice talking to you," then leave.

Lake

THE CAR is up to its headlights in water and indeed, there are frogs swimming around. But the rain is letting up and the water is seeping into the drains along the sides of the street. The parking lot just happens to have its own personal lake with my car in the center of it. I sigh and hope that it's secretly a boat in disguise as a car.

I climb into the driver's seat with only a little bit of seepage getting through. Amazingly enough, the car starts and hauls itself out of the lake and onto the road.

As I drive, I realize what a useless endeavor it all is. For a second, I'm overwhelmed by failure. But before I let myself do anything I'd regret later like bang my head against the steering wheel or cry, I tell myself that I am the only one I can rely on and I should pull myself together or else. I think this in my mother's voice. It always works to calm me down.

Where to now? I'm obviously going about searching all wrong with my haphazard methods. I decide to find a map to make my way to my uncle's house.

Maps

THERE ARE so many different types of maps. There are maps of paper, of blood, of ink, of dirt and sweat. They trace the routes of one's life; they show us where we've been and where we have yet to go. They let us know what we should do and sometimes, why. There are air maps, traced on the wind and maps on vellum, showing us the way to our dreams. There are maps of the cities in our mind, of buried gold and ships of the sky. There are maps that show the skyscrapers of our lives. Every map is a map of the way home.

Right Track

I FIND a map in the glove compartment and there in red, a circle around exit 39W and the words 'Uncle's House'. Unfortunately, there's no circle saying, 'You are here' or 'Mom and Dad'. Those would've been helpful.

So the game plan is this:

1. Go to my uncle's house.

2. Ask my uncle what's going on.

3. If he doesn't know, stay at uncle's house and let him figure everything out.

It's a grand plan. I turn on the radio, hoping for some happy pop music to combat the gloom of the day but instead, find the news on every station.

News

NEWS just in – apparently, a fire started during the downpour in Nassau County and has spread throughout Garden City and adjacent towns. Firefighters have not been able to get to the area due to the incessant rain, the frogs, and the billowing smoke. It's a deadly combination that if inhaled, can often result in croaking and suffocation. A warning has been issued.

Fire

THERE'S A GLOW on the horizon as I near my uncle's town and soon, I see the individual fires on roofs, the ashes floating down. The rain has ceased; a rainbow floats above the fiery horizon. There are frogs littering the streets, dead frogs with their legs splayed like flattened mosquitoes.

When I get to my uncle's street, all I see are the burnt out hulls of houses, fire crackling at their edges. I can't recognize my uncle's. I don't remember the number but the mailboxes are gone anyway. I wonder where the people could have escaped to. Are they still stuck inside? I park the car, step out into the smog-filled air.

The smoke hits me like a wave, clogging my nostrils, my throat. I gasp and cover my mouth with my hands. Breathing is a chore. I open the door of the car, stick my head in for a quick gasp of air, then make my way to the closest house.

The ground is hot through the soles of my sneakers. My eyes are tearing as I near the house, stung by the smoke. There are small fires everywhere. I make my way around them and into the house.

Inside, everything is burnt and completely unrecognizable. I can't tell a chair leg from a human leg. Ashes, ashes everywhere.

I leave, kicking frogs along the way. It's not their fault but I've got to take my frustration out somehow. And frustration is always better than breaking down. If I keep moving, I won't be able to feel what's buzzing around in my head, hovering just out of reach. Give me blind anger, give me obstinance, just don't give me grief.

There's a mostly intact television in the driveway, its plastic only a little warped and it's showing the news.

News

– WELL, Jim, the rain has stopped so the firefighters were able to go into that fiery disaster area. What they found was quite strange.

What'd they find, Jim?

Empty, burnt houses, Jim. The fact that they were burnt wasn't the strange part. It was the fact that every single house was empty. Every single house, Jim. No corpses, no nothing.

Not even a pet?

Only frogs, Jim.

So Jim, do we even know the cause of the fires?

Not a clue, Jim. Some say it might've been caused by highly reactive chemical rain mixing with the skin of the frogs, causing them to spontaneously combust and so, causing fires. Personally, Jim, I don't believe it. There are still plenty of frogs around and none of them seem burnt at all.

Jim, you're absolutely right. I bet frog lovers are having a field day though –

Fireproof

WHEN I GET BACK into the car, my shoes squish and my head feels like someone's been pounding at it with a hammer for several hours. In the car, I watch the frogs hopping around the sidewalks, avoiding the fiery patches. Are frogs fireproof?

I step on the gas, peel out of the street and into the highway.

I don't know where I'm going or what I'm doing but I think I'll know when I get there.

Pretty Soon, Pretty Please

I'M GOING with intuition. Driving east on the L.I.E., from exit 63 up, toward Montauk Point, I'm surprised by how empty the roads are. There are only about five cars on the road, including mine. The highway stretches on and on, no one behind me or ahead of me for miles. The frogs are gone and the sun is high overhead. It's nearing four in the afternoon.

Out east, where the farms and vineyards are. Where the mansions border on the Sound, the lighthouses beckoning the ships to shore. I've never been very far east on the island but because it's the last place my parents would be, it may also be the first.

I switch on the radio.

News

SO, JIM, how's it going out on the east end?

The usual, Jim. Tsunami-like waves and a beached humpback whale on the north side of Montauk Point. It's a pity, Jim, a real pity.

Sounds pretty terrible, Jim. How are the sailboats then?

I've gotta admit, the sailboats have all been smashed to smithereens, Jim. The lighthouse was taken down by the waves and all the sailboats smashed against the rocks.

Jim, have I ever told you that I've always wanted a sailboat? I guess it's the wrong time to get one now.

No, Jim, actually, it's the perfect time to buy a sailboat. Demand is down since they're all getting ripped apart so prices have dropped. That's actually the economic news of the day.

Well, thanks for the advice, Jim. Hear that, folks? Get your sailboats now!

Sand, Stars and Storms

IT'S ALWAYS amazed me how long this island I live on is. The rain has started again, pellets of rain falling like bullets onto my windshield and after two hours of drenched fields, I'm starting to wonder if I'll ever reach the end.

But I do reach the end just as the rain ends, literally driving to the edge. The lighthouse is a few hundred feet away, the water higher than its door. I have a feeling that that's not the way it should be. The waves are huge, crashing against the lighthouse and lapping onto the shore. I stop the car and get out.

The sky is overcast with clouds, dark since the sun has already set but in between the clouds, I can see the dim twinkling of the stars. There is no one here and it feels as if I am the last person on earth, surrounded by the forces of nature with the waves pounding, the sand at my feet, and the stars above.

I lie down in the sand, exhausted, and watch the clouds rush by.

Dream A Little Dream

DREAM OF the sands swallowing me, my bones washed by the ever-changing sea. I dream of earthquakes opening fissures in the ground, hurricanes tearing houses down, mountains spewing lava and ash. Of floods, of fires, of plagues of locusts.

I dream of being alone.

I dream of people disappearing one by one. I watch them as they go.

And away they go.

Almost There

WAKE because of the waves tickling my feet, sucking me down and out. Scrabbling out of the wet sand, I haul myself to my feet and head back to the car.

The car is already sitting in a pool of water a few inches deep and getting it out of the sand and water is not an easy task. Sand and water spray everywhere, traction is almost impossible but somehow, it heaves out of the hole it dug for itself and we head back on the road. Back towards home.

The radio sputters alive but only to give off the sound of static. There are no cars on the road at all but I don't worry. It's pretty late and dark enough that sometimes it's hard to see the white lines in the road. I fly through the night on slick black tires, occasionally hydroplaning on the wet road.

All I can see are silhouettes. Silhouettes of telephone wires and grape vines in vineyards. Silhouettes of houses. Occasionally, a green sign will leap out of the dark, informing me of exit 80 a half mile away or route 247 to my right. But everything is strangely calm. The rain hasn't returned and the night is silent. I crank down the windows but all I can hear is the sound of the engine and my own breath.

And into the darkness I sing.

I sing songs from my childhood, of heartbreak and loss before I knew such things. I sing, like the old cliché, as if no one's listening because I know that, in fact, no one is. And I'm alright with that. My voice is hoarse as I spill other people's secrets and worries out into song. I feel free and unburdened; I know where I'm going and what I'm doing now.

I'm going home.

Home, At Last

WHEN I reach home, it's past the witching hour and my neighborhood is so silent that I imagine I could hear a mouse move. All the lights in the house are out. I park the car in the driveway and walk up to the door. It's a different color than I remember.

But my key fits into the lock, the quiet *snick* as it turns. I open the door, step in, turn on the light, and there they are.

There they are.

Nyarlathotep

H.P. Lovecraft

NYARLATHOTEP... the crawling chaos... I am the last... I will tell the audient void...

I do not recall distinctly when it began, but it was months ago. The general tension was horrible. To a season of political and social upheaval was added a strange and brooding apprehension of hideous physical danger; a danger widespread and all-embracing, such a danger as may be imagined only in the most terrible phantasms of the night. I recall that the people went about with pale and worried faces, and whispered warnings and prophecies which no one dared consciously repeat or acknowledge to himself that he had heard. A sense of monstrous guilt was upon the land, and out of the abysses between the stars swept chill currents that made men shiver in dark and lonely places. There was a demoniac alteration in the sequence of the seasons – the autumn heat lingered fearsomely, and everyone felt that the world and perhaps the universe had passed from the control of known gods or forces to that of gods or forces which were unknown.

And it was then that Nyarlathotep came out of Egypt. Who he was, none could tell, but he was of the old native blood and looked like a Pharaoh. The fellahin knelt when they saw him, yet could not say why. He said he had risen up out of the blackness of twenty-seven centuries, and that he had heard messages from places not on this planet. Into the lands of civilisation came Nyarlathotep, swarthy, slender, and sinister, always buying strange instruments of glass and metal and combining them into instruments yet stranger. He spoke much of the sciences – of electricity and psychology – and gave exhibitions of power which sent his spectators away speechless, yet which swelled his fame to exceeding magnitude. Men advised one another to see Nyarlathotep, and shuddered. And where Nyarlathotep went, rest vanished; for the small hours were rent with the screams of nightmare. Never before had the screams of nightmare been such a public problem; now the wise men almost wished they could forbid sleep in the small hours, that the shrieks of cities might less horribly disturb the pale, pitying moon as it glimmered on green waters gliding under bridges, and old steeples crumbling against a sickly sky.

I remember when Nyarlathotep came to my city – the great, the old, the terrible city of unnumbered crimes. My friend had told me of him, and of the impelling fascination and allurement of his revelations, and I burned with eagerness to explore his uttermost mysteries. My friend said they were horrible and impressive beyond my most fevered imaginings; that what was thrown on a screen in the darkened room prophesied things none but Nyarlathotep dare prophesy, and that in the sputter of his sparks there was taken from men that which had never been taken before yet which shewed only in the eyes. And I heard it hinted abroad that those who knew Nyarlathotep looked on sights which others saw not.

It was in the hot autumn that I went through the night with the restless crowds to see Nyarlathotep; through the stifling night and up the endless stairs into the choking room. And shadowed on a screen, I saw hooded forms amidst ruins, and yellow evil faces peering from behind fallen monuments. And I saw the world battling against blackness; against the waves of destruction from ultimate space; whirling, churning; struggling around the dimming, cooling sun. Then the sparks played amazingly around the heads of the spectators, and hair stood up on end whilst shadows more grotesque than I can tell came out and squatted on the heads. And when I, who was colder and more scientific than the rest, mumbled a trembling protest about 'imposture' and 'static electricity,' Nyarlathotep drave us all out, down the dizzy stairs into the damp, hot, deserted midnight streets. I screamed aloud that I was *not* afraid; that I never could be afraid; and others screamed with me for solace. We sware to one another that the city *was* exactly the same, and still alive; and when the electric lights began to fade we cursed the company over and over again, and laughed at the queer faces we made.

I believe we felt something coming down from the greenish moon, for when we began to depend on its light we drifted into curious involuntary marching formations and seemed to know our destinations though we dared not think of them. Once we looked at the pavement and found the blocks loose and displaced by grass, with scarce a line of rusted metal to show where the tramways had run. And again we saw a tram-car, lone, windowless, dilapidated, and almost on its side. When we gazed around the horizon, we could not find the third tower by the river, and noticed that the silhouette of the second tower was ragged at the top. Then we split up into narrow columns, each of which seemed drawn in a different direction. One disappeared in a narrow alley to the left, leaving only the echo of a shocking moan. Another filed down a weed-choked subway entrance, howling with a laughter that was mad. My own column was sucked toward the open country, and presently felt a chill which was not of the hot autumn: for as we stalked out on the dark moor, we beheld around us the hellish moon-glitter of evil snows. Trackless, inexplicable snows, swept asunder in one direction only, where lay a gulf all the blacker for its glittering walls. The column seemed very thin indeed as it plodded dreamily into the gulf. I lingered behind, for the black rift in the green-litten snow was frightful, and I thought I had heard the reverberations of a disquieting wail as my companions vanished; but my power to linger was slight. As if beckoned by those who had gone before, I half-floated between the titanic snowdrifts, quivering and afraid, into the sightless vortex of the unimaginable.

Screamingly sentient, dumbly delirious, only the gods that were can tell. A sickened, sensitive shadow writhing in hands that are not hands, and whirled blindly past ghastly midnights of rotting creation, corpses of dead worlds with sores that were cities, charnel winds that brush the pallid stars and make them flicker low. Beyond the worlds vague ghosts of monstrous things; half-seen columns of unsanctified temples that rest on nameless rocks beneath space and reach up to dizzy vacua above the spheres of light and darkness. And through this revolving graveyard of the universe the muffled, maddening beating of drums, and thin, monotonous whine of blasphemous flutes from inconceivable, unlighted chambers beyond Time; the detestable pounding and piping whereunto dance slowly, awkwardly and absurdly the gigantic, tenebrous ultimate gods – the blind, voiceless, mindless gargoyles whose soul is Nyarlathotep.

An Introvert at the End of the World

Wendy Nikel

IF THERE'S ONE THING the zombie apocalypse taught me: the living dead are easier to deal with than the still-living.

I came to dread those days when I had to strap on my backpack full of supplies and walk to the nearest commissary. Wading through the fly-infested piles of groaning, half-rotted corpses, I'd often stumble across a zombie that still had both legs or that had figured out how to pull itself along on stub arms, and I'd have to stop and take care of it.

Even worse, though, was running into other survivors.

They'd always ramble on with small-talk pleasantries and inane questions, like how much of the country do you think survived? When do I think the military will clean up the carcasses rotting in the streets?

"How should I know? Do I look like the president?" I'd say (in my head). Outwardly, I'd offer a tight smile and shrug. Then I'd mutter my excuses and escape.

That's why I usually took the back way to the commissary, climbing over backyard fences to avoid the open streets where the living roamed. Unfortunately, this was precisely where I ran into Joan.

"Is that you, Becky?"

I groaned. Maybe if I ignored her and walked stiffly, my former coworker would think I was already dead.

"Oh, it *is* you! I *knew* you'd make it! I told Tom, that Becky Gilroy *must've* made it. I remember way back before *you-know-what*, we'd see you running in the city park, and I'd tell Tom, there's that Becky Gilroy, running like there's a zombie after her." She chortled, one of those awful, tear-your-ears-out laughs that I'd hoped I'd never have to hear again.

I implemented my smile, shrug, escape strategy. My hand tightened involuntarily on my ax when I heard the *thunk-thunk* of her combat boots hurrying after me.

"You know what we ought to do?" Joan asked.

"Go our separate ways and forget we ever saw each other?" I suggested (in my head).

"We ought to team up. You and me. Two survivors, going at it alone. We can share your place; it's got better defenses."

I gaped, grappling for some excuse.

"Don't be coy! Everyone's seen your fences; you've got quite the setup!"

"What about Tom?"

"Zombies got him just last week, the poor guy."

"Poor guy," I muttered.

"What's wrong? Don't you trust me?" She laughed again. The sound of zombies gnawing my ears off would have been preferable.

I had to ditch her – not because I was afraid she'd rob me or kill me in my sleep – but because the thought of being around this insufferable woman 24/7 made me want to strangle *her*. Or myself.

During the early days of the apocalypse, I'd been as anxious as anyone else, worried about what this would mean for humanity's future. Soon, though, I realized that the end of the world was liberating. Sure, society's collapse did away with our infrastructures, but it also did away with inane societal niceties.

No more get-togethers with distant relations who always forget your name. No more girls' nights out with friends who drag you from bar to bar while you'd rather be sleeping. No more strangers on the train commenting on the book you're trying to read. No more work parties. No more company picnics. No more funerals or birthday parties or – the worst of all – *weddings*.

Nowadays, no one cared if I spent all day soaking in my tub (after collecting the rainwater in barrels, boiling it over a campfire, and pumping it through the window into the bathroom, of course) or all night reading by candlelight. If anyone noticed I hadn't been outside in weeks, they'd just think I was being cautious. This post-apocalyptic lifestyle was an introvert's dream.

Joan grabbed my hand. "We'll start a bridge club!"

That did it. I had to get rid of her.

The W and L of the WALMART sign were lit up, indicating that the air force unit that had commandeered its inventory had opened the doors to the public for the afternoon. Before, I'd have avoided the place like the plague, but since the apocalypse, I didn't actually mind it. The parking lot was empty, there were never any lines, and with so few survivors, I could peruse the DVD bargain bin without a single nosy shopper butting in to comment about how underrated the fifth film in the series had been and how the lead actor's replacement was so much better for the role.

"Let's check out the DVDs," Joan said, pulling me along. "I love the bargain bins."

"I'll bet you do," I muttered.

While she was digging through the cheap knockoffs and 80s movies no one liked when they were new, I crept away to sort out my problem. Joan wasn't some zombie I could just decapitate and be done with, but what other options did I have? She already knew where I lived.

"Can I help you, ma'am?" The military guard must've thought I was acting suspiciously. Normally, I'd have offered a polite 'no thanks', but maybe he could help.

"See that lady over there?"

He nodded.

"She's been following me around and…" How could I explain it without sounding like a jerk? "She's alone and looking for a place to stay. Is there some sort of commune or something that you could direct her to?"

"Local one's at max capacity. Why can't she join you?"

"We don't really get along…"

The man balked. "In case you haven't noticed, ma'am, there's a zombie apocalypse going on. Survivors can't afford to be picky about their companions; you never know when you'll be the one getting mauled and in need of a friend. Those of us left, we gotta help each other out."

Obviously, this guy was going to be no help to *me* at all. I wasn't cruel enough to throw Joan to the zombies or leave her defenseless, but the conversation did give me an idea.

* * *

Joan followed me home, yammering the entire way and toting a karaoke machine behind her. I gritted my teeth and strapped my ax to my pack so I wouldn't be tempted to use it on her.

At the house, she gushed over the alarm system, the food stores, the pumps that brought water from the rain barrels to the bathtub upstairs. At each enthusiastic "Ooo!" and "Aaa!" I steeled myself for what I had to do.

* * *

At dusk, the zombies attacked.

They're always more active in the evening, and while I generally would be in bed with a book by dark, Joan apparently was more of a night owl. A Broadway musical blared from my TV and before each song, she urged me to sing along.

Even then, we'd have been okay if someone hadn't forgotten to latch the front gate.

"Do you hear that?" I looked up from the novel I'd been futilely trying to read. Sure enough, the yard was swarming with the stumbling, bloody remains of our neighbors.

"What do we do?" Joan asked.

I shook my head. It looked pretty bad. "There's too many of them. We'll have to run through the back yard before they reach the house. You grab the emergency packs in the back on your way out and I'll grab –"

I opened the door to the front hallway and was greeted by the rotting face of a zombie. Before I could move, it fell on me. I screamed. "It's got me! Run! Get out!"

Joan didn't need to be told twice. She didn't even really need to be told once. At the sight of the baseball cap and guts clad corpse, she'd screeched and high-tailed it out the back door.

I lay still beneath the zombie, waiting for the end.

When I heard the gate slam shut, I shoved the corpse off me. Its hat rolled off its head, exposing the gaping hole where its brains had been. It'd taken me forever to prop it up just right in the front hall, but Joan had been so engrossed in *Rent* that she hadn't even noticed my extended bathroom break.

Unfortunately, the zombies in the yard *were* a real threat. It'd be weeks, maybe months, before they'd wander off someplace else. I grabbed my emergency backpack, gripped my ax, and took off for the next town over.

It was a shame to leave everything behind, but there were plenty of empty houses, and I'd read most of the books in mine anyway. Rain barrels and defense systems were replaceable, but I couldn't live without peace and solitude.

Sure, I'd run into some zombies on my way, but the living dead were a million times easier to deal with than the living.

Turn, World, Turn

Konstantine Paradias

THE MOST important message I've ever gotten is just two words long and scrawled with garish orange spray-paint on the side of the Parliament building:

Sappes, Fall

It starts at about eye-level, bold lines that taper off into squiggles the higher up they go. The curve of the letters is wonky, irregular, as if written on tiptoe. My eyes wander off, following the spatter of paint that's been smeared at the end of the message and I imagine an unexpected gust of wind, blowing burning orange into the eyes of whoever wrote the message, think of them choking and weeping, tossing the can away.

I think of the can clattering across Syntagma Square, sending the pigeons into a panicked frenzy. Right on cue, the hawks and the cats come down on them. There's a tiny massacre, all because of two little words.

Written by someone.

*Any*one.

Click. Click. Whirr. Clack.

"Tom!" Aunt Polly's voice booms from the car speakers for the hundredth thousandth time as the Adventures of Tom Sawyer starts playing all over again. My heart skips a beat and I whirl around, halfway hoping that I'll maybe see the old bag, standing *right there,* leaning against the guard post, her skirt all caked with dirt and her shriveled little mouth scrunched up as she stares at that other person and they'll see me, in my torn t-shirt I've worn for almost two years now and my hair sticking out like a caveman's and they'll laugh and laugh at me but I won't care.

Except, I turn around and there's no one. Just the same old beat up car, stashed with all the canned kibble and the jars and the liquor. Behind it, a trailer piled high with icons and rolled up canvasses and leather bound books with gilded lettering, set on top of a rattling bed of money and baubles that I have zero use for but I still bothered to pack, on the off chance civilization restarted and I wanted to be on the top of the pile this time around.

Then again, that had been…

I start counting down the chill winters spent by the seaside, the summers spent in the suburbs, but time's become a featureless, sprawling thing that stretches on for ever. I check my watch, stopped dead six months into the end of the world and I tap the bezel, but that doesn't accomplish anything.

I search the trees around the square but they're all dead, their leaves blown out from their branches. I sprint toward the Royal Gardens, a mad dash across a kilometer of baking asphalt, my flip-flops biting into the skin between my toes until it bleeds. When I'm there, I check the leaves, search for any hanging fruit.

Some of them are in bloom. Bees infest the treetops. A pair of peacocks strut and coo for the attentions of a bored female. Late summer, has to be. August, maybe? There's still time.

"You're a coward and a pup!" Tom Sawyer's voice comes from the speakers, blaring out across half of Athens and I walk back toward the car, unhitch the trailer. I stash the valuables inside the burnt out shell of what used to be the tearoom of the Grand Bretagne Hotel. That should keep them safe from the rain. Not much I can do about anything else.

When the trailer's all safe, I spend the next four hours tearing down one of the quarantine banners laid out across the edges of Syntagma Square, facing Ermou Street. Written across the thick yellow fabric in bold, red letters are the words:

HIGH LETHALITY ZONE – TRESPASSERS SHOT ON SIGHT

Across it, scrawled in blue and white, someone's calling out for God. Someone else is asking his mother for forgiveness. There's a halfway finished Banksy spray-painting, laid under what looks like a bullet hole. I paint over all the mess until it's nothing but white smoothness and write:

GONE TO SAPPES. ALEXANDROUPOLI IN WINTER.

"Stop her, sir! Ting-a-ling-ling!" the boy calls out from the speakers and I turn the damn thing off. The silence falls so suddenly it jabs at my chest like a knife, so I hop into the car and hit the road as fast as I can. Behind me, the tires howl like something that's dragged itself out of Hell and into daylight. All around Athens, an impromptu chorus of feral dogs begins to howl, calling to their masters, long since extinct.

* * *

Nights on the highway are so thick that the darkness feels like a hungry, clinging thing, reaching for you from all sides. Even with the fog lights on and the sky dotted with stars, I can't see more than a few meters ahead, jerking the wheel every now and then at random to dodge a crack on the asphalt or the abandoned husk of some sports car, crashed into the side of the road sometime during the end of the world.

To keep myself occupied, I practice small talk. Nothing too ambitious; just the first things that come to mind:

"Hey."

"Yo!"

"God… someone… someone else!"

"My name is…" I start to say and the words stick to my throat. Sweat dribbles down from my forehead into my eyes. It stings like a bastard so I wipe at it but I won't open the window, no matter what. Somewhere out there are the mass graves, the places where the government started to pile people up when it got so bad they couldn't even risk a quick funeral. Of course, by the time they got the excavators rolling and the dead all piled up nice and neatly, the death toll had gotten so high that no one actually had the means to put them into the ground.

So they were just left there, in the sun and the rain. To every prowling, crawling thing.

That first summer when I realized I was alone, the stench got so bad that I had to leave the country; dash across the interstate up to God knows where and wait it out. When I got back, just in time for cold season, the sky was thick with vultures.

"God, I miss beef. Remember beef?" I say, my voice sounding too loud in the car. I lick at my lips and taste the sweat that's dripped down across my face, whip the car to the left, dodging a rusted old SUV with its windows blown in. A four-legged thing yowls as it leaps out of the way, narrowly dodging the last car on Earth.

"Where were you?" I say, my voice almost a whimper. A wave of pinpricks rushes across my arm, travelling up from my fingers and I realize that I've been gripping the steering wheel like a madman since I passed Lamia, since I slammed my foot down on the gas pedal and started to scream across the country. Slowly easing off the gas, I start to relax my grip. The words come unbidden:

"What's your name? Just... tell me your name," I plead and in my head, I hear the voice coming from somewhere inside me, a gentle noise like silk across a patch of smooth skin; like crystal clear water, breaking across a mossy rock. It's a woman's name and the sound of it makes my heart beat so fast that I hit the brakes before I know it, the speedometer plunging down from 200 kilometers an hour to almost half that speed in three seconds flat. I fishtail like crazy, tires screeching across the night, headlights whipping around. The steering wheel turns and breaks from my grip and I stare at it uselessly, take in the whizzing blur of asphalt and weeds and sky that's the world around me. Too late, I lean back and brace...

Impact hits me like a steam hammer. The car smashes against the railing, bending the metal as it goes. In the blink of an eye, I'm up in the air, perfectly still among the shattered glass that hangs before my eyes, floating like a host of zero-g angels. When gravity kicks in, I slam into the Earth so hard it feels like my bowels are about to plop right out of me. Under my feet, the car's axles give way. The engine whines, purrs and finally settles for a machine death-knell, leaving a pair of busted headlights to flicker against the dark.

* * *

By the time I've dragged myself out of the wreckage and halfway through the stretch of untilled sunflowers, the sun is peeking over the hills of Paggaio. Standing on tiptoe, wincing against the agony that's shearing across my left leg, I check across the wilted stretch of sunflowers, searching for a sign.

"God, please, a back road will do..." I bellow, fighting back the tears. Before I can stop myself, I've looked down at the tear across my jeans, the bleeding stretch of meat running down across my leg. A little animal whimper rises up from somewhere inside me but I choke it down, push through the dense curtain of sunflower stalks, cracking them as I go.

By noon, I've reached a strip of choked asphalt that locals used to call a road. A gust of wind from the east rustles through the field, bringing the awful carrion-stench with it so I hobble away from it. The sun creeps down the horizon and my stomach starts to rumble, my head begins to swoon as time locks back into place. My watch is busted well beyond repair but I don't have to even glance at it to know it's all moving again. The world's started turning again and my heart starts to pound in that way it used to, back when I had a job I was awful at and bills to pay and someone who'd break my heart just so they could put it back together again.

"Please be real, please, please be real," the little mantra comes unbidden as I hobble across the country road, skipping past combine harvesters that have been left to rust. A murder of crows give me dirty looks as I tiptoe around the bloated corpse of a donkey, its saddle still hanging off its mangy back.

Night falls and I collapse on the side of the road. When day breaks, I start hobbling all over again until I'm at some place without a name, a little row of houses and roads built against the mountain range, overlooking a stretch of land so green it hurts your eyes to look at. Every home has an orchard so I rip the hanging oranges from the branches, bite into their flesh without bothering to peel. I pile cucumbers in my shirt and steal tomatoes from the beaks of cawing birds.

I smash in the window leading into the local pharmacy. When I've patched myself up, I search for a bed without a dead couple clinging to each other under the sheets and let myself collapse into it. Dust rises up like a storm cloud around me the second I hit the mattress but I'm too far gone to even wonder how much of it might be human.

Sleep comes like death: dark and dreamless.

It takes two days to find a car in good working order. It's an old BMW, stashed in a garage like an exhibit piece: raised up on a makeshift platform, its chassis spotless, the faux leather seating still crackling. The engine groans like an old miser and the wheel fights me with everything it's got when I try to steer it, but I force the damn thing into the highway and hug the shore.

"Please, let me be worth you," I pray to no one in particular, as the world zips past me in a blur of endless green.

* * *

Sappes' topsoil is tough and dry, hiding away a bounty of black loam. I while away the days rifling through barns, shifting through banks filled with seeds and planting them at random across the stretch of land I've tilled. Then, I water and watch the sprouts grow like children, kneel and search them, as if I have the slightest idea what I am doing.

In the baking summer heat, I chase off chickens gone halfway feral, coop escapees led by battle-scarred roosters with a mean streak a mile-wide. They lunge at me, fearlessly, when I try to stop them from pecking at my bounty. An alpha male, all rowdy, digs its talons into my shirt sleeve, tears though the fabric and draws blood. It caws in pointless panic as it tries to get free and I wring its neck.

That settles dinner for about three days.

To make sure whoever it is can find me, I spend a week searching for every road sign still standing and spray paint a simple message on the board:

OFF TO SAPPES

Along with a little halfway helpful arrow. Every now and again, I stop to check the road, search for the distant rumble of some car engine, drawing closer. If whoever is on the way, I'd be able to hear them all the way from Komotini, just a distant motor, revving closer like thunder.

Summer slowly fades and the rains come down, an outpour that floods the streets and seeps into my garden, drowning my crop. Thunder crashes all around me and I wait for it inside, huddled like a caveman while the gods have their little tantrum. When it's over, I drive to the city and search for fencing, for pots, anything that will keep my crop someplace safe and high. Halfway through it all, I realize that I don't even know where to start, so I settle for carting off some pots and hoping for the best.

"No, goddamn it no!" I scream at the column of smoke rising from Rodopi. Even from here, I can see the conflagration rising, a wall of fire that laps at the mountainside, reducing the forests into cinder. I spend the next two days praying for rain, for it to run itself out. Instead, the wind blows from the west so hard it almost burns away at my eyebrows, carrying with it a cloud of ash and I know it's time to go.

On the side of the house, across the old interstate, I write a jumbled little message:

KOMOTINI, DOWNWIND

And stuff the seedlings into the pots, and pile them high into the backseat of the BMW, hoping for the best. For a moment, I try to imagine the old man's face, if he could see what his prize car looked like, all covered in mud and dirt, the seats stained with rainwater from when I forgot to pull up the window that one time. All I get is my dad's face, staring up at me from behind the plastic sheeting of the quarantine, nodding about how it's all going to be okay.

Across the forest cover, a herd of wild boars decides to brave the outside world. In the distance, a pack of wolves begins to howl, calling their brothers toward their bounty.

I head east.

* * *

Fall finally comes after the fire's almost stripped Rodopi clean of vegetation. From the east, packs of feral dogs, terriers and sheepdogs and second-generation Beagle mutts flood into the city, hunting for the fowl that have found their way there. The Imaret museum is a nesting ground for rock pigeons, its halls echoing with the cries of a million hungry chicks. Wild rabbits have peppered the high school's yard with warrens. Wolves bicker over their hunting grounds near the old Bulgarian border.

The leaves turn yellow, then red, then brown. They come down like a thick carpet of mulch. My seeds grow into tomato plants, tiny cucumbers, a few varieties of pepper. I plant shallots and garlic in a back yard, but the goats get to them before I can stop them.

When the cold season starts to creep in, the bears start to dare the city. After almost crashing my car into one, I realize it's time to go.

WINTER IN XANTHI. FIND ME.

* * *

In Xanthi, the winter is a biting thing that covers the world in a thick carpet of snow, which forces me to dare the icy roads leading into Kavala.

I while away the winter by the sea, listening to the sounds of old cruise ships rocking themselves into the water across the harbor. One of them has a library filled old tapes, nothing but cheesy old songs. I load them up into the BMW and blast them for the world to hear. Sometimes, I fish for oysters, hoping that they might make me look fancy.

Every now and then, I'll search for a message, the distant sound of a revving engine, but I don't really bother with it anymore.

"Guess that's done with," I say and I imagine some wreck on the side of the road, the distant blare of some car door alarm that no one will ever listen.

Bing, bing, bing…

So I hop into the BMW and pile up my tomatoes and my shallots and my carrots and my peppers and my garlic and onions and head for Nigrita, for Polygyros, Thessaloniki, with the speakers turned to full blast, calling for whomever it might be, hoping that perhaps I'm not too late. Just outside of Thessaloniki, a placard reads:

CAR TROUBLE.

And under that:

FIND ME IN VEROIA

It's springtime in Veroia and the smell of peaches is so rich it makes you almost cry; the streets are bursting with greenery. The windows have shattered after God knows how many winters. The high-rises have been turned into eagle fiefdoms. In the church of St. Anargyroi, where owls hold their screeching Congress, I find the next message, scrawled across the side of the building:

EVROS WAS BURNING. HOPE YOU'RE OKAY. VOLOS?

And I rush down across the world, banging my fist against the roof of my car, howling like a madman. She's gone. He's gone. Did I make them up? Maybe I've gone mad and I've just been going after my own scribbles. No, no can't be; then why can't whomever the hell it is just sit still? Why can't they…

I've torn through Larisa, burning through the E95, when I hear it, barely audible over the BMW's ancient revving noise:

The doppler rumble, coming closer.

The sound of something loud and crude that turns petrol into horsepower.

Careening through an empty road.

I bash the car horn as hard as I can, let it blare out into the emptiness. Geese explode out from the underbrush, driven into a frenzied flight. The noise spreads out all around me, spreading out across the face of the world and I imagine the Earth's shaking, stirred from its slumber.

From the corner of my eye, something whizzes by, a streak of silver that *whooshes* through the air. I brake hard, car fishtailing and turn around after it, searching for the glint of sunlight on chrome, squinting against the divide.

"Heeeey!" I scream, as loud as I can. Stomp on the gas. Flick the cheesy love songs up to 11. Out in the distance, there's the barest glint of sunlight against a windshield. I slow down, just enough to take it in. No, a wreck. Then, a shattered little mess of a car that made the plunge before the end of the world. Then, an upended bus and then…

"Helloooo!" I howl as loudly as I can, slam into the car horn. Brake lights light up ahead. There's the screeching of tires on asphalt. The silver car spins around, uncontrollably and I see the barest hint of a panicked, sweating face fighting against a steering wheel that's spinning with a mind of its own. Out from the back seat, a suitcase shoots out into the abandoned highway, snaps open, spilling out clothes as it goes.

"Don't fight it, just ease it, don't pull the handbrake, come on…" I say as I watch the car spin, swerve and finally slam into the divide, stopping cold. I gun it further up across the highway, make a u-turn through the empty toll booths, bursting through the barricade toward the silver car stopped by the side of the road.

And there.

Stepping out, knees wobbly, hand searching for purchase.

Whoever it is, they look so stunning I have to stop before I've crashed into them. Ease on the brakes, stop the car, take a deep breath before I step out and look...

More beautiful than Michelangelo's *David* and the Pietà both put together. I stare and stare and can't get enough of them and hope that if they talk to me, my heart won't just stop and I won't die. So we stare at each other in the silence and I kill the engine. I try to speak, but no words can come.

"Please tell me you're not mute," the voice comes across the silence and I start to laugh and run toward the silver car, hands outstretched and the world is turning again, but it's turning for us.

The Conversation of Eiros and Charmion

Edgar Allan Poe

EIROS.

Why do you call me Eiros?

CHARMION.

So henceforward will you always be called. You must forget too, my earthly name, and speak to me as Charmion.

EIROS.

This is indeed no dream!

CHARMION.

Dreams are with us no more; – but of these mysteries anon. I rejoice to see you looking life-like and rational. The film of the shadow has already passed from off your eyes. Be of heart and fear nothing. Your allotted days of stupor have expired and, tomorrow, I will myself induct you into the full joys and wonders of your novel existence.

EIROS.

True – I feel no stupor – none at all. The wild sickness and the terrible darkness have left me, and I hear no longer that mad, rushing, horrible sound, like the 'voice of many waters.' Yet my senses are bewildered, Charmion, with the keenness of their perception of the new.

CHARMION.

A few days will remove all this; – but I fully understand you, and feel for you. It is now ten earthly years since I underwent what you undergo – yet the remembrance of it hangs by me still. You have now suffered all of pain, however, which you will suffer in Aidenn.

EIROS.

In Aidenn?

CHARMION.

In Aidenn.

EIROS.

Oh God! – Pity me, Charmion! – I am overburthened with the majesty of all things – of the unknown now known – of the speculative Future merged in the august and certain Present.

CHARMION.

Grapple not now with such thoughts. Tomorrow we will speak of this. Your mind wavers, and its agitation will find relief in the exercise of simple memories. Look not around, nor forward – but back. I am burning with anxiety to hear the details of that stupendous event which threw you among us. Tell me of it. Let us converse of familiar things, in the old familiar language of the world which has so fearfully perished.

EIROS.

Most fearfully, fearfully! – This is indeed no dream.

CHARMION.

Dreams are no more. Was I much mourned, my Eiros?

EIROS.

Mourned, Charmion? – Oh deeply. To that last hour of all, there hung a cloud of intense gloom and devout sorrow over your household.

CHARMION.

And that last hour – speak of it. Remember that, beyond the naked fact of the catastrophe itself, I know nothing. When, coming out from among mankind, I passed into Night through the Grave – at that period, if I remember aright, the calamity which overwhelmed you was utterly unanticipated. But, indeed, I knew little of the speculative philosophy of the day.

EIROS.

The individual calamity was as you say entirely unanticipated; but analogous misfortunes had been long a subject of discussion with astronomers. I need scarce tell you, my friend, that, even when you left us, men had agreed to understand those passages in the most holy writings which speak of the final destruction of all things by fire, as having reference to the orb of the earth alone. But in regard to the immediate agency of the ruin, speculation had been at fault from that epoch in astronomical knowledge in which the comets were divested of the terrors of flame. The very moderate density of these bodies had been well established. They had been observed to pass among the satellites of Jupiter, without bringing about any sensible alteration either in the masses or in the orbits of these secondary planets. We had long regarded the wanderers as vapory creations of inconceivable tenuity, and as altogether incapable of doing injury to our substantial globe, even in the event of contact. But contact was not in any degree dreaded; for the elements of all the comets were accurately known. That among them we should look for the agency of the threatened fiery destruction had been for many years considered an inadmissible idea. But wonders and wild fancies had been, of late days, strangely rife among mankind; and, although it was only with a few of the ignorant that actual apprehension prevailed, upon the announcement by astronomers of a new comet, yet this announcement was generally received with I know not what of agitation and mistrust.

The elements of the strange orb were immediately calculated, and it was at once conceded by all observers, that its path, at perihelion, would bring it into very close proximity with the earth. There were two or three astronomers, of secondary note, who resolutely maintained that a contact was inevitable. I cannot very well express to you the effect of this intelligence upon the people. For a few short days they would not believe an assertion which their intellect so long employed among worldly considerations could not in any manner grasp. But the truth of a vitally important fact soon makes its way into the understanding of even the most stolid. Finally, all men saw that astronomical knowledge lied not, and they awaited the comet. Its approach was not, at first, seemingly rapid; nor was its appearance of very unusual character. It was of a dull red, and had little perceptible train. For seven or eight days we saw no material increase in its apparent diameter, and but a partial alteration in its color. Meantime, the ordinary affairs of men were discarded and all interests absorbed in a growing discussion, instituted by the philosophic, in respect to the cometary nature. Even the grossly ignorant aroused their sluggish capacities to such considerations. The learned now gave their intellect – their soul – to no such points as the allaying of fear, or to the sustenance of loved theory. They sought – they panted for right views. They groaned for perfected knowledge. Truth arose in the purity of her strength and exceeding majesty, and the wise bowed down and adored.

That material injury to our globe or to its inhabitants would result from the apprehended contact, was an opinion which hourly lost ground among the wise; and the wise were now freely permitted to rule the reason and the fancy of the crowd. It was demonstrated, that the density of the comet's nucleus was far less than that of our rarest gas; and the harmless passage of a similar visitor among the satellites of Jupiter was a point strongly insisted upon, and which served greatly to allay terror. Theologists with an earnestness fear-enkindled, dwelt upon the biblical prophecies, and expounded them to the people with a directness and simplicity of which no previous instance had been known. That the final destruction of the earth must be brought about by the agency of fire, was urged with a spirit that enforced every where conviction; and that the comets were of no fiery nature (as all men now knew) was a truth which relieved all, in a great measure, from the apprehension of the great calamity foretold. It is noticeable that the popular prejudices and vulgar errors in regard to pestilences and wars – errors which were wont to prevail upon every appearance of a comet – were now altogether unknown. As if by some sudden convulsive exertion, reason had at once hurled superstition from her throne. The feeblest intellect had derived vigor from excessive interest.

What minor evils might arise from the contact were points of elaborate question. The learned spoke of slight geological disturbances, of probable alterations in climate, and consequently in vegetation, of possible magnetic and electric influences. Many held that no visible or perceptible effect would in any manner be produced. While such discussions were going on, their subject gradually approached, growing larger in apparent diameter, and of a more brilliant lustre. Mankind grew paler as it came. All human operations were suspended.

There was an epoch in the course of the general sentiment when the comet had attained, at length, a size surpassing that of any previously recorded visitation. The people now, dismissing any lingering hope that the astronomers were wrong, experienced all the certainty of evil. The chimerical aspect of their terror was gone. The hearts of the stoutest of our race beat violently within their bosoms. A very few days sufficed, however, to merge even such feelings in sentiments more unendurable We could no longer apply to the strange orb any accustomed thoughts. Its historical attributes had disappeared. It oppressed us with a hideous novelty of emotion. We saw it not as an astronomical phenomenon in the heavens, but as an incubus upon our hearts, and a shadow upon our brains. It had taken, with inconceivable rapidity, the character of a gigantic mantle of rare flame, extending from horizon to horizon.

Yet a day, and men breathed with greater freedom. It was clear that we were already within the influence of the comet; yet we lived. We even felt an unusual elasticity of frame and vivacity of mind. The exceeding tenuity of the object of our dread was apparent; for all heavenly objects were plainly visible through it. Meantime, our vegetation had perceptibly altered; and we gained faith, from this predicted circumstance, in the foresight of the wise. A wild luxuriance of foliage, utterly unknown before, burst out upon every vegetable thing.

Yet another day – and the evil was not altogether upon us. It was now evident that its nucleus would first reach us. A wild change had come over all men; and the first sense of pain was the wild signal for general lamentation and horror. This first sense of pain lay in a rigorous constriction of the breast and lungs, and an insufferable dryness of the skin. It could not be denied that our atmosphere was radically affected; the conformation of this atmosphere and the possible modifications to which it might be subjected, were now the topics of discussion. The result of investigation sent an electric thrill of the intensest terror through the universal heart of man.

It had been long known that the air which encircled us was a compound of oxygen and nitrogen gases, in the proportion of twenty-one measures of oxygen, and seventy-nine of nitrogen in every one hundred of the atmosphere. Oxygen, which was the principle of combustion, and the vehicle of heat, was absolutely necessary to the support of animal life, and was the most powerful and energetic agent in nature. Nitrogen, on the contrary, was incapable of supporting either animal life or flame. An unnatural excess of oxygen would result, it had been ascertained in just such an elevation of the animal spirits as we had latterly experienced. It was the pursuit, the extension of the idea, which had engendered awe. What would be the result of a total extraction of the nitrogen? A combustion irresistible, all-devouring, omni-prevalent, immediate; – the entire fulfilment, in all their minute and terrible details, of the fiery and horror-inspiring denunciations of the prophecies of the Holy Book.

Why need I paint, Charmion, the now disenchained frenzy of mankind? That tenuity in the comet which had previously inspired us with hope, was now the source of the bitterness of despair. In its impalpable gaseous character we clearly perceived the consummation of Fate. Meantime a day again passed – bearing away with it the last shadow of Hope. We gasped in the rapid modification of the air. The red blood bounded tumultuously through its strict channels. A furious delirium possessed all men; and, with arms rigidly outstretched towards the threatening heavens, they trembled and shrieked aloud. But the nucleus of the destroyer was now upon us; – even here in Aidenn, I shudder while I speak. Let me be brief – brief as the ruin that overwhelmed. For a moment there was a wild lurid light alone, visiting and penetrating all things. Then – let us bow down Charmion, before the excessive majesty of the great God! – Then, there came a shouting and pervading sound, as if from the mouth itself of HIM; while the whole incumbent mass of ether in which we existed, burst at once into a species of intense flame, for whose surpassing brilliancy and all-fervid heat even the angels in the high Heaven of pure knowledge have no name. Thus ended all.

In the Way You Should Go

Darren Ridgley

WHEN THEY finally left the apartment, Sally had blindfolded Cory so he couldn't see the ocean of dead crowding their path out of the city, but that had been naïve. Of course the blindfold slipped off and he saw, and he quailed and howled for hours, overwhelmed by their walk through the mass grave that had been their neighbourhood – to say nothing of the constant ducking into dark corners or hiding under rubble whenever any of the many diseased rioters were roving near.

Sally had no idea how this happened, or why. She just knew they needed to find mom.

* * *

Night had long fallen, and the wheat field they were travelling through did little to shield them from the cool wind of the early fall. Cory was holding them up again, and Sally was out of patience.

"Go, Cory. Do it now," Sally's voice was more of a hiss than she meant it to be, but she was tired, too. She kept reminding herself not to hold it against Cory. He was only three, after all.

Cory stifled a whine and finally, blessedly, Sally heard a stream strike the ground, and the scent of urine overpowered the smell of wheat and earth for a moment. Sally didn't want to browbeat him into a pee break, but if she didn't, he'd wet himself, ruining his only pants and making it impossible for him to keep warm wherever they were able to stop for the night. To say nothing of the rash he might get. She had to make sure he stayed healthy. It was all up to her now, and she had to stay vigilant.

"Good, buddy. That's really good. Thank you," she tried to be encouraging now. Cory got his pants up and even in the dark, she could see his face was red with shame, with frustration, with exhaustion. She pulled him in for a hug, and whispered soothing words into his ear.

"We're almost there, buddy, we're finally almost there."

The pit stop had taken longer than she wanted it to. It was long past time to move on. She rested her javelin on her shoulder, took her brother by the hand, and kept walking through the wheat field they were using to conceal themselves.

Sally was too young to be Cory's caretaker, at 13 years old. But dad was gone, like so many others, and mom – well, there was still hope, but the time their trip was taking them gnawed that away all the time. Sally adjusted Cory's backpack, making sure it was still comfortable. Her own pack was getting heavy. It held the bulk of their supplies, mostly bottles of water pilfered from looted stores. Cory's pack contained some lighter rations – crackers, dried fruit – and of course, his stuffed tiger.

They'd been on the march for four days now, stopping often so Cory's little legs could rest, and their stuttering pace was making things more dangerous every moment. Each day, people got more desperate. It had only taken a day for nearly everyone to be killed. Their dad had been in the shower, and Sally had thought he'd slipped when she heard his body slam hard into the porcelain. She called 911 for an ambulance, but nobody answered. She told Cory to play in his room while she stayed with their dad, the shower curtain torn off and landing on him in a makeshift shroud, trying to hold his hand tight enough to save his life. It didn't work. Sally didn't get the benefit of hearing any last words, any final encouragements. When he tried to speak, he just ended up spattering the tub, her hands, her face with the blood being forcefully ejected from his lungs.

"I'll look out for him," she'd told him, her voice stammering as the weight of the situation fell down on her. "I'll do my best. I can handle it, dad."

Her dad's eyes searched for something in her, and seemed to find it. And then his hand let go. She left him in the bathroom as he fell, her hands trembling as she fumbled at the door handle. In the living room, Cody was watching some educational cartoon. She let him keep watching it for hours, while she tried in vain to process the difference between the man who'd raised her, and the limp form one room over.

They stayed put in the apartment building for a whole week, afraid of the screaming and looting down below. Their parents had always been paranoid about the neighbourhood and had installed their own steel door on the apartment's entrance, replete with multiple locks. After the first day, people stopped wasting their energy on the door and left them alone. But the power to the building had failed then, too, severing their home AI's connection to the net and leaving Sally with only her solar-powered phone for information. Sally kept Cory occupied with cartoons on its tiny screen, and fed him everything she found in the pantry until it was empty. They never entered the bathroom though, relieving themselves off the balcony. Sally had stuffed towels under the bathroom door to keep out the smell. When that failed, she had lied to Cory, telling him it was just the odour of their food scraps piling up in the trash.

Sally kept her eyes glued to her social media feeds as speculation ran wild without revealing anything close to a concrete answer. Some people talked about a germ bomb, a terrorist attack, a screw-up at a lab. Other people talked about divine judgment and raptures. But Sally only cared about the result, and not the cause. Some, like their dad, died quickly. Others endured, ravaged by open sores and stinking growths before eventually succumbing to madness. If the violence they descended into didn't kill them, time did the job not long after that point.

She still had a hard time sleeping. She still couldn't shake the sound of the howls that filled their building's corridors, all the time.

"I wanna go to bed," Cory said.

"Not now. Not here. Animals might be around. We have to get inside," Sally pointed to the elevator, still a few hundred yards away. Cory stood there, looking at her in the dark, refusing to absorb what she'd said.

"Fine, then. I'll just go without you. I'll just leave you all by yourself."

Sally started walking through the wheat. After about ten steps, she heard Cory panting, running to catch up. She waited for him, then resumed walking when he reached her.

Sally didn't know why she and Cory survived, untouched by the disease. As far as she'd seen, nobody had escaped entirely unscathed but them. Some of them might be nice, and she'd been taught many times not to judge by appearances, but all the same she kept her distance from everyone. There could be no trusting anyone, but that was fine with Sally.

Their mom's work often took her outside of the city, inspecting grain elevators. She figured if she and Cory survived, maybe their mom was the carrier of whatever gene had allowed that. Sally had just read up about genes, a little bit, in a science text online. It was her best guess.

She looked up above the stalks of wheat and saw the blinking red light atop the elevator. Sally remembered that on the day the bomb hit, her mom was supposed to be home the same day as she left, which meant the elevator she was visiting couldn't be that far. According to the map app, this was the closest elevator to the city. She was thankful for the map app – solar power and self-maintaining servers meant she could still access some information online if she had to. With it she could look up information on poisonous plants, check their route, even let Cory watch a handful of cartoons she'd downloaded, if the battery had plenty of juice and he really needed a distraction. It was her universal tool. It was all she needed.

Sally posted about looking for her the first day, but stopped after that, worried someone might be tracking her movements through the geotags. Her mom never commented on the post anyway, so she deleted it. Social media hadn't gone completely dead, after all; some continued to post, looking for other survivors, but Sally always knew she didn't really mean survivors in the way she and Cory were. When she found one of those accounts, it was always the same: the frantic pleas for help, the increasingly deranged updates, and then silence after they either died or were overtaken by their condition to the point they weren't interested in the net anymore. It wasn't worth trying to establish contact, she realized. A friend today would almost definitely be an enemy tomorrow, and Sally couldn't afford to leave a trail of any kind.

At first she had been lucky enough to score a wagon to pull her brother in when his legs got tired, but despite her attempts to conceal it overnight, while they slept in an abandoned bus, it was stolen. That was two days ago. Now, they trudged through the wheat, Sally pushing the tall stalks aside so Cory could walk unimpeded. He stomped petulantly the whole way, packing mud into the treads of his shoes and destroying any chance at traction.

"Can you carry me?"

"No, Cory. My pack is too heavy, I can't carry you too. I need you to be my big buddy right now, okay? Just a little longer."

Cory whined softly. Sally released an annoyed sigh, rolling her eyes.

"Cory, come *on*, I'm *sick* of this. Just do what I tell you to do and quit your whining. Why do you have to make this so hard?"

She spun around to continue rebuking him, but softened when she saw his face, full of confusion.

"Sally? I love you."

He always did that – said he loved you when he thought he was in trouble and wanted people to stop being mad at him. It always turned mom and dad to mush. Cory still didn't understand why they were doing this, asking her every single day about the details. Dad must have known he would be like this. He must have known it would be so scary Cory would never grasp it. He couldn't even read yet. He came up to her and rested his head on her arm, a pleading half-hug.

Sally was grateful she was strong for her age, but she was still too weary to go much further. With any luck, the elevator would have a high place for them to hide out and rest for a very long time. They had enough food to get through a whole day of rest if they were careful about it.

Two hundred metres further and Cory sat down and refused to get up. Sally threaded her javelin through the straps of her pack to keep her lone weapon in place and heaved him up, using the last of her strength to get him the rest of the way. The door to the office was hanging open, its knob broken off. Someone must have been through here and looked for supplies. Sally hoped they left something behind.

Since the door had been left open, this place at least smelled fresh, though there was a strong smell of grain from the storage area far above them. The front office was small, enough to receive visitors and little else. In the centre of the front counter, a dead AI sphere sat like a corpse's greyed eye, seeing nothing. Sally put her brother down on the floor inside, where he swayed half-asleep. She opened the NightVision app on her phone, noting the battery life was only at 13 per cent. She'd learned since they left that it was unwise to wave their flashlight around in the dark, whereas the app would let her see, albeit imperfectly, without any revealing glare.

She made her way to the storage area and did a sweep, looking at the screen to identify any high places they could rest. She hadn't paid attention to her mom's many sermons on how elevators were built, and was displeased to find getting to the top level would be impossible, between Cory's age and his level of energy. The elevator within the elevator was busted, leaving only the staircase. They would have to sleep in the office area.

She barricaded the door as best she could and unrolled their sleeping bag behind the counter. Cory eagerly crawled inside and in the darkness she heard him begin to suck his thumb.

"No thumb," she smacked his hand away. "We're a big boy now, right?"

"Can you read me a story?" his voice yearned for it more than when he'd asked for food earlier.

"It's dark, Cory, but I'll try." Sally retrieved Cory's stuffie from his pack, then reached into her own and pulled out their flashlight, and along with it, a lone storybook – Cory's favourite one.

Sally held the flashlight in the arm she wrapped around Cory and quietly read the story about a yellow balloon that becomes separated from its bundle, and floats around the world before drifting back down. It's meant to teach kids about the countries and peoples of the world, but Sally wondered if it mattered anymore. If there was still a world out there, they'd never see much of it.

* * *

A rattling sound woke Sally from her rest. Someone was pushing on the door. Her heart stopped beating for a moment as she considered the possibilities, only one of which was good. Had her mom been hiding here and returned after some late-night outing? It was unlikely. She listened for Cory's breathing, and it was slow, relaxed. He was still asleep.

A silently as she could, she wiggled out of the sleeping bag and moved for her javelin, which felt heavier than normal after the day's journey. Sally didn't know why she insisted on detouring to her school to grab it from the gym's storage room. She'd always been good at javelin in track and field, but didn't know how to make that skill carry over to surviving. She just felt better, having something long and sharp to jab at something if she needed to. She hoped she'd never need to – she still wasn't sure if she could.

A rough voice emerged from the other side of the door while her improvised barricade continued to shake from repeated attempts to force it open.

"Door's barred. Someone's in there."

"Hoo boy. Could be fun?"

"Oh I need some fun. Need it bad."

She couldn't see their faces in the dark, and couldn't decide if she was frozen out of fear or a need to properly survey them. Two men, she knew. From the shadows they cast in the moonlight, one of them was pretty big, the other not so much, maybe not much bigger than her. The rattling of the barricade began to slow.

"The hell with this. Might not even be anything in there. Whoever blocked that door might be dead."

"Well I don't mind meat that's been aged a little. That's a classy thing, y'know."

"You're sick, Earl."

"Okay, Saint Luke. You think they got somethin' good in there?"

"They better hope so."

Robbers, Sally thought. They didn't have much, but they couldn't afford to lose it. Plus, there was no telling if stealing from them would really be the end of it. They had to hide.

The shaking stopped, and Cory yawned a high-pitched yawn that felt like glass shattering in contrast to the newly fallen silence. The silence that followed was as ominous as anything Sally had felt since her dad stopped talking.

"You hear that?"

"I heard that, Luke."

A moment's silence more, then a thunderclap. The barricaded chairs and detritus standing between the two children and the strangers shook violently. Sally could see them start to untangle from one another.

She took advantage of the noise of their attempted break-in to shake Cory awake.

"Piggyback ride, Cory, piggyback ride."

"Huh? Mmmmph," Cory turned away, trying to go back to sleep.

"Piggyback ride!"

She forced him to awake and threw him into position. He clung on instinctively, frightened by the noise.

"What's that?" his voice was a shaky whisper.

"Bad men. Very bad men."

She fled into the inner rooms of the elevator, Cory hung around her neck like a stole. She had the advantage of having looked through these rooms before, and while she couldn't ascend, she could take advantage of knowledge of the interior her pursuers wouldn't have. She hid behind a column in the room where a conveyer belt fed upwards into a higher level. She shushed her mewling brother as much as possible, and he went quiet, frozen stiff.

The door flung open in an explosion of force and the intruders guffawed at their victory. Already, she could smell the bleeding sores on their flesh, and was grateful it was too dark to see their faces. Cory gasped a little but contained it. Sally listened for their footsteps. *It's just like a Halloween haunted house,* she told herself. *Your friends couldn't get the jump on you in those, and you'll make it through here, too.*

"C'mon new friends," Earl, the little one, now had a friendly tone to his voice, one he didn't have before. "We're all just trying to survive out here. I know you must be scared. C'mon, we can work together, be a team. Ain't that right, Luke?"

"Oh yeah, that's right. Like a team. I think we'll work real good together." The big one, Luke, had a voice that rumbled through the walls, making Sally's stomach turn.

She listened to them stumble around the darkened room, cursing at each other, calling out to them. Sally said nothing. She felt very proud of her brother, suddenly. He was doing so well. She waited for Earl's lighter footsteps to line up more or less with their column. Luke had gone to the other end of the room. She listened as Earl got to within five or six feet from them, then deliberately pinched Cory's leg. His yelp attracted Earl's attention, and Sally took a hard swallow. She didn't know if she was ready to kill a man, but it was dark. She wouldn't see the blood. She hoped that would help. She could feel the tip of her weapon trembling in time with her hands, her nerves waiting for her mind to decide if she was capable of this.

"There —" Earl's exclamation was cut short as Sally reacted in the moment, a shaky, adrenaline-charged stab thrusting out into the darkness. The sucking sound of her javelin being pulled out of his abdomen replaced whatever he was about to say. She felt the air move around her face as he groped in the darkness to snatch at her, his throat sending out hisses of pain. A terrified roar escaped Sally's mouth, frightening her brother behind her, as she plunged the weapon into him again, piercing his soft belly a second time. Across the room, Luke heard his partner's gurgling cry.

"You're dead, you're dead!" Sally heard a bull's stampeding hooves in the room as Luke shouted at her.

"Stay behind me Cory, stay behind me," Sally choked back a sob as the larger man charged between the columns at her. Cory yanked at his sister's arm and she was knocked off balance. Knowing she wouldn't regain her footing in time to fight her much larger second attacker, she rolled away in the direction Cory was pulling her and felt a huge object barrel past her in the darkness. She heard the sound of muscle slapping the wooden wall and Luke staggered backward, dazed. Sally was knocked down, her head smacking the concrete floor, flooding her with pain. Cory was nearby but she couldn't tell exactly where. All she heard was his desperate little voice crying out *I love you, I love you, I love you.*

She groped at the dark ground for her javelin, and found it as she heard footsteps travel to her. Sitting upright, hurt by the fall, she held the point of the javelin out defensively, her hands shaking.

"You know, we mighta taken it easy on you, if you hadn't gone and done that. All we wanted was your stuff and maybe some labour getting us to the next stop. Now I'm gonna make you pay for what you did to Earl. And your little pup there is going to pay double, just to show you." Sick laughter followed up the threat. The sound of his footsteps got closer.

Cory interrupted his crying to let out a yelp, and Sally heard a confused grunt from Luke. She heard feet stumbling, and her eyes caught the vague shape of some object not far from her. He was standing right over her brother and, one man already dead at her hand, something inside her went numb out of necessity. Her body took the posture she'd practiced, in safer settings, a hundred times. Her throw was strong and straight, and her newfound desensitization regarded the sound of a chest being punctured with curiosity, and not revulsion. Luke fell heavily to the ground, the javelin clacking on the concrete floor with his head.

Something in her brain told her the threat had passed, and she was suddenly able to place everything. Cory had wandered in front of her in the dark. Luke had tripped over him, stopping his approach toward her and revealing his position. The rest had been perpetrated by somebody else, somebody she needed. The two men were dead now, and Sally could be herself again. As much as she would ever be, anyway.

Sally scrambled backward, leaving the dying Luke with the spear penetrating his lung and exiting out the back of his ribcage. He wheezed pitifully, and then went silent. Further away in the room, Earl groaned complaints about his stomach wound, dying slowly. Neither was technically dead yet, and Sally didn't know if she should feel good about that or not.

She stepped over Luke and scooped up Cory, who was sobbing uncontrollably. This time, Sally let herself join in.

"It's okay buddy, it's okay. You were such a good boy. You were such a good brother. I love you. I love you."

"I... want... mommy and... daddy." Every word from Cory's mouth was interrupted by a high gasping sound as he struggled to breathe. She held him closer.

"Me too."

She nearly hyperventilated. She worried she might faint, and leave her brother newly vulnerable. She didn't know if it would ever stop. She'd held up her walls too long, and they'd fallen now.

She felt Cory go still, not asleep but too exhausted to keep wailing. Eventually, she stopped too. She stumbled to her feet, cradling him, his legs wrapped around her waist. She considered trying to retrieve the javelin but couldn't bear to wrench it from the dead man. She left it, resolving to find a new weapon later.

She took them back to the office area and laid him down on the ground with his tiger, which soothed him just a little. After gathering up their gear, she did one more sweep with the flashlight, and something new caught her eye in the area near the corpses. Half-covered by a tarp was a large machine with a pull-cord, a fuel canister beside it.

A generator.

Her arms were shot from the day's travel, and the fighting, and even carrying Cory to the lobby moments before, but if there was a chance to get power in the building, she had to take it. She removed the tarp the rest of the way and yanked the cord. Nothing happened the first time, or the second, or the sixth. Or the ninth. She took a moment, placed the last of her hope into her hand, and yanked again. The generator sputtered to life.

The lights flickered on and off, hesitating to accept the power source, but eventually they remained on. A loud startup noise emerged from the lobby and Sally knew the elevator's AI had been reactivated. She heard its monotonous greetings and put all despair out of her mind for the first time in days. Cory stared attentively at the device, calmed by the brief return to normalcy its colourful display represented.

"Please state how I may assist you... Please state how I may assist you..." the machine projected a holographic display with suggested questions.

"Tell me everything you can about Jacqueline Chartrand's last visit here."

"Searching... Supervisor Chartrand did not complete her scheduled evaluation. Supervisor Chartrand was recorded exiting this facility five days ago."

"Five days?" Sally's heart jumped. Five days. The incident hadn't killed her, at least not at first. It was something. But how to find her?

"Would you like me to contact Supervisor Chartrand?"

"You can do that?"

"This employee possesses a corporate-issued phone. Calling... Calling..."

The seconds took too long to pass.

"No answer."

"AI, do you have GPS data?"

"Searching... GPS report from three days ago. Displaying co-ordinates."

The holographic display placed a pin southwest of them. Sally couldn't tell how many kilometres it was by looking, and the display was beginning to fade as the generator's power waned. She looked at her own phone and saw she only had three per cent battery life. She held the phone up to the AI.

"Copy data to my device."

The AI hummed and the data appeared on her screen. The generator gave up the last of its fuel and the interior abruptly went dark again, with only the phone providing illumination. The marker was 10 kilometres away, and seemed to be in the middle of nowhere. Could she really have gone there? Was she still alive? Would they arrive to find their mother had been ravaged by the illness – was she even safe to be around?

Sally didn't know, but she had nothing else to go on. She switched off the phone, resolved to wait until morning, when the sun could provide a needed charge, to consult the map again.

She knew they couldn't stay in the elevator the rest of the night, and there was no other place to sleep nearby. That was fine with Sally, though. Cory could sleep while she walked, once he calmed down enough. She was full of adrenaline now anyway, and needed to work it off.

She went out into the night, taking deep breaths of cool air. She look around and saw, in the direction of her destination, a blinking light – a radio tower. Sally lifted up the two backpacks, and her brother, and started chasing a new light.

Resurrection Blues

John B. Rosenman

"**ONCE UPON** a time, children," Robot said, "there was a species called humans. And they climbed up out of the seas and onto land and evolved, and eventually, in the amplitude of time, they left apes and other anthropoids behind and established great civilizations. To be exact, these civilizations were great only to them, for they and no one else did the boasting about them. These humans harnessed solar and nuclear energy, though there were some cynics who said that energy harnessed them. Anyway, not to put too fine a gloss on it, eventually space travel hit the scene and these humans prepared to leave for the stars. Only just when they were on the cosmic brink, the Big Boom occurred and when the radioactive clouds and crud dissipated, they were back in the Middle Ages and soon regressed even further into savagery and virtual extinction. If we seek a moral in this, children, it is that right must always accompany might, or that 'Pride goeth before destruction, and an haughty spirit before a fall.'"

Around him in the cave, The Twelve Who Were Machines knelt in thoughtful reverence. Or to be exact, as Robot might put it, they rested on the hard-packed soil of the cave's floor, having retracted their mobilators.

"Sir Robot," one of them said, "is it true that humans were made of flesh and were organic? Actually subject to decay and deterioration?"

"Yes, it is true," Robot replied, identifying Number 3 by his position in the circle around him rather than by any distinguishing marks.

Number 3 nodded mechanically. "Humans aged, fought, had emotions?"

"Affirmative."

"Irrational impulses, drives, neuroses, psychoses, hormonal imbal–"

"Yes, Number 3, as I have told you before. Why do you ask again? To do so is itself irrational."

"Pardon, Reverend Robot Guru," Number 8 interjected in a voice identical to Number 3.

"It's just that such a species seems impossible. According to my computations, the odds against such beings existing are on the order of 83 to the 89th power. Virtually an infinite impossibility."

"Number 8," Robot said, "the phrase, 'Virtually an infinite impossibility,' is not only illogical but verbose. Please check your ionization."

"Probably his Vy Synthesizer," Number 5 mumbled.

Robot straightened and raised his hand. "See this extremite? Like yours, three of its digits contain organic human cells in a super frozen state from the rib of one General of the U.S. Army named Scott. Ezekiel E. Scott, to be exact."

In imitation, all twelve machines raised metallic hands and studied them. "But isn't that insignificant, Great One?" one said. "Ezekiel E. Scott is dead."

Robot pursed his duroplast lips. "'Dead' is a relative term. Not to put too fine a gloss on it, but surely you all must know from your memory banks that hair or fur will sometimes grow on an organic cadaver. And in rotting flesh itself new life-forms are engendered by decomposition." Dramatically, Robot turned his hand so they could see his grey palm. "Why, even though this extremite is made of iridium, it too can be said to be 'dying.' If you adjust your sensors into the extreme ultraviolet, you will detect transformation analogous to rust. True, the process is extremely slow, but it is there. In the amplitude of time, such decomposition would be readily apparent..."

In unison, The Twelve Who Were Machines started fidgeting. Reverend Robot Guru might be loved and worshiped, but his professorial mode bored them. They much preferred his witty and entertaining storytelling mode with its incongruous linguistic elements.

Though he recognized their lack of interest, Robot continued. "But to return to your earlier claim that the colonies of human cells contained in our digits are 'insignificant,' I can only respond that it is not so. True, such cells are inert, existing at a temperature 99.9% of absolute zero, but I am fully capable of reviving them at any time. Not only that, but because they contain a full and detailed DNA blueprint of the original human, along with electronically stored memories, it is quite within my power to recreate General Scott as he once was."

There was silence, during which the cold wind scoured a ravaged world, whistling eerily at the cave's mouth as if seeking entrance. Outside no birds ever flew and only a few hardy species such as cockroaches and scorpions managed to survive in the sterile soil.

"Oh Most Supreme Rabbi Robot Guru," Number 8 of the suspect synthesizer said, "are you saying that you can restore this U.S. Army General Ezekiel E. Scott to life?"

"Affirmative."

They shared looks, ruby everpac eyes electronically blinking in excitement.

"This is hard to believe," Number 8 persisted. "The human's identity has been expunged and he is long dead."

The other robots murmured in agreement. For the first time ever, Robot tasted their disbelief. It had a sharp, bitter flavor.

"Nevertheless, it is so," he said. "I *can* resurrect General Scott."

Another robot, Number 1, spread his hands. "But surely, Robot King of Kings, to be exact, this Ezekiel E. Scott would not be the *same* Ezekiel E. Scott from whom the cells were excised. Not to put too fine a gloss on it, but there would be significant variations, departures from –"

"Only minor variations, Number 1," Robot said, pleased that one of his children had used two of his favorite phrases. "Essentially, the original human would be reborn."

Twelve mouthslits opened in awe.

"Would you care for a demonstration?" Robot asked. But being Robot, he knew the answer and swung with inhuman grace toward the cave's entrance. "Follow me."

* * *

Earth, third from the sun, resembled a giant slagheap on which grass here and there managed a feeble foothold. Above the pitted, desolate surface, blue lightning sheeted in weird bursts. The Twelve Who Were Machines knew the dangerous atmospheric changes responsible for such effects, and the continual flickering made them uneasy. Just a few weeks before, Number 5 had almost been blasted to pieces by a bolt from the sky. Robot alone marched unconcerned across the wasteland, leading them to the laboratory where he had been created.

After he had pressed several buttons and modulated his voiceprint to match that of a long-dead scientist, Robot conducted them into a chamber where he switched on an emergency power unit. Silent, maintaining their proper positions, The Twelve watched him open his hand plate and extract a human cell with a micro-instrument. As he worked, Robot explained the procedure in general terms.

"Now if you will observe, I will combine this single cell with a solution…"

"Sir Most Astonishing Robot Guru, what is the precise nature of this solution?"

Intent on his work, Robot was not disposed to be precise even though, for once, The Twelve would have preferred a lecture. "Number 11, the precise nature is immaterial. What matters is that it *works*." He took the petri dish containing the mixture to a device that resembled a giant oven and placed it inside.

They watched him close the door and adjust a dial, then step back as a somber blue light flooded the interior.

"Majestic One, how did we come to be the repository of such cells?"

Gazing through the glass door of the 'oven,' Robot hesitated. The robots' origin was a subject he'd sensed it was wise not to mention, but the question could not be honestly avoided. "We, uh, were built here, and the cells of General Scott placed in our freezing units nearly three centuries ago. He was an important military leader and humans wanted to reconstruct him in the event of a catastrophe. Unfortunately, in the Great War civilization itself was destroyed, and no one ever brought him back."

But The Twelve had heard only one thing. Several spoke at once.

" *You* were built here too?"

"Affirmative."

"By *humans*?"

"Yes."

The strained silence caused Robot at last to turn, and what he met made him wish he had answered differently. Throughout the three centuries of his existence, it had been an immutable fact that The Twelve Who Were Machines worshiped and revered him, viewed his smallest pronouncement with holy awe. They were his *children*, but what he saw now in their electronic eyes was the waning of faith. In turn, he felt a wholly new emotion, and such was his dismay that it required nearly a thousandth of a second to locate the word in his memory chips.

Fear.

"My origin is not significant," he began. "What matters –"

But another revelation had struck The Twelve, and they all spoke together.

"Then *you* did not build us? *You* are *not* our father?" As one, they turned to the gloomy blue light of the oven. "*Humans* built us? Designed and constructed our systems? And what's more, they constructed *you* too, so that you and we belong to the same category and are essentially equivalent despite your vastly superior –"

"No no no," Robot said quickly. "It's not that way at all. I admit, humans designed us, but…"

He stopped, overwhelmed by their continued attention to the oven and disregard of him. For the first time ever, his peaceful creation threatened to crumble.

Something stirred in the oven's blue light.

He regarded the form growing within it, and at the first sign of a head and arms, a thought occurred. Incredibly, his children doubted him, but he could recover his status if he reestablished himself as the Creator and Life-giver. Slowly he raised his arms and declaimed: "Come forth. *I*, AI Unit 3A7 give you life!"

His superb peripheral vision catalogued The Twelve's reactions. Yes, they were impressed. All he had to do now –

The oven's door opened.

Inside, a pasty-colored creature with a swollen abdomen and spindly legs blinked at them. They watched him rub his grey thatch of hair and rise, then look at his body and then them in confusion. Moments passed.

"I…" Nonsensical words stumbled forth, and Robot wondered if the human had come out too soon and was half-baked. But the man swallowed and tried again, and this time his hoarse voice sounded stronger. "My God, what happened? How did I…"

His mouth sagged. "Of course… we must have gone to war, and you, as programmed, have cloned me. Which means that *I* – the *real* me – is dead." Dazed, he shook his head at the implications, then seemed to harden himself.

"What's the date?" he barked.

Robot hesitated. He remembered obediently answering humans' questions, but the practice was so ancient he barel– No, that was not true. His memory chips functioned perfectly. The fact was, he did not *want* to remember. After all, *He* was *Robot*, and –

"Come on, you blasted hunk of tin, what's the Goddamned date?"

He stiffened. "May 16, 2397."

"2397?" The human's eyes bulged. "For Chrissakes, nearly 300 years have passed! Do you mean to tell me you carried me around for three damn centuries before thawing me out? What the hell's wrong with you? You were programmed to do it immediately!"

Robot looked down at the floor. "I was programmed to use discretion, commence the process only when…" His voice trailed off, hollow even to his ears. Suddenly he recalled the human vices and shortcomings that had caused him not only to shun man-made buildings and live in a cave, but to disobey his directive as well. The only thing he couldn't understand was how he had been able to do it. Originally, he had been programmed to obey unequivocally all directives and commands, and it should have been impossible for him to exercise independent judgement.

"Aw, bull!" The human shook a disgusted fist and tottered to a locker. "Let's see. I ordered a spare uniform stored here. Wonder if it's…" He pulled at the metal door with furious vigor. "Seems stuck. Probably rusted shut after all this time."

Still clumsy, he slipped and banged his shin on a bench. "OW!" Clutching his leg, he glared at them. "Well, c'mon, damnit, don't just stand there like bumps on a log. HELP ME OPEN IT!"

Instinctively, The Twelve looked at Robot, who could only look back as his world continued to crumble.

"Master Supreme Robot Guru," one of them whispered. "What should we…"

"Help me OPEN it, damnit!"

There was a short pause, then The Twelve briefly broke ranks to assist him. Within seconds the door was open, revealing formal dress blues and underwear hanging in plastic bags. The underwear, Robot saw, featured flaming rockets and guided missiles, along with mushroom clouds and various combat rifles.

"Ah!" the General said.

Carefully, his movements becoming ever more proficient, the human put on his uniform. In minutes he stood before them, impeccably garbed from a visored cap to sharply creased pants to glistening black shoes. Rows of different colored ribbons rose above the left pocket of his jacket, which to Robot was a particularly depressing shade of blue.

Above the ribbons was a name: EZEKIEL E. SCOTT, U.S. ARMY.

General Scott stalked toward Robot. He looked commanding now instead of pathetic, his starched uniform radiating power and authority. Robot noticed, though, that the effect was somewhat marred by the fact that he had neglected to zip his fly. It gaped wide open, revealing his illustrated shorts. On them, what looked like a Patriot missile pointed directly between Robot's eyes.

Suddenly Scott halted. Stiffening, he threw back his shoulders, actually swelling with indignation. "What's the *matter* with you, soldier? Don't you know you're supposed to *salute* an officer?"

Robot, who was hardly a soldier, hesitated then swiftly obeyed. The General reciprocated by puffing out his chest and snapping off a curt salute. Unfortunately, he was so awkward and out of practice that he almost broke his own nose. Dripping blood, he clutched it, then spun to The Twelve.

"*Well?*" he thundered.

After a moment's uncertainty, they imitated Robot's precision gesture, though Robot saw with surprise that they did so at different times, and that some performed better than others. Scott, though, glowed with pleasure and saluted in return, this time being more careful. Then he swung back to Robot.

"All right, now report! What's happened in 300 years? How badly did they hurt us? How badly did we hurt *them*? Christ, I hope we nuked the bastards to Kingdom Come!" He scowled. "Say, just how and when did it happen? Do you know? Hell, yes, you must. You were here, whereas I was just a frozen cell you carried."

Confronted by the fusillade of questions, Robot thought it prudent to take them in order. "For 289 years, General Scott, the human race has been virtually extinct. Initially, destruction on both sides –"

"Never mind that. How many are left on both sides *now?*"

Robot hesitated. "In what was the United States, you are the only *organic* survivor."

Scott's eyes widened. "The only..." His eyes flicked to The Twelve, who stood silently. "And on their side, how many?"

"Thirty-two, according to netcon. Fourteen men, twelve women, and six children. Originally, there were only five survivors."

Scott sucked his breath in. "Then... they won. They beat us!"

"I beg your pardon?"

The General rammed a fist into his palm. "They beat us, you metal nitwit! They've got thirty-two, including women. They can repopulate, have already started!"

Number 7 stepped forward. "General, I don't quite see how you can say they won. Billions of lives were lost for no –"

"The bastards won!" Scott roared hoarsely. "What does it matter how many died? Don't you understand? They can regenerate, resurrect their military-industrial complex, start again! Come over here and take over!"

The Twelve exchanged glances. "Take over *what?*" three of them chorused.

Scott impatiently swung his hand. "Take over *this*! This country *America*. 'Land of the free and the home of...'"

Suddenly, Scott clasped his heart and began to sing 'The Star-Spangled Banner' in a cracked, raspy voice. The Twelve stood dumbfounded, their mouthslits hanging open. To Robot, it sounded like a dirge or a demented form of the blues, especially when Scott croaked "twilight's last gleaming" and "the rockets' red glare, the bombs bursting in air," all of which Robot had seen. It was so sad, he almost wanted to cry.

Abruptly Scott's voice broke and he burst into tears.

As he did, Robot looked at The Twelve, who were watching both him and the human. Gradually he realized that if he had fallen in their esteem, General Scott wasn't doing much better.

Just as abruptly, Scott stopped crying. They watched him wipe his eyes, embarrassed even before them.

Then the General's expression changed. It became sly and sneaky, and Robot watched the man actually tiptoe away a few steps as if he were crossing a minefield or was engaged in a dangerous midnight mission.

"Wait a minute," the General almost whispered. Turning, he crept stealthily back, lifting his polished shoes high. "Can't you all revitalize those other cells stored in you? Sure, there must be *thousands* of them. The scientists said there were cells deposited in three of your fingers, plus your brains."

They all touched their heads. "Our... brains?"

"Yeah. Guess they didn't tell you that. I wanted my eggs in as many nests as possible. If someone lopped off your hands, I'd be *gone*."

Scott waved the matter off, his eyes gleaming with calculation. "But the point is, why don't I have you thaw out the rest of my cells? Shit, man, we can have an instant army, thousands just like *me*! Then we can march over to that atheist hellhole and wipe 'em out." He grinned. "'Cept for the women, of course. I'll need them to start over." He licked his lips. "*Twelve* women! Why, in twenty years, I should have myself a nice little platoon."

"But that's insane, totally irrational!" Robot cried. "What's the sense of more destruction, of resorting to even more murder? General, I can't allow..." He stopped, amazed at his outburst.

Scott stepped close, bringing with him unpleasant olfactory sensations. "Not to put too fine a gloss on it, but something's wrong here. You're programmed to follow orders. You *can't* disobey, can't even *question*. Most of all, you're not supposed to have any *emotions*!" He looked at The Twelve. "Come to think of it, there's something fishy about the way you've all been acting. It's just not right."

Robot trembled. *Too fine a gloss...* Had he heard correctly? Had the General actually spoken those words?

The General turned back to him, set his jaw. "Listen. Get this: I don't know what's perkin' in your fuzzy wires, but *I'm* the human, and *I* give the orders. You're just machines that carry them out."

Robot shifted his feet. "What... was that phrase you used earlier?"

The General stepped even closer. "Damnit, listen to me! I said, 'I GIVE THE ORDERS'! Understand? *I'm* the General. *I'm* the Commander." He rapped Robot's metallic chest. "To be exact, *I*, Zeke Scott, am your Lord and Master. So when I say 'Jump!', the only thing I want to hear is 'How high?' Got it?"

To be exact. It was also one of his, *Robot's* phrases, which he had passed on to The Twelve. And yet this human had spoken it too! Slowly, Robot raised both hands and clutched his brainplate. He had thought his language and ability to feel emotion had evolved from his own unique consciousness, but such phrases suggested there was another source. He stifled a cry. Somehow, even though frozen in his cerebral processor, Scott's cells had affected his programming and shaped and influenced his personality. And such cells were stored in the Machines' processors too! That meant that The Twelve were not his children, but that he, *all* of them, were Scott's! His own acquiring of a will, personal identity, and the ability to feel emotion and disobey orders was a sheer accident he owed completely to this despicable man, who in many ways, was *his father*.

"I can do anything," Scott said, turning to other matters. "Establish a dynasty, conquer the world. Why, in the amplitude of time –"

"No," one of The Twelve said.

"Eh?"

Dazed, Robot turned to find Scott staring in disbelief at Number 6. "What do you mean, 'No'? I –"

"No," Number 2 said.

Scott spun to him. "Now just a –"

"No."

"No."

"No." One by one they answered, till it was unanimous. The General clenched his fists, sputtering. "This is insubordination! I'll have you…"

"We are most sorry, General, but Robot is our Most Supreme Jesus Rabbi Guru," one of them said. Listening, Robot felt a shiver, knowing the one who spoke did so for all.

But as his pleasure rose he realized more. Not only had the General's ego created his own ability to disobey, but also that of The Twelve, who had remained submissive until today. In addition, that same ego had led him, an advanced, supposedly superior model, to dominate and control The Twelve's lives as if they were automatons, unable to think for themselves. Yes, he realized now how he had encouraged and basked in their adoration. In fact, pride, the very thing he so often preached against, had been the reason he had brought them here to witness Scott's re-creation. Not content with past veneration, he had wanted to sun himself in their awe, just as Scott, his 'father,' had assumed they all existed just to serve him.

Ashamed, Robot lowered his eyes. Yes, he too was arrogant and selfish. But he could change. Must! For the first time ever, he found that he himself needed to believe in something, needed to have faith. Whatever he was, he had to believe that he was more than what this defective human had made him. The son, despite his faults, was not contained or summarized by the father, but must transcend him in a vital way.

A current of understanding passed from The Twelve to him as they turned, seeking guidance. What should they do with this human that he had created and who would precipitate more tragedy if allowed to live? Should they terminate him? That would be murder, but to let him continue…

Twelve sets of glowing eyes sought instruction from him. His children.

Robot looked at Scott who finally realized that something was very wrong. The General opened his mouth. "What… what are you…"

Twelve of them waiting. Waiting for Robot to step in and direct them to do His bidding. Robot smiled, beginning to see them for the first time as potential individuals, rather than as links in a chain of obedience.

"You make the decision," he said.

* * *

The wind tugged at the cave's mouth, moaning softly.

"Once upon a time, my friends," Robot said, "Robot foolishly raised a human from the grave. And when he and his friends, who were then Machines, saw how arrogant and flawed that human was, Robot –"

"Who to be exact, *Robby*, was rather flawed himself…"

Robby. Yes, that was his new, less imposing name. He turned to the one who had spoken, recognizing him by the gaudy peace symbols he wore.

"Yes, Peacemaker… 'Who, to be exact, *Robby*, was rather flawed himself.' As I was saying, Robot – uh, I mean *Robby* – knew he had to do something and was overjoyed, even reborn when he found that despite his limitations, his friends still loved him. Anyway, not to put too fine a gloss on it, Robby had acted foolishly and was deeply touched when he saw that his children – uh, friends – were still loyal and believed in him. So he in turn, not knowing whether to dispose of this Ezekiel E. Scott, or to risk another eventual Big Super Boom, turned to his friends, formerly The Twelve Who Were Machines, and asked them to decide. And you know what? As one, they seized the human and despite his struggles, placed him in the oven and reversed the regenerative process, reducing him to a single microscopic cell which was then returned to Robby's finger and frozen. Thus, in a sense, General Scott is not dead but remains alive within Robby as an everlasting reminder of the dangerous pride he must avoid."

Slowly, Robby raised his finger and held it up for their attention. "And here General Scott will abide in sure and certain hope that he'll *never* be resurrected and that the surviving humans will come to live in fruitful peace and one day replenish the Earth."

There was a long pause while the wind howled.

"Amen," his congregation said.

Ain't No Sunshine When She's Ash

Zach Shephard

WE WERE HALFWAY up the hill's cracked street when Lee decided it was time for a kickboxing lesson.

"Can we focus on my footwork today?" she asked.

I squinted at the mid-sky sun, its light dimming as I watched. Somewhere in the distance, the bell tolled.

"Let's crest the hill first. See how close we are."

We continued up the middle of the road, between rusted cars and ruined buildings. Lee shadowboxed as we walked, her paintbrush ponytail bobbing.

From the hilltop I spotted the bell: a small light down the long suburban street, its twinkle bright against the darkening sky. It never seemed to get any closer, but I had a feeling we could reach it in a few days.

Days. Maybe not the right term for those few hours of light, but oh well.

"Is my stance right?" Lee asked, still punching.

I shaded my eyes and peered ahead. "We could probably get another mile in before it's dark. Let's see if –"

"I'm worried I don't bend my knees enough."

I faced her. She was bouncing around the pavement, sapphire eyes focused on invisible opponents. My gym had once been full of teenage guys who said they wanted to be fighters, but none worked as hard as the tiny, thirty-something fitness nut with the platinum blonde hair.

It pained me to lose what little daylight we had left, but I couldn't say no to Lee. Besides, it wouldn't hurt to create some fond memories before the dark.

"Stance looks great," I said. "But you could tuck your chin more."

"Better?"

"A little more."

She pinned her chin to her chest.

"*Little* more."

She bent forward at the waist. "I can't go any farther!"

"I know. I'm just seeing if I can get you to somersault."

"Connor! Don't make me laugh!"

"Sorry," I said. "I can see you're very serious about this, like that time we were working on kicks and you started giggling so hard you forgot which leg was your left."

"Stop!" She shoved me and resumed shadowboxing, trying not to smile.

I provided some actual instruction then, and sat on a car's hood to watch her practice. The sun dimmed, the bell tolled. Lee looked happy, which meant I was too.

I kept calling out tips, even when her body burst into violet flames. The sun faded to black and Lee continued boxing, a fiery dancer in the dark. A minute later, she was gone.

I stared at the pile of violet ash, wondering if next time she'd love me back.

* * *

I sat on the car's hood, facing the golden twinkle of the bell. Maybe we'd get there some day, and everything could go back to normal.

Something rattled from across the street. It wasn't loud, but you become sensitive to that sort of thing when you're the last man alive. I put myself between the disturbance and the ash pile, whose violet glow revealed an approaching shape.

The figure was tall and slender, a strip of darkness against the black of night. It advanced slowly and deliberately, like a predator with nothing to fear.

I shook out my arms and rolled my head, loosening myself up. I stepped forward.

"Trouble you for some light?" I asked.

Four lines of fire rose around us, high as my shoulders, framing an area the size of a boxing ring. The figure came into view.

He was half a foot taller than me, with onyx skin and a lean, muscular physique – like the Anubis statue I'd seen at a museum once, but without the jackal head. His joker's grin revealed long white teeth like piano keys, and he wore a harlequin's hat.

"Let's make this quick," I said. "I've got a lot of moping to do."

"You're not funny."

"Never said I was. Although technically, I *am* the funniest man on Earth."

"She only laughs to be polite. You try too hard, and she notices. It wears on her."

As much as I'd have liked to wipe the grin off his face right then and there, I was too far out just yet. We met in the ring's center and circled one another, me in my fighting stance, the onyx jester stepping casually. At that distance I realized the bells on his hat were actually lamprey mouths, their fangs chewing the air.

"Tell me something," he said. "How much of your darktime is spent contemplating what you'll say next? How long do you rehearse your conversations with her, convincing yourself you possess some shred of charm? Do you really believe –"

I threw a jab, straight, hook, all of which were blocked. The jester circled out and I aimed a kick at his ribs, but misjudged his height and slammed my shin against his hip. Bone-on-bone contact is no fun for anyone, but I think he got the worst of it.

We bounced away from each other, resetting. He grinned, the fire drawing sharp shadows across his face.

We met again and I felt his full power: a left hook that glanced off my shoulder and sent me stumbling. Had I not hunched in time, that could have been the end.

I fired back, landing twice to the mouth. One of the jester's teeth spun through the air, like a knife-thrower's dagger at a carnival.

"That reminds me," he said, wiping the blood from his lip. "It's a good thing you couldn't muster the courage to extend her an invitation. She never would have accompanied you to the carnival."

I came in with a flurry. It was reckless, but I was pissed. And besides, I knew I was going to win. I always won, so long as I could survive to the part that never changed.

Two exchanges later the right moment came along, with the jester moving in the exact way Neil Dixon had during my last fight before the lights went out. I flashed back to that day: shiny purple glove, coming straight at me, casino crowd cheering us on...

I slipped the jester's punch and countered with a hard left hook, just like I had with Neil Dixon. The jester went down like a felled tree, shattering into a thousand obsidian pieces. A cloud of black smoke rose from the pavement, eventually clearing to reveal an acoustic guitar.

The flames faded and I returned to the car's hood. I spent the rest of the darktime plucking my favorite Bill Withers song, watching the pile of violet ash.

* * *

Just once, I'd have liked to sleep again – to check out of reality for a while. What was it like to dream? I tried remembering as I sat on the car, listening to the bell.

The first trace of light caught me by surprise. The sun faded into being and I finger-combed my hair, wondering what the hell I looked like. You'd think I'd have sought out a decent mirror during all that darktime to myself, but I didn't like leaving the ash pile unguarded.

I stood and took a breath. What was I going to say to her? I'd had something lined up, hadn't I?

The ashes flared with bright violet light, and from the pile Lee rose. I took a half-step forward before realizing I wasn't sure how to greet her. "Hello"? "Hi"? Too many options, all of them wrong. I sat back down and looked away before she turned toward me.

"Hey, Connor."

I looked over. "Oh – hey. What's new?"

She smiled, squinting against the sun's brightness. "Nothing much. Up for a walk?"

"Sure."

We moved through the barren neighborhood, toward the glowing bell. I thought about asking Lee what was new, but realized I'd already done that.

"Connor?"

"Yeah?"

"What was your best fight?"

"In what way?"

"Most memorable, I guess? If a stranger asks you for a fight story, what do you tell them?"

I didn't have to think long.

"Guy named Neil Dixon. He'd been scheduled to fight at the casino, but his opponent pulled out and I filled in on short notice. Probably shouldn't have."

"Why not?"

What was I supposed to tell her? That I didn't realize the fight would end the world as we knew it? She wouldn't understand.

"There just wasn't enough prep time," I said.

"So why'd you do it?"

I shrugged. "Gave me something to focus on for a few days. Sometimes the distraction of a training camp is just what a guy needs."

She nodded thoughtfully. "I get that. I mean, I'm not a fighter, but even punching a bag is like therapy for me, you know?"

"All too well."

The street widened, flanked on either side by huge, sheltering oaks. The nearby houses were bigger than those we'd passed earlier, but just as decrepit.

"So how'd the fight go?"

"Not great. He was too damned fast – every time I took a swing, his head was somewhere else. I felt like a drugged-up orangutan swatting at an imaginary fly."

She laughed – but did she mean it? *She only laughs to be polite. You try too hard, and she notices.*

I ditched the jokes and continued.

"Dixon beat the hell out of me for two and a half rounds. Knocked me down twice in the third. Once more and the ref would call the fight."

"Jeez – I can't believe he was that much better. You always look sharp when you teach class."

I shrugged. "All the training in the world doesn't matter if your head's not in the game."

"So what happened next?"

"Dixon threw a combination he'd landed earlier, but this time I was ready for it. I slipped the last punch and countered with a left hook. May have been the only clean shot I landed that day, but it was all I needed."

"Wow! That must have felt great."

It probably would have, if my punch hadn't turned off the lights. But I couldn't tell Lee that. She was stuck in the past, oblivious to the fact that reality had fallen apart the exact moment my fist met Dixon's head.

We pressed on. Before long Lee got restless and wanted to train, so we drilled some combos and blocks.

She worked until she burned.

* * *

I was doing pushups in the middle of the road when a woman's voice cut through the dark.

"Well, isn't this a familiar scene? Just like the time she nearly stood you up at the trailhead. How many anxiety-pushups did you pump out *that* day?"

"If that's the best you can do, you're not very good at this." I finished my set and stood. "She was just a little late. We had a great time."

"Lee's friendly enough to have a great time with anyone. Doesn't make you special."

I scanned for the source of the voice, but the ash pile's violet glow revealed nothing. I was about to start a game of Marco Polo when something swooped overhead, cawing.

Black feathers, tall as cornstalks and rimmed in soft blue light, erupted from the ground around me. As per tradition, the area they enclosed was the size of a boxing ring.

The woman in the far corner wore shiny gray shorts and a matching sports bra. Her hair was short and ruffled, and on her right deltoid was a tattoo of a bleeding heart. Dark wings rose from her back, small like Cupid's.

She smirked like she knew something I didn't, the feather-ring giving her the bluish tint of a blacklight. "Do I remind you of her?"

"Of course. I always did say Lee looked like a dead pigeon at a rave."

She shadowboxed around the ring, her movements resembling Lee's. "Remember the first class she took at your gym? From the moment you saw her smile – gosh! You were hooked. It was like you forgot you even had other students."

We met in the ring's center and started feeling each other out.

"Of course, that was just one day," she said, slipping my jab and circling away. "You weren't going to swoon over someone you'd just met, right? Not you – not the guy who'd given up on dating a decade earlier. Not the guy who'd convinced himself he was perfectly happy living a life without love. Whatever you'd felt at the gym was just a temporary thing – right?"

I whiffed on a reckless combo and took a counter to the body. She backed away, smiling. "I know what you're wondering," she said. "'Why Lee?' Out of all the women you'd met at the gym, what about *her* caused that flutter in your chest you hadn't felt in years?" She punched me in the sternum for emphasis.

"Easy answer," I said. "Lee's different."

"But *how?* You spent countless nights wondering what set her apart, but never could come up with an answer. Fact is, no one knows how love works. If they did, it wouldn't be love."

I threw a head-kick she barely blocked, the impact forcing her sideways. She never stopped smiling.

"Face it," she said. "No matter how long you dwell on this, you'll never figure out why you love her. And you *certainly* won't figure out why she doesn't love you back."

I threw another kick that missed. With a birdlike screech the woman lunged in, executing an attack I'd seen a hundred times before: it was the end of the Neil Dixon fight, his purple glove coming my way, looking for the KO. I slipped to the side and fired back with my usual counter hook, a shock shooting through my knuckles.

Feathers burst in every direction as the woman exploded into a flock of crows. The birds cawed and beat their wings at the air, vanishing into the dark.

The guitar this time was a Martin with a mahogany top. I sat and strummed Flogging Molly's 'If I Ever Leave This World Alive.' Halfway through the song, I realized my fretting hand was broken and hadn't actually been playing.

The music continued from no discernible direction. I listened. I waited.

I thought.

* * *

The sun returned and the ashes flared. Lee rose.

"Hey, Connor. Walk with me?"

"Sure."

We resumed our journey down the street, toward the tolling bell. We were quiet for a long time, while I figured out how to say everything I'd been fixated on since the bird-woman's visit. Eventually, I gave up on perfectionism.

"Lee, I've been thinking –"

"I'm leaving."

I stopped. "What?"

"I have to go."

"But you just got here."

"I'm sorry, Connor. Goodbye."

She stood there and burned, violet flames running up her body as we stared at one another.

I wasn't sure what was worse: that she'd left so early, or that she'd finally become aware of her own departure.

* * *

The ice came as the sun left: huge, stalagmite crystals shooting up in a square around me, their pale glow illuminating the vapor they radiated.

My opponent, a powder-white bodybuilder with furry forearms and underbite fangs, said something about the time for cold truths being upon us. I responded with a four-punch combo and a knee to the midsection, being uninterested in the usual banter just then.

My left hand, which I'd broken on the bird-woman's face, felt fine. I wasn't sure when it had healed, but after living in a world of monstrous kickboxers and unexplained guitars, I'd learned not to question that sort of thing.

The ice-man and I threw hard combinations at each other. He knocked me down early, but I was right back up. When he landed a head-kick a few minutes later, he backed away like he was waiting for a ref to count me out.

I went through the numbers in my head, making sure I was on my feet by eight. Things were fuzzy when I moved forward again – I couldn't tell if the crystals' vapor had gotten thicker or if my vision was fogging.

It was a lot like the Neil Dixon fight: knocked down twice in one round, now a little wobbly. Back to the center of the ring. The combo was coming up – I just had to watch for that punch.

The ice-man's fist came forward. I flashed back to the casino, noticing a detail I'd long misremembered: Neil Dixon's glove wasn't purple. It was violet.

The punch landed before I could slip. The world went away.

* * *

I woke under a darktime sky, violet glow of the ash pile nearby. The ice-man and his crystal boxing ring were gone, and the bell's toll had changed: it now produced high-pitched chirps every second, instead of the slow, sepulchral tones of old. I lifted my head off the pavement to see its glow down the road.

It was close – just a few blocks away. And it didn't look the way I'd expected.

I'd always thought it was a bell because of the sounds it made. But what I saw was something else entirely: a glowing golden circle the size of an SUV, hovering just above the road.

I got to my feet. As much as I hated to leave the ashes unguarded, the bell was too close to ignore. I moved down the road.

Inside the portal a scene materialized. I saw a hospital bed, occupied by a purple-faced, swollen-eyed guy with cuts on his brows. Another few steps and I recognized him.

It was me.

The ice-man had promised cold truths, and a big one hit me just then: I hadn't knocked Neil Dixon out. I hadn't even slipped his punch. He'd landed the combo in just the way he'd planned, and that's when the lights had gone out.

In the vision a nurse checked my heart monitor, which produced the sounds I'd long mistaken for bell tolls. Lee entered the room, looking sad.

"Hey, Anne. How is he?"

"Doing great," the nurse said. "You're sure you can't stick around? Doc thinks he could wake up any day now."

Lee shook her head. "We're leaving soon."

"That's too bad. Still, I'm excited for you. Big things ahead, right?"

"Hopefully. I never thought I'd move so far away, but this is a great opportunity for Rick. I want to be there for him."

"Well, with that fancy new job of his, hopefully he'll be able to afford a nice big ring."

Lee mustered a smile. "Fingers crossed."

She went to the bedside table and fiddled with something. My favorite Bill Withers song started playing.

"He really likes this one," she said. "Play it as much as you can, okay?"

"Sure thing."

"And check on him a lot. He always seemed lonely, even at the gym. He needs a friend."

"He's got a great one right by his bed."

There was a high-pitched chime, and Lee pulled out her phone. She wiped her teary eyes and read the text. "Rick's outside with the U-haul," she said. "Gotta go."

The nurse smiled. "Enjoy California."

"Will do."

They embraced. Lee left.

The room's door swung closed, sending a breeze through the portal and into the street. I stood motionless, listening to my song. The nurse shut it off before the end.

I turned, searching for a familiar violet light. The ash-pile was gone, scattered by the breeze.

I stepped away from the portal, bell tolling at my back.

The Purple Cloud
Extract
M.P. Shiel

*[Publisher's Note: At this point in the story Adam Jeffson has decided to
go on expedition to the north pole on board the* Boreal. *The first person
to stand at the North Pole is to receive $175,000,000. Jeffson's fiancée, the
Countess Clodagh, somehow managed to get him a space on the vessel, but
a priest warns him that the expedition will lead him to a terrible fate.]*

THE *BOREAL* left St. Katherine's Docks in beautiful weather on the afternoon of the
19th June, full of good hope, bound for the Pole.

All about the docks was one region of heads stretched far in innumerable vagueness,
and down the river to Woolwich a continuous dull roar and murmur of bees droned from
both banks to cheer our departure.

The expedition was partly a national affair, subvented by Government: and if ever
ship was well-found it was the *Boreal*. She had a frame tougher far than any battle-ship's,
capable of ramming some ten yards of drift-ice; and she was stuffed with sufficient
pemmican, codroe, fish-meal, and so on, to last us not less than six years.

We were seventeen, all told, the five Heads (so to speak) of the undertaking being
Clark (our Chief), John Mew (commander), Aubrey Maitland (meteorologist), Wilson
(electrician), and myself (doctor, botanist, and assistant meteorologist).

The idea was to get as far east as the 100°, or the 120°, of longitude; to catch there
the northern current; to push and drift our way northward; and when the ship could no
further penetrate, to leave her (either three, or else four, of us, on ski), and with sledges
drawn by dogs and reindeer make a dash for the Pole.

This had also been the plan of the last expedition – that of the *Nix* – and of several
others. The *Boreal* only differed from the *Nix*, and others, in that she was a thing of nicer
design, and of more exquisite forethought.

Our voyage was without incident up to the end of July, when we encountered a drift of
ice-floes. On the 1st August we were at Kabarova, where we met our coal-ship, and took
in a little coal for emergency, liquid air being our proper motor; also forty-three dogs,
four reindeer, and a quantity of reindeer-moss; and two days later we turned our bows
finally northward and eastward, passing through heavy 'slack' ice under sail and liquid air
in crisp weather, till, on the 27th August, we lay moored to a floe off the desolate island
of Taimur.

The first thing which we saw here was a bear on the shore, watching for young white-
fish: and promptly Clark, Mew, and Lamburn (engineer) went on shore in the launch, I
and Maitland following in the pram, each party with three dogs.

It was while climbing away inland that Maitland said to me:

"When Clark leaves the ship for the dash to the Pole, it is three, not two, of us, after all, that he is going to take with him, making a party of four."

I: "Is that so? Who knows?"

Maitland: "Wilson does. Clark has let it out in conversation with Wilson."

I: "Well, the more the merrier. Who will be the three?"

Maitland: "Wilson is sure to be in it, and there may be Mew, making the third. As to the fourth, I suppose *I* shall get left out in the cold."

I: "More likely I."

Maitland: "Well, the race is between us four: Wilson, Mew, you and I. It is a question of physical fitness combined with special knowledge. You are too lucky a dog to get left out, Jeffson."

I: "Well, what does it matter, so long as the expedition as a whole is successful? That is the main thing."

Maitland: "Oh yes, that's all very fine talk, Jeffson! But is it quite sincere? Isn't it rather a pose to affect to despise $175,000,000? *I* want to be in at the death, and I mean to be, if I can. We are all more or less self-interested."

"Look," I whispered – "a bear."

It was a mother and cub: and with determined trudge she came wagging her low head, having no doubt smelled the dogs. We separated on the instant, doubling different ways behind ice-boulders, wanting her to go on nearer the shore, before killing; but, passing close, she spied, and bore down at a trot upon me. I fired into her neck, and at once, with a roar, she turned tail, making now straight in Maitland's direction. I saw him run out from cover some hundred yards away, aiming his long-gun: but no report followed: and in half a minute he was under her fore-paws, she striking out slaps at the barking, shrinking dogs. Maitland roared for my help: and at that moment, I, poor wretch, in far worse plight than he, stood shivering in ague: for suddenly one of those wrangles of the voices of my destiny was filling my bosom with loud commotion, one urging me to fly to Maitland's aid, one passionately commanding me be still. But it lasted, I believe, some seconds only: I ran and got a shot into the bear's brain, and Maitland leapt up with a rent down his face.

But singular destiny! Whatever I did – if I did evil, if I did good – the result was the same: tragedy dark and sinister! Poor Maitland was doomed that voyage, and my rescue of his life was the means employed to make his death the more certain.

I think that I have already written, some pages back, about a man called Scotland, whom I met at Cambridge. He was always talking about certain 'Black' and 'White' beings, and their contention for the earth. We others used to call him the black-and-white mystery-man, because, one day – but that is no matter now. Well, with regard to all that, I have a fancy, a whim of the mind – quite wide of the truth, no doubt – but I have it here in my brain, and I will write it down now. It is this: that there may have been some sort of arrangement, or understanding, between Black and White, as in the case of Adam and the fruit, that, should mankind force his way to the Pole and the old forbidden secret biding there, then some mishap should not fail to overtake the race of man; that the White, being kindly disposed to mankind, did not wish this to occur, and intended, for the sake of the race, to destroy our entire expedition before it reached; and that the Black, knowing that the White meant to do this, and by what means, used me – *me*! – to outwit this design, first of all working that I should be one of the party of four to leave the ship on ski.

But the childish attempt, my God, to read the immense riddle of the world! I could laugh loud at myself, and at poor Black-and-White Scotland, too. The thing can't be so simple.

Well, we left Taimur the same day, and goodbye now to both land and open sea. Till we passed the latitude of Cape Chelyuskin (which we did not sight), it was one succession of ice-belts, with Mew in the crow's-nest tormenting the electric bell to the engine-room, the anchor hanging ready to drop, and Clark taking soundings. Progress was slow, and the Polar night gathered round us apace, as we stole still onward and onward into that blue and glimmering land of eternal frore. We now left off bed-coverings of reindeer-skin and took to sleeping-bags. Eight of the dogs had died by the 25th September, when we were experiencing 19° of frost. In the darkest part of our night, the Northern Light spread its silent solemn banner over us, quivering round the heavens in a million fickle gauds.

The relations between the members of our little crew were excellent – with one exception: David Wilson and I were not good friends.

There was a something – a tone – in the evidence which he had given at the inquest on Peters, which made me mad every time I thought of it. He had heard Peters admit just before death that he, Peters, had administered atropine to himself: and he had had to give evidence of that fact. But he had given it in a most half-hearted way, so much so, that the coroner had asked him: "What, sir, are you hiding from me?" Wilson had replied: "Nothing. I have nothing to tell."

And from that day he and I had hardly exchanged ten words, in spite of our constant companionship in the vessel; and one day, standing alone on a floe, I found myself hissing with clenched fist: "If he dared suspect Clodagh of poisoning Peters, I could *kill* him!"

Up to 78° of latitude the weather had been superb, but on the night of the 7th October – well I remember it – we experienced a great storm. Our tub of a ship rolled like a swing, drenching the whimpering dogs at every lurch, and hurling everything on board into confusion. The petroleum-launch was washed from the davits; down at one time to 40° below zero sank the thermometer; while a high aurora was whiffed into a dishevelled chaos of hues, resembling the smeared palette of some turbulent painter of the skies, or mixed battle of long-robed seraphim, and looking the very symbol of tribulation, tempest, wreck, and distraction. I, for the first time, was sick.

It was with a dizzy brain, therefore, that I went off watch to my bunk. Soon, indeed, I fell asleep: but the rolls and shocks of the ship, combined with the heavy Greenland anorak which I had on, and the state of my body, together produced a fearful nightmare, in which I was conscious of a vain struggle to move, a vain fight for breath, for the sleeping-bag turned to an iceberg on my bosom. Of Clodagh was my gasping dream. I dreamed that she let fall, drop by drop, a liquid, coloured like pomegranate-seeds, into a glass of water; and she presented the glass to Peters. The draught, I knew, was poisonous as death: and in a last effort to break the bands of that dark slumber, I was conscious, as I jerked myself upright, of screaming aloud:

"Clodagh! Clodagh! *Spare the man...!*"

My eyes, starting with horror, opened to waking; the electric light was shining in the cabin; and there stood David Wilson looking at me.

Wilson was a big man, with a massively-built, long face, made longer by a beard, and he had little nervous contractions of the flesh at the cheek-bones, and plenty of big freckles. His clinging pose, his smile of disgust, his whole air, as he stood crouching and lurching there, I can shut my eyes, and see now.

What he was doing in my cabin I did not know. To think, my good God, that he should have been led there just then! This was one of the four-men starboard berths: *his* was a-port: yet there he was! But he explained at once.

"Sorry to interrupt your innocent dreams," says he: "the mercury in Maitland's thermometer is frozen, and he asked me to hand him his spirits-of-wine one from his bunk..."

I did not answer. A hatred was in my heart against this man.

The next day the storm died away, and either three or four days later the slush-ice between the floes froze definitely. The *Boreal's* way was thus blocked. We warped her with ice-anchors and the capstan into the position in which she should lay up for her winter's drift. This was in about 79° 20' N. The sun had now totally vanished from our bleak sky, not to reappear till the following year.

Well, there was sledging with the dogs, and bear-hunting among the hummocks, as the months, one by one, went by. One day Wilson, by far our best shot, got a walrus-bull; Clark followed the traditional pursuit of a Chief, examining Crustacea; Maitland and I were in a relation of close friendship, and I assisted his meteorological observations in a snow-hut built near the ship. Often, through the twenty-four hours, a clear blue moon, very spectral, very fair, suffused all our dim and livid clime.

It was five days before Christmas that Clark made the great announcement: he had determined, he said, if our splendid northward drift continued, to leave the ship about the middle of next March for the dash to the Pole. He would take with him the four reindeer, all the dogs, four sledges, four kayaks, and three companions. The companions whom he had decided to invite were: Wilson, Mew, and Maitland.

He said it at dinner; and as he said it, David Wilson glanced at my wan face with a smile of pleased malice: for *I* was left out.

I remember well: the aurora that night was in the sky, and at its edge floated a moon surrounded by a ring, with two mock-moons. But all shone very vaguely and far, and a fog, which had already lasted some days, made the ship's bows indistinct to me, as I paced the bridge on my watch, two hours after Clark's announcement.

For a long time all was very still, save for the occasional whine of a dog. I was alone, and it grew toward the end of my watch, when Maitland would succeed me. My slow tread tolled like a passing-bell, and the mountainous ice lay vague and white around me, its sheeted ghastliness not less dreadfully silent than eternity itself.

Presently, several of the dogs began barking together, left off, and began again.

I said to myself; "There is a bear about somewhere."

And after some five minutes I saw – I thought that I saw – it. The fog had, if anything thickened; and it was now very near the end of my watch.

It had entered the ship, I concluded, by the boards which slanted from an opening in the port bulwarks down to the ice. Once before, in November, a bear, having smelled the dogs, had ventured on board at midnight: but *then* there had resulted a perfect hubbub among the dogs. *Now*, even in the midst of my excitement, I wondered at their quietness, though some whimpered – with fear, I thought. I saw the creature steal forward from the hatchway toward the kennels a-port; and I ran noiselessly, and seized the watch-gun which stood always loaded by the companionway.

By this time, the form had passed the kennels, reached the bows, and now was making toward me on the starboard side. I took aim. Never, I thought, had I seen so huge a bear – though I made allowance for the magnifying effect of the fog.

My finger was on the trigger: and at that moment a deathly shivering sickness took me, the wrangling voices shouted at me, with "Shoot!" "Shoot not!" "Shoot!" Ah well, that latter shout was irresistible. I drew the trigger. The report hooted through the Polar night.

The creature dropped; both Wilson and Clark were up at once: and we three hurried to the spot.

But the very first near glance showed a singular kind of bear. Wilson put his hand to the head, and a lax skin came away at his touch.... It was Aubrey Maitland who was underneath it, and I had shot him dead.

For the past few days he had been cleaning skins, among them the skin of the bear from which I had saved him at Taimur. Now, Maitland was a born pantomimist, continually inventing practical jokes; and perhaps to startle me with a false alarm in the very skin of the old Bruin which had so nearly done for him, he had thrown it round him on finishing its cleaning, and so, in mere wanton fun, had crept on deck at the hour of his watch. The head of the bear-skin, and the fog, must have prevented him from seeing me taking aim.

This tragedy made me ill for weeks. I saw that the hand of Fate was upon me. When I rose from bed, poor Maitland was lying in the ice behind the great camel-shaped hummock near us.

By the end of January we had drifted to 80° 55'; and it was then that Clark, in the presence of Wilson, asked me if I would make the fourth man, in the place of poor Maitland, for the dash in the spring. As I said "Yes, I am willing," David Wilson spat with a disgusted emphasis. A minute later he sighed, with "Ah, poor Maitland..." and drew in his breath with a *tut! tut!*

God knows, I had an impulse to spring then and there at his throat, and strangle him: but I curbed myself.

There remained now hardly a month before the dash, and all hands set to work with a will, measuring the dogs, making harness and seal-skin shoes for them, overhauling sledges and kayaks, and cutting every possible ounce of weight. But we were not destined, after all, to set out that year. About the 20th February, the ice began to pack, and the ship was subjected to an appalling pressure. We found it necessary to make trumpets of our hands to shout into one another's ears, for the whole ice-continent was crashing, popping, thundering everywhere in terrific upheaval. Expecting every moment to see the *Boreal* crushed to splinters, we had to set about unpacking provisions, and placing sledges, kayaks, dogs and everything in a position for instant flight. It lasted five days, and was accompanied by a tempest from the north, which, by the end of February, had driven us back south into latitude 79° 40'. Clark, of course, then abandoned the thought of the Pole for that summer.

And immediately afterwards we made a startling discovery: our stock of reindeer-moss was found to be somehow ridiculously small. Egan, our second mate, was blamed; but that did not help matters: the sad fact remained. Clark was advised to kill one or two of the deer, but he pig-headedly refused: and by the beginning of summer they were all dead.

Well, our northward drift recommenced. Toward the middle of February we saw a mirage of the coming sun above the horizon; there were flights of Arctic petrels and snow-buntings; and spring was with us. In an ice-pack of big hummocks and narrow lanes we made good progress all the summer.

When the last of the deer died, my heart sank; and when the dogs killed two of their number, and a bear crushed a third, I was fully expecting what actually came; it was this: Clark announced that he could now take only two companions with him in the spring: and they were Wilson and Mew. So once more I saw David Wilson's pleased smile of malice.

We settled into our second winter-quarters. Again came December, and all our drear sunless gloom, made worse by the fact that the windmill would not work, leaving us without the electric light.

Ah me, none but those who have felt it could dream of one half the mental depression of that long Arctic night; how the soul takes on the hue of the world; and without and within is nothing but gloom, gloom, and the reign of the Power of Darkness.

Not one of us but was in a melancholic, dismal and dire mood; and on the 13th December Lamburn, the engineer, stabbed Cartwright, the old harpooner, in the arm.

Three days before Christmas a bear came close to the ship, and then turned tail. Mew, Wilson, I and Meredith (a general hand) set out in pursuit. After a pretty long chase we lost him, and then scattered different ways. It was very dim, and after yet an hour's search, I was returning weary and disgusted to the ship, when I saw some shadow like a bear sailing away on my left, and at the same time sighted a man – I did not know whom – running like a handicapped ghost some little distance to the right. So I shouted out:

"There he is – come on! This way!"

The man quickly joined me, but as soon as ever he recognised me, stopped dead. The devil must have suddenly got into him, for he said:

"No, thanks, Jefferson: alone with you I am in danger of my life…"

It was Wilson. And I, too, forgetting at once all about the bear, stopped and faced him.

"I see," said I. "But, Wilson, you are going to explain to me *now* what you mean, you hear? What *do* you mean, Wilson?"

"What I say," he answered deliberately, eyeing me up and down: "alone with you I am in danger of my life. Just as poor Maitland was, and just as poor Peters was. Certainly, you are a deadly beast."

Fury leapt, my God, in my heart. Black as the tenebrous Arctic night was my soul.

"Do you mean," said I, "that I want to put you out of the way in order to go in your place to the Pole? Is that your meaning, man?"

"That's about my meaning, Jefferson," says he: "you are a deadly beast, you know."

"Stop!" I said, with blazing eye. "I am going to kill *you*, Wilson – as sure as God lives: but I want to hear first. Who *told* you that I killed Peters?"

"Your lover killed him – with *your* collusion. Why, I heard you, man, in your beastly sleep, calling the whole thing out. And I was pretty sure of it before, only I had no proofs. By God, I should enjoy putting a bullet into you, Jefferson!"

"You wrong me – you, you wrong me!" I shrieked, my eyes staring with ravenous lust for his blood; "and now I am going to pay you well for it. *Look out, you!*"

I aimed my gun for his heart, and I touched the trigger. He held up his left hand.

"Stop," he said, "stop." (He was one of the coolest of men ordinarily.) "There is no gallows on the *Boreal*, but Clark could easily rig one for you. I want to kill you, too, because there are no criminal courts up here, and it would be doing a good action for my country. But not here – not now. Listen to me – don't shoot. Later we can meet, when all is ready, so that no one may be the wiser, and fight it all out."

As he spoke I let the gun drop. It was better so. I knew that he was much the best shot on the ship, and I an indifferent one: but I did not care, I did not care, if I was killed.

It is a dim, inclement land, God knows: and the spirit of darkness and distraction is there.

Twenty hours later we met behind the great saddle-shaped hummock, some six miles to the S.E. of the ship. We had set out at different times, so that no one might suspect. And each brought a ship's-lantern.

Wilson had dug an ice-grave near the hummock, leaving at its edge a heap of brash-ice and snow to fill it. We stood separated by an interval of perhaps seventy yards, the grave between us, each with a lantern at his feet.

Even so we were mere shadowy apparitions one to the other. The air glowered very drearily, and present in my inmost soul were the frills of cold. A chill moon, a mere abstraction of light, seemed to hang far outside the universe. The temperature was at 55° below zero, so that we had on wind-clothes over our anoraks, and heavy foot-bandages under our Lap boots. Nothing but a weird morgue seemed the world, haunted with despondent madness; and exactly like that world about us were the minds of us two poor men, full of macabre, bleak, and funereal feelings.

Between us yawned an early grave for one or other of our bodies.

I heard Wilson cry out:

"Are you ready, Jeffson?"

"Aye, Wilson!" cried I.

"*Then here goes!*" cries he.

Even as he spoke, he fired. Surely, the man was in deadly earnest to kill me.

But his shot passed harmlessly by me: as indeed was only likely: we were mere shadows one to the other.

I fired perhaps ten seconds later than he: but in those ten seconds he stood perfectly revealed to me in clear, lavender light.

An Arctic fire-ball had traversed the sky, showering abroad, a sulphurous glamour over the snow-landscape. Before the intenser blue of its momentary shine had passed away, I saw Wilson stagger forward, and drop. And him and his lantern I buried deep there under the rubble ice.

* * *

On the 13th March, nearly three months later, Clark, Mew and I left the *Boreal* in latitude 85° 15'.

We had with us thirty-two dogs, three sledges, three kayaks, human provisions for 112 days, and dog provisions for 40. Being now about 340 miles from the Pole, we hoped to reach it in 43 days, then, turning south, and feeding living dogs with dead, make either Franz Josef Land or Spitzbergen, at which latter place we should very likely come up with a whaler.

Well, during the first days, progress was very slow, the ice being rough and laney, and the dogs behaving most badly, stopping dead at every difficulty, and leaping over the traces. Clark had had the excellent idea of attaching a gold-beater's-skin balloon, with a lifting power of 35 pounds, to each sledge, and we had with us a supply of zinc and sulphuric-acid to repair the hydrogen-waste from the bags; but on the third day Mew over-filled and burst his balloon, and I and Clark had to cut ours loose in order to equalise weights, for we could neither leave him behind, turn back to the ship, nor mend the bag. So it happened that at the end of the fourth day out, we had made only nineteen miles, and could still from a hummock discern afar the leaning masts of the old *Boreal*. Clark led on ski, captaining a sledge with 400 lbs. of instruments, ammunition, pemmican, aleuronate bread; Mew followed, his sledge containing provisions only; and last came I, with a mixed freight. But on the third day Clark had an attack of snow-blindness, and Mew took his place.

Pretty soon our sufferings commenced, and they were bitter enough. The sun, though constantly visible day and night, gave no heat. Our sleeping-bags (Clark and

Mew slept together in one, I in another) were soaking wet all the night, being thawed by our warmth; and our fingers, under wrappings of senne-grass and wolf-skin, were always bleeding. Sometimes our frail bamboo-cane kayaks, lying across the sledges, would crash perilously against an ice-ridge – and they were our one hope of reaching land. But the dogs were the great difficulty: we lost six mortal hours a day in harnessing and tending them. On the twelfth day Clark took a single-altitude observation, and found that we were only in latitude 86° 45'; but the next day we passed beyond the furthest point yet reached by man, viz. 86° 53', attained by the *Nix* explorers four years previously.

* * *

Our one secret thought now was food, food – our day-long lust for the eating-time. Mew suffered from 'Arctic thirst.

* * *

Under these conditions, man becomes in a few days, not a savage only, but a mere beast, hardly a grade above the bear and walrus. Ah, the ice! A long and sordid nightmare was that, God knows.

On we pressed, crawling our little way across the Vast, upon whose hoar silence, from Eternity until then, Bootes only, and that Great Bear, had watched.

* * *

After the eleventh day our rate of march improved: all lanes disappeared, and ridges became much less frequent. By the fifteenth day I was leaving behind the ice-grave of David Wilson at the rate of ten to thirteen miles a day.

Yet, as it were, his arm reached out and touched me, even there.

His disappearance had been explained by a hundred different guesses on the ship – all plausible enough. I had no idea that anyone connected me in any way with his death.

But on our twenty-second day of march, 140 miles from our goal, he caused a conflagration of rage and hate to break out among us three.

It was at the end of a march, when our stomachs were hollow, our frames ready to drop, and our mood ravenous and inflamed. One of Mew's dogs was sick: it was necessary to kill it: he asked me to do it.

"Oh," said I, "you kill your own dog, of course."

"Well, I don't know," he replied, catching fire at once, "you ought to be used to killing, Jefferson."

"How do you mean, Mew?" said I with a mad start, for madness and the flames of Hell were instant and uppermost in us all: "you mean because my profession –"

"Profession! Damn it, no," he snarled like a dog: "go and dig up David Wilson – I dare say you know where to find him – and he will tell you my meaning, right enough."

I rushed at once to Clark, who was stooping among the dogs, unharnessing: and savagely pushing his shoulder, I exclaimed:

"That beast accuses me of murdering David Wilson!"

"Well?" said Clark.

"I'd split his skull as clean – !"

"Go away, Adam Jefferson, and let me be!" snarled Clark.

"Is that all you've got to say about it, then – you?"

"To the devil with you, man, say I, and let me be!" cried he: "you know your own conscience best, I suppose."

Before this insult I stood with grinding teeth, but impotent. However, from that moment a deeper mood of brooding malice occupied my spirit. Indeed the humour of us all was one of dangerous, even murderous, fierceness. In that pursuit of riches into that region of cold, we had become almost like the beasts that perish.

* * *

On the 10th April we passed the 89th parallel of latitude, and though sick to death, both in spirit and body, pressed still on. Like the lower animals, we were stricken now with dumbness, and hardly once in a week spoke a word one to the other, but in selfish brutishness on through a real hell of cold we moved. It is a cursed region – beyond doubt cursed – not meant to be penetrated by man: and rapid and awful was the degeneration of our souls. As for me, never could I have conceived that savagery so heinous could brood in a human bosom as now I felt it brood in mine. If men could enter into a country specially set apart for the habitation of devils, and there become possessed of evil, as we were so would they be.

* * *

As we advanced, the ice every day became smoother; so that, from four miles a day, our rate increased to fifteen, and finally (as the sledges lightened) to twenty.

It was now that we began to encounter a succession of strange-looking objects lying scattered over the ice, whose number continually increased as we proceeded. They had the appearance of rocks, or pieces of iron, incrusted with glass-fragments of various colours, and they were of every size. Their incrustations we soon determined to be diamonds, and other precious stones. On our first twenty-mile day Mew picked up a diamond-crystal as large as a child's foot, and such objects soon became common. We thus found the riches which we sought, beyond all dream; but as the bear and the walrus find them: for ourselves we had lost; and it was a loss of riches barren as ashes, for all those millions we would not have given an ounce of fish-meal. Clark grumbled something about their being meteor-stones, whose ferruginous substance had been lured by the magnetic Pole, and kept from frictional burning in their fall by the frigidity of the air: and they quickly ceased to interest our sluggish minds, except in so far as they obstructed our way.

* * *

We had all along had good weather: till, suddenly, on the morning of the 13th April, we were overtaken by a tempest from the S.W., of such mighty and solemn volume that the heart quailed beneath it. It lasted in its full power only an hour, but during that time snatched two of our sledges long distances, and compelled us to lie face-downward. We had travelled all the sun-lit night, and were gasping with fatigue; so as soon as the wind allowed us to huddle together our scattered things, we crawled into the sleeping-bags, and instantly slept.

We knew that the ice was in awful upheaval around us; we heard, as our eyelids sweetly closed, the slow booming of distant guns, and brittle cracklings of artillery. This may have been a result of the tempest stirring up the ocean beneath the ice. Whatever it was, we did not care: we slept deep.

We were within ten miles of the Pole.

* * *

In my sleep it was as though someone suddenly shook my shoulder with urgent "*Up! Up!*" It was neither Clark nor Mew, but a dream merely: for Clark and Mew, when I started up, I saw lying still in their sleeping-bag.

I suppose it must have been about noon. I sat staring a minute, and my first numb thought was somehow this: that the Countess Clodagh had prayed me 'Be first' – for her. Wondrous little now cared I for the Countess Clodagh in her far unreal world of warmth – precious little for the fortune which she coveted: millions on millions of fortunes lay unregarded around me. But that thought, *Be first!* was deeply suggested in my brain, as if whispered there. Instinctively, brutishly, as the Gadarean swine rushed down a steep place, I, rubbing my daft eyes, arose.

The first thing which my mind opened to perceive was that, while the tempest was less strong, the ice was now in extraordinary agitation. I looked abroad upon a vast plain, stretched out to a circular, but waving horizon, and varied by many hillocks, boulders, and sparkling meteor-stones that everywhere tinselled the blinding white, some big as houses, most small as limbs. And this great plain was now rearranging itself in a widespread drama of havoc, withdrawing in ravines like mutual backing curtsies, then surging to clap together in passionate mountain-peaks, else jostling like the Symplegades, fluent and inconstant as billows of the sea, grinding itself, piling itself, pouring itself in cataracts of powdered ice, while here and there I saw the meteor-stones leap spasmodically, in dusts and heaps, like geysers or spurting froths in a steamer's wake, a tremendous uproar, meantime, filling all the air. As I stood, I plunged and staggered, and I found the dogs sprawling, with whimperings, on the heaving floor.

I did not care. Instinctively, daftly, brutishly, I harnessed ten of them to my sledge; put on Canadian snow-shoes: and was away northward – alone.

The sun shone with a clear, benign, but heatless shining: a ghostly, remote, yet quite limpid light, which seemed designed for the lighting of other planets and systems, and to strike here by happy chance. A great wind from the S.W., meantime, sent thin snow-sweepings flying northward past me.

The odometer which I had with me had not yet measured four miles, when I began to notice two things: first that the jewelled meteor-stones were now accumulating beyond all limit, filling my range of vision to the northern horizon with a dazzling glister: in mounds, and parterres, and scattered disconnection they lay, like largesse of autumn leaves, spread out over those Elysian fields and fairy uplands of wealth, trillions of billions, so that I had need to steer my twining way among them. Now, too, I noticed that, but for these stones, all roughness had disappeared, not a trace of the upheaval going on a little further south being here, for the ice lay positively as smooth as a table before me. It is my belief that this stretch of smooth ice has never, never felt one shock, or stir, or throe, and reaches right down to the bottom of the deep.

* * *

And now with a wild hilarity I flew. Gradually, a dizziness, a lunacy, had seized upon me, till finally, up-buoyed on air, and dancing mad, I sped, I spun, with grinning teeth that chattered and gibbered, and eyeballs of distraction: for a Fear, too – most cold and dreadful – had its hand of ice upon my heart, I being so alone in that place, face to face with the Ineffable: but still with a giddy levity, and a fatal joy, and a blind hilarity, on I sped, I spun.

* * *

The odometer measured nine miles from my start. I was in the immediate neighbourhood of the Pole.

I cannot say when it began, but now I was conscious of a sound in my ears, distinct and near, a steady sound of splashing, or fluttering, resembling the noising of a cascade or brook: and it grew. Forty more steps I took (slide I could not now for the meteorites) – perhaps sixty – perhaps eighty: and now, to my sudden horror, I stood by a circular clean-cut lake.

One minute only, swaying and nodding there, I stood: and then I dropped down flat in swoon.

* * *

In a hundred years, I suppose, I should never succeed in analysing *why* I swooned: but my consciousness still retains the impression of that horrid thrill. I saw nothing distinctly, for my whole being reeled and toppled drunken, like a spinning-top in desperate death-struggle at the moment when it flags, and wobbles dissolutely to fall; but the very instant that my eyes met what was before me, I knew, I knew, that here was the Sanctity of Sanctities, the old eternal inner secret of the Life of this Earth, which it was a most burning shame for a man to see. The lake, I fancy, must be a mile across, and in its middle is a pillar of ice, very low and broad; and I had the clear impression, or dream, or notion, that there was a name, or word, graven all round in the ice of the pillar in characters which I could never read; and under the name a long date; and the fluid of the lake seemed to me to be wheeling with a shivering ecstasy, splashing and fluttering, round the pillar, always from west to east, in the direction of the spinning of the earth; and it was borne in upon me – I can't at all say how – that this fluid was the substance of a living creature; and I had the distinct fancy, as my senses failed, that it was a creature with many dull and anguished eyes, and that, as it wheeled for ever round in fluttering lust, it kept its eyes always turned upon the name and the date graven in the pillar. But this must be my madness…

* * *

It must have been not less than an hour before a sense of life returned to me; and when the thought stabbed my brain that a long, long time I had lain there in the presence of those gloomy orbs, my spirit seemed to groan and die within me.

In some minutes, however, I had scrambled to my feet, clutched at a dog's harness, and without one backward glance, was flying from that place.

Half-way to the halting-place, I waited Clark and Mew, being very sick and doddering, and unable to advance. But they did not come.

Later on, when I gathered force to go further, I found that they had perished in the upheaval of the ice. One only of the sledges, half buried, I saw near the spot of our bivouac.

* * *

Alone that same day I began my way southward, and for five days made good progress. On the eighth day I noticed, stretched right across the south-eastern horizon, a region of purple vapour which luridly obscured the face of the sun: and day after day I saw it steadily brooding there. But what it could be I did not understand.

* * *

Well, onward through the desert ice I continued my lonely way, with a baleful shrinking terror in my heart; for very stupendous, alas! is the burden of that Arctic solitude upon one poor human soul.

Sometimes on a halt I have lain and listened long to the hollow silence, recoiling, crushed by it, hoping that at least one of the dogs might whine. I have even crept shivering from the thawed sleeping-bag to flog a dog, so that I might hear a sound.

I had started from the Pole with a well-filled sledge, and the sixteen dogs left alive from the ice-packing which buried my comrades. This was on the evening of the 13th April. I had saved from the wreck of our things most of the whey-powder, pemmican, etc., as well as the theodolite, compass, chronometer, train-oil lamp for cooking, and other implements: I was therefore in no doubt as to my course, and I had provisions for ninety days. But ten days from the start my supply of dog-food failed, and I had to begin to slaughter my only companions, one by one.

Well, in the third week the ice became horribly rough, and with moil and toil enough to wear a bear to death, I did only five miles a day. After the day's work I would crawl with a dying sigh into the sleeping-bag, clad still in the load of skins which stuck to me a mere filth of grease, to sleep the sleep of a swine, indifferent if I never woke.

Always – day after day – on the south-eastern horizon, brooded sullenly that curious stretched-out region of purple vapour, like the smoke of the conflagration of the world. And I noticed that its length constantly reached out and out, and silently grew.

* * *

Once I had a very pleasant dream. I dreamed that I was in a garden – an Arabian paradise – so sweet was the perfume. All the time, however, I had a sub-consciousness of the gale which was actually blowing from the S.E. over the ice, and, at the moment when I awoke, was half-wittedly droning to myself; "It is a Garden of Peaches; but I am not really in the garden: I am really on the ice; only, the S.E. storm is wafting to me the aroma of this Garden of Peaches."

I opened my eyes – I started – I sprang to my feet! For, of all the miracles! – I could not doubt – an actual aroma like peach-blossom was in the algid air about me!

Before I could collect my astonished senses, I began to vomit pretty violently, and at the same time saw some of the dogs, mere skeletons as they were, vomiting, too. For a long time I lay very sick in a kind of daze, and, on rising, found two of the dogs dead, and all very queer. The wind had now changed to the north.

Well, on I staggered, fighting every inch of my deplorably weary way. This odour of peach-blossom, my sickness, and the death of the two dogs, remained a wonder to me.

Two days later, to my extreme mystification (and joy), I came across a bear and its cub lying dead at the foot of a hummock. I could not believe my eyes. There she lay on her right side, a spot of dirty-white in a disordered patch of snow, with one little eye open, and her fierce-looking mouth also; and the cub lay across her haunch, biting into her rough fur. I set to work upon her, and allowed the dogs a glorious feed on the blubber, while I myself had a great banquet on the fresh meat. I had to leave the greater part of the two carcasses, and I can feel again now the hankering reluctance – quite unnecessary, as it turned out – with which I trudged onwards. Again and again I found myself asking: "Now, what could have killed those two bears?"

With brutish stolidness I plodded ever on, almost like a walking machine, sometimes nodding in sleep while I helped the dogs, or manouvred the sledge over an ice-ridge, pushing or pulling. On the 3rd June, a month and a half from my start, I took an observation with the theodolite, and found that I was not yet 400 miles from the Pole, in latitude 84° 50'. It was just as though some Will, some Will, was obstructing and retarding me.

However, the intolerable cold was over, and soon my clothes no longer hung stark on me like armour. Pools began to appear in the ice, and presently, what was worse, my God, long lanes, across which, somehow, I had to get the sledge. But about the same time all fear of starvation passed away: for on the 6th June I came across another dead bear, on the 7th three, and thenceforth, in rapidly growing numbers, I met not bears only, but fulmars, guillemots, snipes, Ross's gulls, little awks – all, all, lying dead on the ice. And never anywhere a living thing, save me, and the two remaining dogs.

If ever a poor man stood shocked before a mystery, it was I now. I had a big fear on my heart.

On the 2nd July the ice began packing dangerously, and soon another storm broke loose upon me from the S.W. I left off my trek, and put up the silk tent on a five-acre square of ice surrounded by lanes: and *again* – for the second time – as I lay down, I smelled that delightful strange odour of peach-blossom, a mere whiff of it, and presently afterwards was taken sick. However, it passed off this time in a couple of hours.

Now it was all lanes, lanes, alas! yet no open water, and such was the difficulty and woe of my life, that sometimes I would drop flat on the ice, and sob: "Oh, no more, no more, my God: here let me die." The crossing of a lane might occupy ten or twelve entire hours, and then, on the other side I might find another one opening right before me. Moreover, on the 8th July, one of the dogs, after a feed on blubber, suddenly died; and there was left me only 'Reinhardt,' a white-haired Siberian dog, with little pert up-sticking ears, like a cat's. Him, too, I had to kill on coming to open water.

This did not happen till the 3rd August, nearly four months from the Pole.

I can't think, my God, that any heart of man ever tholed the appalling nightmare and black abysm of sensations in which, during those four long desert months, I weltered: for though I was as a brute, I had a man's heart to feel. What I had seen, or dreamed, at the Pole followed and followed me; and if I shut my poor weary eyes to sleep, those others yonder seemed to watch me still with their distraught and gloomy gaze, and in my spinning dark dreams spun that eternal ecstasy of the lake.

However, by the 28th July I knew from the look of the sky, and the absence of fresh-water ice, that the sea could not be far; so I set to work, and spent two days in putting to rights the now battered kayak. This done, I had no sooner resumed my way than I sighted far off a streaky haze, which I knew to be the basalt cliffs of Franz Josef Land; and in a craziness of joy I stood there, waving my ski-staff about my head, with the senile cheers of a very old man.

In four days this land was visibly nearer, sheer basaltic cliffs mixed with glacier, forming apparently a great bay, with two small islands in the mid-distance; and at fore-day of the 3rd August I arrived at the definite edge of the pack-ice in moderate weather at about the freezing-point.

I at once, but with great reluctance, shot Reinhardt, and set to work to get the last of the provisions, and the most necessary of the implements, into the kayak, making haste to put out to the toilless luxury of being borne on the water, after all the weary trudge. Within fourteen hours I was coasting, with my little lug-sail spread, along the shore-ice of that land. It was midnight of a calm Sabbath, and low on the horizon smoked the drowsing red sun-ball, as my canvas skiff lightly chopped her little way through this silent sea. Silent, silent: for neither snort of walrus, nor yelp of fox, nor cry of startled kittiwake, did I hear: but all was still as the jet-black shadow of the cliffs and glacier on the tranquil sea: and many bodies of dead things strewed the surface of the water.

* * *

When I found a little fjord, I went up it to the end where stood a stretch of basalt columns, looking like a shattered temple of Antediluvians; and when my foot at last touched land, I sat down there a long, long time in the rubbly snow, and silently wept. My eyes that night were like a fountain of tears. For the firm land is health and sanity, and dear to the life of man; but I say that the great ungenial ice is a nightmare, and a blasphemy, and a madness, and the realm of the Power of Darkness.

* * *

I knew that I was at Franz Josef Land, somewhere or other in the neighbourhood of C. Fligely (about 82° N.), and though it was so late, and getting cold, I still had the hope of reaching Spitzbergen that year, by alternately sailing all open water, and dragging the kayak over the slack drift-ice. All the ice which I saw was good flat fjord-ice, and the plan seemed feasible enough; so after coasting about a little, and then three days' good rest in the tent at the bottom of a ravine of columnar basalt opening upon the shore, I packed some bear and walrus flesh, with what artificial food was left, into the kayak, and I set out early in the morning, coasting the shore-ice with sail and paddle. In the afternoon I managed to climb a little way up an iceberg, and made out that I was in a bay whose terminating headlands were invisible. I accordingly decided to make S.W. by W. to cross it, but, in doing so, I was hardly out of sight of land, when a northern storm overtook me toward midnight; before I could think, the little sail was all but whiffed away, and the kayak upset. I only saved it by the happy chance of being near a floe with an ice-foot, which, projecting under the water, gave me foot-hold; and I lay on the floe in a mooning state the whole night under the storm, for I was half drowned.

And at once, on recovering myself, I abandoned all thought of whalers and of Europe for that year. Happily, my instruments, etc., had been saved by the kayak-deck when she capsized.

* * *

A hundred yards inland from the shore-rim, in a circular place where there was some moss and soil, I built myself a semi-subterranean Eskimo den for the long Polar night. The spot was quite surrounded by high sloping walls of basalt, except to the west, where they opened in a three-foot cleft to the shore, and the ground was strewn with slabs and boulders of granite and basalt. I found there a dead she-bear, two well-grown cubs, and a fox, the latter having evidently fallen from the cliffs; in three places the snow was quite red, overgrown with a red lichen, which at first I took for blood. I did not even yet feel secure from possible bears, and took care to make my den fairly tight, a work which occupied me nearly four weeks, for I had no tools, save a hatchet, knife, and metal-shod ski-staff. I dug a passage in the ground two feet wide, two deep, and ten long, with perpendicular sides, and at its north end a circular space, twelve feet across, also with perpendicular sides, which I lined with stones; the whole excavation I covered with inch-thick walrus-hide, skinned during a whole bitter week from four of a number that lay about the shore-ice; for ridge-pole I used a thin pointed rock which I found near, though, even so, the roof remained nearly flat. This, when it was finished, I stocked well, putting in everything, except the kayak, blubber to serve both for fuel and occasional light, and foods of several sorts, which I procured by merely stretching out the hand. The roof of both circular part and passage was soon buried under snow and ice, and hardly distinguishable from the general level of the white-clad ground. Through the passage, if I passed in or out, I crawled flat, on hands and knees: but that was rare: and in the little round interior, mostly sitting in a cowering attitude, I wintered, harkening to the large and windy ravings of darkling December storms above me.

* * *

All those months the burden of a thought bowed me; and an unanswered question, like the slow turning of a mechanism, revolved in my gloomy spirit: for everywhere around me lay bears, walruses, foxes, thousands upon thousands of little awks, kittiwakes, snow-owls, eider-ducks, gulls-dead, dead. Almost the only living things which I saw were some walruses on the drift-floes: but very few compared with the number which I expected. It was clear to me that some inconceivable catastrophe had overtaken the island during the summer, destroying all life about it, except some few of the amphibia, cetacea, and crustacea.

On the 5th December, having crept out from the den during a southern storm, I had, for the third time, a distant whiff of that self-same odour of peach-blossom: but now without any after-effects.

* * *

Well, again came Christmas, the New Year – Spring: and on the 22nd May I set out with a well-stocked kayak. The water was fairly open, and the ice so good, that at one place I could sail the kayak over it, the wind sending me sliding at a fine pace. Being on the west coast of Franz Josef Land, I was in as favourable a situation as possible, and I turned my bow southward with much hope, keeping a good many days just in sight of land. Toward the evening of my third day out I noticed a large flat floe, presenting far-off a singular and lovely sight, for it seemed freighted thick with a profusion of pink and white roses, showing in its clear crystal the empurpled reflection. On getting near I saw that it was covered with millions of Ross's gulls, all dead, whose pretty rosy bosoms had given it that appearance.

Up to the 29th June I made good progress southward and westward (the weather being mostly excellent), sometimes meeting dead bears, floating away on floes, sometimes dead or living walrus-herds, with troop after troop of dead kittiwakes, glaucus and ivory gulls, skuas, and every kind of Arctic fowl. On that last day – the 29th June – I was about to encamp on a floe soon after midnight, when, happening to look toward the sun, my eye fell, far away south across the ocean of floes, upon something – *the masts of a ship.*

A phantom ship, or a real ship: it was all one; real, I must have instantly felt, it could not be: but at a sight so incredible my heart set to beating in my bosom as though I must surely die, and feebly waving the cane oar about my head, I staggered to my knees, and thence with wry mouth toppled flat.

So overpoweringly sweet was the thought of springing once more, like the beasts of Circe, from a walrus into a man. At this time I was tearing my bear's-meat just like a bear; I was washing my hands in walrus-blood to produce a glairy sort of pink cleanliness, in place of the black grease which chronically coated them.

Worn as I was, I made little delay to set out for that ship; and I had not travelled over water and ice four hours when, to my in-describable joy, I made out from the top of a steep floe that she was the *Boreal*. It seemed most strange that she should be anywhere hereabouts: I could only conclude that she must have forced and drifted her way thus far westward out of the ice-block in which our party had left her, and perhaps now was loitering here in the hope of picking us up on our way to Spitzbergen.

In any case, wild was the haste with which I fought my way to be at her, my gasping mouth all the time drawn back in a *rictus* of laughter at the anticipation of their gladness to see me, their excitement to hear the grand tidings of the Pole attained. Anon I waved the paddle, though I knew that they could not yet see me, and then I dug deep at the whitish water. What astonished me was her main-sail and fore-mast square-sail – set that calm morning; and her screws were still, for she moved not at all. The sun was abroad like a cold spirit of light, touching the great ocean-room of floes with dazzling spots, and a tint almost of rose was on the world, as it were of a just-dead bride in her spangles and white array. The *Boreal* was the one little distant jet-black spot in all this purity: and upon her, as though she were Heaven, I paddled, I panted. But she was in a queerish state: by 9 a.m. I could see that. Two of the windmill arms were not there, and half lowered down her starboard beam a boat hung askew; moreover, soon after 10 a.m. I could clearly see that her main-sail had a long rent down the middle.

I could not at all make her out. She was not anchored, though a sheet-anchor hung over at the starboard cathead; she was not moored; and two small ice-floes, one on each side, were sluggishly bombarding her bows.

I began now to wave the paddle, battling for my breath, ecstatic, crazy with excitement, each second like a year to me. Very soon I could make out someone at the bows, leaning well over, looking my way. Something put it into my head that it was Sallitt, and I began an impassioned shouting. "Hi! Sallitt! Hallo! Hi!" I called.

I did not see him move: I was still a good way off: but there he stood, leaning steadily over, looking my way. Between me and the ship now was all navigable water among the floes, and the sight of him so visibly near put into me such a shivering eagerness, that I was nothing else but a madman for the time, sending the kayak flying with venomous digs in quick-repeated spurts, and mixing with the diggings my crazy wavings, and with both the daft shoutings of "Hallo! Hi! Bravo! I have *been to the Pole!*"

Well, vanity, vanity. Nearer still I drew: it was broad morning, going on toward noon: I was half a mile away, I was fifty yards. But on board the *Boreal*, though now they *must* have heard me, seen me, I observed no movement of welcome, but all, all was still as death that still Arctic morning, my God. Only, the ragged sail flapped a little, and – one on each side – two ice-floes sluggishly bombarded the bows, with hollow sounds.

I was certain now that Sallitt it was who looked across the ice: but when the ship swung a little round, I noticed that the direction of his gaze was carried with her movement, he no longer looking my way.

"Why, Sallitt!" I shouted reproachfully: "why, Sallitt, man...!" I whined.

But even as I shouted and whined, a perfect wild certainty was in my heart: for an aroma like peach, my God, had been suddenly wafted from the ship upon me, and I must have very well known then that that watchful outlook of Sallitt saw nothing, and on the *Boreal* were dead men all; indeed, very soon I saw one of his eyes looking like a glass eye which has slid askew, and glares distraught. And now again my wretched body failed, and my head dropped forward, where I sat, upon the kayak-deck.

* * *

Well, after a long time, I lifted myself to look again at that forlorn and wandering craft. There she lay, quiet, tragic, as it were culpable of the dark secret she bore; and Sallitt, who had been such good friends with me, would not cease his stare. I knew quite well why he was there: he had leant over to vomit, and had leant ever since, his forearms pressed on the bulwark-beam, his left knee against the boards, and his left shoulder propped on the cathead. When I came quite near, I saw that with every bump of the two floes against the bows, his face shook in response, and nodded a little; strange to say, he had no covering on his head, and I noted the play of the faint breezes in his uncut hair. After a time I would approach no more, for I was afraid; I did not dare, the silence of the ship seemed so sacred and awful; and till late afternoon I sat there, watching the black and massive hull. Above her water-line emerged all round a half-floating fringe of fresh-green sea-weed, proving old neglect; an abortive attempt had apparently been made to lower, or take in, the larch-wood pram, for there she hung by a jammed davit-rope, stern up, bow in the water; the only two arms of the windmill moved this way and that, through some three degrees, with an *andante* creaking sing-song; some washed clothes, tied on the bow-sprit rigging to dry, were still there; the iron casing all round the bluff bows was red and rough with rust; at several points the rigging was in considerable tangle; occasionally the boom moved a little with a tortured skirling cadence; and the sail, rotten, I presume, from exposure – for she had certainly encountered no bad weather – gave out anon a heavy languid flap at a rent down the middle. Besides Sallitt, looking out there where he had jammed himself, I saw no one.

By a paddle-stroke now, and another presently, I had closely approached her about four in the afternoon, though my awe of the ship was complicated by that perfume of hers, whose fearful effects I knew. My tentative approach, however, proved to me, when I remained unaffected, that, here and now, whatever danger there had been was past; and finally, by a hanging rope, with a thumping desperation of heart, I clambered up her beam.

* * *

They had died, it seemed, very suddenly, for nearly all the twelve were in poses of activity. Egan was in the very act of ascending the companion-way; Lamburn was sitting against the chart-room door, apparently cleaning two carbines; Odling at the bottom of the engine-room stair seemed to be drawing on a pair of reindeer komagar; and Cartwright, who was often in liquor, had his arms frozen tight round the neck of Martin, whom he seemed to be kissing, they two lying stark at the foot of the mizzen-mast.

Over all – over men, decks, rope-coils – in the cabin, in the engine-room – between skylight leaves – on every shelf, in every cranny – lay a purplish ash or dust, very impalpably fine. And steadily reigning throughout the ship, like the very spirit of death, was that aroma of peach-blossom.

* * *

Here it had reigned, as I could see from the log-dates, from the rust on the machinery, from the look of the bodies, from a hundred indications, during something over a year. It was, therefore, mainly by the random workings of winds and currents that this fragrant ship of death had been brought hither to me.

And this was the first direct intimation which I had that the Unseen Powers (whoever and whatever they may be), who through the history of the world had been so very, very careful to conceal their Hand from the eyes of men, hardly any longer intended to be at the pains to conceal their Hand from me. It was just as though the *Boreal* had been openly presented to me by a spiritual agency, which, though I could not see it, I could readily apprehend.

* * *

The dust, though very thin and flighty above-decks, lay thickly deposited below, and after having made a tour of investigation throughout the ship, the first thing which I did was to examine that – though I had tasted nothing all day, and was exhausted to death. I found my own microscope where I had left it in the box in my berth to starboard, though I had to lift up Egan to get at it, and to step over Lamburn to enter the chart-room; but there, toward evening, I sat at the table and bent to see if I could make anything of the dust, while it seemed to me as if all the myriad spirits of men that have sojourned on the earth, and angel and devil, and all Time and all Eternity, hung silent round for my decision; and such an ague had me, that for a long time my wandering finger-tips, all ataxic with agitation, eluded every delicate effort which I made, and I could nothing do. Of course, I know that an odour of peach-blossom in the air, resulting in death, could only be associated with some vaporous effluvium of cyanogen, or of hydrocyanic ('prussic') acid, or of both; and when I at last managed to examine some of the dust under the microscope, I was not therefore surprised to find, among the general mass of purplish ash, a number of bright-yellow particles, which could only be minute crystals of potassic ferrocyanide. What potassic ferrocyanide was doing on board the *Boreal* I did not know, and I had neither the means, nor the force of mind, alas! to dive then further into the mystery; I understood only that by some extraordinary means the air of the region just south of the Polar environ had been impregnated with a vapour which was either cyanogen, or some product of cyanogen; also, that this deadly vapour, which is very soluble, had by now either been dissolved by the sea, or else dispersed into space (probably the latter), leaving only its faint after-perfume; and seeing this, I let my poor abandoned head drop again on the table, and long hours I sat there staring mad, for I had a suspicion, my God, and a fear, in my breast.

* * *

The *Boreal,* I found, contained sufficient provisions, untouched by the dust, in cases, casks, etc., to last me, probably, fifty years. After two days, when I had partially scrubbed and boiled the filth of fifteen months from my skin, and solaced myself with better food, I overhauled her thoroughly, and spent three more days in oiling and cleaning the engine. Then, all being ready, I dragged my twelve dead and laid them together in two rows on the chart-room floor; and I hoisted for love the poor little kayak which had served me through so many tribulations. At nine in the morning of the 6th July, a week from my first sighting of the *Boreal,* I descended to the engine-room to set out.

The screws, like those of most quite modern ships, were driven by the simple contrivance of a constant stream of liquid air, contained in very powerful tanks, exploding through capillary tubes into non-expansion slide-valve chests, much as in the ordinary way with steam: a motor which gave her, in spite of her bluff hulk, a speed of sixteen knots. It is, therefore, the simplest thing for one man to take these ships round the world, since their movement, or stopping, depend upon nothing but the depressing or raising of a steel handle, provided that one does not get blown to the sky meantime, as liquid air, in spite of its thousand advantages, occasionally blows people. At any rate, I had tanks of air sufficient to last me through twelve years' voyaging; and there was the ordinary machine on board for making it, with forty tons of coal, in case of need, in the bunkers, and two excellent Belleville boilers: so I was well supplied with motors at least.

The ice here was quite slack, and I do not think I ever saw Arctic weather so bright and gay, the temperature at 41°. I found that I was midway between Franz Josef and Spitzbergen, in latitude 79° 23' N. and longitude 39° E.; my way was perfectly clear; and something almost like a mournful hopefulness was in me as the engines slid into their clanking turmoil, and those long-silent screws began to churn the Arctic sea. I ran up with alacrity and took my stand at the wheel; and the bows of my eventful Argo turned southward and westward.

* * *

When I needed food or sleep, the ship slept, too: when I awoke, she continued her way.

Sixteen hours a day sometimes I stood sentinel at that wheel, overlooking the varied monotony of the ice-sea, till my knees would give, and I wondered why a wheel at which one might sit was not contrived, rather delicate steering being often required among the floes and bergs. By now, however, I was less weighted with my ball of Polar clothes, and stood almost slim in a Lap great-coat, a round Siberian fur cap on my head.

At midnight when I threw myself into my old berth, it was just as though the engines, subsided now into silence, were a dead thing, and had a ghost which haunted me; for I heard them still, and yet not them, but the silence of their ghost.

Sometimes I would startle from sleep, horrified to the heart at some sound of exploding iceberg, or bumping floe, noising far through that white mystery of quietude, where the floes and bergs were as floating tombs, and the world a liquid cemetery. Never could I describe the strange Doom's-day shock with which such a sound would recall me from far depths of chaos to recollection of myself: for often-times, both waking and in nightmare, I did not know on which planet I was, nor in which Age, but felt myself adrift in the great gulf of time and space and circumstance, without bottom for my consciousness to stand upon; and the world was all mirage and a new show to me; and the boundaries of dream and waking lost.

Well, the weather was most fair all the time, and the sea like a pond. During the morning of the fifth day, the 11th July, I entered, and went moving down, an extraordinary long avenue of snow-bergs and floes, most regularly placed, half a mile across and miles long, like a Titanic double-procession of statues, or the Ming Tombs, but rising and sinking on the cadenced swell; many towering high, throwing placid shadows on the aisle between; some being of a lucid emerald tint; and three or four pouring down cascades that gave a far and chaunting sound. The sea between was of a strange thick bluishness, almost like raw egg-white; while, as always here, some snow-clouds, white and woolly, floated in the pale sky. Down this avenue, which produced a mysterious impression of Cyclopean cathedrals and odd sequesteredness, I had not passed a mile, when I sighted a black object at the end.

I rushed to the shrouds, and very soon made out a whaler.

Again the same panting agitations, mad rage to be at her, at once possessed me; I flew to the indicator, turned the lever to full, then back to give the wheel a spin, then up the main-mast ratlins, waving a long foot-bandage of vadmel tweed picked up at random, and by the time I was within five hundred yards of her, had worked myself to such a pitch, that I was again shouting that futile madness: "Hullo! Hi! Bravo! *I have been to the Pole!*"

And those twelve dead that I had in the chart-room there must have heard me, and the men on the whaler must have heard me, and smiled their smile.

For, as to that whaler, I should have known better at once, if I had not been crazy, since she *looked* like a ship of death, her boom slamming to port and starboard on the gentle heave of the sea, and her fore-sail reefed that serene morning. Only when I was quite near her, and hurrying down to stop the engines, did the real truth, with perfect suddenness, drench my heated brain; and I almost ran into her, I was so stunned.

However, I stopped the *Boreal* in time, and later on lowered the kayak, and boarded the other.

This ship had evidently been stricken silent in the midst of a perfect drama of activity, for I saw not one of her crew of sixty-two who was not busy, except one boy. I found her a good-sized thing of five hundred odd tons, ship-rigged, with auxiliary engine of seventy horse-power, and pretty heavily armour-plated round the bows. There was no part of her which I did not over-haul, and I could see that they had had a great time with whales, for a mighty carcass, attached to the outside of the ship by the powerful cant-purchase tackle, had been in process of flensing and cutting-in, and on the deck two great blankets of blubber, looking each a ton-weight, surrounded by twenty-seven men in many attitudes, some terrifying to see, some disgusting, several grotesque, all so unhuman, the whale dead, and the men dead, too, and death was there, and the rank-flourishing germs of Inanity, and a mesmerism, and a silence, whose dominion was established, and its reign was growing old. Four of them, who had been removing the gums from a mass of stratified whalebone at the mizzen-mast foot, were quite imbedded in whale-flesh; also, in a barrel lashed to the top of the main top-gallant masthead was visible the head of a man with a long pointed beard, looking steadily out over the sea to the S.W., which made me notice that five only of the probable eight or nine boats were on board; and after visiting the 'tween-decks, where I saw considerable quantities of stowed whalebone plates, and about fifty or sixty iron oil-tanks, and cut-up blubber; and after visiting cabin, engine-room, fo'cas'le, where I saw a lonely boy of fourteen with his hand grasping a bottle of rum under all the turned-up clothes in a chest, he, at the moment of death, being evidently intent upon hiding it; and after two hours' search of the ship, I got back to my own, and half an hour later came upon all the three missing whale-boats about a mile apart, and steered zig-zag near to each. They contained five men each and a steerer, and one had the harpoon-gun fired, with the loose line coiled round and round the head and upper part of the stroke line-manager; and in the others hundreds of fathoms of coiled rope, with toggle-irons, whale-lances, hand-harpoons, and dropped heads, and grins, and lazy *abandon*, and eyes that stared, and eyes that dozed, and eyes that winked.

After this I began to sight ships not infrequently, and used regularly to have the three lights burning all night. On the 12th July I met one, on the 15th two, on the 16th one, on the 17th three, on the 18th two – all Greenlanders, I think: but, of the nine, I boarded only three, the glass quite clearly showing me, when yet far off, that on the others was no life; and on the three which I boarded were dead men; so that that suspicion which I had, and that fear, grew very heavy upon me.

I went on southward, day after day southward, sentinel there at my wheel; clear sunshine by day, when the calm pale sea sometimes seemed mixed with regions of milk, and at night the immense desolation of a world lit by a sun that was long dead, and by a light that was gloom. It was like Night blanched in death then; and wan as the very kingdom of death and Hades I have seen it, most terrifying, that neuter state and limbo of nothingness, when unreal sea and spectral sky, all boundaries lost, mingled in a vast shadowy void of ghastly phantasmagoria, pale to utter huelessness, at whose centre I, as if annihilated, seemed to swoon in immensity of space. Into this disembodied world would come anon waftures of that peachy scent which I knew: and their frequency rapidly grew. But still the *Boreal* moved, traversing, as it were, bottomless Eternity: and I reached latitude 72°, not far now from Northern Europe.

And now, as to that blossomy peach-scent – even while some floes were yet around me – I was just like some fantastic mariner, who, having set out to search for Eden and the Blessed Islands, finds them, and balmy gales from their gardens come out, while he is yet afar, to meet him with their perfumes of almond and champac, cornel and jasmin and lotus. For I had now reached a zone where the peach-aroma was constant; all the world seemed embalmed in its spicy fragrance; and I could easily imagine myself voyaging beyond the world toward some clime of perpetual and enchanting Spring.

* * *

Well, I saw at last what whalers used to call 'the blink of the ice'; that is to say, its bright apparition or reflection in the sky when it is left behind, or not yet come-to. By this time I was in a region where a good many craft of various sorts were to be seen; I was continually meeting them; and not one did I omit to investigate, while many I boarded in the kayak or the larch-wood pram. Just below latitude 70° I came upon a good large fleet of what I supposed to be Lafoden cod and herring fishers, which must have drifted somewhat on a northward current. They had had a great season, for the boats were well laden with curing fish. I went from one to the other on a zig-zag course, they being widely scattered, some mere dots to the glass on the horizon. The evening was still and clear with that astral Arctic clearness, the sun just beginning his low-couched nightly drowse. These sturdy-looking brown boats stood rocking gently there with slow-creaking noises, as of things whining in slumber, without the least damage, awaiting the appalling storms of the winter months on that tenebrous sea, when a dark doom, and a deep grave, would not fail them. The fishers were braw carles, wearing, many of them, fringes of beard well back from the chin-point, with hanging woollen caps. In every case I found below-decks a number of cruses of corn-brandy, marked *aquavit*, two of which I took into the pram. In one of the smacks an elderly fisher was kneeling in a forward sprawling pose, clasping the lug-mast with his arms, the two knees wide apart, head thrown back, and the yellow eye-balls with their islands of grey iris staring straight up the mast-pole. At another of them, instead of boarding in the pram, I shut off the *Boreal's* liquid air at such a point that, by delicate steering, she slackened down to a stoppage just a-beam of the smack, upon whose deck I was thus able to jump down. After looking around I descended the three steps aft into the dark and garrety below-decks, and with stooping back went calling in an awful whisper: "*Anyone? Anyone?*" Nothing answered me: and when I went up again, the *Boreal* had drifted three yards beyond my reach. There being a dead calm, I had to plunge into the water, and in that half-minute there a sudden cold throng of unaccountable terrors beset me, and I can feel again now that abysmal desolation of loneliness, and sense of a hostile and malign universe bent upon eating me up: for the ocean seemed to me nothing but a great ghost.

Two mornings later I came upon another school, rather larger boats these, which I found to be Brittany cod-fishers. Most of these, too, I boarded. In every below-decks was a wooden or earthenware image of the Virgin, painted in gaudy faded colours; and in one case I found a boy who had been kneeling before the statue, but was toppled sideways now, his knees still bent, and the cross of Christ in his hand. These stalwart blue woollen blouses and tarpaulin sou'-westers lay in every pose of death, every detail of feature and expression still perfectly preserved. The sloops were all the same, all, all: with sing-song creaks they rocked a little, nonchalantly: each, as it were, with a certain sub-consciousness of its own personality, and callous unconsciousness of all the others round it: yet each a copy of the others: the same hooks and lines, disembowelling-knives, barrels of salt and pickle, piles and casks of opened cod, kegs of biscuit, and low-creaking rockings, and a bilgy smell, and dead men. The next day, about eighty miles south of the latitude of Mount Hekla, I sighted a big ship, which turned out to be the French cruiser *Lazare Tréport*. I boarded and overhauled her during three hours, her upper, main, and armoured deck, deck by deck, to her lowest black depths, even childishly spying up the tubes of her two big, rusted turret-guns. Three men in the engine-room had been much mangled, after death, I presume, by a burst boiler; floating about 800 yards to the north-east lay a long-boat of hers, low in the water, crammed with marines, one oar still there, jammed between the row-lock and the rower's forced-back chin; on the ship's starboard deck, in the long stretch of space between the two masts, the blue-jackets had evidently been piped up, for they lay there in a sort of serried disorder, to the number of two hundred and seventy-five. Nothing could be of suggestion more tragic than the wasted and helpless power of this poor wandering vessel, around whose stolid mass myriads of wavelets, busy as aspen-leaves, bickered with a continual weltering splash that was quite loud to hear. I sat a good time that afternoon in one of her steely port main-deck casemates on a gun-carriage, my head sunken on my breast, furtively eyeing the bluish turned-up feet, all shrunk, exsanguined, of a sailor who lay on his back before me; his soles were all that I could see, the rest of him lying head-downwards beyond the steel door-sill.

Drenched in seas of lugubrious reverie I sat, till, with a shuddering start, I awoke, paddled back to the *Boreal*, and, till sleep conquered me, went on my way. At ten the next morning, coming on deck, I spied to the west a group of craft, and turned my course upon them. They turned out to be eight Shetland sixerns, which must have drifted north-eastward hither. I examined them well, but they were as the long list of the others: for all the men, and all the boys, and all the dogs on them were dead.

* * *

I could have come to land a long time before I did: but I would not: I was so afraid. For I was used to the silence of the ice: and I was used to the silence of the sea: but, God knows it, I was afraid of the silence of the land.

* * *

Once, on the 15th July, I had seen a whale, or thought I did, spouting very remotely afar on the S.E. horizon; and on the 19th I distinctly saw a shoal of porpoises vaulting the sea-surface, in their swift-successive manner, northward: and seeing them, I had said pitifully to myself: "Well, I am not quite alone in the world, then, my good God – not quite alone."

Moreover, some days later, the *Boreal* had found herself in a bank of cod making away northward, millions of fish, for I saw them, and one afternoon caught three, hand-running, with the hook.

So the sea, at least, had its tribes to be my mates.

But if I should find the land as still as the sea, without even the spouting whale, or school of tumbling sea-hogs – *if Paris were dumber than the eternal ice* – what then, I asked myself, should I do?

* * *

I could have made short work, and landed at Shetland, for I found myself as far westward as longitude 11° 23' W.: but I would not: I was so afraid. The shrinking within me to face that vague suspicion which I had, turned me first to a foreign land.

I made for Norway, and on the first night of this definite intention, at about nine o'clock, the weather being gusty, the sky lowering, the air sombrous, and the sea hard-looking, dark, and ridged, I was steaming along at a good rate, holding the wheel, my poor port and starboard lights still burning there, when, without the least notice, I received the roughest physical shock of my life, being shot bodily right over the wheel, thence, as from a cannon, twenty feet to the cabin-door, through it head-foremost down the companion-way, and still beyond some six yards along the passage. I had crashed into some dark and dead ship, probably of large size, though I never saw her, nor any sign of her; and all that night, and the next day till four in the afternoon, the *Boreal* went driving alone over the sea, whither she would: for I lay unconscious. When I woke, I found that I had received really very small injuries, considering: but I sat there on the floor a long time in a sulky, morose, disgusted, and bitter mood; and when I rose, pettishly stopped the ship's engines, seeing my twelve dead all huddled and disfigured. Now I was afraid to steam by night, and even in the daytime I would not go on for three days: for I was childishly angry with I know not what, and inclined to quarrel with those whom I could not see.

However, on the fourth day, a rough swell which knocked the ship about, and made me very uncomfortable, coaxed me into moving; and I did so with bows turned eastward and southward.

I sighted the Norway coast four days later, in latitude 63° 19', at noon of the 11th August, and pricked off my course to follow it; but it was with a slow and dawdling reluctance that I went, at much less than half-speed. In some eight hours, as I knew from the chart, I ought to sight the lighthouse light on Smoelen Island; and when quiet night came, the black water being branded with trails of still moonlight, I passed quite close to it, between ten and twelve, almost under the shadow of the mighty hills: but, oh my God, no light was there. And all the way down I marked the rugged sea-board slumber darkling, afar or near, with never, alas! one friendly light.

* * *

Well, on the 15th August I had another of those maniac raptures, whose passing away would have left an elephant racked and prostrate. During four days I had seen not one sign of present life on the Norway coast, only hills, hills, dead and dark, and floating craft, all dead and dark; and my eyes now, I found, had acquired a crazy fixity of stare into the very bottom of the vacant abyss of nothingness, while I remained unconscious of being, save of one point, rainbow-blue, far down in the infinite, which passed slowly from left to right before my consciousness a little way, then vanished, came back, and passed slowly again, from left to right continually; till some prick, or voice, in my brain would startle me into the consciousness that I was staring, whispering the profound confidential warning: "*You must not stare so, or it is over with you!*" Well, lost in a blank trance of this sort, I was leaning over the wheel during the afternoon of the 15th, when it was as if some instinct or premonition in my soul leapt up, and said aloud: "If you look just yonder, *you will see...!*" I started, and in one instant had surged up from all that depth of reverie to reality: I glanced to the right: and there, at last, my God, I saw something human which moved, rapidly moved: at last! – and it came to me.

That sense of recovery, of waking, of new solidity, of the comfortable usual, a million-fold too intense for words – how sweetly consoling it was! Again now, as I write, I can fancy and feel it – the rocky solidity, the adamant ordinary, on which to base the feet, and live. From the day when I stood at the Pole, and saw there the dizzy thing that made me swoon, there had come into my way not one sign or trace that other beings like myself were alive on the earth with me: till now, suddenly, I had the sweet indubitable proof: for on the south-western sea, not four knots away, I saw a large, swift ship: and her bows, which were sharp as a hatchet, were steadily chipping through the smooth sea at a pretty high pace, throwing out profuse ribbony foams that went wide-vawering, with outward undulations, far behind her length, as she ran the sea in haste, straight northward.

At the moment, I was steering about S.E. by S., fifteen miles out from a shadowy-blue series of Norway mountains; and just giving the wheel one frantic spin to starboard to bring me down upon her, I flew to the bridge, leant my back on the main-mast, which passed through it, put a foot on the white iron rail before me, and there at once felt all the mocking devils of distracted revelry possess me, as I caught the cap from my long hairs, and commenced to wave and wave and wave, red-faced maniac that I was: for at the second nearer glance, I saw that she was flying an ensign at the main, and a long pennant at the main-top, and I did not know what she was flying those flags there for: and I was embittered and driven mad.

With distinct minuteness did she print herself upon my consciousness in that five minutes' interval: she was painted a dull and cholera yellow, like many Russian ships, and there was a faded pink space at her bows under the line where the yellow ceased: the ensign at her main I made out to be the blue-and-white saltire, and she was clearly a Russian passenger-liner, two-masted, two-funnelled, though from her funnels came no trace of smoke, and the position of her steam-cones was anywhere. All about her course the sea was spotted with wobbling splendours of the low sun, large coarse blots of glory near the eye, but lessening to a smaller pattern in the distance, and at the horizon refined to a homogeneous band of livid silver.

The double speed of the *Boreal* and the other, hastening opposite ways, must have been thirty-eight or forty knots, and the meeting was accomplished in certainly less than five minutes: yet into that time I crowded years of life. I was shouting passionately at her, my eyes starting from my head, my face all inflamed with rage the most prone, loud and urgent. For she did not stop, nor signal, nor make sign of seeing me, but came furrowing down upon me like Juggernaut, with steadfast run. I lost reason, thought, memory, purpose, sense of relation, in that access of delirium which transported me, and can only remember now that in the midst of my shouting, a word, uttered by the fiends who used my throat to express their frenzy, set me laughing high and madly: for I was crying: "Hi! Bravo! Why don't you stop? *Madmen! I have been to the Pole!*"

That instant an odour arose, and came, and struck upon my brain, most detestable, most execrable; and while one might count ten, I was aware of her near-sounding engines, and that cursed charnel went tearing past me on her maenad way, not fifteen yards from my eyes and nostrils. She was a thing, my God, from which the vulture and the jackal, prowling for offal, would fly with shrieks of loathing. I had a glimpse of decks piled thick with her festered dead.

In big black letters on the round retreating yellow stern my eye-corner caught the word *Yaroslav*, as I bent over the rail to retch and cough and vomit at her. She was a horrid thing.

This ship had certainly been pretty far south in tropical or sub-tropical latitudes with her great crowd of dead: for all the bodies which I had seen till then, so far from smelling ill, seemed to give out a certain perfume of the peach. She was evidently one of those many ships of late years which have substituted liquid air for steam, yet retained their old steam-funnels, etc., in case of emergency: for air, I believe, was still looked at askance by several builders, on account of the terrible accidents which it sometimes caused. The *Boreal* herself is a similar instance of both motors. This vessel, the *Yaroslav*, must have been left with working engines when her crew were overtaken by death, and, her air-tanks being still unexhausted, must have been ranging the ocean with impunity ever since, during I knew not how many months, or, it might be, years.

Well, I coasted Norway for nearly a hundred and sixty miles without once going nearer land than two or three miles: for something held me back. But passing the fjord-mouth where I knew that Aadheim was, I suddenly turned the helm to port, almost before I knew that I was doing it, and made for land.

In half an hour I was moving up an opening in the land with mountains on either hand, streaky crags at their summit, umbrageous boscage below; and the whole softened, as it were, by veils woven of the rainbow.

This arm of water lies curved about like a thread which one drops, only the curves are much more pointed, so that every few minutes the scene was changed, though the vessel just crawled her way up, and I could see behind me nothing of what was passed, or only a land-locked gleam like a lake.

I never saw water so polished and glassy, like clarid polished marble, reflecting everything quite clean-cut in its lucid abysm, over which hardly the faintest zephyr breathed that still sun-down; it wimpled about the bluff *Boreal*, which seemed to move as if careful not to bruise it, in rich wrinkles and creases, like glycerine, or dewy-trickling lotus-oil; yet it was only the sea: and the spectacle yonder was only crags, and autumn-foliage and mountain-slope: yet all seemed caught-up and chaste, rapt in a trance of rose and purple, and made of the stuff of dreams and bubbles, of pollen-of-flowers, and rinds of the peach.

I saw it not only with delight, but with complete astonishment: having forgotten, as was too natural in all that long barrenness of ice and sea, that anything could be so ethereally fair: yet homely, too, human, familiar, and consoling. The air here was richly spiced with that peachy scent, and there was a Sabbath and a nepenthe and a charm in that place at that hour, as it were of those gardens of Hesperus, and fields of asphodel, reserved for the spirits of the just.

Alas! but I had the glass at my side, and for me nepenthe was mixed with a despair immense as the vault of heaven, my good God: for anon I would take it up to spy some perched hut of the peasant, or burg of the 'bonder,' on the peaks: and I saw no one there; and to the left, at the third marked bend of the fjord, where there is one of those watch-towers that these people used for watching in-coming fish, I spied, lying on a craggy slope just before the tower, a body which looked as if it must surely tumble head-long, but did not. And when I saw that, I felt definitely, for the first time, that shoreless despair which I alone of men have felt, high beyond the stars, and deep as hell; and I fell to staring again that blank stare of Nirvana and the lunacy of Nothingness, wherein Time merges in Eternity, and all being, like one drop of water, flies scattered to fill the bottomless void of space, and is lost.

The *Boreal's* bow walking over a little empty fishing-boat roused me, and a minute later, just before I came to a new promontory and bend, I saw two people. The shore there is some three feet above the water, and edged with boulders of rock, about which grows a fringe of shrubs and small trees: behind this fringe is a path, curving upward through a sombre wooded little gorge; and on the path, near the water, I saw a driver of one of those Norwegian sulkies that were called karjolers: he, on the high front seat, was dead, lying sideways and backwards, with low head resting on the wheel; and on a trunk strapped to a frame on the axle behind was a boy, his head, too, resting sideways on the wheel, near the other's; and the little pony was dead, pitched forward on its head and fore-knees, tilting the shafts downward; and some distance from them on the water floated an empty skiff.

* * *

When I turned the next fore-land, I all at once began to see a number of craft, which increased as I advanced, most of them small boats, with some schooners, sloops, and larger craft, the majority a-ground: and suddenly now I was conscious that, mingling with that delicious odour of spring-blossoms – profoundly modifying, yet not destroying it – was another odour, wafted to me on the wings of the very faint land-breeze: and "Man," I said, "is decomposing": for I knew it well: it was the odour of human corruption.

* * *

The fjord opened finally in a somewhat wider basin, shut-in by quite steep, high-towering mountains, which reflected themselves in the water to their last cloudy crag: and, at the end of this I saw ships, a quay, and a modest, homely old town.

Not a sound, not one: only the languidly-working engines of the *Boreal*. Here, it was clear, the Angel of Silence had passed, and his scythe mown.

I ran and stopped the engines, and, without anchoring, got down into an empty boat that lay at the ship's side when she stopped; and I paddled twenty yards toward the little quay. There was a brigantine with all her courses set, three jibs, stay-sails, square-sails, main and fore-sails, and gaff-top-sail, looking hanging and listless in that calm place, and wedded to a still copy of herself, mast-downward, in the water; there were three lumber-schooners, a forty-ton steam-boat, a tiny barque, five Norway herring-fishers, and ten or twelve shallops: and the sailing-craft had all fore-and-aft sails set, and about each, as I passed among them, brooded an odour that was both sweet and abhorrent, an odour more suggestive of the very genius of mortality – the inner mind and meaning of Azrael – than aught that I could have conceived: for all, as I soon saw, were crowded with dead.

Well, I went up the old mossed steps, in that strange dazed state in which one notices frivolous things: I remember, for instance, feeling the lightness of my new clothes: for the weather was quite mild, and the day before I had changed to Summer things, having on now only a common undyed woollen shirt, the sleeves rolled up, and cord trousers, with a belt, and a cloth cap over my long hair, and an old pair of yellow shoes, without laces, and without socks. And I stood on the unhewn stones of the edge of the quay, and looked abroad over a largish piece of unpaved ground, which lay between the first house-row and the quay.

What I saw was not only most woeful, but wildly startling: woeful, because a great crowd of people had assembled, and lay dead, there; and wildly startling, because something in their *tout ensemble* told me in one minute why they were there in such number.

They were there in the hope, and with the thought, to fly westward by boat.

And the something which told me this was a certain *foreign* air about that field of the dead as the eye rested on it, something un-northern, southern, and Oriental.

Two yards from my feet, as I stepped to the top, lay a group of three: one a Norway peasant-girl in skirt of olive-green, scarlet stomacher, embroidered bodice, Scotch bonnet trimmed with silver lace, and big silver shoe-buckles; the second was an old Norway man in knee-breeches, and eighteenth-century small-clothes, and red worsted cap; and the third was, I decided, an old Jew of the Polish Pale, in gaberdine and skull-cap, with ear-locks.

I went nearer to where they lay thick as reaped stubble between the quay and a little stone fountain in the middle of the space, and I saw among those northern dead two dark-skinned women in costly dress, either Spanish or Italian, and the yellower mortality of a Mongolian, probably a Magyar, and a big negro in zouave dress, and some twenty-five obvious French, and two Morocco fezes, and the green turban of a shereef, and the white of an Ulema.

And I asked myself this question: "How came these foreign stragglers here in this obscure northern town?"

And my wild heart answered: "There has been an impassioned stampede, northward and westward, of all the tribes of Man. And this that I, Adam Jeffson, here see is but the far-tossed spray of that monstrous, infuriate flood."

* * *

Well, I passed up a street before me, careful, careful where I trod. It was not utterly silent, nor was the quay-square, but haunted by a pretty dense cloud of mosquitoes, and dreamy twinges of music, like the drawing of the violin-bow in elf-land. The street was narrow, pavered, steep, and dark; and the sensations with which I, poor bent man, passed through that dead town, only Atlas, fabled to bear the burden of this Earth, could divine.

* * *

I thought to myself: If now a wave from the Deep has washed over this planetary ship of earth, and I, who alone happened to be in the extreme bows, am the sole survivor of that crew? ... What then, my God, shall I do?

* * *

I felt, I felt, that in this townlet, save the water-gnats of Norway, was no living thing; that the hum and the savour of Eternity filled, and wrapped, and embalmed it.

The houses are mostly of wood, some of them fairly large, with a *porte-cochère* leading into a semi-circular yard, around which the building stands, very steep-roofed, and shingled, in view of the heavy snow-masses of winter. Glancing into one open casement near the ground, I saw an aged woman, stout and capped, lie on her face before a very large porcelain stove; but I paced on without stoppage, traversed several streets, and came out, as it became dark, upon a piece of grass-land leading downward to a mountain-gorge. It was some distance along this gorge that I found myself sitting the next morning: and how, and in what trance, I passed that whole blank night is obliterated from my consciousness. When I looked about with the return of light I saw majestic fir-grown mountains on either hand, almost meeting overhead at some points, deeply shading the mossy gorge. I rose, and careless of direction, went still onward, and walked and walked for hours, unconscious of hunger; there was a profusion of wild mountain-strawberries, very tiny, which must grow almost into winter, a few of which I ate; there were blue gentianellas, and lilies-of-the-valley, and luxuriance of verdure, and a noise of waters. Occasionally, I saw little cataracts on high, fluttering like white wild rags, for they broke in the mid-fall, and were caught away, and scattered; patches also of reaped hay and barley, hung up, in a singular way, on stakes six feet high, I suppose to dry; there were perched huts, and a seemingly inaccessible small castle or burg, but none of these did I enter: and five bodies only I saw in the gorge, a woman with a babe, and a man with two small oxen.

About three in the afternoon I was startled to find myself there, and turned back. It was dark when I again passed through those gloomy streets of Aadheim, making for the quay, and now I felt both my hunger and a dropping weariness. I had no thought of entering any house, but as I passed by one open *porte-cochère*, something, I know not what, made me turn sharply in, for my mind had become as fluff on the winds, not working of its own action, but the sport of impulses that seemed external. I went across the yard, and ascended a wooden spiral stair by a twilight which just enabled me to pick my way among five or six vague forms fallen there. In that confined place fantastic qualms beset me; I mounted to the first landing, and tried the door, but it was locked; I mounted to the second: the door was open, and with a chill reluctance I took a step inward where all was pitch darkness, the window-stores being drawn. I hesitated: it was very dark. I tried to utter that word of mine, but it came in a whisper inaudible to my ears: I tried again, and this time heard myself say: "*anyone?*" At the same time I had made another step forward, and trodden upon a soft abdomen; and at that contact terrors the most cold and ghastly thrilled me through and through, for it was as though I saw in that darkness the sudden eyeballs of Hell and frenzy glare upon me, and with a low gurgle of affright I was gone, helter-skelter down the stairs, treading upon flesh, across the yard, and down the street, with pelting feet, and open arms, and sobbing bosom, for I thought that all Aadheim was after me; nor was my horrid haste appeased till I was on board the *Boreal*, and moving down the fjord.

Out to sea, then, I went again; and within the next few days I visited Bergen, and put in at Stavanger. And I saw that Bergen and Stavanger were dead.

It was then, on the 19th August, that I turned my bow toward my native land.

* * *

From Stavanger I steered a straight course for the Humber.

I had no sooner left behind me the Norway coast than I began to meet the ships, the ships – ship after ship; and by the time I entered the zone of the ordinary alternation of sunny day and sunless night, I was moving through the midst of an incredible number of craft, a mighty and wide-spread fleet.

Over all that great expanse of the North Sea, where, in its most populous days of trade, the sailor might perhaps sight a sail or two, I had now at every moment at least ten or twelve within scope of the glass, oftentimes as many as forty, forty-five.

And very still they lay on a still sea, itself a dead thing, livid as the lips of death; and there was an intensity in the calm that was appalling: for the ocean seemed weighted, and the air drugged.

Extremely slow was my advance, for at first I would not leave any ship, however remotely small, without approaching sufficiently to investigate her, at least with the spy-glass: and a strange multitudinous mixture of species they were, trawlers in hosts, war-ships of every nation, used, it seemed, as passenger-boats, smacks, feluccas, liners, steam-barges, great four-masters with sails, Channel boats, luggers, a Venetian *burchiello*, colliers, yachts, *remorqueurs*, training ships, dredgers, two *dahabeeahs* with curving gaffs, Marseilles fishers, a Maltese *speronare*, American off-shore sail, Mississippi steam-boats, Sorrento lug-schooners, Rhine punts, yawls, old frigates and three-deckers, called to novel use, Stromboli caiques, Yarmouth tubs, xebecs, Rotterdam flat-bottoms, floats, mere gunwaled rafts – anything from anywhere that could bear a human freight on water had come, and was here: and all, I knew, had been making westward, or northward, or both; and all, I knew, were crowded; and all were tombs, listlessly wandering, my God, on the wandering sea with their dead.

And so fair was the world about them, too: the brightest suavest autumn weather; all the still air aromatic with that vernal perfume of peach: yet not so utterly still, but if I passed close to the lee of any floating thing, the spicy stirrings of morning or evening wafted me faint puffs of the odour of mortality over-ripe for the grave.

So abominable and accursed did this become to me, such a plague and a hissing, vague as was the offence, that I began to shun rather than seek the ships, and also I now dropped my twelve, whom I had kept to be my companions all the way from the Far North, one by one, into the sea: for now I had definitely passed into a zone of settled warmth.

I was convinced, however, that the poison, whatever it might be, had some embalming, or antiseptic, effect upon the bodies: at Aadheim, Bergen and Stavanger, for instance, where the temperature permitted me to go without a jacket, only the merest hints and whiffs of the processes of dissolution had troubled me.

* * *

329

Very benign, I say, and pleasant to see, was sky and sea during all that voyage: but it was at sun-set that my sense of the wondrously beautiful was roused and excited, in spite of that great burden which I carried. Certainly, I never saw sun-sets resembling those, nor could have conceived of aught so flamboyant, extravagant, and bewitched: for the whole heaven seemed turned into an arena for warring Hierarchies, warring for the universe, or it was like the wild countenance of God defeated, and flying marred and bloody from His enemies. But many evenings I watched with unintelligent awe, believing it but a portent of the un-sheathed sword of the Almighty; till, one morning, a thought pricked me like a sword, for I suddenly remembered the great sun-sets of the later nineteenth century, witnessed in Europe, America, and, I believe, over the world, after the eruption of the volcano of Krakatoa.

And whereas I had before said to myself: "If now a wave from the Deep has washed over this planetary ship of earth...," I said now: "A wave – but not from the Deep: a wave rather which she had reserved, and has spouted, from her own un-motherly entrails..."

* * *

I had some knowledge of Morse telegraphy, and of the manipulation of tape-machines, telegraphic typing-machines, and the ordinary wireless transmitter and coherer, as of most little things of that sort which came within the outskirts of the interest of a man of science; I had collaborated with Professor Stanistreet in the production of a text-book called *Applications of Science to the Arts*, which had brought us some notoriety; and, on the whole, the *minutiae* of modern things were still pretty fresh in my memory. I could therefore have wired from Bergen or Stavanger, supposing the batteries not run down, to somewhere: but I would not: I was so afraid; afraid lest for ever from nowhere should come one answering click, or flash, or stirring...

* * *

I could have made short work, and landed at Hull: but I would not: I was so afraid. For I was used to the silence of the ice: and I was used to the silence of the sea: but I was afraid of the silence of England.

* * *

I came in sight of the coast on the morning of the 26th August, somewhere about Hornsea, but did not see any town, for I put the helm to port, and went on further south, no longer bothering with the instruments, but coasting at hap-hazard, now in sight of land, and now in the centre of a circle of sea; not admitting to myself the motive of this loitering slowness, nor thinking at all, but ignoring the deep-buried fear of the tomorrow which I shirked, and instinctively hiding myself in today. I passed the Wash, I passed Yarmouth, Felixstowe. By now the things that floated motionless on the sea were beyond numbering, for I could hardly lower my eyes ten minutes and lift them, without seeing yet another there: so that soon after dusk I, too, had to lie still among them all, till morning: for they lay dark, and to move at any pace would have been to drown the already dead.

Well, I came to the Thames-mouth, and lay pretty well in among the Flats and Pan Sands towards eight one evening, not seven miles from Sheppey and the North Kent coast: and I did not see any Nore Light, nor Girdler Light: and all along the coast I had seen no light: but as to that I said not one word to myself, not admitting it, nor letting my heart know what my brain thought, nor my brain know what my heart surmised; but with a daft and mock-mistrustful under-look I would regard the darkling land, holding it a sentient thing that would be playing a prank upon a poor man like me.

And the next morning, when I moved again, my furtive eye-corners were very well aware of the Prince's Channel light-ship, and also the Tongue ship, for there they were: but I would not look at them at all, nor go near them: for I did not wish to have anything to do with whatever might have happened beyond my own ken, and it was better to look straight before, seeing nothing, and concerning one's-self with one's-self.

The next evening, after having gone out to sea again, I was in a little to the E. by S. of the North Foreland: and I saw no light there, nor any Sandhead light; but over the sea vast signs of wreckage, and the coasts were strewn with old wrecked fleets. I turned about S.E., very slowly moving – for anywhere hereabouts hundreds upon hundreds of craft lay dead within a ten-mile circle of sea – and by two in the fore-day had wandered up well in sight of the French cliffs: for I had said: "I will go and see the light-beam of the great revolving-drum on Calais pier that nightly beams half-way over-sea to England." And the moon shone clear in the southern heaven that morning, like a great old dying queen whose Court swarms distantly from around her, diffident, pale, and tremulous, the paler the nearer; and I could see the mountain-shadows on her spotty full-face, and her misty aureole, and her lights on the sea, as it were kisses stolen in the kingdom of sleep; and all among the quiet ships mysterious white trails and powderings of light, like palace-corridors in some fairy-land forlorn, full of breathless wan whispers, scandals, and runnings-to-and-fro, with leers, and agitated last embraces, and flight of the princess, and death-bed of the king; and on the N.E. horizon a bank of brown cloud that seemed to have no relation with the world; and yonder, not far, the white coast-cliffs, not so low as at Calais near, but arranged in masses separated by vales of sward, each with its wreck: but no light of any revolving-drum I saw.

* * *

I could not sleep that night: for all the operations of my mind and body seemed in abeyance. Mechanically I turned the ship westward again; and when the sun came up, there, hardly two miles from me, were the cliffs of Dover; and on the crenulated summit of the Castle I spied the Union Jack hang motionless.

I heard eight, nine o'clock strike in the cabin, and I was still at sea. But some mad, audacious whisper was at my brain: and at 10:30, the 2nd September, immediately opposite the Cross Wall Custom House, the *Boreal's* anchor-chain, after a voyage of three years, two months, and fourteen days, ran thundering, thundering, through the starboard hawse-hole.

Ah heaven! But I must have been stark mad to let the anchor go! For the effect upon me of that shocking obstreperous hubbub, breaking in upon all that cemetery repose that blessed morning, and lasting it seemed a year, was most appalling; and at the sudden racket I stood excruciated, with shivering knees and flinching heart, God knows: for not less terrifically uproarious than the clatter of the last Trump it raged and raged, and I thought that all the billion dead could not fail to start, and rise, at alarum so excessive, and question me with their eyes...

* * *

On the top of the Cross Wall near I saw a grey crab fearlessly crawl; at the end where the street begins, I saw a single gas-light palely burn that broad day, and at its foot a black man lay on his face, clad only in a shirt and one boot; the harbour was almost packed with every sort of craft, and on a Calais-Dover boat, eight yards from my stern, which must have left Calais crowded to suffocation, I saw the rotted dead lie heaped, she being unmoored, and continually grinding against an anchored green brig.

And when I saw that, I dropped down upon my knees at the capstan, and my poor heart sobbed out the frail cry: "Well, Lord God, Thou hast destroyed the work of Thy hand..."

* * *

After a time I got up, went below in a state of somnambulism, took a packet of pemmican cakes, leapt to land, and went following the railway that runs from the Admiralty Pier. In an enclosed passage ten yards long, with railway masonry on one side, I saw five dead lie, and could not believe that I was in England, for all were dark-skinned people, three gaudily dressed, and two in flowing white robes. It was the same when I turned into a long street, leading northward, for here were a hundred, or more, and never saw I, except in Constantinople, where I once lived eighteen months, so variegated a mixture of races, black, brunette, brown, yellow, white, in all the shades, some emaciated like people dead from hunger, and, overlooking them all, one English boy with a clean Eton collar sitting on a bicycle, supported by a lamp-post which his arms clasped, he proving clearly the extraordinary suddenness of the death which had overtaken them all.

I did not know whither, nor why, I went, nor had I the least idea whether all this was visually seen by me in the world which I had known, or in some other, or was all phantasy of my disembodied spirit – for I had the thought that I, too, might be dead since old ages, and my spirit wandering now through the universe of space, in which there is neither north nor south, nor up nor down, nor measure nor relation, nor aught whatever, save an uneasy consciousness of a dream about bottomlessness. Of grief or pain, I think, I felt nothing; though I have a sort of memory now that some sound, resembling a sob or groan, though it was neither, came at regular clockwork intervals from my bosom during three or four days. Meantime, my brain registered like a tape-machine details the most frivolous, the most ludicrous – the name of a street, Strond Street, Snargate Street; the round fur cap – black fur for the side, white ermine for the top – of a portly Karaite priest on his back, whose robes had been blown to his spread knees, as if lifted and neatly folded there; a violin-bow gripped between the thick, irregular teeth of a little Spaniard with brushed-back hair and mad-looking eyes; odd shoes on the foot of a French girl, one black, one brown. They lay in the street about as numerous as gunners who fall round their carriage, at intervals of five to ten feet, the majority – as was the case also in Norway, and on the ships – in poses of distraction, with spread arms, or wildly distorted limbs, like men who, the instant before death, called upon the rocks and hills to cover them.

* * *

On the left I came to an opening in the land, called, I believe, 'The Shaft,' and into this I turned, climbing a very great number of steps, almost covered at one point with dead: the steps I began to count, but left off, then the dead, and left off. Finally, at the top, which must be even higher than the Castle, I came to a great open space laid out with gravel-walks, and saw fortifications, barracks, a citadel. I did not know the town, except by passings-through, and was surprised at the breadth of view. Between me and the Castle to the east lay the district of crowding houses, brick and ragstone, mixed in the distance with vague azure haze; and to the right the harbour, the sea, with their ships; and visible around me on the heights seven or eight dead, biting the dust; the sun now high and warm, with hardly a cloud in the sky; and yonder a mist, which was the coast of France.

It seemed too big for one poor man.

My head nodded. I sat on a bench, black-painted and hard, the seat and back of horizontal boards, with intervals; and as I looked, I nodded, heavy-headed and weary: for it was too big for me. And as I nodded, with forehead propped on my left hand, and the packet of pemmican cakes in my right, there was in my head, somehow, an old street-song of my childhood: and I groaned it sleepily, like coronachs and drear funereal nenias, dirging; and the packet beat time in my right hand, falling and raising, falling heavily and rising, in time.

I'll buy the ring,
You'll rear the kids:
Servants to wait on our ting, ting, ting...
Ting, ting,
Won't we be happy?
Ting, ting,
That shall be it:
I'll buy the ring,
You'll rear the kids:
Servants to wait on our ting, ting, ting...

So maundering, I fell forward upon my face, and for twenty-three hours, the living undistinguished from the dead, I slept there.

* * *

I was awakened by drizzle, leapt up, looked at a silver chronometer which, attached by a leather to my belt, I carried in my breeches-pocket, and saw that it was 10 a.m. The sky was dark, and a moaning wind – almost a new thing now to me – had arisen.

I ate some pemmican, for I had a reluctance – needless as it turned out – to touch any of the thousand luxuries here, sufficient no doubt, in a town like Dover alone, to last me five or six hundred years, if I could live so long; and, having eaten, I descended The Shaft, and spent the whole day, though it rained and blustered continually, in wandering about. Reasoning, in my numb way, from the number of ships on the sea, I expected to find the town over-crowded with dead: but this was not so; and I should say, at a venture, that not a thousand English, nor fifteen thousand foreigners, were in it: for that westward rage and stampede must have operated here also, leaving the town empty but for the ever new-coming hosts.

The first thing which I did was to go into an open grocer's shop, which was also a post and telegraph office, with the notion, I suppose, to get a message through to London. In the shop a single gas-light was burning its last, and this, with that near the pier, were the only two that I saw: and ghastly enough they looked, transparently wannish, and as it were ashamed, like blinking night-things overtaken by the glare of day. I conjectured that they had so burned and watched during months, or years: for they were now blazing diminished, with streaks and rays in the flame, as if by effort, and if these were the only two, they must have needed time to all-but exhaust the works. Before the counter lay a fashionably-dressed negro with a number of tied parcels scattered about him, and on the counter an empty till, and behind it a tall thin woman with her face resting sideways in the till, fingers clutching the outer counter-rim, and such an expression of frantic terror as I never saw. I got over the counter to a table behind a wire-gauze, and, like a numb fool, went over the Morse alphabet in my mind before touching the transmitting key, though I knew no code-words, and there, big enough to be seen, was the ABC dial, and who was to answer my message I did not ask myself: for habit was still strong upon me, and my mind refused to reason from what I saw to what I did not see; but the moment I touched the key, and peered greedily at the galvanometer-needle at my right, I saw that it did not move, for no current was passing; and with a kind of fright, I was up, leapt, and got away from the place, though there was a great number of telegrams about the receiver which, if I had been in my senses, I would have stopped and read.

Turning the corner of the next street, I saw wide-open the door of a substantial large house, and went in. From bottom to top there was no one there, except one English girl, sitting back in an easy-chair in the drawing-room, which was richly furnished with Valenciennes curtains and azure-satin things. She was a girl of the lowest class, hardly clad in black rags, and there she lay with hanging jaw, in a very crooked and awkward pose, a jemmy at her feet, in her left hand a roll of bank-notes, and in her lap three watches. In fact, the bodies which I saw here were, in general, either those of new-come foreigners, or else of the very poor, the very old, or the very young.

But what made me remember this house was that I found here on one of the sofas a newspaper: *The Kent Express*; and sitting unconscious of my dead neighbour, I pored a long while over what was written there.

It said in a passage which I tore out and kept:

"Telegraphic communication with Tilsit, Insterburg, Warsaw, Cracow, Przemysl, Gross Wardein, Karlsburg, and many smaller towns lying immediately eastward of the 21st parallel of longitude has ceased during the night. In some at least of them there must have been operators still at their duty, undrawn into the great westward-rushing torrent: but as all messages from Western Europe have been answered only by that dread mysterious silence which, just three months and two days since, astounded the world in the case of Eastern New Zealand, we can only assume that these towns, too, have been added to the long and mournful list; indeed, after last evening's Paris telegrams we might have prophesied with some certainty, not merely their overthrow, but even the hour of it: for the rate-uniformity of the slow-riding vapour which is touring our globe is no longer doubtful, and has even been definitely fixed by Professor Craven at 100-1/2 miles per day, or fou miles 330 yards per hour. Its nature, its origin, remains, of course, nothing but matter of conjecture: for it leaves no living thing behind it: nor, God knows, is that of any moment now to us who remain. The rumour that it is associated with an odour of almonds is declared, on high authority, to be improbable; but the morose purple of its impending gloom has been attested by tardy fugitives from the face of its rolling and smoky march.

"Is this the end? We do not, and cannot, believe it. Will the pure sky which we today see above us be invaded in nine days, or less, by this smoke of the Pit of Darkness? In spite of the assurances of the scientists, we still doubt. For, if so, to what purpose that long drama of History, in which we seem to see the Hand of the Dramaturgist? Surely, the end of a Fifth Act should be obvious, satisfying to one's

sense of the complete: but History, so far, long as it has been, resembles rather a Prologue than a Fifth Act. Can it be that the Manager, utterly dissatisfied, would sweep all off, and 'hang up' the piece for ever? Certainly, the sins of mankind have been as scarlet: and if the fair earth which he has turned into Hell, send forth now upon him the smoke of Hell, little the wonder. But we cannot yet believe. There is a sparing strain in nature, and through the world, as a thread, is spun a silence which smiles, and on the end of events we find placarded large the words: 'Why were ye afraid?' A dignified Hope, therefore – even now, when we cower beneath this worldwide shadow of the wings of the Condor of Death – becomes us: and, indeed, we see such an attitude among some of the humblest of our people, from whose heart ascends the cry: 'Though He slay me, yet will I trust in Him.' Here, therefore, O Lord! O Lord, look down, and save!

"But even as we thus write of hope, Reason, if we would hear her, whispers us 'fool': and inclement is the sky of earth. No more ships can New York Harbour contain, and whereas among us men die weekly of privations by the hundred thousand, yonder across the sea they perish by the million: for where the rich are pinched, how can the poor live? Already 700 out of the 1000 millions of our race have perished, and the empires of civilisation have crumbled like sand-castles in a horror of anarchy. Thousands upon thousands of unburied dead, anticipating the more deliberate doom that comes and smokes, and rides and comes and comes, and does not fail, encumber the streets of London, Manchester, Liverpool. The guides of the nation have fled; the father stabs his child, and the wife her husband, for a morsel of food; the fields lie waste; wanton crowds carouse in our churches, universities, palaces, banks and hospitals; we understand that late last night three territorial regiments, the Munster Fusiliers, and the Lotian and East Lancashire Regiments, riotously disbanded themselves, shooting two officers; infectious diseases, as we all know, have spread beyond limit; in several towns the police seem to have disappeared, and, in nearly all, every vestige of decency; the results following upon the sudden release of the convicts appear to be monstrous in the respective districts; and within three short months Hell seems to have acquired this entire planet, sending forth Horror, like a rabid wolf, and Despair, like a disastrous sky, to devour and confound her. Hear, therefore, O Lord, and forgive our iniquities! O Lord, we beseech Thee! Look down, O Lord, and spare!"

* * *

When I had read this, and the rest of the paper, which had one whole sheet-side blank, I sat a long hour there, eyeing a little patch of the purple ash on a waxed board near the corner where the girl sat with her time-pieces, so useless in her Eternity; and there was not a feeling in me, except a pricking of curiosity, which afterwards became morbid and ravenous, to know something more of that cloud, or smoke, of which this man spoke, of its dates, its origin, its nature, its minute details. Afterwards, I went down, and entered several houses, searching for more papers, but did not find any; then I found a paper-shop which was open, with boards outside, but either it had been deserted, or printing must have stopped about the date of the paper which I had read, for the only three news-papers there were dated long prior, and I did not read them.

Now it was raining, and a blustering autumn day it was, distributing the odours of the world, and bringing me continual mixed whiffs of flowers and the hateful stench of decay. But I would not mind it much.

I wandered and wandered, till I was tired of spahi and bashi-bazouk, of Greek and Catalan, of Russian 'pope' and Coptic abuna, of dragoman and Calmuck, of Egyptian maulawi and Afghan mullah, Neapolitan and sheik, and the nightmare of wild poses, colours, stuffs and garbs, the yellow-green kefie of the Bedouin, shawl-turbans of Baghdad, the voluminous rose-silk tob of women, and face-veils, and stark distorted nakedness, and sashes of figured muslin, and the workman's cords, and the red tarboosh. About four, for very weariness, I was sitting on a door-steep, bent beneath the rain; but soon was up again, fascinated no doubt by this changing bazaar of sameness, its chance combinations and permutations, and novelty in monotony. About five I was at a station, marked Harbour Station, in and about which lay a considerable crowd, but not one train. I sat again, and rested, rose and roamed again; soon after six I found myself at another station, called 'Priory'; and here I saw two long trains, both crowded, one on a siding, and one at the up-platform.

I examined both engines, and found them of the old boiler steam-type with manholes, heaters, autoclaves, feed-pump, etc., now rare in western countries, except England. In one there was no water, but in that at the platform, the float-lever, barely tilted toward the float, showed that there was some in the boiler. Of this one I overhauled all the machinery, and found it good, though rusted. There was plenty of fuel, and oil, which I supplemented from a near shop: and during ninety minutes my brain and hands worked with an intelligence as it were automatic, of their own motion. After three journeys across the station and street, I saw the fire blaze well, and the manometer move; when the lever of the safety-valve, whose load I lightened by half an atmosphere, lifted, I jumped down, and tried to disconnect the long string of carriages from the engine: but failed, the coupling being an automatic arrangement new to me; nor did I care. It was now very dark; but there was still oil for bull's-eye and lantern, and I lit them. I forgot nothing. I rolled driver and stoker – the guard was absent – one to the platform, one upon the rails: and I took their place there. At about 8.30 I ran out from Dover, my throttle-valve pealing high a long falsetto through the bleak and desolate night.

* * *

My aim was London. But even as I set out, my heart smote me: I knew nothing of the metals, their junctions, facing-points, sidings, shuntings, and complexities. Even as to whether I was going toward, or away from, London, I was not sure. But just in proportion as my first timorousness of the engine hardened into familiarity and self-sureness, I quickened speed, wilfully, with an obstinacy deaf and blind.

Finally, from a mere crawl at first, I was flying at a shocking velocity, while something, tongue in cheek, seemed to whisper me: "There must be other trains blocking the lines, at stations, in yards, and everywhere – it is a maniac's ride, a ride of death, and Flying Dutchman's frenzy: remember your dark five-deep brigade of passengers, who rock and bump together, and will suffer in a collision." But with mulish stubbornness I thought: "They wished to go to London;" and on I raged, not wildly exhilarated, so far as I can remember, nor lunatic, but feeling the dull glow of a wicked and morose Unreason urge in my bosom, while I stoked all blackened at the fire, or saw the vague mass of dead horse or cow, running trees and fields, and dark homestead and deep-slumbering farm, flit ghostly athwart the murky air, as the half-blind saw "men like trees walking."

Long, however, it did not last: I could not have been twenty miles from Dover when, on a long reach of straight lines, I made out before me a tarpaulined mass opposite a signal-point: and at once callousness changed to terror within me. But even as I plied the brake, I felt that it was too late: I rushed to the gangway to make a wild leap down an embankment to the right, but was thrown backward by a quick series of rough bumps, caused by eight or ten cattle which lay there across the lines: and when I picked myself up, and leapt, some seconds before the impact, the speed must have considerably slackened, for I received no fracture, but lay in semi-coma in a patch of yellow-flowered whin on level ground, and was even conscious of a fire on the lines forty yards away, and, all the night, of vague thunder sounding from somewhere.

* * *

About five, or half-past, in the morning I was sitting up, rubbing my eyes, in a dim light mixed with drizzle. I could see that the train of my last night's debauch was a huddled-up chaos of fallen carriages and disfigured bodies. A five-barred gate on my left opened into a hedge, and swung with creaks: two yards from my feet lay a little shaggy pony with swollen wan abdomen, the very picture of death, and also about me a number of dead wet birds.

I picked myself up, passed through the gate, and walked up a row of trees to a house at their end. I found it to be a little country-tavern with a barn, forming one house, the barn part much larger than the tavern part. I went into the tavern by a small side-door – behind the bar – into a parlour – up a little stair – into two rooms: but no one was there. I then went round into the barn, which was paved with cobble-stones, and there lay a dead mare and foal, some fowls, with two cows. A ladder-stair led to a closed trap-door in the floor above. I went up, and in the middle of a wilderness of hay saw nine people – labourers, no doubt – five men and four women, huddled together, and with them a tin-pail containing the last of some spirit; so that these had died merry.

I slept three hours among them, and afterwards went back to the tavern, and had some biscuits of which I opened a new tin, with some ham, jam and apples, of which I made a good meal, for my pemmican was gone.

Afterwards I went following the rail-track on foot, for the engines of both the collided trains were smashed. I knew northward from southward by the position of the sun: and after a good many stoppages at houses, and by railway-banks, I came, at about eleven in the night, to a great and populous town.

By the Dane John and the Cathedral, I immediately recognised it as Canterbury, which I knew quite well. And I walked up Castle Street to the High Street, conscious for the first time of that regularly-repeated sound, like a sob or groan, which was proceeding from my throat. As there was no visible moon, and these old streets very dim, I had to pick my way, lest I should desecrate the dead with my foot, and they all should rise with hue and cry to hunt me. However, the bodies here were not numerous, most, as before, being foreigners: and these, scattered about this strict old English burg that mourning dark night, presented such a scene of the baneful wrath of God, and all abomination of desolation, as broke me quite down at one place, where I stood in travail with jeremiads and sore sobbings and lamentations, crying out upon it all, God knows.

Only when I stood at the west entrance of the Cathedral I could discern, spreading up the dark nave, to the lantern, to the choir, a phantasmagorical mass of forms: I went a little inward, and striking three matches, peered nearer: the two transepts, too, seemed crowded – the cloister-doorway was blocked – the southwest porch thronged, so that a great congregation must have flocked hither shortly before their fate overtook them.

Here it was that I became definitely certain that the after-odour of the poison was not simply lingering in the air, but was being more or less given off by the bodies: for the blossomy odour of this church actually overcame that other odour, the whole rather giving the scent of old mouldy linens long embalmed in cedars.

Well, away with stealthy trot I ran from the abysmal silence of that place, and in Palace Street near made one of those sudden immoderate rackets that seemed to outrage the universe, and left me so woefully faint, decrepit, and gasping for life (the noise of the train was different, for there I was flying, but here a captive, and which way I ran was capture). Passing in Palace Street, I saw a little lampshop, and wanting a lantern, tried to get in, but the door was locked; so, after going a few steps, and kicking against a policeman's truncheon, I returned to break the window-glass. I knew that it would make a fearful noise, and for some fifteen or twenty minutes stood hesitating: but never could I have dreamed, my good God, of *such* a noise, so passionate, so dominant, so divulgent, and, O Heaven, so long-lasting: for I seemed to have struck upon the weak spot of some planet, which came suddenly tumbling, with protracted bellowing and *débâcle*, about my ears. It was a good hour before I would climb in; but then quickly found what I wanted, and some big oil-cans; and till one or two in the morning, the innovating flicker of my lantern went peering at random into the gloomy nooks of the town.

Under a deep old Gothic arch that spanned a pavered alley, I saw the little window of a little house of rubble, and between the two diamond-paned sashes rags tightly beaten in, the idea evidently being to make the place air-tight against the poison. When I went in I found the door of that room open, though it, too, apparently, had been stuffed at the edges; and on the threshold an old man and woman lay low. I conjectured that, thus protected, they had remained shut in, till either hunger, or the lack of oxygen in the used-up air, drove them forth, whereupon the poison, still active, must have instantly ended them. I found afterwards that this expedient of making air-tight had been widely resorted to; and it might well have proved successful, if both the supply of inclosed air, and of food, had been anywhere commensurate with the durability of the poisonous state.

Weary, weary as I grew, some morbid persistence sustained me, and I would not rest. About four in the morning I was at a station again, industriously bending, poor wretch, at the sooty task of getting another engine ready for travel. This time, when steam was up, I succeeded in uncoupling the carriages from the engine, and by the time morning broke, I was lightly gliding away over the country, whither I did not know, but making for London.

* * *

Now I went with more intelligence and caution, and got on very well, travelling seven days, never at night, except it was very clear, never at more than twenty or twenty-five miles, and crawling through tunnels. I do not know the maze into which the train took me, for very soon after leaving Canterbury it must have gone down some branch-line, and though the names were marked at stations, that hardly helped me, for of their situation relatively to London I was seldom sure. Moreover, again and again was my progress impeded by trains on the metals, when I would have to run back to a shunting-point or a siding, and, in two instances, these being far behind, changed from my own to the impeding engine. On the first day I travelled unhindered till noon, when I stopped in open country that seemed uninhabited for ages, only that half a mile to the left, on a shaded sward, was a large stone house of artistic design, coated with tinted harling, the roof of red Ruabon tiles, and timbered gables. I walked to it after another row with putting out the fire and arranging for a new one, the day being bright and mild, with great masses of white cloud in the sky. The house had an outer and an inner hall, three reception rooms, fine oil-paintings, a kind of museum, and a large kitchen. In a bed-room above-stairs I found three women with servants' caps, and a footman, arranged in a strange symmetrical way, head to head, like rays of a star. As I stood looking at them, I could have sworn, my good God, that I heard someone coming up the stairs. But it was some slight creaking of the breeze in the house, augmented a hundredfold to my inflamed and fevered hearing: for, used for years now to this silence of Eternity, it is as though I hear all sounds through an ear-trumpet. I went down, and after eating, and drinking some clary-water, made of brandy, sugar, cinnamon, and rose water, which I found in plenty, I lay down on a sofa in the inner hall, and slept a quiet sleep until near midnight.

I went out then, still possessed with the foolish greed to reach London, and after getting the engine to rights, went off under a clear black sky thronged with worlds and far-sown spawn, some of them, I thought, perhaps like this of mine, whelmed and drowned in oceans of silence, with one only inhabitant to see it, and hear its silence. And all the long night I travelled, stopping twice only, once to get the coal from an engine which had impeded me, and once to drink some water, which I took care, as always, should be running water. When I felt my head nod, and my eyes close about 5 a.m., I threw myself, just outside the arch of a tunnel upon a grassy bank, pretty thick with stalks and flowers, the workings of early dawn being then in the east: and there, till near eleven, slept.

On waking, I noticed that the country now seemed more like Surrey than Kent: there was that regular swell and sinking of the land; but, in fact, though it must have been either, it looked like neither, for already all had an aspect of return to a state of wild nature, and I could see that for a year at the least no hand had tended the soil. Near before me was a stretch of lucerne of such extraordinary growth, that I was led during that day and the succeeding one to examine the condition of vegetation with some minuteness, and nearly everywhere I detected a certain hypertrophie tendency in stamens, calycles, pericarps, and pistils, in every sort of bulbiferous growth that I looked at, in the rushes, above all, the fronds, mosses, lichens, and all cryptogamia, and in the trefoils, clover especially, and some creepers. Many crop-fields, it was clear, had been prepared, but not sown; some had not been reaped: and in both cases I was struck with their appearance of rankness, as I was also when in Norway, and was all the more surprised that this should be the case at a time when a poison, whose action is the arrest of oxidation, had traversed the earth; I could only conclude that its presence in large volumes in the lower strata of the atmosphere had been more or less temporary, and that the tendency to exuberance which I observed was due to some principle by which Nature acts with freer energy and larger scope in the absence of man.

Two yards from the rails I saw, when I got up, a little rill beside a rotten piece of fence, barely oozing itself onward under masses of foul and stagnant fungoids: and here there was a sudden splash, and life: and I caught sight of the hind legs of a diving young frog. I went and lay on my belly, poring over the clear dulcet little water, and presently saw two tiny bleaks, or ablets, go gliding low among the swaying moss-hair of the bottom-rocks, and thought how gladly would I be one of them, with my home so thatched and shady, and my life drowned in their wide-eyed reverie. At any rate, these little creatures are alive, the batrachians also, and, as I found the next day, pupae and chrysales of one sort or another, for, to my deep emotion, I saw a little white butterfly staggering in the air over the flower-garden of a rustic station named Butley.

* * *

It was while I was lying there, poring upon that streamlet, that a thought came into my head: for I said to myself: "If now I be here alone, alone, alone… alone, alone… one on the earth… and my girth have a spread of 25,000 miles… what will happen to my mind? Into what kind of creature shall I writhe and change? I may live two years so! What will have happened then? I may live five years – ten! What will have happened after the five? The ten? I may live twenty, thirty, forty…"

Already, already, there are things that peep and sprout within me…!

* * *

I wanted food and fresh running water, and walked from the engine half a mile through fields of lucerne whose luxuriance quite hid the foot-paths, and reached my shoulder. After turning the brow of a hill, I came to a park, passing through which I saw some dead deer and three persons, and emerged upon a terraced lawn, at the end of which stood an Early English house of pale brick with copings, plinths, stringcourses of limestone, and spandrels of carved marble; and some distance from the porch a long table, or series of tables, in the open air, still spread with cloths that were like shrouds after a month of burial; and the table had old foods on it, and some lamps; and all around it, and all on the lawn, were dead peasants. I seemed to know the house, probably from some print which I may have seen, but I could not make out the escutcheon, though I saw from its simplicity that it must be very ancient. Right across the façade spread still some of the letters in evergreens of the motto: 'Many happy returns of the day,' so that someone must have come of age, or something, for inside all was gala, and it was clear that these people had defied a fate which they, of course, foreknew. I went nearly throughout the whole spacious place of thick-carpeted halls, marbles, and famous oils, antlers and arras, and gilt saloons, and placid large bed-chambers: and it took me an hour. There were here not less than a hundred and eighty people. In the first of a vista of three large reception-rooms lay what could only have been a number of quadrille parties, for to the *coup d'oeil* they presented a two-and-two appearance, made very repulsive by their jewels and evening-dress. I had to steel my heart to go through this house, for I did not know if these people were looking at me as soon as my back was turned. Once I was on the very point of flying, for I was going up the great central stairway, and there came a pelt of dead leaves against a window-pane in a corridor just above on the first floor, which thrilled me to the inmost soul. But I thought that if I once fled, they would all be at me from behind, and I should be gibbering mad long, long before I reached the outer hall, and so stood my ground, even defiantly advancing. In a small dark bedroom in the north wing on the second floor – that is to say, at the top of the house – I saw a tall young lady and a groom, or wood-man, to judge by his clothes, horribly riveted in an embrace on a settee, she with a light coronet on her head in low-necked dress, and their lipless teeth still fiercely pressed together. I collected in a bag a few delicacies from the under-regions of this house, Lyons sausages, salami, mortadel, apples, roes, raisins, artichokes, biscuits, a few wines, a ham, bottled fruit, pickles, coffee, and so on, with a gold plate, tin-opener, cork-screw, fork, etc., and dragged them all the long way back to the engine before I could eat.

* * *

My brain was in such a way, that it was several days before the perfectly obvious means of finding my way to London, since I wished to go there, at all occurred to me; and the engine went wandering the intricate railway-system of the south country, I having twice to water her with a coal-bucket from a pool, for the injector was giving no water from the tank under the coals, and I did not know where to find any near tank-sheds. On the fifth evening, instead of into London, I ran into Guildford.

* * *

That night, from eleven till the next day, there was a great storm over England: let me note it down. And ten days later, on the 17th of the month came another; and on the 23rd another; and I should be put to it to count the great number since. And they do not resemble English storms, but rather Arctic ones, in a certain very suggestive something of personalness, and a carousing malice, and a Tartarus gloom, which I cannot quite describe. That night at Guildford, after wandering about, and becoming very weary, I threw myself upon a cushioned pew in an old Norman church with two east apses, called St. Mary's, using a Bible-cushion for pillow, and placing some distance away a little tin lamp turned low, whose ray served me for *veilleuse* through the night. Happily I had taken care to close up everything, or, I feel sure, the roof must have gone. Only one dead, an old lady in a chapel on the north side of the chancel, whom I rather mistrusted, was there with me: and there I lay listening: for, after all, I could not sleep a wink, while outside vogued the immense tempest. And I communed with myself, thinking: "I, poor man, lost in this conflux of infinitudes and vortex of the world, what can become of me, my God? For dark, ah dark, is the waste void into which from solid ground I am now plunged a million fathoms deep, the sport of all the whirlwinds: and it were better for me to have died with the dead, and never to have seen the wrath and turbulence of the Ineffable, nor to have heard the thrilling bleakness of the winds of Eternity, when they pine, and long, and whimper, and when they vociferate and blaspheme, and when they expostulate and intrigue and implore, and when they despair and die, which ear of man should never hear. For they mean to eat me up, I know, these Titanic darknesses: and soon like a whiff I shall pass away, and leave the world to them." So till next morning I lay mumping, with shivers and cowerings: for the shocks of the storm pervaded the locked church to my very heart; and there were thunders that night, my God, like callings and laughs and banterings, exchanged between distant hill-tops in Hell.

* * *

Well, the next morning I went down the steep High Street, and found a young nun at the bottom whom I had left the previous evening with a number of girls in uniform opposite the Guildhall – half-way up the street. She must have been spun down, arm over arm, for the wind was westerly, and whereas I had left her completely dressed to her wimple and beads, she was now nearly stripped, and her little flock scattered. And branches of trees, and wrecked houses, and reeling clouds of dead leaves were everywhere that wild morning.

This town of Guildford appeared to be the junction of an extraordinary number of railway-lines, and before again setting out in the afternoon, when the wind had lulled, having got an A B C guide, and a railway-map, I decided upon my line, and upon a new engine, feeling pretty sure now of making London, only thirty miles away. I then set out, and about five o'clock was at Surbiton, near my aim; I kept on, expecting every few minutes to see the great city, till darkness fell, and still, at considerable risk, I went, as I thought, forward: but no London was there. I had, in fact, been on a loop-line, and at Surbiton gone wrong again; for the next evening I found myself at Wokingham, farther away than ever.

I slept on a rug in the passage of an inn called The Rose, for there was a wild, Russian-looking man, with projecting top-teeth, on a bed in the house, whose appearance I did not like, and it was late, and I too tired to walk further; and the next morning pretty early I set out again, and at 10 a.m. was at Reading.

The notion of navigating the land by precisely the same means as the sea, simple and natural as it was, had not at all occurred to me: but at the first accidental sight of a compass in a little shop-window near the river at Reading, my difficulties as to getting to any desired place in the world vanished once and for all: for a good chart or map, the compass, a pair of compasses, and, in the case of longer distances, a quadrant, sextant or theodolite, with a piece of paper and pencil, were all that were necessary to turn an engine into a land-ship, one choosing the lines that ran nearest the direction of one's course, whenever they did not run precisely.

Thus provided, I ran out from Reading about seven in the evening, while there was still some light, having spent there some nine hours. This was the town where I first observed that shocking crush of humanity, which I afterwards met in every large town west of London. Here, I should say, the English were quite equal in number to the foreigners: and there were enough of both, God knows: for London must have poured many here. There were houses, in every room of which, and on the stairs, the dead actually overlay each other, and in the streets before them were points where only on flesh, or under carriages, was it possible to walk. I went into the great County Gaol, from which, as I had read, the prisoners had been released two weeks before-hand, and there I found the same pressed condition, cells occupied by ten or twelve, the galleries continuously rough-paved with faces, heads, and old-clothes-shops of robes; and in the parade-ground, against one wall, a mass of human stuff, like tough grey clay mixed with rags and trickling black gore, where a crush as of hydraulic power must have acted. At a corner between a gate and a wall near the biscuit-factory of this town I saw a boy, whom I believe to have been blind, standing jammed, at his wrist a chain-ring, and, at the end of the chain, a dog; from his hap-hazard posture I conjectured that he, and chain, and dog had been lifted from the street, and placed so, by the storm of the 7th of the month; and what made it very curious was that his right arm pointed a little outward just over the dog, so that, at the moment when I first sighted him, he seemed a drunken fellow setting his dog at me. In fact, all the dead I found much mauled and stripped and huddled: and the earth seemed to be making an abortive effort to sweep her streets.

Well, some little distance from Reading I saw a big flower-seed farm, looking dead in some plots, and in others quite rank: and here again, fluttering quite near the engine, two little winged aurelians in the quiet evening air. I went on, passing a great number of crowded trains on the down-line, two of them in collision, and very broken up, and one exploded engine; even the fields and cuttings on either hand of the line had a rather populous look, as if people, when trains and vehicles failed, had set to trudging westward in caravans and streams. When I came to a long tunnel near Slough, I saw round the foot of the arch an extraordinary quantity of wooden *débris*, and as I went very slowly through, was alarmed by the continuous bumping of the train, which, I knew, was passing over bodies; at the other end were more *débris*; and I easily guessed that a company of desperate people had made the tunnel air-tight at the two arches, and provisioned themselves, with the hope to live there till the day of destiny was passed; whereupon their barricades must have been crashed through by some up-train and themselves crushed, or else, other crowds, mad to share their cave of refuge, had stormed the boardings. This latter, as I afterwards found, was a very usual event.

I should very soon have got to London now, but, as my bad luck would have it, I met a long up-train on the metals, with not one creature in any part of it. There was nothing to do but to tranship, with all my things, to its engine, which I found in good condition with plenty of coal and water, and to set it going, a hateful labour: I being already jet-black from hair to toes. However, by half-past ten I found myself stopped by another train only a quarter of a mile from Paddington, and walked the rest of the way among trains in which the standing dead still stood, propped by their neighbours, and over metals where bodies were as ordinary and cheap as waves on the sea, or twigs in a forest. I believe that wild crowds had given chase on foot to moving trains, or fore-run them in the frenzied hope of inducing them to stop.

I came to the great shed of glass and girders which is the station, the night being perfectly soundless, moonless, starless, and the hour about eleven.

I found later that all the electric generating-stations, or all that I visited, were intact; that is to say, must have been shut down before the arrival of the doom; also that the gas-works had almost certainly been abandoned some time previously: so that this city of dreadful night, in which, at the moment when Silence choked it, not less than forty to sixty millions swarmed and droned, must have more resembled Tartarus and the foul shades of Hell than aught to which my fancy can liken it.

For, coming nearer the platforms, I saw that trains, in order to move at all, must have moved through a slough of bodies pushed from behind, and forming a packed homogeneous mass on the metals: and I knew that they *had* moved. Nor could *I* now move, unless I decided to wade: for flesh was everywhere, on the roofs of trains, cramming the interval between them, on the platforms, splashing the pillars like spray, piled on trucks and lorries, a carnal quagmire; and outside, it filled the space between a great host of vehicles, carpeting all that region of London. And all here that odour of blossoms, which nowhere yet, save on one vile ship, had failed, was now wholly overcome by another: and the thought was in my head, my God, that if the soul of man had sent up to Heaven the odour which his body gave to me, then it was not so strange that things were as they were.

I got out from the station, with ears, God knows, that still awaited the accustomed noising of this accursed town, habituated as I now was to all the dumb and absent void of Soundlessness; and I was overwhelmed in a new awe, and lost in a wilder woesomeness, when, instead of lights and business, I saw the long street which I knew brood darker than Babylons long desolate, and in place of its ancient noising, heard, my God, a shocking silence, rising higher than I had ever heard it, and blending with the silence of the inane, eternal stars in heaven.

* * *

I could not get into any vehicle for some time, for all thereabouts was practically a mere block; but near the Park, which I attained by stooping among wheels, and selecting my foul steps, I overhauled a Daimler car, found in it two cylinders of petrol, lit the ignition-lamp, removed with averted abhorrence three bodies, mounted, and broke that populous stillness. And through streets nowhere empty of bodies I went urging eastward my jolting, and spattered, and humming way.

That I should have persisted, with so much pains, to come to this unbounded catacomb, seems now singular to me: for by that time I could not have been sufficiently daft to expect to find another being like myself on the earth, though I cherished, I remember, the irrational hope of yet somewhere finding dog, or cat, or horse, to be with me, and would anon think bitterly of Reinhardt, my Arctic dog, which my own hand had shot. But, in reality, a morbid curiosity must have been within me all the time to read the real truth of what had happened, so far as it was known, or guessed, and to gloat upon all that drama, and cup of trembling, and pouring out of the vials of the wrath of God, which must have preceded the actual advent of the end of Time. This inquisitiveness had, at every town which I reached, made the search for newspapers uppermost in my mind; but, by bad luck, I had found only four, all of them ante-dated to the one which I had read at Dover, though their dates gave me some idea of the period when printing must have ceased, viz. soon after the 17th July – about three months subsequent to my arrival at the Pole – for none I found later than this date; and these contained nothing scientific, but only orisons and despairings. On arriving, therefore, at London, I made straight for the office of the *Times*, only stopping at a chemist's in Oxford Street for a bottle of antiseptic to hold near my nose, though, having once left the neighbourhood of Paddington, I had hardly much need of this.

I made my way to the square where the paper was printed, to find that, even there, the ground was closely strewn with calpac and pugaree, black abayeh and fringed praying-shawl, hob-nail and sandal, figured lungi and striped silk, all very muddled and mauled. Through the dark square to the twice-dark building I passed, and found open the door of an advertisement-office; but on striking a match, saw that it had been lighted by electricity, and had therefore to retrace my stumbling steps, till I came to a shop of lamps in a near alley, walking meantime with timid cares that I might hurt no one – for in this enclosed neighbourhood I began to feel strange tremors, and kept striking matches, which, so still was the black air, hardly flickered.

When I returned to the building with a little lighted lamp, I at once saw a file on a table, and since there were a number of dead there, and I wished to be alone, I took the heavy mass of paper between my left arm and side, and the lamp in my right hand; passed then behind a counter; and then, to the right, up a stair which led me into a very great building and complexity of wooden steps and corridors, where I went peering, the lamp visibly trembling in my hand, for here also were the dead. Finally, I entered a good-sized carpeted room with a baize-covered table in the middle, and large smooth chairs, and on the table many manuscripts impregnated with purple dust, and around were books in shelves. This room had been locked upon a single man, a tall man in a frock-coat, with a pointed grey beard, who at the last moment had decided to fly from it, for he lay at the threshold, apparently fallen dead the moment he opened the door. Him, by drawing his feet aside, I removed, locked the door upon myself, sat at the table before the dusty file, and, with the little lamp near, began to search.

I searched and read till far into the morning. But God knows, He alone…

I had not properly filled the little reservoir with oil, and at about three in the fore-day, it began to burn sullenly lower, letting sparks, and turning the glass grey: and in my deepest chilly heart was the question: "Suppose the lamp goes out before the daylight…"

I knew the Pole, and cold, I knew them well: but to be frozen by panic, my God! I read, I say, I searched, I would not stop: but I read that night racked by terrors such as have never yet entered into the heart of man to conceive. My flesh moved and crawled like a lake which, here and there, the breeze ruffles. Sometimes for two, three, four minutes, the profound interest of what I read would fix my mind, and then I would peruse an entire column, or two, without consciousness of the meaning of one single word, my brain all drawn away to the innumerable host of the wan dead that camped about me, pierced with horror lest they should start, and stand, and accuse me: for the grave and the worm was the world; and in the air a sickening stirring of cerements and shrouds; and the taste of the pale and insubstantial grey of ghosts seemed to infect my throat, and faint odours of the loathsome tomb my nostrils, and the toll of deep-toned passing-bells my ears; finally the lamp smouldered very low, and my charnel fancy teemed with the screwing-down of coffins, lych-gates and sextons, and the grating of ropes that lower down the dead, and the first sound of the earth upon the lid of that strait and gloomy home of the mortal; that lethal look of cold dead fingers I seemed to see before me, the insipidness of dead tongues, the pout of the drowned, and the vapid froths that ridge their lips, till my flesh was moist as with the stale washing-waters of morgues and mortuaries, and with such sweats as corpses sweat, and the mawkish tear that lies on dead men's cheeks; for what is one poor insignificant man in his flesh against a whole world of the disembodied, he alone with them, and nowhere, nowhere another of his kind, to whom to appeal against them? I read, and I searched: but God, God knows ... If a leaf of the paper, which I slowly, warily, stealingly turned, made but one faintest rustle, how did that *reveille* boom in echoes through the vacant and haunted chambers of my poor aching heart, my God! And there was a cough in my throat which for a cruelly long time I would not cough, till it burst in horrid clamour from my lips, sending crinkles of cold through my inmost blood. For with the words which I read were all mixed up visions of crawling hearses, wails, and lugubrious crapes, and piercing shrieks of madness in strange earthy vaults, and all the mournfulness of the black Vale of Death, and the tragedy of corruption. Twice during the ghostly hours of that night the absolute and undeniable certainty that some presence – some most gashly silent being – stood at my right elbow, so thrilled me, that I leapt to my feet to confront it with clenched fists, and hairs that bristled stiff in horror and frenzy. After that second time I must have fainted; for when it was broad day, I found my dropped head over the file of papers, supported on my arms. And I resolved then never again after sunset to remain in any house: for that night was enough to kill a horse, my good God; and that this is a haunted planet I know.

* * *

What I read in the *Times* was not very definite, for how could it be? But in the main it confirmed inferences which I had myself drawn, and fairly satisfied my mind.

There had been a battle royal in the paper between my old collaborator Professor Stanistreet and Dr. Martin Rogers, and never could I have conceived such an indecorous piece of business, men like them calling one another 'tyro,' 'dreamer,' and in one place 'block-head.' Stanistreet denied that the perfumed odour of almonds attributed to the advancing cloud could be due to anything but the excited fancy of the reporting fugitives, because, said he, it was unknown that either Cn, HCn, or K_4FeCn_6 had been given out by volcanoes, and the destructiveness to life of the travelling cloud could only be owing to CO and CO_2. To this Rogers, in an article characterised by extraordinary heat, replied that he could not understand how even a 'tyro'(!) in chemical and geological phenomena would venture to rush into print with the statement that HCn had not commonly been given out by volcanoes: that it *had* been, he said, was perfectly certain; though whether it had been or not could not affect the decision of a reasoning mind as to whether it was being: for that cyanogen, as a matter of fact, was not rare in nature, though not directly occurring, being one of the products of the common distillation of pit-coal, and found in roots, peaches, almonds, and many tropical flora; also that it had been actually pointed out as probable by more than one thinker that some salt or salts of Cn, the potassic, or the potassic ferrocyanide, or both, must exist in considerable stores in the earth at volcanic depths. In reply to this, Stanistreet in a two-column article used the word 'dreamer,' and Rogers, when Berlin had been already silenced, finally replied with his amazing 'block-head.' But, in my opinion, by far the most learned and lucid of the scientific dicta was from the rather unexpected source of Sloggett, of the Dublin Science and Art Department: he, without fuss, accepted the statements of the fugitive eye-witnesses, down to the assertion that the cloud, as it rolled travelling, seemed mixed from its base to the clouds with languid tongues of purple flame, rose-coloured at their edges. This, Sloggett explained, was the characteristic flame of both cyanogen and hydrocyanic acid vapour, which, being inflammable, may have become locally ignited in the passage over cities, and only burned in that limited and languid way on account of the ponderous volumes of carbonic anhydride with which they must, of course, be mixed: the dark empurpled colour was due to the presence of large quantities of the scoriae of the trappean rocks: basalts, green-stone, trachytes, and the various porphyries. This article was most remarkable for its clear divination, because written so early – not long, in fact, after the cessation of telegraphic communication with Australia and China; and at a date so early Sloggett stated that the character of the devastation not only proved an eruption – another, but far greater Krakatoa – probably in some South Sea region, but indicated that its most active product must be, not CO, but potassic ferrocyanide (K_4FeCn_6), which, undergoing distillation with the products of sulphur in the heat of eruption, produced hydrocyanic acid (HCn); and this volatile acid, he said, remaining in a vaporous state in all climates above a temperature of 26.5° C., might involve the entire earth, if the eruption proved sufficiently powerful, travelling chiefly in a direction contrary to the earth's west-to-east motion, the only regions which would certainly be exempt being the colder regions of the Arctic circles, where the vapour of the acid would assume the liquid state, and fall as rain. He did not anticipate that vegetation would be permanently affected, unless the eruption were of inconceivable duration and activity, for though the poisonous quality of hydrocyanic acid consisted in its sudden and complete arrest of oxidation, vegetation had two sources of life – the soil as well as the air; with this exception, all life, down to the lowest evolutionary forms, would disappear (here was the one point in which he was somewhat at fault), until the earth reproduced them. For the rest, he fixed the rate of the on-coming cloud at from 100 to 105 miles a day; and the date of eruption, either the 14th, 15th, or 16th of April – which was either one, two, or three days after the arrival of the *Boreal* party at the Pole; and he concluded by saying that, if the facts were as he had stated them, then he could suggest no hiding-place for the race of man, unless such places as mines and tunnels could be made air-tight; nor could even they be of use to any considerable number, except in the event of the poisonous state of the air being of very short duration.

* * *

I had thought of mines before: but in a very languid way, till this article, and other things that I read, as it were struck my brain a slap with the notion. For "there," I said, "if anywhere, shall I find a man…"

* * *

I went out from that building that morning feeling like a man bowed down with age, for the depths of unutterable horror into which I had had glimpses during that one night made me very feeble, and my steps tottered, and my brain reeled.

I got out into Farringdon Street, and at the near Circus, where four streets meet, had under my furthest range of vision nothing but four fields of bodies, bodies, clad in a rag-shop of every faded colour, or half-clad, or not clad at all, actually, in many cases, over-lying one another, as I had seen at Reading, but here with a markedly more skeleton appearance: for I saw the swollen-looking shoulders, sharp hips, hollow abdomens, and stiff bony limbs of people dead from famine, the whole having the grotesque air of some *macabre* battle-field of fallen marionettes. Mixed with these was an extraordinary number of vehicles of all sorts, so that I saw that driving among them would be impracticable, whereas the street which I had taken during the night was fairly clear. I thought a minute what I should do: then went by a parallel back-street, and came out to a shop in the Strand, where I hoped to find all the information which I needed about the excavations of the country. The shutters were up, and I did not wish to make any noise among these people, though the morning was bright, it being about ten o'clock, and it was easy to effect entrance, for I saw a crow-bar in a big covered furniture-van near. I, therefore, went northward, till I came to the British Museum, the cataloguing-system of which I knew well, and passed in. There was no one at the library-door to bid me stop, and in the great round reading-room not a soul, except one old man with a bag of goître hung at his neck, and spectacles, he lying up a book-ladder near the shelves, a 'reader' to the last. I got to the printed catalogues, and for an hour was upstairs among the dim sacred galleries of this still place, and at the sight of certain Greek and Coptic papyri, charters, seals, had such a dream of this ancient earth, my good God, as even an angel's pen could not half express on paper. Afterwards, I went away loaded with a good hundred-weight of Ordnance-maps, which I had stuffed into a bag found in the cloak-room, with three topographical books; I then, at an instrument-maker's in Holborn, got a sextant and theodolite, and at a grocer's near the river put into a sack-bag provisions to last me a week or two; at Blackfriars Bridge wharf-station I found a little sharp white steamer of a few tons, which happily was driven by liquid air, so that I had no troublesome fire to light: and by noon I was cutting my solitary way up the Thames, which flowed as before the ancient Britons were born, and saw it, and built mud-huts there amid the primaeval forest; and afterwards the Romans came, and saw it, and called it Tamesis, or Thamesis.

* * *

That night, as I lay asleep on the cabin-cushions of my little boat under the lee of an island at Richmond, I had a clear dream, in which something, or someone, came to me, and asked me a question: for it said: "Why do you go seeking another man? – That you may fall upon him, and kiss him? Or that you may fall upon him, and murder him?" And I answered sullenly in my dream: "I would not murder him. I do not wish to murder anyone."

* * *

What was essential to me was to know, with certainty, whether I was really alone: for some instinct began to whisper me: "Find that out: be sure, be sure: for without the assurance you can never be – yourself."

I passed into the great Midland Canal, and went northward, leisurely advancing, for I was in no hurry. The weather remained very warm, and great part of the country was still dressed in autumn leaves. I have written, I think, of the terrific character of the tempests witnessed in England since my return: well, the calms were just as intense and novel. This observation was forced upon me: and I could not but be surprised. There seemed no middle course now: if there was a wind, it was a storm: if there was not a storm, no leaf stirred, not a roughening zephyr ran the water. I was reminded of maniacs that laugh now, and rave now – but never smile, and never sigh.

On the fourth afternoon I passed by Leicester, and the next morning left my pleasant boat, carrying maps and compass, and at a small station took engine, bound for Yorkshire, where I loitered and idled away two foolish months, sometimes travelling by steam-engine, sometimes by automobile, sometimes by bicycle, and sometimes on foot, till the autumn was quite over.

* * *

There were two houses in London to which especially I had thought to go: one in Harley Street, and one in Hanover Square: but when it came to the point, I would not; and there was a little embowered home in Yorkshire, where I was born, to which I thought to go: but I would not, confining myself for many days to the eastern half of the county.

One morning, while passing on foot along the coast-wall from Bridlington to Flambro', on turning my eyes from the sea, I was confronted by a thing which for a moment or two struck me with the most profound astonishment. I had come to a mansion, surrounded by trees, three hundred yards from the cliffs: and there, on a path at the bottom of the domain, right before me, was a board marked: 'Trespassers will be Prosecuted.' At once a mad desire – the first which I had had – to laugh, to roar with laughter, to send wild echoes of merriment clapping among the chalk gullies, and abroad on the morning air, seized upon me: but I kept it under, though I could not help smiling at this poor man, with his little delusion that a part of the earth was his.

Here the cliffs are, I should say, seventy feet high, broken by frequent slips in the upper stratum of clay, and, as I proceeded, climbing always, I encountered some rather formidable gullies in the chalk, down and then up which I had to scramble, till I came to a great mound or barrier, stretching right across the great promontory, and backed by a natural ravine, this, no doubt, having been raised as a rampart by some of those old invading pirate-peoples, who had their hot life-scuffle, and are done now, like the rest. Going on, I came to a bay in the cliff, with a great number of boats lodged on the slopes, some quite high, though the declivities are steep; toward the inner slopes is a lime-kiln which I explored, but found no one there. When I came out on the other side, I saw the village, with an old tower at one end, on a bare stretch of land; and thence, after an hour's rest in the kitchen of a little inn, went out to the coast-guard station, and the lighthouse.

Looking across the sea eastward, the light-keepers here must have seen that thick cloud of convolving browns and purples, perhaps mixed with small tongues of fire, slowly walking the water, its roof in the clouds, upon them: for this headland is in precisely the same longitude as London; and, reckoning from the hour when, as recorded in the *Times*, the cloud was seen from Dover over Calais, London and Flambro' must have been overtaken soon after three o'clock on the Sunday afternoon, the 25th July. At sight in open daylight of a doom so gloomy – prophesied, but perhaps hoped against to the last, and now come – the light-keepers must have fled howling, supposing them to have so long remained faithful to duty: for here was no one, and in the village very few. In this lighthouse, which is a circular white tower, eighty feet high, on the edge of the cliff, is a book for visitors to sign their names: and I will write something down here in black and white: for the secret is between God only, and me: After reading a few of the names, I took my pencil, and I wrote my name there.

* * *

The reef before the Head stretches out a quarter of a mile, looking bold in the dead low-water that then was, and showing to what extent the sea has pushed back this coast, three wrecks impaled on them, and a big steamer quite near, waiting for the first movements of the already strewn sea to perish. All along the cliff-wall to the bluff crowned by Scarborough Castle northward, and to the low vanishing coast of Holderness southward, appeared those cracks and caves which had brought me here, though there seemed no attempts at barricades; however, I got down a rough slope on the south side to a rude wild beach, strewn with wave-worn masses of chalk: and never did I feel so paltry and short a thing as there, with far-outstretched bays of crags about me, their bluffs encrusted at the base with stale old leprosies of shells and barnacles, and crass algae-beards, and, higher up, the white cliff all stained and weather-spoiled, the rock in some parts looking quite chalky, and elsewhere gleaming hard and dull like dirty marbles, while in the huge withdrawals of the coast yawn darksome gullies and caverns. Here, in that morning's walk, I saw three little hermit-crabs, a limpet, and two ninnycocks in a pool of weeds under a bearded rock. What astonished me here, and, indeed, above, and everywhere, in London even, and other towns, was the incredible number of birds that strewed the ground, at some points resembling a real rain, birds of nearly every sort, including tropic specimens: so that I had to conclude that they, too, had fled before the cloud from country to country, till conquered by weariness and grief, and then by death.

By climbing over rocks thick with periwinkles, and splashing through great sloppy stretches of crinkled sea-weed, which give a raw stench of brine, I entered the first of the gullies: a narrow, long, winding one, with sides polished by the sea-wash, and the floor rising inwards. In the dark interior I struck matches, able still to hear from outside the ponderous spasmodic rush and jostle of the sea between the crags of the reef, but now quite faintly. Here, I knew, I could meet only dead men, but urged by some curiosity, I searched to the end, wading in the middle through a three-feet depth of sea-weed twine: but there was no one; and only belemnites and fossils in the chalk. I searched several to the south of the headland, and then went northward past it toward another opening and place of perched boats, called in the map North Landing: where, even now, a distinct smell of fish, left by the old crabbers and herring-fishers, was perceptible. A number of coves and bays opened as I proceeded; a faded green turf comes down in curves at some parts on the cliff-brows, like wings of a young soldier's hair, parted in the middle, and plastered on his brow; isolated chalk-masses are numerous, obelisks, top-heavy columns, bastions; at one point no less than eight headlands stretched to the end of the world before me, each pierced by its arch, Norman or Gothic, in whole or in half; and here again caves, in one of which I found a carpet-bag stuffed with a wet pulp like bread, and, stuck to the rock, a Turkish tarboosh; also, under a limestone quarry, five dead asses: but no man. The east coast had evidently been shunned. Finally, in the afternoon I reached Filey, very tired, and there slept.

* * *

I went onward by train-engine all along the coast to a region of iron-ore, alum, and jet-excavations round Whitby and Middlesborough. By by-ways near the small place of

Goldsborough I got down to the shore at Kettleness, and reached the middle of a bay in which is a cave called the Hob-Hole, with excavations all around, none of great depth, made by jet-diggers and quarrymen. In the cave lay a small herd of cattle, though for what purpose put there I cannot guess; and in the jet-excavations I found nothing. A little further south is the chief alum-region, as at Sandsend, but as soon as I saw a works, and the great gap in the ground like a crater, where the lias is quarried, containing only heaps of alum-shale, brushwood-stacks, and piles of cement-nodules extracted from the lias, I concluded that here could have been found no hiding; nor did I purposely visit the others, though I saw two later. From round Whitby, and those rough moors, I went on to Darlington, not far now from my home: but I would not continue that way, and after two days' indecisive lounging, started for Richmond and the lead mines about Arkengarth Dale, near Reeth. Here begins a region of mountain, various with glens, fells, screes, scars, swards, becks, passes, villages, river-heads, and dales. Some of the faces which I saw in it almost seemed to speak to me in a broad dialect which I knew. But they were not numerous in proportion: for all this country-side must have had its population multiplied by at least some hundreds; and the villages had rather the air of Danube, Levant, or Spanish villages. In one, named Marrick, I saw that the street had become the scene either of a great battle or a great massacre; and soon I was everywhere coming upon men and women, English and foreign, dead from violence: cracked heads, wounds, unhung jaws, broken limbs, and so on. Instead of going direct to the mines from Reeth, that waywardness which now rules my mind, as squalls an abandoned boat, took me somewhat further south-west to the village of Thwaite, which I actually could not enter, so occupied with dead was every spot on which the eye rested a hundred yards about it. Not far from here I turned up, on foot now, a very steep, stony road to the right, which leads over the Buttertubs Pass into Wensleydale, the day being very warm and bright, with large clouds that looked like lakes of molten silver giving off grey fumes in their centre, casting moody shadows over the swardy dale, which below Thwaite expands, showing Muker two miles off, the largest village of Upper Swaledale. Soon, climbing, I could look down upon miles of Swaledale and the hills beyond, a rustic panorama of glens and grass, river and cloudshadow, and there was something of lightness in my step that fair day, for I had left all my maps and things, except one, at Reeth, to which I meant to return, and the earth, which is very good, was – mine. The ascent was rough, and also long: but if I paused and looked behind – I saw, I saw. Man's notion of a Heaven, a Paradise, reserved for the spirits of the good, clearly arose from impressions which the earth made upon his mind: for no Paradise can be fairer than this; just as his notion of a Hell arose from the squalid mess into which his own foolish habits of thought and action turned this Paradise. At least, so it struck me then: and, thinking it, there was a hiss in my breath, as I went up into what more and more acquired the character of a mountain pass, with points of almost Alpine savagery: for after I had skirted the edge of a deep glen on the left, the slopes changed in character, heather was on the mountain-sides, a fretting beck sent up its noise, then screes, and scars, and a considerable waterfall, and a landscape of crags; and lastly a broad and rather desolate summit, palpably nearer the clouds.

* * *

Two days later I was at the mines: and here I first saw that wide-spread scene of horror with which I have since become familiar. The story of six out of ten of them all is the same, and short: selfish 'owners,' an ousted world, an easy bombardment, and the destruction of all concerned, before the arrival of the cloud in many cases. About some of the Durham pit-mouths I have been given the impression that the human race lay collected there; and that the notion of hiding himself in a mine must have occurred to every man alive, and sent him thither.

In these lead mines, as in most vein-mining, there are more shafts than in collieries, and hardly any attempt at artificial ventilation, except at rises, winzes and cul-de-sacs. I found accordingly that, though their depth does not exceed three hundred feet, suffocation must often have anticipated the other dreaded death. In nearly every shaft, both up-take and down-take, was a ladder, either of the mine, or of the fugitives, and I was able to descend without difficulty, having dressed myself in a house at the village in a check flannel shirt, a pair of two-buttoned trousers with circles of leather at the knees, thick boots, and a miner's hat, having a leather socket attached to it, into which fitted a straight handle from a cylindrical candlestick; with this light, and also a Davy-lamp, which I carried about with me for a good many months, I lived for the most part in the deeps of the earth, searching for the treasure of a life, to find everywhere, in English duckies and guggs, Pomeranian women in gaudy stiff cloaks, the Walachian, the Mameluk, the Khirgiz, the Bonze, the Imaum, and almost every type of man.

* * *

One most brilliant Autumn day I walked by the village market-cross at Barnard, come at last, but with a tenderness in my heart, and a reluctance, to where I was born; for I said I would go and see my sister Ada, and – the other old one. I leaned and loitered a long time on the bridge, gazing up to the craggy height, which is heavy with waving wood, and crowned by the Castle-tower, the Tees sweeping round the mountain-base, smooth here and sunlit, but a mile down, where I wished to go, but would not, brawling bedraggled and lacerated, like a sweet strumpet, all shallow among rocks under reaches of shadow – the shadow of Rokeby Woods. I climbed very leisurely up the hill-side, having in my hand a bag with a meal, and up the stair in the wall to the top I went, where there is no parapet, but a massiveness of wall that precludes danger; and here in my miner's attire I sat three hours, brooding sleepily upon the scene of lush umbrageous old wood that marks the long way the river takes, from Marwood Chase up above, and where the rapid Balder bickers in, down to bowery Rokeby, touched now with autumn; the thickness of trees lessening away toward the uplands, where there are far etherealized stretches of fields within hedgerows, and in the sunny mirage of the farthest azure remoteness hints of lonesome moorland. It was not till near three that I went down along the river, then, near Rokeby, traversing the old meadow, and ascending the old hill: and there, as of old, was the little black square with yellow letters on the gate-wall:

HUNT HILL HOUSE

No part, no house, I believe, of this country-side was empty of strange corpses: and they were in Hunt Hill, too. I saw three in the weedy plot to the right of the garden-path, where once the hawthorn and lilac tree had grown from well-rollered grass, and in the little bush-wilderness to the left, which was always a wilderness, one more: and in the breakfast-room, to the right of the hall, three; and in the new wooden clinker-built attachment opening upon the breakfast-room, two, half under the billiard-table; and in her room overlooking the porch on the first floor, the long thin form of my mother on her bed, with crushed-in left temple, and at the foot of the bed, face-downward on the floor, black-haired Ada in a night-dress.

Of all the men and women who died, they two alone had burying. For I digged a hole with the stable-spade under the front lilac; and I wound them in the sheets, foot and form and head; and, not without throes and qualms, I bore and buried them there.

* * *

Some time passed after this before the long, multitudinous, and perplexing task of visiting the mine-regions again claimed me. I found myself at a place called Ingleborough, which is a big table-mountain, with a top of fifteen to twenty acres, from which the sea is visible across Lancashire to the west; and in the sides of this strange hill are a number of caves which I searched during three days, sleeping in a garden-shed at a very rural and flower-embowered village, for every room in it was thronged, a place marked Clapham in the chart, in Clapdale, which latter is a dale penetrating the slopes of the mountain: and there I found by far the greatest of the caves which I saw, having ascended a path from the village to a hollow between two grass slopes, where there is a beck, and so entering an arch to the left, screened by trees, into the limestone cliff. The passage narrows pretty rapidly inwards, and I had not proceeded two yards before I saw the clear traces of a great battle here. All this region had, in fact, been invaded, for the cave must have been famous, though I did not remember it myself, and for some miles round the dead were pretty frequent, making the immediate approach to the cave a matter for care, if the foot was to be saved from pollution. It is clear that there had been an iron gate across the entrance, that within this a wall had been built across, shutting in I do not know how many, perhaps one or two, perhaps hundreds: and both gate and wall had been stormed and broken down, for there still were the sledges and rocks which, without doubt, had done it. I had a lamp, and at my forehead the lighted candle, and I went on quickly, seeing it useless now to choose my steps where there was no choice, through a passage incrusted, roof and sides, with a scabrous petrified lichen, the roof low for some ninety yards, covered with down-looking cones, like an inverted forest of children's toy-trees. I then came to a round hole, apparently artificial, opening through a curtain of stalagmitic formation into a great cavern beyond, which was quite animated and festal with flashes, sparkles, and diamond-lustres, hung in their myriads upon a movement of the eye, these being produced by large numbers of snowy wet stalagmites, very large and high, down the centre of which ran a continuous long lane of clothes and hats and faces; with hasty reluctant feet I somehow passed over them, the cave all the time widening, thousands of stalactites appearing on the roof of every size, from virgin's breast to giant's club, and now everywhere the wet drip, drip, as it were a populous busy bazaar of perspiring brows and hurrying feet, in which the only business is to drip. Where stalactite meets stalagmite there are pillars: where stalactite meets stalactite in fissures long or short there are elegances, flimsy draperies, delicate fantasies; there were also pools of water in which hung heads and feet, and there were vacant spots at outlying spaces, where the arched roof, which continually heightened itself, was reflected in the chill gleam of the floor. Suddenly, the roof came down, the floor went up, and they seemed to meet before me; but looking, I found a low opening, through which, drawing myself on the belly over slime for some yards in repulsive proximity to dead personalities, I came out upon a floor of sand and pebbles under a long dry tunnel, arched and narrow, grim and dull, without stalactites, suggestive of monks, and catacomb-vaults, and the route to the grave; and here the dead were much fewer, proving either that the general mob had not had time to penetrate so far inward, or else that those within, if they were numerous, had gone out to defend, or to harken to, the storm of their citadel. This passage led me into an open space, the grandest of all, loftily vaulted, full of genie riches and buried treasures of light, the million-fold *ensemble* of lustres dancing schottishe with the eye, as it moved or was still: this place, I should guess, being quite half a mile from the entrance. My prying lantern showed me here only nineteen dead, men of various nations, and at the far end two holes in the floor, large enough to admit the body, through which from below came up a sound of falling water. Both of these holes, I could see, had been filled with cement concrete – wisely, I fancy, for a current of air from somewhere seemed to be now passing through them: and this would have resulted in the death of the hiders. Both, however, of the fillings had been broken through, one partially, the other wholly, by the ignorant, I presume, who thought to hide in a secret place yet beyond, where they may have believed, on seeing the artificial work, that others were. I had my ear a long time at one of these openings, listening to that mysterious chant down below in a darkness most murky and dismal; and afterwards, spurred by the stubborn will which I had to be thorough, I went back, took a number of outer robes from the bodies, tied them well together, then one end round the nearest pillar, and having put my mouth to the hole, calling: *"Anyone? Anyone?"* let myself down by the rope of garments, the candle at my head: I had not, however, descended far into those mournful shades, when my right foot plunged into water: and instantly the feeling of terror pierced me that all the evil things in the universe were at my leg to drag me down to Hell: and I was up quicker than I went down: nor did my flight cease till, with a sigh of deliverance, I found myself in open air.

* * *

After this, seeing that the autumn warmth was passing away, I set myself with more system to my task, and within the next six months worked with steadfast will, and strenuous assiduity, seeking, not indeed for a man in a mine, but for some evidence of the possibility that a man might be alive, visiting in that time Northumberland and Durham, Fife and Kinross, South Wales and Monmouthshire, Cornwall and the Midlands, the lead mines of Derbyshire, of Allandale and other parts of Northumberland, of Alston Moor and other parts of Cumberland, of Arkendale and other parts of Yorkshire, of the western part of Durham, of Salop, of Cornwall, of the Mendip Hills of Somersetshire, of Flint, Cardigan, and Montgomery, of Lanark and Argyll, of the Isle of Man, of Waterford and Down; I have gone down the 360-ft. Grand Pipe iron ladder of the abandoned graphite-mine at Barrowdale in Cumberland, half-way up a mountain 2,000 feet high; and visited where cobalt and manganese ore is mined in pockets at the Foel Hiraeddog mine near Rhyl in Flintshire, and the lead and copper Newton Stewart workings in Galloway; the Bristol coal-fields, and mines of South Staffordshire, where, as in Somerset, Gloucester, and Shropshire, the veins are thin, and the mining-system is the 'long-wall,' whereas in the North, and Wales, the system is the 'pillar-and stall'; I have visited the open workings for iron ores of Northamptonshire, and the underground stone-quarries, and the underground slate-quarries, with their alternate pillars and chambers, in the Festiniog district of North Wales; also the rock-salt workings; the tin, copper and cobalt workings of Cornwall; and where the minerals were brought to the surface on the backs of men, and where they were brought by adit-levels provided with rail-roads, and where, as in old Cornish mines, there are two ladders in the shaft, moved up and down alternately, see-saw, and by skipping from one to the other at right moments you ascended or descended, and where the drawing-up is by a gin or horse-whinn, with vertical drum; the Tisbury and

Chilmark quarries in Wiltshire, the Spinkwell and Cliffwood quarries in Yorkshire; and every tunnel, and every recorded hole: for something urged within me, saying: "You must be sure first, or you can never be – yourself."

* * *

At the Farnbrook Coal-field, in the Red Colt Pit, my inexperience nearly ended my life: for though I had a minute theoretical knowledge of all British workings, I was, in my practical relation to them, like a man who has learnt seamanship on shore. At this place the dead were accumulated, I think beyond precedent, the dark plain around for at least three miles being as strewn as a reaped field with stacks, and, near the bank, much more strewn than stack-fields, filling the only house within sight of the pit-mouth – the small place provided for the company's officials – and even lying over the great mountain-heap of wark, composed of the shale and *débris* of the working. Here I arrived on the morning of the 15th December, to find that, unlike the others, there was here no rope-ladder or other contrivance fixed by the fugitives in the ventilating-shaft, which, usually, is not very deep, being also the pumping-shaft, containing a plug-rod at one end of the beam-engine which works the pumps; but looking down the shaft, I discerned a vague mass of clothes, and afterwards a thing that could only be a rope-ladder, which a batch of the fugitives, by hanging to it their united weight, must have dragged down upon themselves, to prevent the descent of yet others. My only way of going down, therefore, was by the pit-mouth, and as this was an important place, after some hesitation I decided, very rashly. First I provided for my coming up again by getting a great coil of half-inch rope, which I found in the bailiff's office, probably 130 fathoms long, rope at most mines being so plentiful, that it almost seemed as if each fugitive had provided himself in that way. This length of rope I threw over the beam of the beam-engine in the bite where it sustains the rod, and paid one end down the shaft, till both were at the bottom: in this way I could come up, by tying one rope-end to the rope-ladder, hoisting it, fastening the other end below, and climbing the ladder; and I then set to work to light the pit-mouth engine-fire to effect my descent. This done, I started the engine, and brought up the cage from the bottom, the 300 yards of wire-rope winding with a quaint deliberateness round the drum, reminding me of a camel's nonchalant leisurely obedience. When I saw the four meeting chains of the cage-roof emerge, the pointed roof, and two-sided frame, I stopped the ascent, and next attached to the knock-off gear a long piece of twine which I had provided; carried the other end to the cage, in which I had five companions; lit my hat-candle, which was my test for choke-damp, and the Davy; and without the least reflection, pulled the string. That hole was 900 feet deep. First the cage gave a little up-leap, and then began to descend – quite normally, I thought, though the candle at once went out – nor had I the least fear; a strong current of air, indeed, blew up the shaft: but that happens in shafts. *This* current, however, soon became too vehemently boisterous for anything: I saw the lamp-light struggle, the dead cheeks quiver, I heard the cage-shoes go singing down the wire-rope guides, and quicker we went, and quicker, that facile descent of Avernus, slipping lightly, then raging, with sparks at the shoes and guides, and a hurricane in my ears and eyes and mouth. When we bumped upon the 'dogs' at the bottom, I was tossed a foot upwards with the stern-faced others, and then lay among them in the eight-foot space without consciousness.

It was only when I sat, an hour later, disgustedly reflecting on this incident, that I remembered that there was always some 'hand-working' of the engine during the cage-descents, an engineman reversing the action by a handle at every stroke of the piston, to prevent bumping. However, the only permanent injury was to the lamp: and I found many others inside.

I got out into the coal-hole, a large black hall 70 feet square by 15 high, the floor paved with iron sheets; there were some little holes round the wall, dug for some purpose which I never could discover, some waggons full of coal and shale standing about, and all among the waggons, and on them, and under them, bodies, clothes. I got a new lamp, pouring in my own oil, and went down a long steep ducky-road, very rough, with numerous rollers, over which ran a rope to the pit-mouth for drawing up the waggons; and in the sides here, at regular intervals, man-holes, within which to rescue one's self from down-tearing waggons; and within these man-holes, here and there, a dead, and in others every sort of food, and at one place on the right a high dead heap, and the air here hot at 64 or 65 degrees, and getting hotter with the descent.

The ducky led me down into a standing – a space with a turn-table – of unusual size, which I made my base of operations for exploring. Here was a very considerable number of punt-shaped putts on carriages, and also waggons, such as took the new-mined coal from putt to pit-mouth; and raying out from this open standing, several avenues, some ascending as guggs, some descending as dipples, and the dead here all arranged in groups, the heads of this group pointing up this gugg, of that group toward that twin-way, of that other down that dipple, and the central space, where weighing was done, almost empty: and the darksome silence of this deep place, with all these multitudes, I found extremely gravitating and hypnotic, drawing me, too, into their great Passion of Silence in which they lay, all, all, so fixed and veteran; and at one time I fell a-staring, nearer perhaps to death and the empty Gulf than I knew; but I said I would be strong, and not sink into their habit of stillness, but let them keep to their own way, and follow their own fashion, and I would keep to my own way, and follow my own fashion, nor yield to them, though I was but one against many; and I roused myself with a shudder; and setting to work, caught hold of the drum-chain of a long gugg, and planting my feet in the chogg-holes in which rested the wheels of the putt-carriages that used to come roaring down the gugg, I got up, stooping under a roof only three feet high, till I came, near the end of the ascent, upon the scene of another battle: for in this gugg about fifteen of the mine-hands had clubbed to wall themselves in, and had done it, and I saw them lie there all by themselves through the broken cement, with their bare feet, trousers, naked bodies all black, visage all fierce and wild, the grime still streaked with sweat-furrows, the candle in their rimless hats, and, outside, their own 'getting' mattocks and boring-irons to besiege them. From the bottom of this gugg I went along a very undulating twin-way, into which, every thirty yards or so, opened one of those steep putt-ways which they called topples, the twin-ways having plates of about 2-1/2 ft. gauge for the putts from the headings, or workings, above to come down upon, full of coal and shale: and all about here, in twin-way and topples, were ends and corners, and not one had been left without its walling-in, and only one was then intact, some, I fancied, having been broken open by their own builders at the spur of suffocation, or hunger; and the one intact I broke into with a mattock – it was only a thin cake of plaster, but air-tight – and in a space not seven feet long behind it I found the very ill-smelling corpse of a carting-boy, with guss and tugger at his feet, and the pad which protected his head in pushing the putts, and a great heap of loaves, sardines, and bottled beer against the walls, and five or six mice that suddenly pitched screaming through the opening which I made, greatly startling me, there being of dead mice an extraordinary number in all this mine-region. I went back to the standing, and at one point in the ground, where there was a windlass and chain, lowered myself down a 'cut' – a small pit sunk perpendicularly to a lower coal-stratum, and here, almost thinking I could hear the perpetual rat-tat of notice once exchanged between the putt-boys below and the windlass-boys above, I proceeded down a dipple to another place like a standing, for in this mine there were six, or perhaps seven, veins: and there immediately I came upon the acme of the horrible drama of this Tartarus, for all here was not merely crowded, but, at some points, a packed congestion of flesh, giving out a strong smell of the peach, curiously mixed with the stale coal-odour of the pit, for here ventilation must have been very limited; and a large number of these masses had been shot down by only three hands, as I found: for through three hermetical holes in a plaster-wall, built across a large gugg, projected a little the muzzles of three rifles, which must have glutted themselves with slaughter; and when, after a horror of disgust, having swum as it were through a dead sea, I got to the wall, I peeped from a small clear space before it through a hole, and made out a man, two youths in their teens, two women, three girls, and piles of cartridges and provisions; the hole had no doubt been broken from within at the spur of suffocation, when the poison must have entered; and I conjectured that here must be the mine-owner, director, manager, or something of that sort, with his family. In another dipple-region, when I had re-ascended to a higher level, I nearly fainted before I could retire from the commencement of a region of after-damp, where there had been an explosion, the bodies lying all hairless, devastated, and grotesque. But I did not desist from searching every other quarter, no momentary work, for not till near six did I go up by the pumping-shaft rope-ladder.

* * *

One day, standing in that wild region of bare rock and sea, called Cornwall Point, whence one can see the crags and postillion wild rocks where Land's End dashes out into the sea, and all the wild blue sea between, and not a house in sight, save the chimney of some little mill-like place peeping between the rocks inland – on that day I finished what I may call my official search.

In going away from that place, walking northward, I came upon a lonely house by the sea, a very beautiful house, made, it was clear, by an artist, of the bungalow type, with an exquisitely sea-side expression. I went to it, and found its special feature a spacious loggia or verandah, sheltered by the overhanging upper story. Up to the first floor, the exterior is of stone in rough-hewn blocks with a distinct batter, while extra protection from weather is afforded by green slating above. The roofs, of low pitch, are also covered with green slates, and a feeling of strength and repose is heightened by the very long horizontal lines. At one end of the loggia is a hexagonal turret, opening upon the loggia, containing a study or nook. In front, the garden slopes down to the sea, surrounded by an architectural sea-wall; and in this place I lived three weeks. It was the house of the poet Machen, whose name, when I saw it, I remembered very well, and he had married a very beautiful young girl of eighteen, obviously Spanish, who lay on the bed in the large bright bedroom to the right of the loggia, on her left exposed breast being a baby with an india-rubber comforter in its mouth, both mother and child wonderfully preserved, she still quite lovely, white brow under low curves of black hair. The poet, strange to say, had not died with them, but sat in the sitting-room behind the bedroom in a long loose silky-grey jacket, at his desk – actually writing a poem! Writing, I could see, furiously fast, the place all littered with the written leaves – at three o'clock in the morning, when, as I knew, the cloud overtook this end of Cornwall, and stopped him, and put his head to rest on the desk; and the poor little wife must have got sleepy, waiting for it to come, perhaps sleepless for many long nights before, and gone to bed, he perhaps promising to follow in a minute to die with her, but bent upon finishing that poem, and writing feverishly on, running a race with the cloud, thinking, no doubt, 'just two couplets more,' till the thing came, and put his head to rest on the desk, poor carle: and I do not know that I ever encountered aught so complimentary to my race as this dead poet Machen, and his race with the cloud: for it is clear now that the better kind of those poet men did not write to please the vague inferior tribes who might read them, but to deliver themselves of the divine warmth that thronged in their bosom; and if all the readers were dead, still they would have written; and for God to read they wrote. At any rate, I was so pleased with these poor people, that I stayed with them three weeks, sleeping under blankets on a couch in the drawing-room, a place full of lovely pictures and faded flowers, like all the house: for I would not touch the young mother to remove her. And finding on Machen's desk a big note-book with soft covers, dappled red and yellow, not yet written in, I took it, and a pencil, and in the little turret-nook wrote day after day for hours this account of what has happened, nearly as far as it has now gone. And I think that I may continue to write it, for I find in it a strange consolation, and companionship.

The complete and unabridged text is available online, *from flametreepublishing.com/extras*

We Make Tea

Meryl Stenhouse

Model: Para-sentient Construct Bipedal v205.0.3
Designation: Plantation Manager
Systems check… OK
Connecting to local area network… success
Connecting to global network… … …no connection available
Reconnecting in 5…

I CANCELLED the reconnection and opened my eyes. Interior Seven contacted me as soon as I emerged from my cupboard with a damage report. Today was Tuesday. Tuesday was baking day.

I made my way through the house to the dining room and surveyed the chaos. Kitchen Four crouched on her tracks in the middle of the room. She scooped her creations off the table and hurled them at the walls.

Bread, cakes, pastries fell like rain. Serving staff rushed to collect ruined crockery, their narrow tracks grinding food into the carpet. K4, twice the mass of the little constructs that formed the wait staff, hefted a cast-iron bread pan with ease and flung it at the wall, showering nearby staff with plaster chips.

I left them to it. The serving staff had something to do now and would not require further input from me. I sent a packet of instructions to the interior staff. Tonight they would plaster and repaint the wall.

In the entranceway I found Attendant Two. He had completed his tasks for the day and was back to circling. One track slow, the other fast, and around he would go, around and around, the drone of his motor the sound of boredom. Around and around, until his energy cells ran down and he retreated to his cubby to recharge.

At least now he picked a different spot every day. The carpet in the conservatory would never be the same. Still, I preferred A2's endless circling to K4's histrionics.

A2 paused, his motor idling. [Man?]

[There is no man. They are gone.]

[Man.] He swung around and rushed to the front door.

I followed him. [No man.]

Outside, the tea bushes in their long rows grew and flourished in the clean bright air. The seasons still turned. In the absence of humans, harvesting, planting, pruning, and manufacturing continued and gave us purpose.

Then I heard it, from the workers on Field Seven. [Man.] [Man.] [Man.] [Man.] I patched into their limited visual network, saw what I thought I would not see again.

A man walked up the long drive. A2, with his early warning system, had seen him first. The rest of us could only see as far as the boundaries of the plantation.

[Man.] [Man.] [Man.] The chorus spread through the field workers and up to the house staff.

K4 burst into the entranceway behind us. [ManManManManManMan.] She charged to the edge of the steps and for a moment I thought she would hurtle down them to land in a heap on the gravel. But she halted, her tracks poking over the edge of the top step.

There was work to be done. Orders flowed, packets were sent, and what had been stagnant and empty was alive as the house staff rushed to perform the duties triggered by the apparent return of the owners.

I stood by the door and waited. The lower-function constructs with their limited understanding would not realise that this was not our owner walking up the drive. This was a visitor. An unknown.

The man limped up the drive, clothes and skin filthy, boots in bad repair. He stared up at the house as he approached. A massive construct of unknown function rumbled along behind him, leaking fluids and bytes in equal quantities. I sent a connection packet, but what came back was corrupt and dirty. I locked down our network connections.

The man stopped when he saw me and a rifle came off his shoulder and into his hands.

I bowed. "Good day, sir. Welcome to Jarrah Dale Farms."

"Whose side are you on?"

"I'm sorry sir, I do not understand your question."

"Who are you with? Affiliate?"

"We are an independent farming operation sir, providing quality tea products to discerning consumers. Our products are available at –"

"Okay, enough. Where's your boss?"

"I'm sorry, sir, the master of the house is not available."

"Where is he?"

"I do not know."

"Anyone else here?"

"We have a staff of –"

"People. Any people here. Humans?"

"No, sir. There are no humans here."

"Huh." He lowered the rifle. "How the hell did you manage to stay out of it?"

"I'm sorry, sir?"

"Never mind. You have food?" He sniffed. "You do. I can smell it."

"Yes, sir. Food is being served, if you would care to come in and wash your hands."

"Wash?" He started to laugh. "Wash! Oh lordy!" He bent over, and the laugh turned into a cough. The cough turned into a sob. Then he was squatting on the gravel with his hands over his head, rocking back and forth, making the strange noises humans make when they cry.

I could hear K4 in my datastream. [Man. Man. Man. Man.] She wasn't the only one. I sent a command for silence and most of the chatter ceased. K4 still babbled on and I was thankful for her limited ability to communicate verbally.

The man on the gravel wiped his nose, leaving a clean streak through the grime. He pushed himself up, leaning on his knees, then straightened. "All right. Lead on, then."

He took the steps slowly, and I realised when he reached me how thin he was. The construct shuddered up to the steps and tried to follow him, tracks biting into the marble.

"No, you wait there," he said to it. The construct buzzed then settled at the foot of the steps. The man turned to me. "You have a jack outside that we can plug him into?"

"Yes, sir. We have one in the maintenance shed." I did not want that chaotic presence plugged into our main system. "We also have repair facilities."

"Yeah?" He turned to the construct. "Go get yourself fixed."

I sent a packet to the damaged machine and braced myself against the garbage returned. It must have understood, because it trundled off towards the maintenance sheds. I sent specific instructions to the repair staff and led our guest inside.

He whistled as we came through the door into the entrance hall. "Hell of a place."

"Thank you, sir. What may I call you?"

"Huh? Oh. Eriksen. Major Eriksen."

"Thank you, sir." I led him to the downstairs bathroom and waited while he blackened a cloth and a towel cleaning his face and hands.

"Sorry about that."

"No problem, sir. Please follow me."

In the dining room the wait staff, all twelve of them, lined up along the wall in perfect formation. The man jerked to a stop and stared. "How many 'bots you got here?"

"We have a staff of fifty-seven, sir."

"Huh." He pulled out the first chair he came to and sat down, ignoring the place set at the head of the table. As soon as he was seated, the wait staff overwhelmed him, placing his napkin, pouring him water, offering wine, resetting the table around him. In moments it was over. Then the kitchen staff flooded in, laying dish after dish.

When the table was covered in food, they swept back, except K4 who hovered around him, picking up dishes and putting them down closer to our guest. I sent a stern command to return to the kitchen and she did, though the refrain of [Man. Man. Man.] filled my datastream.

He ate and ate. While he did, I forked a process to see what was happening to the construct. Through the visual input of the maintenance staff, I could see him in Warehouse 2, hunched beside one of the harvesters. He was plugged into the power but not the mainframe. I retrieved the information packets from maintenance; corruption of the central processing core, missing connections, damaged boards. I sent the order to repair physical damage first.

"Good food."

I transferred my attention to our guest. "Thank you, sir."

"Got a smoke?"

"A cigar, sir?"

He grinned. "That will do." I sent A2 to fetch the box. One of the wait staff approached with port and filled his glass.

"So you're alone here? No people?"

"No, sir."

"How long?"

"1,936 days, sir."

"What's that in years?"

"Five years, sir."

"Lost them in the war, did you?"

"I do not understand, sir."

"Don't know about the war? The bomb? Plague?"

"No, sir."

"Lucky you."

A2 trundled in with a box of cigars and the man took one. A2 lit it for him, and the smoke curled upwards.

"So what do you do with yourselves?"

"We make tea, sir."

"So you said. What else? Food?"

"We maintain the kitchen garden to provide food for the household."

"I see." He blew out some smoke. "Where's my construct?"

"In the maintenance shed, sir."

"Lead on."

I led him out to the gardens, through the little gate to the maintenance sheds and hangars where the big machinery waited for its season to be useful. The man looked around as we walked, asked questions about the plantation: size, water supply, food and resources. I had all the information at hand.

In the shed, he patted the grimy construct. "Poor old boy, you've had a rough time."

"He has significant damage, sir. The maintenance report says that he has a number of unofficial additions and modifications and that some parts from different models have been added to his system."

"'Course they have. Put him back together more times than I can remember. But he's still going."

"Yes, sir. But his memory and subprocessor have an incompatible connection. There is significant data loss occurring during communication."

"Can you fix it?"

"We don't have parts for this model."

"Well, put in some other parts."

"Sir, the maintenance staff advise against it."

"Override. Just use whatever you have to fix him, ok?"

"Yes, sir."

"Right." He straightened, and slung his rifle over his shoulder.

"Would you like me to put that in your room, sir?"

"No, I would not, and tell your staff they're not to touch it."

"Yes, sir. Will you be needing me further, sir?"

"Nope. I'm good."

I went back to my duties. Through the lens of the staff, I followed our guest as he stumbled around the garden, then upstairs to a bath and bed. A2 sent updates until I tuned them out of my datastream.

* * *

The house, so long dead, had come to life. The staff bustled around, purposeful for the first time in years. A2 advised me that our guest slept on, upstairs, so I went to check on the packing staff. They were 62.43% through packing and storage of this year's harvest.

I sent a request for information to Packing One. The response came in: operating parameters normal. I could have received that information from anywhere on the plantation, but I preferred to be here, watching the careful, delicate handling of the tea bags. Each precise movement, each micro-adjustment to ensure perfect placement soothed me, if a para-sentient construct could be soothed.

A2 sent news to my datastream that the man was awake. I found him in the breakfast room, eating toast. He wore clothes that had once belonged to the master of the house. They hung from his wasted frame.

He grunted when he saw me. "You have a name?"

"Plantation Manager, sir."

"That's pretty impersonal."

"That is my designation, sir."

"Fair enough." He wiped his face with a napkin. "I'd like a tour of the house. Can you manage that?"

"Of course, sir."

I led him through the rooms, explaining the history of the plantation and the house as I had done for many visitors before him, in the days when the Master was at home.

"And this is the door to the music room. In July, 2064, the master violinist Pavenecci performed here, to a small audience that included – No sir, don't –"

I was too late. Major Eriksen grabbed the door handles and flung the doors open.

Teabags cascaded from the room, washing over him in a rustling wave. I sent out an emergency command to the house staff.

They appeared to an audible chorus of "Sorry, sir." I reached down and pulled him from under the tide.

"What the hell?" He batted at the attendants as they attempted to brush tea dust from his clothes. "Shut up!" The chorus stopped.

"I do apologise, sir."

"Why is this room full of –" He reached down and grabbed a handful of bags. "Tea bags? Why is the room full of tea bags?"

"We have run out of boxes, sir."

"Run out of –" He flung the bags to the ground. "Don't you have somewhere else to store them?"

"No, sir. Our storage bays are full."

"So you moved into the house? Damn constructs."

"Yes, sir."

"Is this the only room?"

"No, sir."

At his request, I took him to the guest bedroom that was currently being filled and we watched the packing staff for a while.

"How many rooms?"

"Seven so far."

"Well, they'll all have to be emptied."

"Sir?"

"Emptied. Tell these things to stop. No more packing."

"Sir, we still have 36.23% of this year's harvest to pack."

"Forget the harvest. Move these out of the house. Dump them in your recycler."

"No, sir."

"What do you mean 'no'?"

"I'm sorry sir, that goes against the plantation specifications. The harvest has passed quality assessment. Manufactured goods must be produced and stored for distribution."

"What distribution?" He waved his hands. "You're running out of space. No one is coming to pick up the damn tea bags. There's no one out there who gives a damn about your tea. No shops. No businesses. Get it?"

"No, sir."

"No of course you don't." He rubbed his face. "Never mind. Just empty these rooms."

"No, sir."

"I'm giving you an order."

"You are not listed on my authority table, sir."

"Where's your mainframe?"

"I'm sorry sir, I cannot give you that information."

"Oh, so you do have some security?" He snorted. "Fine. We'll find it anyway and reassign your orders. This place isn't going to be a tea plantation much longer."

"I don't understand, sir."

"No, you don't, but you will. Go on. Go back to your – Whatever you do."

He left and I watched him through the lens of the staff. He went to the maintenance shed, unplugged the damaged construct, and the two of them walked down the drive.

I monitored him as I oversaw the packing staff restack the music room, recalculating the packing schedule to allow for this unexpected task. Major Erikson passed the field workers, all busy with pest control, stepped through the front gate and disappeared.

Like the master of the house had done.

Panic erupted in the house staff. I sent a stern command to the data stream. [He will return.] They subsided, but the nervous chatter went on. He would return. Wouldn't he?

I sent a request to A2, the only one of us who could see beyond the gate, whose parameters allowed him knowledge of approaching visitors. He assured me the man was still there. But I could see nothing beyond the boundaries.

He returned in 0:23:34 hours. The staff chatter dropped back to normal levels. K4 made odd noises as she worked, unsettling the rest of the kitchen staff. I acknowledged their alerts, then ignored them. There was nothing wrong with K4 that maintenance could find or fix.

* * *

That night while Major Eriksen slept, I went down to the maintenance shed. The construct hummed, hulking in the shadows. I connected to it.

[What is your designation?]

In response I received a blast of data. A warning. More general questions were needed.

[What is war?]

Images flooded my memory banks. Destruction. Ruin. Machines, humans, cities. I saw farms destroyed by fire, plants burning in the fields. Humans, dead. Dead?

[What is death?]

Humans, bodies, blood and life, decomposition. Now I understood what had happened to our humans. Why they had stopped moving. Why they had disappeared slowly as we watched.

This was waste! This was war. This was what Major Eriksen wanted to bring to my plantation.

I pushed further into the construct's memory banks. There was heavy security, large areas that I could not access. I traced a path through bad connections, access points never meant to be connected. I knew there had to be a way in – no one could connect so many disparate parts and not compromise security.

It turned out to be relatively easy. A set of pins had been removed to allow a motor unit to talk unhindered to the main mobility router. I slipped into his main processor along that path.

Inside was noise. No clear streams of data, no neatly compressed packages. Everything leaked. I filtered out the worst of the junk and started my search, not even sure what I was looking for.

I found it in the communication logs, a corrupted recording of the Major's conversation with an unknown via the construct's radio.

"Found a place. Secure. Up in the highlands. No sign of damage. Water and food uncontaminated. Yes, I've run tests. Coordinates coming now."

I followed the coordinates and found maps. Map after map. The world opened and suddenly I knew there was something beyond the boundaries of the plantation, a world that went on and on.

I had known this, of course, known that we existed on a world of land and ocean and cities, but the terms had been abstract, the locations missing.

Now I understood.

I spent the night repairing the damaged connections, giving orders to the maintenance staff, copying new data over corrupted clusters, replacing scavenged parts with what we had on hand.

At 06:00 I left the maintenance staff to complete the repair and went to attend to my duties. I planned to review the house staff, start calculating the projected harvest biomass figures, and decide where to store the manufactured product.

Instead I found myself walking down the gravelled drive to the wide gates at the entrance to the plantation. I looked out through the gates. Before, my visual sensors had provided no information. Now, with my core memory loaded with new maps, I could see.

A road wound down the slope to disappear into the distant hills. It was in poor repair, potholed and uneven, edges crumbling away. I stood for a long moment, studying it, then I stepped through the gates.

A stone turned under my heel, throwing me off-balance. I corrected, but still felt insecure. The world was wrong. No straight lines, no perfect rows. Trees dotted the uneven ground, some short, some tall, all different, and below them bushes ranked without order, not one the same as the next.

I stumbled back through the gates. I did not like this world.

* * *

Major Eriksen came to me as I was supervising the packing staff. We were 72.83% through the packing of last year's harvest.

"What the hell is going on?"

"I do not understand, sir."

"I asked you to fix my construct, not reprogram him!"

"I'm sorry, sir. We had to replace his central memory. I chose the closest profile from what we had available."

"He's knocking down trees!"

"Yes, sir. He is clearing new fields. After checking his mass and power configuration, I found he most closely matched our –"

"You turned him into a plough?"

"No, sir. He lacks the correct attachment for soil re-profiling. However –"

"The hell!" The major slammed his fist into my midsection, then bent over, nursing his hand. "Fuck."

"Sorry, sir," chorused the packing staff.

He glared up at me. "I told you to stop packing those damn tea bags!"

"No, sir."

"Right." He straightened, and stepped forward into my face. "Now listen up, you brainless, stinking pile of metal. I am taking my construct and I am leaving. And when I get back, I'll have a company with me. And we'll be moving in here, and reprogramming everyone, and there will be no more of this damn tea!"

No more tea. No more tea?

"Now tell my construct to get up here!"

I sent the order and followed him to the entranceway. He was leaving and with him would go our purpose.

"There is no need to leave, sir."

Major Eriksen grunted.

"Would you like to view the arboretum before you go, sir?"

No response.

"Perhaps a bath, sir."

He flung open the front doors. What could I do? I was spewing garbage into the datastream. I could feel the confusion of the staff. I reached for his arm.

"You may not leave, sir."

He swung around and stepped forward, so his face was inches from mine. "Try and stop me."

But I could not and he knew that I could not.

I called the house staff for a formal farewell. They gathered in the entranceway.

"What's this?"

"A farewell is customary, sir."

He grunted and turned away. I could hear his construct coming up the drive. I sent the command for farewell.

"Goodbye, sir. Please come again," chorused the staff.

Major Eriksen made his way down the steps.

A2 sent the first query. [Man?]

[No more man] I told him.

[Man go?] [No man?] [Man?] The questions filled my datastream.

[No man. No more man.] For now. But I knew, when Major Eriksen came back, that there would be men enough to satisfy the household. But I could not predict the shape of that household.

[NoNoNoNoNoNoNo.] Behind me, K4's motor whined. Before I could do anything to stop her, she hurtled past me and off the landing. She was airborne for only a moment before she fell, crashing and tumbling down the marble steps. I saw Major Eriksen turn, eyes wide, then she rolled over him.

"Sorry, sir," chorused the staff.

I made my way down the steps. At the bottom, K4 lay on her side, tracks spinning, digging up the gravel. I sent a command to stop. Major Eriksen lay beneath her.

"Sir?" I waited for an answer. "Sir?"

The maintenance staff came with a crane and lifted K4 upright. The Major lay unmoving on the gravel.

[Man] said K4.

[Yes. Man.] I ordered A2 to carry him around the side of the house and put him back in the guest bedroom, and for the Garden Staff to clean up the trail of blood behind them.

K4 swung from the crane hoist. [Man. Man stay?]

[Man stay.] I ordered the rest of the staff back to their duties.

Major Ericksen's construct trundled to a stop in front of the house and waited for orders. I sent a packet of instructions, listening for the reply. It was clean and free of corruption.

The field staff worked on, secure in their duties. I would need to reallocate resources, reprogram a number of staff from harvest to planting. We had only enough replacement seed for a few new fields. We would need to build more irrigation channels, more service roads for the new fields.

I bent down and picked up Major Eriksen's rifle. A simple design, one that we could easily duplicate. I thought about the house staff, passing their days draining their batteries, without purpose. I knew now that the master of the house would not return. There was no purpose in keeping the house staff in the house.

I followed Major Eriksen's construct down the drive and out the front gates. More constructs were out here now, clearing, furrowing, planting in the clean soil.

I recalled the maps to my access memory, calculated rows and fields and pathways and channels, stretching on and on across the landscape. I would bring order to this unordered world.

One field at a time.

The Fooling of Gylfe
Chapters XVI–XVII
Snorri Sturluson

[Publisher's Note: In this story Gylfe King of Sweden, wants to find out about inhuman races called the asa, so he disguises himself as an old man called Ganglere and visits Asgard. The asa know who he is and disguise themselves too but Jahnhar, Thride and Har agree to answer his questions. Here Gylfe asks his final question about the Ragnarök, or apocalypse.]

Chapter XVI
Ragnarök

THEN SAID Ganglere: What tidings are to be told of Ragnarök? Of this I have never heard before. Har answered: Great things are to be said thereof. First, there is a winter called the Fimbul-winter, when snow drives from all quarters, the frosts are so severe, the winds so keen and piercing, that there is no joy in the sun. There are three such winters in succession, without any intervening summer. But before these there are three other winters, during which great wars rage over all the world. Brothers slay each other for the sake of gain, and no one spares his father or mother in that manslaughter and adultery. Thus says the Vala's Prophecy:

> *Brothers will fight together*
> *And become each other's bane;*
> *Sisters' children*
> *Their sib shall spoil.[1]*
> *Hard is the world,*
> *Sensual sins grow huge.*
> *There are ax-ages, sword-ages –*
> *Shields are cleft in twain, –*
> *There are wind-ages, wolf-ages,*
> *Ere the world falls dead.[2]*

Then happens what will seem a great miracle, that the wolf[3] devours the sun, and this will seem a great loss. The other wolf will devour the moon, and this too will cause great mischief. The stars shall be Hurled from heaven. Then it shall come to pass that the earth and the mountains will shake so violently that trees will be torn up by the roots, the mountains will topple down, and all bonds and fetters will be broken and snapped. The Fenris-wolf gets loose. The sea rushes over the earth, for the Midgard-serpent writhes in giant rage and seeks to gain the land. The ship that is called *Naglfar* also becomes loose. It is made of the nails of dead men; wherefore it is worth warning that, when a man dies with unpared nails, he supplies a large amount of materials for the building of this ship, which both gods and men wish may be finished as late as possible. But in this flood Naglfar gets afloat. The giant Hrym is its steersman. The Fenris-wolf advances with wide open mouth; the upper jaw reaches to heaven and the lower jaw is on the earth. He would open it still wider had he room. Fire flashes from his eyes and nostrils. The Midgard-serpent vomits forth venom, defiling all the air and the sea; he is very terrible, and places himself by the side of the wolf. In the midst of this clash and din the heavens are rent in twain, and the sons of Muspel come riding through the opening. Surt rides first, and before him and after him flames burning fire. He has a very good sword, which shines brighter than the sun. As they ride over Bifrost it breaks to pieces, as has before been stated. The sons of Muspel direct their course to the plain which is called Vigrid. Thither repair also the Fenris-wolf and the Midgard-serpent. To this place have also come Loke and Hrym, and with him all the frost-giants. In Loke's company are all the friends of Hel. The sons of Muspel have there effulgent bands alone by themselves. The plain Vigrid is one hundred miles (rasts) on each side.

While these things are happening, Heimdal stands up, blows with all his might in the Gjallar-horn and awakens all the gods, who thereupon hold counsel. Odin rides to Mimer's well to ask advice of Mimer for himself and his folk. Then quivers the ash Ygdrasil, and all things in heaven and earth fear and tremble. The asas and the einherjes arm themselves and speed forth to the battle-field. Odin rides first; with his golden helmet, resplendent byrnie, and his spear Gungner, he advances against the Fenris-wolf. Thor stands by his side, but can give him no assistance, for he has his hands full in his struggle with the Midgard-serpent. Frey encounters Surt, and heavy blows are exchanged ere Frey falls. The cause of his death is that he has not that good sword which he gave to Skirner. Even the dog Garm, that was bound before the Gnipa-cave, gets loose. He is the greatest plague. He contends with Tyr, and they kill each other. Thor gets great renown by slaying the Midgard-serpent, but retreats only nine paces when he falls to the earth dead, poisoned by the venom that the serpent blows on him. The wolf swallows Odin, and thus causes his death; but Vidar immediately turns and rushes at the wolf, placing one foot on his nether jaw. On this foot he has the shoe for which materials have been gathering through all ages, namely, the strips of leather which men cut off for the toes and heels of shoes; wherefore he who wishes to render assistance to the asas must cast these strips away. With one hand Vidar seizes the upper jaw of the wolf, and thus rends asunder his mouth. Thus the wolf perishes. Loke fights with Heimdal, and they kill each other. Thereupon Surt flings fire over the earth and burns up all the world. Thus it is said in the Vala's Prophecy:

Loud blows Heimdal
His uplifted horn.
Odin speaks
With Mimer's head.
The straight-standing ash
Ygdrasil quivers,
The old tree groans,
And the giant gets loose.
How fare the asas?
How fare the elves?

All Jotunheim roars.
The asas hold counsel;
Before their stone-doors
Groan the dwarfs,
The guides of the wedge-rock.
Know you now more or not?
From the east drives Hrym,
Bears his shield before him.
Jormungand welters
In giant rage
And smites the waves.
The eagle screams,
And with pale beak tears corpses,
Naglfar gets loose.
A ship comes from the east,
The hosts of Muspel
Come o'er the main,
And Loke is steersman.
All the fell powers
Are with the wolf;
Along with them
Is Byleist's brother.[4]
From the south comes Surt
With blazing fire-brand, –
The sun of the war-god
Shines from his sword.
Mountains dash together,
Giant maids are frightened,
Heroes go the way to Hel,
And heaven is rent in twain.
Then comes to Hlin
Another woe,
When Odin goes
With the wolf to fight,
And Bele's bright slayer[5]
To contend with Surt.
There will fall
Frigg's beloved.
Odin's son goes
To fight with the wolf,
And Vidar goes on his way
To the wild beast.[6]
With his hand he thrusts
His sword to the heart
Of the giant's child,
And avenges his father.

> Then goes the famous
> Son[7] of Hlodyn
> To fight with the serpent.
> Though about to die,
> He fears not the contest;
> All men
> Abandon their homesteads
> When the warder of Midgard
> In wrath slays the serpent.
> The sun grows dark,
> The earth sinks into the sea,
> The bright stars
> From heaven vanish;
> Fire rages,
> Heat blazes,
> And high flames play
> 'Gainst heaven itself.[8]
> And again it is said as follows:
> Vigrid is the name of the plain
> Where in fight shall meet
> Surt and the gentle god.
> A hundred miles
> It is every way.
> This field is marked out for them.

Chapter XVII
Regeneration

THEN ASKED Ganglere: What happens when heaven and earth and all the world are consumed in flames, and when all the gods and all the einherjes and all men are dead? You have already said that all men shall live in some world through all ages. Har answered: There are many good and many bad abodes. Best it is to be in Gimle, in heaven. Plenty is there of good drink for those who deem this a joy in the hall called Brimer. That is also in heaven. There is also an excellent hall which stands on the Nida mountains. It is built of red gold, and is called Sindre. In this hall good and well-minded men shall dwell. Nastrand is a large and terrible hall, and its doors open to the north. It is built of serpents wattled together, and all the heads of the serpents turn into the hall and vomit forth venom that flows in streams along the hall, and in these streams wade perjurers and murderers. So it is here said:

> A hall I know standing
> Far from the sun
> On the strand of dead bodies.
> Drops of venom
> Fall through the loop-holes.
> Of serpents' backs
> The hall is made.

> There shall wade
> Through heavy streams
> Perjurers
> And murderers.
> But in Hvergelmer it is worst.
> There tortures Nidhug
> The bodies of the dead.

Then said Ganglere: Do any gods live then? Is there any earth or heaven? Har answered: The earth rises again from the sea, and is green and fair. The fields unsown produce their harvests. Vidar and Vale live. Neither the sea nor Surf's fire has harmed them, and they dwell on the plains of Ida, where Asgard was before. Thither come also the sons of Thor, Mode and Magne, and they have Mjolner. Then come Balder and Hoder from Hel. They all sit together and talk about the things that happened aforetime, – about the Midgard-serpent and the Fenris-wolf. They find in the grass those golden tables which the asas once had. Thus it is said:

> Vidar and Vale
> Dwell in the house of the gods,
> When quenched is the fire of Surt.
> Mode and Magne
> Vingner's Mjolner shall have
> When the fight is ended.

In a place called Hodmimer's-holt are concealed two persons during Surt's fire, called Lif and Lifthraser. They feed on the morning dew. From these so numerous a race is descended that they fill the whole world with people, as is here said:

> Lif and Lifthraser
> Will lie hid
> In Hodmimer's-holt.
> The morning dew
> They have for food.
> From them are the races descended.

But what will seem wonderful to you is that the sun has brought forth a daughter not less fair than herself, and she rides in the heavenly course of her mother, as is here said:

> A daughter
> Is born of the sun
> Ere Fenrer takes her.
> In her mother's course
> When the gods are dead
> This maid shall ride.

And if you now can ask more questions, said Har to Ganglere, I know not whence that power came to you. I have never heard any one tell further the fate of the world. Make now the best use you can of what has been told you.

Then Ganglere heard a terrible noise on all sides, and when he looked about him he stood out-doors on a level plain. He saw neither hall nor burg. He went his way and came back to his kingdom, and told the tidings which he had seen and heard, and ever since those tidings have been handed down from man to man.

Footnotes for *The Fooling of Gylfe*

1. Commit adultery.
2. Elder Edda: The Vala's Prophecy.
3. Fenris-wolf.
4. Loke.
5. Frey.
6. The Fenris-wolf.
7. Thor.
8. Elder Edda: The Vala's Prophecy.

The complete and unabridged text is available
online, *from flametreepublishing.com/extras*

Bleed the Weak

Morgan Sylvia

"IT'S A coincidence," Gerry said, looking at the dusty ground.

"Ain't no coincidence," Maddie pointed at the exact spot Gerry was staring at. "That's right where Michael died."

Maddie looked around. Not that there was much to see: dry, cracked earth, dun-colored hills, rubble, and the withered, pallid skeletons of what had once been trees. Everything around them was lifeless and barren, leached of life and color and vitality.

Everything, that is, but the spot they stood before. There, the soil was a few shades darker. And in the center of that dark patch, a tiny plant had sprouted from the soil, a single spot of green in an endless wasteland.

"Can we eat it?" Bobby asked eagerly. He bent over to get a better look. Gerry put an arm out, stopping him.

"We shouldn't," Maddie said. "Maybe that's her soul."

Gerry spat. "Girl, if the souls of the dead made plants, we'd be standing in a jungle right now. Go on: you got chores."

Maddie pondered this event throughout the day, but she did not mention it until supper, when they gathered inside the old bank vault, and shared a tin of beans. They rarely delved into the canned food these days, but Gerry decided that the sprout, however small, however fragile, was worthy of celebration.

"It makes sense," Maddie said suddenly. "We took all the nutrients from the earth. When Michael died there, he gave his back. Maybe that's what the Mother needs." She looked at them all, her eyes reflecting the light of the lone hurricane lamp. Her voice dropped. "Blood."

"No." Gerry shook his head. "That's nonsense."

Jim chewed the last bit of rat, and swallowed. "The Mother's dead, girl. We're living on a corpse. If blood was what the Mother needed, there'd be green fields stretching from horizon to horizon." He picked a bit of gristle out of his teeth before finishing. "Her blood is oil, and the last of that was pumped out decades ago."

Sandra spoke up, which was rare. "Maybe she's right. It is the same spot." She looked up, her red, watery eyes glittering in the firelight. Her face and hair were both thin and colorless. She looked ghoulish, even by present standards. "We should test it."

"Test it?" Maddie frowned. "How?"

Sandra looked into the shadows on the other side of the room, at the thin form that lay there, unmoving, on the cot. "Papa won't last long," she said. "Isn't it kinder?"

"Murder," Gerry said tightly, "isn't kind."

"It isn't murder," Sandra said, and there was a determination in her voice that was unusual for her. "It's mercy."

"Has he eaten today?" Maddie asked quietly.

Sandra shook her head. "Wouldn't take but a drop of water. He won't last the week. It's not murder if you kill the dying."

"We're all dying," Gerry said. "Some faster 'n others, that's all."

"It should be his choice." Jim said. "Not ours."

A thin, wan voice came to them from the bundle of bones that had once been their hero. "Do it," Papa said. He coughed heavily. When the spasms stopped, he had to draw several deep breaths before he could speak again. "Feed the Mother."

They all heard the death rattle in his lungs.

Papa had saved them, kept them alive. It was he who had brought them here, to the old vault. Taught them how to survive, if one could call it that. The small town had only supported a handful of businesses, and had been almost as deserted in its heyday as it was now. But when the wars burnt the sky and blackened the land, the vault in its lone, tiny bank had proved to be worth far more than the riches it had once contained. And Papa, well, Papa had been worth his weight in gold, as Gerry used to say. Not just because he had keys to the vault, either. Papa knew things. He had grown up in the first world, in the years before the darkening. Long before he'd become a banker, his father had taught him the ways of the woods and the land. That frail skull encased lost, archaic knowledge of trees and crops and hunting, ancient wisdom that had been set aside, replaced by the buzz of computer data. That knowledge that had seen them through those first dark years, when ashes fell from the sky and charnel winds swept the land, and men died not by the thousands, but by the millions.

"Papa," Gerry said. "You know what we're talking about?"

"Yep." The old man's voice was thin and weak, but his eyes glittered with resolve. "She's right. I don't have much time left." A fit of coughing interrupted the old man's words. Maddie went to his side with a cup of rat broth, but he turned away from it. "Kinda just as soon hurry things up a bit. You need the food more than I do."

They sat in silence for a time. In a way, they were debating, but no one spoke.

Usually, after dark, after they had finished whatever supper they'd scavenged, they would gather around the fire barrel, and the bards would speak of the old days, the first world. By then, there were few who truly remembered the first world. There were books, of course, scattered here and there in the ruins. Photos and magazines. Those who could read, did so, but most people just looked at the pictures. The bards, who had sunk to the bottom of the hierarchy of the first world, rose again, became prominent. They told the stories, the stories that reminded them of what they were, and what they had once been. They were important in this new world.

Papa had been the best bard of all. Before his lungs had failed and his breath weakened, he had spoken about the history of man, his words dancing around the firelit vault like fireflies. He had told them about the first world, details that had been burnt away. But he was kind enough to tell them that they were, in some ways, not much worse off than the early tribes, the cave dwellers. Maddie found this comforting.

Outside, the charnel winds howled through an empty world. There were no other sounds. They didn't know, and had long stopped wondering, if there was even anyone or anything left to make noise, other than themselves. Every now and then, some blighted soul would stumble through, starving and bedraggled and half mad. But these nomads were offered no sanctuary. They had long since closed off their small circle: they just retreated into the shadows and let the wanderers shuffle past, staggering into oblivion.

Sometimes Maddie wondered what they were looking for. There was nothing left to find out there anymore, but bones and dust and ruins.

They had all learned that lesson. Hope was cruel, for it lit false fires in their hearts, and made the colorless world around them seem even more hostile. Laughter was pointless: it did not belong here, in this dry, desolate place. Nor did songs, or dancing, or clothes that were pretty rather than practical. The stories, however, they kept, for stories were made for firesides and shadows, and for nights when the poisoned wind screamed over barren fields. They painted their tales on the walls in blood and charcoal and, on occasion, real paint and ink. They were reduced to their beginnings; dark, slender figures huddled around fires in cavernous, echoing rooms, in a world that was strange and wild and terrible.

Papa coughed again. "Pick the spot well. Something that gets sun, but isn't too exposed to the wind. Low ground, for when the rains come, but not too low, in case too much rain comes."

They stared at him silently, their eyes glassy pools of misery.

The silence was broken. This required discussion. It meant a counting of what few scavenged seeds they had left, and a careful selection and planting of the best. They saved the water they could for that spot, as well as their waste. Papa had taught them those tricks, too, the alchemy of the soil, the magic of turning filth into food. Their results had been meager, at best.

They did not weep, when it came time. They did not speak fancy words, or say goodbye. They'd all seen far too much dying to make much of a fuss over it.

Papa's death was quiet and peaceful. A raven came and lit on the withered branch of what had once been an oak tree, but was now little more than twisted scrub brush. Ghosts danced in the wind.

It took only a few days for the sprout to emerge.

Maddie dreamt the old dream that night, of bright gardens and shining seas, and clear skies that were a color she had forgotten the name of.

Papa became a blackberry bush. Maddie tried to guard it, but ravens came and took the berries. She chased them away, at first, until she dreamt that they were flying off with bits and pieces of Papa, taking him into the clouds. She woke frightened that maybe she was trapping Papa here, by keeping the ravens away. After that, instead of chasing the ravens away, Maddie gave them scraps. They grew to know her and flocked around her. And when the fruit ripened, she gave them the berries, though Gerry beat her for it.

She bore this calmly, unperturbed.

Once, she had raged. She had whispered her anger into hellish winds, and screamed her fury to poisoned clouds. The broken, charred bones of what had once been a city bore silent witness to her madness. She had been strong once, and blonde. The frail bundle of madness and rage that Papa had found on the edge of the nowherelands had long since given way to stony silence and acceptance. She no longer thought of words like *tomorrow* or *yesterday*.

But now forgotten words reappeared in her thoughts. *Live*, she wished at the bush. *Grow*.

The bush survived. When the moon grew fat and yellow, one of the ravens flew to Maddie, and dropped a berry at her foot. She ate it, and felt forgotten words bursting in her mouth, words like *sweet* and *ripe* and *fresh*.

In her dreams that night, the Mother whispered to her. *Bleed the weak.*

They decided their course of action, as they always did, by tossing finger bones onto a small patch of asphalt. And so it was decided: they were to become bloodletters. But, after much debate and deliberation, during which words like *right* and *wrong* and *morality* were drudged up from distant memory, they added one caveat.

The weak would decide.

The days passed (there were no seasons in the second world), and, as before, the occasional ragged traveler staggered through. They no longer hid from these wanderers, but approached openly, offering a choice.

Many of these wretched souls opted to become part of the garden. Some were overwhelmed just by the sight of the garden, and stood there in shock, drinking in the sight, gulping eyefuls of it. They raised their sore-covered faces to the sun, and wept from red, crusty eyes, nodding their heads wildly. *Yes*, they would say, *I choose this*. They never told their stories, but they gave their reasons, and these things were writ on the crumbling stone wall that surrounded the meager garden patch. The graffiti was in truth, only bits and pieces of the fragmented last thoughts of the desperate and the mad. *Bessie*, one man wrote. Another had quoted Shakespeare. *Doomsday is near; die all, die merrily*. Others left dates, or battalions, or family names, or song lyrics. But as time went on, it became customary for them to write a single phrase. Three words began to dominate the wall (which they now called the Wall of Truth) dressed in vivid colors they found hiding in rusted paint cans.

For the Mother.

In the first year, only a few bushes grew. But as more and more of the weak and the broken shuffled through the cemetery gate, the garden grew.

Maddie began, one day, as she watered a scrabbly plant that had once been a man named Saul, to understand that something had happened. She couldn't call it hope, exactly. That word was forbidden. But somehow, the Golgotha had become a garden. And the fruit it bore lit sparks in the eyes of those who still stood, however precariously, upon the earth.

Alchemy, she thought, recalling Papa's lessons. *A change. Transmutation.*

Jim found a guitar one day, on a scavenging run. That night, Maddie found her voice and sang to the garden, and more forgotten words slipped through the sweltering air: *music* and *magic*.

After that, they always sang as they bled the weak. It did something; it made a change in the air, the energy of the place. None of them could truly say whether it was good or bad. It did not matter. It was something other than death and decay.

Maddie was in the garden one day, tending the bush that had once been Papa, and the apple tree that she had fed herself, when she glanced up and saw something moving in one of the branches. She looked closer, and found that it had scales. A word rose up through her memory. *Serpent.*

The snake hissed at her.

"Did you come here to die?" Maddie asked it. She could not remember if animals spoke or not. She seemed to recall seeing talking beasts in a brightly colored box, in which lights flashed and music played. But that had belonged to the first world.

The snake had a tumor on its side, and was covered with lesions. As it slithered down the tree, approaching her, Maddie stood frozen, not sure if she should run or stay put. It glided over her foot, and that was when she noticed that a single red fruit had fallen to the ground.

It was the first apple the tree had produced.

The Mother whispered into her thoughts. *Eat the apple.*

And so she did.

The fruit tasted, as everything did, of death, of rotted flesh, like a putrid corpse. There was a worm in the apple, but she had long ago learned that food was food, and she ate that as well.

That night the visions began. Had she lived in the first world, she might have known something of fermented apples, but in this one, there were only a few truths one needed to understand, and most of those had to do with death.

In the morning, Maddie stood before them in pallid sunlight, and her reddened, glazed eyes held a tiny spark of transcendence.

"The Mother spoke to me last night," she said. "In words, and then in visions."

Sandra snickered. Gerry grumbled.

Maddie drew herself up. Somewhere within her, in the part of her that belonged, and would always belong, to the first world, she found words that had long since blown away. *Projection. Authority.* "In the first world," she said, "weak men hurt the Mother. Weak men destroyed our cities and poisoned our seas and burnt our world. In this world, that has to change."

Something moved in the shadows. Sandra jumped back, screaming, but Maddie planted herself before the snake. "He's not to be eaten," she said. "He is sacred."

They developed, in time, a more elaborate ritual. There were words to be spoken, now, questions to be asked. Gerry found a fancy sword in a pile of rubble, and that, too, became part of the rite. And when the weak came forth, they fed the garden with blood that stank of madness and torment, and pomegranates grew from the puddles of their filth.

Maddie guided them in these things.

The wind blew their words, their tales, their miracles, into the distant, miserable corners of the world, where small pockets of thin, dirty survivors huddled around greasy fires. The ravens and the winds and the ragged wanderers sent word, and Maddie's name was whispered beside barrel fires and in toxic shadows. The weak came and bled, as did the mad and the dying. The wall of bone grew higher and higher. They made art of it, understanding death to be both beautiful and terrible.

And so the second world rose. The first was dead: this one was new and primal.

The Mother drank the blood of innocents, and her dirty, cracked flanks bore fruit. There were children born that year, for the first time since the blight. People came from afar, in time, to die with dignity, they who had lived without it for so long. *To give back,* they said, through parched lips. *To make it mean something.*

And so the garden grew, encircled by a wall they built from the bones of the dead, fed by blood and filth. The ravens stayed on the wall, content to eat the weak, the ones who fed the soil. They whispered to Maddie, put words and pictures into her thoughts. When she closed her eyes, her consciousness flew out into a dead world on a thousand black wings. It lit on the top of a tower, and roosted in a forest of bone. It picked the dusty soil, rooting among the empty skulls of a million dead.

The ravens brought her nails and screws and buttons. They brought keys and jewels and bits of shiny glass, the kind Papa said happened sometimes when the bombs hit sand. They brought pretty shards of twisted metal, and finger bones encased in glittering rings. She wore these things in her hair, and around her neck and wrists.

Find me seeds, she told them.

And so they did. They lit out for the four corners of the world, and they returned with seeds. They grew pomegranates and apples and lemons, and grapes and berries and tomatoes. She hung their feathers from her hair, and began to mark spirals on her cheeks.

That summer, the rains came back. But the rains were acid, and burned their skin.

Ash, Maddie said. *We must coat the garden in ash and filth. We must encase it in the bones of those who gave. And we must build a gate.*

They brought barrels to contain the rain. Maddie directed them to fill the barrels with coal and sand and stone, and take water from the bottom. None of them seemed to recall that this had been Papa's way of purifying water. It didn't matter. They whispered of her alchemy, and did what she said.

The ravens brought her berries, and told her this was correct. The serpent whispered jeweled dreams into her thoughts, agreeing.

The Mother guided her in these things.

When the weak came, it was she who held the blade.

When it was time again to harvest the garden, Maddie stopped them before the apple tree.

"Do not eat of this tree," Maddie told them. "You can have the others. But this tree, this one is mine."

The serpent watched all this with jeweled eyes. In the day, it sunned itself on rocks and bones. At night, it slid to the edge of the circle of firelight, and listened to the bards speaking of the wonders of the first world. It ate its share of rats, but it was polite about it, and left plenty for the rest of them.

They did not leave the garden anymore, for they had no need.

In time, the word spread, and a band of warriors approached them. These men – who were, quite clearly *strong* – had aims to take the place, but when they saw the garden, they became hesitant to kill its keepers, for they did not know the sacred, salvaged truths of planting. In the end, they fed it four of their own, the ones who did not agree with their decision. After that, they protected the garden, and helped till the soil and build the walls even higher.

The raiders left Maddie alone, whispering other words, once forgotten. *Witch*, they called her. *Sorceress*. But they kept their distance. They knew the garden responded to her, and the snake, which by then lived mostly around her neck, frightened them. One of them in particular liked that fear, for it reminded him of what it meant to be human, to feel emotions. One night, this man, whose name was Evan, followed Maddie into the garden, and that night more forgotten words returned, words like *love* and *kiss*.

The snake and the ravens kept close as her belly grew.

Sandra became jealous of Maddie and Evan, and turned the others against her. "Why should she have the one tree?" she demanded. "We all worked on this place. She steals from us."

And so Maddie was cast aside. They did not dare exile her, but they shunned her, and would not speak to her or even look at her. Evan stayed with her, and they took up residence in a canvas tent in a dry corner of the compound. They watched quietly as Sandra sang and danced and ate the fruit. Her silver blade flashed in the moonlight, and the garden drank again.

That night, the Mother whispered to Sandra, but her words, this time, were different.

Kill, she said. *Eat*.

Sandra told the raiders. And so they killed, and they ate. In time, in a month that had once been known as August, a raging madness fell upon the last of the wretched survivors. Had they recalled the ways of the first world, they might have known that their particular madness had once been known as *Mad Cow Disease*, but they had forgotten those words.

Maddie and Evan watched quietly from the shadows as the madness took over the camp. When the killings began, they went into the vault, and closed it behind them. They stayed there, huddled together, until only the sound of the wind broke the silence above.

The Worm Moon was full in the sky when Maddie went into labor. For two days and two nights she struggled and sweated and screamed, but the babe would not come. Evan wept and paced and prayed to gods he had forgotten, but it was to no avail.

When the sun sank over a dying world, Maddie looked at her last sunset, her pale face sheened with sweat, and told him what to do. "Take me to the garden," she said. "I am weak now, and my blood is ready. But when it is done, cut down the tree. No one else should taste that fruit but me."

The snake watched with topaz eyes as Evan raised the knife.

The ravens carried her spirit to the moon. A child's thin cry split the night, and then fell silent.

Greif-stricken, Evan went to the plant that had once been Papa, and pulled it from the ground. It screamed when he plucked it. And then he went to the apple tree, and, in a rage, chopped at it with his knife. When the tree fell, he bit into one of the fruits.

And then he, too, heard the voice of the Mother.

The third world belongs to the serpents, the Mother said. *There will be no fourth.*

Before Evan could move, he felt a sharp stabbing pain in his ankle.

The serpent looked up at him once before slithering over his foot and into the shadows.

Only the wind and the moon looked down on the garden after that. In time, untended, it turned to dust again. And then, after many years of silence, a broken star fell to earth. The thick clouds that formed cast the world into eternal darkness, and the plants and animals died. By the time the Earth, sea, and sky became one, and dissipated into the night, the only living things on the planet were the apple tree that held the soul of a woman named Madelyn and the serpent coiled around its branches.

Subsumption

Lucy Taylor

ANIKKA HUNKERS against the empty water tank as Baris twists the lock on Salvation's inner door, two feet of reinforced concrete and steel leading to a mud room with a twelve-foot ladder leading topside. He starts to climb.

Outside the scraping and cracking have begun again, just like last night after the generator failed. Persistent, rhythmic. Something or someone trying to get in?

"Wait!" she says.

He looks down. "What?"

"We don't know what's out there."

"You're right. But we don't have a choice." His lightly accented voice drifts down to her, pure Gujarati, and she's reminded why she loves him; his steady, calming voice and fierce black eyes, his stoic acceptance of the unimaginable. They'd met at the lab where Anikka's father worked (works, she tells herself) in Los Alamos, New Mexico. It was Baris who'd helped them design Salvation, the name her father gave to the forty-two feet of galvanized corrugated pipe buried fifteen feet down in the mountains near Raton Pass north of Chama, New Mexico.

"The end has to come at some point," her father said, while he was laying out the plans for Salvation. "The only question is what form it comes in."

Lucky us, Anikka thinks, *now we've got the chance to find out.*

Outside the sounds are sharper, more invasive. Anikka looks up at Baris on the ladder. "If it's something horrible, something that we can't survive, remember what you promised."

He pats the .9mm Luger on his hip. "You first. I'll be right after."

She feels absurdly comforted.

He engages the automatic lift mechanism. The camouflaged blast hatch powers open to a cacophony of snapping, creaking. Bones breaking on a torture rack, Anikka thinks.

As Baris exits, Anikka begins to climb. A moment later, his laughter shocks her. "A tree fell across the hatch. Just branches, that's all it was!"

She exhales.

Topside, strands of hazy light filter through dusky, dog-turd clouds, but around them spread the pinyon-juniper woodlands, unchanged as far as she can tell. She takes a shallow breath. Frowns. The air has an acrid, raw taste now, a pungent smoky scent, richly fertilized soil underlain with the tang of decay. Baris sniffs cautiously, his right eye twitching as it does when he's confused.

"Smells strange," he says.

"Maybe the fires around Denver."

"Yeah. Chemicals." He mutters something in Gujarati. A prayer, Anikka thinks, and wishes they'd had time to stock the gas masks.

Once it started, there wasn't much time for anything. The first wave of bolides struck the northern hemisphere the day after Memorial Day in the States, late May of 2021. Fireballs at 14 brightness, twice as bright as a full moon, rained like missiles over huge sections of the planet, even as debate still raged whether they were rocky or metallic asteroids or something intelligent, an alien attack. No one agreed. Locked inside Salvation, while the HAM radio still worked, they got news of inconceivable destruction – central Asia, Alaska, everything from Minnesota down to Mexico and east was sheeted in walls of fire hundreds of feet high.

Annika has steeled herself to emerge into a charred moonscape, the Old Earth reduced to ash and bones. What she sees now is so contrary to her expectations that her reeling brain struggles to accept it – darkly verdant hillsides thick with ponderosa pines, junipers and aspen whose silver bark glows like polished pewter.

"How is this possible?" she gasps.

"Who knows? We got lucky. Let's find your dad."

They hoist their packs, check the compass, and head southwest toward Los Alamos. If Anikka's father's still alive, he may be waiting for them.

A few miles on, they find a road that the topo map tells them will intersect with 285 just north of Chama. A breeze picks up. The swirling air grows dense with tiny particles. Anikka tells herself it's pollen from the golden Chamisa that crowd the verge. Baris starts to cough, which is when she hears the voices. She grabs his arm, signals him to hush.

People coming.

A woman's querulous voice and then a harsh male one. Anikka can't make out the words, but she knows anguish when she hears it. They slide among the trees and crouch as a small band, four men and a woman, crests the hill. They trudge single-file, armed with rifles and AK-47's, and all wear black bandannas, but for the stooped man in the lead. His bandanna is a startling emerald green and appears to cause him pain, judging by how he shakes his head back and forth. Still he makes no effort to adjust it.

The group halts on the roadside, and a heated argument ensues with two of the men bellowing invective back and forth. A third man intervenes. Green Bandanna starts limping toward the trees, alone. The woman, young and burly and heavily tattooed, pulls out her pistol, racks the slide, and fires. Green Bandanna's head explodes into scarlet and smoke.

One of the men douses the body with accelerant and throws a match. The woman lingers a few minutes while the others leave. Then she crosses herself and follows after.

Anikka and Baris whisper together and adjust their plan. They'll avoid the roads and bushwhack whenever possible, staying within the shelter of the trees.

They make their way in silence, each stunned by the execution they've just witnessed.

Finally Anikka says, "It was plague wasn't it?"

"We don't know that."

"My father said first impact might not be the worst of this. He said the bolides could bring contaminants that would disperse when they hit."

"That makes it sound like there was intelligence behind this, like something or someone planned it. There wasn't, Nikka. Shit flies through space all the time. Earth just happened to get in the way."

"But they burned the body."

"Maybe he didn't deserve a decent burial. Maybe he was an enemy. Somebody from the wrong tribe."

"So already we're dividing into tribes?" The possibility makes her throat constrict. "What's that, the first step on the way to the Stone Age?"

He laughs and kisses her neck.

She rips cloth from her shirttail to improvise bandannas. They should have stocked gas masks, she thinks. They should have stocked other things, too. Like guava jelly and macadamia nuts and caviar and Brie. So many things she longs for now and wishes she could taste again.

Something flashes in her peripheral vision. She's just fast enough to glimpse a covey of quail, lightning fast as they dart for hiding. She permits herself a tiny gust of pleasure. She's always liked quail. Glad to see that some survived.

* * *

The afternoon looks much like morning, hazy under a parade of low-hanging clouds that pass ponderously, like tamed elephants. At a pond, they purify some water and rest in the shade. Beneath the trees, Anikka notices the soil is soft and spongy, although there's no sign of recent rain. Gazing into the maze of trees, she spies an odd growth, a mottled, oval flower with a striking green center that appears to sprout from a juniper trunk. She blinks, trying to reconcile what she's seeing with what she's *not* seeing.

She nudges Baris.

"What is that?"

It takes him a moment to spot what she's pointing at and become concerned enough to tell her to stay there while he investigates. She goes with him, of course. And when he sucks in his breath and looks away, she studies more intently, willing herself to see something else, to realize it's just a trick of light that causes her to think the spine of the man slumped there is fused with the tree and that the outline of a juniper branch isn't visible through the papery skin of his throat.

He leans against the tree in a way that suggests sleep, except for the roots that snake around his legs and the glimpses of exposed femur that disturb the architectural balance of flesh and root system.

"The tree's absorbing him," she says, her tone replete with the awe and wonder of one who comes upon a nature god inside his leafy temple. But then the ruined legs spasm down and up, a croak issue from the mangled throat, and Anikka claps a hand across her gut and doubles over.

In a surreal display of effort, the head raises, lolls, fights to find a balance point on the engorged neck. The mouth twists and contorts, and a hand paws the eyes where thin green shoots have knit themselves among the brows, lips and lashes, the handiwork of a sadistic seamstress or a darkly comic one.

"Who would do this?" Baris says as what once was human fights to breathe, and Anikka doesn't answer, not knowing how to tell him no one did anything, but that this is now the nature of the world.

"We need to clear his airway," Baris says and slides his thumbs inside the corners of the man's mouth, trying to work free the obstructions. When this fails, he grabs his knife, flicks out the blade.

"No!" Anikka says.

Baris strokes the man's forehead and talks soothingly, as though what he is about to do is normal. "Don't be afraid. I'm only going to cut some of this away."

Bunches of tightly clumped, dark needles fall to the forest floor, but so does blood – a lot of it. An image flashes in Anikka's mind: Green Bandanna executed, his mouth clotted with a vivid green. She yells, "You're cutting him!"

The man convulses, legs kicking out as far as the roots allow, then planking, quivering, and going limp.

"What —?"

"It's part of him. Or he's part of the tree. You can't cut one without cutting the other."

He stares at the blood dripping from the blade.

"We've got to do something," Baris says, even as pliant green filaments weave shut the lashes, sewing off sight, and Anikka only understands the one kind of help they have to offer. She unholsters the Sig and tells Baris to walk away. When she fires, the air explodes with whirring, agitated life, pollen that's insectile, comet shaped. She runs to join Baris, holding her breath as long as she can.

Now instead of staying in the trees, they search for roads of any kind, a highway's what they're hoping for but dirt will do, anything to keep some space between the trees and them.

Evening's coming on. They find a meadow wide enough to offer some distance from the trees and shed their packs, unfold their sleeping bags. Baris spots deer tracks, says they need food and there's still enough light to make a shot. He seems angry, eager to bring down a doe or a buck. Anikka, who's just shot a man to death, feels spent and sick and not keen on killing anything. She waves him off, crawls into her bag, and slips into murky sleep.

She wakes up dreaming that Baris is inside her, thrusting angrily with a cock carved from burled wood and tipped with a black Stone Age arrow. Her twilit brain is trying to makes sense of this, when she feels the warmth between her legs and smells the blood.

Baris' sleeping bag lies empty, but she pounds it with her fist, anger and panic released with every punch. Calm descends. She lies back down, unsnaps her jeans, struggles them down over her thighs. The flashlight shows pale green, six-inch stalks and a clutch of narrow, braided roots. When she runs a finger along the tips, she feels an answering quiver deep inside, a tiny tongue-flick sensation followed by an electric jolt of pain. Her breath hitches and she sinks her front teeth into the meat of her lip, clinging to the pain for sanity.

Gingerly she pinches a stem between two fingers and tugs, praying that this parasite will slide out easily, but the thing holds fast and more blood pours.

She wraps the pliant blades around her fingers, fists her hand, lets out all her breath and yanks before she can change her mind. Her vision pinpricks. She screams to keep from fainting.

* * *

If Baris heard her cry, she knows he'd come to her. Since he does not, she takes the gun and flashlight and moves shakily across the meadow, into the forest.

At first it's just bark and leaves and branches she sees, the junipers and pinyons, regal aspen nodding in the breeze, but the farther she goes the more nuanced her sight becomes, the more adroitly she can parse the liminal threshold of this realm.

She wants to a call out Baris's name, but remembers too vividly those melded vertebrae, the throat crammed with juniper and bits of bark and prefers to keep her silence.

Beneath her feet, lichen-furred roots protrude from loamy soil; they forge meandering, unnatural paths, contrive to cut her off. A twisted juniper, lightning-struck and blackened, dangles grotesque seeds, each composed of five elongated rows, white beads that clink and shake. Then eyes and brain coordinate to give a meaning to this horror, flensed hands and tiny finger bones, the trellis of a wrist. Root systems from surrounding trees intertwine with carpals, skulls and shanks, the basin of a pelvic girdle garlanded with ropey coils of greyish purple meat.

She shuts off the flashlight and pads from one splash of moonlight to the next, wandering these charnel house woods with gun in hand, shuddering each time something drips from overhead.

That Baris is the newest addition to this tableau is evidenced by his relative intactness and the still new look of his tactical jacket and unscuffed Wolverines. His face, once so unspeakably dear to her, is now just unspeakable. She turns away, hating him for what he's done, but hating more the loss of him. Of everything.

For a moment she sways between gusts of grief and fury.

You said I'd go first. You'd be right behind.

The forest shivers, although there is no wind. She hears the mourning of an owl and wonders if animal life is somehow immune to this, if it's no accident she sees no skins or feathers, paws or fur. Perhaps the plants are sentient now and can distinguish among types of prey. Perhaps that is the point.

Baris's gun lies in the underbrush beside him. She starts to leave it, then goes back and tries to pick it up. Vines fight her for possession, but she wins this time, only to discover that the muzzle, trigger guard, and rear sight are already clogged with coarse and tangled weeds. She throws the gun away and tries to find her way back to the meadow, but her halting progress quickly becomes a gauntlet, she's lashed and buffeted, caressed and enmeshed, a spider in a flytrap.

When she stumbles, her foot becomes entangled. Within minutes whole portions of her throat and brain are being colonized. Adrenaline floods her bloodstream. Her heart syncopates, and she goes blind and deaf in seconds. Her brain waves spike, even as a deadly languor surges through her. Only at the last, when she feels the forest infiltrate every damp and open pore of her honeycomb skin does she recall the magic she still wields, the quick death Baris promised and denied her, and reaches for the Sig. She brings it to her head only to find her mind contains no memory of what this object is or how she is supposed to use it or why it even matters…

There are no words.

A sound builds within her and she tries to give it voice, but other life forms own her now, the rich nutrients of her bone and blood divvied up among a million microscopic mouths as her body is repurposed for a grander destiny.

Dog Island

Natalia Theodoridou

"**WHAT DID YOU** say it sounded like?" the Handyman asks, and I try not to roll my eyes at his tone. He screws the lid back onto the air unit and starts climbing down the ladder. He stops midway to rub his back. Like most Handies, he's still young enough to do some of the harder jobs, but the work takes its toll, no doubt.

"Like banging," I say. "Like a bang-bang, bang-bang. Or a thumpa-thumpa. I don't know. It comes and goes."

The Handyman finishes his descent and smoothes back his ruffled hair. It's grey, I notice. For some reason, that makes me feel avenged.

"Well, sir, there's nothing wrong with your air filtration system either," he says.

I show him my palms. "What am I supposed to do, then?"

"Are you sure you didn't imagine it?" He glances around my kitchen – for signs that I've lost my marbles, I'm sure.

I straighten my back. It makes a hollow sound, like two pieces of a puzzle falling reluctantly together. I glare at the handyman. "I may be old, older than you, certainly, but I am not senile," I say. My voice sounds creaky and ancient even to myself.

He reaches out and touches my shoulder. A wrinkled hand, a few blemishes. Paper-thin skin. How old might he be? Seventy? Seventy-five? He must have been a baby.

"Look," he says, "I'm sure it's nothing too serious, or I would have found it. If there are any problems, give me a call and I'll come take another look."

His hand's still resting on my shoulder. I pat it with my own blemished hand, and I find myself wishing that he wouldn't let go.

"Till then, I guess you'll just have to live with it," he continues. "Whatever it is. All right?"

I don't know this man, and yet I hold his hand and I close my eyes for a moment, just a moment. Don't let go, don't let go.

He squeezes my shoulder one last time. "Yeah, you'll be all right," he says. He lets go.

* * *

After the Handyman's gone, I ride the automated train to Annie's. Part of the line is still running, but who knows for how long. I am alone in the carriage, except for two dogs. My hands feel extra empty today as they rest on my lap. I realize I forgot my walking cane. It's OK. I don't need it to walk as much as to feel safe. The dogs seem calm, but I keep my distance, just in case. The female one looks like it's recently given birth, its breasts full and heavy, hanging low under its belly. The city flashes by, a blur of concrete covered in wild green.

I get off the train three blocks from Annie's house; that's as far as the line goes. I take care not to provoke the dogs on the way out. The Sky-V picks up my concern and responds with a nature show about the evolving hunting habits of canines. It covers the sky with images of stalking, chasing, ripping – muscles tensing, sharp teeth doing what they were built for. There's no sound, thankfully. When the targeted news system failed, the sound system went with it. But the rest of the network stayed on, so the Sky-V made do with documentaries and scenes from old movies to match people's interests. Our moods, even.

The sky's watching over us. There are no children in these movies.

I keep covering the distance to Annie's house. It would have made sense for one of us to move closer, to one of the empty apartments in my building, perhaps, but old dogs and new tricks and all that had made us postpone the move until neither one of us could physically pull it off. It's too late now. Besides, I like the city, green and empty like this.

The city's dogs stand alert and motionless, eyeing me from behind thick bushes and unkempt trees. Their staring helps me forget the pain in my knees. The Sky-V is still broadcasting scenes of predatory aggression. Either no one else is around, or they're thinking of being torn apart too.

* * *

Annie is napping when I get there, so I check her food supply and then clean the cages and feed her birds. When I'm done, I fetch a tub of lukewarm water and shake Annie gently.

She opens her eyes and smiles. "Eddie? You're here," she says. The sclera of her eyes is yellow, the brown irises washed out and milky.

"It's time for your bath, little girl," I say. I help her lean forward on the bed and she wraps her arms around my neck. We do our little awkward dance, and I finally land her on the bedroom chair. I sit on the bed to catch my breath. She pats my knee, but she's still too tired to speak.

I nod. "It's okay," I reassure her. "I'm okay." I stand up and position myself behind her chair. I undo the back of her nightie and she pulls away her hair. Her body looks tired, used up – like something past its expiration date. I immediately feel blood rushing to my cheeks. That's not a nice thing to think, boy. I dip my sponge in the tub and start cleaning her parched skin.

"I had a Handy over at the house today," I say, to keep the unkind thoughts away. "That's why I was late."

"Oh? What broke this time?" She chuckles.

I squirt some liquid disinfectant on the sponge and rub her back.

"I've been hearing this sound in the house, like a banging," I explain. "Usually at night. It keeps me up." I pass her the sponge and look away. "It sounds deep, somehow. Like it's coming from down below. Anyway, he didn't find anything."

"Are you sure it's from your building?" she asks while cleaning herself.

"I don't know."

"You can look now," she says. She passes me the sponge, and I dip it in the water. I go over her back one more time, soaking up the soap, then give her the sponge and look away again so she can do the same. Finally, I tie her nightie behind her back and neck. I bend over and kiss her thin hair.

"Bring a chair here," she says. "Sit next to me."

"I'll get our game," I say. I put a chair opposite hers, then drag over the Formica coffee table with the draughts board top.

Annie pulls a bag out of the little table drawer and starts setting out the pieces. She pauses and looks at me, suddenly serious. "Thank you for taking care of me," she says.

I wave her gratitude away. "I like coming here." I lower my eyes, stare at the draughts.

Annie makes her first move. She's playing the dark pieces. I respond quickly, and she moves again. She seems pensive. She lifts her hand and touches the faded scar next to her right eye. I've always wondered how she got it, but I never asked. In the riots, I assumed, and so I didn't want to know.

"Have I ever told you I had a phantom pregnancy back in the day?" she says, catching me off guard. "Right around the time I started running out of students." She stops and thinks about it for a moment. "It was when they decided to destroy the last sperm banks, so about ten years after the national sterilization," she continues. "My Greek grandmother said 'You caught a baby, Annie.' Catching a baby, isn't that a strange phrase?"

"Yes," I say. "Yes it is." Why are you telling me this, Annie? Why now?

"It always sounded to me like something accidental," she says, "like a cold, and at the same time something that required a particular talent, such as capturing a rare bird, or a butterfly." She twists a strand of hair around her index finger, like a little girl. "I watched my belly grow and grow, and in the end all that came out was air."

My face feels flushed. My arm wavers mid-movement, as I am about to take one of her pieces. We never talk about this, about the old times. I lack the vocabulary for it, the social repertoire. What is a proper reaction to such a thing? "I'm sorry," I say, finally. I complete my move.

"Ruthie couldn't handle it. She left soon after that. Went overseas."

"I'm sorry, Annie. You never said."

She takes two of my pieces with one move. I respond.

"It's curious, isn't it? You've been coming here so long, and yet we've said so little. It feels as if all we've ever done is play draughts. I've never asked what you did before, in the early days. I don't imagine your job has always been looking after an old lady."

She fixes her gaze on me, and I shiver, as if something cold and dark just passed between us. "Do I even want to know?" she asks, then laughs it off and makes her move.

I was a propagandist, I almost blurt out. And look at me now, Annie, grasping for words. Who would have thought? But my phone rings, and so I don't say anything.

* * *

"Eddie?"

The voice on the phone sounds distant, as if coming from a place far, far away, full of static. I think I hear dogs barking in the background.

"Yes?"

"It's Sophie." A pause. A bark. Something drowned in the static. "... tell you that Donnie killed himself."

I don't reply right away. What am I supposed to say? Ask why? How?

"Hello? Eddie, are you there?" She yells so I can hear her over the noise.

"Yes. Yes, I'm sorry. I'm here."

"The funeral is tomorrow at two in the afternoon." She sounds disappointed in me. Rightfully. I've never been as good as she was at these things. At any of it.

"Okay."

"Are you going to come?"

She's pushing now. Testing me. My limits. As if we're still at work. "I don't know," I say. I sense she's about to hang up. "Sophie?" I stop her.

"Yes, Eddie."

"Thank you for calling me."

"Sure," is all she says, and the line goes silent.

* * *

It's not the funeral itself that frightens me. I've seen too many dead friends' bodies already – withered, frail, returned to earth in tightly wrapped bundles – it's only natural when you get to ninety. It's the thought of seeing Sophie again, after all these years, my partner in crime.

I spot her in the small crowd across the grave. We don't speak until after the deed is done, the body lowered into the ground, words said, dirt thrown onto Donnie's shrouded form in little handfuls. There is a smell of wet soil in the air. No priest, no cross. There's no religion here. Overhead, a documentary about the funerary rites of lost cultures: images of pyres, sculpted bones, and boiled wheat berries light up the sky.

* * *

We walk the two blocks to Mikey's bar in silence. It's uphill and the paths are narrow and overgrown, so it takes some time, but when we reach the top, the whole city is laid out before us, all the way to the surrounding wall. From up here, it looks like a city slowly being swallowed by its parks. Most of the buildings are covered in ivy or moss. Inch by inch, the roads surrender to the adjacent shrubbery. And every once in a while, the disintegrating sculptures of endangered species poke through foliage: an elephant, a tiger, a whale, the slender neck of a giraffe.

"The smell," Sophie says. "Did you notice? It's gone."

"What smell?"

"Rot. Old age."

I sniff the air like a dog. She's right. "Maybe it's the hill. It doesn't carry all the way up here."

Sophie nods towards Mikey's. "Shall we?" she asks, playful. Carefree. You've always been this way, Sophie, Sophie, like a child.

Inside, it's warm and comfortable. Old tunes make it all better, somehow; places feel brighter, conversation flows easier. If only nostalgia were my thing.

"So, are you still with Johnny?" I ask. I sip my spiked tea. The alcohol stings my eyes.

"Yes. Are you still with Alex?" she asks back.

"Alex died twelve years ago," I respond, dryly. That was vindictive, boy.

She looks at me, and I can almost see my colleague as she was all those years ago, when we were both young and eager. Her hair is thinner, her skin shaggy and yellow, but she hasn't changed at all. Not really.

"I'm so sorry to hear that, Eddie."

I nod, suddenly embarrassed.

We listen to the music for a while. I think of Annie's air-filled belly, growing and growing until she takes flight; an inflatable mother hovering over the city.

Sophie tells me about her and Johnny's hobbies: tinkering with broken gadgets for their neighbours, recycling the city, dehydrating fruit. As you do.

"I used to do calligraphy," she says, "but my eyesight isn't what it was." She stirs her drink. "So? What are you up to?"

I shrug. She rests her hand on the table, not too close to mine, but close enough. As if saying, *I'm here. I'm safe.*

I look at her hand, but I don't dare touch it. Why not tell her, boy? Why not?

"I don't sleep." I look at the few patrons around Mikey's. Dusty old things. "There's this banging sound in the house. Something's broken and I can't get a moment's peace."

Her lips are pressed together into a thin line, but she looks at me with that encouraging stare of hers. The one that says, *keep going, boy. Sophie's here. Sophie knows what you need better than you do.* Maybe she does.

"It's like I live in a movie," I say. "Sometimes I think a nice young person will discover the last human sperm in an ultra-secret facility somewhere in the world and humankind will reemerge from its ashes. But then I remember; there is no nice young person. And the youngest womb in the world is too old to bear children."

Sophie reclaims her hand and takes little sips from her gin and tonic, avoiding my gaze now.

"Did we make a mistake, Sophie?"

"Even if I could bear children, I couldn't bear to bring them into this world. That was my opinion back then, and I have not changed my mind."

"It was fascist."

"Yes. It was also idealistic. And kind. It was the kind thing to do."

Then we talk about the weather and our lives with and without our partners and we finish our drinks with scarcely another word about our work. What would be the point, right?

Outside, we part with a peck on the cheek. It feels normal and familiar, as if all the years since the last time we saw each other were but a long weekend. Surely, we would meet at the office the next day, pick it all up right where we left off. Except all our work is already done. Finished.

"It was good to see you, Eddie," she says.

I smile goodbye.

There are so few of us left to mourn the dead, Sophie, I want to tell her as she turns around and leaves. *Who will mourn the last of us?*

Above me, a pair of giant lips inhale against the night.

* * *

I try to postpone my return home as long as I can, avoid the sleeplessness that awaits me there. I take the long way back, making a small detour to visit the wall. It hugs the city, shadowing its edges, its bulk towering over it, protective and ominous. I haven't been here in months; I've almost forgotten this sense of being enclosed, surrounded.

I place both palms on the cement and bring my ear to the wall's facade. Cold. Behind the cold, the wild rumble of the ocean, the pounding of waves, thunder. I close my eyes, and there I am, watching from a sandy beach, tormented by the phantom of a strong, youthful shoulder breaking the surface of a long-ago sea.

Another wave crashes against the wall, seeps into me through my palms and my ear and my cheekbone. It travels all the way to my core, rocks me. My pulse quickens, thunderous in my ears. I take a step back from the wall and look up, hoping for a black-and-white oldie, perhaps, or a travel show. The Sky-V remains dark.

Later, on my way home, it indulges me with a sunset and I, for once, for a little while, allow myself the reverie, its sharp and spiteful stab.

* * *

The sun was about to set. It was the night before we sealed the city for good, to fend off the rising sea that had already swallowed so many seaside towns and villages. The last segment of the wall would be placed at the top of the southeast section the next morning in an open ceremony. They called it a celebration, but I was not sure why. It was protection, yes, but it was such a final thing to do, so abrupt and irrevocable.

Hundreds of people had gathered to see off those leaving the city to try their luck overseas. The sterilization project was complete everywhere, of course – not always democratically or peacefully, but that didn't matter; what mattered was that there would be no shortage of resources at their final destinations. A dozen ships would sail away that night, each holding more than six thousand people. The rest of us would stay behind, each one carefully evaluated, our existence calculated and summarized as estimates of our needs: how much food, how much water, how much energy. As if that was all that was left for us to do: eat, drink, shit, get warm. But it wasn't. You can't measure out a life like that. The Sky-V offered 24-hour news coverage of the events: diagrams of the wall, analyses of long-term resources for the remaining citizens, interviews and short retrospectives into the lives of those departing. The human side of things.

Alex had stayed home, couldn't bear all the goodbyes, but most of all couldn't come to terms with my role in all of this. Sophie was there. Fittingly. She took my hand in hers and squeezed. She was losing a sister today, but she wouldn't allow herself to tear up. I wasn't even sure if she allowed herself to feel it. Or feel anything at all.

It wasn't just Sophie, though. People seemed oddly calm – almost resigned, complacent. Some did break through their composure, sure, there were a few screams and tears, but mostly it was quiet, and for that all the more irritating, as if all the fight had already been beaten out of them. There would be no more riots here. *Why are you so calm?* I remember thinking. *How can you be so calm? Have I done my job this well?* I wanted to grab each one of them, every sister, every brother, every partner, and shake them. *This is it*, I wanted to say. *Do you get it? There is no going back.* I didn't, though. I wouldn't. This was partly my doing, after all, wasn't it?

The ships sailed soon enough, the crowd dispersed, the sky went blank. Sophie let my hand go.

"I could use a drink," she said.

I nodded. "Wanna go to Mikey's?"

"No." She turned away from the wall and put her hands in her pockets. "Some place without a view."

* * *

I lie in bed waiting, wishing for sleep to finally take hold, when the sound returns and fills the night. *Thumpa-thumpa. Thumpa-thumpa.* The banging drives away the drowsiness. I glance at the clock on my bed stand. It's too late to call the Handy, so I decide to go down and check the mechanical room myself. *Thumpa-thumpa, boy. Thumpa-thumpa.* I leave the apartment in my slippers. I'm not sure what looking at the engines will even tell me – I'm no Handy, after all – but I make my way down to the basement anyway.

The mechanical room is illuminated by yellow fluorescent lamps. There is no banging sound down here, only the low hum of the machinery. It's old but efficient. I put a hand on one of the machines. It feels alive and vibrating, and suddenly I'm flooded with this indescribable exhaustion, this despair – to exist non-stop for so many years. The drudgery of it. "The whole catastrophe," Alex called it.

I walk slowly to the door at the other end of the room. It's unlocked, so I push in and turn on the light switch. It's a storage room, filled with clutter. There's no sound here either. Only clothes in plastic bags, worn shoes, a few old toys. The yellow light makes everything look odd and morbid, like a faded photograph. I catch myself thinking about all these things, these objects that people will leave behind when they're gone. The world will be overflowing with clutter. Just things, without owners, alone on the empty earth. A shanty town of the extinct. The world as landfill.

* * *

I spend the rest of the night sitting at the kitchen table, waiting for the first light to break over the wall and thinking of Annie's belly ballooning with loneliness. I decide I need to tell her about my work in the old days. Try redemption on for size.

On the way to her house, the propagandist in me rehearses his old argument: *We made the right choice. We made the only decision an animal would never make. Don't you see, Annie? In negating our own survival for the sake of all the rest, we became truly human.*

It is the barking that interrupts me.

A man is walking a block ahead of me. He's wearing a raincoat and an old-style hat. He's carrying a plastic bag filled with something heavy. He enters the yard of the abandoned school. There are only dogs there now. Hundreds and hundreds of dogs.

"Hey!" I shout. "Don't go in there!" I hear the metallic sound of the gate closing behind him and start running towards the school as fast as my knees and cane will carry me. I lean against the schoolyard railing, my lungs burning, my breath scraping my throat. I push my hand against my chest. This is certainly not a movie, boy. Hold on to your heart.

"Hey, come out," I try to yell, but a coughing fit seizes me. All I can do is watch while the man takes off his coat and hat and lets them drop on the cement as the dogs gather around him. I count dozens of them. The man unties the top of the plastic bag and takes out what looks like raw, blood-dripping meat. He only needs to toss a couple of shreds for the dogs to respond. The animals growl and fight each other for the meat. They go for the bag first. There are at least fifty, sixty, a hundred dogs around him now. They go for the throat next, but the man doesn't fight. He gives in, offers himself up.

I turn around. I try to block out the sound of gnashing, gnawing, tearing. I push myself to walk fast, faster. I'm almost running when the banging arrests me and I stumble to my knees. The thumping sound, loud and clear, fills the city. I look up, wondering if the sound system was somehow restored, or if I've finally lost my mind like Sophie always said I would. The Sky-V shows a person standing in the middle of a desert, a lonely tree on fire. Then, rooms filled with sand.

"I don't understand," I croak. "What are you showing me?"

Thumpa-thumpa. Thumpa-thumpa.

I lie down on the street, and wait for the sound to relent, for the images to go away.

When the sky gives up, I climb to my feet and walk towards Annie's house under blank weather. The propagandist in me has forgotten what he wanted to say to her. I'll tell her about that person in the schoolyard, I decide. We'll play draughts, and she'll win like she always does. She'll tell me she wants to throw a funeral party. Everyone who's still alive will be invited.

I'm one block away from Annie's building when the banging returns and fills my head like a flood of something solid pushing against the walls of my skull. I realize it's changed since the first time I heard it, slowed down, and growing slower and slower.

My heart thumps hard inside my chest.

Thumpa-thumpa, boy, it says. *Thumpa-thumpa.*

And so, in a final bout of guilt or self-importance, it hits me, and I get it now, what it is, what it's always been – this lub-dub of the world's heart, slowly coming to a halt –

The Eternal Adam

Jules Verne

ZARTOGSOFR-AI-SR – meaning 'Doctor, third male representative of the hundred and first generation in the Sofr Family' – was slowly following the principal street of Basidra, the capital of the Hars-Iten-Schu – otherwise known as 'The Empire of the Four Seas.'

Four seas, indeed: the Tubélone or northern, the Ehone or southern, the Spone or eastern, and the Mérone or western. They bounded that vast irregularly-shaped country, whose most remote points – to use the means of reckoning familiar to the reader – lay respectively in longitude 14° E and 72° W, and in latitude 54° N and 55° S.[1] As for the size of these seas, how was it to be calculated, even approximately, for they all merged together, so that a seaman leaving any one of their shores and always following a straight course was bound to reach the shore diametrically opposite? For nowhere on the surface of the globe did there exist any land other than the Hars-Iten-Schu.

Sofr walked slowly, partly because it was very warm; the torrid season was beginning, and on Basidra, situated on the edge of the Spone-Schu, or Eastern Sea, less than 20° N of the Equator, a terrible cataract of rays was falling from the sun, then almost in the zenith.

But not only lassitude and the heat but also the weight of his thoughts slowed the step of Sofr, the savant Zartog. As he wiped his forehead with a heedless hand he recalled the session held the previous evening, when so many eloquent orators, among whom he had the honour of being counted, had magnificently celebrated the hundred and ninety-fifth anniversary of their empire's foundation.

Some had reviewed its history, which was that of all mankind. They had described the Mahart-Iten-Schu, the Land of the Four Seas, as divided at first between an immense number of savage peoples who knew nothing of one another. It was to them that the most ancient traditions went back. As to what had gone before, nobody knew anything, and the natural sciences had hardly begun to throw a gleam of light into the impenetrable shadows of the past. Certainly those far-distant times evaded critical history, whose earliest vestiges consisted of vague notions regarding these age-old scattered peoples.

For more than eight thousand years, the history of the Mahart-Iten-Schu, gradually getting more complete and more exact, described only conflicts and wars, at first of individual against individual, then of family against family, then of tribe against tribe. Each living creature, each community, small or large, had throughout the course of the ages no other objective than to ensure its own supremacy over its competitors and to strive, with varying and often contradictory fortunes, to subject them to its laws.

After these eight thousand years, human memory had become somewhat more precise. At the opening of the second of the four great ages into which the annals of the Mahart-Iten-Schu were commonly divided, legend had begun appropriately to merit the name of history. Nonetheless, history or legend, the subject-matter of the story hardly changed at all: always massacres and slaughters – no longer, admittedly, of tribe by tribe but henceforth of people by people – so much so, indeed, that on the whole this second period was not so very different from the first.

And it was still the same with the third period which, after having lasted nearly six centuries, had ended hardly two hundred years ago. More atrocious still perhaps, this third period during which, grouped into countless armies, mankind, with its insatiable rage, had watered the earth with its own blood.

Somewhat less than eight centuries, indeed, before the day on which Zartog Sofr was following the principal street of Basidra, humanity had been rent by vast convulsions. Then weapons, fire, violence, having already accomplished much of their inevitable work and the weak having succumbed to the strong, the people of the Mahart-Iten-Schu had formed three distinct nations, in each of which time had lessened the differences between the conquerors and the conquered of the past.

Then it was that one of these nations had undertaken to subdue its neighbours. Situated near the centre of the Mahart-Iten-Schu, the Andarti-Hai-Sammgor, the Men of the Brazen Face, had struggled mercilessly to enlarge their frontiers, within which their spirited and prolific race was being choked.

One after the other, at the cost of age-long wars, they had overcome the Andarti-Mahart-Horis, the Men of the Snow Country, who inhabited the southern lands, and the Andarti-Mitra-Psul, the Men of the Motionless Star, whose empire was situated more towards the north and the west.

Nearly two hundred years had elapsed since the final revolt of these two peoples had been drowned in torrents of blood, and the land had at last known an era of peace. This was the fourth period of its history. One solitary empire having replaced the three nations of olden time, and the law of Basidra having been enforced everywhere, political unity had tended to merge the races. No longer was anything said about the men with the Brazen Faces, the men of the Snow Country, the Men of the Motionless Star. The earth now bore only one unique populace, the Andart'-Iten-Schu, the Men of the Four Seas, which in itself included all the others.

But now, after these two hundred years of peace, a fifth period seemed to be opening. For some time disquieting rumours, arising nobody knew where, had been going the rounds. They suggested that certain thinkers were trying to arouse in the human heart ancestral memories long believed to have been abolished. The ancient emotions of the race were being revived in a novel form characterised by newly-coined words. People were now speaking of 'atavism', 'affinities', 'nationalities', and so forth – all recently created terms which, answering as they did to some new need, had now gained recognition.

Based upon common origin, physical appearance, moral tendency, mutual interest, or simply upon district or climate, groups were appearing, and they were obviously getting larger and showing signs of unrest. Where would this growing evolution lead? Would the empire, scarcely formed though it was, start falling to pieces? Would the Mahart-Iten-Schu be divided, as of old, between a large number of nations? Or would it, to maintain its unity, have to seek recourse to the frightful hecatombs which, lasting for thousands of years, have turned the earth into a charnel house?

With a shake of the head Sofr cast off these thoughts. The future was something which neither he nor anyone else could possibly know. So why depress himself by the prospect of uncertain events? This was no day to brood over these sinister possibilities. Today everybody was in a cheerful mood, and nothing was thought about except the august grandeur of

Mogar-Si, twelfth emperor of the Hars-Iten-Schu, whose sceptre was leading the universe to its glorious destiny.

What was more, a zartog by no means lacked grounds for rejoicing. Not only had the historian retraced the pageant of the Mahart-Iten-Schu; a constellation of savants, to mark this grandiose anniversary, had, each in his own specialty, drawn up the balance-sheet of human knowledge, and had announced the point to which its age-long efforts had brought mankind. And if the former had to some extent aroused distressing thoughts by recalling by what a slow and tortuous route it had freed itself from its bestial origin, the others had stimulated their hearers' legitimate pride.

Yes, in very truth, it was bound to inspire admiration, the comparison between what man had been when he arrived naked and helpless upon the earth and what he was today. Throughout the centuries, in spite of discords and fratricidal hates, never for one instant had he interrupted his struggle against nature; ever had he increased the scope of his victory.

At first slow, during the last two hundred years his triumphant march had been astonishingly accelerated; and the stability of political institutions and the universal peace which this had produced had stimulated a marvellous advance in science. Humanity lived not only by its limbs but by its mind; instead of exhausting itself in senseless wars, it had thought, – and that was why, in the course of the last two centuries, it had advanced ever more rapidly towards knowledge and the taming of material nature.

So, as beneath the scorching sun he followed the long Basidran street, Sofr mentally sketched in bold outline the picture of the conquests man had made.

First of all – though this was lost in the darkness of time – mankind had invented writing, so as to perpetuate his thoughts. Then – the invention went back more than five hundred years – he had found a method of spreading the written word far and wide in an endless number of copies by the aid of a block cast once and for all. It was really from this invention that all the others had sprung. It was thanks to this that so many brains had come into action, that the intelligence of each had grown from that of his neighbour, and that discoveries, both theoretical and practical, had so greatly multiplied that they could no longer be counted.

Man had penetrated into the bowels of the earth and had extracted its coal, the generous donor of heat; he had liberated the latent power of water, so that steam now drew the heavy trains along the iron rails or drove a host of machines, as powerful as they were delicate and precise. Thanks to these machines, he could weave the vegetable fibres and do what he pleased with metal, marble or rock.

In a realm that was less concrete or at all events of less direct and immediate utility, he had gradually unravelled the mystery of numbers and entered ever more deeply into the infinity of mathematical truth. By this means his thought had penetrated into the sky... He knew that the sun was nothing but a star gravitating through space according to rigorous laws, dragging with its flaming orb its escort of the seven planets.[2] He understood the art both of combining certain natural bodies into new substances with which they had nothing in common, and of dividing certain other bodies into their constituent and primordial elements. He had subjected to analysis sound, heat and light, and was beginning to realise their nature and their laws.

Fifty years ago he had learned how to generate that force whose most terrifying manifestations are lightning and thunder, and he had at once made it his slave. Already that mysterious agent transmitted the written thought over incalculable distances; tomorrow it would transmit sound, and next day, no doubt, the light[3]... Yes, man was great, greater than the immense universe of which, on some day yet to come, he would be the master...

But for him to possess the truth in its integrity, one last problem remained to be solved. 'This man, master of the world, who was he? Whence came he? To what unknown ends did his tireless efforts lead?'

It was precisely this vast subject that Zartog Sofr had just discussed during the ceremony from which he had emerged. Admittedly he had done no more than to skim over its surface, for such a problem was at the moment insoluble and would no doubt long remain so.

Yet a few vague gleams had already begun to throw light upon the mystery. And of all these gleams was it not Zartog Sofr who had thrown the most powerful when, by systematising and codifying the patient observations of his predecessors and of himself, he had arrived at his law of the evolution of living matter, a law universally accepted and which had found nobody whatever to contradict it?

This theory rested upon a threefold base.

First there was the science of geology which, born on the day when the bowels of the earth had first been dug into, had reached perfection through the development of mining technique. The earth's crust was now so perfectly known that they had dared to fix its age at four hundred thousand years, and that of Mahart-Iten-Schu, as it was now, at twenty thousand years. This continent had formerly slept beneath the waters of the sea, as was testified to by the thick layer of marine silt which interruptedly covered the rocky beds immediately below. By what force had it been lifted above the waves? Doubtless by the contraction of the cooling globe. But whatever the truth about that, the elevation of Mahart-Iten-Schu from the sea must be regarded as proved.

The natural sciences had furnished Sofr with the two other foundations of his system, by making clear the close interrelationship on the one hand of the plants, on the other of the animals. He had gone still further: he had proved from the available evidence that almost all the plants still in existence were connected with their ancestor, a seaweed, and that all the animals of earth or air were descended from those of the sea. By a slow but incessant evolution, they had gradually adapted themselves to living conditions at first resembling, then more distant from, those of their primitive life. Thus, from stage to stage, they had given birth to most of the living beings which peopled earth and sky.

But this ingenious theory was unfortunately not unassailable. That living beings of the animal or vegetable orders had descended from marine ancestors, that seemed incontestable for almost all of them, but not for all. There still indeed existed a few plants and animals which it seemed impossible to connect with the aquatic types. That was one of the two weak points of his system.

The other weak point – and Sofr never concealed this – was mankind. Between man and the animals there was no point of union. Certainly their primordial functions and properties – such as respiration, nutrition, and movement – were similar and were obviously carried out or showed themselves in a similar manner, but an impassable gulf existed between the exterior forms, the number, and the arrangement of their organs. If, by a chain of which few of the links were missing, the great majority of the animals could be associated with their ancestors from the sea, no such affiliation was admissible as regards man. To preserve the theory of evolution intact, the truth of a hypothesis had to be assumed gratuitously, that of a stock common to the inhabitants of the waters and to man, a stock of which nothing, absolutely nothing, demonstrated the former existence.

At one time Sofr had hoped to find in the ground the arguments that favoured his predilection. At his instigation and under his direction, digging had been carried out over a long succession of years, but only to lead to results diametrically opposed to those he had hoped for.

Below a thin layer of humus formed by the decomposition of plants and animals like or similar to those of every day, there had come the thick bed of silt, and in this these vestiges of the past had changed in nature. Within this silt, no more of the contemporary flora or fauna, but a quantity of fossils exclusively marine resembling types which were still living, most of them in the oceans surrounding the Mahart-Iten-Schu.

What was to be inferred from this, if it were not that the geologists were right in stating that the continent had once served as the floor of those same oceans? And that neither had Sofr been wrong in affirming the marine origin of the contemporary fauna and flora? Since, but for exceptions so rare that they might rightly be regarded as monstrosities, the aquatic and terrestrial forms were the only ones of which any trace had been found, the latter must necessarily have been engendered by the former...

Unfortunately for the generalisation of the system, other finds were made. Scattered throughout the whole thickness of the humus, and even in the most superficial part of the deposit or silt, innumerable human bones were brought to the daylight. Nothing exceptional in the structure of these fragmentary skeletons, and Sofr had to give up asking for intermediate organisms whose existence his theory asserted: these bones were human bones, neither more nor less.

However one fairly remarkable peculiarity was not slow to be realised. Up to a certain antiquity, which could be roughly evaluated as two or three thousand years, the older the ossuaries were the smaller the skulls within them. Beyond that epoch, on the other hand, progress was reversed and thenceforward the further one went back into the past, the bigger was the capacity of the skulls, and the larger therefore were the brains which they had held.

The very largest were found among the debris, somewhat scanty to be sure, found on the surface of the layer of silt. The conscientious examination of these venerable remains admitted of no doubt that the men living at that distant epoch had a cerebral development far superior to that of their successors – including the very contemporaries of Zartog Sofr. So that, during a period of a hundred and sixty or a hundred and seventy centuries, there had been an obvious retrogression, followed by a new ascent.

Disturbed by these strange facts, Sofr pushed his researches further. The bed of silt was dug through and through; its thickness showed that at the most moderate computation it could not have taken less than fifteen or twenty thousand years to form. Beyond, much surprise was felt at the discovery of the scanty remains of another layer of humus. Then, below that humus, there was rock, its nature varying from place to place.

But what raised his astonishment to its height was the discovery of some debris, undoubtedly of human origin, obtained from these mysterious depths. They were some pieces of bones obviously of human type, and also some odds and ends of weapons and implements, potsherds, vestiges of inscriptions in a language unknown, fragments of hard stone exquisitely worked, some sculptured into statues which were still almost intact, and some into the remains of delicately worked architecture, and so forth. Taken together, these discoveries led logically to the conclusion that about forty thousand years earlier, and thus twenty thousand years before the rise – nobody knew how or where – of the first representatives of contemporary man, human beings were already living in the same places and had arrived at a high degree of civilisation.

This was, indeed, the conclusion generally accepted, though there was at least one dissident.

This dissident was no other than Sofr. To admit that other races of men, separated from their successors by a gulf of twenty thousand years, had at one time peopled the earth, was, to his mind, sheer folly. What would have become, in that event, of the descendants of ancestors so long vanished? Rather than welcome so absurd an hypothesis it would be better to suspend judgment. Although these strange facts were unexplained, it did not follow that they were inexplicable; sooner or later, they would be interpreted. Until then it was better to ignore them, and to keep to the following principles, so fully satisfactory to the reason:

Planetary life might be divided into two phases: before and during the age of man. During the first the earth, in a state of perpetual change, was for that very reason unhabitable and uninhabited. During the second the earth's crust had gained enough cohesion to stabilise it. At once, having at last a solid substratum, life had appeared. It had originated in the simplest forms, and became ever more complicated to reach its climax in man, its last and most perfect expression. Hardly had he appeared upon earth than he at once began his endless ascent. At a slow but sure pace he was on his way towards his goal, the perfect knowledge and the absolute domination of the universe...

Borne away by the heat of his convictions, Sofr had gone past his house. He turned round fuming.

"What!" he said to himself, "to admit that man – forty thousand years ago! – had reached a civilisation comparable with – if not superior to – that which we enjoy today? That its knowledge and achievements have vanished, without leaving the slightest trace, so completely that their descendants had to start right at the beginning, as if they were the pioneers in a world as yet uninhabited? ... But that would be to deny the future, to announce that our efforts are all in vain, and that all progress is as precarious and as uncertain as a bubble of foam on the surface of the waves!"

In front of his house he stopped.

"Upsa ni! ... hartchok! (No, indeed o! ...), Andant mir' hoe spha! ... (Man is the master of things...)" – he murmured as he opened the door.

When the Zartog was somewhat rested, he lunched with a good appetite, then stretched himself out for his daily siesta. But the questions over which he had been pondering as he was coming home still obsessed him and drove away sleep.

Greatly as he wished to demonstrate the complete unity of nature's methods, he had too critical a mind to fail to realise how weak his system was when it touched on the problem of man's origin and development. To adapt the facts to agree with a foregone conclusion, that is one way of convincing others, but not of convincing oneself.

If instead of being a savant, a most eminent zartog, Sofr had been classed among the illiterates he would have been less embarrassed. The people, in fact, without wasting their time in deep reflections, were content to accept with their eyes closed the ancient legend which from time immemorial had been handed down from father to son. Explaining one mystery by another, they had ascribed the origin of man to the intervention of a Higher Will. There was a time when that extra-terrestrial power had created out of nothing Hedom and Hiva, the first man and first woman, whose descendants had populated the earth. After that everything followed quite simply.

Too simply! As Sofr reflected. When you have given up trying to understand something, it is only too easy to bring in the intervention of a deity. But that makes it useless to look for an answer to the riddles of the universe, for no sooner are the questions asked than they are suppressed.

If only that legend had even the semblance of a serious basis! ... But it was founded upon nothing. It was only a tradition, born in the epochs of ignorance, and thence transmitted from age to age. As for that name 'Hedom!' – where did that strange vocable come from, for it did not seem to belong to the language of the Andart'-Iten-Schu?

Confronted only with that trifling philological difficulty countless savants had worn themselves out unable to find any satisfactory answer.... All nonsense that was unworthy of a zartog's attention.

Sofr was still agitated as he went into his garden. Still, this was the hour when he usually did so. The setting sun shed a less scorching heat over the earth, and a warm breeze was beginning to blow in from the Spone-Schu. The Zartog wandered along the paths in the shadow of the trees whose trembling leaves murmured in the wind from the open sea, and little by little his nerves regained their accustomed calm. He was at last able to shake off these troublesome thoughts and to enjoy the open air, to feel an interest in the fruits which formed the wealth of his garden, and in the flowers, its ornaments.

His chance footsteps bringing him back towards the house, he stopped on the edge of a deep excavation in which were scattered a number of tools. There, before long, would be laid the foundations of a new building which would double the size of his laboratory. But on this general holiday the workers had abandoned their task, and had gone off to enjoy themselves.

Sofr was rather casually estimating the extent of the work already done and still remaining to do when in the shadows of the excavation a shining point attracted his gaze. Interested, he went down into the depths of the hole, and freed a strange-looking object from the earth which partly covered it.

Returned to the daylight, the Zartog examined his find. It was a sort of container, constructed of some unknown metal of a greyish colour and a granular texture, and whose brightness had been dimmed by its long stay in the ground. At one third of its length, a crack showed that the case consisted of two parts, one inside the other. He tried to open it.

At his first attempt the metal, disintegrated by time, fell into dust and revealed a second object which it contained.

The material of which this object was formed was as great a novelty for the Zartog as the metal which had hitherto protected it. It was a roll of sheets superimposed and covered with strange signs, whose regularity indicated that they were written characters of an unfamiliar type. Sofr had never seen anything like them or even distantly resembling them.

Trembling with emotion, the zartog hunied to shut himself in his laboratory. After carefully spreading out the precious document he began to study it.

Yes, it was indeed writing, nothing could be more certain than that. But it was no less certain that this writing resembled none of those which, since the beginning of historic time, had been used anywhere on the surface of the earth.

Whence came that document? What did it signify? Such were the two questions which at once confronted Sofr's mind.

To reply to the first he had of course to be able to reply to the second. So it was first a question of reading and then of translating – for it could be affirmed *à priori* that the language in which this document was written was as unknown as its writing.

Would that be impossible? The Zartog Sofr did not think so. Without further delay he set feverishly to work.

The work lasted long, very long, for whole years. Sofr did not give up. Without letting himself get discouraged, he continued his methodical study of the mysterious document, advancing step by step towards the light. At last the day came when he grasped the key to this undecipherable riddle, the day when, though still with much hesitation and more trouble, he could translate it into the tongue of the Men of the Four Seas.

And when that day came, Zartog Sofr-Ai-Sr read what follows:

Rosario, May 24th, 2.

I date the opening of my narrative in this way although it was really drawn up much more recently and in very different surroundings. But in such a matter order is to my mind imperiously necessary, and for this reason I have adopted the form of a 'journal' written from day to day.

Thus it is May 24th that opens the narration of those frightful happenings which I propose to describe for the enlightenment of those who come after me – if indeed mankind is still entitled to count on any future whatever.

In what language shall I write? In English or in Spanish, which I speak fluently? No! I shall write in the language of my own country: in French.

That day, May 24th, I had invited a few friends to my villa in Rosario.

Rosario is or rather was a Mexican town, on the shore of the Pacific, a little to the south of the Gulf of California. About ten years previously I had settled there to direct the exploitation of a silver-mine which I owned. My affairs had gone surprisingly well. I was rich, very rich indeed – that word makes me laugh today! – and I was intending before long to go back to my own country, France.

My villa, a very luxurious one, was situated on the highest point of a large garden which sloped down towards the sea and ended abruptly in a steep cliff, over a hundred yards high. To its rear the ground rose still further, and by using the zig-zag roads we could reach the crest of the mountains at a height of more than fifteen hundred yards. It was a very pleasant run – I had often climbed it in my car, a fine powerful open car of thirty-five horse-power, one of the best French makes.

I had been living at Rosario with my son Jean, a fine lad of twenty, when, on the death of some relatives distant by blood but near to my heart I welcomed their daughter Hélène, an orphan totally unprovided for. Since then five years had elapsed. My son Jean was now twenty-five and my ward Hélène twenty; in my secret heart I destined them for one another.

Our wants were attended to by a valet, Germain, by Modeste Simonat, an expert chauffeur, and by two servants Edith and Mary, the daughters of my gardener George Raleigh and his wife Anna.

That day, May 24th, there were eight of us sitting round my table, in the light of lamps fed by electrogenic groups installed in the garden. In addition to the master of the house, his son, and his ward there were five others, three belonging to the Anglo-Saxon race and two to the Mexican peoples.

Dr. Bathurst figured among the former and Dr. Moreno among the latter. Both were savants in the broadest acceptance of the word, but this did not keep them from being very seldom in agreement. At heart they were splendid fellows and the best friends in the world.

The two other Anglo-Saxons were Williamson, the owner of an important fishery in Rosario; and Rowling, an enterprising business man who had founded near the town a number of market gardens from which he was reaping a rich fortune.

As for the last of the guests, it was Señor Mendoza, president of the Rosario law-courts, a worthy man with a cultivated mind and of high integrity.

We reached the end of the meal without any noteworthy incident. What we talked about till then I have forgotten. Not so, on the other hand, regarding what we said as we smoked our cigars.

Not that our remarks were of any importance in themselves, but the brutal commentary soon to be made upon them could not fail to give them a certain piquancy. For this reason I have never been able to get them out of my mind.

We had come – how, it doesn't matter! – to speak of the wonderful progress accomplished by man. Then Dr. Bathurst said:

"It's a fact that if Adam (which naturally, as an Anglo-Saxon, he pronounced Edem) and Eve (which of course he pronounced Iva) were to come back upon the earth, they'd have a nice surprise!"

That was the beginning of the discussion. A fervent Darwinian and a convinced supporter of natural selection, Moreno asked Bathurst ironically if he seriously believed in the legend of the Earthly Paradise. Bathurst replied that at any rate he believed in God and that as the existence of Adam and Eve was stated in the Bible, he refused to question it.

Moreno retorted that he believed in God at least as much as his adversary, but it was quite likely that the first man and the first woman were only myths and symbols. So there was nothing irreligious in supposing that the Bible had meant thus to typify the breath of life introduced by the Creative Power into the first cell, from which all the others had then evolved.

Bathurst retorted that this explanation was specious and that for his part he thought it more complimentary to be the direct work of Divinity rather than to be descended from it by the intermediary of more or less simian primates…

I saw that the time had come for the discussion to get heated, but it suddenly ended, the two adversaries having chanced to find some common ground. It is this way, indeed, that such things usually finish.

This time, returning to their first subject, the two antagonists agreed, whatever might be his origin, in admiring the high degree of culture that man had attained, they enumerated his conquests with pride. We all joined in. Bathurst praised chemistry, brought to such a degree of perfection that it was tending to disappear and merge into physics; the two subjects were now becoming one, whose object was the study of immanent energy. Moreno praised medicine and surgery, thanks to which such researches had been made into the intimate nature of the phenomena of life that in the near future the immortality of living organisms might well be hoped for. They both congratulated themselves on the heights attained by astronomy. Were we not now in communication, failing the stars, with seven of the planets of the solar system? [4]

Wearied out by their enthusiasm, the two snatched some moments' rest. The others, in their turn, took advantage of this to put in a word, and we entered upon the vast field of practical inventions which have so profoundly modified human conditions. We praised the railways and the steamers, used for the carriage of heavy and cumbersome merchandise; the economical aeronefs, used by travellers who are not pressed for time; the pneumatic or electro-ionic tubes that traverse every continent and sea, used by people in a hurry. We praised the countless machines, each more ingenious than the other, of which, in certain industries, one alone can perform the work of a hundred men. We praised printing and the photography of colour and of light, sound, heat, and all the vibrations of the ether. We especially praised electricity, that agent so adaptable, so docile, and so thoroughly understood in its properties and in its nature, which enables us, with-out the slightest mechanical connection, either to work any mechanism whatever or to steer a vessel across or under the sea or through the air; either to write, to converse, or to see one another no matter how great the distance between us.

It was quite a dithyramb in which, I must admit, I took part. We were all agreed that mankind had reached an intellectual level unknown before our time, and that this justified us in believing in its definitive triumph over nature.

"However," broke in the gentle voice of President Mendoza, taking advantage of the silence which followed, "I will venture to say that there may have been peoples, now vanished without leaving the slightest trace, who reached a civilisation equal or analogous to our own."

"Which?" asked everybody at once.

"Oh well! … The Babylonians, for example."

There followed a burst of mirth. To dare to compare the Babylonians with modern man!

"The Egyptians," Don Mendoza went on quietly.

We laughed louder than ever.

"There are the Atlanteans, too – it's only our ignorance that makes us regard them as legendary," the President continued.

"You might add that an infinity of other peoples, older than the Atlanteans themselves, may have appeared, prospered, and died out without our knowing anything about them!"

Don Mendoza insisted on his paradox and, so as not to hurt his feelings, we agreed to pretend to take him seriously.

"But look here, my dear president," Moreno insinuated, in the sort of tone one uses to make a child see reason, "you don't want to claim, I suppose, that any of those ancient peoples could be compared to ourselves? … In morality, I agree that they reached the same degree of culture, but in material things!"

"Why not?" Don Mendoza objected.

"Because," Bathurst hastened to explain, "the great thing about our inventions is that they spread instantaneously over the earth: the disappearance of one people, or even a large number of peoples, would leave the sum of human progress intact. For human achievements to be lost, all mankind would have to vanish at once. Is that, I ask you, an admissible hypothesis? …"

While we were talking in this way, effects and causes went on interacting throughout the infinite universe, and less than a minute after Dr. Bathurst had asked this question, their final result would justify Mendoza's scepticism only too completely.

But we had no suspicion of this, and we went on talking quietly. Some leaning over the backs of their chairs, others with their elbows on the tables, we were all turning pitying glances on Mendoza, who, as we thought, had been completely floored by Bathurst's reply.

"First," the President replied unemotionally, "we can well believe that in the old days the earth had fewer inhabitants than it has now, so that one nation might be the only one to possess universal knowledge. Then I don't see anything absurd, on the face of it, in supposing that the whole surface of the globe should be overwhelmed at once!"

"Nonsense" we exclaimed in chorus.

It was at that very moment that there came the cataclysm.

We had hardly chorused "Nonsense!" when a terrible din broke out. The ground trembled and gave way under our feet, the villa shook on its foundations.

We rose, we jostled together; the victims of an indescribable terror, we rushed outside.

Scarcely had we crossed the threshold than the house collapsed, burying in its ruins President Mendoza and my valet Germain, who had been coming out last. After a few seconds' natural consternation we were going to try to rescue them when we saw Raleigh, my gardener, followed by his wife, rushing from his house at the end of the garden.

"The sea! ... The sea! ..." he was shouting at the top of his voice.

Turning towards the ocean, I stood there motionless, stupefied. It was not that I realised what I was seeing, but I felt at once that my whole surroundings had completely changed. And was not that enough to chill the heart with fright when the whole aspect of nature, that nature which we always think of as essentially changeless, could be so strangely transformed in a few seconds?

Yet I was not slow in regaining my presence of mind. The true superiority of man is not to conquer and dominate nature. It is, for the thinking man, to understand it, to hold the whole universe in the microcosm of his mind. It is, for the man of action, to keep a calm spirit before the revolt of matter. It is to tell himself: 'I may be destroyed, yes! but unnerved, never!'

As soon as I had regained my calm, I realised how the scene before my eyes differed from what I was accustomed to see. The cliff had vanished, simply vanished, and my garden was sloping down to the edge of the sea, whose waves, after destroying the gardener's house, were beating furiously against the lowermost flower-beds.

As it was hardly admissible that the level of the sea had risen, it necessarily followed that that of the land had fallen. The subsidence was more than a hundred yards, for that had hitherto been the height of the cliff but it must have taken place fairly gently, for we had hardly perceived it. This explained the comparative calmness of the ocean.

A few minutes thought told me that my theory was correct; what was more, it showed me that the descent had not yet stopped. Indeed, the sea was continuing to rise with a speed apparently of about six feet a second – roughly four or five miles an hour. Given the distance between us and the foremost of the waves, we should thus be swallowed up in less than three minutes, if the speed of the subsidence stayed the same.

I came to a decision at once:

"My car!" I shouted.

They saw what I meant. We dashed towards the garage, and dragged the car outside. In a twinkling it was filled with petrol, and we crowded pell-mell into it. My chauffeur, Simonat, swung the starting-handle, jumped to the wheel, engaged the clutch, and set off up the road in low gear, while Raleigh, having opened the gate, grabbed the car as it went by and hung on to the back springs.

It was high time! Just at the moment when the car reached the road, a wave broke, washing right up to the centre of the wheels. Bah! Now we could laugh at the pursuit of the sea. Although it was overloaded, my fine car would know how to keep us out of its reach and so long as the descent into the gulf did not go on indefinitely... Indeed, we had plenty of room: two hours' climb at least, to a possible height of about fifteen hundred yards.

But I soon had to realise that it was not yet time to shout victory. After the first leap of the car had carried us about twenty yards beyond the line of foam, it was in vain that Simonat did his utmost: the distance did not increase. There could be no doubt about it: the weight of twelve people was slowing us down. However that might be, our speed was almost exactly that of the advancing water, which always kept the same distance away.

We soon realised our disquieting position and, except for Simonet, who had his hands full driving the car, we turned round towards the road we were leaving behind us. We could see nothing but water. As fast as we conquered it, the road vanished beneath the sea, which was conquering it at the same rate.

The sea itself was calm. A few ripples were quietly dying out against an ever-changing shore. It was a lake which kept on swelling, swelling, with a steady motion, and nothing could be more tragic than our pursuit by that calm sea. It was in vain that we fled before it; the water rose implacably with us...

Simonet was keeping his eyes fixed on the road. When we came to one of the turnings he told us:

"Here we are, half-way up the slope. Still another hour's climb."

We shuddered. What! Within an hour we were going to reach the top, and we should have to go on down, hunted, caught up perhaps, whatever our speed, by the masses of liquid which would crash like an avalanche on top of us! ...

The hour passed without any change in the situation. We could already distinguish the summit of the hill when the car was violently shaken and made a lurch which threatened to smash it against the stones by the side of the way. Meanwhile a great wave rose behind us, rushed forward to attack the hill, overhung and at last broke right over the car, which was surrounded by its foam... Were we going to be swallowed up? ...

No! The water retired, seething, while the motor, suddenly panting more quickly, speeded up.

Where had that sudden acceleration come from? The cry that Anna Raleigh gave told us: the poor woman had just realised that her husband was no longer hanging on the springs. The backwash of the wave had torn the wretched fellow away, and that was why the lightened car was climbing the slope more easily.

Suddenly it stopped dead.

"What's up?" I asked Simonat. "A breakdown?"

Even in these tragic circumstances, professional pride still maintained its rights: Simonat gave a disdainful shrug of his shoulders, by way of letting me know that to a chauffeur of his sort breakdowns were unknown. Then, raising his hand, he silently pointed ahead. Thus the stop was explained.

The road was cut less than ten yards away from us. 'Cut' is the very word; it might have been slashed with a knife. Beyond the sharp crest in which it ended, there was emptiness, a shadowy gulf in whose depths it was impossible to distinguish anything.

We turned round bewildered, sure that our last hour had come. The ocean which had pursued us even on to heights was bound to catch up with us in a few seconds.

Except for the unhappy Anna and her daughters, who were sobbing as though their hearts were breaking, we gave a cry of joyful surprise. No, the water was no longer moving upwards, or, more precisely, the earth had stopped falling. The shaking we had just felt had no doubt been the last manifestation of the phenomenon. The ocean had halted, and its level was still nearly a hundred yards below the point where we were grouped around our car, which was still throbbing, like an animal out of breath after a rapid run.

Shall we be able to get out of this predicament? We cannot know until daybreak. Until then, we shall have to wait. One after another we stretched ourselves out on the ground, and I think, God forgive me, that I must have fallen asleep...

During the night

I am suddenly aroused by a terrible noise. What time is it? I don't know. Moreover, we are still drowned in the shadows of night.

The noise is coming from the impenetrable gulf into which the road has collapsed. What has happened? ... I could swear that masses of water were falling in cataracts, that gigantic waves were violently crashing together... Yes, it must be that, for swirls of foam are reaching us, and we are covered by the spray.

Then gradually calm returns... Silence covers everything... The sky is getting lighter... It's daybreak.

May 25th

What agony, the slow realisation of our actual position! At first we can distinguish only our immediate surroundings, but the circle widens, grows ever wider, as if our disappointed hopes were lifting one after another an infinite number of flimsy veils; – and at last it is broad daylight, which dispels the last of our illusions.

Our situation is quite simple and can be summed up in a few words: we are on an island. The sea surrounds us on every side. Yesterday we should have seen a whole ocean of summits, several higher than the one on which we now find ourselves. These summits have vanished while, for reasons which must remain for ever unknown, our own, though more humble, has been stopped in its gentle fall: in their place is a boundless sheet of water. On all sides, nothing but the sea. We are occupying the only solid point within the immense circle of the horizon.

A glance is enough to reveal the whole extent of the islet upon which some extraordinary chance has found us a refuge. It is indeed quite small: a thousand yards long at most, and five hundred in the other direction. To north, west, and south, its crest, rising only about a hundred yards above the waves, joins them by a fairly gentle slope. To the east, on the other hand, the islet ends in a cliff falling sheerly down into the ocean.

It is above all to that side that we turn our eyes. In that direction we ought to see range upon range of mountains, and beyond them the whole of Mexico. What a change in the space of a short spring night! The mountains have vanished, Mexico has been swallowed up! In their place is a boundless desert, the arid desert of the sea!

We stare at each other, terrified. Penned up, without food, without drinking-water, on this bare narrow rock, we cannot cherish even the faintest hope. We grimly lie down on the ground and set ourselves to wait for death.

On board the 'Virginia', June 4th

What happened during the next few days? I can't remember. Presumably I ended by at last losing conciousness; I only came back to my senses on board the *vessel which picked us up. Then only did I learn that we had spent ten whole days on the islet, and that two of our number, Williamson and Rowling, had died of hunger and thirst. Of the fifteen people whom my home had sheltered at the moment of the disaster, there were now only nine: my son Jean and my ward Hélène, my chauffeur Simonat, inconsolable at the loss of his machine, Anna Raleigh and her two daughters, Dr. Bathurst and Dr. Moreno – and lastly myself, I who hasten to jot down these lines for the edification of future peoples, assuming, that is, that they will ever be born.*

The Virginia, which is carrying us, is a 'mixed' vessel – with steam and sails – of about two thousand tons, devoted to merchant traffic. She is a fairly old ship, rather a slow sailer. Captain Morris has twenty men under his command; he and his crew are English.

The Virginia left Melbourne under ballast a little over a month ago, sailing for Rosario. No incident had marked her voyage except, on the night of May 24th, a series of deep-sea waves rising to a prodigious height; but they were of a proportionate length and this made them inoffensive. However strange they might be, these waves could not have forewarned the captain of the cataclysm which was taking place at that time.

So he was amazed to find nothing but the sea where he had expected to make Rosario and the Mexican coast. Of that shore, there remained nothing but an islet. One of the Virginia's boats put off to that islet, on which eleven inanimate bodies were found. Two were only corpses; the nine others were taken on board. It was in this way we were saved.

On land – January or February

An interval of eight months separates the last of the preceding lines from the first which follow. I date these January or February because it is impossible to be more precise, for I have no longer any exact notion of time.

These eight months formed the most atrocious of our trials, those during which, getting ever more strictly rationed, we realised the full extent of our misfortune.

After picking us up, the Virginia cruised on at full steam towards the east. When I regained my senses, the islet where we had barely escaped death had long been below the horizon. According to our bearings, which the captain obtained from a cloudless sky, we were then sailing exactly over the place where Mexico should have been. But of Mexico there remained not a trace – no more than they had been able to find, while I was unconscious, of its central mountains; no more than any land whatever could be distinguished anywhere, no matter how far they looked. Everywhere, nothing but the infinity of the sea.

The realisation of this was indeed terrifying. We feared that our minds would give way. What! All Mexico swallowed up! ... We exchanged horrified glances, silently asking one another how far the ravages of this frightful cataclysm extended...

Wishing to clear this matter up, the captain steered towards the north: even if Mexico no longer existed, it was unthinkable that this could be true of the whole continent of America.

Yet true it was. We cruised vainly northwards for twelve days without sighting land, nor did we sight it when we put about and steered southwards for nearly a month. However paradoxical it might appear, we had to give way to the evidence: yes, the whole of the American continent had been engulfed by the waves!

THE ETERNAL ADAM

Then had we been saved only to experience the agonies of death a second time? We had certainly good reason to fear so. Without speaking of the food, which would give out sooner or later, a more urgent danger threatened us: what would become of us when our engines came to a standstill for lack of fuel? So the heart of an animal stops beating for lack of blood.

This was why, on July 14th – we were then almost at the former position of Buenos Ayres – Captain Morris let the fires die out and hoisted the sails. That done, he mustered all the personnel of the Virginia, passengers and crew, explained the position to us in a few words, and asked us to think it over and to make any suggestions we could at the council he meant to hold next day.

I do not know whether any of my companions in misfortune could think of any more or less ingenious expedient. For my part, I must admit, I was still hesitating, quite uncertain what to suggest, when the question was settled by a tempest that sprang up during the night. We had to fly westwards, swept along by a tempestuous gale, always on the point of being swallowed up by a raging sea.

The hurricane lasted thirty-five days, without a minute's interruption, or even a momentary lull. We were beginning to despair of its ever ending when, on August 19th, the fine weather returned as suddenly as it had stopped. The captain seized the opportunity to take our bearings: his calculations showed 40° north latitude and 114° east longitude. These were the co-ordinates of Pekin!

Thus we had sped over Polynesia, and perhaps even over Australia, without realising it. There where we were, now floating, had once been the capital of an empire numbering four hundred million souls!

Then Asia had suffered the fate of America?

We were soon convinced of this. The Virginia, still heading for the south-west, reached the latitude of Tibet and then that of the Himalayas. Here ought to have towered the highest summits of earth. Yet wherever we looked, nothing emerged from the surface of the sea. We had to believe that there no longer existed, anywhere on earth, any solid land other than the islet which had saved us – that we were the only survivors of the cataclysm, the last inhabitants of a world wrapped in the moving shroud of the sea!

If this were so, it would not be long before we too in our turn would perish. In spite of our strict rationing, our store of provisions was diminishing, and we had to give up all hopes of renewing them…

I will not dwell on the record of that frightful voyage. If, to describe it in detail, I were to try to relive it day by day, its memory would drive me mad. However strange and terrible were the events which preceded and followed it, however distressing the future seems – a future which I shall never see – it was during that infernal voyage that we reached the height of our fear.

Oh, that eternal cruise over an endless sea! To expect every day to get somewhere, and to see the end of the journey for ever receding!

To live poring over the maps on which human hands had traced the irregular line of the coast, and to realise that nothing, absolutely nothing, remained of these lands which had once been thought eternal! To tell ourselves that the earth, quivering with innumerable lives, that the millions of men and the myriads of animals which had traversed it in every direction or had soared through the air, had gone out like a tiny flame in a breath of wind! To look everywhere for our fellows and to look in vain!

To become little by little convinced that nowhere around us was any living thing, to realise ever more clearly our loneliness in the midst of a pitiless universe! ...

Have I found words suitable for expressing my anguish? I do not know. In no language whatever are there terms adequate for so completely unprecedented a situation.

After ascertaining that where the Indian peninsula had once been the sea now flowed, we headed to the north-west. Without the slightest change in our condition, we crossed the Ural chain – which had now become a submarine range of mountains – and sailed on over what once had been Europe. We then descended southwards, to twenty degrees beyond the Equator. Next, weary of our fruitless search, we made our way back towards the north and traversed, even over the Pyrenees, the sheet of water which covered Africa and Spain.

To tell the truth, we were beginning to get used to our terror. Wherever we went, we marked our route on our charts, and said to one another: "Here, this was Moscow... Warsaw... Berlin... Vienna... Rome... Tunis... Timbuctoo... St. Louis... Oran... Madrid..." But we spoke with growing indifference and, having become habituated to it, we were at last able to pronounce these words, really so full of tragedy, without the slightest emotion.

But so far as I was concerned I had not yet exhausted my capacity for suffering. I can see it still, that day – it was about December 11th – when Captain Morris told me "Here, this was Paris..." At these words I felt that my heart was being torn out. That the universe might be swallowed up, well and good. But France – my France! – and Paris, which symbolised her!

From beside me came something like a sob. I turned round; it was Simonat who was weeping.

For another four days we pushed on towards the north; then, having reached the latitude of Edinburgh, we turned towards the southwest in search of Ireland, and then towards the east... We were really wandering about at random, for there was no reason to go in one direction rather than in any other...

We sailed above London, whose liquid tomb was saluted by the whole crew. Five days later, when we were at the latitude of Danzig, the captain decided to go about and gave orders that we were to head to the south-west. The helmsman obeyed passively. What difference could that make to him? Wasn't it the same on every side?

It was when we had sailed in that direction for nine days that we swallowed our last scrap of biscuit.

As we stared at one another with haggard eyes, Captain Morris unexpectedly ordered the fires to be lighted. What notion was he giving way to? I still ask myself that; but the order was obeyed; the speed of our vessel increased...

Two days later we were suffering cruelly from hunger. After another two days, almost everyone obstinately refused to leave his bunk; there was only the captain. Simonat, a few members of the crew, and myself, with enough energy to keep the ship on course.

The next day, the fifth of our fast, the number of well-disposed steersmen and stokers had decreased still further. Another twenty-four hours and none of us would have the strength to stand.

We had then been travelling for more than seven months. For more than seven months we had been furrowing the sea in every direction. I think it must have been

January 8th – I say 'I think' for I cannot possibly be more precise, for by now the calendar had lost much of its meaning for us.

And it was on that day, while I was at the wheel and devoting all my flagging attention to the compass, that I started to make out something towards the west. Thinking that I was the play thing of some error, I stared…

No, I was not mistaken!

I gave a veritable roar, then, hanging on to the wheel, I shouted at the top of my voice: "Land on the starboard bow!"

What a magic effect those words had! All those dying men revived at once, and their haggard faces lined the starboard rail.

"Yes, land it is," said Captain Morris, after scrutinising the cloud rising above the horizon.

Half-an-hour later, it was impossible to feel the slightest doubt. It was certainly land which, after seeking it in vain all over the former continents, we had found in the midst of the Atlantic Ocean!

About three in the afternoon we could make out the details of the coast which barred our way, and we sank back into despair. In very truth this shore was unlike any other, and not one of us could remember ever seeing a coast so completely, so absolutely wild.

In the countries where we had lived before the disaster, green had always been the most abundant colour. Not one of us had ever known a coast so forsaken, a country so arid, that we could not find upon it a few shrubs, even if only a few tufts of gorse, or a few trails of lichen or moss. Here, nothing of the sort. All we could distinguish was a tall blackish cliff, at whose foot lay a chaos of rocks, without a plant, without a solitary blade of grass. It was the most complete, the most total, desolation that one could imagine.

For two days we coasted that abrupt cliff without finding the smallest gap. It was only towards the evening of the second day that we discovered a large bay, well sheltered against the winds of the open sea, in whose depths we let fall the anchor.

After reaching land in our boats, our first care was to collect some food from the shore, which was covered with turtles by the hundred and shellfish by the million. In the crevices of the rocks we found fabulous quantities of crabs and lobsters, to say nothing of innumerable fish. To all appearances this sea was so richly inhabited that, failing any other resources, it would suffice to assure our subsistence for an indefinite time.

When we were restored, a gap in the cliff enabled us to reach the plateau, which we found to cover a wide expanse. The appearance of the coast had not deceived us: on all sides, in every direction, there was nothing but arid rocks, covered with sea weed and wrack – most of it dried up – without the smallest blade of grass, with no living thing either on the ground or in the sky. Here and there were tiny lakes, or rather ponds, gleaming in the sunshine, but when we sought to quench our thirst, we realised that they were salt.

To tell the truth, this did not surprise us. It confirmed what we had thought right from the outset, that this unknown continent was born yesterday and had risen, in one solid mass, from the depths of the sea. This explained both its aridity and its utter loneliness. It moreover explained this thick layer of mud, uniformly spread, which as the result of evaporation was beginning to crack and to fall into dust.

Next day, at noon, our bearings showed 17° 30' north latitude and 23° 55' west longitude. On consulting the map, we found that this was right in the open sea, nearly on a level with Cape Verde. And yet towards the west the land, and towards the east the sea, now extended out of sight.

However repulsive and inhospitable was this continent upon which we had set foot, we should have to be satisfied with it. For this reason the unloading of the Virginia *was begun without further delay. We carried on to the plateau, at random, everything she contained. First, however, the ship had been securely moored with four anchors, in fifteen fathoms of water. In this quiet bay she was in no danger, and we could quite safely leave her to herself.*

As soon as the unloading was complete, our new life began. In the first place we had to…

When he reached this point in his translation Zartog Sofr had to pause. In this place the manuscript had the first of its *lacunae*; this seemed to involve a large number of pages, and it was followed by several others which to all appearances were larger still. No doubt, in spite of the protection given by the case, many of the sheets had been attacked by damp; there remained only a few more or less lengthy fragments, their context having been destroyed. They were in the following order:

…beginning to get acclimatised.

How long is it since we landed on this coast? I no longer know. I asked Dr. Moreno, who keeps a calendar of the days as they flow by. He told me: "Six months…" Then added "Within a few days," for fear of being mistaken.

So there we arc already! It's only needed six months for us not to be sure of keeping an exact count of time. That promises well!

But on the whole there is nothing surprising in our negligence. It takes all our attention, all our efforts, to keep ourselves alive. To feed ourselves is a problem whose solution takes the whole day. What do we eat? Fish, when we can find any, and every day that gets harder, for our ceaseless hunt is scaring them. We also eat turtle's eggs and a few edible seaweeds. By evening we have fed, but we are exhausted, and all we think about is sleep.

We have improvised some tents out of the Virginia's *sails. I expect that soon we'll have to build some better shelter.*

Sometimes we shoot a bird; the air is not so completely deserted as we had thought, and a dozen known species are represented on this new continent. They are one and all migratory birds: the swallow, albatross, and so forth. Presumably they can find no food on this land, devoid of vegetation as it is, for they never stop flying round our camp, and this helps to eke out our wretched meals. Sometimes we are able to pick up one that has died of hunger, which saves our powder and shot.

Fortunately, however, there is a possibility that our situation will become less wretched. We have found a sack of wheat in the Virginia's *hold, and we sowed half of it. That will help us greatly when the wheat grows. But will it sprout? The ground is covered with a thick sheet of alluvium, a sandy mud enriched by the decomposition of the seaweeds; poor though its quality may be, it is soil all the same. When we landed it was impregnated with salt; but since then torrential rains have washed copiously over the surface, and all the depressions are now full of fresh water.*

Yet the alluvial layer has been freed from its salt only on its surface; the streams and the very rivers which are beginning to form are all strongly brackish, and this shows that its depths are still saturated.

To sow the corn and keep the other half of it in reserve, we almost had to fight. Some of the Virginia's *crew wanted to make all of it into bread at once. We have had to...*

...that we had on board the Virginia. *The two pairs of rabbits have run off into the interior and we haven't seen them since. I suppose they've found something to live on. Then does the land, unknown to us, produce...*

...two years, at least, that we've been here! ... The wheat had grown splendidly. We have almost as much bread as we want, and our fields are always getting wider. But what a struggle against the birds! They have multiplied amazingly, and all around our crops...

In spite of the deaths I mentioned, our little tribe is no smaller. On the contrary. My son and my ward have three children, and each of the three other households likewise. All these kids are in radiant health. Presumably the human species has a greater vigour, a more intense vitality, now that it is so much less numerous. But what causes...

...here for ten years, and we knew nothing about this continent. All we had seen of it was a distance of several miles round our camp. It was Dr. Bathurst who made us ashamed of our weakness: at his suggestion we got the Virginia *into service, which took nearly six months, and made a voyage of exploration.*

We got back the day before yesterday. The voyage lasted longer than we thought, because we wanted to carry it out thoroughly.

We went all round this continent which, everything makes us think, must be, with our islet, the only stretch of solid land that now exists on the earth's surface. Its shores seemed much the same everywhere, very craggy and very wild.

Our voyage was interrupted by several excursions into the interior; we especially hoped to find traces of the Azores and Madeira – situated, before the cataclysm, in the Atlantic Ocean, which certainly ought to make them a part of the new continent. – We could not recognise even the smallest vestige of them. All that we could find is that everywhere round their position the ground is upheaved and covered with a thick layer of lava; no doubt they were the centre of some great volcanic eruption.

Yet, if we failed to find what we were looking for, we found something we were not looking for at all! Half buried in the lava, in the latitude of the Azores, some evidences of human handiwork caught our eye – but not the handiwork of the inhabitants of these islands, our contemporaries of yesteryear. These were the remains of some columns and pottery, such as none of us had ever seen before. After studying them, Dr. Moreno put forward the theory that these remains must have come from ancient Atlantis, and that it was the volcanic flow that restored them to the light of day.

Dr. Moreno may be right. If it ever existed, the legendary Atlantis must certainly have been somewhere near the new continent. If so it is certainly very strange that three different races of man have followed one another in the same region.

However this may be, I declare that the problem leaves me cold: we have plenty to keep us busy in the present, without worrying about the past.

As soon as we got back to our camp, it struck us that, compared with the rest of the country, the region we occupied seems much favoured. This is due solely to the fact that the colour green, formerly so abundant in nature, is not completely unknown here, while it seems to have been radically suppressed elsewhere in the continent. We had not noticed this before, but it cannot be denied. Some blades of grass, which never existed at all before we landed, are now growing around us in fairly large numbers. They belong only to a few of the most common species, whose seeds were doubtless brought here by the birds.

It must not be inferred, however, that except for these familiar species there is no vegetation. Through the strangest work of adaptation, on the other hand, a vegetation in at least a rudimentary and promising state exists all over the continent.

The marine plants which covered it when it emerged from the waves have mostly died in the sunlight. A few, however, persisted in the lakes, the ponds, and the puddles of water which the heat has gradually dried up. But at that time rivers and rivulets began to flow, and these were the more suited for the existence of wracks and seaweeds in that their waters were salt. When the surface, and then the depths, of the soil were deprived of their salt, and the water became fresh, most of these plants were destroyed.

A few, however, able to adapt themselves to the new living conditions, flourished in the fresh water just as they had in the salt. But the process did not stop there: a few of these plants, gifted with an even greater power of accommodation, adapted themselves first to fresh water and then to the open air. At first along the banks and then further and further away from them they have spread into the interior.

We surprised this transformation in the very act, and we can see how their structures are getting modified along with their physiological functions. Already a few stems are rising timidly towards the sky. We can foresee that one day a flora of great variety will thus be created and that a fierce struggle will begin between these new species and those surviving from the ancient order of things.

What is true of the flora is true also of the fauna. Along the watercourses we can see the former marine animals, mostly molluscs and crustaceans, in process of becoming terrestrial. The air is furrowed by flying fish, birds rather than fish, their wings having enlarged beyond all reason and their incurved tails allowing them to...

The last of the fragments contained, intact, the end of the manuscript:

...all old. Captain Morris is dead. Dr. Bathurst is sixty-five; Dr. Moreno sixty; myself, sixty-eight. We shall all soon have done with life. First, however, we mean to finish the task we resolved on, and, so far as is in our power, we shall come to the aid of future generations in the struggle that awaits them.

But will they see the day, these future generations?

I should be tempted to say yes, if I considered only how my fellows are multiplying: the children are swarming, and, for the rest, in this healthy climate, in this country where wild animals are unknown, life is long. Our colony has tripled in size.

On the other hand I am tempted to say no, if I consider the deep intellectual decadence of my companions in distress.

Yet our little group of survivors was in a favourable position to share in human knowledge: it included one exceptionally energetic man – Captain Morris, who died today – two men more cultivated than is usual – my son and myself – and two real savants – Dr. Bathurst and Dr. Moreno. With such components we ought to have been able to accomplish something. We have done nothing. Right from the outset the maintenance of our material life has always been, and is still, our sole care. As at first we spend all our time looking for food, and in the evening we fall exhausted into a heavy sleep.

It is, alas! only too certain that mankind, of which we are the only representatives, is in a state of rapid retrogression and is tending to revert to the animal. Among the sailors of the Virginia, *men originally uncultivated, the brutal characteristics have become more marked; my son and I, we have forgotten what we knew; Dr. Bathurst and Dr. Morena have put their brains on the shelf. One might say that our cerebral life is abolished.*

How lucky it is that, so many years ago, we made a survey of this continent! Today we shouldn't have the courage.... And besides, Captain Morris, who led the expedition, is dead – and dead also, or rather decayed, is the Virginia *which carried us.*

At the beginning of our stay a few of us decided to build some houses. They were never finished and now they are falling in ruins. We sleep, as before, on the ground, whatever the season.

For a long time not a vestige has been left of the garments which covered us. For several years we contrived to replace them by seaweeds woven together in a style that was at first ingenious but soon became coarser. At last we got tired of making the effort, which the mild climate renders needless: we go naked, like those whom we used to call savages.

Eating, eating, that is our perpetual aim, our sole preoccupation.

Yet there still remains some remnants of our former ideas, our former feelings. My son John, now a grown man and a grandfather, has not lost all his affection, and my ex-chauffeur, Modeste Simonat, keeps a vague memory that I used to be his master.

But for them, for us, these faint traces of the men we once were – for in very sooth we are no longer men – will vanish for ever. The people of the future, who were born here, have never known any other existence. Mankind will be reduced to these adults – even as I write I have them before my very eyes – who do not know how to write or to count, who hardly know how to speak; and to these sharp-toothed youngsters who seem to be nothing but an insatiable stomach. And after them there will be other adults and other children, and then still more adults and still more children, ever nearer to the animal, ever further away from their thinking ancestors.

I can almost see them, these future men, forgetting all articulate language, their intelligence extinct, their bodies covered with coarse fur, wandering about this sad wilderness...

Well, we want to try to avoid this. We want to do everything in our power to ensure that the achievements of the men among whom we once were shall not be completely lost.

Dr. Moreno, Dr. Bathurst and I, we are going to revive our stupefied minds, we are going to make ourselves recall what we once knew. We are going to share the task, and on this paper and with this ink which came from the Virginia *we are going to set out all that we remember of the various branches of science, so that, later men, if they still exist, and if, after a more or less long period of savagery, they feel a revival of their thirst for light, will find a summary of what their predecessors have done. May they then bless the memory of those who strove, at all costs, to shorten the sorrowful road to be trodden by the brothers whom they will never see!*

At death's door

It is now nearly fifteen years since the above lines were written. Dr. Bathurst and Dr. Moreno are no more. Of all those who landed here, I, one of the oldest, I am almost the only one left. But death will soon take me in my turn. I can feel it rising from my frozen feet to my heart, which is about to stop.

Our work is done. I have entrusted the manuscripts which contain this summary of human knowledge into an iron chest landed from the Virginia, *and which I have buried deeply in the earth. At its side I am going to bury these few pages rolled up in an aluminium container.*

Will anyone ever find this material committed to the earth? Will anyone ever so much as look for it?

That is for fate to decide. À Dieu vat!

As Zartog Sofr translated this strange document, a sort of terror seized upon his soul.

What! So the Andart'-Iten-Schu people were descended from these men who, after having wandered for long months across the desert of the ocean, had at last been washed up on this point on the shore where Basidra now stood? So these wretched creatures had formed part of a glorious race of men, compared with which modern man could scarcely babble! Yet for the knowledge and even the memory of these peoples to be destroyed, what was needed? Less than nothing; an imperceptible shudder had run through the earth's crust.

What an irreparable misfortune that the manuscripts the document spoke of had been destroyed, along with the iron chest that contained them! But great though that misfortune was, it was impossible to cherish the slightest hope: while digging the foundations the workmen had turned up the earth in every direction. There could be no doubt that the iron had been corroded away by time, which the aluminium container had triumphantly resisted.

For the rest, it needed no more than this for Sofr's optimism to be irretrievably overthrown. Although the manuscript gave no technical details, it was full of general indications and showed quite unmistakably that mankind had at one time advanced further in the quest for truth than it had done since. Everything was there in this narrative, the notions that Sofr had cherished, and others that he had not dared to imagine – even to the explanation of the name of Hedom, over which so many vain quarrels had broken out! …Hedom, it was a corrupt form of Edem – itself a corrupt form of Adam – the said Adam being perhaps nothing more than the corrupt form of some other word more ancient still.

Hedom, Edem, Adam – that was the perpetual symbol of the first man, and it was also an explanation of his appearance on earth. Then Sofr had been wrong to deny that ancestor, whose reality the manuscript had proved once and for all, and it was the people who had been right in giving themselves such an ancestry. But, not only in that but in everything else, the Andart'-Iten-Schu had invented nothing. They had been content to repeat what had been said before.

And perhaps, after all, the contemporaries of the author of the narrative had likewise invented nothing. Perhaps they too had done nothing but to retrace the road traversed by other races of man who had preceded them on earth. Did not the document speak of a people whom it called the Atlanteans? It was these Atlanteans, no doubt, of whom Sofr's excavations had disclosed a few impalpable traces below the marine silt. What knowledge of the truth had that age-old nation attained when the invasion of the sea had swept them from the earth?

However that might be, none of their work had remained after the catastrophe, and mankind had again to start at the foot of the hill in climbing towards the light.

Perhaps it would be the same for the Andart'-Iten-Schu. Perhaps it would again be the same after them, until the day...

But would the day ever come when the insatiable desire of mankind would be satisfied? Would the day ever come when they, having succeeded in climbing the slope, would be content to rest upon the summit they had at last conquered?

Such were the meditations of Zartog Sofr, as he bent over this venerable manuscript.

This narrative from beyond the tomb enabled him to imagine the terrible drama which is forever played throughout the universe, and his heart overflowed with pity. Bleeding from the countless wounds from which those who had ever lived had suffered before him, bending beneath the weight of these vain efforts accumulated throughout the infinity of time, Zartog Sofr'-Ai-Sr gained, slowly and painfully, an intimate conviction of the eternal recurrence of events.

Footnotes for *The Eternal Adam*

1. From the neighbourhood of Berlin to near Cape Horn.
2. The Andart'-Iten-Schu thus knew nothing of Neptune.
3. It will be seen that, at the time when Zartog Sofr-Ai-Sr was indulging in these reflections, though the Andart'-Iten-Schu knew the telegraph, they were still ignorant of the telephone and the electric light.
4. From these words it must be assumed that at the time when this journal will be written, the solar system will include more than eight planets, and that man will have discovered one or several beyond Neptune.

The World Set Free
Prelude–Chapter II
H.G. Wells

Prelude
The Sun Snarers

THE HISTORY of mankind is the history of the attainment of external power. Man is the tool-using, fire-making animal. From the outset of his terrestrial career we find him supplementing the natural strength and bodily weapons of a beast by the heat of burning and the rough implement of stone. So he passed beyond the ape. From that he expands. Presently he added to himself the power of the horse and the ox, he borrowed the carrying strength of water and the driving force of the wind, he quickened his fire by blowing, and his simple tools, pointed first with copper and then with iron, increased and varied and became more elaborate and efficient. He sheltered his heat in houses and made his way easier by paths and roads. He complicated his social relationships and increased his efficiency by the division of labour. He began to store up knowledge. Contrivance followed contrivance, each making it possible for a man to do more. Always down the lengthening record, save for a set-back ever and again, he is doing more.... A quarter of a million years ago the utmost man was a savage, a being scarcely articulate, sheltering in holes in the rocks, armed with a rough-hewn flint or a fire-pointed stick, naked, living in small family groups, killed by some younger man so soon as his first virile activity declined. Over most of the great wildernesses of earth you would have sought him in vain; only in a few temperate and sub-tropical river valleys would you have found the squatting lairs of his little herds, a male, a few females, a child or so.

He knew no future then, no kind of life except the life he led. He fled the cave-bear over the rocks full of iron ore and the promise of sword and spear; he froze to death upon a ledge of coal; he drank water muddy with the clay that would one day make cups of porcelain; he chewed the ear of wild wheat he had plucked and gazed with a dim speculation in his eyes at the birds that soared beyond his reach. Or suddenly he became aware of the scent of another male and rose up roaring, his roars the formless precursors of moral admonitions. For he was a great individualist, that original, he suffered none other than himself.

So through the long generations, this heavy precursor, this ancestor of all of us, fought and bred and perished, changing almost imperceptibly.

Yet he changed. That keen chisel of necessity which sharpened the tiger's claw age by age and fined down the clumsy Orchippus to the swift grace of the horse, was at work upon him – is at work upon him still. The clumsier and more stupidly fierce among him were killed soonest and oftenest; the finer hand, the quicker eye, the bigger brain, the better balanced body prevailed; age by age, the implements were a little better made, the man a little more delicately adjusted to his possibilities. He became more social; his herd grew larger; no longer did each man kill or drive out his growing sons; a system of taboos made them tolerable to him, and they revered him alive and soon even after he was dead, and were his allies against the beasts and the rest of mankind. (But they were forbidden to touch the women of the tribe, they had to go out and capture women for themselves, and each son fled from his stepmother and hid from her lest the anger of the Old Man should be roused. All the world over, even to this day, these ancient inevitable taboos can be traced.) And now instead of caves came huts and hovels, and the fire was better tended and there were wrappings and garments; and so aided, the creature spread into colder climates, carrying food with him, storing food – until sometimes the neglected grass-seed sprouted again and gave a first hint of agriculture.

And already there were the beginnings of leisure and thought.

Man began to think. There were times when he was fed, when his lusts and his fears were all appeased, when the sun shone upon the squatting-place and dim stirrings of speculation lit his eyes. He scratched upon a bone and found resemblance and pursued it and began pictorial art, moulded the soft, warm clay of the river brink between his fingers, and found a pleasure in its patternings and repetitions, shaped it into the form of vessels, and found that it would hold water. He watched the streaming river, and wondered from what bountiful breast this incessant water came; he blinked at the sun and dreamt that perhaps he might snare it and spear it as it went down to its resting-place amidst the distant hills. Then he was roused to convey to his brother that once indeed he had done so – at least that some one had done so – he mixed that perhaps with another dream almost as daring, that one day a mammoth had been beset; and therewith began fiction – pointing a way to achievement – and the august prophetic procession of tales.

For scores and hundreds of centuries, for myriads of generations that life of our fathers went on. From the beginning to the ripening of that phase of human life, from the first clumsy eolith of rudely chipped flint to the first implements of polished stone, was two or three thousand centuries, ten or fifteen thousand generations. So slowly, by human standards, did humanity gather itself together out of the dim intimations of the beast. And that first glimmering of speculation, that first story of achievement, that story-teller bright-eyed and flushed under his matted hair, gesticulating to his gaping, incredulous listener, gripping his wrist to keep him attentive, was the most marvellous beginning this world has ever seen. It doomed the mammoths, and it began the setting of that snare that shall catch the sun.

* * *

That dream was but a moment in a man's life, whose proper business it seemed was to get food and kill his fellows and beget after the manner of all that belongs to the fellowship of the beasts. About him, hidden from him by the thinnest of veils, were the untouched sources of Power, whose magnitude we scarcely do more than suspect even today, Power that could make his every conceivable dream come real. But the feet of the race were in the way of it, though he died blindly unknowing.

At last, in the generous levels of warm river valleys, where food is abundant and life very easy, the emerging human overcoming his earlier jealousies, becoming, as necessity persecuted him less urgently, more social and tolerant and amenable, achieved a larger community. There began a division of labour, certain of the older men specialised in knowledge and direction, a strong man took the fatherly leadership in war, and priest and king began to develop their roles in the opening drama of man's history. The priest's solicitude was seed-time and harvest and fertility, and the king ruled peace and war. In a hundred river valleys about the warm, temperate zone of the earth there were already towns and temples, a score of thousand years ago. They flourished unrecorded, ignoring the past and unsuspicious of the future, for as yet writing had still to begin.

Very slowly did man increase his demand upon the illimitable wealth of Power that offered itself on every hand to him. He tamed certain animals, he developed his primordially haphazard agriculture into a ritual, he added first one metal to his resources and then another, until he had copper and tin and iron and lead and gold and silver to supplement his stone, he hewed and carved wood, made pottery, paddled down his river until he came to the sea, discovered the wheel and made the first roads. But his chief activity for a hundred centuries and more, was the subjugation of himself and others to larger and larger societies. The history of man is not simply the conquest of external power; it is first the conquest of those distrusts and fiercenesses, that self-concentration and intensity of animalism, that tie his hands from taking his inheritance. The ape in us still resents association. From the dawn of the age of polished stone to the achievement of the Peace of the World, man's dealings were chiefly with himself and his fellow man, trading, bargaining, law-making, propitiating, enslaving, conquering, exterminating, and every little increment in Power, he turned at once and always turns to the purposes of this confused elaborate struggle to socialise. To incorporate and comprehend his fellow men into a community of purpose became the last and greatest of his instincts. Already before the last polished phase of the stone age was over he had become a political animal. He made astonishingly far-reaching discoveries within himself, first of counting and then of writing and making records, and with that his town communities began to stretch out to dominion; in the valleys of the Nile, the Euphrates, and the great Chinese rivers, the first empires and the first written laws had their beginnings. Men specialised for fighting and rule as soldiers and knights. Later, as ships grew seaworthy, the Mediterranean which had been a barrier became a highway, and at last out of a tangle of pirate polities came the great struggle of Carthage and Rome. The history of Europe is the history of the victory and breaking up of the Roman Empire. Every ascendant monarch in Europe up to the last, aped Caesar and called himself Kaiser or Tsar or Imperator or Kasir-i-Hind. Measured by the duration of human life it is a vast space of time between that first dynasty in Egypt and the coming of the aeroplane, but by the scale that looks back to the makers of the eoliths, it is all of it a story of yesterday.

Now during this period of two hundred centuries or more, this period of the warring states, while men's minds were chiefly preoccupied by politics and mutual aggression, their progress in the acquirement of external Power was slow – rapid in comparison with the progress of the old stone age, but slow in comparison with this new age of systematic discovery in which we live. They did not very greatly alter the weapons and tactics of warfare, the methods of agriculture, seamanship, their knowledge of the habitable globe, or the devices and utensils of domestic life between the days of the early Egyptians and the days when Christopher Columbus was a child. Of course, there were inventions and changes, but there were also retrogressions; things were found out and then forgotten again; it was, on the whole, a progress, but it contained no steps; the peasant life was the same, there were already priests and lawyers and town craftsmen and territorial lords and rulers, doctors, wise women, soldiers and sailors in Egypt and China and Assyria and south-eastern Europe at the beginning of that period, and they were doing much the same things and living much the same life as they were in Europe in A.D. 1500. The English excavators of the year A.D. 1900 could delve into the remains of Babylon and Egypt and disinter legal documents, domestic accounts, and family correspondence that they could read with the completest sympathy.

There were great religious and moral changes throughout the period, empires and republics replaced one another, Italy tried a vast experiment in slavery, and indeed slavery was tried again and again and failed and failed and was still to be tested again and rejected again in the New World; Christianity and Mohammedanism swept away a thousand more specialised cults, but essentially these were progressive adaptations of mankind to material conditions that must have seemed fixed for ever. The idea of revolutionary changes in the material conditions of life would have been entirely strange to human thought through all that time.

Yet the dreamer, the story-teller, was there still, waiting for his opportunity amidst the busy preoccupations, the comings and goings, the wars and processions, the castle building and cathedral building, the arts and loves, the small diplomacies and incurable feuds, the crusades and trading journeys of the middle ages. He no longer speculated with the untrammelled freedom of the stone-age savage; authoritative explanations of everything barred his path; but he speculated with a better brain, sat idle and gazed at circling stars in the sky and mused upon the coin and crystal in his hand. Whenever there was a certain leisure for thought throughout these times, then men were to be found dissatisfied with the appearances of things, dissatisfied with the assurances of orthodox belief, uneasy with a sense of unread symbols in the world about them, questioning the finality of scholastic wisdom. Through all the ages of history there were men to whom this whisper had come of hidden things about them. They could no longer lead ordinary lives nor content themselves with the common things of this world once they had heard this voice. And mostly they believed not only that all this world was as it were a painted curtain before things unguessed at, but that these secrets were Power. Hitherto Power had come to men by chance, but now there were these seekers seeking, seeking among rare and curious and perplexing objects, sometimes finding some odd utilisable thing, sometimes deceiving themselves with fancied discovery, sometimes pretending to find. The world of every day laughed at these eccentric beings, or found them annoying and ill-treated them, or was seized with fear and made saints and sorcerers and warlocks of them, or with covetousness and entertained them hopefully; but for the greater part heeded them not at all. Yet they were of the blood of him who had first dreamt of attacking the mammoth; every one of them was of his blood and descent; and the thing they sought, all unwittingly, was the snare that will some day catch the sun.

* * *

Such a man was that Leonardo da Vinci, who went about the court of Sforza in Milan in a state of dignified abstraction. His common-place books are full of prophetic subtlety and ingenious anticipations of the methods of the early aviators. Durer was his parallel and Roger Bacon – whom the Franciscans silenced – of his kindred. Such a man again in an earlier city was Hero of Alexandria, who knew of the power of steam nineteen hundred years before it was first brought into use. And earlier still was Archimedes of Syracuse, and still earlier the legendary Daedalus of Cnossos. All up and down the record of history whenever there was a little leisure from war and brutality the seekers appeared. And half the alchemists were of their tribe.

When Roger Bacon blew up his first batch of gunpowder one might have supposed that men would have gone at once to the explosive engine. But they could see nothing of the sort. They were not yet beginning to think of seeing things; their metallurgy was all too poor to make such engines even had they thought of them. For a time they could not make instruments sound enough to stand this new force even for so rough a purpose as hurling a missile. Their first guns had barrels of coopered timber, and the world waited for more than five hundred years before the explosive engine came.

Even when the seekers found, it was at first a long journey before the world could use their findings for any but the roughest, most obvious purposes. If man in general was not still as absolutely blind to the unconquered energies about him as his paleolithic precursor, he was at best purblind.

* * *

The latent energy of coal and the power of steam waited long on the verge of discovery, before they began to influence human lives.

There were no doubt many such devices as Hero's toys devised and forgotten, time after time, in courts and palaces, but it needed that coal should be mined and burning with plenty of iron at hand before it dawned upon men that here was something more than a curiosity. And it is to be remarked that the first recorded suggestion for the use of steam was in war; there is an Elizabethan pamphlet in which it is proposed to fire shot out of corked iron bottles full of heated water. The mining of coal for fuel, the smelting of iron upon a larger scale than men had ever done before, the steam pumping engine, the steam-engine and the steam-boat, followed one another in an order that had a kind of logical necessity. It is the most interesting and instructive chapter in the history of the human intelligence, the history of steam from its beginning as a fact in human consciousness to the perfection of the great turbine engines that preceded the utilisation of intra-molecular power. Nearly every human being must have seen steam, seen it incuriously for many thousands of years; the women in particular were always heating water, boiling it, seeing it boil away, seeing the lids of vessels dance with its fury; millions of people at different times must have watched steam pitching rocks out of volcanoes like cricket balls and blowing pumice into foam, and yet you may search the whole human record through, letters, books, inscriptions, pictures, for any glimmer of a realisation that here was force, here was strength to borrow and use.... Then suddenly man woke up to it, the railways spread like a network over the globe, the ever enlarging iron steamships began their staggering fight against wind and wave.

Steam was the first-comer in the new powers, it was the beginning of the Age of Energy that was to close the long history of the Warring States.

But for a long time men did not realise the importance of this novelty. They would not recognise, they were not able to recognise that anything fundamental had happened to their immemorial necessities. They called the steam-engine the 'iron horse' and pretended that they had made the most partial of substitutions. Steam machinery and factory production were visibly revolutionising the conditions of industrial production, population was streaming steadily in from the country-side and concentrating in hitherto unthought-of masses about a few city centres, food was coming to them over enormous distances upon a scale that made the one sole precedent, the corn ships of imperial Rome, a petty incident; and a huge migration of peoples between Europe and Western Asia and America was in Progress, and – nobody seems to have realised that something new had come into human life, a strange swirl different altogether from any previous circling and mutation, a swirl like the swirl when at last the lock gates begin to open after a long phase of accumulating water and eddying inactivity....

The sober Englishman at the close of the nineteenth century could sit at his breakfast-table, decide between tea from Ceylon or coffee from Brazil, devour an egg from France with some Danish ham, or eat a New Zealand chop, wind up his breakfast with a West Indian banana, glance at the latest telegrams from all the world, scrutinise the prices current of his geographically distributed investments in South Africa, Japan, and Egypt, and tell the two children he had begotten (in the place of his father's eight) that he thought the world changed very little. They must play cricket, keep their hair cut, go to the old school he had gone to, shirk the lessons he had shirked, learn a few scraps of Horace and Virgil and Homer for the confusion of cads, and all would be well with them....

* * *

Electricity, though it was perhaps the earlier of the two to be studied, invaded the common life of men a few decades after the exploitation of steam. To electricity also, in spite of its provocative nearness all about him, mankind had been utterly blind for incalculable ages. Could anything be more emphatic than the appeal of electricity for attention? It thundered at man's ears, it signalled to him in blinding flashes, occasionally it killed him, and he could not see it as a thing that concerned him enough to merit study. It came into the house with the cat on any dry day and crackled insinuatingly whenever he stroked her fur. It rotted his metals when he put them together.... There is no single record that any one questioned why the cat's fur crackles or why hair is so unruly to brush on a frosty day, before the sixteenth century. For endless years man seems to have done his very successful best not to think about it at all; until this new spirit of the Seeker turned itself to these things.

How often things must have been seen and dismissed as unimportant, before the speculative eye and the moment of vision came! It was Gilbert, Queen Elizabeth's court physician, who first puzzled his brains with rubbed amber and bits of glass and silk and shellac, and so began the quickening of the human mind to the existence of this universal presence. And even then the science of electricity remained a mere little group of curious facts for nearly two hundred years, connected perhaps with magnetism – a mere guess that – perhaps with the lightning. Frogs' legs must have hung by copper hooks from iron railings and twitched upon countless occasions before Galvani saw them. Except for the lightning conductor, it was 250 years after Gilbert before electricity stepped out of the cabinet of scientific curiosities into the life of the common man.... Then suddenly, in the half-century between 1880 and 1930, it ousted the steam-engine and took over traction, it ousted every other form of household heating, abolished distance with the perfected wireless telephone and the telephotograph....

* * *

And there was an extraordinary mental resistance to discovery and invention for at least a hundred years after the scientific revolution had begun. Each new thing made its way into practice against a scepticism that amounted at times to hostility. One writer upon these subjects gives a funny little domestic conversation that happened, he says, in the year 1898, within ten years, that is to say, of the time when the first aviators were fairly on the wing. He tells us how he sat at his desk in his study and conversed with his little boy.

His little boy was in profound trouble. He felt he had to speak very seriously to his father, and as he was a kindly little boy he did not want to do it too harshly.

This is what happened.

"I wish, Daddy," he said, coming to his point, "that you wouldn't write all this stuff about flying. The chaps rot me."

"Yes!" said his father.

"And old Broomie, the Head I mean, he rots me. Everybody rots me."

"But there is going to be flying – quite soon."

The little boy was too well bred to say what he thought of that. "Anyhow," he said, "I wish you wouldn't write about it."

"You'll fly – lots of times – before you die," the father assured him.

The little boy looked unhappy.

The father hesitated. Then he opened a drawer and took out a blurred and under-developed photograph. "Come and look at this," he said.

The little boy came round to him. The photograph showed a stream and a meadow beyond, and some trees, and in the air a black, pencil-like object with flat wings on either side of it. It was the first record of the first apparatus heavier than air that ever maintained itself in the air by mechanical force. Across the margin was written: "Here we go up, up, up – from S.P. Langley, Smithsonian Institution, Washington."

The father watched the effect of this reassuring document upon his son. "Well?" he said.

"That," said the schoolboy, after reflection, "is only a model."

"Model today, man tomorrow."

The boy seemed divided in his allegiance. Then he decided for what he believed quite firmly to be omniscience. "But old Broomie," he said, "he told all the boys in his class only yesterday, 'no man will ever fly.' No one, he says, who has ever shot grouse or pheasants on the wing would ever believe anything of the sort...."

Yet that boy lived to fly across the Atlantic and edit his father's reminiscences.

* * *

At the close of the nineteenth century as a multitude of passages in the literature of that time witness, it was thought that the fact that man had at last had successful and profitable dealings with the steam that scalded him and the electricity that flashed and banged about the sky at him, was an amazing and perhaps a culminating exercise of his intelligence and his intellectual courage. The air of 'Nunc Dimittis' sounds in same of these writings. 'The great things are discovered,' wrote Gerald Brown in his summary of the nineteenth century. 'For us there remains little but the working out of detail.' The spirit of the seeker was still rare in the world; education was unskilled, unstimulating, scholarly, and but little valued, and few people even then could have realised that Science was still but the flimsiest of trial sketches and discovery scarcely beginning. No one seems to have been afraid of science and its possibilities. Yet now where there had been but a score or so of seekers, there were many thousands, and for one needle of speculation that had been probing the curtain of appearances in 1800, there were now hundreds. And already Chemistry, which had been content with her atoms and molecules for the better part of a century, was preparing herself for that vast next stride that was to revolutionise the whole life of man from top to bottom.

One realises how crude was the science of that time when one considers the case of the composition of air. This was determined by that strange genius and recluse, that man of mystery, that disembowelled intelligence, Henry Cavendish, towards the end of the eighteenth century. So far as he was concerned the work was admirably done. He separated all the known ingredients of the air with a precision altogether remarkable; he even put it upon record that he had some doubt about the purity of the nitrogen. For more than a hundred years his determination was repeated by chemists all the world over, his apparatus was treasured in London, he became, as they used to say, 'classic,' and always, at every one of the innumerable repetitions of his experiment, that sly element argon was hiding among the nitrogen (and with a little helium and traces of other substances, and indeed all the hints that might have led to the new departures of the twentieth-century chemistry), and every time it slipped unobserved through the professorial fingers that repeated his procedure.

Is it any wonder then with this margin of inaccuracy, that up to the very dawn of the twentieth-century scientific discovery was still rather a procession of happy accidents than an orderly conquest of nature?

Yet the spirit of seeking was spreading steadily through the world. Even the schoolmaster could not check it. For the mere handful who grew up to feel wonder and curiosity about the secrets of nature in the nineteenth century, there were now, at the beginning of the twentieth, myriads escaping from the limitations of intellectual routine and the habitual life, in Europe, in America, North and South, in Japan, in China, and all about the world.

It was in 1910 that the parents of young Holsten, who was to be called by a whole generation of scientific men, 'the greatest of European chemists,' were staying in a villa near Santo Domenico, between Fiesole and Florence. He was then only fifteen, but he was already distinguished as a mathematician and possessed by a savage appetite to understand. He had been particularly attracted by the mystery of phosphorescence and its apparent unrelatedness to every other source of light. He was to tell afterwards in his reminiscences how he watched the fireflies drifting and glowing among the dark trees in the garden of the villa under the warm blue night sky of Italy; how he caught and kept them in cages, dissected them, first studying the general anatomy of insects very elaborately, and how he began to experiment with the effect of various gases and varying temperature upon their light. Then the chance present of a little scientific toy invented by Sir William Crookes, a toy called the spinthariscope, on which radium particles impinge upon sulphide of zinc and make it luminous, induced him to associate the two sets of phenomena. It was a happy association for his inquiries. It was a rare and fortunate thing, too, that any one with the mathematical gift should have been taken by these curiosities.

* * *

And while the boy Holsten was mooning over his fireflies at Fiesole, a certain professor of physics named Rufus was giving a course of afternoon lectures upon Radium and Radio-Activity in Edinburgh. They were lectures that had attracted a very considerable amount of attention. He gave them in a small lecture-theatre that had become more and more congested as his course proceeded. At his concluding discussion it was crowded right up to the ceiling at the back, and there people were standing, standing without any sense of fatigue, so fascinating did they find his suggestions. One youngster in particular, a chuckle-headed, scrub-haired lad from the Highlands, sat hugging his knee with great sand-red hands and drinking in every word, eyes aglow, cheeks flushed, and ears burning.

"And so," said the professor, "we see that this Radium, which seemed at first a fantastic exception, a mad inversion of all that was most established and fundamental in the constitution of matter, is really at one with the rest of the elements. It does noticeably and forcibly what probably all the other elements are doing with an imperceptible slowness. It is like the single voice crying aloud that betrays the silent breathing multitude in the darkness. Radium is an element that is breaking up and flying to pieces. But perhaps all elements are doing that at less perceptible rates. Uranium certainly is; thorium – the stuff of this incandescent gas mantle – certainly is; actinium. I feel that we are but beginning the list. And we know now that the atom, that once we thought hard and impenetrable, and indivisible and final and – lifeless – lifeless, is really a reservoir of immense energy. That is the most wonderful thing about all this work. A little while ago we thought of the atoms as we thought of bricks, as solid building material, as substantial matter, as unit masses of lifeless stuff, and behold! These bricks are boxes, treasure boxes, boxes full of the intensest force. This little bottle contains about a pint of uranium oxide; that is to say, about fourteen ounces of the element uranium. It is worth about a pound. And in this bottle, ladies and gentlemen, in the atoms in this bottle there slumbers at least as much energy as we could get by burning a hundred and sixty tons of coal. If at a word, in one instant I could suddenly release that energy here and now it would blow us and everything about us to fragments; if I could turn it into the machinery that lights this city, it could keep Edinburgh brightly lit for a week. But at present no man knows, no man has an inkling of how this little lump of stuff can be made to hasten the release of its store. It does release it, as a burn trickles. Slowly the uranium changes into radium, the radium changes into a gas called the radium emanation, and that again to what we call radium A, and so the process goes on, giving out energy at every stage, until at last we reach the last stage of all, which is, so far as we can tell at present, lead. But we cannot hasten it."

"I take ye, man," whispered the chuckle-headed lad, with his red hands tightening like a vice upon his knee. "I take ye, man. Go on! Oh, go on!"

The professor went on after a little pause. "Why is the change gradual?" he asked. "Why does only a minute fraction of the radium disintegrate in any particular second? Why does it dole itself out so slowly and so exactly? Why does not all the uranium change to radium and all the radium change to the next lowest thing at once? Why this decay by driblets; why not a decay en masse? … Suppose presently we find it is possible to quicken that decay?"

The chuckle-headed lad nodded rapidly. The wonderful inevitable idea was coming. He drew his knee up towards his chin and swayed in his seat with excitement. "Why not?" he echoed, "why not?"

The professor lifted his forefinger.

"Given that knowledge," he said, "mark what we should be able to do! We should not only be able to use this uranium and thorium; not only should we have a source of power so potent that a man might carry in his hand the energy to light a city for a year, fight a fleet of battleships, or drive one of our giant liners across the Atlantic; but we should also have a clue that would enable us at last to quicken the process of disintegration in all the other elements, where decay is still so slow as to escape our finest measurements. Every scrap of solid matter in the world would become an available reservoir of concentrated force. Do you realise, ladies and gentlemen, what these things would mean for us?"

The scrub head nodded. "Oh! Go on. Go on."

"It would mean a change in human conditions that I can only compare to the discovery of fire, that first discovery that lifted man above the brute. We stand today towards radio-activity as our ancestor stood towards fire before he had learnt to make it. He knew it then only as a strange thing utterly beyond his control, a flare on the crest of the volcano, a red destruction that poured through the forest. So it is that we know radio-activity today. This – this is the dawn of a new day in human living. At the climax of that civilisation which had its beginning in the hammered flint and the fire-stick of the savage, just when it is becoming apparent that our ever-increasing needs cannot be borne indefinitely by our present sources of energy, we discover suddenly the possibility of an entirely new civilisation. The energy we need for our very existence, and with which Nature supplies us still so grudgingly, is in reality locked up in inconceivable quantities all about us. We cannot pick that lock at present, but –"

He paused. His voice sank so that everybody strained a little to hear him.

" – we will."

He put up that lean finger again, his solitary gesture.

"And then," he said…

"Then that perpetual struggle for existence, that perpetual struggle to live on the bare surplus of Nature's energies will cease to be the lot of Man. Man will step from the pinnacle of this civilisation to the beginning of the next. I have no eloquence, ladies and gentlemen, to express the vision of man's material destiny that opens out before me. I see the desert continents transformed, the poles no longer wildernesses of ice, the whole world once more Eden. I see the power of man reach out among the stars…"

He stopped abruptly with a catching of the breath that many an actor or orator might have envied.

The lecture was over, the audience hung silent for a few seconds, sighed, became audible, stirred, fluttered, prepared for dispersal. More light was turned on and what had been a dim mass of figures became a bright confusion of movement. Some of the people signalled to friends, some crowded down towards the platform to examine the lecturer's apparatus and make notes of his diagrams. But the chuckle-headed lad with the scrub hair wanted no such detailed frittering away of the thoughts that had inspired him. He wanted to be alone with them; he elbowed his way out almost fiercely, he made himself as angular and bony as a cow, fearing lest some one should speak to him, lest some one should invade his glowing sphere of enthusiasm.

He went through the streets with a rapt face, like a saint who sees visions. He had arms disproportionately long, and ridiculous big feet.

He must get alone, get somewhere high out of all this crowding of commonness, of everyday life.

He made his way to the top of Arthur's Seat, and there he sat for a long time in the golden evening sunshine, still, except that ever and again he whispered to himself some precious phrase that had stuck in his mind.

"If," he whispered, "if only we could pick that lock…"

The sun was sinking over the distant hills. Already it was shorn of its beams, a globe of ruddy gold, hanging over the great banks of cloud that would presently engulf it.

"Eh!" said the youngster. "Eh!"

He seemed to wake up at last out of his entrancement, and the red sun was there before his eyes. He stared at it, at first without intelligence, and then with a gathering recognition. Into his mind came a strange echo of that ancestral fancy, that fancy of a Stone Age savage, dead and scattered bones among the drift two hundred thousand years ago.

"Ye auld thing," he said – and his eyes were shining, and he made a kind of grabbing gesture with his hand; "ye auld red thing…. We'll have ye YET."

Chapter I
The New Source of Energy

THE PROBLEM which was already being mooted by such scientific men as Ramsay, Rutherford, and Soddy, in the very beginning of the twentieth century, the problem of inducing radio-activity in the heavier elements and so tapping the internal energy of atoms, was solved by a wonderful combination of induction, intuition, and luck by Holsten so soon as the year 1933. From the first detection of radio-activity to its first subjugation to human purpose measured little more than a quarter of a century. For twenty years after that, indeed, minor difficulties prevented any striking practical application of his success, but the essential thing was done, this new boundary in the march of human progress was crossed, in that year. He set up atomic disintegration in a minute particle of bismuth; it exploded with great violence into a heavy gas of extreme radio-activity, which disintegrated in its turn in the course of seven days, and it was only after another year's work that he was able to show practically that the last result of this rapid release of energy was gold. But the thing was done – at the cost of a blistered chest and an injured finger, and from the moment when the invisible speck of bismuth flashed into riving and rending energy, Holsten knew that he had opened a way for mankind, however narrow and dark it might still be, to worlds of limitless power. He recorded as much in the strange diary biography he left the world, a diary that was up to that particular moment a mass of speculations and calculations, and which suddenly became for a space an amazingly minute and human record of sensations and emotions that all humanity might understand.

He gives, in broken phrases and often single words, it is true, but none the less vividly for that, a record of the twenty-four hours following the demonstration of the correctness of his intricate tracery of computations and guesses. "I thought I should not sleep," he writes – the words he omitted are supplied in brackets – (on account of) "pain in (the) hand and chest and (the) wonder of what I had done…. Slept like a child."

He felt strange and disconcerted the next morning; he had nothing to do, he was living alone in apartments in Bloomsbury, and he decided to go up to Hampstead Heath, which he had known when he was a little boy as a breezy playground. He went up by the underground tube that was then the recognised means of travel from one part of London to another, and walked up Heath Street from the tube station to the open heath. He found it a gully of planks and scaffoldings between the hoardings of house-wreckers. The spirit of the times had seized upon that narrow, steep, and winding thoroughfare, and was in the act of making it commodious and interesting, according to the remarkable ideals of Neo-Georgian aestheticism. Such is the illogical quality of humanity that Holsten, fresh from work that was like a petard under the seat of current civilisation, saw these changes with regret. He had come up Heath Street perhaps a thousand times, had known the windows of all the little shops, spent hours in the vanished cinematograph theatre, and marvelled at the high-flung early Georgian houses upon the westward bank of that old gully of a thoroughfare; he felt strange with all these familiar things gone. He escaped at last with a feeling of relief from this choked alley of trenches and holes and cranes, and emerged upon the old familiar scene about the White Stone Pond. That, at least, was very much as it used to be.

There were still the fine old red-brick houses to left and right of him; the reservoir had been improved by a portico of marble, the white-fronted inn with the clustering flowers above its portico still stood out at the angle of the ways, and the blue view to Harrow Hill and Harrow spire, a view of hills and trees and shining waters and wind-driven cloud shadows, was like the opening of a great window to the ascending Londoner. All that was very reassuring. There was the same strolling crowd, the same perpetual miracle of motors dodging through it harmlessly, escaping headlong into the country from the Sabbatical stuffiness behind and below them. There was a band still, a women's suffrage meeting – for the suffrage women had won their way back to the tolerance, a trifle derisive, of the populace again – socialist orators, politicians, a band, and the same wild uproar of dogs, frantic with the gladness of their one blessed weekly release from the back yard and the chain. And away along the road to the Spaniards strolled a vast multitude, saying, as ever, that the view of London was exceptionally clear that day.

Young Holsten's face was white. He walked with that uneasy affectation of ease that marks an overstrained nervous system and an under-exercised body. He hesitated at the White Stone Pond whether to go to the left of it or the right, and again at the fork of the roads. He kept shifting his stick in his hand, and every now and then he would get in the way of people on the footpath or be jostled by them because of the uncertainty of his movements. He felt, he confesses, 'inadequate to ordinary existence.' He seemed to himself to be something inhuman and mischievous. All the people about him looked fairly prosperous, fairly happy, fairly well adapted to the lives they had to lead – a week of work and a Sunday of best clothes and mild promenading – and he had launched something that would disorganise the entire fabric that held their contentments and ambitions and satisfactions together. 'Felt like an imbecile who has presented a box full of loaded revolvers to a Creche,' he notes.

He met a man named Lawson, an old school-fellow, of whom history now knows only that he was red-faced and had a terrier. He and Holsten walked together and Holsten was sufficiently pale and jumpy for Lawson to tell him he overworked and needed a holiday. They sat down at a little table outside the County Council house of Golders Hill Park and sent one of the waiters to the Bull and Bush for a couple of bottles of beer, no doubt at Lawson's suggestion. The beer warmed Holsten's rather dehumanised system. He began to tell Lawson as clearly as he could to what his great discovery amounted. Lawson feigned attention, but indeed he had neither the knowledge nor the imagination to understand. "In the end, before many years are out, this must eventually change war, transit, lighting, building, and every sort of manufacture, even agriculture, every material human concern –"

Then Holsten stopped short. Lawson had leapt to his feet. "Damn that dog!" cried Lawson. "Look at it now. Hi! Here! Phewoo – phewoo phewoo! Come HERE, Bobs! Come HERE!"

The young scientific man, with his bandaged hand, sat at the green table, too tired to convey the wonder of the thing he had sought so long, his friend whistled and bawled for his dog, and the Sunday people drifted about them through the spring sunshine. For a moment or so Holsten stared at Lawson in astonishment, for he had been too intent upon what he had been saying to realise how little Lawson had attended.

Then he remarked, "WELL!" and smiled faintly, and – finished the tankard of beer before him.

Lawson sat down again. "One must look after one's dog," he said, with a note of apology. "What was it you were telling me?"

* * *

In the evening Holsten went out again. He walked to Saint Paul's Cathedral, and stood for a time near the door listening to the evening service. The candles upon the altar reminded him in some odd way of the fireflies at Fiesole. Then he walked back through the evening lights to Westminster. He was oppressed, he was indeed scared, by his sense of the immense consequences of his discovery. He had a vague idea that night that he ought not to publish his results, that they were premature, that some secret association of wise men should take care of his work and hand it on from generation to generation until the world was riper for its practical application. He felt that nobody in all the thousands of people he passed had really awakened to the fact of change, they trusted the world for what it was, not to alter too rapidly, to respect their trusts, their assurances, their habits, their little accustomed traffics and hard-won positions.

He went into those little gardens beneath the over-hanging, brightly-lit masses of the Savoy Hotel and the Hotel Cecil. He sat down on a seat and became aware of the talk of the two people next to him. It was the talk of a young couple evidently on the eve of marriage. The man was congratulating himself on having regular employment at last; "they like me," he said, "and I like the job. If I work up – in'r dozen years or so I ought to be gettin' somethin' pretty comfortable. That's the plain sense of it, Hetty. There ain't no reason whatsoever why we shouldn't get along very decently – very decently indeed."

The desire for little successes amidst conditions securely fixed! So it struck upon Holsten's mind. He added in his diary, 'I had a sense of all this globe as that....'

By that phrase he meant a kind of clairvoyant vision of this populated world as a whole, of all its cities and towns and villages, its high roads and the inns beside them, its gardens and farms and upland pastures, its boatmen and sailors, its ships coming along the great circles of the ocean, its time-tables and appointments and payments and dues as it were one unified and progressive spectacle. Sometimes such visions came to him; his mind, accustomed to great generalisations and yet acutely sensitive to detail, saw things far more comprehensively than the minds of most of his contemporaries. Usually the teeming sphere moved on to its predestined ends and circled with a stately swiftness on its path about the sun. Usually it was all a living progress that altered under his regard. But now fatigue a little deadened him to that incessancy of life, it seemed now just an eternal circling. He lapsed to the commoner persuasion of the great fixities and recurrencies of the human routine. The remoter past of wandering savagery, the inevitable changes of tomorrow were veiled, and he saw only day and night, seed-time and harvest, loving and begetting, births and deaths, walks in the summer sunlight and tales by the winter fireside, the ancient sequence of hope and acts and age perennially renewed, eddying on for ever and ever, save that now the impious hand of research was raised to overthrow this drowsy, gently humming, habitual, sunlit spinning-top of man's existence....

For a time he forgot wars and crimes and hates and persecutions, famine and pestilence, the cruelties of beasts, weariness and the bitter wind, failure and insufficiency and retrocession. He saw all mankind in terms of the humble Sunday couple upon the seat beside him, who schemed their inglorious outlook and improbable contentments. 'I had a sense of all this globe as that.'

His intelligence struggled against this mood and struggled for a time in vain. He reassured himself against the invasion of this disconcerting idea that he was something strange and inhuman, a loose wanderer from the flock returning with evil gifts from his sustained unnatural excursions amidst the darknesses and phosphorescences beneath the fair surfaces of life. Man had not been always thus; the instincts and desires of the little home, the little plot, was not all his nature; also he was an adventurer, an experimenter, an unresting curiosity, an insatiable desire. For a few thousand generations indeed he had tilled the earth and followed the seasons, saying his prayers, grinding his corn and trampling the October winepress, yet not for so long but that he was still full of restless stirrings.

'If there have been home and routine and the field,' thought Holsten, 'there have also been wonder and the sea.'

He turned his head and looked up over the back of the seat at the great hotels above him, full of softly shaded lights and the glow and colour and stir of feasting. Might his gift to mankind mean simply more of that?

He got up and walked out of the garden, surveyed a passing tram-car, laden with warm light, against the deep blues of evening, dripping and trailing long skirts of shining reflection; he crossed the Embankment and stood for a time watching the dark river and turning ever and again to the lit buildings and bridges. His mind began to scheme conceivable replacements of all those clustering arrangements....

'It has begun,' he writes in the diary in which these things are recorded. 'It is not for me to reach out to consequences I cannot foresee. I am a part, not a whole; I am a little instrument in the armoury of Change. If I were to burn all these papers, before a score of years had passed, some other man would be doing this...'

* * *

Holsten, before he died, was destined to see atomic energy dominating every other source of power, but for some years yet a vast network of difficulties in detail and application kept the new discovery from any effective invasion of ordinary life. The path from the laboratory to the workshop is sometimes a tortuous one; electro-magnetic radiations were known and demonstrated for twenty years before Marconi made them practically available, and in the same way it was twenty years before induced radio-activity could be brought to practical utilisation. The thing, of course, was discussed very much, more perhaps at the time of its discovery than during the interval of technical adaptation, but with very little realisation of the huge economic revolution that impended. What chiefly impressed the journalists of 1933 was the production of gold from bismuth and the realisation albeit upon unprofitable lines of the alchemist's dreams; there was a considerable amount of discussion and expectation in that more intelligent section of the educated publics of the various civilised countries which followed scientific development; but for the most part the world went about its business – as the inhabitants of those Swiss villages which live under the perpetual threat of overhanging rocks and mountains go about their business – just as though the possible was impossible, as though the inevitable was postponed for ever because it was delayed.

It was in 1953 that the first Holsten-Roberts engine brought induced radio-activity into the sphere of industrial production, and its first general use was to replace the steam-engine in electrical generating stations. Hard upon the appearance of this came the Dass-Tata engine – the invention of two among the brilliant galaxy of Bengali inventors the modernisation of Indian thought was producing at this time – which was used chiefly for automobiles, aeroplanes, waterplanes, and such-like, mobile purposes. The American Kemp engine, differing widely in principle but equally practicable, and the Krupp-Erlanger came hard upon the heels of this, and by the autumn of 1954 a gigantic replacement of industrial methods and machinery was in progress all about the habitable globe. Small wonder was this when the cost, even of these earliest and clumsiest of atomic engines, is compared with that of the power they superseded. Allowing for lubrication the Dass-Tata engine, once it was started cost a penny to run thirty-seven miles, and added only nine and quarter pounds to the weight of the carriage it drove. It made the heavy alcohol-driven automobile of the time ridiculous in appearance as well as preposterously costly. For many years the price of coal and every form of liquid fuel had been clambering to levels that made even the revival of the draft horse seem a practicable possibility, and now with the abrupt relaxation of this stringency, the change in appearance of the traffic upon the world's roads was instantaneous. In three years the frightful armoured monsters that had hooted and smoked and thundered about the world for four awful decades were swept away to the dealers in old metal, and the highways thronged with light and clean and shimmering shapes of silvered steel. At the same time a new impetus was given to aviation by the relatively enormous power for weight of the atomic engine, it was at last possible to add Redmayne's ingenious helicopter ascent and descent engine to the vertical propeller that had hitherto been the sole driving force of the aeroplane without overweighting the machine, and men found themselves possessed of an instrument of flight that could hover or ascend or descend vertically and gently as well as rush wildly through the air. The last dread of flying vanished. As the journalists of the time phrased it, this was the epoch of the Leap into the Air. The new atomic aeroplane became indeed a mania; every one of means was frantic to possess a thing so controllable, so secure and so free from the dust and danger of the road, and in France alone in the year 1943 thirty thousand of these new aeroplanes were manufactured and licensed, and soared humming softly into the sky.

And with an equal speed atomic engines of various types invaded industrialism. The railways paid enormous premiums for priority in the delivery of atomic traction engines, atomic smelting was embarked upon so eagerly as to lead to a number of disastrous explosions due to inexperienced handling of the new power, and the revolutionary cheapening of both materials and electricity made the entire reconstruction of domestic buildings a matter merely dependent upon a reorganisation of the methods of the builder and the house-furnisher. Viewed from the side of the new power and from the point of view of those who financed and manufactured the new engines and material it required the age of the Leap into the Air was one of astonishing prosperity. Patent-holding companies were presently paying dividends of five or six hundred per cent and enormous fortunes were made and fantastic wages earned by all who were concerned in the new developments. This prosperity was not a little enhanced by the fact that in both the Dass-Tata and Holsten-Roberts engines one of the recoverable waste products was gold – the former disintegrated dust of bismuth and the latter dust of lead – and that this new supply of gold led quite naturally to a rise in prices throughout the world.

This spectacle of feverish enterprise was productivity, this crowding flight of happy and fortunate rich people – every great city was as if a crawling ant-hill had suddenly taken wing – was the bright side of the opening phase of the new epoch in human history. Beneath that brightness was a gathering darkness, a deepening dismay. If there was a vast development of production there was also a huge destruction of values. These glaring factories working night and day, these glittering new vehicles swinging noiselessly along the roads, these flights of dragon-flies that swooped and soared and circled in the air, were indeed no more than the brightnesses of lamps and fires that gleam out when the world sinks towards twilight and the night. Between these high lights accumulated disaster, social catastrophe. The coal mines were manifestly doomed to closure at no very distant date, the vast amount of capital invested in oil was becoming unsaleable, millions of coal miners, steel workers upon the old lines, vast swarms of unskilled or under-skilled labourers in innumerable occupations, were being flung out of employment by the superior efficiency of the new machinery, the rapid fall in the cost of transit was destroying high land values at every centre of population, the value of existing house property had become problematical, gold was undergoing headlong depreciation, all the securities upon which the credit of the world rested were slipping and sliding, banks were tottering, the stock exchanges were scenes of feverish panic; – this was the reverse of the spectacle, these were the black and monstrous under-consequences of the Leap into the Air.

There is a story of a demented London stockbroker running out into Threadneedle Street and tearing off his clothes as he ran. "The Steel Trust is scrapping the whole of its plant," he shouted. "The State Railways are going to scrap all their engines. Everything's going to be scrapped – everything. Come and scrap the mint, you fellows, come and scrap the mint!"

In the year 1955 the suicide rate for the United States of America quadrupled any previous record. There was an enormous increase also in violent crime throughout the world. The thing had come upon an unprepared humanity; it seemed as though human society was to be smashed by its own magnificent gains.

For there had been no foresight of these things. There had been no attempt anywhere even to compute the probable dislocations this flood of inexpensive energy would produce in human affairs. The world in these days was not really governed at all, in the sense in which government came to be understood in subsequent years. Government was a treaty, not a design; it was forensic, conservative, disputatious, unseeing, unthinking, uncreative; throughout the world, except where the vestiges of absolutism still sheltered the court favourite and the trusted servant, it was in the hands of the predominant caste of lawyers, who had an enormous advantage in being the only trained caste. Their professional education and every circumstance in the manipulation of the fantastically naive electoral methods by which they clambered to power, conspired to keep them contemptuous of facts, conscientiously unimaginative, alert to claim and seize advantages and suspicious of every generosity. Government was an obstructive business of energetic fractions, progress went on outside of and in spite of public activities, and legislation was the last crippling recognition of needs so clamorous and imperative and facts so aggressively established as to invade even the dingy seclusions of the judges and threaten the very existence of the otherwise inattentive political machine.

The world was so little governed that with the very coming of plenty, in the full tide of an incalculable abundance, when everything necessary to satisfy human needs and everything necessary to realise such will and purpose as existed then in human hearts was already at hand, one has still to tell of hardship, famine, anger, confusion, conflict, and incoherent suffering. There was no scheme for the distribution of this vast new wealth that had come at last within the reach of men; there was no clear conception that any such distribution was possible. As one attempts a comprehensive view of those opening years of the new age, as one measures it against the latent achievement that later years have demonstrated, one begins to measure the blindness, the narrowness, the insensate unimaginative individualism of the pre-atomic time. Under this tremendous dawn of power and freedom, under a sky ablaze with promise, in the very presence of science standing like some bountiful goddess over all the squat darknesses of human life, holding patiently in her strong arms, until men chose to take them, security, plenty, the solution of riddles, the key of the bravest adventures, in her very presence, and with the earnest of her gifts in court, the world was to witness such things as the squalid spectacle of the Dass-Tata patent litigation.

There in a stuffy court in London, a grimy oblong box of a room, during the exceptional heat of the May of 1956, the leading counsel of the day argued and shouted over a miserable little matter of more royalties or less and whether the Dass-Tata company might not bar the Holsten-Roberts' methods of utilising the new power. The Dass-Tata people were indeed making a strenuous attempt to secure a world monopoly in atomic engineering. The judge, after the manner of those times, sat raised above the court, wearing a preposterous gown and a foolish huge wig, the counsel also wore dirty-looking little wigs and queer black gowns over their usual costume, wigs and gowns that were held to be necessary to their pleading, and upon unclean wooden benches stirred and whispered artful-looking solicitors, busily scribbling reporters, the parties to the case, expert witnesses, interested people, and a jostling confusion of subpoenaed persons, briefless young barristers (forming a style on the most esteemed and truculent examples) and casual eccentric spectators who preferred this pit of iniquity to the free sunlight outside. Every one was damply hot, the examining King's Counsel wiped the perspiration from his huge, clean-shaven upper lip; and into this atmosphere of grasping contention and human exhalations the daylight filtered through a window that was manifestly dirty. The jury sat in a double pew to the left of the judge, looking as uncomfortable as frogs that have fallen into an ash-pit, and in the witness-box lied the would-be omnivorous Dass, under cross-examination....

Holsten had always been accustomed to publish his results so soon as they appeared to him to be sufficiently advanced to furnish a basis for further work, and to that confiding disposition and one happy flash of adaptive invention the alert Dass owed his claim....

But indeed a vast multitude of such sharp people were clutching, patenting, pre-empting, monopolising this or that feature of the new development, seeking to subdue this gigantic winged power to the purposes of their little lusts and avarice. That trial is just one of innumerable disputes of the same kind. For a time the face of the world festered with patent legislation. It chanced, however, to have one oddly dramatic feature in the fact that Holsten, after being kept waiting about the court for two days as a beggar might have waited at a rich man's door, after being bullied by ushers and watched by policemen, was called as a witness, rather severely handled by counsel, and told not to 'quibble' by the judge when he was trying to be absolutely explicit.

The judge scratched his nose with a quill pen, and sneered at Holsten's astonishment round the corner of his monstrous wig. Holsten was a great man, was he? Well, in a law-court great men were put in their places.

"We want to know has the plaintiff added anything to this or hasn't he?" said the judge, "we don't want to have your views whether Sir Philip Dass's improvements were merely superficial adaptations or whether they were implicit in your paper. No doubt – after the manner of inventors – you think most things that were ever likely to be discovered are implicit in your papers. No doubt also you think too that most subsequent additions and modifications are merely superficial. Inventors have a way of thinking that. The law isn't concerned with that sort of thing. The law has nothing to do with the vanity of inventors. The law is concerned with the question whether these patent rights have the novelty the plantiff claims for them. What that admission may or may not stop, and all these other things you are saying in your overflowing zeal to answer more than the questions addressed to you – none of these things have anything whatever to do with the case in hand. It is a matter of constant astonishment to me in this court to see how you scientific men, with all your extraordinary claims to precision and veracity, wander and wander so soon as you get into the witness-box. I know no more unsatisfactory class of witness. The plain and simple question is, has Sir Philip Dass made any real addition to existing knowledge and methods in this matter or has he not? We don't want to know whether they were large or small additions nor what the consequences of your admission may be. That you will leave to us."

Holsten was silent.

"Surely?" said the judge, almost pityingly.

"No, he hasn't," said Holsten, perceiving that for once in his life he must disregard infinitesimals.

"Ah!" said the judge, "now why couldn't you say that when counsel put the question? ..."

An entry in Holsten's diary-autobiography, dated five days later, runs: 'Still amazed. The law is the most dangerous thing in this country. It is hundreds of years old. It hasn't an

THE WORLD SET FREE

idea. The oldest of old bottles and this new wine, the most explosive wine. Something will overtake them.'

* * *

There was a certain truth in Holsten's assertion that the law was 'hundreds of years old.' It was, in relation to current thought and widely accepted ideas, an archaic thing. While almost all the material and methods of life had been changing rapidly and were now changing still more rapidly, the law-courts and the legislatures of the world were struggling desperately to meet modern demands with devices and procedures, conceptions of rights and property and authority and obligation that dated from the rude compromises of relatively barbaric times. The horse-hair wigs and antic dresses of the British judges, their musty courts and overbearing manners, were indeed only the outward and visible intimations of profounder anachronisms. The legal and political organisation of the earth in the middle twentieth century was indeed everywhere like a complicated garment, outworn yet strong, that now fettered the governing body that once it had protected.

Yet that same spirit of free-thinking and outspoken publication that in the field of natural science had been the beginning of the conquest of nature, was at work throughout all the eighteenth and nineteenth centuries preparing the spirit of the new world within the degenerating body of the old. The idea of a greater subordination of individual interests and established institutions to the collective future, is traceable more and more clearly in the literature of those times, and movement after movement fretted itself away in criticism of and opposition to first this aspect and then that of the legal, social, and political order. Already in the early nineteenth century Shelley, with no scrap of alternative, is denouncing the established rulers of the world as Anarchs, and the entire system of ideas and suggestions that was known as Socialism, and more particularly its international side, feeble as it was in creative proposals or any method of transition, still witnesses to the growth of a conception of a modernised system of inter-relationships that should supplant the existing tangle of proprietary legal ideas.

The word 'Sociology' was invented by Herbert Spencer, a popular writer upon philosophical subjects, who flourished about the middle of the nineteenth century, but the idea of a state, planned as an electric-traction system is planned, without reference to pre-existing apparatus, upon scientific lines, did not take a very strong hold upon the popular imagination of the world until the twentieth century. Then, the growing impatience of the American people with the monstrous and socially paralysing party systems that had sprung out of their absurd electoral arrangements, led to the appearance of what came to be called the 'Modern State' movement, and a galaxy of brilliant writers, in America, Europe, and the East, stirred up the world to the thought of bolder rearrangements of social interaction, property, employment, education, and government, than had ever been contemplated before. No doubt these Modern State ideas were very largely the reflection upon social and political thought of the vast revolution in material things that had been in progress for two hundred years, but for a long time they seemed to be having no more influence upon existing institutions than the writings of Rousseau and Voltaire seemed to have had at the time of the death of the latter. They were fermenting in men's minds, and it needed only just such social and political stresses as the coming of the atomic mechanisms brought about, to thrust them forward abruptly into crude and startling realisation.

* * *

Frederick Barnet's Wander Jahre is one of those autobiographical novels that were popular throughout the third and fourth decades of the twentieth century. It was published in 1970, and one must understand Wander Jahre rather in a spiritual and intellectual than in a literal sense. It is indeed an allusive title, carrying the world back to the Wilhelm Meister of Goethe, a century and a half earlier.

Its author, Frederick Barnet, gives a minute and curious history of his life and ideas between his nineteenth and his twenty-third birthdays. He was neither a very original nor a very brilliant man, but he had a trick of circumstantial writing; and though no authentic portrait was to survive for the information of posterity, he betrays by a score of casual phrases that he was short, sturdy, inclined to be plump, with a 'rather blobby' face, and full, rather projecting blue eyes. He belonged until the financial debacle of 1956 to the class of fairly prosperous people, he was a student in London, he aeroplaned to Italy and then had a pedestrian tour from Genoa to Rome, crossed in the air to Greece and Egypt, and came back over the Balkans and Germany. His family fortunes, which were largely invested in bank shares, coal mines, and house property, were destroyed. Reduced to penury, he sought to earn a living. He suffered great hardship, and was then caught up by the war and had a year of soldiering, first as an officer in the English infantry and then in the army of pacification. His book tells all these things so simply and at the same time so explicitly, that it remains, as it were, an eye by which future generations may have at least one man's vision of the years of the Great Change.

And he was, he tells us, a 'Modern State' man 'by instinct' from the beginning. He breathed in these ideas in the class rooms and laboratories of the Carnegie Foundation school that rose, a long and delicately beautiful facade, along the South Bank of the Thames opposite the ancient dignity of Somerset House. Such thought was interwoven with the very fabric of that pioneer school in the educational renascence in England. After the customary exchange years in Heidelberg and Paris, he went into the classical school of London University. The older so-called 'classical' education of the British pedagogues, probably the most paralysing, ineffective, and foolish routine that ever wasted human life, had already been swept out of this great institution in favour of modern methods; and he learnt Greek and Latin as well as he had learnt German, Spanish, and French, so that he wrote and spoke them freely, and used them with an unconscious ease in his study of the foundation civilisations of the European system to which they were the key. (This change was still so recent that he mentions an encounter in Rome with an 'Oxford don' who 'spoke Latin with a Wiltshire accent and manifest discomfort, wrote Greek letters with his tongue out, and seemed to think a Greek sentence a charm when it was a quotation and an impropriety when it wasn't.')

Barnet saw the last days of the coal-steam engines upon the English railways and the gradual cleansing of the London atmosphere as the smoke-creating sea-coal fires gave place to electric heating. The building of laboratories at Kensington was still in progress, and he took part in the students' riots that delayed the removal of the Albert Memorial. He carried a banner with 'We like Funny Statuary' on one side, and on the other 'Seats and Canopies for Statues, Why should our Great Departed Stand in the Rain?' He learnt the rather athletic aviation of those days at the University grounds at Sydenham, and he was fined for flying over the new prison for political libellers at Wormwood Scrubs, 'in a manner calculated to exhilarate the prisoners while at exercise.' That was the time of the attempted suppression of any criticism of the public judicature and the place was crowded with journalists who had ventured to call attention to the dementia of Chief Justice Abrahams. Barnet was not a very good aviator, he confesses he was always a little afraid of his machine – there was excellent reason for every one to be afraid of those clumsy early types – and he never attempted steep descents or very high flying. He also, he records, owned one of those oil-driven motor-bicycles whose clumsy complexity and extravagant filthiness still astonish the visitors to the museum of machinery at South Kensington. He mentions running over a dog and complains of the ruinous price of 'spatchcocks' in Surrey. 'Spatchcocks,' it seems, was a slang term for crushed hens.

He passed the examinations necessary to reduce his military service to a minimum, and his want of any special scientific or technical qualification and a certain precocious corpulence that handicapped his aviation indicated the infantry of the line as his sphere of training. That was the most generalised form of soldiering. The development of the theory of war had been for some decades but little assisted by any practical experience. What fighting had occurred in recent years, had been fighting in minor or uncivilised states, with peasant or barbaric soldiers and with but a small equipment of modern contrivances, and the great powers of the world were content for the most part to maintain armies that sustained in their broader organisation the traditions of the European wars of thirty and forty years before. There was the infantry arm to which Barnet belonged and which was supposed to fight on foot with a rifle and be the main portion of the army. There were cavalry forces (horse soldiers), having a ratio to the infantry that had been determined by the experiences of the Franco-German war in 1871. There was also artillery, and for some unexplained reason much of this was still drawn by horses; though there were also in all the European armies a small number of motor-guns with wheels so constructed that they could go over broken ground. In addition there were large developments of the engineering arm, concerned with motor transport, motor-bicycle scouting, aviation, and the like.

No first-class intelligence had been sought to specialise in and work out the problem of warfare with the new appliances and under modern conditions, but a succession of able jurists, Lord Haldane, Chief Justice Briggs, and that very able King's Counsel, Philbrick, had reconstructed the army frequently and thoroughly and placed it at last, with the adoption of national service, upon a footing that would have seemed very imposing to the public of 1900. At any moment the British Empire could now put a million and a quarter of arguable soldiers upon the board of Welt-Politik. The traditions of Japan and the Central European armies were more princely and less forensic; the Chinese still refused resolutely to become a military power, and maintained a small standing army upon the American model that was said, so far as it went, to be highly efficient, and Russia, secured by a stringent administration against internal criticism, had scarcely altered the design of a uniform or the organisation of a battery since the opening decades of the century. Barnet's opinion of his military training was manifestly a poor one, his Modern State ideas disposed him to regard it as a bore, and his common sense condemned it as useless. Moreover, his habit of body made him peculiarly sensitive to the fatigues and hardships of service.

'For three days in succession we turned out before dawn and – for no earthly reason – without breakfast,' he relates. 'I suppose that is to show us that when the Day comes the first thing will be to get us thoroughly uncomfortable and rotten. We then proceeded to Kriegspiel, according to the mysterious ideas of those in authority over us. On the last day we spent three hours under a hot if early sun getting over eight miles of country to a point we could have reached in a motor omnibus in nine minutes and a half – I did it the next day in that – and then we made a massed attack upon entrenchments that could have shot us all about three times over if only the umpires had let them. Then came a little bayonet exercise, but I doubt if I am sufficiently a barbarian to stick this long knife into anything living. Anyhow in this battle I shouldn't have had a chance. Assuming that by some miracle I hadn't been shot three times over, I was far too hot and blown when I got up to the entrenchments even to lift my beastly rifle. It was those others would have begun the sticking….

'For a time we were watched by two hostile aeroplanes; then our own came up and asked them not to, and – the practice of aerial warfare still being unknown – they very politely desisted and went away and did dives and circles of the most charming description over the Fox Hills.'

All Barnet's accounts of his military training were written in the same half-contemptuous, half-protesting tone. He was of opinion that his chances of participating in any real warfare were very slight, and that, if after all he should participate, it was bound to be so entirely different from these peace manoeuvres that his only course as a rational man would be to keep as observantly out of danger as he could until he had learnt the tricks and possibilities of the new conditions. He states this quite frankly. Never was a man more free from sham heroics.

* * *

Barnet welcomed the appearance of the atomic engine with the zest of masculine youth in all fresh machinery, and it is evident that for some time he failed to connect the rush of wonderful new possibilities with the financial troubles of his family. 'I knew my father was worried,' he admits. That cast the smallest of shadows upon his delighted departure for Italy and Greece and Egypt with three congenial companions in one of the new atomic models. They flew over the Channel Isles and Touraine, he mentions, and circled about Mont Blanc – 'These new helicopters, we found,' he notes, 'had abolished all the danger and strain of sudden drops to which the old-time aeroplanes were liable' – and then he went on by way of Pisa, Paestum, Ghirgenti, and Athens, to visit the pyramids by moonlight, flying thither from Cairo, and to follow the Nile up to Khartum. Even by later standards, it must have been a very gleeful holiday for a young man, and it made the tragedy of his next experiences all the darker. A week after his return his father, who was a widower, announced himself ruined, and committed suicide by means of an unscheduled opiate.

At one blow Barnet found himself flung out of the possessing, spending, enjoying class to which he belonged, penniless and with no calling by which he could earn a living. He tried teaching and some journalism, but in a little while he found himself on the underside of a world in which he had always reckoned to live in the sunshine. For innumerable men such an experience has meant mental and spiritual destruction, but Barnet, in spite of his bodily gravitation towards comfort, showed himself when put to the test, of the more valiant modern quality. He was saturated with the creative stoicism of the heroic times that were already dawning, and he took his difficulties and discomforts stoutly as his appointed material, and turned them to expression.

Indeed, in his book, he thanks fortune for them. 'I might have lived and died,' he says, 'in that neat fool's paradise of secure lavishness above there. I might never have realised the gathering wrath and sorrow of the ousted and exasperated masses. In the days of my own prosperity things had seemed to me to be very well arranged.' Now from his new point of view he was to find they were not arranged at all; that government was a compromise of aggressions and powers and lassitudes, and law a convention between interests, and that the poor and the weak, though they had many negligent masters, had few friends.

'I had thought things were looked after,' he wrote. 'It was with a kind of amazement that I tramped the roads and starved – and found that no one in particular cared.'

He was turned out of his lodging in a backward part of London.

'It was with difficulty I persuaded my landlady – she was a needy widow, poor soul, and I was already in her debt – to keep an old box for me in which I had locked a few letters, keepsakes, and the like. She lived in great fear of the Public Health and Morality Inspectors, because she was sometimes too poor to pay the customary tip to them, but at last she consented to put it in a dark tiled place under the stairs, and then I went forth into the world – to seek first the luck of a meal and then shelter.'

He wandered down into the thronging gayer parts of London, in which a year or so ago he had been numbered among the spenders.

London, under the Visible Smoke Law, by which any production of visible smoke with or without excuse was punishable by a fine, had already ceased to be the sombre smoke-darkened city of the Victorian time; it had been, and indeed was, constantly being rebuilt, and its main streets were already beginning to take on those characteristics that distinguished them throughout the latter half of the twentieth century. The insanitary horse and the plebeian bicycle had been banished from the roadway, which was now of a resilient, glass-like surface, spotlessly clean; and the foot passenger was restricted to a narrow vestige of the ancient footpath on either side of the track and forbidden at the risk of a fine, if he survived, to cross the roadway. People descended from their automobiles upon this pavement and went through the lower shops to the lifts and stairs to the new ways for pedestrians, the Rows, that ran along the front of the houses at the level of the first story, and, being joined by frequent bridges, gave the newer parts of London a curiously Venetian appearance. In some streets there were upper and even third-story Rows. For most of the day and all night the shop windows were lit by electric light, and many establishments had made, as it were, canals of public footpaths through their premises in order to increase their window space.

Barnet made his way along this night-scene rather apprehensively since the police had power to challenge and demand the Labour Card of any indigent-looking person, and if the record failed to show he was in employment, dismiss him to the traffic pavement below.

But there was still enough of his former gentility about Barnet's appearance and bearing to protect him from this; the police, too, had other things to think of that night, and he was permitted to reach the galleries about Leicester Square – that great focus of London life and pleasure.

He gives a vivid description of the scene that evening. In the centre was a garden raised on arches lit by festoons of lights and connected with the Rows by eight graceful bridges, beneath which hummed the interlacing streams of motor traffic, pulsating as the current alternated between east and west and north and south. Above rose great frontages of intricate rather than beautiful reinforced porcelain, studded with lights, barred by bold illuminated advertisements, and glowing with reflections. There were the two historical music halls of this place, the Shakespeare Memorial Theatre, in which the municipal players revolved perpetually through the cycle of Shakespeare's plays, and four other great houses of refreshment and entertainment whose pinnacles streamed up into the blue obscurity of the night. The south side of the square was in dark contrast to the others; it was still being rebuilt, and a lattice of steel bars surmounted by the frozen gestures of monstrous cranes rose over the excavated sites of vanished Victorian buildings.

This framework attracted Barnet's attention for a time to the exclusion of other interests. It was absolutely still, it had a dead rigidity, a stricken inaction, no one was at work upon it and all its machinery was quiet; but the constructor's globes of vacuum light filled its every interstice with a quivering green moonshine and showed alert but motionless – soldier sentinels!

He asked a passing stroller, and was told that the men had struck that day against the use of an atomic riveter that would have doubled the individual efficiency and halved the number of steel workers.

"Shouldn't wonder if they didn't get chucking bombs," said Barnet's informant, hovered for a moment, and then went on his way to the Alhambra music hall.

Barnet became aware of an excitement in the newspaper kiosks at the corners of the square. Something very sensational had been flashed upon the transparencies. Forgetting for a moment his penniless condition, he made his way over a bridge to buy a paper, for in those days the papers, which were printed upon thin sheets of metallic foil, were sold at determinate points by specially licensed purveyors. Half over, he stopped short at a change in the traffic below; and was astonished to see that the police signals were restricting vehicles to the half roadway. When presently he got within sight of the transparencies that had replaced the placards of Victorian times, he read of the Great March of the Unemployed that was already in progress through the West End, and so without expenditure he was able to understand what was coming.

He watched, and his book describes this procession which the police had considered it unwise to prevent and which had been spontaneously organised in imitation of the Unemployed Processions of earlier times. He had expected a mob but there was a kind of sullen discipline about the procession when at last it arrived. What seemed for a time an unending column of men marched wearily, marched with a kind of implacable futility, along the roadway underneath him. He was, he says, moved to join them, but instead he remained watching. They were a dingy, shabby, ineffective-looking multitude, for the most part incapable of any but obsolete and superseded types of labour. They bore a few banners with the time-honoured inscription: 'Work, not Charity,' but otherwise their ranks were unadorned.

They were not singing, they were not even talking, there was nothing truculent nor aggressive in their bearing, they had no definite objective they were just marching and showing themselves in the more prosperous parts of London. They were a sample of that great mass of unskilled cheap labour which the now still cheaper mechanical powers had superseded for evermore. They were being 'scrapped' – as horses had been 'scrapped.'

Barnet leant over the parapet watching them, his mind quickened by his own precarious condition. For a time, he says, he felt nothing but despair at the sight; what should be done, what could be done for this gathering surplus of humanity? They were so manifestly useless – and incapable – and pitiful.

What were they asking for?

They had been overtaken by unexpected things. Nobody had foreseen –

It flashed suddenly into his mind just what the multitudinous shambling enigma below meant. It was an appeal against the unexpected, an appeal to those others who, more fortunate, seemed wiser and more powerful, for something – for INTELLIGENCE. This mute mass, weary footed, rank following rank, protested its persuasion that some of these others must have foreseen these dislocations – that anyhow they ought to have foreseen – and arranged.

That was what this crowd of wreckage was feeling and seeking so dumbly to assert.

'Things came to me like the turning on of a light in a darkened room,' he says. 'These men were praying to their fellow creatures as once they prayed to God! The last thing that men will realise about anything is that it is inanimate. They had transferred their animation to mankind. They still believed there was intelligence somewhere, even if it was careless or malignant.... It had only to be aroused to be conscience-stricken, to be moved to exertion.... And I saw, too, that as yet THERE WAS NO SUCH INTELLIGENCE. The world waits for intelligence. That intelligence has still to be made, that will for good and order has still to be gathered together, out of scraps of impulse and wandering seeds of benevolence and whatever is fine and creative in our souls, into a common purpose. It's something still to come....'

It is characteristic of the widening thought of the time that this not very heroical young man who, in any previous age, might well have been altogether occupied with the problem of his own individual necessities, should be able to stand there and generalise about the needs of the race.

But upon all the stresses and conflicts of that chaotic time there was already dawning the light of a new era. The spirit of humanity was escaping, even then it was escaping, from its extreme imprisonment in individuals. Salvation from the bitter intensities of self, which had been a conscious religious end for thousands of years, which men had sought in mortifications, in the wilderness, in meditation, and by innumerable strange paths, was coming at last with the effect of naturalness into the talk of men, into the books they read, into their unconscious gestures, into their newspapers and daily purposes and everyday acts. The broad horizons, the magic possibilities that the spirit of the seeker had revealed to them, were charming them out of those ancient and instinctive preoccupations from which the very threat of hell and torment had failed to drive them. And this young man, homeless and without provision even for the immediate hours, in the presence of social disorganisation, distress, and perplexity, in a blazing wilderness of thoughtless pleasure that blotted out the stars, could think as he tells us he thought.

'I saw life plain,' he wrote. 'I saw the gigantic task before us, and the very splendour of its intricate and immeasurable difficulty filled me with exaltation. I saw that we have still to discover government, that we have still to discover education, which is the necessary reciprocal of government, and that all this – in which my own little speck of a life was so manifestly overwhelmed – this and its yesterday in Greece and Rome and Egypt were nothing, the mere first dust swirls of the beginning, the movements and dim murmurings of a sleeper who will presently be awake....'

* * *

And then the story tells, with an engaging simplicity, of his descent from this ecstatic vision of reality.

'Presently I found myself again, and I was beginning to feel cold and a little hungry.'

He bethought himself of the John Burns Relief Offices which stood upon the Thames Embankment. He made his way through the galleries of the booksellers and the National Gallery, which had been open continuously day and night to all decently dressed people now for more than twelve years, and across the rose-gardens of Trafalgar Square, and so by the hotel colonnade to the Embankment. He had long known of these admirable offices, which had swept the last beggars and matchsellers and all the casual indigent from the London streets, and he believed that he would, as a matter of course, be able to procure a ticket for food and a night's lodgings and some indication of possible employment.

But he had not reckoned upon the new labour troubles, and when he got to the Embankment he found the offices hopelessly congested and besieged by a large and rather unruly crowd. He hovered for a time on the outskirts of the waiting multitude, perplexed and dismayed, and then he became aware of a movement, a purposive trickling away of people, up through the arches of the great buildings that had arisen when all the railway stations were removed to the south side of the river, and so to the covered ways of the Strand. And here, in the open glare of midnight, he found unemployed men begging, and not only begging, but begging with astonishing assurance, from the people who were emerging from the small theatres and other such places of entertainment which abounded in that thoroughfare.

This was an altogether unexampled thing. There had been no begging in London streets for a quarter of a century. But that night the police were evidently unwilling or unable to cope with the destitute who were invading those well-kept quarters of the town. They had become stonily blind to anything but manifest disorder.

Barnet walked through the crowd, unable to bring himself to ask; indeed his bearing must have been more valiant than his circumstances, for twice he says that he was begged from. Near the Trafalgar Square gardens, a girl with reddened cheeks and blackened eyebrows, who was walking alone, spoke to him with a peculiar friendliness.

"I'm starving," he said to her abruptly.

"Oh! Poor dear!" she said; and with the impulsive generosity of her kind, glanced round and slipped a silver piece into his hand....

It was a gift that, in spite of the precedent of De Quincey, might under the repressive social legislation of those times, have brought Barnet within reach of the prison lash. But he took it, he confesses, and thanked her as well as he was able, and went off very gladly to get food.

* * *

A day or so later – and again his freedom to go as he pleased upon the roads may be taken as a mark of increasing social disorganisation and police embarrassment – he wandered out into the open country. He speaks of the roads of that plutocratic age as being 'fenced with barbed wire against unpropertied people,' of the high-walled gardens and trespass warnings that kept him to the dusty narrowness of the public ways. In the air, happy rich people were flying, heedless of the misfortunes about them, as he himself had been flying two years ago, and along the road swept the new traffic, light and swift and wonderful. One was rarely out of earshot of its whistles and gongs and siren cries even in the field paths or over the open downs. The officials of the labour exchanges were everywhere overworked and infuriated, the casual wards were so crowded that the surplus wanderers slept in ranks under sheds or in the open air, and since giving to wayfarers had been made a punishable offence there was no longer friendship or help for a man from the rare foot passenger or the wayside cottage....

'I wasn't angry,' said Barnet. 'I saw an immense selfishness, a monstrous disregard for anything but pleasure and possession in all those people above us, but I saw how inevitable that was, how certainly if the richest had changed places with the poorest, that things would have been the same. What else can happen when men use science and every new thing that science gives, and all their available intelligence and energy to manufacture wealth and appliances, and leave government and education to the rustling traditions of hundreds of years ago? Those traditions come from the dark ages when there was really not enough for every one, when life was a fierce struggle that might be masked but could not be escaped. Of course this famine grabbing, this fierce dispossession of others, must follow from such a disharmony between material and training. Of course the rich were vulgar and the poor grew savage and every added power that came to men made the rich richer and the poor less necessary and less free. The men I met in the casual wards and the relief offices were all smouldering for revolt, talking of justice and injustice and revenge. I saw no hope in that talk, nor in anything but patience...'

But he did not mean a passive patience. He meant that the method of social reconstruction was still a riddle, that no effectual rearrangement was possible until this riddle in all its tangled aspects was solved. 'I tried to talk to those discontented men,' he wrote, 'but it was hard for them to see things as I saw them. When I talked of patience and the larger scheme, they answered, "But then we shall all be dead" – and I could not make them see, what is so simple to my own mind, that that did not affect the question. Men who think in lifetimes are of no use to statesmanship.'

He does not seem to have seen a newspaper during those wanderings, and a chance sight of the transparency of a kiosk in the market-place at Bishop's Stortford announcing a 'Grave International Situation' did not excite him very much. There had been so many grave international situations in recent years.

This time it was talk of the Central European powers suddenly attacking the Slav Confederacy, with France and England going to the help of the Slavs.

But the next night he found a tolerable meal awaiting the vagrants in the casual ward, and learnt from the workhouse master that all serviceable trained men were to be sent back on the morrow to their mobilisation centres. The country was on the eve of war. He was to go back through London to Surrey. His first feeling, he records, was one of extreme relief that his days of 'hopeless battering at the underside of civilisation' were at an end. Here was something definite to do, something definitely provided for. But his relief was greatly modified when he found that the mobilisation arrangements had been made so hastily and carelessly that for nearly thirty-six hours at the improvised depot at Epsom he got nothing either to eat or to drink but a cup of cold water. The depot was absolutely unprovisioned, and no one was free to leave it.

Chapter II
The Last War

VIEWED FROM the standpoint of a sane and ambitious social order, it is difficult to understand, and it would be tedious to follow, the motives that plunged mankind into the war that fills the histories of the middle decades of the twentieth century.

It must always be remembered that the political structure of the world at that time was everywhere extraordinarily behind the collective intelligence. That is the central fact of that history. For two hundred years there had been no great changes in political or legal methods and pretensions, the utmost change had been a certain shifting of boundaries and slight readjustment of procedure, while in nearly every other aspect of life there had been fundamental revolutions, gigantic releases, and an enormous enlargement of scope and outlook. The absurdities of courts and the indignities of representative parliamentary government, coupled with the opening of vast fields of opportunity in other directions, had withdrawn the best intelligences more and more from public affairs. The ostensible governments of the world in the twentieth century were following in the wake of the ostensible religions. They were ceasing to command the services of any but second-rate men. After the middle of the eighteenth century there are no more great ecclesiastics upon the world's memory, after the opening of the twentieth no more statesmen. Everywhere one finds an energetic, ambitious, short-sighted, common-place type in the seats of authority, blind to the new possibilities and litigiously reliant upon the traditions of the past.

Perhaps the most dangerous of those outworn traditions were the boundaries of the various 'sovereign states,' and the conception of a general predominance in human affairs on the part of some one particular state. The memory of the empires of Rome and Alexander squatted, an unlaid carnivorous ghost, in the human imagination – it bored into the human brain like some grisly parasite and filled it with disordered thoughts and violent impulses. For more than a century the French system exhausted its vitality in belligerent convulsions, and then the infection passed to the German-speaking peoples who were the heart and centre of Europe, and from them onward to the Slavs. Later ages were to store and neglect the vast insane literature of this obsession, the intricate treaties, the secret agreements, the infinite knowingness of the political writer, the cunning refusals to accept plain facts, the strategic devices, the tactical manoeuvres, the records of mobilisations and counter-mobilisations. It ceased to be credible almost as soon as it ceased to happen, but in the very dawn of the new age their state craftsmen sat with their historical candles burning, and, in spite of strange, new reflections and unfamiliar lights and shadows, still wrangling and planning to rearrange the maps of Europe and the world.

It was to become a matter for subtle inquiry how far the millions of men and women outside the world of these specialists sympathised and agreed with their portentous activities. One school of psychologists inclined to minimise this participation, but the balance of evidence goes to show that there were massive responses to these suggestions of the belligerent schemer. Primitive man had been a fiercely combative animal; innumerable generations had passed their lives in tribal warfare, and the weight of tradition, the example of history, the ideals of loyalty and devotion fell in easily enough with the incitements of the international mischief-maker. The political ideas of the common man were picked up haphazard, there was practically nothing in such education as he was given that was ever intended to fit him for citizenship as such (that conception only appeared, indeed, with the development of Modern State ideas), and it was therefore a comparatively easy matter to fill his vacant mind with the sounds and fury of exasperated suspicion and national aggression.

For example, Barnet describes the London crowd as noisily patriotic when presently his battalion came up from the depot to London, to entrain for the French frontier. He tells of children and women and lads and old men cheering and shouting, of the streets and rows hung with the flags of the Allied Powers, of a real enthusiasm even among the destitute and unemployed. The Labour Bureaux were now partially transformed into enrolment offices, and were centres of hotly patriotic excitement. At every convenient place upon the line on either side of the Channel Tunnel there were enthusiastic spectators, and the feeling in the regiment, if a little stiffened and darkened by grim anticipations, was none the less warlike.

But all this emotion was the fickle emotion of minds without established ideas; it was with most of them, Barnet says, as it was with himself, a natural response to collective movement, and to martial sounds and colours, and the exhilarating challenge of vague dangers. And people had been so long oppressed by the threat of and preparation for war that its arrival came with an effect of positive relief.

* * *

The plan of campaign of the Allies assigned the defence of the lower Meuse to the English, and the troop-trains were run direct from the various British depots to the points in the

Ardennes where they were intended to entrench themselves.

Most of the documents bearing upon the campaign were destroyed during the war, from the first the scheme of the Allies seems to have been confused, but it is highly probable that the formation of an aerial park in this region, from which attacks could be made upon the vast industrial plant of the lower Rhine, and a flanking raid through Holland upon the German naval establishments at the mouth of the Elbe, were integral parts of the original project. Nothing of this was known to such pawns in the game as Barnet and his company, whose business it was to do what they were told by the mysterious intelligences at the direction of things in Paris, to which city the Whitehall staff had also been transferred. From first to last these directing intelligences remained mysterious to the body of the army, veiled under the name of 'Orders.' There was no Napoleon, no Caesar to embody enthusiasm. Barnet says, 'We talked of Them. THEY are sending us up into Luxembourg. THEY are going to turn the Central European right.'

Behind the veil of this vagueness the little group of more or less worthy men which constituted Headquarters was beginning to realise the enormity of the thing it was supposed to control....

In the great hall of the War Control, whose windows looked out across the Seine to the Trocadero and the palaces of the western quarter, a series of big-scale relief maps were laid out upon tables to display the whole seat of war, and the staff-officers of the control were continually busy shifting the little blocks which represented the contending troops, as the reports and intelligence came drifting in to the various telegraphic bureaux in the adjacent rooms. In other smaller apartments there were maps of a less detailed sort, upon which, for example, the reports of the British Admiralty and of the Slav commanders were recorded as they kept coming to hand. Upon these maps, as upon chessboards, Marshal Dubois, in consultation with General Viard and the Earl of Delhi, was to play the great game for world supremacy against the Central European powers. Very probably he had a definite idea of his game; very probably he had a coherent and admirable plan.

But he had reckoned without a proper estimate either of the new strategy of aviation or of the possibilities of atomic energy that Holsten had opened for mankind. While he planned entrenchments and invasions and a frontier war, the Central European generalship was striking at the eyes and the brain. And while, with a certain diffident hesitation, he developed his gambit that night upon the lines laid down by Napoleon and Moltke, his own scientific corps in a state of mutinous activity was preparing a blow for Berlin. 'These old fools!' was the key in which the scientific corps was thinking.

The War Control in Paris, on the night of July the second, was an impressive display of the paraphernalia of scientific military organisation, as the first half of the twentieth century understood it. To one human being at least the consulting commanders had the likeness of world-wielding gods.

She was a skilled typist, capable of nearly sixty words a minute, and she had been engaged in relay with other similar women to take down orders in duplicate and hand them over to the junior officers in attendance, to be forwarded and filed. There had come a lull, and she had been sent out from the dictating room to take the air upon the terrace before the great hall and to eat such scanty refreshment as she had brought with her until her services were required again.

From her position upon the terrace this young woman had a view not only of the wide sweep of the river below her, and all the eastward side of Paris from the Arc de Triomphe to Saint Cloud, great blocks and masses of black or pale darkness with pink and golden flashes of illumination and endless interlacing bands of dotted lights under a still and starless sky, but also the whole spacious interior of the great hall with its slender pillars and gracious arching and clustering lamps was visible to her. There, over a wilderness of tables, lay the huge maps, done on so large a scale that one might fancy them small countries; the messengers and attendants went and came perpetually, altering, moving the little pieces that signified hundreds and thousands of men, and the great commander and his two consultants stood amidst all these things and near where the fighting was nearest, scheming, directing. They had but to breathe a word and presently away there, in the world of reality, the punctual myriads moved. Men rose up and went forward and died. The fate of nations lay behind the eyes of these three men. Indeed they were like gods.

Most godlike of the three was Dubois. It was for him to decide; the others at most might suggest. Her woman's soul went out to this grave, handsome, still, old man, in a passion of instinctive worship.

Once she had taken words of instruction from him direct. She had awaited them in an ecstasy of happiness – and fear. For her exaltation was made terrible by the dread that some error might dishonour her....

She watched him now through the glass with all the unpenetrating minuteness of an impassioned woman's observation.

He said little, she remarked. He looked but little at the maps. The tall Englishman beside him was manifestly troubled by a swarm of ideas, conflicting ideas; he craned his neck at every shifting of the little red, blue, black, and yellow pieces on the board, and wanted to draw the commander's attention to this and that. Dubois listened, nodded, emitted a word and became still again, brooding like the national eagle.

His eyes were so deeply sunken under his white eyebrows that she could not see his eyes; his moustache overhung the mouth from which those words of decision came. Viard, too, said little; he was a dark man with a drooping head and melancholy, watchful eyes. He was more intent upon the French right, which was feeling its way now through Alsace to the Rhine. He was, she knew, an old colleague of Dubois; he knew him better, she decided, he trusted him more than this unfamiliar Englishman....

Not to talk, to remain impassive and as far as possible in profile; these were the lessons that old Dubois had mastered years ago. To seem to know all, to betray no surprise, to refuse to hurry – itself a confession of miscalculation; by attention to these simple rules, Dubois had built up a steady reputation from the days when he had been a promising junior officer, a still, almost abstracted young man, deliberate but ready. Even then men had looked at him and said: "He will go far." Through fifty years of peace he had never once been found wanting, and at manoeuvres his impassive persistence had perplexed and hypnotised and defeated many a more actively intelligent man. Deep in his soul Dubois had hidden his one profound discovery about the modern art of warfare, the key to his career. And this discovery was that NOBODY KNEW, that to act therefore was to blunder, that to talk was to confess; and that the man who acted slowly and steadfastly and above all silently, had the best chance of winning through. Meanwhile one fed the men. Now by this same strategy he hoped to shatter those mysterious unknowns of the Central European command. Delhi might talk of a great flank march through Holland, with all the British submarines and hydroplanes and torpedo craft pouring up the Rhine in support of it; Viard might crave for brilliance with the motor bicycles, aeroplanes, and ski-men among the Swiss mountains, and a sudden swoop upon Vienna; the thing was to listen – and wait for the other side to begin experimenting. It was all experimenting. And meanwhile he remained in profile, with an air of assurance – like a man who sits in an automobile after the chauffeur has had his directions.

And every one about him was the stronger and surer for that quiet face, that air of knowledge and unruffled confidence. The clustering lights threw a score of shadows of him upon the maps, great bunches of him, versions of a commanding presence, lighter or darker, dominated the field, and pointed in every direction. Those shadows symbolised his control. When a messenger came from the wireless room to shift this or that piece in the game, to replace under amended reports one Central European regiment by a score, to draw back or thrust out or distribute this or that force of the Allies, the Marshal would turn his head and seem not to see, or look and nod slightly, as a master nods who approves a pupil's self-correction. "Yes, that's better."

How wonderful he was, thought the woman at the window, how wonderful it all was. This was the brain of the western world, this was Olympus with the warring earth at its feet. And he was guiding France, France so long a resentful exile from imperialism, back to her old predominance.

It seemed to her beyond the desert of a woman that she should be privileged to participate. . . .

It is hard to be a woman, full of the stormy impulse to personal devotion, and to have to be impersonal, abstract, exact, punctual. She must control herself. . . .

She gave herself up to fantastic dreams, dreams of the days when the war would be over and victory enthroned. Then perhaps this harshness, this armour would be put aside and the gods might unbend. Her eyelids drooped. . . .

She roused herself with a start. She became aware that the night outside was no longer still. That there was an excitement down below on the bridge and a running in the street and a flickering of searchlights among the clouds from some high place away beyond the Trocadero. And then the excitement came surging up past her and invaded the hall within.

One of the sentinels from the terrace stood at the upper end of the room, gesticulating and shouting something.

And all the world had changed. A kind of throbbing. She couldn't understand. It was as if all the water-pipes and concealed machinery and cables of the ways beneath, were beating – as pulses beat. And about her blew something like a wind – a wind that was dismay.

Her eyes went to the face of the Marshal as a frightened child might look towards its mother.

He was still serene. He was frowning slightly, she thought, but that was natural enough, for the Earl of Delhi, with one hand gauntly gesticulating, had taken him by the arm and was all too manifestly disposed to drag him towards the great door that opened on the terrace. And Viard was hurrying towards the huge windows and doing so in the strangest of attitudes, bent forward and with eyes upturned.

Something up there?

And then it was as if thunder broke overhead.

The sound struck her like a blow. She crouched together against the masonry and looked up. She saw three black shapes swooping down through the torn clouds, and from a point a little below two of them, there had already started curling trails of red. . . .

Everything else in her being was paralysed, she hung through moments that seemed infinities, watching those red missiles whirl down towards her.

She felt torn out of the world. There was nothing else in the world but a crimson-purple glare and sound, deafening, all-embracing, continuing sound. Every other light had gone out about her and against this glare hung slanting walls, pirouetting pillars, projecting fragments of cornices, and a disorderly flight of huge angular sheets of glass. She had an impression of a great ball of crimson-purple fire like a maddened living thing that seemed to be whirling about very rapidly amidst a chaos of falling masonry, that seemed to be attacking the earth furiously, that seemed to be burrowing into it like a blazing rabbit....

She had all the sensations of waking up out of a dream.

She found she was lying face downward on a bank of mould and that a little rivulet of hot water was running over one foot. She tried to raise herself and found her leg was very painful. She was not clear whether it was night or day nor where she was; she made a second effort, wincing and groaning, and turned over and got into a sitting position and looked about her.

Everything seemed very silent. She was, in fact, in the midst of a vast uproar, but she did not realise this because her hearing had been destroyed.

At first she could not join on what she saw to any previous experience.

She seemed to be in a strange world, a soundless, ruinous world, a world of heaped broken things. And it was lit – and somehow this was more familiar to her mind than any other fact about her – by a flickering, purplish-crimson light. Then close to her, rising above a confusion of debris, she recognised the Trocadero; it was changed, something had gone from it, but its outline was unmistakable. It stood out against a streaming, whirling uprush of red-lit steam. And with that she recalled Paris and the Seine and the warm, overcast evening and the beautiful, luminous organisation of the War Control....

She drew herself a little way up the slope of earth on which she lay, and examined her surroundings with an increasing understanding....

The earth on which she was lying projected like a cape into the river. Quite close to her was a brimming lake of dammed-up water, from which these warm rivulets and torrents were trickling. Wisps of vapour came into circling existence a foot or so from its mirror-surface. Near at hand and reflected exactly in the water was the upper part of a familiar-looking stone pillar. On the side of her away from the water the heaped ruins rose steeply in a confused slope up to a glaring crest. Above and reflecting this glare towered pillowed masses of steam rolling swiftly upward to the zenith. It was from this crest that the livid glow that lit the world about her proceeded, and slowly her mind connected this mound with the vanished buildings of the War Control.

"Mais!" she whispered, and remained with staring eyes quite motionless for a time, crouching close to the warm earth.

Then presently this dim, broken human thing began to look about it again. She began to feel the need of fellowship. She wanted to question, wanted to speak, wanted to relate her experience. And her foot hurt her atrociously. There ought to be an ambulance. A little gust of querulous criticisms blew across her mind. This surely was a disaster! Always after a disaster there should be ambulances and helpers moving about....

She craned her head. There was something there. But everything was so still!

"Monsieur!" she cried. Her ears, she noted, felt queer, and she began to suspect that all was not well with them.

It was terribly lonely in this chaotic strangeness, and perhaps this man – if it was a man, for it was difficult to see – might for all his stillness be merely insensible. He might have been stunned....

The leaping glare beyond sent a ray into his corner and for a moment every little detail was distinct. It was Marshal Dubois. He was lying against a huge slab of the war map. To it there stuck and from it there dangled little wooden objects, the symbols of infantry and cavalry and guns, as they were disposed upon the frontier. He did not seem to be aware of this at his back, he had an effect of inattention, not indifferent attention, but as if he were thinking....

She could not see the eyes beneath his shaggy brows, but it was evident he frowned. He frowned slightly, he had an air of not wanting to be disturbed. His face still bore that expression of assured confidence, that conviction that if things were left to him France might obey in security....

She did not cry out to him again, but she crept a little nearer. A strange surmise made her eyes dilate. With a painful wrench she pulled herself up so that she could see completely over the intervening lumps of smashed-up masonry. Her hand touched something wet, and after one convulsive movement she became rigid.

It was not a whole man there; it was a piece of a man, the head and shoulders of a man that trailed down into a ragged darkness and a pool of shining black....

And even as she stared the mound above her swayed and crumbled, and a rush of hot water came pouring over her. Then it seemed to her that she was dragged downward....

* * *

When the rather brutish young aviator with the bullet head and the black hair close-cropped en brosse, who was in charge of the French special scientific corps, heard presently of this disaster to the War Control, he was so wanting in imagination in any sphere but his own, that he laughed. Small matter to him that Paris was burning. His mother and father and sister lived at Caudebec; and the only sweetheart he had ever had, and it was poor love-making then, was a girl in Rouen. He slapped his second-in-command on the shoulder. "Now," he said, "there's nothing on earth to stop us going to Berlin and giving them tit-for-tat.... Strategy and reasons of state – they're over.... Come along, my boy, and we'll just show these old women what we can do when they let us have our heads."

He spent five minutes telephoning and then he went out into the courtyard of the chateau in which he had been installed and shouted for his automobile. Things would have to move quickly because there was scarcely an hour and a half before dawn. He looked at the sky and noted with satisfaction a heavy bank of clouds athwart the pallid east.

He was a young man of infinite shrewdness, and his material and aeroplanes were scattered all over the country-side, stuck away in barns, covered with hay, hidden in woods. A hawk could not have discovered any of them without coming within reach of a gun. But that night he only wanted one of the machines, and it was handy and quite prepared under a tarpaulin between two ricks not a couple of miles away; he was going to Berlin with that and just one other man. Two men would be enough for what he meant to do....

He had in his hands the black complement to all those other gifts science was urging upon unregenerate mankind, the gift of destruction, and he was an adventurous rather than a sympathetic type....

He was a dark young man with something negroid about his gleaming face. He smiled like one who is favoured and anticipates great pleasures. There was an exotic richness, a chuckling flavour, about the voice in which he gave his orders, and he pointed his remarks with the long finger of a hand that was hairy and exceptionally big.

"We'll give them tit-for-tat," he said. "We'll give them tit-for-tat. No time to lose, boys...."

And presently over the cloud-banks that lay above Westphalia and Saxony the swift aeroplane, with its atomic engine as noiseless as a dancing sunbeam and its phosphorescent gyroscopic compass, flew like an arrow to the heart of the Central European hosts.

It did not soar very high; it skimmed a few hundred feet above the banked darkness of cumulus that hid the world, ready to plunge at once into their wet obscurities should some hostile flier range into vision. The tense young steersman divided his attention between the guiding stars above and the level, tumbled surfaces of the vapour strata that hid the world below. Over great spaces those banks lay as even as a frozen lava-flow and almost as still, and then they were rent by ragged areas of translucency, pierced by clear chasms, so that dim patches of the land below gleamed remotely through abysses. Once he saw quite distinctly the plan of a big railway station outlined in lamps and signals, and once the flames of a burning rick showing livid through a boiling drift of smoke on the side of some great hill. But if the world was masked it was alive with sounds. Up through that vapour floor came the deep roar of trains, the whistles of horns of motor-cars, a sound of rifle fire away to the south, and as he drew near his destination the crowing of cocks....

The sky above the indistinct horizons of this cloud sea was at first starry and then paler with a light that crept from north to east as the dawn came on. The Milky Way was invisible in the blue, and the lesser stars vanished. The face of the adventurer at the steering-wheel, darkly visible ever and again by the oval greenish glow of the compass face, had something of that firm beauty which all concentrated purpose gives, and something of the happiness of an idiot child that has at last got hold of the matches. His companion, a less imaginative type, sat with his legs spread wide over the long, coffin-shaped box which contained in its compartments the three atomic bombs, the new bombs that would continue to explode indefinitely and which no one so far had ever seen in action. Hitherto Carolinum, their essential substance, had been tested only in almost infinitesimal quantities within steel chambers embedded in lead. Beyond the thought of great destruction slumbering in the black spheres between his legs, and a keen resolve to follow out very exactly the instructions that had been given him, the man's mind was a blank. His aquiline profile against the starlight expressed nothing but a profound gloom.

The sky below grew clearer as the Central European capital was approached.

So far they had been singularly lucky and had been challenged by no aeroplanes at all. The frontier scouts they must have passed in the night; probably these were mostly under the clouds; the world was wide and they had had luck in not coming close to any soaring sentinel. Their machine was painted a pale gray, that lay almost invisibly over the cloud levels below. But now the east was flushing with the near ascent of the sun, Berlin was but a score of miles ahead, and the luck of the Frenchmen held. By imperceptible degrees the clouds below dissolved....

Away to the north-eastward, in a cloudless pool of gathering light and with all its nocturnal illuminations still blazing, was Berlin. The left finger of the steersman verified roads and open spaces below upon the mica-covered square of map that was fastened by his wheel. There in a series of lake-like expansions was the Havel away to the right; over by those forests must be Spandau; there the river split about the Potsdam island; and right ahead was Charlottenburg cleft by a great thoroughfare that fell like an indicating beam of light straight to the imperial headquarters. There, plain enough, was the Thiergarten; beyond rose the imperial palace, and to the right those tall buildings, those clustering, beflagged, bemasted roofs, must be the offices in which the Central European staff was housed. It was all coldly clear and colourless in the dawn.

He looked up suddenly as a humming sound grew out of nothing and became swiftly louder. Nearly overhead a German aeroplane was circling down from an immense height to challenge him. He made a gesture with his left arm to the gloomy man behind and then gripped his little wheel with both hands, crouched over it, and twisted his neck to look upward. He was attentive, tightly strung, but quite contemptuous of their ability to hurt him.

No German alive, he was assured, could outfly him, or indeed any one of the best Frenchmen. He imagined they might strike at him as a hawk strikes, but they were men coming down out of the bitter cold up there, in a hungry, spiritless, morning mood; they came slanting down like a sword swung by a lazy man, and not so rapidly but that he was able to slip away from under them and get between them and Berlin. They began challenging him in German with a megaphone when they were still perhaps a mile away. The words came to him, rolled up into a mere blob of hoarse sound. Then, gathering alarm from his grim silence, they gave chase and swept down, a hundred yards above him perhaps, and a couple of hundred behind. They were beginning to understand what he was. He ceased to watch them and concentrated himself on the city ahead, and for a time the two aeroplanes raced....

A bullet came tearing through the air by him, as though some one was tearing paper. A second followed. Something tapped the machine.

It was time to act. The broad avenues, the park, the palaces below rushed widening out nearer and nearer to them. "Ready!" said the steersman.

The gaunt face hardened to grimness, and with both hands the bomb-thrower lifted the big atomic bomb from the box and steadied it against the side. It was a black sphere two feet in diameter. Between its handles was a little celluloid stud, and to this he bent his head until his lips touched it. Then he had to bite in order to let the air in upon the inducive. Sure of its accessibility, he craned his neck over the side of the aeroplane and judged his pace and distance. Then very quickly he bent forward, bit the stud, and hoisted the bomb over the side.

"Round," he whispered inaudibly.

The bomb flashed blinding scarlet in mid-air, and fell, a descending column of blaze eddying spirally in the midst of a whirlwind. Both the aeroplanes were tossed like shuttlecocks, hurled high and sideways and the steersman, with gleaming eyes and set teeth, fought in great banking curves for a balance. The gaunt man clung tight with hand and knees; his nostrils dilated, his teeth biting his lips. He was firmly strapped....

When he could look down again it was like looking down upon the crater of a small volcano. In the open garden before the Imperial castle a shuddering star of evil splendour spurted and poured up smoke and flame towards them like an accusation. They were too high to distinguish people clearly, or mark the bomb's effect upon the building until suddenly the facade tottered and crumbled before the flare as sugar dissolves in water. The man stared for a moment, showed all his long teeth, and then staggered into the cramped standing position his straps permitted, hoisted out and bit another bomb, and sent it down after its fellow.

The explosion came this time more directly underneath the aeroplane and shot it upward edgeways. The bomb box tipped to the point of disgorgement, and the bomb-thrower was pitched forward upon the third bomb with his face close to its celluloid stud. He clutched its handles, and with a sudden gust of determination that the thing should not escape him, bit its stud. Before he could hurl it over, the monoplane was slipping sideways. Everything was falling sideways. Instinctively he gave himself up to gripping, his body holding the bomb in its place.

Then that bomb had exploded also, and steersman, thrower, and aeroplane were just flying rags and splinters of metal and drops of moisture in the air, and a third column of fire rushed eddying down upon the doomed buildings below....

* * *

Never before in the history of warfare had there been a continuing explosive; indeed, up to the middle of the twentieth century the only explosives known were combustibles whose explosiveness was due entirely to their instantaneousness; and these atomic bombs which science burst upon the world that night were strange even to the men who used them. Those used by the Allies were lumps of pure Carolinum, painted on the outside with unoxidised cydonator inducive enclosed hermetically in a case of membranium. A little celluloid stud between the handles by which the bomb was lifted was arranged so as to be easily torn off and admit air to the inducive, which at once became active and set up radio-activity in the outer layer of the Carolinum sphere. This liberated fresh inducive, and so in a few minutes the whole bomb was a blazing continual explosion. The Central European bombs were the same, except that they were larger and had a more complicated arrangement for animating the inducive.

Always before in the development of warfare the shells and rockets fired had been but momentarily explosive, they had gone off in an instant once for all, and if there was nothing living or valuable within reach of the concussion and the flying fragments then they were spent and over. But Carolinum, which belonged to the beta group of Hyslop's so-called 'suspended degenerator' elements, once its degenerative process had been induced, continued a furious radiation of energy and nothing could arrest it. Of all Hyslop's artificial elements, Carolinum was the most heavily stored with energy and the most dangerous to make and handle. To this day it remains the most potent degenerator known. What the earlier twentieth-century chemists called its half period was seventeen days; that is to say, it poured out half of the huge store of energy in its great molecules in the space of seventeen days, the next seventeen days' emission was a half of that first period's outpouring, and so on. As with all radio-active substances this Carolinum, though every seventeen days its power is halved, though constantly it diminishes towards the imperceptible, is never entirely exhausted, and to this day the battle-fields and bomb fields of that frantic time in human history are sprinkled with radiant matter, and so centres of inconvenient rays.

What happened when the celluloid stud was opened was that the inducive oxidised and became active. Then the surface of the Carolinum began to degenerate. This degeneration passed only slowly into the substance of the bomb. A moment or so after its explosion began it was still mainly an inert sphere exploding superficially, a big, inanimate nucleus wrapped in flame and thunder. Those that were thrown from aeroplanes fell in this state, they reached the ground still mainly solid, and, melting soil and rock in their progress, bored into the earth. There, as more and more of the Carolinum became active, the bomb spread itself out into a monstrous cavern of fiery energy at the base of what became very speedily a miniature active volcano. The Carolinum, unable to disperse, freely drove into and mixed up with a boiling confusion of molten soil and superheated steam, and so remained spinning furiously and maintaining an eruption that lasted for years or months or weeks according to the size of the bomb employed and the chances of its dispersal. Once launched, the bomb was absolutely unapproachable and uncontrollable until its forces were nearly exhausted, and from the crater that burst open above it, puffs of heavy incandescent vapour and fragments of viciously punitive rock and mud, saturated with Carolinum, and each a centre of scorching and blistering energy, were flung high and far.

Such was the crowning triumph of military science, the ultimate explosive that was to give the 'decisive touch' to war….

* * *

A recent historical writer has described the world of that time as one that 'believed in established words and was invincibly blind to the obvious in things.' Certainly it seems now that nothing could have been more obvious to the people of the earlier twentieth century than the rapidity with which war was becoming impossible. And as certainly they did not see it. They did not see it until the atomic bombs burst in their fumbling hands. Yet the broad facts must have glared upon any intelligent mind. All through the nineteenth and twentieth centuries the amount of energy that men were able to command was continually increasing. Applied to warfare that meant that the power to inflict a blow, the power to destroy, was continually increasing. There was no increase whatever in the ability to escape. Every sort of passive defence, armour, fortifications, and so forth, was being outmastered by this tremendous increase on the destructive side. Destruction was becoming so facile that any little body of malcontents could use it; it was revolutionising the problems of police and internal rule. Before the last war began it was a matter of common knowledge that a man could carry about in a handbag an amount of latent energy sufficient to wreck half a city. These facts were before the minds of everybody; the children in the streets knew them. And yet the world still, as the Americans used to phrase it, 'fooled around' with the paraphernalia and pretensions of war.

It is only by realising this profound, this fantastic divorce between the scientific and intellectual movement on the one hand, and the world of the lawyer-politician on the other, that the men of a later time can hope to understand this preposterous state of affairs. Social organisation was still in the barbaric stage. There were already great numbers of actively intelligent men and much private and commercial civilisation, but the community, as a whole, was aimless, untrained and unorganised to the pitch of imbecility. Collective civilisation, the 'Modern State,' was still in the womb of the future....

* * *

But let us return to Frederick Barnet's Wander Jahre and its account of the experiences of a common man during the war time. While these terrific disclosures of scientific possibility were happening in Paris and Berlin, Barnet and his company were industriously entrenching themselves in Belgian Luxembourg.

He tells of the mobilisation and of his summer day's journey through the north of France and the Ardennes in a few vivid phrases. The country was browned by a warm summer, the trees a little touched with autumnal colour, and the wheat already golden. When they stopped for an hour at Hirson, men and women with tricolour badges upon the platform distributed cakes and glasses of beer to the thirsty soldiers, and there was much cheerfulness. 'Such good, cool beer it was,' he wrote. 'I had had nothing to eat nor drink since Epsom.'

A number of monoplanes, 'like giant swallows,' he notes, were scouting in the pink evening sky.

Barnet's battalion was sent through the Sedan country to a place called Virton, and thence to a point in the woods on the line to Jemelle. Here they detrained, bivouacked uneasily by the railway – trains and stores were passing along it all night – and next morning he marched eastward through a cold, overcast dawn, and a morning, first cloudy and then blazing, over a large spacious country-side interspersed by forest towards Arlon.

There the infantry were set to work upon a line of masked entrenchments and hidden rifle pits between St Hubert and Virton that were designed to check and delay any advance from the east upon the fortified line of the Meuse. They had their orders, and for two days they worked without either a sight of the enemy or any suspicion of the disaster that had abruptly decapitated the armies of Europe, and turned the west of Paris and the centre of Berlin into blazing miniatures of the destruction of Pompeii.

And the news, when it did come, came attenuated. 'We heard there had been mischief with aeroplanes and bombs in Paris,' Barnet relates; 'but it didn't seem to follow that "They" weren't still somewhere elaborating their plans and issuing orders. When the enemy began to emerge from the woods in front of us, we cheered and blazed away, and didn't trouble much more about anything but the battle in hand. If now and then one cocked up an eye into the sky to see what was happening there, the rip of a bullet soon brought one down to the horizontal again....

'That battle went on for three days all over a great stretch of country between Louvain on the north and Longwy to the south. It was essentially a rifle and infantry struggle. The aeroplanes do not seem to have taken any decisive share in the actual fighting for some days, though no doubt they effected the strategy from the first by preventing surprise movements. They were aeroplanes with atomic engines, but they were not provided with atomic bombs, which were manifestly unsuitable for field use, nor indeed had they any very effective kind of bomb. And though they manoeuvred against each other, and there was rifle shooting at them and between them, there was little actual aerial fighting. Either the airmen were indisposed to fight or the commanders on both sides preferred to reserve these machines for scouting...'

After a day or so of digging and scheming, Barnet found himself in the forefront of a battle. He had made his section of rifle pits chiefly along a line of deep dry ditch that gave a means of inter-communication, he had had the earth scattered over the adjacent field, and he had masked his preparations with tussocks of corn and poppy. The hostile advance came blindly and unsuspiciously across the fields below and would have been very cruelly handled indeed, if some one away to the right had not opened fire too soon.

'It was a queer thrill when these fellows came into sight,' he confesses; 'and not a bit like manoeuvres. They halted for a time on the edge of the wood and then came forward in an open line. They kept walking nearer to us and not looking at us, but away to the right of us. Even when they began to be hit, and their officers' whistles woke them up, they didn't seem to see us. One or two halted to fire, and then they all went back towards the wood again. They went slowly at first, looking round at us, then the shelter of the wood seemed to draw them, and they trotted. I fired rather mechanically and missed, then I fired again, and then I became earnest to hit something, made sure of my sighting, and aimed very carefully at a blue back that was dodging about in the corn. At first I couldn't satisfy myself and didn't shoot, his movements were so spasmodic and uncertain; then I think he came to a ditch or some such obstacle and halted for a moment. "GOT you," I whispered, and pulled the trigger.

'I had the strangest sensations about that man. In the first instance, when I felt that I had hit him I was irradiated with joy and pride....

'I sent him spinning. He jumped and threw up his arms....

'Then I saw the corn tops waving and had glimpses of him flapping about. Suddenly I felt sick. I hadn't killed him....

'In some way he was disabled and smashed up and yet able to struggle about. I began to think....

'For nearly two hours that Prussian was agonising in the corn. Either he was calling out or some one was shouting to him....

'Then he jumped up – he seemed to try to get up upon his feet with one last effort; and then he fell like a sack and lay quite still and never moved again.

'He had been unendurable, and I believe some one had shot him dead. I had been wanting to do so for some time....'

The enemy began sniping the rifle pits from shelters they made for themselves in the woods below. A man was hit in the pit next to Barnet, and began cursing and crying out in a violent rage. Barnet crawled along the ditch to him and found him in great pain, covered with blood, frantic with indignation, and with the half of his right hand smashed to a pulp. "Look at this," he kept repeating, hugging it and then extending it. "Damned foolery! Damned foolery! My right hand, sir! My right hand!"

For some time Barnet could do nothing with him. The man was consumed by his tortured realisation of the evil silliness of war, the realisation which had come upon him in a flash with the bullet that had destroyed his skill and use as an artificer for ever. He was looking at the vestiges with a horror that made him impenetrable to any other idea. At last the poor wretch let Barnet tie up his bleeding stump and help him along the ditch that conducted him deviously out of range....

When Barnet returned his men were already calling out for water, and all day long the line of pits suffered greatly from thirst. For food they had chocolate and bread.

'At first,' he says, 'I was extraordinarily excited by my baptism of fire. Then as the heat of the day came on I experienced an enormous tedium and discomfort. The flies became extremely troublesome, and my little grave of a rifle pit was invaded by ants. I could not get up or move about, for some one in the trees had got a mark on me. I kept thinking of the dead Prussian down among the corn, and of the bitter outcries of my own man. Damned foolery! It WAS damned foolery. But who was to blame? How had we got to this? ...

'Early in the afternoon an aeroplane tried to dislodge us with dynamite bombs, but she was hit by bullets once or twice, and suddenly dived down over beyond the trees.

"'From Holland to the Alps this day," I thought, "there must be crouching and lying between half and a million of men, trying to inflict irreparable damage upon one another. The thing is idiotic to the pitch of impossibility. It is a dream. Presently I shall wake up." ...

'Then the phrase changed itself in my mind. "Presently mankind will wake up."

'I lay speculating just how many thousands of men there were among these hundreds of thousands, whose spirits were in rebellion against all these ancient traditions of flag and empire. Weren't we, perhaps, already in the throes of the last crisis, in that darkest moment of a nightmare's horror before the sleeper will endure no more of it – and wakes?

'I don't know how my speculations ended. I think they were not so much ended as distracted by the distant thudding of the guns that were opening fire at long range upon Namur.'

* * *

But as yet Barnet had seen no more than the mildest beginnings of modern warfare. So far he had taken part only in a little shooting. The bayonet attack by which the advanced line was broken was made at a place called Croix Rouge, more than twenty miles away, and that night under cover of the darkness the rifle pits were abandoned and he got his company away without further loss.

His regiment fell back unpressed behind the fortified lines between Namur and Sedan, entrained at a station called Mettet, and was sent northward by Antwerp and Rotterdam to Haarlem. Hence they marched into North Holland. It was only after the march into Holland that he began to realise the monstrous and catastrophic nature of the struggle in which he was playing his undistinguished part.

He describes very pleasantly the journey through the hills and open land of Brabant, the repeated crossing of arms of the Rhine, and the change from the undulating scenery of Belgium to the flat, rich meadows, the sunlit dyke roads, and the countless windmills of the Dutch levels. In those days there was unbroken land from Alkmaar and Leiden to the Dollart. Three great provinces, South Holland, North Holland, and Zuiderzeeland, reclaimed at various times between the early tenth century and 1945 and all many feet below the level of the waves outside the dykes, spread out their lush polders to the northern sun and sustained a dense industrious population. An intricate web of laws and custom and tradition ensured a perpetual vigilance and a perpetual defence against the beleaguering sea. For more than two hundred and fifty miles from Walcheren to Friesland stretched a line of embankments and pumping stations that was the admiration of the world.

If some curious god had chosen to watch the course of events in those northern provinces while that flanking march of the British was in progress, he would have found a convenient and appropriate seat for his observation upon one of the great cumulus clouds that were drifting slowly across the blue sky during all these eventful days before the great catastrophe. For that was the quality of the weather, hot and clear, with something of a breeze, and underfoot dry and a little inclined to be dusty. This watching god would have looked down upon broad stretches of sunlit green, sunlit save for the creeping patches of shadow cast by the clouds, upon sky-reflecting meres, fringed and divided up by masses of willow and large areas of silvery weeds, upon white roads lying bare to the sun and upon a tracery of blue canals. The pastures were alive with cattle, the roads had a busy traffic, of beasts and bicycles and gaily coloured peasants' automobiles, the hues of the innumerable motor barges in the canal vied with the eventfulness of the roadways; and everywhere in solitary steadings, amidst ricks and barns, in groups by the wayside, in straggling villages, each with its fine old church, or in compact towns laced with canals and abounding in bridges and clipped trees, were human habitations.

The people of this country-side were not belligerents. The interests and sympathies alike of Holland had been so divided that to the end she remained undecided and passive in the struggle of the world powers. And everywhere along the roads taken by the marching armies clustered groups and crowds of impartially observant spectators, women and children in peculiar white caps and old-fashioned sabots, and elderly, clean-shaven men quietly thoughtful over their long pipes. They had no fear of their invaders; the days when 'soldiering' meant bands of licentious looters had long since passed away....

That watcher among the clouds would have seen a great distribution of khaki-uniformed men and khaki-painted material over the whole of the sunken area of Holland. He would have marked the long trains, packed with men or piled with great guns and war material, creeping slowly, alert for train-wreckers, along the north-going lines; he would have seen the Scheldt and Rhine choked with shipping, and pouring out still more men and still more material; he would have noticed halts and provisionings and detrainments, and the long, bustling caterpillars of cavalry and infantry, the maggot-like wagons, the huge beetles of great guns, crawling under the poplars along the dykes and roads northward, along ways lined by the neutral, unmolested, ambiguously observant Dutch. All the barges and shipping upon the canals had been requisitioned for transport. In that clear, bright, warm weather, it would all have looked from above like some extravagant festival of animated toys.

As the sun sank westward the spectacle must have become a little indistinct because of a golden haze; everything must have become warmer and more glowing, and because of the lengthening of the shadows more manifestly in relief. The shadows of the tall churches grew longer and longer, until they touched the horizon and mingled in the universal shadow; and then, slow, and soft, and wrapping the world in fold after fold of deepening blue, came the night – the night at first obscurely simple, and then with faint points here and there, and then jewelled in darkling splendour with a hundred thousand lights. Out of that mingling of darkness and ambiguous glares the noise of an unceasing activity would have arisen, the louder and plainer now because there was no longer any distraction of sight.

It may be that watcher drifting in the pellucid gulf beneath the stars watched all through the night; it may be that he dozed. But if he gave way to so natural a proclivity, assuredly on the fourth night of the great flank march he was aroused, for that was the night of the battle in the air that decided the fate of Holland. The aeroplanes were fighting at last, and suddenly about him, above and below, with cries and uproar rushing out of the four quarters of heaven, striking, plunging, oversetting, soaring to the zenith and dropping to the ground, they came to assail or defend the myriads below.

Secretly the Central European power had gathered his flying machines together, and now he threw them as a giant might fling a handful of ten thousand knives over the low country. And amidst that swarming flight were five that drove headlong for the sea walls of Holland, carrying atomic bombs. From north and west and south, the allied aeroplanes rose in response and swept down upon this sudden attack. So it was that war in the air began. Men rode upon the whirlwind that night and slew and fell like archangels. The sky rained heroes upon the astonished earth. Surely the last fights of mankind were the best. What was the heavy pounding of your Homeric swordsmen, what was the creaking charge of chariots, beside this swift rush, this crash, this giddy triumph, this headlong swoop to death?

And then athwart this whirling rush of aerial duels that swooped and locked and dropped in the void between the lamp-lights and the stars, came a great wind and a crash louder than thunder, and first one and then a score of lengthening fiery serpents plunged hungrily down upon the Dutchmen's dykes and struck between land and sea and flared up again in enormous columns of glare and crimsoned smoke and steam.

And out of the darkness leapt the little land, with its spires and trees, aghast with terror, still and distinct, and the sea, tumbled with anger, red-foaming like a sea of blood....

Over the populous country below went a strange multitudinous crying and a flurry of alarm bells....

The surviving aeroplanes turned about and fled out of the sky, like things that suddenly know themselves to be wicked....

Through a dozen thunderously flaming gaps that no water might quench, the waves came roaring in upon the land....

* * *

'We had cursed our luck,' says Barnet, 'that we could not get to our quarters at Alkmaar that night. There, we were told, were provisions, tobacco, and everything for which we craved. But the main canal from Zaandam and Amsterdam was hopelessly jammed with craft, and we were glad of a chance opening that enabled us to get out of the main column and lie up in a kind of little harbour very much neglected and weedgrown before a deserted house. We broke into this and found some herrings in a barrel, a heap of cheeses, and stone bottles of gin in the cellar; and with this I cheered my starving men. We made fires and toasted the cheese and grilled our herrings. None of us had slept for nearly forty hours, and I determined to stay in this refuge until dawn and then if the traffic was still choked leave the barge and march the rest of the way into Alkmaar.

'This place we had got into was perhaps a hundred yards from the canal and underneath a little brick bridge we could see the flotilla still, and hear the voices of the soldiers. Presently five or six other barges came through and lay up in the meer near by us, and with two of these, full of men of the Antrim regiment, I shared my find of provisions. In return we got tobacco. A large expanse of water spread to the westward of us and beyond were a cluster of roofs and one or two church towers. The barge was rather cramped for so many men, and I let several squads, thirty or forty perhaps altogether, bivouac on the bank. I did not let them go into the house on account of the furniture, and I left a note of indebtedness for the food we had taken. We were particularly glad of our tobacco and fires, because of the numerous mosquitoes that rose about us.

'The gate of the house from which we had provisioned ourselves was adorned with the legend, Vreugde bij Vrede, "Joy with Peace," and it bore every mark of the busy retirement of a comfort-loving proprietor. I went along his garden, which was gay and delightful with big bushes of rose and sweet brier, to a quaint little summer-house, and there I sat and watched the men in groups cooking and squatting along the bank. The sun was setting in a nearly cloudless sky.

'For the last two weeks I had been a wholly occupied man, intent only upon obeying the orders that came down to me. All through this time I had been working to the very limit of my mental and physical faculties, and my only moments of rest had been devoted to snatches of sleep. Now came this rare, unexpected interlude, and I could look detachedly upon what I was doing and feel something of its infinite wonderfulness. I was irradiated with affection for the men of my company and with admiration at their cheerful acquiescence in the subordination and needs of our positions. I watched their proceedings and heard their pleasant voices. How willing those men were! How ready to accept leadership and forget themselves in collective ends! I thought how manfully they had gone through all the strains and toil of the last two weeks, how they had toughened and shaken down to comradeship together, and how much sweetness there is after all in our foolish human blood. For they were just one casual sample of the species – their patience and readiness lay, as the energy of the atom had lain, still waiting to be properly utilised. Again it came to me with overpowering force that the supreme need of our race is leading, that the supreme task is to discover leading, to forget oneself in realising the collective purpose of the race. Once more I saw life plain….'

Very characteristic is that of the 'rather too corpulent' young officer, who was afterwards to set it all down in the Wander Jahre. Very characteristic, too, it is of the change in men's hearts that was even then preparing a new phase of human history.

He goes on to write of the escape from individuality in science and service, and of his discovery of this 'salvation.' All that was then, no doubt, very moving and original; now it seems only the most obvious commonplace of human life.

The glow of the sunset faded, the twilight deepened into night. The fires burnt the brighter, and some Irishmen away across the meer started singing. But Barnet's men were too weary for that sort of thing, and soon the bank and the barge were heaped with sleeping forms.

'I alone seemed unable to sleep. I suppose I was over-weary, and after a little feverish slumber by the tiller of the barge I sat up, awake and uneasy….

'That night Holland seemed all sky. There was just a little black lower rim to things, a steeple, perhaps, or a line of poplars, and then the great hemisphere swept over us. As at first the sky was empty. Yet my uneasiness referred itself in some vague way to the sky.

'And now I was melancholy. I found something strangely sorrowful and submissive in the sleepers all about me, those men who had marched so far, who had left all the established texture of their lives behind them to come upon this mad campaign, this campaign that signified nothing and consumed everything, this mere fever of fighting. I saw how little and feeble is the life of man, a thing of chances, preposterously unable to find the will to realise even the most timid of its dreams. And I wondered if always it would be so, if man was a doomed animal who would never to the last days of his time take hold of fate and change it to his will. Always, it may be, he will remain kindly but jealous, desirous but discursive, able and unwisely impulsive, until Saturn who begot him shall devour him in his turn....

'I was roused from these thoughts by the sudden realisation of the presence of a squadron of aeroplanes far away to the north-east and very high. They looked like little black dashes against the midnight blue. I remember that I looked up at them at first rather idly – as one might notice a flight of birds. Then I perceived that they were only the extreme wing of a great fleet that was advancing in a long line very swiftly from the direction of the frontier and my attention tightened.

'Directly I saw that fleet I was astonished not to have seen it before.

'I stood up softly, undesirous of disturbing my companions, but with my heart beating now rather more rapidly with surprise and excitement. I strained my ears for any sound of guns along our front. Almost instinctively I turned about for protection to the south and west, and peered; and then I saw coming as fast and much nearer to me, as if they had sprung out of the darkness, three banks of aeroplanes; a group of squadrons very high, a main body at a height perhaps of one or two thousand feet, and a doubtful number flying low and very indistinct. The middle ones were so thick they kept putting out groups of stars. And I realised that after all there was to be fighting in the air.

'There was something extraordinarily strange in this swift, noiseless convergence of nearly invisible combatants above the sleeping hosts. Every one about me was still unconscious; there was no sign as yet of any agitation among the shipping on the main canal, whose whole course, dotted with unsuspicious lights and fringed with fires, must have been clearly perceptible from above. Then a long way off towards Alkmaar I heard bugles, and after that shots, and then a wild clamour of bells. I determined to let my men sleep on for as long as they could....

'The battle was joined with the swiftness of dreaming. I do not think it can have been five minutes from the moment when I first became aware of the Central European air fleet to the contact of the two forces. I saw it quite plainly in silhouette against the luminous blue of the northern sky. The allied aeroplanes – they were mostly French – came pouring down like a fierce shower upon the middle of the Central European fleet. They looked exactly like a coarser sort of rain. There was a crackling sound – the first sound I heard – it reminded one of the Aurora Borealis, and I supposed it was an interchange of rifle shots. There were flashes like summer lightning; and then all the sky became a whirling confusion of battle that was still largely noiseless. Some of the Central European aeroplanes were certainly charged and overset; others seemed to collapse and fall and then flare out with so bright a light that it took the edge off one's vision and made the rest of the battle disappear as though it had been snatched back out of sight.

'And then, while I still peered and tried to shade these flames from my eyes with my hand, and while the men about me were beginning to stir, the atomic bombs were thrown at the dykes. They made a mighty thunder in the air, and fell like Lucifer in the picture, leaving a flaring trail in the sky. The night, which had been pellucid and detailed and eventful, seemed to vanish, to be replaced abruptly by a black background to these tremendous pillars of fire....

'Hard upon the sound of them came a roaring wind, and the sky was filled with flickering lightnings and rushing clouds....

'There was something discontinuous in this impact. At one moment I was a lonely watcher in a sleeping world; the next saw every one about me afoot, the whole world awake and amazed....

'And then the wind had struck me a buffet, taken my helmet and swept aside the summerhouse of Vreugde bij Vrede, as a scythe sweeps away grass. I saw the bombs fall, and then watched a great crimson flare leap responsive to each impact, and mountainous masses of red-lit steam and flying fragments clamber up towards the zenith. Against the glare I saw the country-side for miles standing black and clear, churches, trees, chimneys. And suddenly I understood. The Central Europeans had burst the dykes. Those flares meant the bursting of the dykes, and in a little while the sea-water would be upon us....'

He goes on to tell with a certain prolixity of the steps he took – and all things considered they were very intelligent steps – to meet this amazing crisis. He got his men aboard and hailed the adjacent barges; he got the man who acted as barge engineer at his post and the engines working, he cast loose from his moorings. Then he bethought himself of food, and contrived to land five men, get in a few dozen cheeses, and ship his men again before the inundation reached them.

He is reasonably proud of this piece of coolness. His idea was to take the wave head-on and with his engines full speed ahead. And all the while he was thanking heaven he was not in the jam of traffic in the main canal. He rather, I think, overestimated the probable rush of waters; he dreaded being swept away, he explains, and smashed against houses and trees.

He does not give any estimate of the time it took between the bursting of the dykes and the arrival of the waters, but it was probably an interval of about twenty minutes or half an hour. He was working now in darkness – save for the light of his lantern – and in a great wind. He hung out head and stern lights....

Whirling torrents of steam were pouring up from the advancing waters, which had rushed, it must be remembered, through nearly incandescent gaps in the sea defences, and this vast uprush of vapour soon veiled the flaring centres of explosion altogether.

'The waters came at last, an advancing cascade. It was like a broad roller sweeping across the country. They came with a deep, roaring sound. I had expected a Niagara, but the total fall of the front could not have been much more than twelve feet. Our barge hesitated for a moment, took a dose over her bows, and then lifted. I signalled for full speed ahead and brought her head upstream, and held on like grim death to keep her there.

'There was a wind about as strong as the flood, and I found we were pounding against every conceivable buoyant object that had been between us and the sea. The only light in the world now came from our lamps, the steam became impenetrable at a score of yards from the boat, and the roar of the wind and water cut us off from all remoter sounds. The black, shining waters swirled by, coming into the light of our lamps out of an ebony blackness and vanishing again into impenetrable black. And on the waters came shapes, came things that flashed upon us for a moment, now a half-submerged boat, now a cow, now a huge fragment of a house's timberings, now a muddle of packing-cases and scaffolding. The things clapped into sight like something shown by the opening of a shutter, and then bumped shatteringly against us or rushed by us. Once I saw very clearly a man's white face....

'All the while a group of labouring, half-submerged trees remained ahead of us, drawing very slowly nearer. I steered a course to avoid them. They seemed to gesticulate a frantic despair against the black steam clouds behind. Once a great branch detached itself and tore shuddering by me. We did, on the whole, make headway. The last I saw of Vreugde bij Vrede before the night swallowed it, was almost dead astern of us....'

* * *

Morning found Barnet still afloat. The bows of his barge had been badly strained, and his men were pumping or baling in relays. He had got about a dozen half-drowned people aboard whose boat had capsized near him, and he had three other boats in tow. He was afloat, and somewhere between Amsterdam and Alkmaar, but he could not tell where. It was a day that was still half night. Gray waters stretched in every direction under a dark gray sky, and out of the waves rose the upper parts of houses, in many cases ruined, the tops of trees, windmills, in fact the upper third of all the familiar Dutch scenery; and on it there drifted a dimly seen flotilla of barges, small boats, many overturned, furniture, rafts, timbering, and miscellaneous objects.

The drowned were under water that morning. Only here and there did a dead cow or a stiff figure still clinging stoutly to a box or chair or such-like buoy hint at the hidden massacre. It was not till the Thursday that the dead came to the surface in any quantity. The view was bounded on every side by a gray mist that closed overhead in a gray canopy. The air cleared in the afternoon, and then, far away to the west under great banks of steam and dust, the flaming red eruption of the atomic bombs came visible across the waste of water.

They showed flat and sullen through the mist, like London sunsets. 'They sat upon the sea,' says Barnet, 'like frayed-out waterlilies of flame.'

Barnet seems to have spent the morning in rescue work along the track of the canal, in helping people who were adrift, in picking up derelict boats, and in taking people out of imperilled houses. He found other military barges similarly employed, and it was only as the day wore on and the immediate appeals for aid were satisfied that he thought of food and drink for his men, and what course he had better pursue. They had a little cheese, but no water. 'Orders,' that mysterious direction, had at last altogether disappeared. He perceived he had now to act upon his own responsibility.

'One's sense was of a destruction so far-reaching and of a world so altered that it seemed foolish to go in any direction and expect to find things as they had been before the war began. I sat on the quarter-deck with Mylius my engineer and Kemp and two others of the non-commissioned officers, and we consulted upon our line of action. We were foodless and aimless. We agreed that our fighting value was extremely small, and that our first duty was to get ourselves in touch with food and instructions again. Whatever plan of campaign had directed our movements was manifestly smashed to bits. Mylius was of opinion that we could take a line westward and get back to England across the North Sea. He calculated that with such a motor barge as ours it would be possible to reach the Yorkshire coast within four-and-twenty hours. But this idea I overruled because of the shortness of our provisions, and more particularly because of our urgent need of water.

'Every boat we drew near now hailed us for water, and their demands did much to exasperate our thirst. I decided that if we went away to the south we should reach hilly country, or at least country that was not submerged, and then we should be able to land, find some stream, drink, and get supplies and news. Many of the barges adrift in the haze about us were filled with British soldiers and had floated up from the Nord See Canal, but none of them were any better informed than ourselves of the course of events. "Orders" had, in fact, vanished out of the sky.

'"Orders" made a temporary reappearance late that evening in the form of a megaphone hail from a British torpedo boat, announcing a truce, and giving the welcome information that food and water were being hurried down the Rhine and were to be found on the barge flotilla lying over the old Rhine above Leiden...'

We will not follow Barnet, however, in the description of his strange overland voyage among trees and houses and churches by Zaandam and between Haarlem and Amsterdam, to Leiden. It was a voyage in a red-lit mist, in a world of steamy silhouette, full of strange voices and perplexity, and with every other sensation dominated by a feverish thirst. 'We sat,' he says, 'in a little huddled group, saying very little, and the men forward were mere knots of silent endurance. Our only continuing sound was the persistent mewing of a cat one of the men had rescued from a floating hayrick near Zaandam. We kept a southward course by a watch-chain compass Mylius had produced....

'I do not think any of us felt we belonged to a defeated army, nor had we any strong sense of the war as the dominating fact about us. Our mental setting had far more of the effect of a huge natural catastrophe. The atomic bombs had dwarfed the international issues to complete insignificance. When our minds wandered from the preoccupations of our immediate needs, we speculated upon the possibility of stopping the use of these frightful explosives before the world was utterly destroyed. For to us it seemed quite plain that these bombs and the still greater power of destruction of which they were the precursors might quite easily shatter every relationship and institution of mankind.

'"What will they be doing," asked Mylius, "what will they be doing? It's plain we've got to put an end to war. It's plain things have to be run some way. THIS – all this – is impossible."

'I made no immediate answer. Something – I cannot think what – had brought back to me the figure of that man I had seen wounded on the very first day of actual fighting. I saw again his angry, tearful eyes, and that poor, dripping, bloody mess that had been a skilful human hand five minutes before, thrust out in indignant protest. "Damned foolery," he had stormed and sobbed, "damned foolery. My right hand, sir! My RIGHT hand..."

'My faith had for a time gone altogether out of me. "I think we are too – too silly," I said to Mylius, "ever to stop war. If we'd had the sense to do it, we should have done it before this. I think this –" I pointed to the gaunt black outline of a smashed windmill that stuck up, ridiculous and ugly, above the blood-lit waters – "this is the end."'

* * *

But now our history must part company with Frederick Barnet and his barge-load of hungry and starving men.

For a time in western Europe at least it was indeed as if civilisation had come to a final collapse. These crowning buds upon the tradition that Napoleon planted and Bismarck watered, opened and flared 'like waterlilies of flame' over nations destroyed, over churches smashed or submerged, towns ruined, fields lost to mankind for ever, and a million weltering bodies. Was this lesson enough for mankind, or would the flames of war still burn amidst the ruins?

Neither Barnet nor his companions, it is clear, had any assurance in their answers to that question. Already once in the history of mankind, in America, before its discovery by the whites, an organised civilisation had given way to a mere cult of warfare, specialised and cruel, and it seemed for a time to many a thoughtful man as if the whole world was but to repeat on a larger scale this ascendancy of the warrior, this triumph of the destructive instincts of the race.

The subsequent chapters of Barnet's narrative do but supply body to this tragic possibility. He gives a series of vignettes of civilisation, shattered, it seemed, almost irreparably. He found the Belgian hills swarming with refugees and desolated by cholera; the vestiges of the contending armies keeping order under a truce, without actual battles, but with the cautious hostility of habit, and a great absence of plan everywhere.

Overhead aeroplanes went on mysterious errands, and there were rumours of cannibalism and hysterical fanaticisms in the valleys of the Semoy and the forest region of the eastern Ardennes. There was the report of an attack upon Russia by the Chinese and Japanese, and of some huge revolutionary outbreak in America. The weather was stormier than men had ever known it in those regions, with much thunder and lightning and wild cloud-bursts of rain...

**The complete and unabridged text is available
online,** *from flametreepublishing.com/extras*

Lost and Found

Shannon Connor Winward

THERE ISN'T so much a sunrise on these mountains; it's more a lessening of the dark. I imagine someone turning a giant dimmer switch to brighten the valley.

Maybe I've been thinking too much about my mom.

Sometimes when I was little, we'd have dinner in the den. Candles on the table, real cloth napkins, cheesy VH1 music and the hanging lamp set to low – the 'shandahleeeer,' as she would say, with a smile and a roll of her fingers. "We will be fancy tonight, Danae. We will be la*dies.*"

I like how the leaves tell the time. Right now, they are black as bat wings, but in a few hours they will begin to glow. I like when the sun gets higher and the canopy becomes so iridescent you can see veins, capillaries in the undersides. In the spring and summer, it'll all be neon green. Now it's reds and yellows and spiky blades of pine. Makes it almost worth the cold.

I am shivering.

For the moment there's only the rumbling in the earth to tell me morning is coming. I can feel it coursing down the mountain, bubbling in the stream. A bird calling. The temperature rising. I can feel it.

But there's no message for me in it. The mountain doesn't care that we're here. I don't know where we're supposed to go, no more than I knew yesterday. Or the day before that. There is no pull. No whispers. Nothing but –

– dirt. I have a handful of dirt in my glove. I let it loose, mouthing prayers, but the dirt falls straight to the ground.

"Anything?"

Howard has come up behind me. He's gotten good at stalking, but still I should have heard him. *What good am I?* My senses are dull. All of them. I'm dead weight. I shake my head.

"Then we go east." He has the map out. He stabs a gloved finger at the folded section in his hand – neither of us can see it in this light, but we don't have to. I know where he means.

We hear there's a pocket open to travelers a day's walk from here, a few miles off I-180. We're low on supplies, and I'm lonely for conversation that isn't Howard's.

I miss the others.

Howard puts a hand on my shoulder, pulls me close. I hear him sniffle, his nose running from the cold. He kisses me on the forehead.

He hasn't offered a word of reproach, in all this time. It's been months. A year maybe. I am lost, empty. Adrift.

It's not a big deal to Howard. The wilderness is his playground. Even without my help, we're getting by. Actually, I think he likes being the one to say where we go, where we stop. Where we hide. In the early days, I think he was afraid of me. He used to joke about it, to the others, even just to me after they were gone. "Listen to Danae, if you want to survive." He'd laugh, like it was funny.

He's quieter now. Confidence does that. He's a man who's found his calling, even while I'm losing mine. *Have lost. I don't know.*

But he knows how much it means to me. *Meant. Means.* He asks, every morning, and if the answer is "nothing," he takes over. Easy. He moves off down the trail, back towards the campsite. Whistling.

* * *

"Thread," I tell him. Now that we have crested the hill, I can see the movie theater marquee.

Howard is already checking his watch, and picking up my wrist to check mine. "Right."

"Booze."

"Naturally."

"Bread."

"We don't need bread. Oh-sixteen-hundred."

"I want bread. Or cookies. And shampoo. Do you have a list?"

He throws me a pained look. I have insulted his manhood.

"You forgot the first aid tape in Eagle Town."

"One time."

"And my tampons in Columbia."

"Your people used strips of leather in the old days. I can get you leather."

"*My people* used Tampax. Kotex. As long as there are women, they'll have supplies. Ask."

"Fine." He turns his back to me and saunters off down Main Street. According to the travelers we bunked with in the Catskills, there's a trade store in an old elementary school a few blocks west.

"Painkillers!" I shout after him. We're down to half a bottle of Aspirin. His migraines have been bad.

"What am I, a rich man?" Howard calls over his shoulder. But he'll try. He has a stash of batteries and a couple of bags of hand-rolled cigarettes. He's ready for a bargain.

I check the map in my hands, once an afterthought in Howard's glove compartment, now a bible. Under Howard's shorthand and hieroglyphics in red ink, I look at Trachtenberg, Pennsylvania and then glance up for comparison.

The town appears structurally unaffected. Mountain pockets tend to be. There's a rift in the road, some obvious earthquake damage, but the county library is where we were told it would be – a tall, gray, fancy-looking building visible beyond the spires of what was once a Roman Catholic church. But the names and what's of things are always unreliable.

We've been noticed. There's a trio of women in puffy coats standing outside of an old diner, catty-corner to me. Judging from the smell wafting across the street it is still a place for food. My stomach growls. I peek at Howard's retreating form, wondering what I'd have to offer up tonight in apology if I splurged on a home-cooked meal.

The women seem friendly-ish. None of that pinched, suspicious look. Just curious.

I wave. Step off the curb. As I do, one of the women ducks back into the diner. It's dark inside; the afternoon sun is hiding behind the buildings now, but I can see little flickering lights through the window.

"What's your business?" one of the remaining women asks. She is middle-aged. The third woman isn't a woman at all, just a really tall girl.

"Barter," I answer. I smile.

The girl's face blossoms in a grin. "Where you come down from?" she asks. She has white-blonde hair done up in a messy bun and freckles sprinkled across her nose. She can't be more than fourteen.

"We've been tracking along the creek." I sniff the air. "Is that…?"

"French-fries. Want some?"

"You in the market for some dried sunnies?"

Freckles wrinkles her nose. "Not really. But you don't have to trade for it. We have plenty. Don't we, Mom?"

"Gabby."

"Come on, Mom. It's Veteran's Day. We can spare."

"It's what now?" Mom is surprised into a laugh. "How do you even know that?"

Gabby shrugs. "It's in my calendar."

"Well we don't just go giving out food to…" Gabby's mother glances at me. "Travelers."

"It's OK," I interject. "I'm not a veteran anyway."

"We're all veterans," says a woman from the doorway. She's wearing a turtleneck sweater and an apron, her arms crossed. Her ponytail is pure white. Gabby's grandmother, maybe. Something around the eyes.

"You want fries?"

Uh. "Sure. I'd love some."

Grandmother nods and turns away again. She didn't invite me in, and the others are still standing here, so I wait with them. Inside, I can see necks craning to look at me, staring white faces, but no one has gotten up out of their seats. They've got manners here, or travelers aren't so infrequent as I thought.

The old woman returns with a small bundle – a handful of french-fries wrapped in a towel. They're fresh. I can feel the heat through the cloth and through my glove. *Sweet Mother.* The aroma is almost too much to bear.

"Thank you," I manage. The women nod.

"What are you shopping for?" Gabby asks, as I unwrap the towel and put a fry in my mouth. It scalds my tongue, but I don't care. I'm already sticking in the next one.

"Mmph," I say, and gesture in the direction that Howard disappeared. *Grease. Hot. Potato. Gods.* I might melt with pleasure right here. Gabby is smiling at me, bemused. "Stuff," I tell her, swallowing another bite. "The usual. My man is doing the trading. I'm looking for the library."

"Oh, the Lost and Found?" Gabby asks, her brows dancing in graceful blonde arcs.

"Yeah."

"It's right down there," she tells me, pointing. "I'll go with you, if you want."

"Gabby," scolds her mother.

"Well it's… it's fine," I say. And it is. It's nice to have people to talk to. Women, especially. Not so nice as these fries, rapidly disappearing, but nice. A novelty.

Grandmother has already vanished back into the diner. Gabby's mom says she can go, but she has to promise to be back in an hour – she's needed for the evening meal.

Gabby walks alongside me, watching with bright eyes as I polish off the rest of my windfall. For once I'm glad for the cold mountain breezes – maybe it will blow the telltale smell of French-fries away from me. Howard won't approve.

I wish I had a breath mint. I have to settle for water from my flask.

"Are you spending the night?" Gabby asks, as we navigate a complex array of potholes. She's wearing fuzzy white boots that seem audaciously impractical to me, but they're cute. It's been a long time since I considered fashion.

"No, just passing through."

"But you must be camping nearby. It won't be long 'til sundown."

"I suppose."

"Where are you going next?"

"Don't know."

"Where you been?"

"West." I look at her. "Haven't been out of town much, have you."

"I've been trekking with my Grumper in the foothills," she says, "but no. Not really. Who are you looking for at the El and Eff?"

I don't answer. *No one. Everyone.* Gabby is too young to realize what a landslide could be kicked loose by such a question.

The library door lets out a painful squeal as we come inside. We pass through a lobby where once there would have been tables of leaflets and community boards peppered with local announcements, but the furniture and corkboards have been removed. We open the inner door, sweeping aside crisp, brown leaves.

Gabby calls out in a high, sing-song voice. "Mr. Merriweather! Company, Mr. Merriweather! We've got a traveler!"

Aside from the inevitable musty smell and some boarded up windows, the place is in remarkable shape. A skylight overhead has survived tremors, hail, wind. It bathes the stacks in cool sunlight. The shelves are orderly and well-stocked. If it weren't for the lack of heat and electricity, I could imagine I've walked into any small town library before The Chain – before small towns across the world fell like dominoes.

There are books spread across the checkout counter. I pick one up – a calculus textbook – and smell it. I close my eyes, and I am seven years old again, curled up in the mythology aisle of the Appoquinimink Public Library.

"Mr. Merriweather!"

"Coming," calls a voice from a side hall, followed by an unmistakable flushing sound.

I turn to Gabby. "You've got plumbing?"

"Uh-huh." She grins at me, like this is her own personal accomplishment.

Footsteps, another creaking door, and a man enters the library proper. He's spectacled, walks with a slight dowager's hump and has thinning blonde hair – so quintessential a librarian I find myself smiling. He's pulling a parka on over his cardigan, though, a concession for the cold. His nose and cheeks are pink – either he's got a heat source somewhere, or he's been nipping at something alcoholic. Maybe both. He's smiling at me, all dimples and teeth, and I'm nearly overcome with the urge to ask if I can join him back there, but Howard will be waiting for me.

Howard's literary interests are limited.

"Hello! Hello!" Mr. Merriweather exclaims. He juts out a hand to take mine; I pull off the glove and give it to him. His grip is strong and warm. "I don't know how long it's been since the last time we had a traveler. "Welcome," he adds, with a cute little bow of his head. I feel like royalty.

"She wants to register with the El and Eff," Gabby informs him, boosting herself onto the counter.

"Of course she does." Merriweather's gaze is full of sympathy, camaraderie. It's that look I've come to crave in these perennial trips to civilization. Howard doesn't get it – he was a loner, before. A weekend survivalist. The Chain, for him, was a renaissance.

"Now then." The librarian searches under his counter, then takes off his glasses and checks again. "Where did I put that paper…"

"I have a list." I have it ready in the inside pocket of my coat. I pull it out and hand it to him. He withdraws the slip of paper from its protective sandwich baggie and unfolds it; solemnly, as if this were a ritual. It is.

"Danae Perez?" He reads from the top line and glances at me. I nod. He draws a pen from behind his ear and uses it to copy down my information – name, date of birth, last pre-Chain address (I list my hometown, not college. Anyone who would be looking for me would know me from home.)

When he is finished, Merriweather runs his finger down the rest of the page, the names of my missing. He hums a little. I can see the mental wheels turning, already consulting his archives.

He looks up at me. "Well let's see, shall we?"

The librarian steps away from the counter and begins the necromancy of his work – the pulling of file drawers, the lift and thump and reverent page-turning of ledgers. I've seen it dozens of times now, a hundred – how many pockets have we passed through, how many libraries, schools, museums, church basements? Never a word in any of them for me, but still I keep looking. Expectation has nothing to do with it.

"What kind of name is Perez?" asks Gabby.

"What do you mean, 'what kind'. What's your last name?"

"Hoefflefinger."

"Huh. Are you Mennonites?"

She shakes her head. "They're further north. We have a trading pact, though." She's still looking at me, openly assessing, trying to puzzle me out.

"My dad was Puerto Rican. Don't you have Latinos around here?"

"The influenza and everything hit us pretty bad. We don't have much of anybody." She ponders. "There's a homestead out behind the Walmart by the name of Rios. The Pa was from Mexico, I think. But you don't look like them."

"Yeah, well."

"What was your Mom?"

What was Mom?

A nurse, I answer, silently. *A song-writer. A witch. A dreamer. A fan of* Days of Our Lives *and Stephen King and* The Rocky Horror Picture Show. *A tarot card reader, queen of peanut butter sandwiches. Would any of that mean anything to you?*

"A little bit of everything," is what I tell her. "Scots-Irish. French. Nanticoke."

Gabby is quiet for almost a minute. Then: "Was Puerto Rico in Mexico?"

"Do you even read these books, Gabby?"

"Some."

Merriweather chuckles from a desk nearby. He is holding up a candle and checking between a ledger and the contents of a strongbox. Drivers licenses. Knowing where those IDs came from, I look away.

"Your grandfather was half Jewish," I say to Gabby, before I even know it's coming. "His mother survived the…"

I trail off, glancing at the librarian. He doesn't seem to have heard me.

"The First One," Gabby whispers, eyes wide. "How did you know that?"

It happens this way sometimes, when I'm off my guard. It's been so long, I'd almost forgotten.

"Are you… *psychic?*" she asks, sotto voce. Vigorously, I shake my head. I can tell she doesn't believe me.

Merriweather closes the box and moves onto a massive black file cabinet. It looks like it's survived not only The Chain but both previous world wars. It sticks, but with a grunt and a practiced choreography of pulls, Merriweather wrestles it open.

Gabby is still staring, a flush of excitement creeping over her freckled face. "I heard…"

"It was just a lucky guess," I shrug, keeping my voice light, disinterested.

I check my watch. Howard will be expecting me to join him in twenty minutes. He tolerates my habit; he understands on a cerebral level why it is important, even if there's no one he's missed himself, no one whose whereabouts have cost him a moment's sleep. But he doesn't like for it to slow us down. "In and out. Don't ask what isn't necessary, don't give too much away." And he's right. *Shit.* As nice as these folks seem in Trachtenberg, we can't afford to be too friendly. I have to remember Maria and Santos, trussed up in a town hall for loitering and paganism.

Pockets are for settlers. They only look out for their own.

But, still. People wouldn't put their resources into places like this – the Lost and Founds, the hostels, the roadside shrines – if there wasn't a sense of something bigger still running through us. *A national identity? Maybe? I don't know.* Maybe it's just nostalgia.

Merriweather has left his glasses on the counter. I am working myself into knots with this. I'm itching to leave, to get back to Howard. Merriweather's glasses are just sitting there in front of me, on top of a stack of books. I can't help myself. I pick them up, turn to Gabby, and mime dropping them. I make a cracking noise.

"Oh no!" I croon. "All these books, and all the time in the world to read them! It's not fair!"

Gabby looks at me as if I've grown another head.

Merriweather has returned to the circulation desk. "Don't think I haven't considered that," he says. "Fortunately, my prescription is not uncommon."

I smile, replace the spectacles, and hike my backpack higher on my shoulder. Then I notice Merriweather has something in his hands besides my list. He's reaching across the desk, holding it out for me. A packet of folded squares of paper, about an inch thick and tied with twine. I blink, confused, ready to tell him *that's not mine*, when Merriweather mentions a name. "Looks like you're a lucky one," he says. "Passed through a little over a year ago, left this for you. Danae Perez. Imagine that."

I take the packet, and my list. I tuck them both inside my coat.

A year.

I have to remind myself to breathe.

Landslide.

* * *

Howard is waiting for me in the school parking lot. He has a smirk on his face. A good trade, then.

The sun is setting. Howard swings an arm around my shoulder and ushers me away from Trachtenberg, the apartment buildings and row homes and basketball courts choked with weeds, trees. Over the turnpike of rusting hulks, past the reservoir, a marshland. Back into the hills.

He tells me what he has gleaned from the traders: north of here is Jesus-land, from Straughberg to Hollenfield. They won't be welcoming. But there's a civil pocket growing in Puxtawney working to get a system of steam power going. If we skirt the foothills west, barring too-heavy snowfall, we could get there before the Solstice.

I nod, distracted. My heart is a fist in my throat. I stuff my hands in my coat to keep from touching the letters in my pocket. I don't know how to tell him. Jesus-land, of course, is exactly where you would be heading.

* * *

He found me oatmeal cream pies. Little Debbie's. Helluva lot past expiration, but kept airtight in some industrial freezer.

I don't hear him when he brags about how little he got them for. I break open the box, pop the plastic, eat them with a pasted-on grin while he beams at me over the campfire. After a dinner of roast groundhog, they taste like soiled mattress.

Howard is in good spirits. He struts, banking the fire. He makes love like a warrior. He doesn't even notice my heart's not in it.

You're alive. Oh, Gods, you're alive.

* * *

Now I'm thinking of my mother again, but in a distant way, beneath a cacophony of panic and gratitude (*you're alive, you're alive*). Like I can hear her telling me that one time, when she met you, "There's a wanderlust in that one. You can see it in his eyes."

I had no idea what wanderlust looked like, back then, but I believed her. My dad was not the first guy to disappear on her, and hardly the last. If there were a look that promised leaving, she would know.

I didn't tell her much about you; not what I felt, or how far it went, and nothing about the God stuff. She would have thought it hysterical that I found me a religious man.

There was a Magic: The Gathering card called *Wanderlust* – it dealt a point of damage for every turn, death by attrition. I took it out of the deck and kept it taped to my mirror because I never had any pictures of you.

I used to wonder what it felt like, to be touched by God, or Spirit, whatever you wanted to call it. I envied your specialness. You said He spoke to you, and I believed you.

You said I should repent my false gods, my tarot and divining, all my mother's wanton, idolatrous influence. You said the End of Days were coming. When the blazing light of the Lord came to purge the sinners and shepherd the righteous to a new Eden, you planned to walk among His chosen.

I keep thinking about that night in the school parking lot. Not so Godly then, with your hand down the front of my jeans, though His name was surely on my lips. I ripped a tear in the shoulder seam of your jacket, gripping so hard like I could keep you from falling. I thought I was touching something special, and if you left you'd take a piece of me with you.

Isn't it ironic, in the end, it was me who did the leaving.

* * *

Dawn bleeds over the mountain. Harold grumbles in his sleep, turns over. I am out of the tent, sitting on a rock, watching stars blink out through evergreen branches.

I have barely slept.

* * *

When Maria and Santos were taken, I blamed myself. I was the one who said "go to Lutherville" after the truck finally died. Harold used to hold me at night, wiping my tears with my braids, kissing my wet cheeks. "He was dying," he'd say, reminding me how Santo's eyes had turned yellow weeks before, how he'd been coughing up blood and bile. In Lutherville, we found the suitcase full of penicillin, birth control ("Thank the gods," Harold had laughed. "Hallelujah!") and oxy. "Boy was out of his mind, didn't feel a thing. You gave him that, Danae. Stoned, violent and quick is better than the alternative."

He'd meant to comfort me. He forgets that I saw the body, a sixteen-year-old suspended two stories above the ground. One of the telephone poles that held him was carved with 'IDOLATER.' 'CATHOLIC SPIC,' was emblazoned on the other.

Once, just once, I pointed out, "Maria wasn't sick." Sweet Maria, my college roommate, my best friend. She'd been a nursing student before The Chain and a healer after, tending to the lost and the broken. The first to believe in me. "Danae has the Sight," she'd say. "Danae talks to God. Listen to Danae."

"You told her not to go back for him." Harold's shrug was eloquent in the dark.

* * *

I have barely slept, but – I have been dreaming. Visions of Maria and her brother, of heaven and hell. Visions of Gabby, slinking this way down the mountainside with a backpack and stolen hiking boots. Visions, most of all, of you. You preaching from the college roof, from hospital steps, straddling telephone poles. You, far ahead on a road flanked with old letters. You calling, *Let's go. This way. Let's go.*

Who's to say it means anything? Wide awake now, my mind is a jumble. The mountain is stirring, Harold is snoring, and you're alive, or you were a year ago.

I touch the packet inside my coat. It's too dark to see, but I don't need to. I have already memorized every word, the one's you wrote and those you didn't.

"Don't go looking for your Mom," you said. *She was home when the bombs dropped.*

"I pray every night for a sign of you." *I know you're out there. I can feel you.*

"I hear there's a resurgence forming among the Amish." *Finally, I am following my calling.* In my gut, I feel it stirring. The pull. The knowing. But it could just be this. It might be...

I bend down to brush aside pine needles, leaves from the base of the rock. I remove my glove and scratch the ground with my nails, scooping a fistful of red earth into my hands. I say a prayer, words bubbling up from a great well inside me, things I'd forgotten were ever there.

I open my fingers. For a moment, in the shadows of the shivering pines, the earth swirls in a downward spiral. Particles hover, the wind holding its breath. A sigh, a yanking in my heart. *This way. Go this way.* Dirt settles on the ground, arranging itself in an inarguable pattern.

* * *

When Howard emerges, the coffee and gruel are already hot. He sees I've made extra.

"We're getting company."

"What have you done, Danae?"

"I can't stop them from coming." I fiddle with my coffee. "The visions are back."

"Where?" His voice cracks on the question.

"North."

Howard is quiet for a long time, struggling. In the early days, he never would have asked, but now –

"Why?"

I am cruel. "Because I feel it," is all I give him. And it is true, if not the whole story.

He stands, fists clenched. Then, with a breath, Howard sits to consult the map. His shoulders drop. He plots a course.

Harold is a simple man. Maybe not a good one, but there are worse. Harold would kill for me. Has. He will go where I tell him.

So we're going. Where travelers, outsiders like us are unwelcome. Where we have no business other than a fool's errand… a dream vision. My vision.

For Howard, this has always been a march of faith. Faith in survival, faith that the earth provides. That I am Her voice, a compass to some new world order.

I don't think he has ever figured out – for me it isn't so much about the future. It's just… a need to know if what was lost can be found again. At whatever cost.

I watch the leaves trembling over my head, read the sparkle of sunrise with all its shady promises. I remember explosions on the horizon, cities burning, smoke rising. I remember home, the rasp of your cheek under my hand.

Howard coughs, searching his sack for a cigarette. He sounds like an old man.

I think of regret, and love, and all it can drive a person to.

Biographies & Sources

Mike Adamson
Flight of the Storm God
(First Publication)
Mike Adamson holds a PhD in archaeology from Flinders University of South Australia, where he has both studied and taught for some twenty-four years. Born in England, his family emigrated in 1971; after early aspirations in art and writing, Mike secured degrees in marine biology and archaeology. Mike currently lectures in anthropology, is a passionate photographer, master-level hobbyist and journalist for international magazines. Recently, Mike has rediscovered a passion for speculative fiction and has placed some forty stories with magazines and anthologies to date. Interests embrace science fiction, fantasy, horror, historical and military fields.

Stephen Vincent Benét
By the Waters of Babylon
(Originally Published in *The Saturday Evening Post* as 'The Place of the Gods', 1937)
Stephen Vincent Benét (1898–1943) was an American poet, novelist, and short story writer. Following his family's military tradition, he studied at the United States Military Academy, but eventually found his calling in literature. He went on to study English at Yale University, where he contributed to their published periodicals including Yale Literature Magazine and more humorous Yale Record. He was awarded with the Pulitzer Prize for Poetry in 1929 and posthumously in 1944. By the Waters of Babylon is one of Benét's most notable works. Inspired by the 1937 bombing of Spanish Guernica, the poignant story explores themes of war and humanity's deadly desire for power.

J.D. Beresford
Goslings (chapters IX–XV)
(Originally Published by William Heinemann, 1913)
John Davys Beresford (1873–1947) was an English writer known for his science fiction, horror, and mystery stories. Beresford's novel *The Hampdenshire Wonder* was greatly inspired by H.G. Wells and he was the first to write a critical study of Wells in 1915. Reflected in his writings is Beresford's extraordinary capability of a compassionate observation of society. Goslings explores the themes of sexism, free love, power structures, and religion in the world where most of the male population of England is wiped out by a plague, creating areas under matriarchal rule.

Lord Byron
Darkness
(Written in July 1816)
A poet and politician, George Gordon Byron (1788–1824) was one of the leading figures of the Romantic period in England. As many noble gentlemen at the time, he spent a chunk of his short life abroad in Italy and traveling around Mediterranean countries. In 1923 Byron joined the Greek War of Independence aiming at defeating the Ottoman Empire. He died less than a year later, weakened by serious illness. Hailed as a Greek national hero,

Byron was refused a burial at Westminster Abbey due to his well-known promiscuity. A memorial at the Abbey was placed 145 years after his death. Written in 1816, 'Darkness' draws inspiration from the low temperatures and dark skies experienced in Europe that year. It is praised not only as a post-apocalyptic vision, but also for its historical context and anti-biblical nature.

Bill Davidson

A Brief Moment of Rage
(First Publication)
Bill Davidson is a Scottish author living in Dorset and hoping to find a publisher for his novel(s). He got the short story bug in earnest about a year ago and since then has been writing like a demon. Maybe two of them. Still, he's had stories accepted by Storyteller, Dark Lane Books, *Under the Bed*, *Emerging Worlds*, *Metamorphose*, Tigershark Publishing and *Storgy Magazine*. If he had to pick two writers who have influenced him, he'd choose the King fella and Elmore Leonard.

Arthur Conan Doyle

The Poison Belt
(Originally Published in *The Strand Magazine*, 1913)
Arthur Conan Doyle (1859–1930) was born in Edinburgh, Scotland. As a medical student Doyle was so impressed by his professor's powers of deduction that he was inspired to create the illustrious and much-loved figure of Sherlock Holmes. Doyle became increasingly interested in spiritualism and the supernatural, leaving him keen to explore fantastical elements in his stories. His vibrant and remarkable characters have breathed life into all of his stories, engaging readers throughout the decades. *The Poison Belt* continues the story of Professor Challenger after the events in *The Lost World*. As the Earth is heading toward a belt of poisonous ether, Challenger and his friends observe the apocalypse from a safe location.

George Allan England

The Vacant World (chapters I–XII)
(First Published in *Cavalier*, 1912)
George Allan England (1877–1936) was an American writer and explorer, best known for his speculative science fiction inspired by authors such as H.G. Wells and Jack London. After a period of translating fiction he published his first story in 1905, leading to over 330 pieces now accounted for. England attended Harvard University and later in life ran for Governor of Maine. Though unsuccessful in that endeavour, he transferred his interest in politics into his writing, where themes of socialist utopia often appear.

Michael Paul Gonzalez

City of Emerald Ash
(First Publication)
Michael Paul Gonzalez is the author of the novels *Angel Falls* and *Miss Massacre's Guide to Murder and Vengeance*. His newest creation is the audio drama podcast 'Larkspur Underground', a serialized horror story, available for free on iTunes. He resides in Los Angeles, a place full of wonders and monsters far stranger than any that live in the imagination. Find him online at MichaelPaulGonzalez.com.

Michael Haynes
Written on the Skin
(First Publication)
Michael Haynes lives in Central Ohio. An ardent short story reader and writer, Michael has had stories appear in periodicals such as *Ellery Queen Mystery Magazine*, *Beneath Ceaseless Skies*, and *Nature* and also in anthologies such as *Deep Cuts*, *Not Our Kind: Tales of Not Belonging*, and *Heroic Fantasy Short Stories*. He is the chair of the Cinevent classic film convention and enjoys photography, geocaching, and travel. His website is michaelhaynes. info and he can be found on Twitter as @mohio73.

William Hope Hodgson (1877–1918)
The Night Land (chapters I–V)
(First Published by Eveleigh Nash, 1912)
William Hope Hodgson (1877–1918) was born in Essex, England but moved several times with his family, including living for some time in County Galway, Ireland – a setting that would later inspire *The House on the Borderland*. Hodgson made several unsuccessful attempts to run away to sea, until his uncle secured him some work in the Merchant Marine. This association with the ocean would unfold later in his many sea stories. After some initial rejections of his writing, Hodgson managed to become a full-time writer of both novels and short stories, which form a fantastic legacy of adventure, mystery and horror fiction.

Liam Hogan
Silent Night
(Originally Performed at Liars' League Leeds, 2011, and Originally Published in *O Little Town of Deathlehem*, 2013)
Liam Hogan is an Oxford Physics graduate and award winning London-based writer. His short story 'Ana' appears in *Best of British Science Fiction 2016* (NewCon Press) and his twisted fantasy collection *Happy Ending Not Guaranteed* is published by Arachne Press. 'Spectrum' appears in Flame Tree's *Sword & Steam*, and 'How to Build a Mass Murderer' in *Murder Mayhem*. And if you look hard enough you can find him on stage, as the host of the monthly literary event, Liars' League. More details at happyendingnotguaranteed.blogspot.co.uk, or tweet @LiamJHogan.

Jennifer Hudak
Changed
(First Publication)
Jennifer Hudak has been dreaming about other worlds ever since she was a girl staying up past her bedtime to read Madeleine L'Engle and Ursula LeGuin by flashlight. Her fiction, creative nonfiction, and personal essays appear online in publications ranging from *Runners World* to *Literary Mama*. She lives with her husband and children in upstate New York where, in addition to writing, she teaches yoga, collects cookbooks, and knits tiny pocket-sized animals. Find her on Twitter @writerunyoga.

Jake Jackson
The Deluge
(Originally Appeared Online on These Fantastic Worlds, 2017)
With a particular interest in human origin, cosmology and early civilisation Jake Jackson has written and edited a number books and is General Editor of *Myths and Legends*,

and series editor of *Celtic Myths*, *Native American Myths*, *Norse Myths* and *Greek Myths*. Jackson is also a science fiction and dark fantasy author whose work explores the interplay between dreams, memory and imagination. He runs a podcast of flash fiction ('These Fantastic Worlds').

Curt Jeffreys
Dust Devil
(First Publication)
Curt Jeffreys has been writing speculative fiction since 1996. He has had stories published both online and in print, in publications including *Aofe's Kiss*, *Dark Fire Fiction*, *Galaxy Ezine*, *Millenium Science Fiction and Fantasy*, *Mysterical-e*, *Shadowkeep*, *SNM Horror Magazine*, *The Absent Willow Review*, and the *Science Fiction Museum*. His short story collection *Walking the Edge* is available on Amazon, Smashwords, and elsewhere in both print and electronic form. His work has been influenced by diverse authors from Asimov to Poe to King. Curt lives in Arvada, Colorado, with his lovely wife, handsome son, and a slightly odd cat called Eric.

Su-Yee Lin
Away They Go or Hurricane Season
(Originally Published in *A Cappella Zoo*, 2013)
Su-Yee Lin is a writer from New York with a B.A. in Literary Arts from Brown University. Her work has been published in *Day One*, *Strange Horizons*, Tor.com, *Electric Literature*, *Bennington Review*, *The Offing*, *NANO Fiction*, and other literary journals. A 2012 Fulbright Fellow to China, she was also a 2014 fellow at the Center for Fiction. She's currently working on a collection of magical-realist short stories and enjoys bicycling in foreign cities and hiking. Her website is suyeelin.com.

H.P. Lovecraft
Nyarlathotep
(Originally Published in *The United Amateur*, November 1920)
Master of weird fiction Howard Phillips Lovecraft (1890–1937) was born in Providence, Rhode Island. Featuring unknown, extra-terrestrial and otherworldly creatures, gods and beings, his stories were one of the first to mix science fiction with horror. His inspiration came predominantly from mythology, astronomy and the supernatural and gothic writings of such authors as Edgar Allan Poe. Plagued by nightmares from an early age, he was inspired to write his dark and strange fantasy tales; and the isolation he must have experienced from suffering frequent illnesses, can be felt as a prominent theme in his work. Lovecraft inspired many other authors, and his most famous story *The Call of Cthulhu* has gone on to influence many aspects of popular culture.

Florian Mussgnug
Foreword: Endless Apocalypse Short Stories
Dr. Florian Mussgnug is Reader in Italian and Comparative Literature at University College London. Educated at the Universities of Oxford (BA, MSt) and Pisa (PhD), he has been Visiting Lecturer at Oxford and Visiting Professor at the University of Rome. He has published widely on twentieth and twenty-first century literature in German, Italian and English, including *The Eloquence of Ghosts* (2010, winner of the 2012 Edinburgh Gadda Prize) and *The Good Place:*

Comparative Perspectives on Utopia (2014, with Matthew Reza). He is currently writing a book about apocalypse fiction, parental responsibility and global existential risk.

Wendy Nikel
An Introvert at the End of the World
(First Publication)
Wendy Nikel is a speculative fiction author with a degree in elementary education, a fondness for road trips, and a terrible habit of forgetting where she's left her cup of tea. Her short fiction has been published by *Fantastic Stories of the Imagination*, *Daily Science Fiction*, *Nature: Futures*, and elsewhere. Her time travel novella, *The Continuum*, is available from World Weaver Press. For more info, visit wendynikel.com.

Konstantine Paradias
Turn, World, Turn
(First Publication)
Konstantine Paradias is a writer by choice and a member of the SFWA by compulsion. At the moment, he's published over 100 stories in a bunch of languages and has written, edited and posed for videogames, screenplays and anthologies. People tell him he's got a writing problem but he can, like, quit whenever he wants, man. His latest book, *Sorry, Wrong Country*, is published by Rooster Republic Press.

Edgar Allan Poe
The Conversation of Eiros and Charmion
(Originally Published in *Burton's Gentleman's Magazine*, 1839)
Versatile writer Edgar Allan Poe (1809–49) was born in Boston, Massachusetts. Poe is well known for being an author, poet, editor and literary critic during the American Romantic Movement. He is generally considered the inventor of the detective fiction genre as well as being an important influence on early science fiction, and his works are famously filled with terror, mystery, death and haunting. The dark, mystifying characters from his tales have captured the public's imagination and reflect the struggling, poverty-stricken lifestyle he lived his whole life.

Darren Ridgley
In the Way You Should Go
(First Publication)
Darren Ridgley is a journalist and speculative fiction writer residing in Winnipeg, Manitoba, Canada. His work has previously appeared in anthologies such as *Fitting In: Historical Accounts of Paranormal Subcultures and Memories of the Past,* and magazines including *Empyreome*, *Fantasia Divinity*, *Polar Borealis*, and *Mad Scientist Journal*. Darren believes life experience provides the best inspiration, and so has dabbled in a wide range of pursuits, including stand-up comedy and amateur boxing. To this day, he can't determine which of the two was most painful.

John B. Rosenman
Resurrection Blues
(Originally Published in *Planet Relish E-zine* in March 2001)
John B. Rosenman is a retired English professor from Norfolk State University in Norfolk, Virginia. He has published three hundred stories in *Weird Tales*, *Whitley Strieber's Aliens*,

Galaxy and elsewhere. He has also published SF novels such as *Speaker of the Shakk* and *Beyond Those Distant Stars* (Mundania Press), and *Alien Dreams, A Senseless Act of Beauty*, and (YA) *The Merry-Go-Round Man* (Crossroad Press). MuseItUp Publishing has published his first four novels in the *Inspector of the Cross* series. John's time-travel story 'Killers' received Musa Publishing's 2013 Editor's Top Pick award. Some of John's books are available as audio books from Audible.com.

Zach Shephard

Ain't No Sunshine When She's Ash
(First Publication)
Zach Shephard lives in Enumclaw, Washington, where he's written stories that have appeared in *Fantasy & Science Fiction, Galaxy's Edge*, the *Unidentified Funny Objects* anthology series, and similar publications. He spends a lot of time at his local MMA gym, learning the most efficient ways to swing his bones into defenceless targets. (He then makes sure to pass that knowledge on to his students, because it never hurts to have an army of blindly loyal kickboxers at your side.) Zach's favourite author is Roger Zelazny, whose works have been a huge influence on his writing.

M.P. Shiel

The Purple Cloud (extract)
(Originally Published by Chatto & Windus, 1901)
Matthew Phipps Shiel (1865–1947) was born in Montserrat, West Indies. Upon his arrival in Britain in 1885, Shiel had been educated in Barbados at Harrison College. He wrote numerous science fiction, supernatural, horror and, later in his career, romance stories. Praised at length by H.G. Wells and H.P. Lovecraft, *The Purple Cloud* remains Shiel's best known and most often reprinted novel. A story of the last man on Earth slowly descending into madness, it is believed to have begun the future history genre.

Meryl Stenhouse

We Make Tea
(Originally Published in *Shimmer Magazine* #14, 2011)
Meryl Stenhouse lives in subtropical Queensland where she curates an extensive notebook collection and fights a running battle with the Lego models trying to take over the house. She's currently revisiting Le Guin's Earthsea and finding it just as magical as when she first read it. She has stories in *Shimmer, Aurealis* and upcoming in the *Mother of Invention* anthology. She's currently co-writing a book on writing science fiction with two other scientists. You can find her on Twitter @merylstenhouse.

Snorri Sturluson

The Fooling of Gylfe (chapters XVI–XVII)
(Written in the 13th century, Published by Scott, Foresman and Company, 1901)
A poet, historian, and politician, Snorri Sturluson (1179–1241) was the first Icelandic author known by name. He is best known for his writings on Norse mythology and the medieval Scandinavian history, remaining one of the main sources of insight into medieval culture. The 'Fooling of Gylfe', also known as 'Gylfaginning', is one of three books that make up Sturluson's *Prose Edda*, a collection recording and standardising Norse mythology and the language of poetry. Gylfaginning focuses on the story of creation and destruction of the

world of the Nordic gods. It is thought that there was a previous edition called the *Elder Edda*, which Sturluson quotes in his *Prose Edda*, however it has never been confirmed. There is also a collection of poetry from the same era, called the *Poetic Edda*.

Morgan Sylvia
Bleed the Weak
(First Publication)
Morgan Sylvia is an Aquarius, a metalhead, a coffee addict, a beer snob, and a work in progress. A former obituarist, she is now working as a full-time freelance writer. Her fiction and poetry have appeared in several places, including *Wicked Witches, Wicked Haunted, Northern Frights*, and *Twice Upon an Apocalypse*. In 2013, she released *Whispers from the Apocalypse*, a horror poetry collection. Her first novel, *Abode*, was released from Bloodshot Books in July 2017. She also writes for *Antichrist Metalzine* when time allows. She lives in Maine with her boyfriend, two cats, and a chubby goldfish.

Lucy Taylor
Subsumption
(First Publication)
Lucy Taylor is the author of the Stoker-award-winning novel *The Safety of Unknown Cities*, which is currently being reprinted in illustrated form by The Overlook Connection Press. Her short stories have appeared in over one hundred publications, including her short story collection *Fatal Journeys*. Most recently, her work can be found at Tor.com ('Sweetlings'; 'In the Cave of the Delicate Singers'), *Painfreak* ('He Who Whispers the Dead Back to Life'), *The Beauty of Death 2: Death by Water* ('You Will Come to No Harm in Water'), and *Fright Mares* ('Dead Messengers'). She lives in the high desert outside Santa Fe, New Mexico.

Natalia Theodoridou
Dog Island
(First Publication)
Natalia Theodoridou is a media & cultural studies scholar and a writer of strange stories. Originally from Greece, she is currently based in Devon, UK. Her work has appeared in *Clarkesworld, Beneath Ceaseless Skies, Strange Horizons, Apex, Shimmer*, and elsewhere. She is also the dramaturge of Adrift Performance Makers (@adriftPM), alongside whom she experiments with interactive fiction and digital performance. Her first interactive novel will be published by Choice of Games. For details, visit her website, www.natalia-theodoridou.com, or follow @natalia_theodor on Twitter.

Jules Verne
The Eternal Adam
(First Published in *Yesterday and Tomorrow*, 1905)
Jules Verne (1828–1905) was born in Nantes, France. As a novelist, poet and playwright, he wrote adventure novels and had a big impact on the science fiction genre. Along with H.G. Wells, Verne is considered to be one of the founding fathers of science fiction. His most famous adventure novels formed the series *Voyages Extraordinaires*, and include *Journey to the Centre of the Earth* and *Twenty Thousand Leagues Under the Sea*. His works continue to be popular today, and Verne ranks as the most translated science fiction author to date, with his works often reprinted and adapted for film.

H.G. Wells

The World Set Free (prelude–chapter II)
(Originally Published by *Macmillan & Co.*, 1914)

Herbert George Wells (1866–1946) was born in Kent, England. Novelist, journalist, social reformer, and historian, Wells is one of the greatest ever science fiction writers and along with Jules Verne is sometimes referred to as a 'founding father' of the genre. With Aldous Huxley and, later, George Orwell he defined the adventurous, social concern of early speculative fiction where the human condition was played out on a greater stage. Wells wrote over 50 novels, including his famous works *The Time Machine, The War of the Worlds, The Invisible Man,* and *The Island of Doctor Moreau*, as well as a fantastic array of short stories. *The World Set Free* is a consideration of both the positive and the destructive nature of the then recent invention of atomic energy.

Shannon Connor Winward

Lost and Found
(Originally Published in *Persistent Visions*, 2016)

Shannon Connor Winward is the author of the Elgin-Award winning chapbook *Undoing Winter.* Her writing has earned recognition in the Writers of the Future Contest and the Delaware Division of the Arts Individual Fellowship in Literature, and appears in *Fantasy & Science Fiction, Analog, Pseudopod, StoryHack Action & Adventure, Killing It Softly 2: The Best by Women in Horror, Flash Fiction Online, Heiresses of Russ: The Year's Best Lesbian Speculative Fiction,* and elsewhere. In between parenting, writing, and other madness, Shannon is also a poetry editor for *Devilfish Review* and founding editor of *Riddled with Arrows Literary Journal*.